The Waters of Destiny

The Waters of Destiny

Ian Watson & Andy West

Containing both
Assassins' Legacy & Assassins' Endgame

Steel Quill Books
England

First published in the UK by Steel Quill Books
An imprint of NewCon Press
41 Wheatsheaf Road, Alconbury Weston, Cambs, PE28 4LF

SQ010 (paperback)

10 9 8 7 6 5 4 3 2 1

ISBN:

978-1-912950-10-2

Cover art and design by Ian Whates

Minor Editorial meddling by Ian Whates
Text layout by Storm Constantine

Preface by the Humanity Futures Institute

How critical can any single event be in shaping the broad course of history? Especially a tiny event? Surely momentous natural, biological, and cultural forces have much more impact upon populations. Droughts, diseases, dogmas!

For instance war always has its roots in pre-existing, prevailing social conditions; individual battles and kings are merely surface features. People love to record that surface in great graphic detail, consequently our fussy historical accounts persuade us that innumerable single events are crucial. Yet even when messiahs or dictators play a role, the true agents of change are generally powerful currents hidden beneath the surface.

Nevertheless, the mathematical Law of Truly Large Numbers insists that given a huge enough sample size of events, a circumstance which seems to verge on the impossible is sooner or later *inevitable*. This allies with the Yokohama interpretation of quantum mechanics, whereby a random event at the atomic level may effectively result in a whole new parallel world, due to a *cascade* of changes. The result is a divergent timeline that is radically different, even though stemming from a common root.

Early in 1989 the inevitable came to be; our global destiny was balanced very precariously upon a single criticality, involving – by the thinnest of threads, indeed sub-microscopic – a peripheral society of fanatics half a millennium bygone, and their astounding creation. Within that creation was stored immense biological power, which could have engulfed our world, igniting a holocaust whose victorious survivors would have imposed a fanatical religious reign, halting what remained of modern civilisation. The world we occupy today is one in which, thankfully, the thread broke.

This book chronicles the long and costly original investment in the created 'fluid', and the dire consequences of its first deployment long ago. Likewise in narrative form, our sophisticated model projections of what would have unfolded in *an alternative modern world*, had the crucial thread remained intact.

How the US government obtained all the research data and remaining samples of vital fluid remains unknown to the Humanity Futures Institute. What *is* known is that huge efforts were devoted to unravelling the whole scientific story, and the detailed social story too. Religious terrorists who sought to raise a terrible spectre of history had access to the best biolab facilities for their project, carried out in Tehran. They kept meticulous records, right down to the full medical histories of their test subjects, the usage of every tiny drop of material, reams of mass spectrogram analyses and blood test results; a veritable mountain of documentation.

A *pair* of fluids was involved, one containing a highly dangerous virus, the other something more benign. Secrecy beyond our ability to penetrate still surrounds work on the latter fluid, from which we deduce those samples are still viable. Inside the former, the thread of fate wound through strands of DNA that had dwindled over the centuries to a critical threshold.

Amazing biotechnology developed for genetic assessment and manipulation can now reach down to the level of individual molecules and, via the slow transformation of carbon isotopes and other markers, accurately backtrack the degradation history of small samples kept in a sealed and temperature-stable environment. So regarding the most robust sample of the lethal liquid, the final loss of viability was shown to occur just when that sample was being assessed by terrorists in their Tehran lab. The chief US researcher (who must remain nameless) speculated in full seriousness that viability versus non-viability at that date may have hung upon a single molecule, indeed a single atom. Thus quantum uncertainty decided whether the original deadly purpose would fulfil itself or fail – spawning a fork in global history.

Whereupon we realised that we could project events forward from the fork, since all the players were known, as well as interested parties who would be sucked in. Only one fact changes: the viability of the lethal fluid. 'Projection' isn't prophecy, yet overall *something very similar would happen*. Parallels are close enough such that in the following account of an alternate modern unfolding it was necessary to shuffle some dates and locations in a minor way, plus alter the names and/or certain characteristics of various people, publications, and organizations. This is so that these entities are better protected from identification or inquiry, or indeed prejudice regarding behaviour which would not occur outside the context of the alternate unfolding.

Our medieval account relates real events, and of course everyone from that era is long dead. Yet even here we have disguised certain religiously significant places and graves in order to protect these from violation. Besides which, when highlighting historic events that were deliberately camouflaged, some educated guesswork is indispensable.

Hence the narrative which follows is necessarily dressed as fiction. We are obliged to its 'ghost' writers.

Humanity Futures Institute.

Elburz Mountains, Northern Iran: July 1986

Out in the fierce sun, Mahmoud was writhing on the rough ground, whimpering. His hands clutched a strip of cloth which Yasuf had evidently bound over his eyes. Not for Mahmoud any sight of the stark peaks surrounding them, nor the heavens beyond, which now he must seek in a different way.

"Let him go to Paradise," commanded Jafar. "We're a long way from medical help. A soldier of God can't be blind."

Yasuf pulled out Mahmoud's own pistol. The candidate for eternity screamed a plea and waved his arms frantically.

A single shot rang out. This echoed, amplified, around the empty mountains, becoming many reverberating shots, just as the *waters of life* and of *death* would multiply...

An hour earlier, the slow clicking of the metal detector had risen suddenly to a continuous buzz, like a Geiger counter near a radioactive source. Except that what they searched for here was potentially much more deadly; yet contained salvation too, Jafar hoped. He'd chosen this type of detector as it could also be used underwater. Its mechanical vibrator made his hand quiver, though his heart quivered more.

"Here!" he called urgently. "I think we've found it!"

After almost seven centuries, the floor of the cave as illuminated by the men's torch beams was a seamless sea of dusty rubble. Even back in the distant past, it would probably have taken a practised eye to detect that a hole had been hacked out and then camouflaged.

The predecessors had been cunning. Burial deep inside an isolated cave not only hid the item twice over, but protected the fragile apocalypse it contained from freezing during bitter winters. And a constant level of moderate cold helped with preservation; the blazing heat of summers never reached inside this dark sanctum. Outside in the trembling air of July, sunshine baked a scrub-covered mountainside; but the cave's interior was cool, almost chill.

Even armed with a painstakingly assembled list of clues, it had taken a very long while indeed to locate this secret place. Or maybe it had taken *exactly the right length of time*. Enough for the rise of molecular biology, and too for Islam to rouse itself at last, once more becoming militant... here at least in Iran, where Ayatollah Khomeini reigned from his house in Tehran; also in Afghanistan, of course, where the Mujahideen Alliance used rockets and guns from the stupid infidel CIA to slaughter atheist Russians. All this allowed them to hijack certain sympathies and facilities for their own hidden agenda, pursuing the pure route that long ago Islam *should* have taken.

"Allah be praised." The buzz of the detector almost drowned Mahmoud's murmur, and he repeated more loudly, "Be praised!" Quite so; to make this discovery now was surely His Will. And to find this *must be* to make use of it, otherwise why the finding? Two of the four men in the cave, Yasuf and Ali, were armed. Discarding the metal detector, Jafar knelt. With gloved hands, he and Mahmoud began lifting aside stones large and small, until both men sweated.

Half an hour later, torchlight played upon a Samarkand carpet, costly in its time and now a rare if musty antique. Carefully unfolding the delicate but intact fabric revealed a chest of black wood. The lid was exquisitely inlaid with silver Arabic, its style of calligraphy medieval.

"Beware," read Jafar. "For the *water of death* is within."

"Let us hope the *water of life* too, praise the Prophet," said Ali. "I don't suppose there could be two chests? Another, hidden elsewhere?"

Underneath the carpet's mustiness, Jafar scented fear borne on sweat. His own? Or Mahmoud's, who crouched next to him? Cold apprehension, blended with triumph, stretched all their faces into ambivalent grins.

"Obviously they inscribed a *warning* on the lid," he responded, "not an *invitation*, in case someone ignorant stumbled upon this."

"You mean someone who couldn't read? As used to be the case for the majority." Ali could sound flippant at times. Perhaps this was the young man's personal way of coping with the exigencies of holy war and of death, and consequently of being reliable in that war, but Mahmoud frowned at him reproachfully.

It took three of them to heave the chest out of its stone bed and place it gingerly on a level space of the cave floor. They propped their torches on rocks and gathered about the dark artefact. A carved knot of writhing monkeys, with staring pits of eyes, surrounded a large keyhole. Underneath, inlaid in humble copper turned green and in a less elaborate script than the silver, were the words 'pray to me'.

Jafar's veins thrummed. He scarcely believed this was real and not myth, yet he felt chosen, nominated as God's warrior for the ultimate task. He fished from his bag the Key of the Imams, which featured seven teeth of varying lengths. Months earlier, it had proved difficult to retrieve the weighty brass object; onlookers at the local beauty spot of Lake Evan, crouched at the feet of the mountains, had been intensely curious about a search of its muddy bottom. But eventually and discreetly the precious item was found, sealed inside a glazed pot of Persian blue.

It was much better to have the key. Forcing their way inside not only risked losing the contents, but also their lives in a terrible disaster. Yet at that moment his hand hung in doubt before the sacred chest.

"What does it mean?" he questioned earnestly of his God.

Ali's eyes shone devilishly in the upward pointing beams.

"Open it!" he urged.

Still Jafar hesitated.

"Our brethren of old were trained in the arts," he cautioned, "even as we are."

Jafar recollected the Black Stone secured by a silver band and silver nails to the eastern corner of the Ka'aba in Mecca. Rarely for an Ismaili, he'd been on the Hajj. When the pilgrims were perambulating around the great cube, Jafar had been able to quickly stoop and kiss the sacred stone that was the same colour as this chest.

Pray to me.

Towards Mecca? But the elite of the ancient Nizari Order, those who had hidden this terrible power from the world, would surely not have bowed towards Mecca in their prayers. They had transcended such things.

Impatiently, Mahmoud plucked the key from Jafar's hand and knelt before the chest. He inserted the object and, with some difficulty, twisted it. A loud click issued forth.

"Two more to go," exclaimed Ali. Yet even as he spoke, a peculiar whine and a simultaneous sigh emanated from inside the aged walls of wood. Mahmoud snapped up straight.

"Dust!" he spluttered, rubbing his eyes.

Jafar breathed a sigh of relief. Nothing serious.

"Turn it again."

But Mahmoud was blinking furiously now, and gasping too.

"Shit! It hurts. Aah it… ahh…"

Pray to me.

They should have obeyed!

Mahmoud clutched at his eyes and squealed.

"Water!" yelled Jafar. Their water was outside. "Get him to the entrance! Get him out!"

Yasuf dragged Mahmoud up and pulled him away. Moments later, blood-curdling screams filled the cave, echoing around within. But even as the cries of pain diminished, Jafar's keen mind dismissed them.

Pray to me.

When the fourth Master of Alamut, Hasan Ali, declared the *qiyama*, the new age, the Resurrection, he'd done so with his back to Mecca, emphasising the overthrow of dogmatic *Shari'ah* law, which insisted that worshippers face the holy city. Yet in subsequent centuries the true Nizari faith couldn't always be practised openly. Harsh political realities had at times forced the Nizaris into *taqiyyah*, dissimulation, their tactic to avoid persecution. In such cruel times they'd pretended to once again obey *Shari'ah* law, the pedantic law of the vast Sunni majority. Was this chest buried during the blessed decades of the *qiyama*? Or later, *after* Jalal al-Din Hasan, the sixth Master, had re-imposed *Shari'ah* practices?

"Do you have your compass?" he asked Ali.

Jafar reasoned and fervently hoped that, whether or not dissimulation was in force, the super-elite of the Nizari Ismailis would still have prayed with their backs to the *mihrab*, the niche that pointed to Mecca. This would demonstrate their pure spiritual state, their high ascent above ordinary rules. And most likely their booby-traps were designed to harm lowly initiates and the over-eager and despised unbelievers alike, as Ali had unfortunately just discovered. *Only the super-elite were ever intended to regain this buried power.*

For once without comment, Ali had drawn a bush-knife from his boot and flipped the compass out from its hilt. Under Jafar's direction, they got the deadly chest as level as they could using a makeshift plumb-line, then turned it so that the front precisely faced Mecca. To kneel before the keyhole, was now to have one's back to the holy city.

"We aren't meant to *actually* pray to the box," Jafar explained. "That'd be blasphemy. But in a physical sense we must obey its instruction literally, *and in exactly the same fashion as our ancient brethren.* Then we'll be safe."

Ali nodded nervously. "Sure," he said. "Whatever. Just don't expect *me* to turn that key again!"

Jafar considered covering the chest with their shirts and shemaghs, particularly those monkeys' eyes. But a sudden calm settled upon him and an inner light filled his mind, a gleam of the *Nur*, God's light, granted him at this critical time. He was *chosen* for this ritual, and he knew he'd interpreted the signs. He must take this test, *and he would pass it.* He knelt as though to pray and, open-eyed, he turned the key once more.

Once more came the click, and to his momentary dismay the whining sigh too. But no dust issued from the staring simians, and his shock soon passed.

A third sequence, just the same, except that this time the lid shifted noticeably.

Jafar bent forward and opened the chest. Ali peered over his shoulder.

The unexpected size and weight were explained. Thick copper lined the inside. Waxed and twisted cables held a casket suspended in the centre.

The mechanism of the booby trap was also laid bare. Thin wires ran from the lock up to three copper tubes, down which glass or steel balls had no doubt dropped to create a pulse of air. Fed to narrower piping for an increase in pressure, and of course to pick up the poisonous powder, these led to the front of the chest. A paper-thin gap separated them from the holes of the monkey's eyes, and into this gap, by way of a fluted channel, had slid a wafer of ivory so thin it was transparent, preventing the toxic cloud from blowing out. The wafer was attached to a large and primitive needle-compass, suspended by a thin thread. Only on the current and *exact* geographic orientation of the chest would the simple trap be disabled in this way.

Dazed and high on reaction to shock, Jafar thanked the true Imam and God profusely. On that centuries-old thread, his sight had hung.

Sensing that danger had passed, Ali knelt by his comrade.

Jafar failed to steady his shaking hands, as he unlatched and opened the inner casket. Inside were two further lids, covered with embroidered red velvet. One was labelled '*life*', the other, '*death*'.

"They're both here!" rejoiced Ali.

Jafar took a pen from his top pocket and flipped open the *life* lid. A row of hand-blown bottles in greenish glass lay snug in padded beds. Clear liquid within them reflected back glimmers of torchlight. The bottles appeared to be sealed with a honey-coloured wax.

More cautiously, he peeked into *death*. It looked no different, except that those bottles were sealed with black wax.

Jafar was tense with passion. "Behold the gift of the Assassins, the gift of God," he whispered.

"Allah Akbar," responded Ali reverently. He reached forward, clearly intent on grasping one of those delicate, fascinating vessels, holding water that could save or damn entire populations.

The moment shattered.

Jafar grabbed the young man's arm. "*No*! We don't know whether the seals are fully intact!"

Ali snatched back his hand and leapt away, fear spilling from his eyes.

"Go back," shouted Jafar. "Get the gloves and medical cases. The medium-sized aluminium ones should do."

As the echoes of that gunshot died away, Jafar felt nearer to heaven, and powerful. By way of their ancient brethren, whom only the weight of the Mongol hordes had been able to humble, God had granted them the gift of an ultimate weapon: intricate essences bequeathed from the very first global conflict.

According to the most persuasive interpretation of their secret writings, the ingenuity of the Assassins had produced something beyond their own wildest dreams and nightmares, the use of which the Assassins themselves couldn't possibly have optimised or controlled, all those centuries ago.

Unlike now…

Now the time was ripe. A black tide would devour their enemies as the *water of death* swept away the very foundations of Sunni and Christian and heathen civilisations alike, thus revealing the golden grains of the one true people.

Mahmoud was in heaven now. The gunshot that had sent him there celebrated his sacrifice and the future victory. Had anyone else in these mountains heard the thundering of the shot, and wondered? Perhaps, perhaps not. Let the world pay no further attention for twenty years or more…!

Radcliffe Institute for Advanced Study, Cambridge, Massachusetts: April 2008

From her office window, Abigail Leclaire admired the burgeoning spring greenery of Radcliffe Yard. The peaceful oval was flanked by modest buildings in old red brick, watched over by their ordered rows of windows. Those could almost be houses; like *an academical village*, to use Thomas Jefferson's phrase.

Sadly, at the end of May, her two semesters as a stipendiary fellow would finish. Come late September, the extended contract for her apartment at the graduate centre finished too. Before then she'd need to confront the future. Her original plan of reclaiming her teaching post for freshman history back in Canada, at Montreal's McGill University, would no doubt cause a big problem for Terry. Well, her spirit yearned for something better, something more exciting. Anyhow, September was still far off.

Her first book, *The Medieval Woman*, based on her doctoral thesis, had been well received; and her application for one of the fifty annual stipends of $60,000 plus project expenses had, to her joy, succeeded. Radcliffe, once a women's college and now part of Harvard, prided itself on matters female, as the huge holdings of old cookbooks in its Shlesinger Library bore witness; though Abigail never mentioned *that* to most men, in case they got a wrong impression about female scholarship.

Just as Terry may have got the wrong impression of her?

In theory, Radcliffe no longer prioritised women's issues, but the theme of her project application couldn't have harmed her chances, especially these days: *Troubadours and Arab Women Poets: the Gentling of Europe.*

Her premise was that the poets of al-Andalus, the Arab name for the huge swathe of Spain which they'd ruled, greatly influenced the troubadours of southern France, not least in a new sensitivity to male-female relationships and emotions; thus respect and politeness and courtly love were born – and Queen Eleanor of Aquitaine groomed her somewhat thuggish knights to become chivalrous. More generally, Arabic culture mellowed Christian Europe, especially regarding attitudes to women, even as militant Christians were gearing up to drive the Arabs out of Spain and destroy Islamic civilisation there.

Her own angle was that the *women* poets of al-Andalus, the 'poetisas', played a major role in the gentling process, their work included in the many poems from al-Andalus that were translated into Provençal. Though few women authors in Arab Spain were famous – due to a general lack of opportunity much bemoaned by Arab intellectuals at the time – one historian had listed more than forty poetisas. Unfortunately, much of their work appeared to have been lost. Yet there were stars such as Walladah bint al-Mustakfi of Córdoba, or the renowned Fatima who was also a rare book collector *par excellence* on behalf of Caliph Hakam II, a ruler who'd devoted his life to establishing public libraries.

Abigail was determined to make a case for the poetisas, and Harvard's Centre for Middle Eastern Studies had texts in its library which scholars had scarcely yet examined.

True, the topic was quite specialised and mightn't result in a second *book* as such, but at least a monograph of 50 or 60 pages for an academic journal; and who knows what she might yet find?

Having only just started to learn Arabic, she reluctantly acknowledged this was a hurdle, but she relished challenges. Unfortunately, so far, Arabic seemed to be largely eluding her.

Terry had once said she needed 'impossible' challenges! What made him say that?

She'd been coming at the subject from the French side, being from Montreal and raised bilingually. That first book of hers might more accurately have been titled *The French Medieval Woman*! She could read medieval French easily and cope with medieval Provençal too, nor was her Spanish bad after long holidays in Mexico; just as well, considering the amount of scholarly works in Spanish about the various Arab Emirates and Caliphates of al-Andalus.

Also, handily, Boston's Roxbury district had become home to the most expensive mosque in the North-Eastern United States. Promoted by the Islamic Society of Boston and costing $24 million, it was built on city land sold at a fraction of market value, to help create a centre for moderation and dialogue as well as a place of prayer. Clerics and staff there, especially her friend Walid, helped her with Arabic translations and interpretations of religious poetry. Harvard itself was particularly keen on intellectual outreach to Islam and the Muslim community. A long-standing programme of outreach had been set in place after the 9/11 acts of terrorism.

Only a couple of weeks ago a reporter from the *Boston Globe*, a guy with a goofy grin and ringletty hair, who'd been hanging around the mosque, had more or less kidnapped her into a brief interview about her interest. What was his name? Paul Something. Summers, that was it. He was into Islamic outreach, at least for the moment. She'd told him about her work, since the *Globe* was a prestigious newspaper, though there was nothing about her in his subsequent story. Probably much too fringe; she presumed reporters liked stuff they could manipulate into drama, or at least into this week's simple myths and messages.

And Terry had lately accused her *of being manipulative!* On top of earlier counts of being idealistic to the point of naivety, as well as obsessive. To her own mind she was simply enthusiastic and committed; an idea could capture and invigorate her. As for Terry, he couldn't commit to anything, so perhaps the commitment of others frightened him. And it was completely beyond her how one could be manipulative and naive at the same time!

There was a loud knock on her office door.

"Come," she called.

A man, maybe in his early thirties, very short blond hair, blue-eyed, clean-shaven, dark blue suit and lilac shirt, open-necked. He smiled in a briskly professional way.

"Dr Leclaire? Abigail Leclaire?"

"That's me."

"My name's Jack Turner." He produced ID. A photo of him. His name. And above those: US Immigration & Customs Enforcement. *www.ice.gov.*

That was the outfit that targeted illegal immigrants. And kept watch on foreign nationals too? Back in Canada last year there'd been an outcry in the press about a guy with dual Iraqi-Canadian nationality – wasn't that it? – whom, yes, ICE had arrested in New York when he'd briefly visited there. ICE accused him of being a terrorist sympathiser and promptly put him on a plane to the Middle East. She remembered a headline: **The ICEman Cometh**. Now the ICEman had come calling on her. *Why in hell's name?*

"I think you have the wrong Leclaire," she said frostily.

"*I* don't think so. May we talk?"

Was this intrusion because she frequently visited the Roxbury mosque? It was unfortunately true that the mosque was linked to controversy. There'd been stories in the *Boston Globe* fingering the *original* founder of the Islamic Society of Boston as an al-Qaeda fund-raiser. Two *former* ISB trustees were also Islamist hotheads. Three apparently bad apples in a rather big barrel. Or *allegedly* bad apples. Was *she* now tainted too?

These days in the States, it seemed one could end up in trouble for very bizarre reasons supposedly connected with national security; farewell, Land of Liberty!

But Jack Turner completely surprised her by saying, "You just had a little piece published in the on-line *American Annals of Medieval History*, about some old stuff you found in the Harvard library." From his pocket he produced a printout. "A Lost Poetisa of al-Andalus."

Abigail clearly remembered her excitement when she came across two pieces of paper, folded up in the back of an early printed chapbook of

Provençal verse such as were sold in medieval street-markets. Each paper was in the hand of a different scribe, evidently no connection between them. The first sheet contained a fragmentary account of what Abigail took to be an outbreak of plague in Provence, with an odd comment scrawled at the bottom: *Hospitaller Have Pity.* The second was the gem, a torn scrap from a poem. Although penned in Provençal script, it was *actually ascribed* on the sheet to Safiyya bint Yusuf al-Ballisiyya. This poetisa lived in Granada in the early 14th century, when the Alhambra palace complex was being completed. Only one other poem by her survived. Though the early 14th was a bit late to affect the original troubadours, whose tradition was in decline as well as under attack from the Dominican Inquisition trying to stamp out heresy, the 1320s saw a revival in Toulouse.

Abigail had no desire to touch material proffered by someone from a spooky agency such as ICE, so she quickly accessed that same item at www.aamh.edu. There was the fragment in medieval Provençal, followed by her own translation:

> ...*mort*
> *se cofla, e de riba sort*
> *mentre l'agla forta*
> *qui molt leisons ensenha*
> *d'amont a bas agaita*
> *per la vezion jutjar*
> *que fem de la vertat*
> *abans lo terme acabat*

> ...*death*
> *swells and overflows*
> *while the strong eagle*
> *teacher of many lessons*
> *watches down from high*
> *with the vision to judge*
> *what we make of the truth*
> *before our term is ended*

Little enough! Yet accompanied by a longish comment about the female poets of al-Andalus, it made the on-line *AAMH*. And somehow attracted the attention of the US Immigration and Customs Enforcement...? Uninvited, Jack Turner sat in the black leather swivel chair opposite her desk, twin to her own.

"This may be a long shot," he said, "but I wonder what the phrase 'eagle teacher' might suggest to you?"

"Just those two words, out of context? That sounds to me more like a native American medicine-man rather than anything connected with an early medieval Arab woman's poem!"

"I wasn't thinking Redskins."

"Native Americans," she corrected him.

He just stared hard at her. "What does *eagle* evoke to you?"

"The Eagle has landed," she replied, "on the Moon. I dunno, the bald eagle on the Great Seal of the US government. Endangered species," she added.

"The US government is an endangered species?" he enquired.

"I didn't mean that. There's no punctuation of course, but there *is* a line-break between *eagle* and *teacher*," she pointed out tartly.

He ignored this. "If not Redskins, how about greenbacks? You may have noticed there's an eagle on every US Federal Reserve currency bill."

"I don't *study* money, I spend it."

"60,000 good US dollars. Your stipend. I know. What's *Eagle Teacher* in Arabic?"

"I've no idea."

"Oh, I kind of assumed…"

"But I'm learning," she said defensively, and regretted it right away.

"Going to classes?"

Classes *where* exactly? Taught by *which* Arabic speakers? Hatefully, he was contriving to make her feel, or seem, guilty of something. How many people felt, when they saw a cop, that they were guilty of some indefinable crime?

"Audio CD and book," she told him.

The ICEman's cold eyes appraised.

How did this badge-carrying intruder see her? Snub nose with a bridge of faint freckles, though could he see her skin flushing? Tumbly goldilocks hair that was *natural;* no doubt he'd mark this as her best feature. Eyes levelled and vanitied with greeny multi-focal contact lenses over pupils that were rather more grey, a strong chin but no obvious lipstick; it was *subtle*. Reasonably slim. And thank god for modest-sized boobs; she despised breast-fixated men, at least Terry wasn't one of those, and she despised still more those women who deliberately dysfunctioned themselves to appease this fixation. Was Turner's appraisal the ordinary male kind, or was he looking for signs of guilt, or at least of non-compliance?

"Just how did you…?" she began. Ah, but of course. High-speed computers were constantly scanning websites, e-mails, everything on-line, searching for key words or phrases, supposedly defending the USA in a war, 'the war against terror'. She tried a likely guess. "*Eagle Teacher* is a code-name for some terrorist plot, is that it?"

"You reckon so, Dr Leclaire? Supposing so, why would you choose it?"

"I certainly *didn't* choose it."

"Why would *one* choose it?"

"Teach the bald eagle a lesson? Meaning the government?"

"Specifically? Assassination maybe?"

"How would I know?"

"Or maybe an attack on American money? Some way to make the dollar sick?"

"I thought most money already had cocaine on it."

He bulled onward. "*Eagle Teacher* might signify that you teach the eagle, or that the eagle does the teaching. In which case, who or what might the eagle be? What does this bit of verse suggest to you, historically, you know?"

She shrugged. "It's only a fragment."

"Come on, you're the expert."

"If it's a literal translation from Arabic into Provençal, perhaps the teacher is a religious figure. The phrase 'from high' may mean at or near the top of the hierarchy, somebody like an Imam maybe. I don't see how this has any connection with anything of interest to you nowadays. I mean, if somebody is using *Eagle Teacher* as, as..."

"A code-name for a plan, just for instance?" he supplied, as if taunting her.

"Well, obviously they didn't take it from this."

"There wasn't any more than those seven lines, preceded by 'death'?"

"Nothing recoverable. I'd have published it if so!"

"I bet you would. If anything more does occur to you, we'd appreciate..." He held out a card bearing only his name and a phone number. Hastily she tucked the card under a book entitled *The Forgotten Queens of Islam*.

"It's highly unlikely anything will occur to me, Mr Turner."

She half expected him to say *we never had this conversation*. Since he didn't, maybe he hoped she'd call someone at the mosque, just for instance, which in turn might cause them to do something out of profile... Paranoia! For that, they'd have to tap her phone. Anyhow, she wasn't even going to phone Terry to tell him.

As soon as the door closed on the ICEman, she googled www.ice.gov. Jesus, it was the men from ICE who'd nailed the founder of the Islamic Society of Boston. ICE's Mission: "to protect against terrorist attacks." Set up in 2003 as the *largest* investigative branch of Homeland Security!

She clicked links. Joint Terrorism Task Force… Uhuh, and the US Secret Service were buddies under the banner of Homeland Security, although not the FBI nor the CIA, thanks for small mercies. And the Secret Service was founded first of all to protect American money, only adding the protection of presidents to their job description later on…

Eagle, she thought to herself. Islamist eagle, terrorist eagle? It seemed blindingly obvious that there couldn't be any connection with the early Middle Ages. On impulse she typed *eagle teacher* into Google, and got millions of hits. Ah, but ICE must have gone for an exact phrase search. This produced 12,000 hits, still far too many! A quick scan revealed that most hits were about schoolteachers associated with 'eagle' awards or courses or some such, so she added *-school* to remove these. Much less, but still a few thousand.

She'd been visited *in person*. ICE must have put something extra into their search. What, what? Abigail re-read the fragment of poem. Struck by an awful inspiration, she typed *+death* as an extra search term.

Only 79 hits. Right at the top of the first page, staring coldly at her from the screen, was her contribution to the *American Annals of Medieval History*. There she was at number one. She sat back, shocked and shaking.

Back Bay, Boston, Massachusetts: April 2008

She'd needed to get out of her office, out of Harvard itself, see fresh faces. Inside Tealuxe, sunshine highlighted the faces of Boston's chattering connoisseurs of the beverage: old ladies in scarves, trendy students with lip-rings or shemaghs or brightly coloured beanie caps, a chap in a long black coat with a dove-grey scarf reading *Newsweek*. It was still chilly outside, and the warm haven was crowded.

Abigail sipped at her Lady Grey, pushing away uncomfortable thoughts about Terry; to no avail, he always crept back.

Perhaps they'd both got the wrong impression of each other from the get-go. From her perspective at least, she saw now that *she* certainly had. She'd always been a sucker for charm, and Terry's winning smile, smooth courtesy and lavish attention soon crashed through her flimsy defences. Yet his easy charm turned out to be just a mask, behind which lived an insecure and home-loving boy, who wouldn't commit to anything that would force him to take responsibility and grow up.

And what had *he* seen in her? She didn't know, but at the moment he probably saw an obsessive and argumentative woman, who pushed him where he didn't always want to go. A woman who was never going to stay in Boston forever, no matter that it was a lovely place to live. This made her seem cruel, which in turn made her feel bad, yet it had all started so well.

After the stipendiary at Radcliffe came up, she arrived a couple of months early to settle in, only to find herself desperately lonely. Boston had a small town mentality; it seemed surprisingly hard to break in. She asked Terry about the city when he served her a drink. He expounded. Soon he was taking her on whirlwind tours. He knew every inch of the place, introducing her to head waiters and chefs and barmen in all the fanciest venues; an instant circle of local and useful friends. He bought her meals and delightful little gifts. The intense shared experience had rolled heedlessly into romance.

She should have known from the first encounter that Terry's roots went deep, as deep as the roots of Boston itself, despite new structures built above. He'd even said then, almost with an odd kind of pride, that he'd never spent more than a fortnight away from home. Abruptly, it came to her that he would *never* leave Boston. Therefore they should end this now, before a worse ending was forced upon them. She felt nauseous, abandoned some tea undrunk, and headed out into crisp air and the hope offered by a bright blue sky.

She turned down Clarendon Street and paused where it crossed St.

James Avenue, to take in a view that always fascinated her; Trinity Church reflected in the mirror-glass wall of the Hancock Tower. The old reflected in the new.

Jack Turner's odd questions returned to prick her. Could the words of the old poem by Safiyya bint Yusuf al-Ballisiyya be reflected in some new and destructive purpose? Hijacked by terrorists to serve their violent ends? Or had someone dug down to find an *old* purpose, then built anew upon it?

The whole thing seemed ridiculous. Safiyya al-Ballisiyya had penned her words more than five hundred years ago. Apart from the fact that it was unsettling to receive personal interest from Immigration and Customs Enforcement, Jack Turner's bizarre visit heightened an unresolved problem which had been niggling her for quite a while. The fragment by Safiyya was obscure, to say the least. Abigail simply didn't know what it was really about. With only a single other work by the same writer, and that one romantic in nature, there was very little context to work with.

It seemed overwhelming likely that ICE were clutching at any Islamic straw to support some flimsy case. Nevertheless, she had to get ahead of them on this poem, if only to fend off any further unwarranted government intrusion. She headed down St. James and towards the public library, determining to make Safiyya al-Ballisiyya and her curious verse a priority, even above introducing reality to Terry.

Later, when she emerged from the library into its courtyard of Italianate columns, that same guy who'd been in Tealuxe was leaning against one, still intent on *Newsweek*. Coincidence?

Cairo, the Fatimid Caliphate: 1145

Hakim, the Arabic name for doctor, was the name he now determined to use as his own. This gave no information about either his lineage or his birthplace, shearing him of all associations but the high purpose he was about to dedicate his whole life to.

As a medical student freshly arrived in Cairo, bursaried by the charity of the Nizari Ismaili community in Syria, Hakim was determined to fit in. He didn't want the same fate as the pious fellow student named Sadiq. Poor Sadiq was tolerated, just, yet was socially excluded and, though that young man surely had a very similar background to himself, Hakim made no overtures to Sadiq for many months. That wasn't the way to advance.

Before long, the popular Abdul and his crony Naguib sidled up to Hakim to ask, "Would you care to put some milk into a cow tonight, along with us?"

Cow was what you called a whore. So-called milk cows gave you sex outdoors; free cows went to the rooms of their clients; wild cows used their own rooms; and then there were the farm cows who worked in brothels.

"Of course," and Abdul had winked, "we examine the cows carefully first of all, to make sure they're clean."

Down by the wax candle market, beside the mosque of Aqmar, Hakim had seen whores clad in red leather trousers coughing suggestively to draw the attention of prospective clients. He forced himself to smile, sharing the joke. "That isn't for me," he said. "I need to watch my purse."

"Surely you can afford thirty dirhams for admittance to the gateway of joy?

"Thirty dirhams," repeated Hakim, thinking of the money generously gifted him for his education, raised by tithes and donations.

"Yes, dirhams. I didn't say gold dinars! Or are you a prude, like poor Sadiq?"

"No, I'll come with you," agreed Hakim.

Later that same evening, as a half-moon shone upon the splendours and squalors of Cairo, mirroring itself like a bright silver sail upon the Nile, Hakim went with his two fellow students of anatomy to a certain house with lattice windows.

Silks hung around the walls of a large room, covering doorways. The three students shared a sprawl of tasselled cushions with another patron, a burly man. They all paid an old woman five dirhams for cool sherbet, an extra cost which Abdul had neglected to mention. Gleaming brass oil-lamps seemed to invite a caress, which might magically cause the flame to leap up and become a fiery enchantress.

The enchantresses, four of them, faces rouged, eyelids shadowed with kohl, shimmied through the silks from separate doorways. They too were scantily clad in silk; their private parts were concealed, though barely so. Bangles on their wrists and ankles jangled, slippers with up-curving toes glittered on their feet. Two were plump and two were slim. One had skin of coffee with milk, another was almost white, a third was African ebony, Nubian undoubtedly, and the fourth was cinnamon. Lewdly, languidly, they began to dance while the old woman clapped her hands rhythmically.

Almost at once the burly fellow arose, gesturing at the plump woman who was almost white. She stood still and recited, "I have allowed you."

He replied, "I have accepted. For a dowry of thirty dirhams, for one hour."

As soon as she nodded, he paid the old woman and followed his temporary wife through red silk to take his delight.

Although scandalised by this highly abbreviated legitimisation of imminent copulation, Hakim was nevertheless glad to know the exact words used. He reminded himself that the Prophet, peace be upon him, had allowed such formulas, so that soldiers or merchants or other men far from home might gain relief.

Naguib stood up and indicated the plump ebony woman; the same transaction then occurred. As the two remaining women continued to dance, Abdul eyed Hakim.

"Be my guest," he murmured, although he wouldn't actually be paying. Yes, Hakim should indeed choose, not allow the choice to be dictated for him. He arose and pointed at the young woman whose skin was the hue of cinnamon.

Within a small lamp-lit chamber beyond blue silk, its door now shut, much of the space was occupied by a bed. Incense smouldered headily. Cinnamon shed her bangles, and turned provocatively to Hakim.

Apprehension assailed Hakim, not an emotion familiar to him. His manhood had swollen under his flowing *jellaba*, though only somewhat. If he failed to bed the whore manfully, Abdul might learn of this even if Hakim later lied and bragged; though what basis of knowledge could he brag upon? Hakim strongly suspected that Abdul or Naguib would question him. Therefore he must *desire* as totally as possible the body that swayed before him like a supple snake piped from a basket. Desire must exclude any other distracting thoughts, as with an animal on heat. Or maybe like a martyr gone to Paradise; yes, here was Paradise in advance, God's reward for unknown accomplishments yet to be achieved. It was paradise that she should surrender herself to him, his slave so vulnerable, soft and delicate, baring her breasts, opening wide her legs, to be pierced by his shaft that now stiffened more.

Her silks were loose and falling. He stared transfixed at the swell of her thighs, and her cleft crowned by a dark tuft below her naked, scarcely rounded belly. Oh the little peaches of her breasts, to gently squeeze.

Yes, surely to squeeze first of all, for he mustn't simply impale her impetuously all at once! What had Abdul said about causing ecstasy in a woman? Abdul might wish to know of this, by hearing tell of the signs of ecstasy from Hakim's own report.

As though aware of his perplexity, or perhaps impatient, Cinnamon silently slid a finger down her belly to her cleft, then within so that half of her finger disappeared. Thrusting forward her pubes, she rubbed herself slowly, as if she sought relief from itchy worms; yet surely her vagina must be deeper between her legs. Evidently, she was showing him what he should do to her, and how. Hakim refrained from speaking in case what he said was stupid, and she seemed disinclined to speak, as though mouths were intended for other purposes. Swiftly he shed his clothing. He was... He *was* in Paradise, blessed by God for what he had, for what he *would*, achieve!

She must have moistened herself liberally with an unguent, he decided presently after she positioned his finger to replace hers. He massaged a small bump, which caused her to moan, then cry out and toss her head from side to side.

Before long she gripped his shaft and guided him to where he fitted perfectly. As his weight bore down upon her, she hoisted her legs to grip him, ankles locking together. How she gasped at his thrusting, until deliriously he spent himself in pulsing surges. Too soon his organ was limp and he withdrew, kneeling between her splayed legs, assessing in the lamplight her wet, flushed openness.

She chuckled with a kind of patronising complicity. And quite suddenly a great emptiness was within Hakim, a hollow sadness as of waste and futility: the waste of some of the carefully gathered funds of his community. The waste too of the sheer *tension*, as of a taut bow that had been within him so recently, all its accumulated potential now lost.

Nevertheless, Hakim revisited the brothel twice more with Abdul and Naguib, choosing a different woman each time for comparison. After successfully establishing his 'normality', he allowed himself to become privately more friendly with Sadiq, not so that others would remark on it. As a result, Sadiq seemed almost to fall in love in a spiritual way; their friendship was to be special and confidential. Then Hakim focused upon mightier matters, his mind cleansed, not least because by now his studies in medicine had shown him many grotesque examples of disease and malignancy, both externally and also internally. He knew full well that anyone's body, even the fairest, could become hideous.

He immersed himself in the great medical texts by Ibn Sina, ar-Razi, Jabir ibn Hayyan, and Abu al-Qasim al-Zahrawi. A lecturer pointed out that ancient Greek doctors made claims based on insufficient observation, claims which ar-Razi disproved. Controlled, systematic experimentation was essential. Commissioned to choose the best site for a hospital in Baghdad, ar-Razi had famously hung up meat throughout the city to discover where it decomposed least quickly, thus to pinpoint the most hygienic place. Animal testing was important, even though a drug might not affect a dog in the same way as a human being.

Hakim paid particular attention to theories of contagious disease, to Ibn Sina's idea of bodily secretions being contaminated by foul foreign bodies, and that water could carry such bodies, as could garments. These foreign bodies were far too small to be seen, though their serious effects belied the size of the cause; therefore patients with similar serious symptoms should be kept separate from others. Mercurial compounds and sulphur and pure alcohol were surely efficacious, Hakim reasoned, because they destroyed or hindered that which could not be seen by any gaze less acute than God's, who saw all.

Hakim couldn't but note ar-Razi's insistence that a doctor's aim is to do good, *'even to our enemies'*. Yet if those enemies were also accursed antagonists of Allah, surely this didn't apply!

Dissections of abandoned or unclaimed corpses needed to be carried out from time to time, otherwise how could one truly learn anatomy? By pretending that a dead pig is a human being? Ay, the vital work was carried out in utmost secrecy, in case the religious authorities heard that the body of a servant of Allah was being abused. A doctor soon learned to keep secrets.

It was the duty of a doctor to heal, if possible. To bring relief. To limit suffering. This he solemnly swore when he was finally granted his licence to practise medicine.

Yet below a calm exterior, always a tempest of ambition raged within Hakim…

To be a doctor was to practise the art which brought one closest to God. Surely God wished the world purged of those who denied and offended Him, such a host of infidels and heretics! *Surely* it would be Godly to use not the clumsy sword forged by Man, but the subtle instruments created and therefore legitimised by God Himself, if those could be sufficiently understood and applied. The ultimate instrument, for instance, of plague...

Armies had catapulted corpses over the battlements of besieged cities, yet no general had ever used disease itself in his armoury with any true understanding. Sickness often trailed behind the ravages of war. Why should disease not precede, and itself ravage enemies, thus sparing many faithful servants of God from being sent to Heaven prematurely by their infidel enemies? A doctor who could assist in this would be saving lives. Hakim dreamed of a future when war might be fought not with swords but with deadly sickness, to the glory of God and the salvation of the faithful, so that true faith might dominate the world, and its higher initiates might unlock the secrets of creation and apprehend the mind of God. Surely for this higher purpose God granted him exemption from his licence, the writ of well-meaning but limited men...

Radcliffe Institute for Advanced Study, Cambridge, Massachusetts: April 2008

Two days after Jack Turner's visit, Abigail was winnowing a crop of almost uniformly negative replies to urgent emails she'd sent to colleagues and contacts all over the world, requesting any further information whatever on Safiyya bint Yusuf al-Ballisiyya. The only glimmer of light came from an old friend now resident in Oxford, England.

Abigail, how's the new book coming on? How is your charming bartender? Has your masterful father done away with him yet?
I have a snippet for you. Not much I'm afraid, but hard-won after mining the Bodleian, so you owe me!
It turns out that the long-term lover of Safiyya bint Yusuf al-Ballisiyya was one Sinan al-Din ibn Nasir. An Ismaili and a man 'of rank' apparently.
Sorry, no other details. Hope it's useful,

Love Jen XX

Abigail smiled. Jen admired older men, especially those with power and money. When introduced five years ago or so, Abigail's own father had evoked a blush in her friend's cheeks just by his presence. Typically, Jen hadn't even offered a polite denial of her attraction.

Rising, Abigail gazed at the graceful bud-bursting greenery of Radcliffe Yard, mulling over Jen's snippet. This could indeed be useful. The once powerful Ismailis formed a sect within the Shi'a wing of Islam, recognising Ismail son of Jafar as-Sadiq as the disputed seventh Imam, the seventh divinely inspired and infallible religious guide for Muslims after the death of the Prophet. Ismailis had spawned a rich poetic tradition of their own. Maybe Safiyya al-Ballisiyya had borrowed from them some convention whereby a *teacher of many lessons* would indeed be an Imam, which might in turn explain the religious context in which death *swells and overflows*.

This was off the edge of her field. She'd need help. The Ismaili connection teased her memory, touching upon something unsavoury at the edge of recollection.

Movement in the yard below caught her attention. A young man, black coat, grey scarf, ducked into a doorway. Sudden fire flashed over Abigail's cheeks as cold wrapped her spine. Had that ICEman prick set a watch on her? Her logic dismissed the idea as ludicrous, but her anger was alight and not so easily doused. The young man didn't reappear.

Centre for Middle Eastern Studies, Cambridge, Massachusetts: April 2008

The reception was boring. Abigail usually found them so. This one was a CMES do, the Centre for Middle Eastern Studies at Harvard, thrown to welcome a new associate to its heart. A free buffet though, inclusive of plonk.

The beaming professor being honoured was taking over a regular seminar series, *Islam in the West*. So, when the ring of eager admirers thinned, she hoped to make contact. He'd astutely combined the CMES event with a PR push for his book, *Guilt, Manipulation and Misunderstanding: the Hand of The West in the Palestinian-Israeli Conflict*.

Pending access to the worthy professor, she sauntered about like a thief spotting for opportunities, wielding her smile like a crowbar to break into the most promising of other people's conversations. Sadly, a great deal of schmoozing was necessary to remain afloat in the treacherous ocean of academia. Conscious of staying sharp and with a busy afternoon ahead too, she sipped her wine slowly. She spotted that reporter guy from the *Boston Globe*, Paul Summers, talking into his phone, though not with the usual animation people have when chatting to someone else, so he was probably just confiding audio notes. She had no wish to hobnob with him right now and hoped he wouldn't recognize her. Crazily, he was wearing a long white kaftan over blue jeans, as if out of solidarity with the occasion. Or maybe not so crazily. CMES boasted a healthy ethnic range of participants: Mediterranean and North African, Arab and Turkic and Anglo-Saxon and more, dressed in Western suits and brightly coloured robes, T-shirts and hijabs and silk scarves and baseball caps.

Of a sudden, there leapt out at her an urgent hiss; *eagle-teacher*. She whirled in a desperate attempt to discover who'd said that, and her wine flew in a wide arc, her glass smashing spectacularly on the floor. Most conversation ceased. Abigail felt terribly exposed under the glare of lights and the glare of those nearby, although Paul Summers was grinning sympathetically at her across the room; maybe he was a connoisseur of social gaffes. A post-grad she'd seen around before, a South-East Asian who sported a puckered old scar just like a supplementary eyebrow, looked shocked and angry; maybe the wine had splashed him. A handsome, well-groomed, middle-aged Arab gentleman next to him smiled quizzically; he probably thought Abi was drunk. She lamely explained to the room in general that she'd lost her footing, then said sorry a lot as one of the catering staff came to clear up the mess. Did Jack Turner have someone snooping around here, asking the same improbable questions of other targets within CMES? A sense of unreality gripped her, a feeling of being adrift on an unknown sea.

Get some perspective, girl.

Her gentle history tutor back home in Montreal had said she should never reprove herself like that. *Girl* revealed disbelief in her own maturity. She circled as discretely as she could, hoping to hear the phrase again; but in vain. After making such an exhibition of herself, she decided this mightn't be the best time to approach that professor.

Tehran, Iran: February 1989

Jafar had hurried to the observation booth as soon as he was told that at last the prisoner was showing the first signs of plague. This was most excellent. Until right now they'd had nagging doubts that any of the liquids from the chest were still viable and potent.

Subject Number Two was also a subject of that impostor who called himself the Aga Khan and who weighed himself in diamonds, so-called Commander-in-Chief of the so-called Nizari Ismailis, whose great-great-grandfather long ago hijacked a lineage and a true faith that had persisted in secret for centuries. How appropriate that the first experimental prisoner to show the desired signs should be one of those false Nizaris.

Doctor... *think of him not by his name, but as the Hakim of our time...* was gazing through the toughened glass at his subject within the padded cell, a naked flabby brown man who suddenly spewed out water which he had only just gorged himself on, as though this might empty himself of what *plagued* him. Was that what his body was trying vainly to do?

The prisoner clutched his head. His neck looked swollen. Moments later, blood began trickling from his nose. His chest flushed with a rash like a blushing girl.

"Very fast onset," commented The Doctor approvingly, scribbling in his notebook. "Extremely satisfactory."

The prisoner staggered. His eyes glared madly at his observers. His bloodied lips mouthed something theatrically; the glass was soundproof but he'd probably screamed the words out. Possibly 'shoot me'.

"In olden times," said The Doctor levelly, "people drowned themselves or jumped off cliffs... the pain and thirst were so great. Still very early days, we have years ahead of us, but I think this is indeed the same disease."

I'll be needing a new identity before long, reflected Jafar, a new name.

Boston, Massachusetts: April 2008

Abigail felt quite ridiculous weaving through downtown Boston, lurking in bookshop aisles with views of the street, leaving by alternative exits if possible, plunging into crowds then doubling back and slipping suddenly down side-streets. No man in a grey scarf appeared to be tailing her, though that didn't mean that someone else wasn't. Apart from taking great exception to Jack Turner knowing her business, she didn't want Walid to suffer similar attention.

She took the subway to Ruggles, then marched briskly into the grounds of North-Eastern University. Entering the foyer of the Behrakis Health Sciences Center, she checked from behind the glare of sunshine on blue glass. All seemed okay, just a few students wandering around. Shabby garb with pseudo-military pockets and zips plus arty beads, or winter coats thrown over bright tee-shirts and jogging bottoms or jeans.

A shame Walid wasn't closer to hand; more of a shame that she'd felt forced to take a long detour into downtown for no other reason than ICEman Jack *might* be watching her! Quelling a spasm of anger, she found a rear exit and wended her way to the intersection of Malcolm X Boulevard and Tremont Street.

The golden dome of the Roxbury mosque was a mirror of the bright sun, nestling on ember-red columns and arches and curtains of brick, although for Abigail its tall minaret spoiled an otherwise exotic effect, looking as it did like a nineteenth century factory chimney. The brickwork architecture had apparently been chosen to fit in with Bostonian style.

"I'm here to see Walid al-Areqi," she told an attendant at the main entrance. "He's expecting me." The man nodded and she stepped inside, then he moved noiselessly away to a shadowed interior.

Abigail browsed the notice board, spotting Walid's name on several committees and support groups. If ever there was anyone on a mission to help the whole of humanity, it was Walid. And after fifteen years of dedicated effort towards the Roxbury mosque project, he certainly deserved his position here.

"Abigail… Abigail, it's good to see you again. Wonderful!"

They hugged warmly, by no means a conventional way for an Islamic man to greet a woman not of his family.

Walid's deep, mellow tones always seemed in contrast with his slight build and thin, restless features, just as his wrinkled and nut-brown skin contrasted with the silky white of his hair and beard. During their previous meetings, Abigail had occasionally found herself asking him a question just so that she could be enfolded in the downy duvet of his answering voice.

"It's good to see you," she responded with feeling. "Are you busy?"

Walid shrugged and smiled. "This place doesn't run itself. But I always have a little time for a beautiful French lady."

"French-Canadian," corrected Abigail, grinning and colouring at the same time. Walid was a star.

"I suppose you need a little help with your research?" Every line of his face showed an intense eagerness to put his substantial knowledge to service.

"I'm afraid so," Abigail admitted.

"Come in, come in."

They passed through the echoing main hall and under the dome, with its curved web of struts trapping a mysterious globe of gloom, then to a small side-room.

"It's about the fragment," Abigail said once they were seated. "I think it may be Ismaili, or at least influenced by the Ismailis. But I'm not too familiar with Ismailism and I need to know more, urgently. What it's really about, why death overflows, the eagle reference?"

"Ah, the famous fragment." He frowned. "Ismaili, eh? That puts a different light on things." A mischievous smile leaked out of him. "When is something *not* urgent for you?"

"Oh, but…"

Walid held up his hand to halt her. "Now, I'm no expert on Ismaili poetry…"

"But?"

Abigail knew his pause was for dramatic effect. Walid *always* said he wasn't an expert, yet she had never yet seen him stumped.

"But I do know their works are usually devotional in nature. Take Ibn Hani for instance." And he quoted in English a couple of verses about salvation, burdens removed, tomorrow bringing forth the day of Resurrection.

"Not an expert, huh? But you can quote the stuff! Presumably that's Ibn Hani al-Andalusi?"

"Yes. He had to flee anti-Ismaili persecution in Andalusia and was mysteriously murdered, around 970 AD I believe. A great loss."

She sensed a touch of bitterness in Walid's voice, as though the poet had died just last month and not a thousand years ago.

"Because of the Spanish connection, I came across Ibn Hani myself," said Abigail. "Given that Safiyya lived in Granada and it now appears had Ismaili sympathies herself, she probably knew his works backwards. Yet she doesn't seem to write in the same style." She passed Walid a copy of her translation from the Provençal, to jog his memory. He searched in vain for his glasses.

"Your poetisa would have cloaked her sympathies, in order to avoid Ibn Hani's fate! Four centuries separate him and her, but righteous anger at fringe beliefs hadn't diminished. Andalusia was a stronghold of orthodoxy until the end."

"Hmmm… I hadn't thought of that."

"Perhaps her poem is deliberately obscure for that very reason."

Glasses discovered, under a mass of draft leaflets, Walid perused the fragment. Abigail had to consciously stop holding her breath. She desperately needed some clues to fend off the ridiculous attention of Jack Turner.

The wrinkles around Walid's eyes tightened in concern or distaste, or maybe like her he was just puzzled.

"I'm afraid I didn't pay enough attention before," he muttered. "Even so I should have realised… Senility setting in, I expect."

"Realised what?" ventured Abigail.

"About the Ismaili connection." He took his glasses off and waved them in vague circles. "The Ismailis were rather militantly organised you know, in medieval times."

The unsavoury association she hadn't been able to recall burst forth like vinegar of the mind. Of course! Extremists at the mountain fortress of Alamut, just south of the Caspian sea, had once led the Ismaili community. An embarrassing period in the history of the sect.

"The Assassins of Alamut," she gasped.

"Quite. Though I think Alamut had been in ruins for quite a while when your poetisa was writing… Mid-fourteenth you said?"

Abigail nodded.

"Nevertheless, that's where you'll find your eagle connection. The place was even called the Eagle's Nest, ages before a certain deplorable German Führer used that same name for his mountain retreat."

She made a mental note to check these things out later; she didn't want to stop Walid in mid-flow.

"Maybe the verses praise a figure or a period historical to Safiyya. But the one who *watches down from high*, who has *the vision to judge*, is an Imam of course. It's a reference to his status of divine appointment. Nizari Quhistani employs the phrase, *the one above them all*, but Nasir-i-Khusraw is much more explicit in the last verse of his work, *The Master and the Disciple*. Ahem: *The master said, He is the Lord of the time, chosen by God from men and jinns.* Unfortunately, none of this poetry works well in English. Come to think of it, I guess Safiyya's style *is* reminiscent of Khusraw. He's another leading light in Ismaili poetry. Eleventh century. You don't have the fragment in Arabic, do you?" Walid peered hopefully over his lenses.

"Only in Provençal, so we can't be sure the translation from Arabic is accurate. I'd actually worked out the Imam bit, but the part about death overflowing is a real mystery."

"Indeed. *Our term is ended* could be a reference to the end of everything, the Resurrection, when revived bodies of the dead come up from the earth to be reunited with their souls. That isn't related to the Christian Resurrection of Jesus. No, it's when the great Judgement takes place."

"Hmm... I translated *de riba sort* as *overflows*, but literally it's *from the bank comes out*, as in a river overflowing its banks. Maybe it should've been *from the earth comes out?* And *mort* could be *dead*, not *death*. It's a pity we haven't got the words just before *mort* to set the context."

Walid frowned. "It doesn't feel right. I think you're bending the words to fit my suggestion. *Swells* is peculiar, despite the dead supposedly regaining their flesh. I've never come across such phrasing as this before." He fell silent, drumming his fingers on the desk. For once maybe he *was* stumped. Then he gave a sigh of exasperation.

"If only we had a little more material! The Ismailis believe in religious cycles, so maybe *our term* means one of those cycles. In fact resurrection, *qiyama*, can also have a special meaning for them, as in the start of a new cycle, like the one announced by Hasan II at Alamut where Shari'ah law was abandoned. Or it could be a personal spiritual renewal. And yet *death* is rarely mentioned directly, though there's a reference in that same poem about the master and disciple by Khusraw. *Since he made me drink from the water of life, death has become quite insignificant to me.*"

"What's 'the water of life'?"

"It's a metaphor. It features in Sufi poetry too, and usually refers to the wellspring of esoteric knowledge – esoteric in the sense of being for initiates only. Or it could refer to an Imam who holds the knowledge, or to Ali himself, the Prophet's son-in-law and the spiritual leader of all Shi'a sects. Al-Khidr is often a kind of intermediary associated with such quotes."

"The green one?" ventured Abigail hesitantly.

"In literal translation, yes. He's the personification of esoteric inspiration, probably adapted from a pre-Islamic figure."

"Well it's certainly powerful water, if it makes death insignificant."

"Esoteric knowledge is a precious treasure, life itself to the Ismailis of old. Khusraw wrote that *the esoteric is like pearls for people who are wise.* Whereas ordinary wisdom is just brackish water."

It seemed as if they'd reached a dead end, or at least were wandering off the point, but Abigail was too polite to interrupt Walid.

"Some interpret the water of life theme more literally. The Baha'is say something like… the water of life flows from the pen of the Exalted, and the water of death flows from the pen of Satan, one drop of which is poison. Oh people, do not mistake the waters of life and death."

"Who on Earth are the *Baha'is*?"

"A splinter group of a splinter group of Twelver Shi'ites, formed only about 150 years ago. I came across a still more literal interpretation quite recently. Coincidentally it may be a fantasy from the last mad days of Alamut, but…"

Walid stopped abruptly. Abigail hoped her impatience wasn't showing.

"I'm sorry, I'm rambling. A habit of age."

She smiled warmly. "There's always something to learn from your ramblings. I ought to record them!"

"If only we knew what was written immediately before the word *death*."

He suddenly frowned, then looked really quite worried. Maybe he wasn't used to scholarly defeat.

"Time for tea?" suggested Abigail.

"Oh yes. Earl Grey the English way, with cake!"

They rose. Walid rubbed his hands on his long robes, as though wiping off something unclean. Maybe he was phobic about cleanliness, something she hadn't noticed before.

"I'll work on this, Abigail. There's a visitor with us here at the moment who may be able to help, a professor. He's giving some lectures over at Harvard too. I'll try to introduce you."

She squeezed his arm. "Thanks. I always seem to be in your debt."

She knew there'd be no more talk of Ismailis or poetry. Walid liked to process things in background mode. He'd come up with something, hopefully sooner rather than later. Meanwhile there was plenty to catch up on. Eagle's nest, eagle teacher…

Cairo, the Fatimid Caliphate: May, 1155

In a courtyard drenched with the scent of orange blossom, a cool glass of sherbet by his side to refresh his spirit, Hakim reread pages from a Greek manuscript, the *History of the Wars*, which he'd paid an Alexandrian living in Cairo to translate scrupulously into Arabic. Doctoring for rich Cairo clients since he graduated had provided Hakim with a healthy income, most of which he saved to finance his visions. In a year all would be ready for him to depart in company with Sadiq, whereupon he must swap such luxuries as sherbet for hardship, perhaps forever.

The almost forgotten conflicts which the *History* recorded had been fought six centuries earlier in Persia, Africa, and Italy, during the reigns of the Christian emperors of Byzantium, Justinus and Justinian. Its author was a Palestinian Greek named Procopius.

The old wars in themselves were of no interest to Hakim. All that mattered were the dozen or so sheets he held in his hands, along with the distilled *idea* of war itself.

The pages described a terrible plague that had almost annihilated the whole human race. Procopius claimed that this plague started among Egyptians living in Pelusium at the easternmost mouth of the Nile delta, and then spread westward throughout Egypt and also north-easterly through Palestine. The affliction had travelled remorselessly onward like a voracious fire, burning a vast forest of a myriad people in many lands and reducing those to a barren landscape of fallen corpses. Plague always began at the coast, wrote Procopius, and moved inland.

Surely this flesh-eating sickness couldn't appear from out of thin air or, as many writers believed, spontaneously due to foul air. Nor could the fire of plague hide unnoticed for decades in such a populated city as Pelusium. Pestilence must arrive like an unwanted traveller from elsewhere more remote and isolated, yet with which nevertheless there was some trade – somewhere where its fire could smoulder unseen, until it put forth a malignant tongue.

Hakim had consulted many sources and wracked his brains. To one Arabic author, the fact that the river Nile reached the Middle Sea at Pelusium was a clue. Surely the plague had arrived from higher up the Nile, which brought goods to Egypt from as far away as the dripping jungles in the heart of Africa. Paradoxically, this fatal fire must have come to Pelusium by way of fire's contrary, water. In other words, the tongue of plague must have hidden itself in a boat.

Although enormous loads could be carried by the great river, travel was still sedate, taking many weeks from the higher reaches. And never forget about the foaming cataracts of the upper Nile, which must be circumvented by the tedious process of unloading and reloading boats! So if the forked tongue that licked lethally at Pelusium had indeed come by way of the Nile, then plague must *already* have been raging in Upper Egypt, which wasn't the case.

Yet the remoter wilds of Africa might hide this terror, and the boat theory explained so much.

Perhaps plague came by the swifter route of the Red Sea to the narrow gulf between Egypt and the Sinai, so finally overland by caravan to Pelusium. At the time of the Plague of Justinian, it was the empire of Axum that controlled the trade routes of the Red Sea. Axum was now a forgotten power, but had once ranked along with Persia, Rome, and China as one of the four great kingdoms of the world, exporting gold and grain, rhino horns, monkeys and animal skins, ivory and frankincense. Only the rise of Islam and the subsequent whirlwind of Arab victories had wrested control of those trade routes which started from...

Ethiopia!

Recessed rills of water cooled the courtyard, bubbling from white marble sources that reminded Hakim momentarily of breasts, liquid overflowing forever from the nipples. He thrust that random thought brusquely aside, purged by the fire of his duty, to God.

His great task drew him irresistibly, yet laid a great burden of responsibility and even fear upon him too. Deeply he inhaled the scent of orange blossom, to fix it indelibly in his memory. What strange jungly smells might assault his nostrils before too long, what strange sights assail his eyes?

Radcliffe Institute for Advanced Study, Cambridge, Massachusetts: April 2008

Back at her desk after visiting Walid, Abigail was keen to get started. But Terry's photograph stared hard at her, inducing serious guilt. She hadn't spoken to him in four days, despite his messages, and couldn't really put it off again. With a resigned sigh, she reached for the phone.

Just as her fingers touched, it rang.

Damn! She muttered. If that's him, I'll have to be even more apologetic.

"Hello Abigail. It's Jack, Jack Turner."

Caught by surprise, Abigail struggled to switch her psychological context from Terry to the ICEman snooper.

"Dr. Leclaire," she managed, acidly.

"Yeah. Okay. I followed your tip, about an Imam."

Why did she have to talk to this man? Why was the government suspicious of anything and everything Islamic? Why couldn't she just live her life without burden or interference?

Anger erupted from Abigail. "Did you have me followed?" she yelled.

"What? What are you talking about?" He sounded shocked, even worried.

Abigail's anger collapsed as quickly as it had flared up. She felt cold, and at a loss.

"Oh, I thought…"

"Why would I do that? Maybe someone at the office got over-zealous. It's unlikely, but I'll check."

"What tip did you say?"

"About the *teacher of many lessons* being an Imam maybe. Not much luck with anyone modern so far, but it's easy enough to find a historic connection. Have you heard of the *Assassins of Alamut?*"

Damn! He was right on her tail. How could she explain that she was only just aware of a link herself? Would he believe her?

"Dr. Leclaire? Have you heard of them?"

"Yes… yes I have. But…"

He talked over her. "Did you know that their fortress at Alamut, the base of an Imam, was known as *the eagle's nest?*"

Even though she should focus on getting control of this call, her brain raced. The link between Alamut and Safiyya couldn't be a direct one. The fortress was in ruins when Safiyya was writing, not to mention Safiyya was more than three thousand miles away in anti-Ismaili Granada. But where had the Ismaili Imamate passed to? And where had Sinan al-Din come from?

Safiyya's Ismaili lover and a man of rank; what knowledge for initiates might he have shared with his poetisa, which maybe she used to build the poem, *knowledge that could be retrievable*? Puzzles abounded and maybe Sinan al-Din was a key, yet this was purely a *medieval* matter, not a modern one. It should not interest ICE! No doubt the word *assassin* had over-excited them.

"Are you there, Dr. Leclaire?"

She was flustered. Her throat was dry.

Why did Jack Turner make her feel guilty? Why did Terry make her feel guilty?

"No, I mean yes."

"Yes you're there? Or yes to the eagle's nest? Why do I get the feeling that you're hiding something?"

"Look, this is absurd. Alamut was twelfth and thirteenth century for God's sake. It's all just medieval history!"

"Then I need a history lesson. We should meet."

"Why should we?"

"Do you intend to obstruct my investigation?"

"No... No of course not."

"Well then, this evening."

Panic ran unchecked through Abigail's veins.

"No... No, I'm busy. Make it next week, Monday."

"Okay Dr. Leclaire, I'll be there Monday morning."

"No, not here," she practically squealed. She didn't want him in her office, in her space. "We could have lunch," she suggested, with as much warmth as she could muster. "At Totally Thai."

"Where?"

"On Walden, one P.M."

"It's a date," answered Jack smoothly. He rang off.

"Shit!" She banged her fist on the desk. "*Shit!*"

It was a couple of minutes before her mind stopped reeling. When it did, she turned Terry's photo over so that he wouldn't watch her. She simply *couldn't* wait for more from Walid. It was *paramount* to stay ahead of Jack, so she needed a short-cut, preferably at least a couple of hard facts. A blunt attack was called for, to uncover anything that might help, however unlikely that seemed and however long it took!

She put her phone on hold, then tapped furiously at her keyboard, connecting to the private Harvard libraries and CMES archives, plus the public web too. She kicked off half a dozen searches centred on Sinan al-Din ibn Nasir, using all acceptable variants and including various tags to filter the inevitable high hit-rates. It was a pretty common name structure.

Then she leapt up and got the coffee machine going, fuel for a long session. She opened some boxes of books at the back of her office, which she'd never got around to unpacking, and scooped out volumes until they littered the floor, searching for half-remembered works that contained references to the Ismailis and Alamut.

Much of the time she cursed herself under her breath, ignoring her old tutor's advice. If she'd researched this poem and its sources properly in the first place, she could have trotted out innocent medieval reality to Immigration and Customs Enforcement, then no doubt never seen them again. She brought up an image of the original fragment on her second screen, to remind herself of the target.

The best image was in infra-red, though they'd tried UV and powerful back-lighting too. The linen-paper was in a pretty bad state, especially near the ragged edges at the top. The dim marks of six more words slid partly into the tear, tantalising yet not discernible, although the fourth might be the single letter 'e', signifying 'and'.

Hours passed. High on caffeine, she growled at cleaners and colleagues alike who dared to put their head around the door. Later still, she lost all track of time. She felt low now, and chill too in the empty building. The screen was starting to swim before her eyes.

Then something curious made her alert. It was in Provençal; she'd only absorbed names and the general gist. Now she reread again, much more carefully, scribbling down a translation as she scanned the lines.

...and so Sinaldin and Guy de Dieulefit journeyed long together from Jerusalem, renewing it is said the friendship of their grandfathers. Yet Sinaldin was sorely wounded in a quarrel with a Saljuq, enemies of his kind in Syria and Persia. Wherewith Guy gave succour, and raised Sinaldin slowly back to life. The two parted in Maselha (i.e. modern Marseilles, she glossed*), though the Arab begged Guy to journey onward, being strangely afraid that the eastern plague would descend upon such a busy area of trade and shipping. In this his fear was soon proved true, yet Guy was called back to our Order here and knew full well his duty. Whereupon Sinaldin, bound for the diminished realm of Granada, bade him farewell and gave to him a great gift. Yet this gift was not of land or gold or other such substance of wealth of this earth, but of most precious Holy Water, which had the most miraculous power. So came Guy de Dieulefit back home, bringing news of the Holy Land and many messages of import from our brethren on the isle of Rhodes.*

She knew of Dieulefit, a town in Provence. What bell did it ring? And what *was* this document?

She flicked to the top and discovered that she was looking at the administrative records for a village called Montlume, digitised only months ago. The item was dated 1350 AD, but seemed to be confirming details of land transfers actually made two and three years before that. Montlume was quite close to Dieulefit, so Guy was indeed coming home. It was very fortunate for historians and researchers that scribes often got bored, adding gossip on the side. How had her frantic efforts managed to pull up this particular text?

She backed up a page, and realised that her last search of the *Medieval French Land Records (Provence, Orange and Burgundy)*, a long shot indeed, was mistyped. Her tired fingers had skipped two characters; she'd entered 'Sina l-din'. The search engine had no doubt tried with and without the dash and the space characters, so *Sinaldin* was valid.

And why not? Given that the great philosopher Abu Nasr Muhammad al Farabi was known in the medieval West as Alfarabius, then surely Sinan al-Din ibn Nasir could be *Sinaldin*. And the dates *were* contemporary with Safiyya, albeit at the later part of her life.

Then it hit her, with a shock so sudden that she physically jumped. She gasped out loud, still barely able to comprehend what her instinct had divined. *Our Order*. She remembered clearly now: Dieulefit was unusual in being ruled jointly for centuries, half of the administration being provided by the Knights Hospitaller!

Guy de Dieulefit was a Hospitaller, and he'd come home to his Order in Provence. Sinan al-Din had travelled with him to modern Marseilles before going on to Granada where his lover waited, the poetisa Safiyya bint Yusuf al-Ballisiyya. There was a bond between the Ismaili and the Christian knight. *And so the two sheets of paper she'd found in the chapbook must be linked!*

What exactly had that note said? With shaky fingers she eventually brought up an image of the plague document, then focused down upon the Provençal scrawl at the bottom.

Hospitaller

Have Pity

She'd lay a hundred to one that this Hospitaller was Guy. And both he and Safiyya were bound to the Ismaili man of rank, Sinan al-Din ibn Nasir, *Sinaldin*.

She leaned back, trying to still her mind and think carefully. Having ignored her watch for hours, she now checked it. 2.23 am.

Did the chapbook once belong to Guy himself? Why keep those two pieces of paper together? The poem of his friend's lover, and an account of plague scribbled with a direct plea. At least *someone* had kept them together, someone aware of the relationships involved.

She checked dates. The plague mentioned in Montlume's records was the first great wave of the Black Death to strike Europe, reaching Marseille in 1347 AD. Was the poem about plague? ...*death / swells and overflows*: swells within the victims and overflows the land? Had Safiyya given literary expression to *the* major disaster of her era? If so, was esoteric Ismaili wisdom irrelevant? Yet why would the Imam be so central?

Disciplined by many years in academia, Abigail put speculation firmly aside. Information had to come first; figuring it out came second. Having got her teeth upon a thread, she wasn't going to let go until she'd pulled it all the way. Recharging with more coffee, she launched back into information space.

The thread of Sinaldin and Guy pulled and pulled, unravelling the tapestry of history to reveal complex subplots.

Guy's father had been a knight of the Templars, transferring to the Hospitallers when the Templars were forcibly disbanded, around 1312 AD. Guy's grandfather was a Templar too, very high in the Order, a Grand Prior. So if Sinaldin and Guy were *renewing the friendship of their grandfathers*, why on Earth had a Grand Prior from Christianity's leading military monastic order been consorting with a Muslim? And why had their offspring continued the relationship?

She drew a blank on Sinaldin's family and history. However, she had clues. He was Ismaili, a man of rank, and his enemy was *a Saljuq*, no doubt a Seljuk Turk. Plus, she now knew he probably came from Syria or Persia, or had connections there.

Soon she discovered that the Nizari Ismailis, a secretive medieval sect, had created a network of well-defended fortresses throughout Syria and northern Persia. Regarded as heretics by most Sunni Muslims and probably by some Shi'a too, the Nizaris had many enemies, though their traditional foes were Seljuk Turks.

Shit! This was bad, for it would pique Jack's interest. The Nizaris' chief castle was at Alamut, none other than the *eagle's nest* Jack had already picked up on, the place from which the sect and its leader had gained their lurid title, *the Assassins of Alamut*. From the early twelfth century, the Imams there had claimed leadership over all Ismailis.

Alamut was overrun by the Mongol hordes in 1256 AD, long before Safiyya wrote her poem. Though Nizari fortresses further west survived longer, most historians considered this period the end for the Assassins. Yet it didn't take much digging to find newer research, theorising an extended or even permanent survival of the murderous sect.

If so, it seemed plausible that Sinaldin's family had occupied positions 'of rank' in the Nizari hierarchy. As a youth, his grandfather may even have been at Alamut and seen the Imam there, shortly before the Mongol conquests. Alas, it looked as though Jack's superficial connection via the word *eagle* could be confirmed by real evidence, even if circumstantial at the moment.

"Damn him!" Abigail muttered to the chill air of her office. "He'll think he's on to something." It wasn't right she should be racing a secretly racist cop to the resolution of medieval puzzles and poetic meaning. The security services had gone mad. The American government had gone mad!

She ignored fatigue and furiously opened more search windows, in the process opening a Pandora's Box of shocking historical happenings.

Though the Templars and the Assassins apparently alternated between conflict and truce, Abigail smelled a strange reek of complicity about their relationship. Various modern scholars pointed out a close alignment between their hierarchies and rituals, even their robes; white with a red cross for the Templars, and white with red trim for the Assassins.

Other writers claimed that these similarities were superficial, yet both organisations rode roughshod over the proclaimed belief-systems of their respective religions. Both too cherished mystical secrets often bundled up in the name Gnosticism; and seemingly that's what eventually sealed the fate of the Templars.

Jealous of the Templars' hundreds of castles, their 35,000 utterly loyal brethren, their seaports, fleet, hospitals and secret drugs, plus their vast banking system, Phillip the Fair of France and Pope Clement V combined forces to bring the Order down. They arrested 15,000 on a single day. Under torture, some confessed to trampling and spitting on the cross during initiation ceremonies, as well as other un-Christian acts and doctrines including a denial of Christ.

A few of the elite, knights and priors and the Grand Master himself, Jacques de Molay, were burnt at the stake. Over a period of five years or so, thousands of Templars were gruesomely interrogated. Most were just sergeants or lay brethren, not privy to the inner rituals. The soles of their feet were burned off, or lead weights placed on their chests until they were slowly crushed. Some had their teeth ripped out and steel needles jammed into the raw nerves, or were gradually filled with water via a funnel until they suffocated.

A scattering of Templar knights from Castille and Provence were so horrified that they fled to Islamic Granada in southern Spain, *the home of Safiyya*, where they became Muslims. An interesting insight into Templar mentality, mused Abigail, considering that Muslims were supposed to be mortal enemies of the warrior monks!

King Phillip couldn't be seen to take everything. A good portion of Templar property was officially made over to the Hospitallers, and some knights discreetly transferred to that Order. Apparently Guy's father had been clever enough or lucky enough to manage this, and so avoided persecution.

The loyalty of the Nizaris to mainstream religious practice was even more questionable than that of the Templars. Most of their assassinations were carried out against other Muslims. Abigail was shocked to find that at one time they even offered to turn Christian and ally permanently with Crusader forces in the Holy Lands. On several occasions they'd fought alongside Frankish armies against the Saracens.

The proposed alliance never got off the ground. Had it done so, the Nizaris would probably have interpreted Christian beliefs as idiosyncratically as they did those of Islam. For the Nizaris considered the Sunni Saracens and most other Muslims as no nearer to religious truth than the Christians; effectively infidels. Only their own mystical doctrines counted, their own relationship with God.

And what about the 2,000 Bezels a year paid by Syrian Nizaris to the Templars for about twenty years in the late twelfth century? A tidy sum! Some said a tribute; some said a *subsidy* from the greater organisation to the lesser; some said payment for services rendered.

Abigail sighed and tried to stretch the stiffness out of her shoulders. What a fascinating maze of impiety, power, and military sectarianism. Though what relevance had any of this to the papers in the chapbook?

At the very least it seemed that the families of Guy and Sinaldin had a long association of some kind. Even before Guy saved Sinaldin's life, probably there was great trust between the two men. Might both be steeped in the secrets of their respective traditions, the Templars and the Assassins? Might their families have been part of an alliance of survival for these theoretically terminated organisations? Might they share arcane beliefs that transcended both Christianity and Islam? Was there Gnosticism in the poem? If only she had the rest of it!

Abigail felt that the strangeness of the early hours was leading her into fantasy. Yet her oft-proven instinct for hidden truths burned bright. There was *something* here!

Maybe the Holy Water was part of a Gnostic ritual. Surely there was more to the gift than revealed by Montlume's scribe. Ordinary folk would be fooled by 'miraculous' holy water, but well-travelled men of lordly rank, returning from the Holy Lands? Maybe there was some special symbolism in this Water.

Abigail refocused on the screen and forced her weary brain to digest more.

Through sustained contact with the Assassins, the Templars absorbed Ismaili philosophies, acting as a conduit to inject these into Europe. Individual Templars, who escaped the destruction of their Order, covertly continued to teach the Gnostic-Ismaili doctrines and mystical techniques they had acquired and augmented in the Holy Lands; the true secrets of the once powerful knights of the Temple. Like fungi in the dark of a forest floor, these teachings flourished beneath the canopy of Christianity, gradually giving rise to the occult arts in Europe...

There were diagrams of eight-pointed stars, a crescent and Byzantine cross combined, other strange symbols. Abigail flicked to another window and read of Hasan II announcing the spiritual Resurrection at Alamut. As Walid had mentioned, Shari'ah law was annulled, replaced by feasting during Ramadan and the abandonment of sexual restrictions. She moved on to tales of Assassin initiates, high on hashish, being shown the Garden of Paradise...

As though she'd taken hashish herself, visions began to occupy the screen: pentangles and swords and cups of blood, white-robed Arabs and Europeans deep in ritual, tortured men with ragged mouths and silent screams, the plunging arc of the assassin's knife, plague sweeping through populations like a blight through wheat, Holy Water sparkling in a vial.

Her head slammed onto the keyboard and woke her. It was 5.26am. God, she must get back to her flat!

Cronkite Graduate Center, Cambridge, Massachusetts: April 2008

The phone rudely pushed Abigail into wakefulness. Sweating and confused, she grabbed the intruding device.

"Hello?"

"Hell, at last!"

"Oh, hello."

"Well there's no need to sound so disappointed!"

"Sorry. I'm not disappointed, just tired. I worked late last night. Research stuff."

"Hey, I miss you, Bee, and you didn't return my calls!"

Guilt flushed Abigail's face. It was a good job he couldn't see her. It seemed her most commonly used word to him these days was *sorry*.

"Sorry, my mobile's playing up again. Doesn't always charge properly." This was true, but not the whole truth. "And I never know when you're sleeping or at college during the day. I wish you'd give up that bar job, or at least work someplace that actually closes before morning!" *Unlike, say, her office?*

But this was an old bone of contention between them. Terry had started working in bars before they'd met, to support his tardy and protracted bid for a college degree. The hours didn't clash with lectures. But the nearer he got to those qualifications he supposedly needed, the less progress he actually seemed to make. Further requirements would mysteriously appear. After a trek of many years through business studies, computer engineering, even philosophy, Abigail realised Terry was never going to finish. The truth was that he loved pleasing people, loved charming them. And as long as it was inside a swanky hotel or club, or maybe a fashionable downtown restaurant, he absolutely loved working in bars.

"It's good money," replied Terry defensively. "You could've emailed from work or something, I was worried about you."

"Sorry." *Damn.* "I'm on to something new with Safiyya al-Ballisiyya. You know how I am, I've got to unravel it." She admitted this much, but decided it wasn't wise to mention about Jack Turner and the ICE interest. Terry would leap to her defence of course, but he'd be hugely angry too and would probably ring everyone from the local police to the president. That was a complication she didn't need.

"I *do* know how you are. Obsessed!"

His voice was light though. She thought she'd got away with it. But then…

"Is that all, Bee? You *are* telling me everything?"

She knew that low tone well, the one that descended almost into a growl. It was the surfacing of Terry's jealousy.

"Yes," she answered, swiftly and flatly. It was liaisons with imagined lovers he was probing for, not arrangements to meet government agents with imagined plots, which stretched fantastically back into medieval history and poetic literature.

"Jesus! You're seeing someone, aren't you?"

"Terry. Don't be ludicrous. I don't do affairs. I have one lover, and it's you, and I'll see you tonight. Sean's got your shift, right?"

"Right." Diminished, but not puppy-dog.

"Okay. Later."

She hung up.

It was 10.37 am. She'd only got to bed around 6.30 am. She flopped back down onto her pillow, and wondered why life was so difficult sometimes.

Southern Ethiopia: October 1156

The Priest-Witch's name was Arwe, and he was reputed to be a hundred years old. From Yaqob, their interpreter between Arabic and Oromifa, the common local language, Hakim and Sadiq learned that Arwe took his name from a potent 'serpent king' of ancient times, who was killed by an ancestor of Bilqis, the Queen of Sheba. Arwe was both famous and feared in this rain-forested region of southern Ethiopia, a vast land of great contrasts. Indeed, once Yaqob had grasped that Hakim's mission was to discover any traditions concerned with pestilence, their guide-interpreter fell into a strange mood, brooding overnight. Only the next day did he finally recommend a long journey to consult the redoubtable Arwe, though for an increased payment due to risk. Yet Yaqob's modest greed had reassured Hakim, rather than irritating him.

So eventually Yaqob had brought Hakim and Sadiq and their three slave porters to a distant village of tall straw huts surrounded by banana groves, close to a sluggish river where crocodiles basked. At first sight a rather backward village, although extensive and visibly armed with spears and bows.

And at first sight the famed Priest-Witch seemed decrepit, as one might reasonably expect if he were truly so ancient. Bald but for a few white hairs, Arwe's face was rutted with wrinkles. His limbs looked like knotty sinew dried in the sun and wrapped around bones, as though, with potions and conjurations and purifying encounters with spirits that only he could see, he had slowly mummified himself alive. His only finery was a belt of bright beads over a whitish sleeveless robe, which appeared on him more like the shroud for a victim of starvation. Yet his dark, piercing eyes!

Hakim presented a fine brass tray as a gift, uncertain whether the value was too high. Or maybe too low?

Hospitality proved to be the boiled meat of some forest creature, steeped in a sauce made from fiery hot peppers and pungent onions. This stew was poured onto the brass tray itself to be shared, each man scooping with torn pieces of a red and spicy pancake-shaped sourbread. Was the tray used out of politeness, or as a rebuke? Was the burning of one's mouth by the sauce a culinary treat or a trial by ordeal? Or maybe a way of making the meat safer to eat? Hakim perspired; he certainly felt it as a trial!

There followed interminable chewing of bitter green leaves, apparently to enliven the mind.

Arwe listened intently rather than responding, head cocked, as beady-eyed as a parrot who seemed determined to memorise the words of these strangers from afar. Hakim spoke with a customary passion he suspected

Yaqob couldn't or didn't convey in translation, though both speakers were hampered by the cud in their mouths.

From time to time, Arwe asked questions of Sadiq, as though addressing these directly to Hakim might allow Hakim's responses to cast some influence over him, perhaps letting his principal visitor achieve too much presence. Was this a form of respect, or was it insulting?

Sadiq described himself as a colleague and close friend of Hakim, though his tone suggested that *disciple* was closer to the truth. Only by exposing his apocalyptic vision to Sadiq, by adding fuel to existing religious fervour, had Hakim acquired a necessary and dedicated companion for this scientific venture.

As the afternoon wore on, Arwe's questioning of Sadiq about what Arab doctors did to heal their sick intensified; and sometimes the ancient man grinned toothlessly in a superior way. With a great effort of will, Hakim remained composed, yet it seemed hours before Arwe deigned to react directly, fully acknowledging him.

Translated by Yaqob, Arwe said enigmatically, "Spirits from the other world live in monkeys. Let us go to the house of the monkeys and listen to their cries."

Hakim was taken aback, mentally groping for a connection. Would he need to repeat what he had already said all over again, *to monkeys*?

Arwe uttered an order. Within a minute, strong young men brought a carved throne of black wood to his door, portable on thick bamboo poles, to which Arwe hobbled. Although he moved awkwardly, his gait seemed more spry than enfeebled.

They wended past a dozen huts until they came to a great bamboo cage where monkeys at once commenced an outcry, then fell strangely silent. The animals had thick brownish fur, though on some it was as if ochre or crushed nettles were rubbed in. Strangely man-like hands and feet were black-skinned, the faces too, these adorned by white brows and wispy white beards. The males sported blue scrotal sacs and red penises. Access for food, without risk of the confined monkeys escaping, was a bamboo door opening into a much smaller inner cage, itself equipped with a door. A big clay bowl held water. Hakim couldn't see much excrement, so dung must be raked out regularly. A villager armed with a spear stood guard.

Arwe addressed the monkeys in his local language, which Yaqob couldn't translate.

Next, the old man seemed to go into a trance, his eyelids fluttering.

Several monkeys rushed to the bars, baring teeth, then crying out raucously. One chattering male masturbated, jerking semen from itself.

Presently Arwe returned to himself and spoke, evidently in Oromifa, for Yaqob translated: "Our Gods permit you to stay."

Southern Ethiopia: May 1157

One morning, the Priest-Witch and his visitors were talking over coffee. The brass pot and glass cups they used were another gift from Hakim to the old man. Two further pots of local manufacture had also been filled. Hakim was glad Arwe had chosen coffee to enliven their minds and not the bitter green leaves, for one of his molars had developed a nagging twinge that was made worse by prolonged chewing.

Sitting cross-legged with them and twitching his feet, was Guba, a man perhaps in his forties, Arwe's assistant and already appointed as his future successor. Guba's eyes bulged as though magnified by curved glass. Obviously a defect in the glands at the base of his neck was responsible, and a good cure was to eat seaweeds, unavailable here. Hakim had in his baggage a bottle of the stinging violet liquid produced from seaweed, which he used to stop wounds from festering. Diluted down, this would control Guba's condition, but Arwe had brusquely rejected Hakim's offer of treatment. Those protruding orbs of eyes made Guba appear... visionary, a quality which evidently Arwe wished for in his successor. Restless activity was also associated with the complaint. Maybe before Arwe died, the Priest-Witch would confide to his heir which plants from what soils could lessen the symptoms. Or perhaps Guba already knew, yet preferred to appear urgently perceptive.

By now Hakim had seen Arwe banish malarial fever from a woman, by using a potion and incantations. She soon stopped shaking and sweating and claimed that her pounding headache had vanished. With a poultice and more of his spells, he cured a wounded foot that had looked gangrenous. While Hakim thought the rituals of magic might provide a mental benefit for patients who were certain of the shaman's spiritual powers, he nevertheless fully acknowledged the impressive range and depth of Arwe's understanding of the body and of natural remedies.

In a cautious exchange of knowledge with Hakim, Arwe had begun to confide some explanations of his spirit-inspired choices. All the while, Hakim had to bear in mind the Priest-Witch's certainty that spirits resided in animals, in plants, even in rocks, a belief very different from the Qu'ran's declarations that *jinn* were created from smokeless fire and inhabited an immaterial world. As often as Hakim deemed diplomatic, he would mention plague and its signs and its possible sources.

The coffee was less than half drunk when a runner came to Arwe's door and jabbered.

Having heard the man's gasped words, Arwe went into a semi-trance while he took the messenger's head in his hands, and licked delicately at his face like a snake, and sniffed him, and chanted for a long while, his eyes rolling up whitely. Then he issued orders.

The black throne on its bamboo poles was brought.

"What interests you," Yaqob translated, "has come to… it's the name of a village half a day's travel from here, I think. You'll see what you most wish, *if* you dare."

"Surely the old man means plague!" exclaimed Sadiq. "Allah is great to let us witness this so soon. It might have taken years. And surely He will protect you and me, otherwise He would not offer this example so willingly, that we may probe and seek understanding."

Hakim nodded, yet thought to himself: *If it is His will, Allah shall indeed safeguard me because of my mission. But you too, good Sadiq? Not inevitably.*

A big woven basket containing bread hung from the back of Arwe's throne as his four porters bore him from the village, accompanied by Hakim, Sadiq, and Yaqob. Spears and bows lay alongside the throne on either side, in case the porters suddenly needed to set down their burden and become warriors. A couple of other armed villagers paced alongside, also one of the Arabs' slaves, burdened with gourds of water stoppered with leaves. Men clutching bows were now guarding the approach to the village with much more vigilance than Hakim had previously seen. There'd been a lull for many months in sporadic hostilities with a community an hour away to the west; evidently the runner's news from the south had caused Arwe to alert the sentries.

The Priest-Witch chuckled dryly, for he had noticed Hakim noticing.

By way of Yaqob: "From today if a stranger approaches, even if he appears full of health, the guards will shout once, *Go away!* If the stranger ignores this, then they will kill him with arrows and leave his body where it lies for a moon and a week."

Hakim's heart leapt within his chest. At last! Arwe was displaying rare knowledge on the subject of plague. The Priest-Witch understood the period between plague putting its seed into a person, and the harvest of that seed suddenly flaring up! Typically, Arwe had refrained from saying this directly but only dropped a hint, no doubt to see whether Hakim would beg for clarification. At times the old man could be so miserly with information! Well, hard-won wisdom was after all Arwe's source of power. Yet occasionally he would offer a surprise nugget of knowledge, as if perhaps he wished to spin out his visitors' stay for his own stimulation. *What more did the Priest-Witch know about plague?* Possibly much more than Hakim had gleaned from the libraries of the civilised world!

"Guba isn't with us," commented Sadiq. "We say that it's foolish to carry both eggs in the same hand." Which Yaqob translated.

"I shall never die from plague," declared Arwe, "even though my death is surely due."

Considering Arwe's greatly advanced years, in fact overdue, Hakim reluctantly admitted this. *Allah, preserve this useful pagan a while longer!*

"Nor will my successor ever die from plague!"

How could he be so sure? But Hakim believed the Priest-Witch, ecstatically sensing great knowledge and power nearly within his own grasp.

Hakim beheld the aftermath of a hell-on-Earth. The survivors, if any there were, must have fled into the forest.

Red-mouthed hyenas were feeding on scores of corpses sprawled higgledy-piggledy among deserted huts; corpses that even from a distance looked ugly and suppurating, and seemed to have been tossed hither and thither as though by demons who had also foully tormented them. Beside this scene even the massacres of war might seem clean, almost merciful yet also, Hakim knew, far less effective. Carrion birds hopped about, vile scraps hanging from their beaks.

Jabbering, Arwe's bearers' set him down, their limbs trembling not from the extended exertion of the journey, but in abject fright.

The Arabs' slave moaned in terror, and Yaqob shuddered. "I not go more," he said, grammar driven from his mind.

Arwe seemed unconcerned. Toting a bag, he rose from his black seat and directed an abrupt order at Hakim.

"Yaqob!" snapped Hakim. "Translate!"

"He said, *support me.*"

Arwe had darted glances at Hakim and at the others, yet he was cocking his head towards the yapping of hyenas rather than staring directly at the terrible spectacle. It occurred to Hakim then that the old man's piercing eyes must actually be quite short-sighted. If so, the horrors that Hakim saw clearly must still be quite blurred for the Priest-Witch. Maybe the spirit-world was easier to see, or to imagine, in a luminous blur!

Aware of the precaution he should take, Hakim tied a fabric mask in place over his mouth and nose, then duly clutched the wizened Priest-Witch under one armpit, easily taking his pathetic weight as Arwe set one bare foot before the other. More brusque words in Oromifa. Yaqob's tremulous voice. "Come to feast your eyes! *Come!*"

And to feast Arwe's eyes too, once he was close enough to focus.

Hakim realised that he wasn't propelling the Priest-Witch so much as being dragged forward against his will. With a prayer, Hakim advanced, breathing deeply to calm himself and quell his fears. Such would be the scene if his quest succeeded, he reminded himself, yet vastly multiplied in many lands. God's enemies would be felled by God's own instrument.

Let it be!

"Stay where you are, Sadiq," Hakim called out behind him, serene now as they drew closer, becoming coolly observant...

His professional eye picked out angry red spots and black sores, festering boils and slimy pustules, swellings, limbs twisted askew, liquefied guts and unidentifiable deliquescing organs seeping through hyena-torn bellies. The festering vomit wasn't merely dark with flies, but blackened. The smell was fouler than the contents of any diseased and shit-filled bowel, yet laced too with a nauseating sweetness.

Arwe hissed like a cat at hyenas that bared their yellow teeth, and he gestured splay-fingered, hypnotically, until the animals whined and reluctantly withdrew to worry at more distant corpses. Some way off, Hakim spied a pile of charred branches, the remains of what must have been a big bonfire. Probably evidence of fearful villagers burning the earliest kin to fall victim, before the situation became uncontrollable.

Evidently unafraid, Arwe hobbled among the dead bodies, pointing at ghastly signs they'd discussed before and uttering single words, some of which Hakim knew by now. Then the Priest-Witch stopped by the ruined corpse of a young man, jerking a knobbed finger demandingly at the sharp knife Hakim always wore. Hakim handed over the blade, after which Arwe mimed being helped to kneel. Hakim complied, then was gestured back a pace or two. Oh yes, in case pressure of gas in the body caused foul liquids to spray.

Arwe slit open the abdomen, laid down the knife, then with his bare hands tugged yielding flesh wide. Exerting himself far more than Hakim had believed possible, the old man proceeded to break ribs and wrench them apart. This laid bare what Hakim, stepping closer again and bending, could identify as a livid, bluish heart and lungs that were blotched black. Lower down the corpse and deep within, he scrutinised what must be a liver, yet swollen to twice the usual size. Below this, the gall-bladder leaked thick and fatty black bile. The writhe of pale guts, resembling the dissolving arms and legs of tiny infants, knees and elbows all bent and jumbled together in an obscene stew, bore a thousand black spots as though being consumed by feasting beetles.

Arwe took from his bag a container of bamboo not quite as wide as his wrist, and removed its stopper, a plug of clay. The bamboo, its top rim sharp, looked greased inside. Then the old man thrust this device at the victim's scrotum, twisted to cut, and captured the soft black oyster of a testicle, for what private purpose of witchcraft Hakim had no idea.

This done, Arwe seemed utterly exhausted. Hakim had to practically carry him back to his throne.

And so having seen the unimaginable, they departed, much to the relief of the rest of the party.

An hour later, a fit of coughing shook the old man as he was borne along, Hakim pacing alongside. Finally Arwe spat out a gob of dirty phlegm, and then, breathing hard, he began to gasp words, as though of a sudden mortality haunted him, and he wished in Guba's absence to confide some legacy of wisdom to Hakim.

Yaqob translated. "Plague. From evil spirit. Makes home in monkey."

"Yes?" urged Hakim and Sadiq, almost with one voice.

"Most spirits in monkeys… benign. Some sublime. So we worship. Others naughty. Make mischief, small mischief. A few *very bad*. Often monkey with evil spirit… weeps, so very sad because made to do evil. Weeps and weeps."

Hakim reinforced all this in his memory, hoping soon to make notes, repeating to himself: *plague lives in monkeys, and those monkeys that harbour it often weep.* What did this signify? A few months earlier Hakim might have dismissed this as a fanciful tale. Not now. He was all too aware of Arwe's depth of experience and insight. *Merciful Allah, preserve this old pagan a while more!* Even so, an evil spirit in a monkey…?

At that moment, it was as though a muezzin wailed from a minaret within his mind: *From Ethiopia the empire of Axum exported along the Red Sea gold and grain, rhino horns, and MONKEYS!*

'Totally Thai', Cambridge, Massachusetts: April 2008

The crisp atmosphere and inspiring light of recent days had gone, sealed off from New England by a leaden lid of cloud. Rain streaks chased each other down the windows of Totally Thai, distorting the hurrying humanity of Cambridge into ungainly creatures with poorly applied blotches of colour.

Abigail had arrived early, trying to claim the military high ground. She removed soaking outer layers and hoped the restaurant's warmth would soon evaporate uncomfortable damp patches from the rest of her clothes. A meaty aroma sharpened by exotic herbs awoke her hunger. Jack came in. The downpour had left him unscathed, Abigail noted sourly. He was folding up an enormous golfing umbrella.

He spotted her, coming over and sitting down without a greeting. "Your nose is wet," he then observed with a grin.

Patriarchal crap, thought Abigail, but the approach of a waiter prevented her from spitting out a rude reply.

She ordered a super-spicy green curry because its sweet coconut milk would mislead until the chillies hit hard, and *green* seemed a harmless word compared with *red*. Without even looking at the menu, Jack ordered the same, as she'd hoped.

"Glad you could make it," he offered.

"Did I have a choice?"

"I thought you'd relish the opportunity to instruct on medieval history, and maybe help America too of course. We've always been big buddies with Canada."

Abigail got the message and gave a noncommittal grunt. No doubt he had the power to get her thrown out of the country. She swallowed her pride and bit down on her resentment at narrow-minded government agencies.

"What do you want to know?" she asked, managing a business-like if not actually pleasant tone.

Jack's face crinkled with supercilious amusement.

"Our language folks tell me that *Alamut* derives from the Arabic for *teaching of the eagle*."

"That would figure. An eagle is supposed to have shown Hasan as-Sabah, the first Master of the Assassins, where to build his fortress."

"They also said that the word *assassin* originally meant *those who take hashish*, and these particular ones specialised in high-risk missions to murder political and religious leaders. Apparently they took out the Christian King of Jerusalem in 1192." Jack leaned forward. All trace of humour had left him and his blue eyes seemed cold and accusatory. "Are we facing a bunch of drug-crazed suicidal killers here?"

Abigail felt her jaw drop. She struggled to make it work again but words spluttered at her lips.

"Not unless they're ghosts!" she finally and indignantly got out.

The food arrived quickly.

"You're being ridiculous!" hissed Abigail. "The Mongols…"

"Yeah yeah, I know. The mighty Mongol hordes wiped out Alamut in 1256. And practically everything else in their path too, like army ants."

Jack was relaxed now and his eyes gleamed. His mouth pulled into a boyish curl. She realised with dismay he'd been trying to rattle her. It had worked.

"But it wouldn't be the first time an old tradition had been resurrected and bent to modern aspirations," he casually continued. "What about the Freemasons claiming lineage from the Templars and borrowing their rituals? Anyhow, if that old poem of yours *is* a link to all this, your own research has it as almost a hundred years after Alamut, at least *mid-fourteenth* century."

Normally Abigail would have ordered an accompanying jasmine rice, but she wanted revenge. As she spooned a mouthful of food, her thoughts racing, warmth invaded her cheeks and neck. Jack's stumbling guesses had brought him far too close to territory she'd only explored herself the other night. Could he tell a guilty flush from spice-heat?

He couldn't *possibly* know about Sinaldin and Guy and their grandfathers and knightly Orders and the plague, she told herself. Nor did she want him to know, until she'd sorted out all the connections and implications herself. And there couldn't *possibly* be a modern connection. Yet an image of Trinity church in the Hancock Tower came to mind; hadn't she thought herself about old purpose and old words serving new aims?

Get a grip Abby. It seemed more than likely that ICE might be hoping to justify an increased persecution of Islam by scaring elected officials with horror stories of ancient militant sects rising up from the past. She hid her reaction inside anger, easy enough to do.

"If you have your own *language people* and no doubt *history people* too, why do you need *me*?" she demanded.

"I like a wide range of sources," mumbled Jack through a full mouth. "They rarely agree, hence the cracks through which an investigation might proceed are quickly revealed." He swallowed, then gasped and reached for water. "Hey, this is *hot*. Besides, to be frank, my people lack imagination."

Abigail couldn't resist. "Hell, you more than make up for them. You've got *far* too much. Or maybe it's just paranoia," she added tartly.

Jack glared over the edge of his glass as his Adam's apple bobbed.

Abigail lightened her tone and spoke hurriedly on.

"Well here's one small crack for you. The word *assassin* probably doesn't come from *hashashin*, the literal Arabic for *those who eat hashish. Hashashin* was used as a general term for disreputable people. I guess it was bad to take drugs even then. That survived into modern times as the Egyptian *hashasheen*, meaning riotous or rowdy. I guess the Nizaris' enemies might have used it in that sense. But the sect itself considered they were the *guardians of knowledge*, or perhaps more accurately *guardians of secrets*. The Arabic *assasseen* means 'guardian'. A much closer match, don't you think?"

"You see you're damn useful already! Did the concept of assassins and assassination not exist before this cult, then? Leaving aside bumping off Julius Caesar and such."

"Oh yes. Another earlier Shi'a group were called *the stranglers*, for instance. But the Nizari sect was simply the most systematic and dedicated at exercising this um… method of control. You might say they laid the ground-rules for the assassination industry, and their name became the label for that industry. It crept into European use via Italy's contacts with the Levant. The first well-known association of a wicked killer with the word *assassin* is in Dante's *The Divine Comedy*."

"Wow. Diabolical operators." Jack was sweating and his cheeks were flushed. He was clearly finding the Green Curry out of his culinary league. Uncharitable but satisfying amusement leaked over Abigail's thoughts.

"No worse than many at the time and more since. In the grand competition of history, you might regard the Nizaris as a targeted instrument of surgical precision. By comparison the so-called Holy Inquisition was a blunt tool for torture and extermination used indiscriminately."

Abigail flashed what she hoped was a superior smile. She'd used this example purely to attack Jack's prejudice and remind him that Christianity too had nasty skeletons in the cupboard. She was beginning to enjoy herself, though faintly heard instinct told her this was dangerous.

Jack sucked in more water and pulled out a handkerchief to dab at his neck.

"You called them Nizaris," he wheezed. Clearing his throat, he carried on in more normal tones, though his voice still scraped. "So what precisely does that mean and what secrets were they guarding? And what drove them? What especially drove them to carry out political killings?"

Cooled by damp clothes and well used to Thai spices, Abigail finished a mouthful and gazed at him with perfect composure. Well, she acknowledged, he earned a mark for attentiveness at least.

"You know about the Sunni and Shi'a branches of Islam, I take it?"

"Sure. Been tearing each other apart in Iraq for years."

"The Shi'a only amount to about ten percent of all Muslims." Jack's eyes registered mild surprise, but he wasn't going to admit this and remained silent. "Yet they are themselves split into several divisions," continued Abigail. "These arose from schisms over the succession of the Imamate." She paused, wondering how to compress centuries of religious diversification into just a few sentences.

"I'm all ears," prompted Jack.

"Okay, well there were just twelve lineal Imams after the Prophet Muhammad, the Messenger of God. Twelve divinely inspired guides, descended in the line of the Prophet's blood. The first was Muhammad's son-in-law, Ali. The second and third were Ali's sons by the Prophet's daughter, Fatimah. Most Shi'ites acknowledge all twelve, and also believe the twelfth will return one day – he went into hiding you see, but over a thousand years ago."

"Heck, that's a great act of faith."

"Isn't all religion just an act of blind faith?"

"Acceptance of God is *a certainty*, nothing blind about it! Uh… sorry, carry on."

Abigail briefly wondered whether she'd touched a nerve.

"Anyhow, the bulk of the Shi'ites are called Twelvers for their belief in the full line. A smaller group think this line went wrong after the sixth Imam. They believe the Imamate should have passed through Ismail, the sixth Imam's eldest son, who in fact died before his father but had eligible offspring.

"These dissenters are known as Ismailis or Seveners, since they dispute the seventh Imam and the line thereafter. And because of an earlier dispute over two brothers, another schismatic group are known as Fivers. Are you keeping up?"

Jack was frowning.

"Yeah, but get to the Nizaris, and don't make it so dry."

Abigail shrugged. "You wanted a history lesson… Well, the Twelvers and the Seveners both spawned several sub-groups over the years. The Seveners peaked in the Middle Ages when the Fatimids, an Ismaili dynasty, conquered Egypt and ruled it for about two hundred years. Halfway through, around the end of the tenth century, schism struck again.

"At that date leadership of all the Ismailis went along with the Fatimid throne. Nizar, the rightful heir, was pushed aside by his younger brother and put to death. That was just the excuse Ismailis in Syria and Palestine needed to break away from Egyptian Fatimid control. Their rather inspired leader,

Hasan as-Sabah, he of the *eagle's nest*, claimed that Nizar was merely 'hidden'. Hasan set himself up as the only 'gate' to Nizar, whom his people still followed; hence of course *Nizaris*. Hasan created a power-base among mountain tribes, and propagated a mystical form of Ismaili doctrine that became increasingly divorced from practically any mainstream ideas. Said doctrine was backed by fortresses and tactical acts of political murder. The sect of the Assassins was born. Later Ismailis rewrote history to make Hasan *himself* an Imam, which for their sect means *the* Imam, since there can only be one at a time in direct descent."

"There's more fractures than a piece of ancient pottery," Jack complained.

"There's as many if not more fractures within Christianity. I guess you could say most religions age in a similar way, becoming more brittle. Usually geography or population shift or imbalance in military technology leads to politics that provoke a schism. The amount of pomposity in church becomes the rival flags for Protestants versus Catholics, then Puritans versus Protestants. How silly is that?"

Jack had abandoned almost half of his food and was cooling down, but if anything he looked still more uncomfortable.

"You can only think like that if you don't believe. Different expressions of religion are channels which men try to navigate towards their God. But men are fallible, so may take wrong turns, and the Devil sets up diversions, perhaps even whole routes that are wrong."

Abigail was astonished. Her opinion of Jack, that she thought couldn't possibly get any lower, dropped off the bottom of the scale. An immigration enforcer *and* a religious fundamentalist.

"Let me guess," she ventured. "Your interpretation is the right one. Which church are you?"

Jack didn't look as if he'd heard. His discomfort was gone and his poise was one of carved triumph. His eyes gleamed with an odd mix of determination and desire, reminding her of grooms who stood at the altar.

"God rewards those who seek him truly."

Abigail managed to keep her face straight, but quivered inside. This was scary before. Now it seemed far worse. Fundamentalists didn't adhere to logic. She decided it was best to move on.

"You asked about the Nizari policy of political murders," she stated neutrally. "You have to understand that the sect was stateless, or at most a scattered state – their small territorial islands were strewn over the countries or empires of the time. Each island was impregnable in itself – at least until the military tsunami of the Mongols crashed through – but they couldn't even travel between their islands without considerable armed support. Personal threat aimed at Kings and Caliphs was a way of ensuring that their powerful hosts left them alone. For the threat to work, it had to be *demonstrated* now and again.

"Even Saladin went in constant fear of the Assassins, surrounding himself with loyal guards he personally knew. The Syrian branch of the Nizaris did make a couple of attempts on his life, wounding him once.

"Overall, Nizari power and distribution of resources…"

Abigail abruptly stopped herself. She was about to say, was much like that of the Crusading Orders. Maybe the Templars would have been left alone if they'd threatened to assassinate Phillip the Fair, or the Pope. But she didn't want to lead Jack back to the Templars or indeed to the Hospitallers, not until she'd resolved the puzzles surrounding Guy and his Holy Water and his friendship with Sinaldin.

"Yes?" queried Jack sharply. His eyes tried to enter her.

"Aren't you bored yet?" asked Abigail lamely. "There's nothing for you here!"

"What about the secrets? What were they hiding? This *Gnostic* stuff?"

"Guarding," emphasised Abigail. "Gnosticism is a big subject. The root of the word comes ultimately from the ancient Greek *to know*. Gnostics tend to think they know certain esoteric truths that are crucial to salvation. These are often linked to rejection of materialism, or a rejection of the standard rules and limits binding whichever religion spawned the Gnostic body. The ancient Nizaris completely abandoned Shari'ah law at times.

"It's possible," she admitted, "that Safiyya's poem is built on esoteric Ismaili truths. Anyhow, Gnosticism frequently goes hand in hand with dualism, the theory that there may be two aspects to God, even that one of these aspects is evil. Dualism also allows for the *divine on Earth*, for example in the person of an Imam.

"I'll grant you it's mystic. And though there are a few million Ismailis around today, the Nizari line died out, so we may *never* know their deepest secrets."

"Maybe someone stumbled across those secrets, or reinvented the Assassins, or both," mused Jack.

"I guess that's your department. But both Christian and Islamic mainstreams have usually viewed their respective Gnostic fringes as heretical, which is certainly the case for the Assassins. I think modern Islam would absolutely *abhor* the return of such a body and its sacrilegious mystique, quite apart from its unacceptable policy of violence. Neither would the Pope encourage a return of the Gnostic Cathars, who were thoroughly stamped out because of their challenge to orthodoxy, despite in this case their beliefs being closer to what real Christianity was originally supposed to be. So can we stay real here?"

"You're the one with your head stuck into poetry and oblivious to reality," parried Jack calmly.

Abigail glared. Jack returned a knowing smile.

"To propose God has an evil side, is itself evil," he said as though talking about the weather. "No true Christian group would do such a thing. And routes to God should be open, not obscured by mystic shrouds. Else the Devil may more easily twist the minds of an elite and so twist the path."

Abigail suppressed a mocking groan. Through religious indoctrination, this enforcer was someone's pawn. But frustration welled up in her too, bursting acidly out.

"Of course openness is desirable. Do you think Islam a false route to God, then? *A diversion of the Devil*, as you put it?"

Jack looked as though she'd slapped him in the face. His shoulders hunched, but his clear eyes regained their focus in only a second or so and continued to probe her. His flushed skin had returned to what she assumed was its normal pallor, yet still glistened with sweat. Short hair bristled and his jaw was thrust forward, a creature ready to strike, one that had slid from under a rock to prey on those in the sun.

"It doesn't matter what I think," he answered casually. "I don't let anything get in the way of the job. Tell me why you went to the mosque."

Abigail's nerve-system plunged into cold shock. She gripped the edge of the table to stop her hands shaking. She suddenly felt she was looking at herself in a movie.

"I... I thought you said you... you didn't have me followed!"

"I didn't need to. We monitor everyone who visits the mosque."

Abigail's shock transmuted to anger. Enormous fury. How could he abuse people's rights that way? Her rights! She instinctively rose, knocking her chair over. She couldn't remember *ever* being so angry. She felt her teeth grind. Her head pounded and a mist clouded her vision. She wanted to punch Jack, wanted to tear those glassy eyes from his snooping fundamentalist face. *He was ignorant and biased and unjustly empowered!*

"Dr. Leclaire." Jack's voice was subdued but steely. "Can a Nizari connection be confirmed? Is it in fact the case that your poem fragment reflects the secrets and survival of the Assassins of Alamut? What is the death that it speaks of?"

"I don't know, *I don't know*," she yelled, long past caring that this was not entirely true, at least for the first question.

"This is a serious matter, Dr. Leclaire, not just an academic question of history."

"You're *fucking* with history! And you want me to give you credibility. Well I won't do that, I won't!"

Barely able to focus on the exit, Abigail left Jack to pay and stormed out, followed by the gaze of all the other customers.

When she'd gone, looks of pity or sympathy shifted over to Jack. He was oblivious, already on the phone.

"Yes, I am still digging up history," he snapped. Then he breathed deeply as he forced a look of resigned patience upon into his features. Collecting himself, he lowered his voice.

"No, I'm not just chasing her tail, attractive though it is. You'll get to see a lot of it yourself. Yes. Stop whinging. This time, the plan is *not* to spook her, *not* to show yourself. We know where she runs to now. Yeah. Yeah, you can ditch the ridiculous scarf. Grey isn't your colour anyhow. And don't screw up. She's on high alert, and very touchy. *Not* in that sense. More like a shapely knee in the groin."

And, reflected Jack, he'd told her something that maybe he shouldn't have let slip. To get himself off a hook? Or to intimidate? Minor mistake, hopefully, even if it incensed her just now. What oh-so-clever Dr Leclaire needed was a bucket of cold water.

Southern Ethiopia: July 1157

Though weeks had passed, Arwe continued to survive obstinately. Strips of dark dried meat seemed woven around the knobbly-jointed poles of his limbs, the empty-looking bone barrel of his body and the full jug of his head – full of insights that Hakim desperately desired to possess.

Hakim's molar sometimes ached badly these days, sabotaging clear thought. To find relief and to further explore Arwe's medical technique, he'd asked the Priest-Witch about remedies for toothache. Arwe peered and felt inside Hakim's mouth, then announced by way of Yaqob, "The tooth must leave your mouth at once, or poison will damage the jaw. Also the coming rites would be spoiled, the spirits shunning you because of this malady."

The purpose of the impending ceremony was to honour and induct Hakim in some way; apparently a 'monkey-spirit' ritual enacted by firelight, which it seemed he must experience in order to be primed for further progress. A cow would be slaughtered and the whole village would feast, though so far Arwe had been oddly reluctant to pick or reveal the exact day this would take place.

"I will remove the offending tooth right now," continued Yaqob as the voice of Arwe, "and we'll enact the rites afterwards, this very evening."

"But Hakim," whispered Sadiq, "I can do that. Why didn't you say it was so bad?"

"*I* will take the tooth out," repeated Arwe firmly. He must have understood Sadiq's tone and expression, if not the Arabic words.

Hakim frowned. Why hadn't he told Sadiq about his problem? Because he wished to seem impeccable?

"Sadiq, now that the old man has offered, I can't risk offending him."

"If only we'd brought extraction forceps with us. Abu al-Qasim al-Zahrawi's design, of course."

Yes, reflected Hakim, as pioneered in Córdoba by the great physician and described in his masterful thirty-volume encyclopaedia, published by Abu al-Qasim fifty years ago. Al-Zahrawi's name and reputation would surely process down the centuries. With a sudden thrill Hakim realised that, by the end of times, his own reputation might well soar above those of all other physicians!

He came back down to Earth. Hindsight was wonderful. An abscess indeed. He'd feared as much. Now he'd be punished for not taking enough heed. His own health was a priority, so that God's work would not be hindered.

Arwe clapped his hands and gave incomprehensible orders in the local language.

First, Guba brought a small gourd, from which Arwe poured a measure of brown liquid into a bowl, which he gave Hakim to drink. The taste was sharp like quince, yet spicy too. Soon Hakim's head was swimming and he had to lie back, only foggily aware of what Guba was now holding out for Arwe. A knife, yes, a blade. And wooden tools. A chisel of wood? A mallet? The objects wavered before Hakim and he couldn't be sure. He wanted to ask, but his jaw had become huge and paralysed.

Experimentally, he moved his legs, only to discover that his limbs were tiny and feeble, his torso too, compared with his vast yet vague head. Of course his face must enlarge enormously, to make it easier for Arwe to enter! By now his head was so large that his senses and sensations were much diluted. In fact the hut *was* his mouth, in which Arwe and Guba and Sadiq all crouched. Then no, the hut wasn't really a hut at all. It was a great tent pitched in the desert. Someone was banging on a tent peg within the tent that was Hakim.

Blood ran down Hakim's chin, leaking past lips that seemed to be the size of bananas. As his tongue probed a soft emptiness, metallic-tasting blood oozed throughout his numbed mouth. He spat red saliva like a sticky sauce onto his palm, perceiving with a professional eye that clotting would soon start, as already there was a slight thickening. He wondered if the Priest-Witch had smeared something into the wound that would help.

Full awareness returned. His head and upper back were raised by some uncomfortable support. Arwe and Guba hunched over the dirt floor, from which they'd pulled back the matting. Guba dug a hole with the knife, then Arwe pushed something inside, after which earth and matting were both replaced.

"They just buried your molar," Sadiq informed him. "Or rather what pieces are left of it, wrapped in a leaf. How do you feel?"

Hakim struggled to sit upright. Sadiq's arm helped him, then held him as the world swam, before suddenly stabilising. He could feel blood in his throat! Not to worry, the flow would soon cease. More delicate probing revealed that the edge of the hole amid his molars was loose, a flap.

"First they cut your gum," Sadiq commented. "And then…"

"Later, later." Burying the extracted tooth must be a rite of witchcraft, presumably benevolent, perhaps to assist healing? Or maybe Arwe simply liked to keep trophies under his floor. Alternatively, the Priest-Witch didn't wish such things to fall into the wrong hands, if to Arwe's mind possession of part of a living person conveyed some power over that same person. Clearly he didn't intend to exercise any such power malignly, since he hadn't tried to hide where he was putting the fragments of demolished molar.

Ah, Hakim told himself, I can think fully again, without constant interruption by that incessant, nagging ache. He spat once more. Arwe shuffled closer, still on his knees, and sniffed at him. Satisfied, the Priest-Witch hummed tunelessly, nodding to himself. Guba provided leaves for wiping oneself and spitting into if necessary.

A few hours later, flickering flames roasted the joints and ribs of a skinny cow. Tumultuous villagers danced and sang until sweat sheened their bodies. The moon was full and bright. By its silver light, older women were scraping the hide of the slaughtered animal, rendering offal that couldn't be eaten into tallow, boiling out some dye from the gall bladder, slicing meat for drying. Hakim's gum and accompanying hole still leaked blood occasionally, but his remaining discomfort was much less than that persistent jinnee of a toothache.

Arwe sat in his black throne, on supports to raise him up. Goggle-eyed Guba stood proudly by Arwe's side like a vizier, or a hybrid of medical orderly and pagan acolyte, since he held a knife and an inverted monkey skull doing duty as bowl. Hakim, Sadiq, and Yaqob sat cross-legged to Arwe's left as the old man swayed and chanted, eyes rolled upward.

At a shout from nearby, dancing and singing abruptly ceased. The villagers, perhaps two hundred in all, gathered around the Priest-Witch and his guests, craning to get the best view.

Then two young men, bodies and faces daubed ghostlike with white pigment, came rushing through, bearing the struggling figure of a small child... no, it was leaner and longer-limbed, not quite human. *A demon*, declared Hakim's shocked thought. No, it was a monkey, its fur made hoary by the moonlight. A muzzle was tied over its mouth.

The ghost-men knelt before the black throne, holding out the panicking monkey by its stretched arms. The animal jerked impotently and its feet scrabbled for purchase. Arwe made gestures and soothing noises, which seemed to calm the animal somewhat. Still it darted fearful glances at the circle of spectators, at the nearby tongue-tips of flame and bat-wings of smoke.

Guba passed the knife to his master and crouched forward, carefully positioning the bone bowl. Arwe bent and slipped the blade under the monkey's neck, raising its chin so that their sight met. His human eyes engaged the animal's gleaming eyes that did not know what a knife was or what it could do.

Arwe intoned what might be a prayer.

"What does he say?" whispered Sadiq to Yaqob.

65

"I don't understand," was the reply.

Suddenly Arwe slashed, and Guba was catching blood that poured from the monkey's severed throat as it convulsed.

Ululating, the ghost-men bore the dying animal away to hurl its body onto the bonfire to complete its death. Guba thrust the bowl at Hakim. He took this gift without hesitation and raised it to his lips. It couldn't be so bad; after all, the taste of blood was already in his mouth! Having swallowed half of the warm contents, he offered the bowl to Arwe, but the Priest-Witch gestured Hakim to drain it dry. At which the crowd leapt up and down, yelling encouragement. He finished drinking and wiped his lips.

"Translate this carefully, Yaqob. You honour me, great Priest. Am I now a blood-brother of those who worship monkeys?"

The exact reply eluded the translator. "He says something about *monkey* and *spirit within you* and *protect*. But many of the words aren't Oromifa, or maybe I never heard them before."

"Ask him to repeat what he said more simply."

Elusive as ever, Arwe called instead for meat, which came quickly, chopped up and served on banana leaves as plates. First the old man sucked the juices from chunks in his toothless mouth, then with a slobbery kiss he transferred these to a young woman with prominent breasts, for her to masticate more before returning them to Arwe lip-to-lip to swallow.

Southern Ethiopia: September 1157

All of Hakim's expertise, and Arwe's redoubtable will-power and witchcraft, were unable to delay the inevitable. The old man was simply *far too old*, his organs worn out, although the Priest-Witch's mind was still mischievous enough to keep Hakim in suspense until *almost* the last moment. He, Hakim, God's chosen vessel for the secrets of blood and plague, was reduced to begging for more clues, was nearly reduced to despair.

Until just before the last, death-bed moment.

Then, finally, *praise be to God the Merciful who had heeded his prayer*, the pagan gasped out long-guarded knowledge. Yaqob's whispered translation was, "Good monkey-spirit… can protect… from plague. Rare monkey-spirit…"

"*How do I know which is a good monkey?*" Hakim implored, on his knees by the old man's head.

"Look… for monkey… *old* before its time." So saying, Arwe cackled, the sound diminishing into his death-rattle.

A monkey old before its time? Arwe had left him a teasing legacy.

Guba kept a night-long vigil beside his former master's corpse, banging loudly on a gourd-drum to begin with, then less noisily until finally towards dawn he was merely tapping intermittently, as if echoing the departure of Arwe's spirit into a far distance which finally became immeasurable.

After sunrise, wearing a monkey skin draped over his head and down his back, grizzled by the dust of mourning thrown over it by young women, Guba led an ululating procession to the river. Laid upon a reed mat and partly covered by Guba's monkey-cape, the corpse was launched out upon sluggish water, to be torn apart soon enough by contending crocodiles. Thus no trace nor trophy of Arwe would remain, which might be misused or abused.

And so began goggle-eyed Guba's reign. Hakim persuaded the younger successor to sample, much diluted with water, the violet liquid derived from seaweed. This medicine soon calmed Guba's restlessness, his rapid heartbeat, his tremors of the fingers and sweating, both relieving these afflictions and lending Guba greater dignity. An alliance with Hakim resulted, which saw the village embark upon new practises regarding captive monkeys, the better to honour the monkey-spirits, of course.

Many more monkeys should be captured, Hakim cunningly advised. For the more monkeys, the greater the spirit of the village! Was this not so?

Indeed it was. Inhabitants of other villages sharing the same language and beliefs began to visit, led by their own lesser priest-witches, paying homage and bringing lavish gifts of food. The growing size and complexity of the monkey shrine was making Guba's village a little Mecca for the pagans. And it seemed too that Arwe's redoubtable reputation now attached itself to Guba, yet without the dread which the old man had also inspired.

Monkeys with weeping eyes, monkeys that sneezed and coughed, were segregated to breed, for Hakim sought to concentrate those evil spirits that Arwe had said seeded plague, or rather, as Hakim thought to himself, concentrate the bad humours in such monkeys. Surely their offspring would also sneeze and cough and have watery eyes, thus providing him with a pure and predictable supply of animals to experiment with.

Yet, except for one isolated instance, this was not so.

"Why not, why not?" Hakim demanded of Sadiq in vain.

"You're beyond me in most of your thinking," confessed Sadiq.

In one matter, Guba followed Arwe's canny precedent. The catching of monkeys was a strictly religious matter, so Hakim should not witness nor learn the actual method. Yet in all other regards, there was the fullest co-operation.

As soon as Hakim gained Guba's complete confidence, naturally he asked about 'monkeys old before their time', only to discover to his chagrin that the skin sported by Guba for Arwe's funeral had come from just such a monkey, hairs grizzled while not even fully grown. Due to how dusty the fur had been on account of the funeral rites, Hakim had seen, yet did not see at all! As Arwe had no doubt envisioned, when he cackled his last. That precious skin, which Hakim could have studied, was squandered as food for crocodiles.

And then a realisation stunned him. The young monkey whose blood Arwe gave him to drink during the pagan ceremony... in the moonlight *its* fur had been hoary! Silver though the moonlight was, moonlight alone was not enough to transform the usual brown coat of these creatures!

Had Arwe somehow conferred on him protection against plague? Or at least given what Arwe *believed* to be protection. Was that what his mysterious words after the ceremony meant? Why was that done with blood? Realisation became a thrill, a cautious belief, or at least almost a belief. Had the pagan Arwe truly been God's tool? Was he, Hakim, now properly armed for God's ultimate work?

Sadiq was certainly not protected, however, nor Yaqob. Hakim decided it would serve no useful purpose to alert his colleagues to this. He would have to be cautious about his speculations, yet he couldn't resist some discussion, some revelation about the ideas that were bursting up inside him, as though al-Khidr the Intercessor himself was calling forth a fountain of knowledge in his head.

"So," said Hakim to Sadiq, "according to our departed Priest-Witch, a youngish monkey with grey fur may give protection against plague. Because, I deem, that monkey itself *is already protected.*"

"Obviously not by a jinnee!"

"Quite so. Protected by a substance which must surely be in the monkey's blood. For blood is the plentiful river of the body, which circles around and around, pumped by the heart."

"*Pumped?*"

"Galen's views are plainly wrong. The blood certainly lies still *after* death, but not before. How else can blood gush from a wound, unless it is being pumped? Air does not displace this blood."

"You should write a treatise about this!"

"I must leave that to some other physician. God has appointed me to study plague and to make of plague His scimitar."

"There does exist another river. Or rather stream. I refer to urine."

"Oh Sadiq, if a substance protects, would it regularly be pissed out?"

"But how can that which protects make the monkey die young?"

"The monkey *looks* old before its time. The cure must carry some cost, some chronic ailment perhaps. Yet not necessarily a *fatal* cost."

To Hakim's great frustration, younger monkeys with greying hair were not yet among those captured.

Southern Ethiopia: March 1158

The tribe an hour to the west had become jealous of Guba's prospering community. Raids on cattle began. When warriors from Guba's village retaliated, lives were lost on both sides, provoking further bloodshed.

"The Igwe are scum," Guba informed Hakim. "They worship hyenas and eat their shit. Their women don't know who sires their babies. They hate everyone."

Hakim wondered whether this assessment was quite accurate, and what the Igwe opinion might be of Guba's people.

"Instead of killing Igwe warriors," Hakim suggested, "maybe they can be captured and brought back here alive."

"For torture?" asked Guba.

"Not exactly… but yes, to die horrible deaths. The monkey-spirits we venerate should be allowed to exact their vengeance upon the vile Igwe, and this I believe they will do, in the most terrible manner."

Guba eagerly agreed.

At last, thought Hakim, he would be able to experiment upon men; he could have them drink the blood of weeping monkeys. And may God be merciful to them, although they were pagans, for their awful suffering would be to His glory! Hakim had thought the theory through and through. He was confident now that the blood of weeping monkeys would seed plague, whereas the blood of prematurely aged monkeys conferred protection from the very same affliction.

And so it was that three Igwe youths were soon held captive in a newly built cage of strong bamboo, adjoining the monkey cages. They were daily objects of mockery for Guba's people, although not targets for physical abuse. Hakim bled a weeping monkey, and by threat of burnings, conveyed enthusiastically by a villager who spoke Igwe, he compelled the three youths to drink cups of blood, with the direst consequence for any one of them who spilled so much as a single drop. Then Hakim waited patiently, inspecting the prisoners three times a day in case the guard failed to notice the earliest signs. Yet a whole month and more went by, without any of the youths developing tokens of plague. Too long!

Hakim doubted both himself and Arwe's knowledge, so tenuously passed on. He sought inspiration in prayer, and questioned himself. What if the seed of plague wasn't in the blood, after all? Loath as he was to sacrifice a captive monkey, he ordered one animal to be killed, then with Sadiq's assistance dissected it. Again by threat of torments, he compelled one of the Igwe to eat its raw brains, a second the heart, a third the liver. He watched those youths for several hours afterwards, in case they vomited, involuntarily or deliberately.

And he waited again, day after day, week after week, to no avail.

With blades of dry grass, Hakim swabbed the tears from a weeping monkey that was restrained by villagers, then compelled the prisoners to lick the swabs. Still no success.

Increasingly, Guba had been grumbling at the failure of the Igwe prisoners to succumb to the promised fatal torments. It wasn't that Guba didn't respect Hakim's peculiar approach to bodily matters, not after the success of the violet liquid. However, Guba had his own status to sustain. So finally stern justice must be meted out to the Igwe trio, the sterner in view of all the delay.

Guba ordained a feast of punishment, which Hakim and Sadiq must attend.

In the past, both doctors had witnessed horrible pain caused by disease, accident, and violence, and had maintained professional detachment, but never previously had they been privy to torture. Not until that afternoon of the disembowelments.

Wood was piled low, with much kindling to ignite it. The naked Igwe were fastened to three upright frames of stout bamboo, secured to bases fitted with rollers contrived from cylindrical gourds. Thus, with a bit of effort, the contraptions could be trundled close to a fire, or pulled away. At first, the three prisoners were positioned equidistantly and very close to the as-yet unlit wood, while a mass of men, women and children looked on avidly, hurling occasional insults at the despised Igwe. Then Guba produced a knife.

"He's going to mutilate their genitals," whispered Sadiq. "Burn their pipes and their balls before their eyes. Or else stuff those in their mouths, to choke on while their ravaged flesh roasts. The Igwe warriors will try to be stoical, until they finally fail and lose all further dignity."

Hakim forbore to comment on such speculation. He felt morose. This ceremony didn't serve God's purpose, and it robbed him of his subjects too. Yet he acknowledged that in witnessing whatever would transpire, he was like a knife blade himself, being honed to greater sharpness on a whetstone, being purged of any remaining mundane sensitivities, as was necessary in a tool for the ultimate work.

Sadiq's guess was wrong...

Guba stood atop the wood then, one by one, he opened the lower abdomens of the three youths, from the navel downwards. Each flinched and bit their lips bloody, but not one cried out. With rags soaked in a bowl of some yellow substance, Guba somehow minimised the blood-flow. Then he slid his hand into each wound and wrenched free the intestine. He cut through this to separate it from the rectum, brown liquid and lumps oozing over his hands, then he pulled out an arm's length of pale tubing; and now each warrior squealed gaspingly like a child as his inner essence was removed from him. The audience whooped and jeered.

Guba pranced around on the wood, pulling out yet more intestine. Hakim was well aware that the intestines are ten times the length of a human body, and the adults were experienced at gutting animals, but to the children in the audience Guba might have seemed like a conjuror. The tormented Igwe issued piercing squeals. Guba wrapped the leaking ends of their three innards around one another and united them with a band of thorns, which he fixed to a stout post beyond the wood-pile. Then he signalled for assistants to roll back the frames. Inevitably this wrenched out more wet tubing and had the doomed prisoners screeching and writhing on their frames; but more importantly this procedure lifted the joined entrails quite high above the intended fire, tautening them.

Only then was the kindling lit, so that the victims, if perception still held sway, could soon behold juices from the cooking of their agonised bowels dripping into the flames. The hissing of liquids was background to a cacophony of torment, and the pervasive smell of tripes assaulted Hakim's nostrils.

Word reached the Igwe village soon enough. One of Guba's warriors, who was very fleet of foot, sneaked near, deposited a tangle of cooked and thorn-spiked intestine, bellowed a few swift words of what had happened as a taunt, then sped away.

For Hakim, the result of this was to bring disaster, yet also, subsequent triumph...

Southern Ethiopia: April 1158

Igwe warriors slipped into the village just before dawn, grey shadows in a world drained of definition and colour. The first that Hakim, Sadiq and Yaqob knew of this was hullabaloo, so that they seized their swords and were quickly at the door of their hut in the quarter-light. The tall thatch of a hut near Guba's took fire as cries rent the air. Like great dark moths, the three men headed for that illumination.

Warriors were jabbing at one another with spears. The intruders wore the heads of hyenas as hats and across their backs carried one or two additional spears in bamboo quivers. Guba stood unsteadily, clutching the weight of one already thrown that had lodged in his shoulder. His two guards lay dead – no, one was still moving unless that was an illusion of dancing firelight. Villagers were beginning to flock, with whatever weapon they had snatched up.

"Protect Guba at all costs!" Hakim shouted. Sadiq rushed forward, swinging his scimitar, though Yaqob slipped away. Hakim reached Guba to pull him back inside his hut, but an Igwe hyena spied an opening and bounded, thrusting his spear deep into the Priest-Witch's navel. Guba buckled, clutching at the agonising shaft, even as Sadiq sliced through the killer's neck. Hakim dragged Guba into the hut, only to hear Sadiq cry out, for a spear thrown true outranked his sword. Sadiq fell, the first daylight painting blood upon him. Hakim stared and saw no movement from his companion. Sadiq was dead.

Guba would soon join him, dying slowly in agony, no matter that Hakim had poured the rest of the violet liquid into the belly wound, no matter what else he attempted.

This was a disaster for God's purpose, disaster for the proud villagers too. As tradition demanded, immediately after Arwe's death Guba himself had taken the most suitable youth as his own apprentice, a young man named Garbu, so called because his mother had given birth while on a lake in a fishing boat. The afterbirth had been thrown to a crocodile because its smell attracted the reptile, an auspicious event. But Garbu only possessed a little knowledge as yet and, with Guba dead, the apprentice would have no way of acquiring more. So the villagers would have to accept the suzerainty of an experienced Priest-Witch from another community, who might or might not choose to continue Garbu's training.

Sadiq's death was likewise a disaster. Even in his grief, though, Hakim realised that losing Yaqob would have been worse. A translator was essential

73

to the work of forging an ultimate weapon to sweep the world clean of unbelief. Yaqob's cowardice must be overlooked.

Hakim saw to Sadiq's speedy burial, while corpses of the overwhelmed Igwe raiders were dragged into the forest for hyenas to eat in a kind of poetic justice. One raider without serious injury had been captured. The dying Guba could decide nothing, so the enraged population thrust their captive into the cage of weeping monkeys. The monkey spirits might make their own judgement and exact a vicious revenge on behalf of the ravaged village.

Guba hung on for two days, but when his spirit departed Hakim no longer had an official sponsor, though he did have credit with the villagers, and fortunately the almost useless Garbu treated Hakim as a kind of advisor… until such time as the elders would yield to the inevitable.

South End, Boston, Massachusetts: April 2008

It had seemed entirely reasonable to Abigail to meet Paul Summers at a café in South End, on Tremont Street. She could hardly expect a comparative stranger to come out to Harvard on her say-so, especially when she hadn't felt able to say very much over the phone. So, to him the choice of venue.

Jack's obnoxious personality still left a bad taste in her mouth. She'd no doubt the ICEman would stoop to anything to dig up dirt, whether on her or within medieval history. He might just as easily manufacture dirt. About that she could do nothing, but she could preserve some privacy, so she made doubly sure that no tail was stuck to her on the journey out from Radcliffe. She'd turned off her mobile too; though she wasn't technical, she recalled that they gave one's position away.

She'd got off the subway at Copley, just to see her favourite Boston vision again: Trinity church captured in its entirety by the glass of the Hancock tower. Then she hurried on down Clarendon Street towards Tremont, throwing in a few more twists and turns for good measure. Having a little time to kill, she circumnavigated leafy Union Park. Despite her preoccupations, she admired the ornamental ironwork on the surrounding houses. She loved the combination of chasing shadows and sun and rain, which made the leaves shine and the urban scenery dynamic. Finally she arrived at the Café Lorca, a name that seemed propitious in view of the poetisa of Granada, until she recalled how the 20th century poet Lorca had been murdered, by fascists, there in his own home town in Spain.

She was still a little early. A couple of bronzed young blond guys in white tee-shirts and blue jeans with big belt-buckles were chatting quietly over the remains of some croissants. Otherwise there was no one except for a languid, dark-haired man behind the counter who sported a head-to-thighs plastic apron adorned with a Jackson Pollock splash-art painting.

A big poster on a side wall advertised a Spanish bullfight, a tight-buttocked torero splendidly clad in silks and sequins. Neat butt, thought Abigail, though disapproving of that sport.

She ordered a camomile tea to calm herself and took from her bag *The Forgotten Queens of Islam*. When Jackson Pollock brought her tea, he glanced and murmured whimsically, "Queens of Islam, eh? Well, what do you know."

It dawned on Abigail then that Café Lorca was a gay hang-out. Lorca had been homosexual, hadn't he? That macho torero's neat butt on the wall was being mischievously misinterpreted!

Just then, ringleted Paul Summers arrived, wearing a crumpled creamy suit and orange-red striped shirt, carrying a laptop case.

"Hi, Dr Leclaire. Tea for me too," he called to Jackson Pollock, then sat close. "You sounded kinda conspiratorial and bottled-up-angry on the phone," he murmured.

"I sounded both those things? I thought I sounded neutral."

He grinned. "Didn't work. Er, why neutral? Do you think your phone's bugged? Dr Leclaire, you can rely on my discretion."

"Call me Abigail."

"Well, I'm Paul. So what's bugging you, in either sense of the word?"

Momentarily, she glanced at the gorgeous torero.

"Don't you feel comfortable here, Abigail?"

She shrugged.

"Hey, it isn't totally my scene either, but it's calm at this time of day, and the intrepid reporter goes everywhere. I have to see someone at the Center for the Arts down the street."

He hushed as Jackson Pollock brought another camomile.

"Are you familiar with ICE?" she asked.

"As in with tea in summertime?"

"What I mean is the US Immigration…"

"And Customs Enforcement," he concluded for her.

Tight-lipped, "What would you say if I told you that ICE are covertly filming everyone who visits the Roxbury mosque?"

He mused a moment. "I'd say that's invasive and paranoid and maybe illegal behaviour, unless there's a specific reason, in which case I'd *love* to know what that reason is. But I'd also ask how you know about this covert activity, and why you're telling me."

"Because it makes my blood boil that innocent people can be spied upon by some fascist government acronym with millions of undeserved dollars obtained for so-called homeland security!"

A burst of sunlight opened up onto Paul's face. His curly hair shone like a halo and his eyes twinkled. "Canadian accent, right? Feeling some righteous ire about Uncle Sam's Big Brother ways?."

"Look, I've been practically threatened with deportation by –!"

"ICE?"

For a surreal moment, Abigail imagined that he was offering cubes to cool herself.

"Threatened," continued Paul, "based on filming you visiting the mosque, you mean? So you got asked by ICE *why* you were visiting the mosque, is that it?"

Abigail suddenly felt defensive. Talking to the press was a double-edged sword, and she wanted to keep her research out of this.

"The details aren't important. I have a good friend at the mosque… a cleric, but also a scholar. He's helping me with some research into a medieval poem. But it's the *principle* that counts, spying on people illicitly. You have to tell the public about this!"

Paul pulled out a notebook, but his expression was sheepish. "Abigail, I take it you have no proof whatsoever, which means it'd be very dangerous for us to publish."

Abigail's principles evaporated. She turned on a seductive gaze. "It's a noble cause." As he looked down to write, was he hiding a blush?

"I know people, I'll do some digging." He grinned lopsidedly. "If I can get a reasonable hint of corroboration, I'll publish."

Terry felt wounded, frustrated and angry, yet terribly guilty too. What he was doing was wrong; there ought to be a better way. Yet he had to know, he *had* to. It wasn't his fault that Abigail was being evasive. Lately, his relationship with the woman he loved seemed as much torture as joy. A cool determination in his veins alternated with fury.

The weather was unstable, like his mood. A high altitude wind was breaking up sullen grey above. Occasional ragged gaps appeared, sending waves of brilliance washing over the buildings. Massed windows were briefly transformed to jewels before the light moved swiftly on, or disappeared as jealous clouds stopped up the hole again. In between such bursts of sun, spatters of wind-blown rain flew.

Another guy was kicking his heels further down the street. Blue jeans, short beige rain-jacket, good-looking, muscular, sandy-haired. No doubt waiting for his girl too; no doubt to greet her warmly. Terry swallowed back bile that rose in his throat. If all was well, what he was doing wouldn't harm Abigail, he schooled himself. But in his heart, he knew that things were *far* from well.

Only the other night she'd needled him yet again about his college courses, then made noises about leaving Boston when her stipendiary finished. *Did he like Spain? The lost poetisas of al-Andalus cry out to be discovered!* What on Earth would *he* do in Spain? He'd reacted badly, counter-attacked. But she *was* obsessive about her work these days, and *was* devoting less and less time to him!

His aromatic cassoulet had saved them from a full-scale row. Her favourite dish and not too easy to find even in Boston's diverse restaurants; it had taken him months to learn the perfect recipe for the Québecois style of the dish. But later, conversation was stilted and sex mechanical, almost embarrassing. Yet he still loved her, yearning for moments of shared joy that might already be history, certainly *would* be history if her domineering father used his wealth to shield her. He knew he wasn't approved of at all, and suspected that previous boyfriends in the same position, possibly *all* of Abigail's boyfriends, had found impossible barriers to a relationship mysteriously appearing. Perhaps the manipulative old tyrant had offered to fund an extended research trip to Spain.

Abigail appeared, at the Radcliffe doorway where they'd often rendezvoused before sharing a late lunch together. One of the few times their schedules could regularly overlap. Yet she hadn't wanted to meet him today. *Important appointment. Critical research.* That evasive tone he was coming to know so well had cut through his love and loyalty, to reach raw anger beneath.

It had to be another man! Why else would she keep stuff from him?

Abigail paused to assess the weather. She was wearing her red retro-coat with the big belt. Good, an easy beacon to follow. Staying well back, he followed his love. He noticed that Beige-jacket-man was also on the move. Perhaps the guy had been stood up after all. Terry sympathised.

Almost immediately, something felt wrong. Abigail was walking far faster than she usually did, and took apparently pointless turns. Where was she headed? Had she realised he was behind her?

After a zigzag through several streets, it became obvious that the beige-jacket guy was following her *too*. Utterly perplexed, Terry dropped back a little. Fortunately the stranger didn't appear to have spotted him. But who the hell was he? Another cheated boyfriend resorting to the same plan as himself? Was everything he thought he knew about Abigail completely wrong?

Confusion temporarily overrode Terry's other emotions. In a quiet side-street, Abigail glanced behind her. After that, Beige-guy stayed much further back and was more cautious at corners. Terry was obliged to fall still further behind, following the follower rather than Abigail herself.

Whatever was going on, Abigail had kept him completely in the dark. Terry's fists clenched and his teeth ground as he walked.

They ended up at Porter subway station. It was tough keeping them both in sight through to the platform, but Terry's seething emotion kept him sharp. Clever Beige-guy pulled level with Abigail, but some distance to her left and hidden by a knot of students. Her continued glances behind, usually made from her right side, would never pick him up.

Terry risked the same carriage as Beige-guy, one behind Abigail's. He kept his head down, nevertheless feeling as though everyone in the packed space was aiming a stare directly at him, probing his debased mood and exposing him. An alien desire to scream his frustration, and lash out at other travellers, was surprisingly difficult to suppress.

In a narrow field of vision threaded through a dozen intervening bodies, Terry saw the mysterious follower take off his jacket and discreetly turn it inside-out. Now he was Blue-jacket guy, silently mocking Terry for his lack of knowledge or expertise. Terry thought about pushing up the aisle and challenging him right there, but then the train screeched to a halt and Abigail had hopped off.

He clung to them both through a change of train and the exit from Copley station, but covert pursuit was much harder among the swarming shoppers and tourists in central Boston. In only a minute or so, he lost them. Sweating and desperate and dropping all pretence of subtlety, he barged through the crowds in an attempt to catch up.

Then he slammed right into someone. They both tumbled to the hard pavement, though Terry landed on his hands and knees and was up again in a moment. The other man was face down, possibly winded, struggling to rise.

"Sorry sorry, sorry," Terry offered speedily, torn between continuing his frantic search and ensuring that the man was all right. But then realisation dawned as he took in the blue jacket, the sandy hair.

The mysterious follower regained his feet, immediately glancing off to his right instead of at the person who'd just bowled him over. Terry followed the man's gaze. Abigail was there, some way off and with her back to them, standing stock-still between rivers of faces, her head tilted back, apparently hypnotised by the mirrored Hancock tower before her. As though ignited by Abigail's scarlet coat, Terry's barely suppressed fury flared.

Grey eyes now stared at him in annoyance. "Watch where you're going, *buddy!*" That last word sarcastically. But then belated recognition widened the stare.

"*Stay away from her!*" snarled Terry. His pent-up emotions burst out in a massive release, and he smashed a tight fist as hard as he could into Blue-jacket's face. The man staggered backwards and hit the deck for a second time.

Shoppers scattered. Someone yelled for the police. Fortunately, Abigail didn't appear to have noticed. He caught sight of her striding south down Clarendon. Sudden flurries of rain split the whole scene with beaded curtains. He hurried after her, still trembling with rage, but his knuckles stung and he was more puzzled than ever. Blue-jacket guy had almost certainly recognised him! What was going on?

Agent Leviticus struggled to a sitting position and waited for the world to stop reeling. Then panic pierced his confused state. His gun! He reached into the pocket of his jacket, the special pocket that could be accessed from both sides of the reversible garment. The hard outlines of his Sig Sauer P229 brought immediate comfort. He recalled cub agent Nehemiah being drummed out of the Service for losing his weapon to a suspect. Yet the comfort was short-lived. There'd be hell to pay from Jack.

The stares and comments of a surrounding crowd suddenly burst in on him. And he felt the warmth of blood around his nose and mouth. Getting to his feet, he fished out a hanky to clean up his face, then pushed through the ring of spectators and quickly away. His embarrassment would be even worse if he had to explain to slow-minded uniforms and expose the business of ICE.

Welcome rain stung his skin and brought him clarity. Abigail must have detailed her boyfriend to take out any followers, which meant she was going somewhere important and he'd missed it. There was no excuse. He'd anticipated an easy mission and had been lax. Even recognising Terry Fox from his mug-shot, just two seconds earlier, might at least have saved him from complete failure.

He found a quiet spot and called his much-feared boss on a Service mobile. Jack's outrage nearly split his eardrum.

Somehow, Terry hung on to his fleeing love through the twists and turns. But, as the shoppers looking for novelties thinned, this became harder. Soon he shared the pavement with Abigail alone, and the red of her coat both dazzled and frightened him. He maintained a long distance, even losing sight of her occasionally. He prayed he wouldn't lose her permanently, and sure enough the scarlet signal, desire and pain, always showed up again.

For some bizarre reason she circled Union Park, perhaps still hoping to catch out the likes of Blue-jacket-guy, but Terry discovered he had a kind of instinct for what Abigail would do at each junction, and it didn't fail him.

She slipped into a brightly coloured café. Café Lorca. Terry sheltered in a doorway across the street and saw her take a table alone, fortunately near the windowed front of the camp-looking joint.

Terry bet himself she wouldn't be alone for long. Confusion and suspicion constricted his throat so much that he could barely swallow. His knuckles ached. Sure enough, a man soon turned up, seating himself opposite Abigail. Terry moved in closer, trying to look casual, edging up from behind the direction of her gaze to get a good look at the guy. He took out his mobile, pretending to answer it, giving him an excuse to loiter while he mouthed *Yes* and *Okay* and *Great* to nobody.

The two were talking earnestly already, yet neither the place nor the mood spoke in the slightest of important academia. An obliging shaft of sunlight revealed a goofy smile and curly hair. Not a match for the reversible jacket guy. Surely not even a match for himself!

Terry was on the point of sneaking a phone-photo when shame stung him. This was Abigail! Why would he need evidence? He felt dirty. Yet despite his lack of trust and despite his ignoble action today, he still oscillated between the bitterness of exclusion and the rage of jealousy.

He swore foully, not realising this was out loud until an old couple passing by stared apprehensively at him. An image of Abigail cuddled up to him in bed escaped from his memory with *such* reality. He could feel her warmth and softness again, could almost smell her scent. Confused still further by the gentle spirit this evoked and feeling like a kicked dog, he slunk off towards home.

Tehran, Iran: September 2007

"In Rome, this says beware pickpockets on crowded trains."

"We have zip pockets. Our jackets have."

The four men were speaking in English for practise, surrounded by the dozens of country maps and guide books and city plans they'd been studying for months now. Ali, Amin, Bashir, and Muhammad. One of the fluorescent strips in the windowless room began to flicker. Bashir picked up the internal phone and in Farsi demanded a replacement tube, then closed his eyes protectively, or because he was tired.

"Which two of us will be chosen?" mused Ali.

"As God wills," replied Muhammad.

"And the extent of our knowledge," added Amin. "And a medical." He rubbed his shoulder. "The gym aches me today. But the pain is of fitness."

"In London," said Ali, "*knowledge* is the name drivers of taxis say for a test about which routes are fastest. Soon we have knowledge together of half the world!"

"And half that knowledge," said Bashir, "will be no use, when one is sent only west or only east."

"Would you only memorise half the Qu'ran because you might die half way through reciting? Two of us might fall ill before departure day, whenever that may be, as God wills."

Immigration and Customs Enforcement, Downtown Boston, Massachusetts: April 2008

The article burned into Jack's brain as though the text was made from fire.

ICE around Roxbury mosque, it declared.

His neck flushed, his hands trembled with the effort of maintaining control. The familiar rage that had kept him tirelessly fighting on the frontline as a soldier of God, and a defender of the country's borders, occasionally let him down too. He pulled back the top-right drawer of his desk and slipped his hand inside, gripping the solid comfort of the Bible there.

Gradually, his muscles relaxed and his heartbeat slowed till it became the steady drum of a march again, a march filled with God's purpose. His vision cleared and he contemplated how orderly his office was: to the right thick carpet, traditional wood, expensively framed pictures and awards above rows of leather-bound books. The desk where he sat was polished oak. To the left, computers fed two dominating wall-screens that gave him a sense of power and control; his eyes and ears. Those screens and a couple of lamps provided the only light; he could concentrate much better in a dim environment and never opened the blinds.

At least the article was only on page five. Nevertheless, it could cause him a lot of trouble. There'd be public pressure, and the legal department would suddenly find a conscience again. For a few months at least, he'd have to stop monitoring visitors to the mosque. This could mean a serious loss of intelligence. Illegals or conspirators would be warned; the latter would meet elsewhere.

So, one point to Abigail Leclaire. He had little doubt she was the *reliable source* quoted, even if the reporter had managed to gain surreptitious confirmation from within ICE itself. This was due to his own misjudgement in letting slip the information at Totally Thai, as part of his attempt to pressure her. Yet he'd really thought she would crumble, not fight back! Undoubtedly there was strong stuff inside the girl; but *why* was she fighting?

He'd crushed many a liberal idealist who'd unwisely decided to turn and nip at the ankles of authority, yet he sensed there was more to Abigail's resistance. She knew stuff; she might be seriously involved. If not directly recruited by the agents of *Eagle Teacher*, then at least an indirect tool.

Direct pressure on Abigail wouldn't work. She'd only clam up, or fight harder, and neither did he have anything on her, as yet. She might call for big industrialist daddy to help too, and that'd mean some serious heat, maybe an ultimatum to lay off. Already he'd been denied a tap on her mobile. 'We don't want to offend Canada,' the high-ups had said. More likely, they couldn't afford to offend Daddy and his powerful friends in the U.S. Her landlines, on university property, were altogether a different matter…

At the very least, Jack surmised, Abigail was a lens through which the origin and motives behind *Eagle Teacher* might be discerned, a lens he very much needed to see through. *And she could still be taught that resisting him wasn't at all wise.*

He punched a button on his desk-phone.

"Leviticus," he said slowly. Using code-names, even in the office, added to the aura of fear he liked to project.

"Quit fawning! I'm giving you a break. You're back on the street. Yeah, thank me later, *if* you don't screw up! I'm sure you remember the guy who damaged your nose. Yeah, him. Search his apartment. And while you're about it, trash the place. Hey, I'm offering you revenge and a second chance too, all in one shot! Yeah. No. Find anything you can to do with the case, and whatever else that might be embarrassing. If there's anything even remotely dodgy, make sure some uniforms find it too. Come to think of it, even if there's *nothing* dodgy, make sure uniforms find something. Unregistered gun, small stash… Yeah, Yeah. That's the idea. Do it today, now… as soon as he goes out to work or whatever."

He would start by isolating Abigail. That was the way to go. She'd recruited her boyfriend to the cause, whatever her cause might actually be, so he was fair game.

He punched the phone again.

"Hi, Jenny." She didn't have a code name, of course, although he'd thought of some, mostly very un-biblical.

"Yeah, rain again. Yeah, tough. Look, I want you to start a new subject file. Er… Paul Summers, reporter at the *Boston Globe*. Yeah, anything and everything you can, just to kick us off. Okay. That'll be fine. Okay, thanks."

Southern Ethiopia: July 1158

Hakim surveyed the naked prisoner huddled in the main monkey cage. Subjected to daily spear-jabs, aimed only to torment him yet never to injure too much, afflicted by numerous monkey bites and scratches, subsisting on whatever monkey food he could scavenge, he was a pathetic figure. In fact absolutely wretched, his scrawny flesh covered in scabs and suppurations.

Ah, the indomitable nature of the human spirit, thought Hakim. *How ironic, how vile, that the doomed will still struggle for survival.*

Yet, in this prisoner's position, what would he do? Would he have the courage to starve himself? Or refrain from drinking the unclean water? Maybe try to swallow his own tongue in order to choke himself?

Allah forbade that anyone should take away his own life, thus rejecting Allah's gift of life, and therefore rejecting Allah Himself. For Hakim there could be no such so-called courage, since courage this would not be, but *blasphemy!*

The prisoner blasphemed simply by existing.

Beacon Hill, Boston, Massachusetts: April 2008

Abigail felt trapped. She wanted to be anywhere but here, in Terry's car, quite apart from the fact that it always smelled musty to her.

"Sorry about the meal, babe," he apologised for the third time. "They're a man down, I have to go in later."

She'd spent months trying to wean him off that patronising word, yet he still slipped easily back to it.

"You should get a real job," she sniped, instantly wishing she hadn't.

He parried, deflecting the attack. "You didn't like the movie then?"

She bit back the sharp *no* that formed on her tongue. Why was she being so acid? It was nice of him to take her out, and he'd done his best. A film about the Crusades she hadn't even known was playing. It was to have been followed by fine home-cooking too, before the current bar he worked at had called him in.

"Very dramatic," she conceded. "But the history was all wrong."

He slipped a quirky smile her way. "Y'know, you could suspend your rationality a bit more often. *Have some fun.* I thought it was real good."

Their talk was dancing within the strict and tiring rules of a duel. Yet neither of them wanted to really wound the other, so silence then reigned inside the car. Abigail was relieved. But she'd put off broaching the big issues for far too long. Collectively, those hung above like the sword of Damocles.

Terry pulled up outside his apartment on Myrtle Street, and turned to face her. A critical moment made itself felt, like the sword's point intruding.

"You could stay over anyhow." His voice scraped slightly in its effort to be gentle.

"Spend hours alone with nothing to do, then have you wake me up at 2.30 am? Thanks but no thanks! I'd prefer to go out and grab some dinner, then work at home with my papers, on *my own* computer."

Terry's brow furrowed. "And not alone? Not for dinner anyhow?"

All gentleness in his voice had evaporated. Why was he always so suspicious? Amazingly, she had once thought his jealousy sweet. Now it infuriated her.

"I do have friends, you know, *if* I needed to eat in company!"

"Oh yeah, I know, *I know that.* Friends!"

Abigail realised the spat had left its normal course behind. His voice was full and dripping with irony, his mouth bitterly twisted, as though there was deeper meaning behind his words that she ought to grasp. But she couldn't. In some confusion, she backed down. The point of that sword was far too close; all she could think about was continuing to avoid it.

"Hey look, let's not get mad," she soothed. "I have to come in for my bag. I'll stay until you need to go. If I get the subway later, you won't use up time having to run me home. There's still an hour or more to chill out, and have a glass of that wine you were going to treat me to."

She finished with a bright smile. It worked, but only just. Trouble still stalked behind Terry's eyes. Something had taken him to the edge, and, though she frantically searched her memory, she couldn't think what she might have done.

The fact that the apartment door was unmistakably open didn't compute at first. Terry stopped dead and gaped, the key already raised in his hand. Abigail bumped into his back. The door was ajar a couple of inches, and light streaming through the gap seemed to mesmerise them both. Abigail recovered first.

"Careful!" she hissed. "Don't go in. *Someone* might still be inside." Terry charged in regardless. Abigail followed.

Terry yelled an aggressive challenge as they burst from the small entrance into the main living area. Yet his voice died as they both gazed at the transformation of his familiar and cosy room. It looked as though a pocket tornado had made a very unsociable visit.

The floor was a sea of paper that sucked in smashed picture-frames and ornaments, along with most of the once-orderly miscellany of Terry's life. Beached hulks of bookcases reared from half-submersion in the mess, while stuffing from slashed cushions floated like froth above angry waves. A bottle of red wine on its side jutted precariously from a shelf; the stopper Terry had put in only hours before now loose, allowing its contents to drip into a shocked silence, spattering onto a metal tray below.

Terry made a croaking sound, but actual words failed him.

"They might still be here," whispered Abigail urgently.

He yelled again, though weakly now, and moved cautiously off to check the other rooms. Abigail fought her fear and stepped further inside. At a couple of places, broken glass crunched under the heels of her leather boots. She attempted to tiptoe, aware of her own shallow breathing, of tension in her neck and shoulders, a readiness to flee.

"No one here," announced Terry as he reappeared. There was obvious relief in his voice. "But it's *all* like this!" And dismay too.

Abigail relaxed a little. "Is anything missing?"

He waved his arms around. "How the fuck would I know?"

"Oh... yeah."

He fished a picture of his parents out from the jumble and tried to rescue the old photo from behind its cracked glass.

"We should call the police." She grasped his shoulder to show support. The muscles were bunched-up. He grunted.

87

"I guess, for all the good they're likely to be."

"And we shouldn't really touch anything. You know, fingerprints and all that."

Terry carried on with the mission to save his smiling parents of thirty years back. He succeeded, but the glass plate fell apart and cut his finger.

"FUCK!"

Blood dripped down, like the wine, but darkening a swathe of earth where it touched; this shed from a plant-pot that must have been flung across the room, ejecting its cactus.

"Hey, hey. It's okay," soothed Abigail, though it probably wasn't. She found a clean tissue and stemmed the flow, but not before a crimson circle had blossomed on the sleeve of her white blouse.

"Here, hold onto that. Why do you think someone would do all this? I mean, burglars don't usually make such a mess, do they?"

"I dunno. Maybe they were drugged-up, out of their heads." Terry was still in shock, staring around in disbelief.

"You're not *involved* in anything are you?"

"ME!" he bellowed, his eyes suddenly blazing. "*Me* involved in something?"

Terry's abrupt rage caught Abigail completely by surprise. She scrabbled about for some defence.

"Well, that loudmouth you banned from the bar put a brick through your window at Christmas, and what about those diamonds you hid for that other customer?"

Terry spluttered with fury before finding his voice. "He just didn't want his wife to find them! It's hardly a nefarious *involvement*. But what are *you* involved in? Huh? How can you accuse *me* of stuff, with your secrets?" He flung words like darts, thoughtlessly reaching for the next ammunition while there was still something left to throw. "*What about that guy who was following you? What was that all about?*"

The tap of dripping wine on tin measured a long and awful silence. Abigail found herself staring at him, while her brain struggled to catch up. The anger was sucked from his eyes, along with the blood from his cheeks. His lips quivered, as though they would tug back what was said. She felt her own anger and suspicion inexorably rising.

Somewhere a pivotal point was passed, which somehow they both knew.

"What guy?" Her softly spoken question nevertheless thrust into Terry like a knife.

"Abigail, Bee, please I…"

"What guy?"

Terry blinked to hold back tears. His slack face admitted... what? Despair? Loss? She didn't care.

"I'm sorry, I'm sorry... I knew something was going on. I got jealous... *only because I love you so much.* I... I followed you. To Café Lorca. You met that dorky guy."

Rage and abhorrence erupted deep inside Abigail. At that moment she loathed everything that Terry was. His limited horizons, his pathetic job, his pretence at college, his aversion to travel, above all his incurable jealousy. He'd deliberately fooled her with his thin mask of charm, yet now truths were out! She could identify her deeper disquiet. Terry was a stalker!

"You're despicable!" she screeched. "*How could you do that?*"

"Bee, please forgive me... I wasn't thinking properly that day. I..."

"That's it! *WE'RE FINISHED.*" A small part of Abigail was amazed by what she was doing, amazed by the uncontrollable intensity of her own mood. But this fragment of consciousness made no effort to interfere. She didn't want to deal with Terry ever again, didn't want to touch him ever again.

Terry was crushed. Streaks of wetness shone upon his pasty cheeks. He didn't even have the spirit to plead.

"*Someone else* was following you too," he insisted weakly. "I've no idea who. Perhaps... Perhaps you're in some kind of danger?"

Abigail was past caring. "Then it's a bit late to tell me!" she snapped furiously. "I can look after myself. I *will* look after myself!"

Terry hung his head in shame.

For just a split second, Abigail thought about grabbing her stuff. But given the state of the flat, she'd never find it. Well, there was nothing she couldn't do without. She stomped through the mess, heading for the door, crushing and scattering goodness knows what.

"Don't call me," she flung bitterly over her shoulder.

"Bee," wailed Terry. "Abbeeegaaail..."

The air outside felt like a breath of freedom to Abigail, yet it didn't cool her mood. She stalked at speed down the sidewalk, her mind a churning engine of wrath. *How could he do that? How could I have been fooled by him for so long? A stalker!*

As she turned the first corner, heading for the Charles MGH station, she didn't notice a police vehicle pulling into the street behind her. In her current state, she might well not have registered even if its lights and siren had been on.

Terry was on his knees amid the sea of destruction. He tasted the salt of tears on his lips, and peered through shifting distortions at the old photo of his parents.

"What kind of son did you raise?" he asked them desperately. Maybe it really was all his fault. Maybe he really was hopeless, the way Abigail thought.

He took a long, shuddering breath, and tried to think of practicalities. He ought to call the police. But it was no use, he probably couldn't even talk without sobbing. He'd lost his beautiful girl. For all he knew, he might have lost half his possessions too. The rest were floating in this chaos, which would take days to clean up. He wouldn't make it to work now either, he'd be letting the guys down.

Life didn't get worse than this. Fresh tears burst forth.

And then two policemen walked in. Terry was confused. He hadn't even called them yet. He stood up and hurriedly wiped his face with his sleeve. The police guys gazed around the room. One took off his cap and scratched the scalp under his thinning blonde hair.

"Sir? We had reports of a serious disturbance."

"I just had a row with my girlfriend, but…"

"I'll say! Some row!"

"No! No, I mean that wasn't the disturbance, we didn't make a disturbance!"

"Well, someone sure disturbed this place pretty bad. Are you injured, sir?"

Terry looked down at his hand. Blood was leaking through the tissue. One of the police guys spoke into his radio.

"I… I just cut my finger. Look… I've been burgled, my place is trashed!"

"So this is your apartment?"

"Yes."

"Well, sir, I have to tell you… This doesn't look like a burglary exactly. I'd say someone was searching for something in particular. Something valuable to them. Really valuable."

A third policeman walked in, accompanied by a menacing-looking German Shepherd on a tight leash.

"I haven't got anything valuable," protested Terry. "Not really valuable."

"Value can be a reflection of need."

"What? What are you talking about?"

"You don't mind if we check then, do you sir?"

"Hey! I'm the victim here!"

But the big dog was already unleashed. It bounded about the room, almost immediately picking out a bulky old computer screen lying on its side.

The dog pawed at the plastic casing and whined.

"What's it doing?" asked Terry, a knot of fear already forming in his gut.

"It's trained to find stuff like cocaine, sir. Perhaps we'd better have that casing off."

Terry collapsed to his knees again. He wondered if this was a nightmare, if he was really asleep. He beat his head with the palm of his hand, hoping to wake up, or disappear into oblivion, or get any result but having to remain here.

"Sir? Sir! Hey Jim, grab his arms."

Abigail was riding the subway by the time her anger abated. The carriage was almost empty, only two other passengers, both apparently too tired to keep their eyes open.

She realised she'd been harsh, leaving Terry like that, with such hate, at such a time. No doubt he'd already felt vulnerable, the lock on his front door broken and his place trashed by some low-life.

In retrospect, she realised her subconscious had long been waiting for its chance to strike, and this chance had been perfect. She'd pulled out with her own psyche intact, with no complications, able to stand on high moral ground and direct all blame towards Terry.

Guilt grew in her mind. She felt manipulative, as he'd sometimes said she was. She stared at the circle of Terry's blood on her sleeve, already dried-out and darkened. She thought about calling him and fished out her mobile, but of course it wouldn't work underground.

Then, perhaps as a counter-balance to guilt, the prospect of freedom and excitement, of exotic places and exotic men, spurted up from some deep source to flood Abigail's consciousness.

She knew herself well. Loyalty and guilt could easily tie her to Terry again, *if* she allowed any opportunities for them to take hold. Without her even knowing, the mobile slipped back into her bag. In the end, Terry *had* tailed her, when she'd given no cause whatever for jealousy.

Only then did she wonder about the other guy who'd been following her. No doubt that was one of Jack's minions. Perhaps this shouldn't be a surprise after their row at Totally Thai, yet she still found it hard to believe that he considered her so important.

She thought about having her father fall on Jack from a great height, but decided against it. Right now she was still full of anger; she needed someone to hate, someone to fight against, especially in a good cause. Bigoted, fundamentalist, spy-master, unacceptable face-of-the-state Jack was the perfect candidate. Already she hated him with a passion.

And then she noticed a newspaper lying abandoned, on the seat next but one to her left. Surely it was a *Boston Globe*, but was it today's? Would Paul have anything in there?

She leaned over and grabbed what indeed turned out to be that morning's *Globe*. She swiftly scanned the first pages… nothing. And then, low down on page five: 'ICE around Roxbury mosque'. A short piece, but enough. Her mouth involuntarily curled to a grim smile. She must thank Paul. It was clearly her day for striking back.

Charlestown, Boston, Massachusetts: April 2008

Jack Turner shut off the phone, then threw it across the room. He swore, then felt guilty as the Reverend Collins was staring intently at him from the wide-screen TV. He restarted the inspirational sermon, only to halt the DVD again seconds later. He couldn't concentrate, and the familiar order of his Swedish-style flat was little comfort. It was bad enough to be roasted by his boss; to get roasted at home, on a Sunday of all days, was unprecedented and deeply unsettling. Very little passed unnoticed by the chief of the Investigations Division of Boston ICE, apparently even when he'd just returned from vacation. Yet ultimately, it was all Mam'zelle Leclaire's fault.

Leclaire had given the mosque story to Paul Summers, but no reporter would've published it without confirmation. From whom? Grunty Hogan of the Intelligence Division, most likely. For three hundred bucks in a plain envelope, either out of Summer's own pocket or more likely reimbursed afterwards by the *Globe*. Hogan did have his uses in other regards, which was why Jack tolerated the man; he was a channel for information or disinformation that Jack wanted leaked, and Hogan knew not to overstep certain bounds. In this case, though, Hogan must have thought that watching a mosque where *foreigners* gathered was a routine precaution, which any sensible mosque should probably expect; besides, if a reporter already had wind of ICE surveillance, it wouldn't stay much of a secret for long…

Now, to add insult to injury, he'd been told in no uncertain terms to lay off her. *Daughter of Leclaire Enterprises, eh?* Whatever Daddy's goddam little empire was called in French. And he'd already lost two days physical watch on her because handling the critical Afghan passport scam had eaten all his resource. For all he knew, she could be consorting with terrorists right now!

Well, Jack wasn't going to let this go. A big bad fish was moving somewhere just under the surface, he could sense it, and Mam'zelle was his only line to the critter. Maybe he could even turn this situation to his advantage? He retrieved the phone, fortunately unbroken, and called Grunty Hogan at home.

"Grunty, Jack Turner here… Yeah, right, *not* a social call. You've been a naughty boy, confirming the mosque surveillance to that *Globe* reporter… Come on, I know it was you. And there's heat coming down on account of it… Yeah, on *me*… But you can make things right instead…You're damn right you'll have to! What I want you to do is contact that *Globe* guy, Summers. Say you have something else of interest for him, meet him wherever you do. Tell him, sell him, same thing in your case, that the boss has cancelled surveillance of the mosque. Yes, I know… but here's the bit where you need to be clever. I want you to let slip that *all* surveillance of a female professor at Radcliffe Ladies College... no, I know it isn't called *that*... Okay okay, just say Harvard, has been cancelled. Yeah, that's the assignment number, I see you're *over-informed* as usual, but *don't* mention her name. Yeah, she's into medieval research. There's no need to give a reason... just mention she has heavyweight connections. Yeah, like it's just chatter. Do you think you can manage that? Good."

Jack hung up.

And now, though this needed to be done in a black way, unauthorised, Paul Fucking Summers' phones would be bugged. Confident that Mam'zelle herself wasn't bugged, Summers would have no reason to suspect that he himself was. That way, clever Jack could follow *part* of the story at least. With luck, he ought to be able to work out what Mam'zelle was up to, as long as she trusted Summers, told him stuff, which seemed to be the case. And maybe, just maybe, she'd let something slip if she thought the heat was off. In a week or so, he'd quietly restore the taps on her landlines too; theoretically, at least, official buildings required lesser approval and, stretching a point or two, the university was official.

Dan Siegel was the guy to call next; a little dull but loyal and reliable, codename Chronicles. Not that Jack would be using a codename when calling the guy at home during the day that should be set aside for rest and prayer.

"Sorry to spoil your Sunday, Dan, if indeed I'm spoiling it... Glad to hear not... This business about Abigail Leclaire... We need to stop following her around right now, and I've already seen to that, but I need to have a little chat with you about Press guys who abuse their freedom, and about phones..."

Two minutes later Jack hung up again, and sighed heavily. All this was definitely spoiling *his* Sunday.

Southern Ethiopia: August 1158

The scrawny, scabbed, suppurating Igwe had survived for a month in the cage, the object of jibes and sharp jabs. Hakim refrained from speculation about how he himself might have fared there, and peered studiously. To his surprise, the youth suddenly scrabbled to his feet and staggered towards the doctor, a baleful rage burning in his eyes. Monkeys leapt up the bamboo poles, screaming and chattering. Collapsing upon the container of dirty water near the bars, the Igwe immersed his forehead, then lapped like a beast. Moments later, the prisoner turned aside and vomited. Blood issued from the Igwe's nostrils and one of his ears, as though his head was trying to burst.

Hakim spied a rash of purple spots amid the dirt and sores on the Igwe's dark chest. And surely the youth's neck was swollen too.

The signs of plague! Which could only have been caught in the monkey cage! Caught from a monkey! No villager showed such signs, nor had come closer to the prisoner than a spear's length.

An amazed Hakim rejoiced. Despite all the setbacks, his planning and patience had not been in vain. Here was his first reward. *Praise God!* At least one of the monkeys in the cage must carry the seed of plague within it, without itself dying. To that extent, Arwe was proved right! Yet the mechanism of transference couldn't be from ingesting the blood or tears of a weeping monkey. *Was it from biting?* The Igwe had several monkey bites upon his flesh. Yet if so, why did Arwe have Hakim *drink* blood in the protection ceremony?

Hakim's mind raced like a steed, then he hurried to find Yaqob. Whatever the explanation, they must alert the villagers at once, claiming credit for the event.

The villagers danced ecstatically, hooting and jeering as they witnessed the mounting agony and bizarre delirium of the Igwe, horribly tortured by his own body.

By noon the next day the prisoner was dead, a disgusting bag of flesh upon the floor of the cage. Black boils protruded in his groin and armpits, like toads trying to burst through the skin. Orange spots infested his thighs like beetles. When a warrior speared one of those boils in the groin, a foul-smelling liquid spilled out. Sniffing suspiciously, the monkeys had drawn as far back from the corpse as they could.

Only the very next day, a hunter brought into the village a small monkey tethered to a pole, a *young* monkey, whose hair was *grey*.

"Oh!" effused Hakim to Yaqob, to God, to anyone who would hear, "this is most excellent indeed!"

95

Scarcely a week passed after the death of the prisoner than a young warrior displaying unmistakable tokens of plague staggered into Hakim and Yaqob's hut. Swaying and dizzy, he demanded that this foreign Priest-Witch cure him.

This was all that Yaqob translated before he made an urgent excuse and darted from the hut, leaving Hakim no option but to behave as a charlatan, making passes with his hands and chanting verses from the Qu'ran as though those were magic spells. After pacifying the doomed man somewhat, Hakim hustled his 'patient' to the thorny corral for cattle at the edge of the village.

Women and children, some men too, had followed Hakim and his unsteady charge, curious or anxious. Opening the bamboo gate to the cattle compound, Hakim half-carried the plague victim inside, then began waving his arms and shouting to expel all the skinny humpbacked cows.

This was all that he could think of by way of quarantine, as recommended by some Arab physicians. Isolation seemed instinctively the best course of action. Hakim's mind worked furiously. Centuries earlier, Procopius had stated that contact with people already displaying symptoms wasn't dangerous. The dangerous time was the dormant period, while the seed of plague grew in a man before its harvest of symptoms came forth; as Arwe indeed had known.

This sick hunter must have been carried plague for a long time unawares. Mixing and mingling. Could he somehow have passed the seed on already? Was it far too late for quarantine?

The man displaying the deadly tokens had prodded the Igwe prisoner with his spear on at least two occasions witnessed by Hakim, and, yes, he'd then licked the bloody tip of his spear, sneering.

Blood on the spear had somehow transferred seeds of plague in its infancy to the owner's body.

But how? By ingestion? Or had the young warrior perhaps nicked his lips or tongue on the sharp point...?

With the shafting clarity of lightning in the night, and the vision of a bloodied spearhead between parted lips dazzling his inner mind, Hakim understood *exactly why* his experiments hadn't succeeded – and how Arwe had cunningly protected him.

Forcing the previous prisoners to consume blood and organs from weeping monkeys had failed to give them plague, *because the seeds had no way to enter their own blood, only their gut! And those three Igwe mustn't have had any cuts or wounds in their mouths.*

The essence of plague harboured in either monkey or man, Hakim realised, must enter the bloodstream *directly* in order to take hold! And invulnerability to plague must be subject to this same rule. There'd been an open wound in his mouth on that evening of the protection ceremony. Arwe had seen to that by knocking out the tooth; an acute observer, he'd probably been aware of the condition for weeks. No doubt the cunning Priest-Witch would otherwise have resorted to an alternate plan, maybe nicking Hakim's lips with a sharp edge of the monkey skull.

Right now Hakim couldn't concentrate on this realisation. Some women and older children were taking charge of the expelled cattle to stop them from wandering off. All other eyes were upon him. He shut the bamboo gate, then spied Yaqob at the edge of the crowd.

"Come here at once!" Hakim bellowed.

Sheepishly Yaqob pushed his way forward.

"You dog, you deserted me!" Immediately Hakim regretted his hotly spat words, and contrived a smile. "If you had gone from me, as dear Sadiq went from me, I would have been inconsolable. Oh I feared you had run from the village."

Yaqob looked shamefaced. "I beg forgiveness. I was overcome by fear. But bands of Igwe scouts are lurking in the forest. I realized that my place is here, so that we may protect one another."

"So then, good Yaqob," replied Hakim. "Which is the greater fear? Of possible disease here, or almost certain capture and torture? Come now, we must organise our hosts to protect themselves." Now at least he could issue instructions that would be understood.

Ian Watson & Andy West

Roxbury, Boston, Massachusetts: April 2008

Walid al-Areqi pulled his robe closely about him as he strolled along Columbus Avenue. The late night air was quite nippy, more like fall than spring, and rain seemed to be threatening as dark, raggy clouds hid the stars. An empty yellow cab cruised by at no great speed, but Walid could tell that the vehicle was registered in Cambridge, thus it couldn't legally pick him up in Boston even if he waved; and anyway he ought to walk home, for the exercise. A sudden downpour wouldn't harm him. Years ago, he might have interpreted a vacant cab ignoring a signalling man, dressed such as he was, as ethnic prejudice. Now, he knew much better. How many rages and acts of violence in the world were due to mere misunderstandings?

So he was very pleased he could help Abigail to cast some enlightenment and also to further their blossoming friendship. Via her publications, a greater understanding of Islamic literature would penetrate western minds. And how curious that the obscure topic she was currently pursuing with such tenacity was connected to the perplexing scholarly problem he'd been wrestling with himself – the alternative and mysterious, almost buried Ismaili interpretation of *the waters of life*. Yet it seemed this was so, and it gratified him to have made some reportable progress. He should also introduce her to Kamal as soon as may be. It gratified him too to flatter Abigail a little, emphasising her Frenchness, her looks. Then a wry smile escaped him. How ridiculous! For a man his age to act so, just because she was pretty.

Rain began to spit. Though only to spit. Under a streetlamp a king-size discarded pizza box grinned, graphic eyes of sliced pepperoni, nose of chilli pepper, smiley tomato paste mouth. Walid felt a sudden, childlike impulse to kick the box along the sidewalk. That wouldn't be very dignified! Besides, maybe a rat had slunk inside the gaudy cardboard, smelling a faint odour of food. Even so, his feet performed a little jig and he recalled games of football long ago in dusty, war-damaged places.

He passed a parked black SUV in which someone was sitting. Momentarily their eyes met. A round-faced Asian of some sort, with light-chocolate skin, so it seemed in the poor light. Maybe Filipino or Indonesian or from somewhere thereabouts. The man seemed to have one eyebrow above another on the right side of his face, which looked a bit weird; though the Asian then looked away.

Walid proceeded in a reverie and turned into a dark alley that was his usual short cut. He was a third of the way along when bright lights flooded the narrow corridor of brick and concrete from behind him, the glaring main beams of some vehicle. As he glanced back it accelerated with a roar, filling the alley with its rushing bulk, just as fear filled his mind. The driver was mad! Cars normally ambled down here, so as to avoid pedestrians.

Gesturing a warning, Walid flattened himself up against the nearest wall. Dazzle that pained his eyes was accompanied by an aghast and paralysing bafflement; the vehicle didn't intend to avoid him! Just seconds later, a moment of crushing agony, almost too brief for any thought.

Downtown Boston, Massachusetts: April 2008

Paul emerged into sunshine from Haymarket station and cut across the vastness of City Hall Plaza, paved with nearly two million dull red bricks. He headed for the John F. Kennedy Federal Building, which rose up as a blunt statement of modernity, twin high-rise towers of concrete and glass joined at right angles to one another, their bands of windows rounding at the corners, plus a lower four-storey building, its vicinity blessed by the only trees and shrubs in sight. This was home to the IRS and other government agencies, including the various divisions of ICE.

Paul walked on by, towards the curve of Cambridge Street and Center Plaza, which resembled a matching curved skyscraper on its side. Grunty Hogan favoured the Kinsale Irish Pub there. Being mid-afternoon by now, the enthusiastic lunch trade should all have departed back to their business and government offices.

Grunty had said he had interesting news *about a certain matter*.

Presently Paul was seated on a high bar stool at a table-top curving around a wooden pillar, which disappeared into the likeness of a hooped barrel below. A glass of the dark stuff was before him, and a cracked-open paperback history of the Middle Ages, since that was Abigail's thing. The bar area was hardly quarter-full. A particularly authentic Irish pub, the Kinsale, having been manufactured in Ireland and shipped over in crates.

Grunty entered, somewhat podgy and red-faced, wearing a lightweight grey suit, though he'd loosened his green tie and opened his top shirt button. After a minute's chat with the barman, he steered towards Paul, glass in hand, and mounted the neighbouring stool.

"*Unk*," he expressed, "your very good health, young man."

Paul had never been quite sure whether Grunty habitually cleared the back of a stuffed-up nose with an *unk*, or whether the tic was his version of *hmm* or *um*.

"So what do you have to tell me about *the matter?*"

"And what would you be having, *unk*, for me?"

Paul slid a flat envelope from his pocket, although he kept his hand resting upon the offering.

"It's like this. All surveillance of the mosque has been called off."

"As a direct result of my piece in the *Globe?* Or due to complaints received?"

"I'd say, *unk*, there have been certain *enquiries*."

He'd say... but was that a fact?

"I'd say, Grunty, that what you're telling me is a bit predictable. I don't think it really merits…" Paul's hand pressed more firmly upon the envelope.

Grunty looked aggrieved. "Here was me thinking you'd be pleased to hear. Grateful."

"I am for the confirmation in the first place, but we already cleared that slate."

"What else am I supposed to tell you about surveillances, or cancelled ones? Ain't much. Some prof woman at Harvard cancelled, some Afghans ongoing but you'd better not print *that*. Neither print nor hint. I thought you'd be glad to hear about the mosque."

"What's that about Harvard?" asked Paul.

"Some foreign research female, *unk*, with heavyweight connections. British… No, Canadian. Investigation office had to lay off, no following her, no messing with her phones, whatever for. Getting back, *unk*, to the mosque cancellation, I'd say I deserve an acknowledgement."

Oh richly deserve. Though not for that.

Judiciously Paul pulled the envelope towards him, slipped it open, extracted two bills which he pocketed, then thrust the remaining acknowledgement Grunty's way.

"Right," he said. "An acknowledgment in proportion."

Southern Ethiopia: September 1158

The village descended into chaos, yet Hakim's thought was consumed more by intricate puzzles about transference of plague than by the plight of the villagers. All the old writings agreed as regards rampant contagion – and the devastating progress of plague through nations, with its virtual erasure of entire cities, is what made the disease so attractive as the ultimate weapon against unbelief. Hakim was now convinced that the bloodstream must become seeded. Yet the villagers were certainly not biting each other, nor transferring bodily fluids into the veins of others by a different route. A paradox!

At first Hakim's authority was sufficient that he could tour the village constantly, inspecting for signs of plague and, if found, ordering the afflicted person to proceed forthwith to the former cattle corral, or in some cases be carried there. He had the corral guarded, and its occupants supplied with food and water. Believing himself protected, Hakim shirked no contact, often carrying or tending to victims himself.

Yet, as the weeks went by and the corral became a place of hideous death, the terrified villagers began to disobey him and abuse him. Manifestly, the foreign Priest-Witch was failing to save them. Malevolent monkey spirits must be to blame, maybe offended at having been confined with the Igwe for so long. Or angry at being confined in the first place.

Hakim kept meticulous records of the whole event, down to every date and symptom and individual and hut location. Hence, reading these back by the wavering light of an oil-lamp, he realised that the spread was primarily through family lines, with cousins or cross-matings connecting the leap of sickness between huts. Somehow, *somehow*, without bites or scratches or even in most cases sexual coupling, the infant seeds of plague were finding their way into the blood of those closest to the victim. Clearly this was possible between people, if not between men and monkeys even when trapped in the same cage. He ordered all contact between each hut to cease, with each obtaining their own water and grain independently. But it was too late; the villagers ignored him.

Just two days later, an old warrior and some younger companions freed all the monkeys, even the precious grey one that was kept separately. When Hakim tried to intervene, he was threatened by spears, although no one went so far as to prick him. The day might not be far off, Hakim realised, when they would do so! Order had almost collapsed. Infected people decamped deliriously into the forest, despite the nightly whooping cries of hyenas. In daylight, uninfected people fled the village too, leaving even less of the able-bodied to cope.

And then Yaqob succumbed. Hakim offered what aid he could, which was useless, so he observed carefully until the end. This came quickly, for the first paroxysm proved fatal. Now there was no way to communicate, nor achieve anything more. Taking only what he could easily carry, Hakim slipped out of the village just before dawn. The Igwe scouts had hopefully been scared away long before, but he couldn't go anywhere near their territory. Nor anywhere he might be recognized by previous visitors to the village during its time of glory as a monkey Mecca, for word of the plague had undoubtedly spread and he would almost certainly be killed out of hand. He struck out into unknown woodland.

Cronkite Graduate Center, Cambridge, Massachusetts: April 2008

When the doorbell of her apartment woke Abigail, she squinted at the bedside clock, bleary-eyed, imagining for a moment that the alarm had rung. 8.00 a.m. Was she forgetting something important? But then the doorbell rang again. A faint echo of interrupted dream still chased around her memory; Jack Turner stabbing her with questions. Was it him standing outside, shoving an acoustic ice-pick into her brain! Surely that bastard knew that she'd only meet him on neutral territory. Or was it Terry? At 8 a.m.? Impossible! Then Friday's events flooded back...

Their terrible break-up. Leaving him among all that chaos. A pall of guilt and depression forced a groan from her. She slipped out of bed, half hoping *it was* Terry. Perhaps she could retrieve some friendship and honour from the emotional wreckage; offer to help him clean up the apartment.

Impelled by another insistent ring, she pulled a green silk dressing-gown over her shortie pyjamas, belting the gown as she padded into the tiny hallway, bumping the door-jamb on the way. *Be careful of your toes, a banged toe hurts like hell.* The floors of these residences in the Cronkite Graduate Center on Brattle Street were hardwood throughout, and she hadn't put down any rugs.

It wasn't Terry, nor Jack. The peephole fish-eyed a dark-complexioned, middle-aged man with a trim salt-and-pepper beard, dressed in a pin-stripe suit and plain grey tie. Who on Earth? Then amazed recognition dawned on Abigail; it was that fairly dishy, sophisticated-looking academic who'd been at the CMES reception, yeah, standing nearby when she'd lost control of her glass. But... What...? Her sleepy brain gave up even trying to form the question and she opened the door, though keeping the chain on.

As soon as she did so, she could see what hadn't been obvious due to the distortion of the lens; the man wore a reluctant and troubled expression.

"Dr Abigail Leclaire?"

"Yes?"

"My name is Kamal al-Mustafa Abu al-Bashir. I'm an acquaintance of Walid al-Areqi."

He must be the selfsame academic Walid had said he might introduce her to... Why ever should he be standing at her door at eight in the morning? Walid mentioning her name couldn't possibly cause the man to pay her a personal visit at home, never mind at such an hour!

"I do apologise," said her visitor, "for intruding upon you so early." Now he looked compassionate, she thought, and faint apprehension whispered inside her. "But I gathered that you were quite close to Walid, a good friend in fact. So I took it upon myself… Your phone number was in Walid's notebook, and an operator was helpful with the address." His English was excellent and almost courtly, the accent softly vibrant in a very attractive way. "I felt that a personal visit was best. A phone call to you would have been… inadequate."

"What's wrong?" she demanded. "What's *wrong*?"

"May I come inside? I do realise you're probably alone, but if we could overlook the offence to etiquette. Walid spoke very highly indeed of you, and of your admirable desire to understand aspects of our faith."

Could dear Walid have rather over-emphasised the scope of her interest, the better to further her cause? She slipped the chain and stood back then, after he'd entered the hallway, closed the front door.

"What's wrong?" she whispered, grasping already that something serious must be.

"It is that your friend Walid, our beloved and wise colleague, has tragically died."

"Died? But how?"

"He was *knocked down*, I think the expression goes in English. It sounds so innocent, doesn't it? In reality the vehicle brutally crushed Walid, peace be upon him in the name of Allah the Merciful. That was last night, on his way home."

Abigail's jaw dropped. Words failed her.

"He was slain by the hand of a drunkard, is my belief. Such an evil of our modern times. I felt it beholden upon me to spare you from perhaps learning this unawares from local television or the newspapers. And to invite you to the funeral, as well as to the litanies of remembrance at the mosque in Roxbury, though that will not be for forty days."

Abigail felt chill and confused. Still struggling to absorb yesterday's drama and loss, her thought couldn't grasp the enormity of this new and much crueller loss. She was suddenly aware of her life teetering on free-fall. She fought against dizziness.

"Crushed?"

Kamal seemed to gather himself, and Abigail sensed within him an aura of great competence in relationships, a warm confidence, as though he was more than an ordinary man yet at the same time serenely concealed that fact.

"There is mercy in this," he softly intoned. "Walid would not have felt anything. Do not be afraid for him, his soul is safe, and on the Day of Judgement will gain paradise. The pain and suffering will be borne by those left behind. We must share our loss, and share our strength."

Kamal firmly clasped Abigail's shoulder, and indeed his touch seemed like a lifeline. She lurched against her visitor, as though a gale of horrors was blowing and he was a great boulder that could shelter her. Kamal held her, his strong muscles a comfort, his odour of sandalwood. Then he led her to her small kitchen, with scarcely a glance at her abandoned bed. After helping seat her in the upright Shaker chair, which he seemed to intuit that she favoured, he glanced around and then to her utter surprise brought down a cognac glass and a half-full bottle of Martell, from which he proceeded to pour a half-inch for her, which she gladly drained.

Kamal seated himself opposite. Self-conscious and shaking, Abigail pulled her silk gown tight around herself, but the Arab gentleman looked only to her face or towards the window, beyond which the crown of a horse-chestnut tree bore white candelabra in bud, offered to a fluffy sky. Gulls winged past, crying mournfully. To Abigail the familiar scene seemed now to hint at candles, at souls.

"Around midnight one of our own…ah, congregation… came across the body. He ran first to the mosque for assistance. It may help you," he suggested, "to reminisce about Walid, whom you surely knew better than I. It is a way of letting his merits live afresh a little longer. It will console."

As he, already, was consoling her in such a noble way.

"I guess you know why I was consulting Walid in the first place," Abigail began.

Her visitor spreads his hands. "No, I *don't*. It was just the other day that Walid spoke about you, in glowing terms I might add, though only briefly. Which is partly why I'm here. Walid and I didn't go into details. We both had so many calls on our time."

Time, that Walid had so unstintingly devoted to Abigail's little quest!

"Time," said Kamal almost telepathically, "which was tragically to be cut so short. Walid simply expressed his admiration for your work and said you'd uncovered something important and puzzling."

To this kindly man, Abigail said, "You must still be very busy. I don't want to use up *your* precious time." Another reason why he'd arrived at her door so early, yet had the courtesy not to mention.

"I have," replied Kamal with evident sincerity, "absolutely as much time for you, as Walid himself had."

Roxbury, Boston, Massachusetts: April 2008

For a hundred dollars, Abigail had hired a long black dress with hat and veil. Her first thought had been to find something suitable knocked down by 75% in Filene's Basement, but then she didn't feel at all like rummaging with eager bargain hunters to equip herself for such a sad occasion. She hardly wished to keep the sombre outfit afterwards; she wasn't planning on any more funerals in the near future.

As she scanned the gathered mourners in the assembly hall, to her surprise she saw ringleted hair. Paul Summers? Why should he be here? She walked over, relieved there was someone else here that she knew.

"Paul?"

It was him indeed, in a charcoal grey suit, complete with goofy grin as soon as he saw her. Then realisation visibly washed across his face, erasing the grin.

"I'm so sorry Abigail, I didn't realise. That cleric friend you talked about... it was Walid al-Areqi?"

A tight band of melancholy gripped Abigail. "Yes," she mumbled, "yes it *was*."

"I had no way to know. I'm so sorry," he repeated.

Abigail breathed deeply to fend off her sadness. "It's okay. But what are *you* doing here?"

"More mosque-related news, among other reasons. My territory at the *Globe*." He blushed slightly. "Oh, as you know, of course."

Poor Paul seemed more uncomfortable and out of place than she did, mused Abigail. She beamed to instil confidence. "I'm *very* grateful for your story. You got my email?"

"Oh, yes." Paul shuffled his feet. "Hey, it's quite an achievement for our M.E.'s office to manage an autopsy and release the body within just a couple of days. Maybe the medical examiner's heedful of Muslim sensitivities."

"Perhaps. But that doesn't make up for other officials who are grossly *insensitive*, or worse!"

Paul smiled conspiratorially. "Well, we did something about that." He frowned. "Which reminds me, I've something pretty important to tell you, but not just now, I guess the service will be starting in a few minutes. Afterwards?"

Abigail nodded, and at that point Kamal appeared. His place was with the other Muslim mourners, but he came to condole with Abigail for a short while, once again promising whatever help he could provide towards her researches.

"Not that I could ever replace such a scholar as Walid in any sense! Yet in attempting to fill the breech, I'd feel that I'm honouring Walid's memory. And I may be of some use." He contemplated dark-suited, crazy-haired Paul, whom Abigail had merely introduced by name. "Hmm… I believe you're that valiant reporter… the one who broke the news about a certain government agency carrying out surveillance of the mosque here in Roxbury."

Paul grinned. "How did you work that out?"

"Your photograph was with your by-line, in the *Globe*. I presume you're here today professionally."

Paul nodded. "Yeah. There'll be a small column with some obituary. Walid was a pillar of the community, as I'm sure you know."

"So you aren't precisely a mourner, unlike your companion."

"Oh, I mourn such a murder all right, make no mistake."

"Murder?" Kamal's eyes widened in shock.

"It amounts to that, doesn't it? I ran the *Globe's* campaign against hit and runs a couple of years back, after that spate of them. Most of the drivers were DUI, or stoned."

"Ah, so you argue that getting into their car forms the deliberate act. I'm inclined to agree, especially as this has robbed us of one so dear." Kamal's gaze lingered on Paul and Abigail, but then he needed to rejoin his group. "Excuse me, Dr Leclaire, Mr Summers."

"Weird," commented Paul. "It's as if he was trying to suss out our relationship, but wouldn't ask outright."

"Relationship?" queried Abigail.

"For want of a better word."

"He was just being courteous. Are reporters suspicious of every darn thing?"

Paul shrugged. "Just, I'm used to phrasing questions to gain a desired result."

"I'd better be careful of you, then." Abigail flashed a smile, in case she might have caused offence; but then the occasion erased that smile, and indeed epitaphs for gentle Walid, many spoken in English as if for her benefit, soon brought tears, which continued to flow as they filed outside for the actual burial.

Afterwards, tissues still in hand, Abigail was keen to find out what Paul had to tell her.

"I discovered something just recently, Abigail. It's important, I mean important *to you*. I was going to arrange to see you anyhow. Shall we walk a while?"

They strolled off in a direction that offered minimal traffic noise. Paul spoke quietly. "My contact, whom I checked with about the mosque surveillance... Well, yesterday afternoon I saw him again. He told me that surveillance is finished, cancelled, kaput."

"Why, that's great! Well done, you. The power of the press!"

"That's not all. We got talking about other surveillances. And he happened to mention a 'prof woman at Harvard'."

Abigail groaned.

"Exactly," said Paul. "To think when we were in Café Lorca the other day I made that daft joke about you being bugged. But it was true."

"I've certainly been followed, by ICE."

"Not any more you aren't. My source didn't seem to know you by name, or what this is all about, but I made the connection all right. *Surveillance of the woman prof has also been cancelled*, he said, *from on high*. Because, it seems, of her 'weighty connections'. Maybe the mosque snooping getting uncovered helped a bit. So you aren't being followed anymore! No one's listening in on any of your phone calls, if in fact they were doing so before."

"Oh, that's *such* a relief to know. Thank you so much, Paul. I really owe you for this."

She beamed hugely at him, but his returned gaze was troubled.

"Is there anything else you'd like to tell me about all this?" he said. "I know that must sound inquisitive! Questions, desired results, I said it myself... I don't mean to be intrusive but... Well, I haven't gotten the whole story here. I mean, why were you being followed in the first place? Even ICE wouldn't do that just because you visited the mosque. And you mentioned a medieval poem – is that connected somehow?"

Abigail shook her head, then stared into the distance.

"I can't think straight today. I do miss Walid. I have to do a lot of serious thinking."

"Okay..." Paul's tone was conciliatory, even gentle. "But can you say what your heavyweight connections are?"

Abigail gave a wry smile. "That'll be my Papa. Leclaire Enterprises."

Paul's eyes bulged. "Fu... er, wow! Industrial technology, advanced hydraulics, military vehicles, system integrator, US government defence contracts, that's you?"

"My Papa," insisted Abigail, "not me! It's usually a burden, but for once it came in handy. Oh I hope he doesn't find out personally what's been going on... He worries, he tries to protect me too much."

"Well..." said Paul. But for once he was lost for words. "Well..."

Tehran, Iran: February 2008

Blood gushed from Bashir's nose as he gritted his teeth to avoid howling. Surely his nose was broken!

"What have you *done*, Amin?" demanded the instructor angrily. "Medic!" he called.

"I apologise," said Amin earnestly. "Oh Bashir, I'm so sorry, I…"

To score his point, Amin should have halted the strike of his knife-hand a fraction of an inch short of the base of Bashir's nose. The nasal bone might have been driven into the frontal sinus if the blow had fully carried through. Amin had indeed stopped his strike, but an instant too late.

"You want to make my face a sight to see at passport checks?" bellowed Bashir, as a first aider rushed onto the practice mat. "What if we are called upon earlier than we expect?"

"No no no no, I swear in God's name. You're my comrade, not a competitor! I curse learning combat."

"You may need combat," snapped the instructor, "to evade capture! Hopefully you'll never need to… Yet you must be as prepared as possible."

As the first aider examined Bashir's injury, the masseur came to rub herbal cream onto Amin's hands…

Radcliffe Institute for Advanced Study, Cambridge, Massachusetts: May 2008

When Kamal phoned Abigail at her desk a couple of days after Walid's funeral, she'd only just been thinking about him – and how much more competent, courteous and compassionate he seemed than the creature of chaos that was Terry, *for sure* now relegated permanently to the past tense! A truly international personage. Terry couldn't even cope in his own backyard. Yet Kamal probably wouldn't find much time for Abigail's puzzles, so she shouldn't badger him.

But then the phone rang.

"Dr Leclaire, this is Kamal al-Mustafa Abu al-Bashir. Be assured I haven't forgotten my promise. I need to be in Back Bay soon and I was wondering whether we might talk over lunch, if you're able to pop down from Harvard? This would give me a fine excuse to enjoy what you might call my native cuisine, at the excellent Jewel of Newbury restaurant."

"Oh, I've heard of it." *Not* the most graceful reply; she should have said: *it's so kind of you to find the time.*

"You'd be my guest, of course."

Abigail frantically searched for something intelligent to say, but her head had emptied.

"Well, thank you…"

"No, I thank *you*. I couldn't possibly indulge myself on my own."

The perfect gentleman! The Jewel of Newbury was pricey.

"In fact tomorrow would be fine, if that isn't too soon."

"So I'll make a reservation for twelve-thirty, if that's suitable. I'll give you my mobile number in case you have any problems. Oh, and please do call me *Kamal*, for simplicity…"

"In that case, you must call me Abigail."

He read out the number. "Until tomorrow, Abigail." He hung up.

God, what should she wear? Just two days after she'd mourned at Walid's funeral… The black dress was still awaiting return. Maybe that, obviously minus veil and hat, but with a modest flower-spray pinned on to lessen the severity? Though Kamal seemed willing to 'indulge' himself, as he gallantly put it; so maybe something informal, though business-like. Slacks, blouse, and a jacket. Yes, and something to indicate sensitivity: a black chiffon scarf.

Southern Ethiopia: October 1158

The cries of monkeys mocked Hakim as he staggered onward through the steamy forest. Was he simply thrashing futile circles through the dense tangles of twisted trees draped with moss and bearded with woolly creepers?

Due to some quirk of weather, sunlight shafted down through the dripping leaf canopy like golden spears stabbing at the broken ant that was Hakim. God's light, the *Nur* from which the world had been made! The light in which the Prophet, peace be upon him, had been forged! The light which shone through the Imams, making them the bright lamps of heaven and Earth! The light that revealed truth!

Sinking to his knees, Hakim vomited a thin, bitter gruel of berries and snails. Radiance wheeled dizzily around him. Surely he was on his knees to pray. How many weeks had he been lost? A bird, whose name he did not know, flew by in a blur of bright wings.

Did he recite his prayers in the right order? In his mind the voice of a Yemeni muezzin seemed to cry, *Hayya 'ala khayri-l-amal*, Rise up for the Best of Works!

Yes, for the Best of Works he must indeed rise up, stinking and shaking, from his soiled and filthy knees! Remember, remember! Before he became so sickly, so lost in this wet and tangled forest, home to predators, had he not been engaged in the Best of Works?

Swaying on his feet, Hakim spied a movement of reddish-brown amid the tumbling green mosses and pale tree-beards. Perhaps he was seeing double, although one of the two shapes in tentative motion seemed to be much smaller than the other. Instinctively he unscabbarded his sword and, with failing muscles, flung it wherever the blade might choose to go, yet with a word of prayer he hoped would recommend its course to heaven. It flew in a lazy arc, turning over and over.

A squeal! As Hakim stumbled forward, the larger shape took flight but a young bushbuck lay with its legs kicking, struggling to rise, pierced by blessed steel through its russet, white-spotted flank, which blood was swiftly blemishing. As the animal's small face jerked towards him, wide-eyed and panting, Hakim threw himself upon the hilt of the sword, thrusting and twisting.

The young antelope's death came soon. Hakim was aware of the mother watching from nearby cover, yet she lacked horns so could do nothing. An angel of Allah had guided the sword, sacrificing her child.

Hakim's butchery was cursory. Soon he was chewing raw meat and sucking blood. He did not vomit because the nourishing blood was angel-sent. A voice seemed to sing:

As sperm from man's backbone
reposes itself in a womb
so divine knowledge from God
settles within the Imam
trustee of authority and blood!

Trustee of blood, trustee of the knowledge of blood... Surely he, Hakim, was that; surely he was trustee of the knowledge of blood which would cleanse, which would wash away the unfaithful from the world.

A week after he had gorged himself on the bushbuck, by Allah's mercy and hopes for him, Hakim heard an Arabic word shouted far away.

How long had he been wandering like an animal? A month? He slapped his hand to his scabbard, momentarily convinced that beside it he wore a stoppered bottle in which he had captured plague like a jinnee. Yet alas, that was an illusion borne of the utter conviction that such was possible. And *would be* possible! Only, he would need more companions, more supplies, more funds.

He combed his hair and beard as best he could with his fingers. He could do little about the filthy rags hanging off him, yet he tore some away. And he still wore his sword, which an angel had guided. He croaked, then spoke his full name aloud, before heading towards the source of that Arabic word.

A Muslim hunting camp. Tents. Horses. Arabs and their slaves. Fire and food. Blessèd, sacred hospitality. Hygiene and clothes. Prayers.

Hakim was very floridly well-spoken and courteous in his gratitude, as befitting a scholar of the famous al-Azhar University in Cairo, sent on a mission of botanical exploration by the Caliph, which was the role he dissembled. Alas, he related, disaster had overtaken the expedition.

Inside, Hakim seethed impatiently while his recovery granted him new strength, and he dreamed about millions of the people of opposition being consumed by plague, but he betrayed none of this.

The Jewel of Newbury restaurant, Boston, Massachusetts: May 2008

Even though Abigail turned up five minutes early, Kamal was already waiting outside. His smile immediately set her at ease.

The restaurant was in a boutique hotel, a restored 19th century town house exalted into a luxurious and elegant evocation of North Africa and the Middle East. As dark-suited Kamal escorted her inside, she admired stained-glass panelling and tiles, ceramics and antique furniture. A bar was Art Deco: mirrors, metal, crystals.

"A preliminary cocktail for you, Abigail?"

"No, thank you. With the meal, some squeezed orange juice perhaps."

Soon they were seated at a round white marble table, being attended by a waiter who behaved more like a private butler. Kamal suggested roasted aubergine, to be followed by a lamb tagine flavoured with olives and prunes. Abigail wondered whether he was married, whether he had children. She saw no ring, should that be the custom.

He smiled, showing good teeth. "I do hope you can do justice to the food, even if you're on a diet like so many young women these days, except for those who would benefit by a diet! A lunchtime meeting seemed more suitable to me than a dinner, even though this place has a rooftop garden especially beloved by couples for its views of the city at night."

Abigail found herself imagining what that rooftop garden might be like of an evening, accompanied by such a man.

"On the phone you said 'native cuisine', Kamal. If I'm not being impudent, does that mean you're from North Africa originally?"

"Abigail, these days I travel around so much, sometimes I think I'm from half a dozen countries! But I was born Syrian."

"Where Sinan... Rashid al-Din, had his stronghold..."

"You are well-versed in history! Have you been to Syria?"

Their orange juices arrived.

"Unfortunately not. I'd love to see Krak des Chevalier and such places."

"The finest Crusader castle anywhere."

"Actually, my urgent problem is the Syrian and Iranian background to a fragment of Provençal poetry I found, which refers to an 'eagle teacher'..."

Kamal set down his orange juice much too close to the edge of the table. "Your glass!"

Reacting almost instantly, he caught the glass even as it tipped. Some juice slopped on to his hand, which he proceeded to dry with the linen napkin.

"Apologies for my clumsiness."

"No way, I wish I had such fast reflexes."

"At my age, no less?" he queried ironically.

"Give me maturity any day, rather than frustrating *immaturity*." Terry, maybe even Paul, would likely have sent orange juice flying all over the floor.

"Well, I'm all ears, Abigail. Do tell me everything."

Tehran, Iran, May 2008

The Doctor, with latex gloves and an air-tight mask his only protection other than a white lab coat, held the hypodermic syringe on open palms as though it were a poison-tipped dagger of old being presented to bare-armed Ali, Assassin of the Unfaithful. From the chair alongside Ali, the other supremely privileged courier of death, Muhammad, a sleeve likewise rolled up, watched raptly, as did two senior witnesses seated further away, one of whom was videoing so that the two suicide martyrs could be commemorated in years to come. This was at the prompting of Jafar, who had warned from doomed America to advance the date. Jafar should have been here as witness too. He'd very much wish to watch that hallowed video when he returned.

"At last the day has come," the Doctor said solemnly, "as willed by God long ago, when my inspired and blessed predecessor created and preserved the waters of death, and of life, for our use when time and our God-given skills became ripe..."

Radcliffe Institute for Advanced Study, Cambridge, Massachusetts: May 2008

When the phone rang, Abigail was glad of a break; she'd been so intensely absorbed in books on early Ismaili culture and poetry, as recommended by Kamal, that she felt dizzy when she raised her head. The caller was Paul Summers, in theory to tell her about readers' letters regarding the mosque surveillance piece, but really sniffing for a deeper story as well as sniffing out an eligible female. She smirked. Nice to be chased again, even if she wasn't interested. Paul made a polite query about Kamal.

"Kamal's being incredibly helpful with my research," she said, "considering how busy he is."

"You're a very persuasive woman, Abi."

"I don't think *woman* has anything at all to do with it." *Though did it? Could it conceivably?*

"Sorry. *Person*. But since you're a woman too, may I take you out to dinner?"

"Journalist's ulterior motive? You want to pump me for more about my medieval mystery?" She'd known at the funeral that he'd ask sooner or later. A funeral was the wrong moment, though, and besides the revelation about her Papa had seemed to intimidate him. Not the first time *that* had happened. In Paul's case this didn't matter; no romance at stake.

"I'm deeply hurt, but anyhow haven't I earned the right?"

Abigail smiled. He had. Then something occurred to her.

"I'd love to be taken for dinner, but can I choose the place?"

"Hmm... unusual rules, but I'm a flexible guy."

"The Sabra restaurant, Eliot Square off J.F.K. Street. Middle Eastern, shawarma and shish-kebab on the menu. Won't break the budget."

Paul readily agreed, and they hung up.

She'd been thinking of the Sabra for a reciprocation with Kamal. Though at just five or six dollars for dishes, he'd be slumming it. The waiters wouldn't be butlers. Despite modest prices, the invitation could be a charming gesture, and proof she wasn't a parasite. *Now* she could test the place in advance. If it seemed mediocre to her, Kamal would find it dire. But if it seemed good, or even great...

Sabra restaurant, Cambridge, Massachusetts: May 2008

At seven that evening the Sabra was bustling, though it was the kind of bustle where you could be private at your own little table due to all the conflicting noisy chatter.

"Baba Ghanoush sounds interesting," commented Abigail to Paul. "Puréed smoked eggplant. Says it's exotic."

"The exotic isn't necessarily *nice*."

"Aphorism of the day? Well, I think I'll try it. Drinks? Oh, there's no wine."

"Or beer. Homemade lemonade for me. I don't think I need zesty carrot juice." Paul wrinkled his nose, rabbit-like, but then suddenly he was serious. "Look, Abi, my newsman's nose says there's a whole lot going on with you that I don't know about, and maybe you're out of your depth."

"I can cope," returned Abigail. But could she? Men like Jack didn't just give up.

"Who in ICE is hassling you, and why? Why is that old poem such a big deal?" His questions sounded like entreaties. He gazed at her earnestly, like a loyal dog.

Abigail wavered. "He's called Jack Turner. He seems a big-size fish, in Boston at least, but… misguided."

"I already helped you, Abi. Maybe I can help you again."

The Press was a powerful ally, and Paul could make a good friend. It was as if a dam burst inside Abigail. Safiyya's fragment. *Eagle Teacher.* The insights that sweet gentle Walid had given her… until his untimely death. The Assassins of Alamut. Paul had swiftly pulled out his smartphone as well as a notebook, setting the former into audio record mode. "Hang on, go back," he'd interrupted. "Don't know if our voices will pick up too well with all this background…" He scribbled valiantly. 'Hospitaller have pity'. Holy Water. Jack Frost's crazy notion about a terrorist plot…

Their food and lemonade arrived, and he could cope with listening and eating and note-taking all at once. Abigail was mostly neglecting her puréed smoked aubergine, and Paul didn't care to interrupt her flow.

So who exactly was Sinaldin? And where did he get his Holy Water from? And what exactly *was* his Holy Water? And did the Hospitaller Guy de Dieulefit leave any records or legacy or just even a tomb, to find more out about him? Safiyya likewise? What did all this have to do with plague? Finally, Abigail gulped lemonade.

"Wow," said Paul. "But Mrs Lincoln, did you enjoy the Baba Ghanoush?"

Abigail noticed her toyed-with meal. "I don't know," she said. "How about yours?"

"Great. Succulent. And the feta in the salad went well."

"That's all right, then." She could safely invite Kamal.

Drawing a line under serious matters, they made small talk during dessert, Abigail consuming hers with more enthusiasm than her main dish. But later as they parted company at Harvard station, Abigail insisting she could walk the rest of the way home on her own, she felt a stab of guilt. Paul couldn't imagine she was romantically encouraging him, could he? So was she just using him?

Boston, Massachusetts: May 2008

As Paul travelled homeward towards his eventual destination of Revere Beach in the north-east, he pulled out his notebook, intending to make additions while Abi's tale was still fresh in his mind. But his pen soon faltered and he found himself wondering why on Earth he'd told her explicitly that he lived with a Retriever and a dad. Sure, this showed he was unattached, but you wouldn't think he was a hot-shot journalist accustomed to honing his phrases. Just as well he hadn't also blurted out the dog's name – Rudolph. Rudolph the Retriever, like some kiddies' cartoon character. Abigail would've laughed, though she mightn't be so amused by his home environment. Three males, one of them canine, in a house without womanly presence; piles of old mags and newspapers on the floors, all the higgledy-piggledy books! Tidying would ruin their highly informal filing system. Which didn't mean you could tell Rudolph: "Good boy, fetch me the atlas."

Each time he met Abigail, it seemed he admired and desired her more. He would turn cartwheels for her. No, that would make him look like a clown. He'd help her all he could. That tumbling golden hair and those intelligent greeny eyes; her assertive chin; her cushioned slimness; breasts evident though far from trying to burst her clothes. Ideal, really.

Should he mention to Abigail that his mother ran off with a charismatic and seductive preacher, of all people? Apparently the pair were now making a tidy income from their crusade in Kansas. Or mention that his desolated, *insulted* dad did his best, and never brought another woman near their home? Although Paul had done so a couple of times. No, no. That would all sound as if he was trying to push a sympathy button.

He was *normal.* Just, things never lasted... The relationships were too shallow. Yet Abigail... for better or worse, Abigail was deep. In those depths she was hiding things, maybe even from herself. So would it be appropriate concern, or *obsession*, if he looked into more than just her medieval mystery? Walid's death niggled. Inappropriately timed, as regards Abigail's research! *Or not?* Great though it had been to see her at the funeral, odd connections and coincidences always bugged him. Would it be naked jealousy to check out Kamal al-whatever?

The Nile: November 1158

They slipped down the Upper Nile, the raucous dawns of lush jungle far behind them. Hakim sat by the bow and listened to the ripple of water, which gave him hope of a swift return to civilisation, hope of progress. The new sun rose into a purple sky, a vast silk tent anchored left and right at distant black banks like sleeping dogs stretched out. The boat sliced through burnished water, its single sail engorged on the dawn breeze.

Much later in the morning, Hakim observed bleached villages trying to hide under scattered palms. The boatmen ate bread and fish. Hakim didn't associate much with them. Like many people outside the major towns of Egypt they were Sunnis, despite two centuries of Ismaili dominance under the Fatimid dynasty. It was in this very country, in Cairo, that the Ismaili cause itself had faltered, when some sixty-five years ago the light of the one true Imam had flickered out. That light was championed now only by the Nizaris of Mid-Syria and Persia, while a puppet Caliph, a false Imam, was virtually imprisoned in the Fatimid palace by his own army.

Cairo was a necessary stop-over. His old colleagues at the university would provide him with clothes and a little money. He could earn more by doctoring for men of rank. He would rewrite his damaged journal that was still tucked beneath his robes, organise his knowledge from its precious medical notes. But he could invite no official assistance for his mission. What, put such power into the hands of a degenerate pretender? Never! Nor could he expect help from the religious leaders, the da'is, whose feet had strayed along the wrong path.

He pitied the people of this land, following their leaders into darkness. Once, they were the *people of graduation, ahl al-tarattub*, acknowledging the truth if not fully perceiving the spiritual reality of the Imam. Now they'd drifted away from the truth, perhaps unable to be rescued. Consequently, they were the *people of opposition, ahl al-tadadd,* and doomed.

The boatmen made many stops and haggled incessantly over goods and shipping fees. Days had become weeks. Yet finally the great river was approaching Egypt's beating heart, whose lifeblood it was. Traffic steadily increased. Barges and dhows and clumsy rafts, and even dainty pleasure boats for the rich, all plied the massive artery that nourished this ancient, wealthy land... which throughout history had leaked plague into the Mediterranean as if from a giant bottle with a loose stopper.

By the time the first slender minarets arose above the wooden wharves and hotchpotch warehouses of a major port, Hakim had his plan clear. This would require enormous amounts of money, no less of faith from those not blessed with his own vision and hard-won knowledge. To obtain backing, he must purify his spirit and rise in the religious hierarchy of his Syrian birthplace. He must become one of the super-elite, *akhass-i khass*. Only thus could he eventually approach the Master of Alamut himself, for there was no one higher in the whole Ismaili world, no other nearer to the hidden Imam, nor to Allah.

Whatever the sacrifice, his rise needed to be swift. He was only a lowly *rafiq*, a comrade in the Ismaili faith. His medical skills and knowledge of plague had taken years of dedication, leaving no time to gain even the lowest ranks of the da'i.

Yet he had his burning faith, his keen mind, and his grand vision of plague as the ultimate weapon against the enemies of Allah, a vision he now *knew* was realisable. At times he felt Godlike. God grants the gift of life, and in accord with His purpose also takes it away. The taking away is as necessary for God's design on Earth as the giving. So God's will permits diseases as well as their cures, and by way of a devastating disease the world might progress towards a state of perfection when everyone's belief in God would be true and all men that survived would be enlightened. The mirror of mankind would at last reflect God's forbidden face, which is all-consuming radiance. Then the world would cease, its purpose at last fulfilled.

At last he came to bustling Cairo. As the solid ground rocked under Hakim's legs that were used to the river, he presently came across a commotion in a busy square. A veiled lady lay on the cobbles. A panicky eunuch companion was supporting her head and shoulders, while a tubby black-clad servant woman called her name and pinched her arm. Two guards stood uncertainly by.

"I can help," asserted Hakim confidently.

Reluctantly, the guards allowed him near.

"May I lift the veil?"

"I shall," said the servant woman.

Quickly Hakim assessed the lady's signs, then fished some potent smelling salts out from his pouch, one of the last two medical items he still possessed, the other being a vial of poppy extract.

In moments the lady's eyes opened. Her pupils focused. The companions expressed relief.

"Who are you?" she asked.

Hakim smiled.

"I am the doctor appointed by Allah, and I will cut out the canker of unfaith from the world."

Her veil swiftly restored, the eunuch raised his lady to a sitting position, then gratefully gave Hakim two dinars.

"Let her sit for five minutes longer."

"Where do you reside?" the eunuch asked.

"I'm newly arrived from Upper Egypt, although I studied at the university here."

"Hmm, I have a problem of some delicacy... Might I escort you to a lodging I know after we have seen my lady safely home?"

Truly, Allah provided.

Sabra restaurant, Cambridge, Massachusetts: May 2008

When Abigail had phoned Kamal, it transpired he was working at the Center for Middle Eastern Studies up in Cambridge all day. So of course her invitation to the Sabra for the evening, couched in tones of mock apology, made perfect sense.

When Abigail and Kamal entered the restaurant, the same waiter greeted her with, "Hullo again, Madam! Two nights in a row. We must be doing something right."

Kamal looked at her enquiringly, and Abigail wasn't sure if she blushed as she quickly whispered to him, "I thought I'd test this place in case it mightn't be up to your standards. Though maybe it isn't." She hoped the waiter didn't hear.

"How charming of you! Just like the taster of a sultan's food, in case it's poisonous!"

Seating her courteously, and then himself, Kamal surveyed the Sabra appreciatively, perhaps amused. "It has… character." A man two tables away was actually reading a newspaper while waiting for his food. "Oh, I read a letter to the editor in the *Globe* that was very supportive of Paul Summers, regarding his ICE surveillance article. Do you know Mr Summers well?"

"Actually, hardly at all." *Keep your options open girl! No need for any unnecessary male complications.* "In fact we just met to make that story." She couldn't help a slight smirk. "I was the main source of Paul's information."

"*You?* Goodness. But how were you privy to ICE operations?"

"I'm not. They've been hassling me, and it slipped out during…" She remembered her shock and then fury at Totally Thai, Jack's steely pressure. "During an interaction."

"Do you mean to say these ICE people have been pressuring you in some way?"

"And how. But they can go jump in the sea."

"Yet why would they…?" Kamal spread his hands, wide-eyed and lost for words.

"Oh, they imagine there's a connection between the ancient Assassins of Alamut and some modern nefarious plot, goodness knows what. They think Safiyya's fragment is a link."

Kamal picked up a menu and fanned himself.

"How absurd and bizarre."

"Utterly absurd! But look, I want to forget all that. At least Paul reckons they've stopped bugging me or following me now. He has contacts."

"Bugging? How… cloak and dagger. Medieval studies is not what it was!

I blame the movies." He displayed a wide grin, then studied the menu and chose stuffed vine leaves. Abigail copied Paul's choice from the evening before. After she'd ordered, Kamal sighed.

"I did mention I need to travel a lot. Well, it's happening again. I have a half-day conference in Tehran on the 26th, but stopping over in Cairo for a couple of days on the way. I'd hoped to avoid this, but it seems that my presence…." He gestured dismissively. "Tedious."

"The terrible lot of an international scholar!" Abigail gave a mock grimace. "I'm jealous."

"*Lot?*"

"Destiny. What fate gives you."

"Ah, I see. Remember that English isn't my first language."

"Kamal, no one would think it isn't."

"You're too kind. Anyway, Abigail, what I'm going to say might seem 'far out' or unsuitable, but the fact is that my home university is very generous. Oil money, you know! They pay first class air travel for attending conferences, and the accommodation allowance is more than adequate for a simple scholar. The fact is, I can change my ticket to *two* regular tickets without any problem. Likewise, regarding *two* rooms in hotels. I realise that this is extremely short notice, but I wondered if you might actually care to accompany me on this trip, for some intelligent conversation? Iran is perfectly safe at the moment." He held up his hand, in case she might object prematurely. "What comes to my mind is that *Alamut* is very close to Tehran… An extra couple of days, and I could show it to you."

Abigail was flabbergasted. "I'd *die* to see Alamut!"

Kamal seemed relieved; he must have been worried about the etiquette of his proposal.

"Do I take that for a 'yes'? We might be away for ten days. It'll be an ideal opportunity to delve into a bit of the background history connected with Safiyya's intriguing piece of verse."

To be able to see such a place with her own personal expert! This outweighed any petty prejudiced qualms about visiting alleged "axis of evil" nations. Besides, what better bodyguard than Kamal?

"I do insist on paying my own plane fare and hotel. It's more than enough that you're willing to show me Alamut, never mind what's en route there. My fellowship's meant to cover some travel. You need first class to sleep comfortably and stretch out."

"To avoid deep vein thrombosis? Your concern is delightful, but I keep fit."

"I can see that much."

"Abigail," and his voice was stern but his eyes gleamed, "me flying first class and you in tourist defeats the purpose of intelligent conversation. So let's compromise. I'll arrange the flights and you pay for your own hotel rooms. Meals are negotiable."

"Done! Oh Kamal, this is wonderful. I feel so privileged."

Was he married? *Did that matter?* Hastily Abigail put the thought aside, as he added: "Also this will take you, and myself as well, away from brooding about the tragic matter of Walid."

Abigail shivered. "It's felt as if there's a shadow over me since Walid... as though the world's fundamentally changed. I must have appreciated him much more than I realised."

Kamal beamed. "The bright sun of the Middle East will dispel that shadow."

Immigration and Customs Enforcement, Downtown Boston, Massachusetts, May 2008

Jack seethed. That damn journalist had got hold of his name. A call from Paul's smartphone to his editor: they were thinking of revealing Jack's identity in print. Could only have come from one place; Leclaire and Summers were closer than sardines in a can! He'd have to lean on the *Globe*.

Jack took out the Bible from his desk drawer, shut his eyes and opened the book at random, then jabbed his finger at a page. Only then did he look: Psalm 57. *The words of his mouth were smoother than butter, but war was in his heart...*

Maybe he ought to have been smoother with Mam'zelle Abigail: that could be the meaning. However, war was in his heart. Precisely! The war against America and the war against God. The ultimate war. In his experience, opening the Bible always yielded a truth, although sometimes the words might turn out later to bear a different interpretation.

His phone rang.

"Brother George? Great to hear from you!

"...Fact is, I'm dithering about going to the IAAT thing next week. There's a lot of extra workload at the moment, and I've a feeling the you-know-what investigation here might break open any time.

"...Yeah, I realise if I go to the Omaha gabfest I'm only an hour away from you. You really feel it's so important I meet up with the Elders?

"...I know how important it is to the Lord! I used the wrong word. I mean, is it *essential*, just at the moment?

"...Okay, I'll book flight and hotel, and you'll send a car. I guess it's another tick on my career profile.

"...and God bless you too, Brother George."

Thoughtfully, Jack cradled the phone, then lifted it again to summon Chronicles. The staff did his bidding more faithfully if he looked them in the eye.

Dan Siegel came soon enough, to be told, "Look, I'm off to Omaha for an IAAT meeting next Monday." *Aye Double-A Tee*, was how he said it.

Siegel looked momentarily blank.

"Inter-Agency Action on Terrorism. Are you with me now?"

"Ah, it sounded like some medical conference, I dunno, International Association for Alzheimer Therapy..."

"Did it indeed. In total I'll be gone four days. Regarding Dr Leclaire, there's still no *proof* of a medieval connection to *Eagle Teacher*, or any proof yet that she's involved in anything, but my gut tells me *both* are true." Jack drilled his gaze into Dan. "So you keep alert to any hints via the Paul Summers taps while I'm away!"

Cronkite Graduate Center, Cambridge, Massachusetts: May 2008

Abigail knew it was too much to hope that she could escape to sunnier climes before ICEman Jack hassled her again. At least this time it was only a minion who invaded her office, a guy named Dan Siegel. He asked questions about her research, her sources, who had custody of the Safiyya fragment. Reluctantly, she gave Dr Friedman's name, the chief archivist at the Harvard library – not exactly a secret, yet redirecting ICE to a colleague felt mean. She said it would take time to collate her sources – don't make it too easy for ICE! Dan Siegel didn't have Jack's grit; he acquiesced.

During the next couple of days, along with hard if frustrating work at the computer, Abigail attempted to teach herself a bit more Arabic. If only she'd stepped up her efforts a month earlier after the ICEman first called on her! She wanted to give Kamal a surprise when they arrived in Egypt.

'*Uriidu 'aSiir al-burtuqaal,*' said the CD. Dutifully though she repeated such sentences, they slipped from her memory; she wasn't going to get *orange juice* that way. In fact, face it: she wasn't going to master elementary Arabic any day soon, apart from some nouns and greetings she already knew and stuff such as *an-najda an-nadja!* help help!

On the plus side, she was finding that the connected-up variable squiggles and dots of the Arabic alphabet and the horizontal vowel lines above or below and the backward e *damma* were less daunting than she'd supposed. She was beginning to decode even if she couldn't understand the meaning; and this capacity *did* stay in her mind. Must be a matter of pattern perception. It had been easy for her to correct the proofs of *The Medieval Woman*. Something similar applied in the case of Arabic. Patterns made sense. If only she could plumb the pattern of Safiyya's verse and Sinaldin and such!

Since there were other preparations to make, Abigail's thoughts drifted from Arabic patterns to Middle Eastern lands, to what suitable hot-weather clothing she might or mightn't find in Filene's bargain basement or on its upper floors. Maybe she'd check out Macy's too.

Despite a rich dad, she generally had a functional attitude to what she wore, the informal academic look. She mustn't disgrace Kamal, though, who always dressed so smartly; nor of course must she appear provocative in Muslim countries. Ticking away in a basement of her mind was a desire to have rather less functional underwear and nightwear, not that anyone but herself would be privy to such items… Still, good for morale. Oh, and she must get a lightweight hat with a broad brim, one that wouldn't crumple in a suitcase.

Three days after Dan Siegel's visit, guilt finally overcame her and she emailed a list of research sources to the address he'd given. She certainly didn't want a sterner visit from Jack himself.

And then another task not wholly without guilt, calling Paul to break the news that she'd be disappearing for a while. He'd been contacting her every chance he got, and they'd met for drinks a couple of times. Paul was so sweet and helpful, but maybe she'd encouraged him too much. She doubted he'd take her departure well, and indeed he seemed flummoxed.

"It's not the end of the world, Paul, we can email… and I'll be seeing Assassin HQ with my own eyes!"

"Abi, that's completely crazy, you can't go there! *Iran*, I mean."

"I have a *Canadian* passport. Don't worry, I'll be with Kamal. He knows the ropes."

"Abi, about Kamal, I…"

"No Paul, don't say any more. You're such a good friend, and I don't want us to part in anger."

Last time they met, Paul had started to express some concern about Kamal, even casting doubt upon his academic credentials. Men were so predictable – promise undying support, and smear any other male in range!

"I'll spend every spare moment on your medieval mystery, Abi, honest injun!"

Abigail smirked, though her reply was sincere. "You're sweet, and I'm sure that'll be invaluable."

Papa had to come next.

"Qu'est-ce-qui se passe, ma mignonne?"

"Nothing bad, Papa," she replied in French, "I'm sorry I haven't phoned home as much as I should lately. Now, would you believe, I'm flying to Cairo in a few days, so I'm rushing around trying to fit everything in."

"Of you I believe anything, but why on Earth Cairo?"

"Well, I'm accompanying an Arab scholar who has taken my research under his wing. There are important Middle Eastern ramifications, so we'll visit Iran after Egypt –"

Papa's initial reaction was similar to Paul's, only more so. Once she had mollified him about the dangers of the Middle East, he demanded: "What kind of Arab? Daughter mine, you're sounding to me suspiciously like the British Princess Diana with her Dodi Fayed."

"It's nothing like that, Papa. It's research."

"What, into the *Kama Sutra*?" Her father could sometimes be very outspoken.

"That's Indian, not Arab, as you probably know full well."

"Indeed... that was uncalled for on my part. But really, I do wonder at your taste in men. That Terry individual, as you've described him..."

"He's *gone*." Perhaps she should not have admitted this.

"And what is the name of this Arab *scholar*? Omar Shariff?"

"Papa, you're showing your age!" Abigail lied: "And Professor Kamal is no spring chicken either. His full name's Kamal al-Mustafa Abu al-Bashir. He's a close colleague of Walid al-Areqi whom I was consulting about my work..." *Until he was slaughtered by some hit and run merchant*. Best not to mention that, no point worrying Papa unnecessarily. Then again, why would that worry him?

"Hmm," said her father. "So when are you coming home again for a weekend? It isn't exactly far."

Since arriving at Radcliffe, she'd only been back home for Christmas, and in March for her Papa's birthday.

"After this trip, probably," she temporised. Five minutes later she managed to extricate herself.

Radcliffe Institute for Advanced Study, Massachusetts: May 2008

"Actually," confided Kamal to Abigail while they took a stroll around tree-girt Radcliffe Yard, "I must confess when I said that my home university are lavish with first class air travel, I might have added that in any case personally I'm quite wealthy."

He paused, breathing deep and appreciating the sweet air, then gazing at the Ionic portico of Agassiz House. "You see, I was a businessman before I became involved in academic life... mainly importing hi-tech novelties into the richer parts of the Middle East. Back then, Islamic history and literature and poetry were just passionate hobbies, until I became wealthy enough to pursue them formally and full-time, although I do still keep an eye on the business side. If I'd said that right off, you might have thought of me as, I don't know, some sort of intellectual playboy sheikh."

"I hardly think so!" protested Abigail.

So Kamal was rich as well as cultured...

"Since you're now committed to coming along on this trip, Abigail, I was thinking that it isn't too late to upgrade to first class. The big advantage is arriving less jet-lagged. Whichever carrier we use, it's a thirteen hour flight with one change. In the end I opted for Air France, changing in Paris, because London Heathrow is so crowded. Charles de Gaulle is much more civilised. And you can use your French!"

"Isn't there a direct flight from JFK to Cairo?"

"We'd still need to fly from Logan to JFK to start with."

"That's true. And JFK is always over-crowded."

"Thirteen hours, with a stretch of the legs in Charles de Gaulle. As a favour, would you permit me to upgrade? Of course, if you prefer the democracy of economy, we'll certainly fly thus. Just, it isn't financially necessary at all."

"You're very considerate, Kamal."

In fact she'd never before met anyone so considerate...

He grinned. "Oh, it's an Arab hospitality thing! You're visiting my part of the world as my guest. So I must slaughter the best camel for a feast, as it were. Otherwise what will my tribe think of me?"

She had to laugh. "Kamal's flying camel...! Oh, you've twisted my arm."

"I'm sorry... Do you mean you're hurt by my suggestion?"

"No, the very opposite! How can I possibly refuse?"

Immigration and Customs Enforcement, Downtown Boston, Massachusetts: May 2008

Only minutes into Jack's first day back at the office after his trip, Chronicles, aka Dan Siegel, rushed in, looking at once anxious and self-important. Jack barely held back a groan; this was going to be significant news then, but not good news.

"Guess what? Abigail Leclaire has flown off to Cairo!"

"Say that again."

Dan Siegel gave a defensive shrug. "Via the Summers tap we got warning she was going, but we had no cause to hold her. I tried to contact you, but…"

"Next time, *invent* a cause," cut in Jack. "Not gone on her own, I presume?"

"No. The details are here." Dan Siegel handed over a printout.

Jack could scarcely believe what he was reading.

"Let me get this straight. Her ticket was *paid for* by a Kamal et cetera et cetera, a *Syrian Arab*, who was seated beside her in first class… And he was admitted to the US a month ago, after a couple of previous visits for academic reasons… Dates?"

Dan helpfully leaned over and pointed those out, further down the page.

"Okay, both those occasions *preceded* our Mam'zelle becoming a fellow at Radcliffe. So it's probable Mam'zelle never knew him until last month. Yet now they swan off together first class to the Middle East! Two academics flying first class?"

"What about the rich daddy?"

"She won't have money off her papa. Far too proud. Get me a transcript of all text and voice exchanges from Summers' phone to her numbers. Right now. Then figure out who's in charge of the archives at the Harvard library. We need to grab the original poem Leclaire wrote about. They've got that booklet thing it came inside too…"

"Chapbook, it's called. And I already know he's Dr Friedman."

"Good. I want you to impound the poem and chapbook whatever under the Patriot Act, which we surely have a right to do, so don't take no shit from this Friedman. We can get higher tech analysis done than any library. But do take a lockable case and a sealtite baggy. This ain't something to cram in your pocket. You'll find the shelving numbers on the system, in the *Eagle Teacher* folder, look at the first footnote of her article. Now please!"

However, Chronicles remained, gazing at another printout he had brought, from which Jack deduced there was still more news, which *surely* couldn't be as bad. He raised his eyebrows and subjected Siegel to a withering glare.

"One of Leclaire's research sources turns out to be a cleric guy called... er... Walid al-Areqi, who just so happens to have been killed in a hit-and-run two or three weeks back."

Jack would have raised his eyebrows further if they'd hadn't already run out of room.

"Two or three weeks! How come we didn't know this sooner?"

"Sir, you know we're doing this in the breathers between other jobs... and the lady's still been playing hard to get. Anyhow, three days back the BPD found the vehicle involved, burned out, but they traced it back to a rental outfit. They got a suspect photo from the rental place's CCTV, not good quality... but something to go on."

"Let me guess, he isn't just some drunk, this actually matters."

"Dead right. Forensics found a piece of paper tucked into the vehicle manual, which was in the glove compartment and partially survived the fire. At least seven web addresses. Two can't be recovered, three are bus and rail timetables, one is www.cdc.gov and one..." Siegel gave a triumphant grin, "is the *AAMH*, the very page with Leclaire's poetry fragment on it."

Jack rubbed his chin. "Useful, Chronicles, if very late. CDC, Centres for Disease Control in Atlanta. So this isn't assassination then, it's bio-terrorism. Yeah, useful. Forward me the photo and details. And make sure Summers doesn't get an inkling we're onto this angle, via Grunty or anyone else! If *he* knows, so will Mam'zelle Leclaire, and if *she* knows, her Arab fancy-man will too, and for all *we* know he could be *Mr Eagle Teacher* himself. In fact, Chronicles, keep this to yourself for now, the department doesn't need to know."

As Dan Siegel hurried away to execute orders, Jack murmured to his retreating back, "*Mam'zelle is up to her eyeballs.*"

The Jebel Bahra, Syria: May 1161

Hakim rejoiced in the keen air and rugged vistas of the Jebel Bahra, the mountains of Syria where he had lived as a child, east of the sea and west of the great Orontes River. The sky was an intense and inspiring blue this day, deeper and more vivid than even lapis lazuli or fine tiles of Persian blue, indeed befitting God's heavenly mantle for the world.

He paused to catch his breath, since he had climbed continuously for an hour and now the slope was becoming even steeper. Turning, he viewed the great channel of the rocky valley that ploughed its way down to distant patchwork greens. How far below were the fields! How high he was already!

How high he had climbed in life too, Hakim contemplated, how swiftly. Only twenty-five years ago he'd watched over goats in this valley. Then, his only goal had been to read properly, to which end he'd smuggled a tattered and poorly executed copy of the Koran out in his food-satchel.

Yet by the age of ten he was encouraged to read, on account of his talent for curing sick animals, which was sold by his father to their farming and herding neighbours. Amid the liquorice-bushes, tall spiky asphodel, and cane-brakes, each medicinal herb caught his eye, and his parents hoped that an increased knowledge of potions and anatomy would also increase their income, especially when he moved on to the cure of people. People who carded cotton in their balconied houses were vexed at times by scrofula sores or colic or dropsy. Hakim used vipers drowned in vinegar to relieve dropsy, vinegar to purge the dust from carders' throats, glasswort and ashes in olive oil and yet more vinegar to treat scrofula pustules. He was a young prodigy. People spoke of him as the new Ibn Butlan, famous even after a century for his clinic in Aleppo to the north.

For a while things worked out just as his parents had hoped, despite he'd bartered for books and scrolls that weren't even medical in nature, and read a lot of hocus-pocus besides. Hakim smiled while recalling his boyish deceit and this happy time, but then his pleasant memories were soured and his smile turned to a grimace. His parents were killed by Christian pillagers, probing inland from their fortresses near the coast. It was small comfort that the excellent Ismaili charitable system which took him in fostered and focussed his talents still more. He'd craved for a suitable revenge even as he studied sacred writings alongside the medical texts.

He seated himself on the sun-warmed surface of a level piece of weathered stone, unfolding a cloth containing goat's cheese and olives, dark bread and fruit. Memories of childhood lingered as he dangled his legs over a long drop. Minerals in the cool mountain water from his flask made it an elixir his tongue still welcomed daily, even now, although it was over a year since his return from the oppressive airs and tasteless warm water of Cairo. Tasteless at best in fact, often tainted.

Even within that year, Hakim had risen significantly, as though Allah was smoothing his way. Having reacquainted himself with the local Nizari Ismaili community and made himself useful to them, he also submerged himself in purification and prayer and religious studies. From a comrade and learner, he'd risen quickly to the role of teacher, for he had a powerful intellect and consequently powerful insights of his own, which traits Ismailis never stifled but directed upwards in their hierarchy.

Of course, his adoption of the name Hakim had intrigued the Nizaris who'd known his parents and himself as an orphan.

"The murderous Franks erased my lineage!" Hakim had declared. "For this reason I prefer to be called only by the name which signifies Doctor, and modestly serve the whole community. I have no other family. In choosing this name I also pay homage to our sixteenth Imam, the illustrious caliph of Cairo, al-Hakim bi-Amrillah, who struck such a blow to the Franks by destroying their main church in Jerusalem, where Christians falsely claim Isa ibn Maryam was buried after his supposed crucifixion."

"In that case, *Hakim*," said one grizzled elder, "beware of the Sons of Grace, the Druzes. Since our neighbours here in the Jebel Bahra actually worship the sixteenth Imam, they might kill you as an impostor!"

Hakim hadn't known this, for the one people more secretive than his own Ismailis were the Druze. Yet neither did he care; they too would one day be reaped by plague.

Hakim had settled as near as he could to the great stone stronghold of al-Kahf, the seat of Abu Muhammad who guided the Syrian Nizari community. Soon he came across another newcomer to the area who was residing in the castle itself, Sinan, a skilful young man who like himself did occasional work as a physician. Sinan behaved as one of the people, yet many men made subtle obeisance to this Sinan, even men of rank, from which Hakim realised that all was not as it first seemed.

Taking an inspired gamble, he had made every effort to befriend Sinan, suspending his own doctoring and instead making all his medical knowledge available to the mysterious young man. One day, Hakim had told himself, this gamble would pay off.

Sinan was a man with piercing eyes, with swift yet subtle judgement, with patient yet boundless ambition, a man filled with God's light, a man from whom it was not wise to hide anything. Yet in the narrow field of medicine Hakim was now second to none, having incorporated Arwe's deep insights into the framework of advanced Islamic science.

It seemed that Sinan's purpose was to gain popularity in the community, in the scattered mountain villages and the virtually impregnable Ismaili castles, the qa'lats of Kahf and Masyaf, Rusafa, Maniqa, Qabat and the rest. Hakim greatly aided Sinan in this goal, to the point where some believed the younger man could actually perform miracles. So eventually there was great gratitude, and mutual revelation too.

On a night flavoured by fermented goat's milk and honey, a night warmed and ruddily lit by embers in the small hearth of Hakim's simple cottage, the two men of vision exchanged their hopes and plans for the triumph of the Ismaili faith and the greater glory of God.

"Blessed Abu Muhammad has been an excellent guide for our community here in Jebel Bahra these last forty years," explained Sinan. "We have no wish for his soul to follow its appointed course to Allah, though this must surely happen in due time as Allah wishes." He hesitated momentarily and his eyes scanned Hakim's face. "And also I'm not sent here by the Master of Alamut, but by Hasan his son, who before long will be ascendant. So timing is... delicate. Until Hasan rises to his inheritance, until he is the true *hand of power*, I have no real authority."

Hakim appreciated Sinan's delicate position. The two young candidates for power intended to usher in a new cycle of leadership, no doubt one of spiritual revelation, with Sinan leading the flock in Syria and subject only to the holy word of Hasan in Alamut. But if Abu Muhammad should die before Sinan's sponsor gained the leadership in Alamut... the succession in Syria could be disputed.

"As you know," said Hakim, "I support you without reservation."

They clasped hands in fealty and friendship across the rough boards of the table, then Sinan refilled their shallow bowls that served as cups, smiling a knowing smile.

"Good Hakim, you are wise indeed to aid me, where others would have flaunted such astounding ability. For I see that some high ambition burns within you, though this thing is not to lead men or become their gate to Allah. Also you are devout and unflinching, so your goal must be exceptionally difficult to achieve or by now you would already hold the fruits of success in your hand. So I will help you, if I can, for surely you toil towards something invaluable for our faith, something that will make our Ismaili brotherhood shine still greater before God?"

Hakim was amazed that Sinan had guessed so closely.

"Not only shine," breathed Hakim. "Triumph! Over *all* our enemies."

That was the proudest hour of Hakim's life. He revealed his grand vision of plague as a scimitar to fell the enemies of Allah, the enemies of the Ismailis, expounding all its glorious detail and holding nothing back. Sinan was at first spellbound, but then sceptical, subjecting Hakim to sharp questions. Yet when Hakim described how far he'd progressed in Ethiopia, the unique knowledge gleaned from Arwe and then synthesised with the written experience of past civilisations, finally Sinan was amazed. As a man of high vision himself, Sinan perceived the power of the concept, and his own medical knowledge helped him grasp Hakim's proposed methods.

"It can be done!" gasped Sinan. "We can capture the jinnee of plague in a bottle, and release it within the heart of our enemies. Its fire will utterly consume them! Hakim, my own place and purpose is here. But I will help you, I swear it. Have faith!"

A movement caught Hakim's eye: off to his right an eagle was rising on a pillar of air. Minutely adjusting its wings, it hovered just below the level of Hakim's improvised seat, intent on a patch of ground far below. The feathers on its back ruffled and strained upwards, as though the very air desired to pull the bird further up. Then, perhaps catching sight of him, the noble hunter wheeled away, disappearing behind a large bluff.

Hakim's own rise must ultimately lead to the eagle's nest of Alamut in Persia. That could be a year away or more, yet surely Allah desired to pull him up! He restarted his climb to qa'lat al-Kahf, though his legs ached much more than he remembered when he was a boy herding goats.

Qazvin, Iran: May 2008

Abigail breezed along the streets of Qazvin in a haze of sunlight and traffic fumes and euphoria. She was free! Free of Terry, free of Jack's arrogant intrusions, out of her father's range too. Even Walid's sudden death now seemed distant, unreal. The Eagle's Nest was tantalisingly close, perched in the mountains beyond the town.

The pieces of the medieval puzzle churned at the back of her mind while powerful emotions made her feet light and her thoughts soar, as well as painting a silly grin across her features. Ignoring a warning voice that bleated *this is too soon*, Abigail was seriously contemplating romance. She savoured the name, Kamal al-Mustafa Abu al-Bashir. How exotic!

They'd come here to Iran via Cairo, where Kamal had some business to attend to. But in four days he'd only been absent for two mornings and one evening. The rest of the time he'd swept her through a kaleidoscopic tour: colourful bazaars, the majestic Nile, fancy restaurants offering the best of local cuisine, Cairo's medieval walls, and of course museums. Not to mention an obligatory visit by taxi to the pyramids, including a short amble on the backs of two snooty camels led by raggy young boys. Abigail had giggled during that ride, and when Kamal called out to her, "What is amusing you?" she'd exclaimed, "Kamal's camel! I'm on it!"

All the time, like the support of a magic carpet, was Kamal's courtesy and gleaming smile, his self-assurance in any circumstance and his seemingly inexhaustible knowledge of Islamic history. Abigail felt a little unworldly beside him, most unusual for her! She'd tried out her own humble smattering of Arabic with only patchy success, although Kamal graciously pronounced himself impressed by her effort.

And too, thought Abigail as colour came to her cheeks, there was Kamal's maleness. For a businessman turned academic he had a trim figure with hard muscle. His manner was unapologetically firm with pushy stall-tenders or lax waiters. His clean yet musky scents pulled at her. Behind intelligent eyes something powerful and animal lurked, something she might want to see unleashed upon herself.

Excitement coursed through Abigail. Yet Kamal remained the perfect gentleman. So much so, she'd worried he wasn't interested in her. It was then, of course, that she realised she was *very much* interested in him.

Now, just this morning, as he'd dropped her off in the centre of Qazvin, she'd pecked him on the cheek, quite without thought as it happened, but an answering warm touch on her arm and a sparkle in his eyes stilled her worries. He *was* interested, but traditional; she needed to give him permission, perhaps assure him that the age-gap didn't bother her.

With difficulty, she forced her thoughts back down to earth. Noisy traffic threaded through a jumble of architecture ancient and modern. A low concrete barrier topped by steel railings bounded a park. The concrete crawled with graffiti in Arabic script in cherry-red and green, too stylised for Abigail to pick out words which in any case would surely be Farsi. Inside the park young couples strolled or sat on the grass, some holding hands. The women's headscarves were almost off their heads. It seemed that the conservatives didn't have everything their own way. One couple kissed, and Abigail found her silly grin reasserting itself. She tried to banish it by taking a swig of water, then checked that her own headscarf was firmly in place.

Only a minute or two later, Abigail located the small museum at the edge of the park, which Kamal had recommended the day before. "Rather a hole in the wall kind of place," he had said, frowning as he wondered whether he'd picked the right figure of speech, "but worth a look."

There were indeed just three small and somewhat shabby rooms, none with windows. Artefacts from right across Qazvin's long history were displayed in dimly lit cabinets: part of a gilded chariot wheel from the city's glory days as capital of the ancient Persian empire, a rusted Mongol sword, fine plates from the Saffavid era, a highly decorated musket.

Disconcertingly, the young female assistant, who seemed to have sole charge, followed Abigail to each exhibit. She was slight and wore a full burkha in black, only her brown eyes visible to Abigail. Wide and unfocussed, those eyes roved restlessly from side to side. Having determined that her only visitor of the moment spoke English, the girl occasionally offered hushed comments that seemed speculative at best.

"This musket, gift from famous Sultan, never fired," came a whisper through the dark cloth where a mouth should be. "It is said... who fires it first... will die *himself*."

In the third room, Abigail came across a scale-model of Alamut. Or at least a model of what people decades ago thought Alamut *might* have looked like; the battlements were covered in dust and paint was peeling from the sheer walls. Only a trace of green remained in the fake grass at the foot of the model's mountain slopes. A faded wall-panel gave a brief history of the Nizaris in several languages.

"*Evil* men," hissed the assistant. "Unholy. Their assassins... they could pass unseen through locked doors. Their masters made dangerous poisons... no I mean, hmm, *potions*. Gaining power over disease... perhaps even power over death. Holding many... hmm, spellbound... many who would harm them otherwise."

Abigail smiled, revising the girl's age downwards in her mind. Though her English was pretty good. "Surely that's just myth. Shouldn't a museum stick to the facts?" she chided gently.

The girl's eyes rolled.

"Allah *used* the Mongols to... hmm, *erase* these bad men. The only force on Earth strong enough! Nizaris were heretics. Yet they held *a power*. Their power was a fact."

The girl was clearly dotty, not to mention in the wrong job. She'd probably do well on the stage, though she'd need to shed that burkha.

On a shelf by the model were a couple of cracked terracotta storage jars and a line of small bottles, apparently uncovered quite recently at Alamut.

"May I touch?" asked Abigail. But the strange young assistant had slipped away, perhaps back to her post near the door.

Abigail picked up one of the bottles. The glass was thick, with a faint tinge of green. Around the neck were patches of some black substance. She couldn't be sure, but it looked like hardened black wax, perhaps the remains of a seal around the stopper. *What would they want to store so meticulously?*

An intense "Take care!" followed her out from the lair of the young woman who tended ancient artefacts, as Abigail emerged into dazzling sun and honking horns.

Along the road she visited a small store to grab some chocolate before continuing on her way. Abigail always felt guilty consuming a whole bar, no matter how hard she tried not to be. This didn't stop her eating it, but she certainly wouldn't be telling Kamal about the habit. Neither had she mentioned her constant email contact with Paul Summers, or indeed anything more about the journalist. An undercurrent of guilt niggled her for this too, though some instinct kept her silent. *Kamal is so formal, so manly,* she reasoned with herself; *he might get jealous.* It'd certainly be hard to disguise the fact that poor Paul clearly mooned after her.

She smiled again, this time smugly. With half a bar already working its magic and the ecstasy of another half to go, she considered it absolutely essential for a woman to have a queue of male interest.

She consulted her crumpled tourist map for the next target, a historic area where books and prints and antiques were sold, at greatly inflated prices according to Kamal. She went by way of the famous Imamzadeh Hossein, a mausoleum, a divine work of 16th century architecture, added to in the 19th century. Yet it wasn't the building that moved Abigail, but the multitude of memorials to martyrs from the Iran-Iraq war arranged in neat rows beside it. Set into the headstone of each was a faded photograph; a whole harvest of young male faces reaped by the ambition of Saddam Hussein and the pussyfooting of the West.

As she proceeded down the funerary aisles in horrid fascination, Walid came to mind, sweeping away the last of her buoyant mood. Then she recalled what he'd said about the Islamic Resurrection. Would the bodies of all these martyred men one day rise in ghostly ranks? All leeched of colour by time, as the merciless Middle-Eastern sun was slowly erasing the hues and definition from their captured images too. Rise to rejoin their souls, up past the gleaming blue tile-work of the great dome, its apex pointing to heaven?

Abigail banished her imaginings, taking another swig of water. Unfortunately, the chocolate was all gone. She doubted the Islamic Resurrection as much as the Christian one, but more importantly for her right now it didn't seem to provide a plausible context for the words *death swells and overflows* that Safiyya had written. The highly modified Nizari concept of Resurrection was even less likely to supply an explanation.

A connection with plague did seem strong but was wholly circumstantial. Even if Safiyya *had* woven in the big event of her time, she would surely have remained within traditional forms. So what core Nizari symbolism had *death swelling and overflowing*, and what special vision to judge did the *teacher of many lessons*, the Imam, have within this context?

The words of the fragment had stumped Kamal as much as they had Walid. His interest in her medieval mystery had been intense since they'd reached Cairo, perhaps the irresistible pull of an academic challenge, as with herself. Nevertheless, she'd fed him only fractions of her knowledge so far, just one drop of intellectual nectar at a time. She wasn't sure why. *Oh come off it girl, you're teasing him on!* Maybe she did need all her womanly wiles to capture a prize like Kamal but, soon enough, she thought as a warm feeling rushed up inside her, the busy bee that was Kamal might have sweeter nectar to sip at.

A while later, in a market street, small doors became entrances to enticing caves filled with brass and silver and polished wood, gilded manuscripts and antique prints. People drifted idly. Vendors tried to snare her with their calls. Vehicles nosed their way through, their tyres just inches from the goods heaped up to right and left. Old books were on offer in a minority of the many tiny establishments.

Another hour passed, and Abigail had just one prize to show for an intensive search; according to the vendor's broken English a volume of early medieval love poetry from across the Islamic world, itself published in Arabic in the 1890s, a more innocent time perhaps. She thought it would be fun for Kamal to translate some of the verses for her. Despite this minor triumph, real prizes eluded her. It wasn't easy searching for works in languages one scarcely knew, including non-Arabic texts printed in Arabic script. She'd found just three books on the Ismailis, one of them in English, another with dramatic illustrations suggesting it was as much a novel as a history. All seemed standard fare.

Yet fate threw her a final chance. The last shop on the street, at the shabbier end, was entirely a bookshop. Oddly relieved, it dawned on her how she was determined to show Kamal that she could pursue her goals independently, even out here. If there was going to be romance, she preferred to start from a position of relative equality.

Tatty books and papers crammed the long corridor of the shop's dim space. The straining shelves supporting walls of literature were untreated wood polished by long use. At the far end, an old man with a flowing grey beard sat at an antique desk. He nodded to Abigail, though said nothing. The thick black rims of his glasses seemed too heavy for his emaciated face and pinched nose to support. Behind him, red and gold and green spines of the more valuable volumes gleamed.

Abigail always felt at home surrounded by words, but these were still very foreign to her; she could make little headway on the large and confusing tapestry of titles. She pulled out a few works and checked for illustrations and style, after some minutes managing to identify the poetry and history sections.

The old man's black slippers appeared before Abigail as she gazed at the volumes nearest to the floor, and she looked up. His sharp frame jutted through a thin robe of pale blue.

"Puis-je vous aider, Madame?" His heavily accented voice was hoarse and very quiet, a rustle of desiccated stalks on an early autumn breeze.

French was a good guess, thought Abigail, or maybe he just didn't speak any English. Headscarf notwithstanding, she must look very obviously a Westerner. Abigail explained her quest for Ismaili poetry and religious texts. She didn't know how much he understood.

"Vous cherchez les perles, les choses ésotériques. Mais ces gens laissaient seulement des vieilles pierres et mythes indistincts. Ils partirent il y a beaucoup de siècles."

She was looking for pearls, esoteric pearls. But those guys only left old stones and vague myths behind. They left centuries ago...

Then he hunkered awkwardly down and indicated one slim volume, before padding silently back to his desk. A collection of poetry. Not just old stones and shadowy myths; they left behind poetry too. She recalled her last ever talk with Walid and his quote from Nasir-i-Khusraw; she'd read much Khusraw since, in translation. The old cleric's chocolate voice echoed in her thoughts… *the esoteric is like pearls*. What pearl was she seeking precisely?

She wasn't sure what was in the poetry book, but decided to buy it anyway. On the next shelf she spotted a group of titles in French. She pulled one out, *Les légendes des montagnes Elburz*. Legends of the Elburz Mountains, by a Professor J Ruffie. Poor quality print on yellowed foxed paper, published in Beirut in 1934. Perhaps the self-styled professor had funded it himself. One chapter of the seemingly rambling work covered the Ismailis, even containing the line of succession at Alamut. The whole book was strewn with small maps and drawings of ruined castles, descriptions of mountain trails and flora, local anecdotes and legends and even folk-remedies. The professor must have spent a great deal of time in the area. One paragraph spoke of a brilliant physician who'd stayed at Alamut, probably in the late twelfth century; *al-Hakim, the sword of Allah, the shield of Allah, the possessed*. What odd appellations for a physician! How could he be all of these things?

In Cairo, Kamal had shown her the medieval mosque of an allegedly mad Ismaili Caliph named al-Hakim, next to a surviving section of old city wall. Hakim was the man who destroyed the church of the Holy Sepulchre in Jerusalem, enraging Christians. Yet Kamal said he died in the early eleventh century; so there must be *two* strange, high-profile men by the name of Hakim in Ismaili history.

She read: in the early thirteenth century, a new legend about the origin of the name Alamut arose. For a while this challenged the earlier wisdom about 'the teaching of the eagle', yet the tale faded after the Mongol invasion and became almost forgotten. This legend insisted that Alamut was a corruption of 'al mawt', meaning death. Tatty though this book looked, she must have it.

The Jebel Bahra, Syria: July 1161

A servant led Hakim along a dim corridor in the guts of the castle. A door swung open and a servant boy emerged, burdened with a tray of cups and bottles. In that moment Hakim saw within. An array of candles on a long table illuminated what perhaps were maps. Hakim was surprised to see that some of the men in this well-appointed room were pale. One had hair like flax, another's was the colour of bright rust. They must be Franks, Christians! All but one of the infidel wore surcoats above chain-mail, white adorned with red crosses. The other was wrapped in a black cloak, a white cross stitched upon it. An open casket on the floor was piled high with gold coins. The boy hastily nudged the door shut.

Bitterness and outrage overturned Hakim's optimistic mood, unravelling the careful phrases and spiritual calm he'd spent all day achieving for this meeting with Sinan. Unholy Christians, here in Kahf of all places! He was still struggling to get himself under control when he was ushered into a modest chamber. Sunlight slanted in from a narrow opening and brightly illuminated hands that were folded upon a table, Sinan's hands, which it was said could work wonders not merely medically but by directing fortunes, as God willed. The rest of him was somewhat veiled by shadow.

"Dear Hakim, welcome! I must first apologise for the deplorable number of weeks since our last meeting. Abu Muhammad grows frail and has started to rely upon me, which I welcome, yet high position is a thief of time... But Hakim, what is amiss? Your eyes smoulder and your brow is furrowed." Sinan leant forward, plunging his face into the light, a face radiant with concern. "Has some wrong been done to you?"

Somehow, Hakim already felt comforted.

"Wrong, yes, though long ago. Yet my pain was recalled to me just now. Our brotherhood is consorting with infidel Christians, inside this very castle!"

Sinan's concern relaxed into a kindly smile, like that of a supportive father to an erring child. He leant back again.

"Hakim, Hakim," he chided gently, "Allah expects more wisdom from his chosen few. Don't let old wounds impair your good judgement. Our enemies here are many and we can't fight them all at once. These particular Christians aren't like the mass of the infidel. They're trained and resourceful, and lift themselves above the herd. They even practice their own dissimulation, *taqiyyah*, beneath which they reject much Christian practice. This makes them attractive as allies of convenience, and we've found that these... these orders, the Templars and Hospitallers, are very dangerous as enemies."

Hakim's logic and faith reasserted themselves, like a ship emerging from the waves after a near capsize. His heart still held bitterness for the Christians, but *nothing* was more important than the survival of the brotherhood. His anger melted away.

"Oh forgive me dear Sinan, my lord and my guide."

Sinan reached out to touch Hakim's hand.

"There's nothing to forgive. Potions are your forte, not politics. The situation here is complex and fluid. The Templars are from Tortosa, the Hospitallers from the old qa'lat al-Akrad, Krak as they call it. Both are too close for comfort, much too close to ignore. But in their hearts these orders admire us. Perhaps they've been granted a faint glimpse of the true light that shines through our Nizari brotherhood. For decades we've encouraged this admiration, and of their own accord they've taken up some of our own ways. Did you notice their attire?"

"Most had surcoats like the robes of our initiates, although the red formed a cross."

"Yes," mused Sinan. "Like, but not identical. And they're a useful thorn in the side of the Sunni enemy, whose strength in Syria has waxed these last years. Yet if your high purpose is achieved, good Hakim, there'll be no further need for any such distasteful alliances! By grant of Allah, our power would approach that of His own hand, and none could then stand against us. To this end I have the authority to raise you to a da'i, which I will do this very day."

"Oh Sinan," breathed Hakim, genuinely overcome. "You have my eternal gratitude."

Sinan beamed magnanimously.

"Having helped each other we will both help the brotherhood triumph within this turbulent world. And you haven't heard the rest… In reply to my urgings, Hasan himself has asked to see you! Tomorrow you'll leave with a small escort to the very fount of our Nizari Ismaili faith, to Alamut. I cannot *guarantee* you'll receive the resources you need, but I think your personal dedication and skill and hard work will do this for you."

Hakim's jaw dropped. He was speechless. So soon! Truly Allah was great.

Qazvin, Iran: May 2008

They were staying in a house owned by one of Kamal's colleagues, who was away. A business colleague rather than an academic, Abigail assumed, considering how expensive the place must be. Wide verandas looked out onto trees and trailing greenery. Airy rooms featured dark wood and tiles with raised knot-work patterns: gold on blue, gold on green, blue on white. The bathroom was a watery cave of smoky grey and mirrored surfaces, adorned by gold taps and fitments. The bed in her guestroom was the softest imaginable. Of course there were exquisite Persian rugs too.

Adding to Abigail's feeling of being bathed in luxury, Kamal had cooked their evening meal. To start there was an aubergine salad with diced tomato, onion, garlic, lemon and parsley. Then Kamal served the main course with a proud flourish; a 'double chicken' dish with rice. The lower layer was broiled in stock with aromatic spice, the upper roasted with pine-nuts and almonds. Abigail tried to guess the spices, but apart from confirming cinnamon Kamal wouldn't reveal anything.

"A secret recipe," he whispered, "known only to the culinary elite."

"Is there no end to your skills?" Abigail felt her laughter descend into girlish giggles and tried frantically to arrest it.

"Well, I've cheated a little. Although we're in Iran these dishes are actually Syrian, from my homeland. The salad is called *father's favourite*."

Their conversation danced light-heartedly around throughout the meal. *Dancing around the obvious, perhaps*, thought Abigail. Beneath the polite smiles there was certainly something deeper, an animal tension she was still a little afraid to let loose. Maybe Kamal was wary too.

As the wine lit a fire in her belly, the tension eased. Selling and consuming alcohol was banned in Iran, but home-brewed beer and wine were available to those with a little local knowledge. Kamal had picked up this fruity little number from behind the counter at a petrol-station in Qazvin. Abigail realised only belatedly that it was pretty strong stuff.

They left the table and settled on a large leather sofa, glasses in hand. Abigail picked up her book of Arabic love poetry, which she'd deliberately seeded there earlier.

"Dear Kamal, *please* read me some poetry."

Kamal raised his hands, his eyebrows too, Abigail noted with amusement.

"The pleasure of Arabic poetry comes largely from harmonies of sound and striking turns of phrase. It can't easily be rendered into English, especially on the spur of the moment and by one with so little talent as I."

"I doubt your talent is little," grinned Abigail. Then she pouted and made eyes. *"Pleeease..."*

Kamal sighed and took the book.

A giddy, teasing mood had grasped Abigail. Wine-fuelled perhaps, or love-fuelled. Her cheeks flushed, but fortunately Kamal was scanning the pages and hadn't noticed.

His face was so noble in profile! The sharp nose hooked over very slightly; a dark eye flicked across the words. A tilted black brow lent an impression of strength, even fierceness. Like an eagle, she thought. Grey in his trim beard advertised experience and authority. Yet the strength was contained by impeccable manners, allied to immense knowledge, tempered by sophistication. She realised with a shock that her father would like Kamal; since they'd both been successful in business, perhaps like him a lot. *Well that would be a first for any man of hers!*

"Oh. I've seen this one before Abigail. The fifth verse is often quoted. It's by Hafiz.

> *My friend, before you wander into the street of love*
> *Do not forget to take along a guide*
> *It is perilous for your undirected feet*
> *Such twists and turns once you are inside."*

The fourteenth century warning wafted impotently over Abigail.

"Hasn't he something more optimistic, more mysterious, more... Oh I don't know, more committed to love?" Abigail drained her wineglass and slipped down into the smooth softness of the sofa.

"Well, here's a likely candidate..."

Kamal muttered a few practice runs under his breath, trying to order the words for best effect and introduce some rhyme, so that even in English it might actually sound a little like poetry. Then he started off, his tone gentle, yet earnest:

> *"On this holy night, stay with me*
> *Until the morning, do not leave*
> *On this night so dark,*
> *My course, how will I weave?*
> *Oh breath of life, this night help me*
> *So come morning, I make a start*
> *In my love for you, I will*
> *My pride and my ego kill*

Like Hafiz, be able at love
I long to master this skill."

Abigail clapped. "Oh, you're so clever!"

Kamal, unflustered as always, permitted himself a small grin.

"If only Safiyya's fragment was so easy to understand. We might have had more chance with the original Arabic."

"*You* might have. That would be much worse for me!"

"So how much have you actually told this *iceman*, this Jack whatever his name is?"

"Jack Turner. Very little. He's paranoid. A religious nut too, most likely. I didn't even tell him about Sinaldin."

"Sinaldin? That sounds like... Well it's an intriguing name." Kamal frowned. "But just who is this Sinaldin?"

"Sinan al-Din ibn Nasir. He's an Ismaili, and something to do with all this I'm sure. He was Safiyya's lover." Abigail waved an arm vaguely; she was having trouble thinking straight. "He came by ship to Provence around the time of the Black Death, then went on to Spain." Her arm landed on Kamal's shoulder. He leaned over and stared at her intently.

"Then your Andalusian poetisa had an exotic Arab lover?" he said softly.

"Yes, possibly younger than her. I've no evidence for that, but I always imagine it so. She must have been at least in her forties by the time Sinaldin returned to her from that trip. Age doesn't have to be a barrier to love, does it?"

She pulled him a little closer. Their gazes locked.

"No, indeed not."

Then his firm lips were pushing against hers. Her tongue tingled at the touch of his, sending pleasant pins and needles in a swift wave all the way down her body. Her nostrils widened to pull in his scents, the musk of sandalwood, the clean smell of his skin. His strength seemed all around her. Her head spun.

Minutes of blessed relief and tight hugs and urgent kisses later, they were stumbling up the stairs. Abigail couldn't stop giggling. She couldn't direct her feet and clung to Kamal. The heat of excitement coursed through her, yet then spawned cold shocks of apprehension. Her stomach began to feel queasy.

They made it awkwardly to her bedroom door. The air seemed close. Abigail had trouble getting her breath.

"Hey Kamal, look I... I'm sorry... I'm not feeling too good. It's been a lovely evening, but maybe it's moving a bit fast, maybe I'm not ready yet.

I'm sorry, I…"

A lopsided smile tugged Kamal's manly features into a moment of boyishness.

"There's no hurry. In my love for you I will, my pride and my ego kill."

He made sure she could stand before fully letting go of her, then lightly kissed her forehead.

"Good night, Abigail."

Qa'lat al-Alamut, Elburz Mountains, Persia: 1162

Alamut was loftier than Kahf, both spiritually and physically. Nestled high in the Elburz mountains, which rose to pierce the sky while their roots seemed to drink from the Caspian sea, the castle was both nearer to Allah and more inaccessible to the enemies of the Nizaris. Yet being nearer to God did not seem to bring Hakim close to Hasan.

The heir apparent of Alamut welcomed Hakim warmly, but then kept him at arm's length. All Hakim's needs were catered for, *except* for the near desperate need to expound his theories, to obtain Hasan's favour and backing. So once again Hakim prayed, and learned still more about the art of patience.

Yet, as months slipped by, he learned other things too. Alamut boasted an extensive library that he visited almost daily, containing copies of many ancient works in translation and the latest scientific and medical texts from across the Islamic world. Hakim's thirsty intellect drank at this great pool of knowledge until he was dizzy, which somewhat soothed his frustration at the delay. After his breakthroughs in Africa, Hakim concentrated mostly upon references to blood and diseases involving blood – he even stumbled across and read in its entirety *On the Secrets of Women*, an eighth century Arab work, for it contained lengthy discourses on menstrual blood – as well as anything he could find about the mechanisms of disease transference.

From one Arab treatise, he noted that incense makers were said rarely to suffer the ravages of various plagues, since their constant exposure to powerful scents transferred good humours into their blood via the nasal passages, which rendered them more resistant, or even immune, to the bad humours that would strike down others. On the same topic, a Persian writer stated: 'The nasal passages are porous, like an exceeding thin and un-oiled skin. Hence either noxious or beneficial herbs may be passed into the blood via fumes or smokes breathed through the nose'.

Hakim had used the aromas of heated oils on his rich clients back in Egypt, to remove aches, or to induce sleep in insomniacs. Did this work via blood? Was the nose a gateway to the blood?

Between intense bouts of study, Hakim strolled around the castle and observed its workings, or savoured the fragrances of mountain flowers and herbs in the gardens. *Do they enter my blood?*

The advanced water engineering truly impressed him, surpassing even the arrangements at Kahf and the other Syrian castles of the Nizaris. Great catchment areas were scooped out of the mountain above the castle, from which underground pipes led to cisterns deep within the foundations. An efficient distribution network provided for the needs of the castle's occupants and also irrigated the gardens. Along with huge, cool storerooms next to the cisterns, the whole system would enable a siege to be resisted for years.

Occasionally Hakim came across Hasan meditating or praying alone in the garden, staring at the sky, his features immobile, as though of fine wood, his eyes glassy and unblinking. Hasan would acknowledge Hakim, and even talk with him though, unlike Sinan, Hasan did not exactly invite intimacy.

The heir to Alamut was a shining enigma, a being of divine intensity, a force at the centre of things, surrounded by an aura of danger and demand and worship. Often Hasan's eyes were focussed far away, yet he could touch a heart directly and fill it with leaping inspiration. Men would do anything to feel that touch again. As would Hakim himself.

Hasan might speak of the path to Allah, of the fountainhead of knowledge, in an unpredictable yet profound way such that Hakim found his own mind racing to keep up. Yet always Hasan steered away from plague and the application of Hakim's theories.

"All things must wait for their time," was all Hasan would say.

Indeed, all Alamut seemed to be waiting, seemed to be holding its breath, for just as within the castle of Kahf in Syria, and yet more so, change seemed ready to crystallise straight out of the clear mountain air. Old men, senior da'is, came and went on the bidding of Hasan's father, but Hasan himself was revered and all the community felt his time approaching.

And when finally the Master died and Hasan automatically ascended to this position, news spread through the community, indeed all the communities of the Ismailis around the Caspian, like a fire through drifts of dry leaves. From Adharbayjan, Khurasan, Quhistan and further, islands of Ismailis both open and hidden within the sea of Sunnis sent their acknowledgements and devotion.

Only one week after Hasan's accession, a message arrived from far to the west, from Syria. The spirit of Abu Muhammad had left the physical domain, and Sinan now led all the Ismailis in that part of the world, subject to the guidance of Alamut.

"The miraculous start of a new spiritual cycle," announced Hasan at a celebratory meal, "a cycle of change!"

Two days later, Hakim was called to a private audience in the new Master's rooms.

"I am aware of your impatience to serve our cause," Hasan began, "but have you added to your knowledge in the meantime, and has our faith sustained you?"

Hakim acknowledged both these; and this was true.

"You may speak in detail."

Rejoicing, Hakim did not try to hide the expense involved, nor the long distance both medically and physically he would need to travel, with a sizable company too.

"A journey is a quest for true knowledge," concluded Hakim. Hasan nodded, his focus seemingly elsewhere. "To travel is a spiritual as well as a physical process, such that the traveller finally discovers the innermost secrets of existence. Is that not so, my Lord?"

"A journey towards... *Resurrection*," mused Hasan. "Towards the transforming moment. You speak with insight, Doctor. Human existence consists of several cumulative phases. Each phase reaches its zenith, only to be replaced by another phase of a higher order, possessing greater potency."

Hakim cleared his throat, which was dry. This moment was so important. Every phrase carried a hidden meaning. Hasan was speaking both of the esoteric process of initiation through the Nizari hierarchy, towards becoming one of the super-elite, and of the quest of discovery for power over plague, and therefore over mankind.

"I have completed one cycle of my journey," Hakim continued. "Now a new cycle would indeed bring great potency. The inner secrets of physical existence await me in Africa, which in the esoteric world will bring overwhelming power, and triumph, to our faith."

"I see this *exactly*," replied Hasan.

Hearing this, Hakim's heart rose like a nightingale. Then Hasan gazed directly at him, for the first time ever, and Hakim trembled both with adoration and responsibility.

"Yet for now you will still need patience, Hakim. We await other great matters, that will confer all the... freedoms we will need for ultimate triumph."

Hakim bowed, out of his depth and not wishing to show his lack of understanding.

"Leave me now."

Hakim proceeded to the door, joy thrumming through his every fibre. He could accommodate more waiting, more patience, now he knew that the Master would sanction his mission. Then Hasan called after him.

"You may well be the sword of the time, Doctor."

Hakim turned. "Only," he replied, "if I follow the commands of the Lord of the time."

The Master of Alamut gazed through the window into a dusty distance, perhaps seeing a stretch of time and not of space.

"I am not that person, exactly. Merely a servant of the Hidden One."

"As are we all," agreed Hakim. "Yet certainly you are chief among the servants of Allah. Not just master of our brotherhood, but the very source of our light." An inspiration struck Hakim. "Only *the hand of power* may wield the ultimate sword."

Hasan smiled. "I shall raise your rank, Doctor, as befits one with such knowledge and understanding of our faith."

Qazvin to Alamut, Iran: May 2008

Eight a.m., and the light was dull, the sun hidden.

The house benefited from Wi-Fi, so, in between tooth-brushing and hair-drying, Abigail fired up her laptop and checked on her messages via email. From Paul:

Hi Abigail. Where are you now?

Something weird. I found out through a guy who owes me at BPD that ICE grabbed all the case details for Walid's hit and run. But all other sources are tight shut. My journalist's nose smells something bad, I just don't know what.

Still trying to dig up clues on your medieval mystery. Pulled in some favours and have a couple of European ex-colleagues on the case, searching records and stuff. Impressive huh? A lordly knight like Guy must have left some echoes behind. Any luck your end?

Paul XX.

She dashed off an answer:

Paul, the bad smell is probably Jack – he'll be thrashing around. Be careful of riling him. Nothing worthwhile here on the medieval front so far. Dark hints about the Assassins, but more legend than fact. Maybe a different slant to legends in the West though: potions, power over death, a physician guy called al-Hakim.

Anyhow, off to Alamut itself today. Stayed in a heavenly house in Qazvin overnight. Kamal cooked dinner. He's suuuch a gentleman!

Btw, came across an alternative name interpretation: Alamut = Al-mawt = 'the death'. Scary huh?

Abi.

And to her old friend Jen, whom she'd been keeping up to date on romantic progress with Kamal, she merely wrote:

Hi Jen, teetering on the brink. Stay tuned.
Love Abi.

Kamal had hugged her warmly earlier, but their conversation in the car was light, avoiding any mention of the previous evening's romantic contact. The consequent void was filled with a kind of tight confusion that made Abigail feel like a shy girl on her first date.

With Qazvin some distance behind and heading upwards on winding mountain roads, they met a bank of pale grey rolling downwards and became cocooned within, tightening the atmosphere in the car still further. Given such poor visibility, it was almost impossible to pass elderly coaches and the overloaded and straining light trucks. They endured two hours of this before more of the road became visible and the grey walls surrounding them became less substantial. Sullen hills lurked behind thinning veils and occasional buttresses of rock leaned over the road. Higher still, and hazy light forced its way through from above, placing them in the midst of pearly luminescence. Then the white veils shredded to tattered banners and blew away. A flood of sunlight illuminated buff scarps and lush green slopes dotted with hosts of mountain flowers. Distant peaks protruded into rich blue.

"Oh Kamal, it's beautiful!"

Kamal reached out and patted Abigail's knee. "I think Lake Evan will be very pleasant after all."

And so the lake proved to be; a rich sapphire in an emerald setting, jealously guarded by hills all around, its waters shining with an inner radiance that fired the imagination.

"It's almost as though there's a secret treasure beneath," breathed Abigail excitedly. "A jewel of light that the depth of water can't mask!"

"A blue treasure," murmured Kamal. "Perhaps a key to power. There are several legends of magical objects placed for safety in Evan's sacred waters. Whether these things are still there or not, maybe the water remembers them."

Scattered groups of locals gazed out at the hypnotic surface of the lake, or wandered around its grassy fringes. Further back, a couple of purple tents huddled up to some poplar trees. There were twisted fruit trees too, cherry or apple maybe, and willows sipping the still water that was such a gift at this altitude. Two men in black seemed a little out of place. One had binoculars and both seemed to be scanning the nearby area rather than the water or the hilltops, almost as though they were checking out the people. Maybe they were bird watchers.

"There'll be more people later, as it warms up," explained Kamal. "It's a popular place for picnics. But we should push on for Alamut."

They drove back to the main road and then headed east for Gazorkhan, the village below Alamut. For an hour and a half the car climbed still more.

From a distance, Gazorkhan was a cluster of tiny rectangles, the miniscule handiwork of man sheltering inside one hollow out of hundreds within the rugged immensity of nature's carvings. Nearer to, the village appeared shabby and weather-beaten, although screens of dwarf trees protected some aspects. They nosed their way through, pausing for frail old men in black skull-caps, shapeless black bundles with the tanned faces of women, darting motor-bikes, and careless, colourfully dressed children.

Outside the village, Kamal found a good place to pull over so they could look across and upwards to Alamut itself. The fortress was perfectly located, on a massive promontory of rock with a single steep access. A guard of majestic peaks marched around it, blue-grey with distance and clad in misty robes. Kamal smiled. Abigail's hand found his, and in silence they drank in the view. Seeing this place, so physically close to the roof of the world, so spiritually high for the Nizaris during their first 166 years, Abigail at last began to realise what extreme defences the Order had needed to survive against great odds. *What a spirit of persistence, of self-discipline and self-inspiration they must have developed!* She wondered whether they had bequeathed this down the ages to the modern Ismaili community, still a tiny minority in the often hostile sea of Islam.

"I'm amazed that even the Mongols could take this place," she commented.

Kamal frowned. "In fact they didn't. The Nizari leader at the time was Rukn al-Din. He was naïve and insecure, so he didn't believe anyone or anything could battle the mighty Mongol war-machine. No one could make a deal with them either, but Rukn tried. He killed his own father to claim leadership. Ala al-Din would have struck severely disabling blows against the enemy, but his traitorous son ordered a surrender before any major conflict happened. The majority of Nizaris simply walked away from their many castles in this area, and most walked straight into betrayal and death. A couple of sites disobeyed Rukn al-Din, resisting right until the end. One fortress held out for fourteen years."

Abigail whistled softly. "Now that's what I call will-power!"

She opened her window. Though it was the latter half of May, the mountain atmosphere that flooded their car was chill, smelling clean, of rock and herbs with a metallic edge like the scent of snow, though no snow was visible and Kamal said that even on the tops it would have melted away a few weeks back. The sun was hot on her arm.

A road to a car park just a few minutes from the castle made the old exposed winding trail unnecessary. After sandwiches, they assaulted Alamut more easily than any Mongol could have dreamed.

Alamut was so well-crafted to the contours of the natural rock; it seemed like an expression of the land itself, a clenched fist of resistance. Kamal brushed his hand reverently along a rimy wall.

"I haven't been here for many years," he commented. "I'd forgotten how magical it is."

Abigail smiled warmly, but in truth she was rather disappointed. Only roots of stone showed where much of the castle had been, and some sections of the surviving walls were covered in scaffolding. Yet the view from the remaining battlements was awesome. Only a handful of visitors were present, seeming subdued, perhaps spell-bound. The peaks were thunderously silent. *It would be easy to feel equal to God here*, thought Abigail, *or at least far above other religions; breathing thin air and Gnostic poetry, wrapped often in cloud and always in secret knowledge.*

Kamal picked up a handful of fine dirt and let it stream out of his fist on the breeze as he recited:

> *"My God, what difference can it make*
> *between my good and my bad*
> *if both are as grains of dust to You?"*

"Not the good Kamal al-Mustafa Abu al-Bashir I think, so who are you quoting?"

Kamal smirked. "Hasan as-Sabah, the visionary founder of the Nizari Ismailis, the man who took this castle and made it their home."

Abigail's disappointment was ebbing away, as the mood of the place seeped into her.

"Just think, we're standing in the very place where Hasan the Second declared *qiyama*, instructing the Nizaris to turn their backs to Mecca, to turn their backs on Shari'ah law."

"Indeed! Though he probably did so from the courtyard over there." Kamal jabbed a finger. "There's a lot of clever engineering here, you know."

He proceeded to explain the Alamut water system in great detail, identifying the catchment scoops in the mountain slopes above the castle. Abigail managed to repress a girlish grin, but felt warm inside. He was so handsome when animated like this! A boyish look came into his distinguished features; the best of both worlds. He pointed to where excavations had taken place a few years earlier by the north gate, with some artefacts unearthed.

Descending to the base of the walls, they edged carefully down a steep slope half carpeted with hardy grass. Kamal was looking for evidence of the huge underground water-storage chambers. Finding a faint and somewhat more level girdle on the hill, they followed it until they came face to face with a guard.

The man smiled, but barred their way and spoke firmly. His uniform was dishevelled; grey hair protruded from under a casually placed cap. Beyond were scaffolding and platforms, piles of earth and stones, a muddy wheelbarrow, shovels and small trowels, wooden crates. Above these was an intriguing dark hole in the hillside.

Kamal answered the man smoothly and cheerfully in his fluent Farsi, following up with something that seemed like a question. The guard shrugged. Then Kamal pulled out a hip-flask and offered the guard a drink. A hip-flask! Clearly she still had a lot to learn about Kamal. His seemed to be a good call though, as, despite Iran's official ban on alcohol, the guard grinned and gladly accepted. In under a minute he was chatting amiably, while Abigail was becoming frustrated at not knowing what was going on. While the guard took a second pull on the flask, Kamal hurriedly flung some words at her.

"Yet another dig! It's almost as if they're looking for something specific. I had no idea about this one. Apparently the dig team are all down in Tehran, showing off some of their finds and begging for funding. I'm trying to get us a look inside."

The conversation in Farsi changed tone; hands were waved. Abigail willed Kamal to succeed; it would be so exciting to enter the dark mystery of that hole, to peer into Nizari history. Eventually Kamal handed over some banknotes; she couldn't see how much value. The guarded turned and headed away past the scaffolding.

"He said it isn't his fault if he needs a pee. We have ten minutes!"

Abigail squealed with delight. "How clever you are! Let's hurry!"

They scrambled up to the entrance. A short passage led through the skin of the mountain into a large hollow within the rock. Only a couple of metres in it became too dark to see much at all, but Kamal found a switch beside a stack of car batteries. A string of small bulbs warmed into modest illumination.

The space they entered was perhaps a natural cave that had been enlarged. Under dirt and debris they saw evidence of trimmed rock, carved pillars, even some tile-work. Piles of rubble showed where much of the ceiling had collapsed. To one side were big iron cages resembling cells or secure storage, still fairly intact. An unpleasant, musty odour caught hold of Abigail's nose. She imagined that long-dried excrement might smell so.

One cage door was open, a floodlight strung to the bars, not in use. Kamal and Abigail crouched and peered into shadows. He pointed. Half excavated, were two skulls and a scattering of bones. *Children! Had the Nizaris kept child slaves?* But the proportions of the skulls were wrong, the brow ridges too prominent.

"They're monkeys!"

Kamal's normal composure seemed to have deserted him. His shoulders were hunched and he muttered a string of words in Arabic, no doubt forgetting that Abigail couldn't understand. He rose and moved towards the back of the space, perhaps searching for a passage up to the castle proper. Abigail spotted a worktable on which stood a lamp and a bowl, along with brushes and tools for removing grime. A stained cloth on the table clearly covered something. Immediately curious, she moved over and lifted the edge of the cloth, revealing a broken bottle and three odd but identical items of bone.

It took some time to figure this out. Each of the three items was a snake's upper jawbone, complete with vicious-looking fangs. Assembling the pieces of bottle in her mind, she realised it was exactly the same as those she'd seen in the museum at Qazvin.

Of a sudden the snake fangs jumped towards her fingers. Her knees buckled even as she registered shocked surprise. Curtains of dirt cascaded from the roof.

"Quake!" yelled Kamal. "Out! Get out!"

He grabbed her from behind and half lifted, half pushed her towards the exit.

The guard looked worried, but grinned when he saw them emerging. No more shocks followed; the Earth had just turned in its sleep.

"Quite common in this area," commented Kamal. "A big one back in 2002 badly damaged Qazvin." Fresh air and sunshine seemed to restore his mood, and he flashed a winning smile. Abigail's racing heart had slowed. Kamal's strength might have saved her from an untimely end in a dark hole if the cave had collapsed...

As they headed towards the car park, Abigail said, "Why on Earth did they have a menagerie at Alamut, do you think?"

"Perhaps that's what really made the legend!" He laughed heartily, but said no more. Abigail grabbed his wrist with one hand and proceeded to punch his shoulder with the other. She may as well have punched an ox.

"Tell me, tell me! What do you mean?"

"Maybe *that* is how their Assassins came and went unseen, despite locked doors. They sent *trained monkeys* in through the windows!"

Abigail laughed too, and they went arm in arm back to the car.

Gazorkhan, Elburz Mountains, Iran: May 2008

The first place the shopkeeper in Gazorkhan recommended had no rooms left. The second was a large ramshackle house painted in a faded flaking hue that once was probably bright terracotta. The sagging slant of the roof extended over a boarded wide veranda, and was held up by sturdy grey poles that looked like old and untreated tree-limbs. White window frames, also flaking, and lace curtains behind the glass, donated a hint of Western suburbia and made Abigail feel comfortable about the place.

Kamal negotiated with a smiling woman, whose deeply carved face seemed outsized above a body like a gangly girl's. A dress the same colour as her house stuck out from the bottom of her burkha. Below were thick black boots.

"She only has one room." Kamal's voice betrayed no hint of hope or hunger, or even humour, yet his eyes twinkled. "Is that all right?"

Abigail flushed and many butterflies fluttered in her tummy, yet lower still something pleasant pulled inside her. She tried to keep her voice light. "It's fine."

She'd already been wearing a wedding ring since Tehran. On her own, a ring deterred unwanted attention. In company with Kamal, it avoided awkward questions.

The room was cramped, but cosy and clean and warm. The second the door was closed, there was no thought of anything else. They both knew what had to take its course, immediately, urgently. Indeed, it was overdue. The cries of children and revving of scramble-bikes, filtering in from outside, quickly receded from their attention.

Clothes seemed to drop away of their own volition; certainly Abigail wasn't too aware of that phase. Her mind was filled with Kamal's princely face, the depth of his eyes, the taste of his kisses, the intensity that was locked within him. Suddenly there was the tingle of his skin up and down her, all around her. She gasped and clutched him tighter. Looking down, she saw the taught muscles of his dusky thigh pressed against her own soft whiteness. He seemed so exotic, almost alien. A moment of panic grasped her. She was still tense inside, unready. She hoped he wouldn't rush.

An arm grabbed her shoulders and she felt her feet swept from under her.

"Kamal!"

He said nothing, but placed her gently on the bed, as though she were a child. He climbed up beside her. She closed her eyes. His lips found a nipple, a surprisingly rough hand stroked her belly. The sensations were good. And she wanted this, needed this. Yet she couldn't relax. She felt like a stick, waiting to be snapped.

Somehow, he knew. He flipped her over, easily and gracefully. His powerful hands began to massage her. Firm fingers ploughed down her neck, then dug into the muscles of her shoulders. Abigail groaned with satisfaction, and at last she felt her body begin to unwind.

Kamal didn't hurry. When he parted her legs and forcefully squeezed her right thigh, desire overtook mere satisfaction; she felt ready. He followed up with the left thigh, then a gorgeous prickly feeling ran swiftly down her spine. An involuntary cry escaped her, and at the same moment she was abruptly aware of her own moistness between her legs. Kamal was using his beard to massage her!

He rolled her back, face up again, then once more spread her thighs. He was manipulating her like a doll, but she was a willing doll, so *so* willing. She kept her eyes shut and revelled in the luxury of total attendance, not having to do a thing. It was so different to the scenes with Terry, his alternate hesitancy and blundering.

"Aaahh…"

The soft slippiness of Kamal's tongue had found her slit, and he seemed to know exactly what to do there. Waves of wonderful sensation washed upward to almost swamp her consciousness. She gasped like a struggling swimmer, but still the surges came. She arched back and her thighs bunched but, whenever she came too near to the ultimate intensity, Kamal slackened off, only to follow up with more waves a minute or so later. Stars and colours danced in front of her closed eyes; she sensed her skin going slick with sweat. Kamal was drowning her in delight!

Then, as his tongue continued to work, she felt his finger slip inside her too. In just seconds, he found a place she was not too expert with herself. But Kamal clearly was. An explosion of ecstasy ripped through her. She cried out as her thighs jerked right up into the air, temporarily disconnecting Kamal. Aftershocks rippled up her, causing her to moan even though she tried to speak instead, tried to ask for a rest.

But Kamal had no mercy. A strong arm anchored her waist, preventing her lower body from moving at all. Then the beautiful waves started again, and then…

She screamed long and hard at the top of her voice as another explosion hit her. Never had she done such a thing before. She fought against the pleasure, it was too much for her! She thrashed her arms, but to no avail. More came. It was as though Kamal had connected a pressure hose of pleasure right into her, and refused to turn it off. Agonising orgasms poured into her. And yet somehow, in all this, he kept her *just* below a final climax that would set her free, that would desensitise her even beyond his skill.

Eventually, he pulled back. Abigail opened her eyes. A mischievous grin split Kamal's features. She weakly raised herself. She was drenched, her thighs still trembling. She gasped and attempted to clear her dry throat. This pause was a blessed ease, but she wasn't done; amazingly, her body still craved climax, and the sight of his dark member sent a shock of anticipation through her.

Once more Kamal manipulated her. She felt like a rag doll now, unresisting, indeed she didn't want to resist. He flipped her face down again, then yanked her waist upwards and got her knees under her. She arched her back. Her head was buried against a pillow. He entered from behind, firmly, in a single movement. But she was *far more* than ready now. The relief of something for her muscles to grip on at last, was ecstasy in itself. A deep grunt of satisfaction was pushed out of her.

He didn't try to hold back. He used powerful thrusts, butting hard into her yielding flesh at the end of each. Yet his right arm reached around and a knowing finger gently rubbed her too. Abigail had never felt so feminine, so animal, so opened, so beautifully used. She squealed as her dam of passion rose, yet uttered a loud, low wail when the dam burst and her climax came, surprising herself with her own strange voice that seemed to swell right up from the depths of her gut.

Kamal had timed himself to her moment, and she seemed to feel as much as hear his triumphant grunts when his last spasms strained against her soft insides.

She collapsed. Kamal got some covers over them, then kissed her. His taste pleasantly reminded her of where he'd recently been. She cuddled up to him, embedding her hand in the mat of hairs on his chest.

"Oh Kamal, I didn't think it would be like that. I didn't know it *could* be like that!"

Kamal chuckled softly. "And you a French woman, or nearly."

That reminded her of Walid, but nicely. Beautiful sleep drifted over her drained and tingling body.

Gazorkhan, Elburz Mountains, Iran: May 2008

Breakfast was provided by the thin woman, who glared disapprovingly at Abigail.

"Probably your screams yesterday evening," whispered Kamal mischievously. Abigail's cheeks burned.

After they'd eaten, Kamal suggested that she explore the village for an hour while he made some business calls. The sun-gilded streets of Gazorkhan welcomed Abigail. With her heart leaping, a secret warmth inside, a slight and gorgeously-earned soreness between her legs, the world seemed full of light and love. She finished tying her headscarf and ran for a little way, for the sheer joy of it, ending by prancing breathlessly down the street like a pony, an action that incredibly her muscles still seemed to remember from childhood.

After wandering for a bit, she spotted a sign saying INTERNET over a small store, and ducked inside.

Two screens were tucked away at the back, and the place sold hot chocolate too. She availed herself of web access and the wonderful liquid.

Paul's inevitable message told how he was reading up on Ismaili history – he'd got two books and ordered a third from Amazon. True dedication, the better to serve her! She sent a swift reply, but kept it business-like. He was so sweet, so helpful, but she had to take care not to encourage him in the wrong way, especially now that love had wrapped her in its beautiful blanket. To Jen she sent a whole page of almost poetic text, spilling out her feelings and her love for Kamal, some of her worries too. Experience suggested that love was never straightforward, but then she'd never met such a sophisticated and magnificent man as Kamal.

She got a little lost on the way back, and ended up approaching the faded terracotta house of ecstasy (for as such she would now always think of it) from a tiny side-street. She spotted two men peering into the car Kamal had hired, and instinctively hung back. *Were they trying to steal it?* Both snoopers wore black T-shirt and black jeans; both looked athletic.

A photo, take a photo, in case they were intent on mischief...

This quickly done, Abigail took a deep breath and clenched her fists. She was just about to run at them, yelling and waving her arms, when the men moved off. They paused at a silver Mercedes a few cars back, from which one of them extracted a jacket, then they disappeared around a corner. How odd! Take a photo of the Mercedes too... Kamal could read the licence plate, if that mattered.

Abigail darted forward and, keeping half a cautious eye on the corner, she peered into *their* car. Empty cans of soft drinks. Pamphlets in Arabic and English, one titled 'ional Water Projects'; perhaps *national* or *international*. A holder for some kind of computing device or electronic navigator. Then, in the rear foot-well below her, she saw binoculars, and remembered the birdwatchers at Evan. *Possible* birdwatchers. Might easily be these same men. Puzzled and suspicious, Abigail hurried back to tell Kamal.

The moment she walked in, Kamal grabbed her and kissed her, sending thrilling shocks chasing around her body and delaying delivery of her story somewhat.

"What did they look like?" he asked rather sharply as soon as he heard.

"Not obviously foreign, I mean not foreign to Iran that is. Black jeans and T-shirts. See for yourself! I took photos of them and their car just in case."

"Clever girl!" Taking the camera, he pressed and stared at the latest image then at the preceding one, zooming it. After a few moments study, though their window faced the rear, Kamal nonetheless peered through the lace.

"They had binoculars in the back of the Mercedes. I think I saw the same men at lake Evan, down near the water when we arrived."

"*Very* clever girl!"

That did grate somewhat with Abigail, even though she used *girl* on herself. Kamal must have seen upset marring her face. He came over to hold her and his voice softened.

"It isn't unusual for the government to keep an eye on foreign academics here. Especially if their studies involve religious or historical or political positions disagreeable to the party line."

He frowned. His dark eyes seemed to search far away.

"But government minions aren't usually like that. T-shirts. Both leaving the stake-out together, if it *is* a stakeout. Very unprofessional. I thought a silver Mercedes was trailing us from Alamut, but I wasn't sure."

Abigail was a little shaken. "They won't kidnap us, will they?"

Kamal laughed, and Abigail was immediately comforted.

"I hope not! Odd place to pick up on us, though, Evan. Unless…" He shrugged. "There are lots of factions here. It could be anyone! My business activities have sailed close to the wind from time to time." He grinned a wicked grin. "Or maybe someone's keeping an eye on *you*. A Western academic who promotes the position of women in Arabic poetry. Not approved of here, I shouldn't think."

"Oh my God!" Maybe she was risking arrest just by being here.

"Don't worry," whispered Kamal huskily. "I'll protect you." He hugged her tightly.

As they left their room, Abigail paused in the doorway for a final check that they hadn't left anything. The place seemed so cosy, so safe. It would stay in her memory forever, the place where she and Kamal first made love. Then it occurred to her to help memory. She pulled out her camera and took a shot.

Alamut Valley, Elburz Mountains, Persia: August 1164

The dozen escorts on their long-necked chestnut chargers looked splendid in white garments and golden girdles, sheathed swords at their waists, wooden hilts tightly covered in leather, double-edged daggers in their boots, and a sheaf of reed-hafted spears each, streamers fluttering. Nasir al-Aziz and his three companions were more travel-stained, having come all the way from al-Kahf, Rashid al-Din Sinan's principal castle in Syria, though they rode Khafaja thoroughbreds too.

The further they rode along the valley, the more Nasir marvelled at the many defences both man-made and natural that protected the heart of the Nizari faith. Castles and smaller forts looked down from jagged crags, as did skilfully placed watch-towers. Impregnable peaks arose behind, and behind again, some touched with snow, although here in the valley the heat was intense. Hidden gorges, from which ambush might spring, divided the stony plateaux over which eagles circled. Fortresses looked unassailable, so steep and scree-covered were the slopes. It would require a host of demons, not mere human soldiers, ever to invade this territory! Ever!

"Look, grapevines!" Umar called to Nasir, pointing.

A wealth of living emeralds against the prevailing red-brown rock, along with walnut and poplar trees. Although the horses' hooves stirred pebbles and dry sand, an icy grey-green river flowed through the desolation, so that pockets of bounty blossomed. Already they'd passed irrigated fields of young green rice, fields of melons, of onions, and nearer to villages knots of goats and sheep grazing under the eye of watchful boys as guardians.

"Allah be praised for the gift of water!" Nasir shouted in return. "Otherwise the world would be hell." Truly the heat of the day was stunning.

Despite a landscape mostly barren, the villages of the valley obviously supported themselves, and one another, and even the hundreds, no, *thousands* of warriors commanded by the Master of Alamut, Hasan Ali, now two years in office, just as with Sinan in Syria. What mysterious event was Hasan Ali planning in the midst of the month of Ramadan, that summoned Nasir to Alamut to represent his master Sinan and the Syrian Nizaris?

"Soon now," Hussain, leader of the escort, told Nasir as their horses paced together, "you'll see the castle of Alamut, from the walls of which privileged Fida'een leapt to their deaths when the first Hasan so commanded, to amaze visiting emissaries."

Indeed! The ultimate warning. The senders of those emissaries would forever live in dread of Hasan as-Sabah's assassins going forth against them in disguise with poisoned knives, if they challenged the will of Alamut's

Master, *knowing absolutely* that those killers had no fear of their own death and would stop at nothing. By sheer willpower the first Hasan had inspired such total dedication, and single-handedly had raised the Nizaris to power.

"Hasan as-Sabah's death was awesome too," replied Nasir.

"What do people tell of it in Syria, now that fifty years has passed?"

"That Hasan announced he would soon leave this life. Consequently he wished to spend three days undisturbed in solitary meditation. Only at the end of three days might anyone enter his private chamber. However, those who entered found no human being there, but only a glossy-coated raven! The bird cried out and flew away, transporting Hasan as-Sabah's soul to heaven within its body."

"*That isn't the whole of it*," confided Hussain so that only his companion could hear. "The raven was *already* within the chamber, and so too was a bath full of oil of vitriol secretly prepared by Hasan. When left alone, Hasan uncaged the raven and then – oh such willpower! – he submerged himself in the atrocious bath, bearing the agony until it surpassed his mind and consciousness fled. Over the course of three days the vitriol dissolved not only his flesh but his bones, so that Hasan seemed to have vanished miraculously from existence. Rather as the Hidden Imam disappeared, continuing in supernatural existence invisible to mankind, until the day when he will reveal himself as Lord of the Age and Ruler of the Universe!"

Nasir slapped his thigh in amazement. How could the second Hasan, grandson of Kiya Buzurgumid, successor to the great founder, match such an achievement? And yet the message summoning the Syrians had implied something overwhelming.

"The bath was drained away, so that the mystery would remain." Hussain spurred his horse on to the front of their short column and shouted at his men to tighten formation.

At long last, as the sun was setting to end the day and prefigure a new one, here was the qa'lat al-Alamut, sprawled upon a great, soaring grey rock that reminded Nasir in shape of a kneeling camel with its neck thrust forward. Alamut's uncompromising presence dominated. A half-circle of huge peaks formed an impregnable wall of giants to guard its rear. To the front were such steep drops, such absence of cover for any besieger! Tall turrets were faced with hard stone; the curtain-walls were massive.

By the time bright stars gleamed in the vault of heaven, the new arrivals were safely inside the castle. A senior da'i, a Summoner to Wisdom, brought them to a large and well-lit chamber. Vivid rugs covered the floor, low tables were laden with turquoise lustreware. The fine plates and dishes were loaded with cooked lamb and saffron rice, barley and millet bread, apricots and grapes. And there was cool water, so sweet, so inviting. The Syrians had of course been sanctioned to eat and drink during their day of strenuous travel, but they'd refrained apart from a minimum of tepid water gulped from flasks.

Many Nizari leaders were present in the room. From Iraq, from Khurasan. From the nearer Caspian regions. Only the Master of Alamut himself appeared to be absent, keeping secluded high in his tower. After exchanges of courtesies, hunger and thirst had to be blunted. Soon the eating became more leisurely, and between mouthfuls news was traded. From Nasir and Umar, news of the Frankish knights of Christendom, and a flux of alliances and intrigues.

"Death to the heretic sultans and their viziers!" exclaimed a leader from Iraq. "For those are the enemies of true faith. These Frankish upstarts are but a devilish trick if they distract us."

"That," agreed Nasir, "is why we treat with the Grand Master of those Knights of the Temple, so their hostility aims elsewhere and does not divert us from our true task."

"Why not simply send a specialist to eliminate this leader of *temple men?*" asked a da'i from Khurasan, who evidently failed to understand the situation in the west.

"Because," said Nasir, "the Knights of the Temple are not as other groups of men, where to cut off the head causes confusion and disarray. Another Grand Master of equal calibre would immediately be appointed. We would gain nothing, and we might lose much."

He paused significantly. "Never forget the principle of *taqiyyah*, dissimulation. Sinan is speculating that we can achieve a powerful alliance with the Knights of the Temple, the Knights of the Hospital too, if we put on the cloak of Christianity."

There was momentary uproar, but Nasir raised his hand.

"I said the *cloak*. The concealment! Did not the Prophet hail *Isa ibn Maryam*, Jesus son of Mary, as a Spirit from God, as the Word of God, who will return at the end of time? Beneath this cloak, consisting of but a few rituals and observances regarding the holy Isa ibn Maryam, we would of course retain our true faith. Yet, by this ruse, the Christian knights would *always* fight with us against the Sunni enemy!"

"*Observances?*" came a sceptical voice.

"Such as pretending to accept the delusion that Jesus rose from the dead, and is himself divine, God in a man's body. Historical errors and failures of understanding cause this delusion, yet the Prophet condones Christian observances, those of the Jews too, since their misunderstandings nevertheless embrace authentic revelations."

Servants brought coffee, which sustains the mind.

All present knew that dissimulation was permitted if professing one's faith could lead to persecution or harm. Inevitably, Nizaris in areas controlled by Sunnis had to dissimulate, just as an assassin would, occasionally for years, so as to place himself close to his target, supposing that the target protected himself as carefully as could be. But to use such a huge dissimulation in order to produce a hypothetical military advantage? Debate about this idea of Sinan's continued for some while, stimulated by the *qahveh* beverage which excited the heart and the brain and the mouth.

"Whence this wonderful drink?" asked a man from a remote northern region.

At which, most people laughed.

"It is the same," said the Summoner to Wisdom, "as the medicine and the meditation wine made from the bright red cherries of a bush cultivated in Yemen, though originally from Ethiopia. Except that the berries are dried and then roasted. Everything valuable and useful comes to Alamut, including persons of great scientific calibre…"

It seemed to Nasir that the Summoner, inspired by the beverage, was tempted to add something more, but the da'i restrained himself.

Gazorkhan to Bandar-e-Anzali, Iran: May 2008

Kamal had a business meeting in Rasht, after which he'd promised Abigail a Caspian Sea sunset. They descended from the heights back past Qazvin, thence to Mulla Ali, Rūdbar, and so to Rasht. The traffic's light flow followed the ancient course of rivers that had carved their way through to the land-locked sea. Green and gold rolled by for hours while the blue-dark mountains marched constantly alongside.

Yet the grand vistas were spoiled for Abigail, as she constantly checked the side mirror for glimpses of the silver Mercedes. Often it seemed to have fallen away behind; always it reappeared. Kamal seemed calmly unconcerned. He put on some music and finally Abigail dozed.

Their silver tail clung to them right through the busy streets of Rasht and beyond, where the town straggled northwards up to its airport.

"Determined," commented Kamal.

"Very!" But Abigail's grin masked worry.

Kamal turned into an area of light industry on the side of the highway opposite to Rasht's modest airport. He pulled up beside a long grey building, devoid of windows but brightened by two metal doors painted orange.

"It's usefully close to the airport. I'll be inside about an hour."

"Oh, okay." She tried to display a relaxed smile, but couldn't help glancing behind where the Mercedes had parked in plain sight.

Kamal patted her arm. "Don't worry. If they'd wanted to trouble us, they would have by now. But give a blast on the horn if they approach, or anything else happens."

With that, he exited the car and pushed a button by one of the orange doors, to be promptly admitted.

The moment Kamal had disappeared, panic started to creep over Abigail. She adjusted the driver's mirror and glared at the threat reflected in its small frame. *Why am I never free of interference?* Her throat became dry and her neck prickled. *Get a grip, girl.* After several minutes, in which absolutely nothing happened, she calmed down and tore her gaze from the mirror. To keep herself busy, she fished Professor Ruffie's book out from her bag on the back seat and flicked through for more references to the Nizaris.

Deprived of their castles by the irresistible Mongol invasion, the Nizaris slowly diminished in Persia. They sent missionaries to safer areas in the distant south-east, within modern India, growing a sizeable community there over the centuries that now is led by his Highness the Aga Khan. In a faraway land, those sky-wrapped homes in the beautiful Elburz, so close to God, remained only as a cultural memory....

The professor then went on to describe in considerable detail the state of each site where a Nizari fortress had stood; Abigail skipped to the end of the section:

The Mongols are universally viewed as a nemesis for true Nizaris, yet the poem 'The Triumph' implies that the Nizaris achieved some great revenge or damage upon the Mongols. Known only through the late fifteenth century comments of 'Abd Allah Ansar, but probably penned well over a century earlier, 'The Triumph' may simply be exulting that the Mongols had converted en masse to Sunni Islam, after which they proved no more capable of **truly** *erasing Ismaili heresy than generations of other Sunnis before them...*

Annoyingly, no lines of 'The Triumph' were quoted. Nor did the professor's book include any bibliography or index. Abigail clucked her tongue. Unprofessional! She chewed her lip thoughtfully while gazing at the mirror again.

She'd insisted to Jack that the Nizaris had died out, bequeathing nothing to the Aga Khan's benign community of modern Ismailis. Yet what if there *was* some more direct survival? Some secret thread in the tapestry of Ismaili history that led right back to the old elite of Alamut, to a power that had prompted the name *Al Maut*, the Death.

To her great relief, Kamal emerged, and they were soon back on the main highway, headed for the nearby port and tourist town of Bandar-e-Anzali. They took a small hotel within sight of the Caspian, then wandered hand in hand along the beach to appreciate the promised sunset. Not a breath of wind touched their faces; the water barely murmured. The western sky was candy pink, striped with dark-gold syrup, laid upon a blue velvet cocktail. They kissed as all was ignited to molten orange, which spilled across the stilled sea and threatened to put the entire world to fire.

After which, Kamal effortlessly produced a yet more romantic setting, treating her to dinner in a converted Caravanserai. Brick arches stretched from warm spheres of candlelight to subtle shadows, fountains teased the eyes and comforted the soul, waiters in felt slippers moved noiselessly on the tiled floor.

Kamal's exchange with the waiter sounded different from the speech of Qazvin or Tehran.

"Were you talking Farsi there?"

"It's Giliki, the language of about three million people between the mountains and the sea."

"So of course you can speak that too!"

Kamal smiled. "I can get by. This place has often been invaded," he went on swiftly. "Sometimes by more than one army at a time. The British Empire fought the Bolsheviks here between 1918 and 1920."

After the meal, the evening air outside had lost much of its earlier warmth. Abigail went up to their room while Kamal chatted to a group of youths on the street. She thought it cool that a man of his age and stature could still hang out with young people, and used the time to prepare herself and the atmosphere. Fortunately, she had some baby-oil.

Soon after Kamal joined her, Abigail returned his gift of ecstasy given at Gazorkhan. She slowly massaged his whole body, kneading the firm muscle as hard as she could, then ending much more gently with his member. She didn't use oil for his eager manhood, instead providing lubrication with her tongue and finally taking his smooth glans into her mouth. Kamal was curiously silent throughout, but she was fully aware of his building tension and his petit-spasms of pleasure that made her feel surprisingly powerful, made her feel that at last she had a way to control this potent man, if only for a little while.

At last he murmured as his muscles tensed and she felt his moment coming. But she immediately pulled her mouth away and pressed her thumb firmly against his swollen helmet, forcing it back a little. She'd learned this trick to stop Terry's premature ejaculation, and sure enough Kamal slowly subsided too. She cupped and softly caressed his balls while his muscles relaxed, keeping a different kind of pleasant sensation going. Then once more she took him up, yet again denied him release, and then a third time she did the same. He moaned now and writhed as she stroked him.

The fourth time, she freed him. As his dark, straining member started its contractions, she didn't want to risk any disturbance by pulling her mouth away again. She stayed put and let the pressured liquid of his love flood over her tongue, something she'd never done before, nor even contemplated doing! The warmth and salty taste surprised her, triggering a shiver of kinky excitement, but she discreetly used a tissue moments later; she certainly wasn't up to swallowing, or at least not yet.

For once Kamal was speechless, his wit and sophistication temporarily overwhelmed. However, he had enough energy left to ensure Abigail didn't have to sleep unsatisfied.

Bandar-e-Anzali to Rasht, Iran: May 2008

The next morning was one of the most unreal in Abigail's life. It started sanely enough, and pleasantly, with a leisurely breakfast after making love again. Later, Kamal started the car and edged into the busy main road outside the hotel; Abigail turned around to see whether their silver shadow was still in place. Indeed the Mercedes pulled out too, yet a leather-jacketed young man on a moped seemed to appear right out of nowhere and ran straight into the vehicle's protruding wing. Abigail gasped as man and moped hit the road surface.

"Kamal! Someone…"

"Yes. I saw in the mirror."

"We can get away!"

Instead of doing so, Kamal calmly drove around the block and came up to the Mercedes from behind. A large group of youths had gathered around the silver car, all remonstrating angrily with the unfortunate driver. Some were shaking their fists while others aggressively slapped the bodywork. A couple more were helping the guy on the ground.

Kamal smirked and accelerated away, as realisation dawned on Abigail.

"This is your doing! But if they're government, things could get nasty. They might stop us leaving Iran!"

"I doubt those men are government minions." A look of contempt flickered briefly over Kamal's features. "Whoever they belong to, they couldn't keep *me* in this country." He flashed her a rakish grin. "Don't worry Abigail, you're safe with me."

Even deep inside, Abigail felt certain this was true. Yet something still bothered her, something she couldn't quite put her finger on. Eventually, another thought took over.

"Will the young man be okay, the moped guy?"

"Ha, of course! It's an old trick. Apply brakes at the last second, then kick out at the car to make it sound like a bad impact. You do need to hit the deck, but with barely any velocity."

Kamal was driving leisurely, as if deliberately frittering away his advantage. Abigail itched to ask, but she knew there'd be a clever reason. Sure enough, the Mercedes soon caught them up again, crazily overtaking the traffic behind.

"So much for your gang of youths."

Kamal merely smiled. After only a few minutes, their tail began to fall behind again. Vehicles began to pass the lagging Mercedes. As Abigail peered over her shoulder through the rear window, distantly she saw the

173

silver car pulling off the road.

"Why on Earth would they give up?"

"In the confusion, my little *gang* levered the petrol cap and put sugar in their tank," commented Kamal casually. "That car will need some very serious repairs."

Abigail was dumbfounded. Life with Kamal was going to be anything but mundane.

She'd assumed that their only option was the long road back to Tehran and a flight out from the International Airport there. Yet Kamal soon surprised her by turning off the main road. She recognised the area, just north of Rasht close to the industrial district they'd visited the day before. This time Kamal exited the highway on the opposite side to that grey building; moments later they were entering Rasht airport.

"Oh, we're going to fly to Tehran and leave the car here!"

"All is arranged." Just the hint of a smile played at the edges of his mouth. Abigail glared back in mock anger and poked him in the ribs.

They relinquished their car at a tiny auto-rental booth, then Kamal made a quick call on his mobile before urging her towards the main airport building, their luggage in tow.

"Hey, slow down!" as Abigail's wheelie-case slewed. Kamal grinned back over his shoulder, but didn't slacken the pace.

The terminal was almost empty as they rushed through. A screen advertised scheduled departures in Farsi and English; just two, Bandar Abbas and Tehran.

"Hang on, that departure time can't be right! Hey let me read…"

Kamal strode purposefully on, Abigail trotting to keep up. He approached a man in uniform, who nodded, then opened a side door and waved them through. A dim corridor, doors to one side, daylight at the other end.

"Kamal! Where the hell are we going?"

"Ah, my dearest, you will soon see."

And she did. They burst out into sunlight, and on to tarmac.

"What are you doing? We're on the airfield!"

"Ah, so we are."

"But…" Abigail realised she didn't know what to say.

Then they were standing beside an aircraft with a propeller, just *one* propeller. A young guy in blue overalls grinned hugely at her, she instinctively smiled back, then he grabbed her wheelie-case and Kamal's piece of luggage to put on board.

"He's our pilot?"

"Climb up, Abigail. Climb aboard."

She did so. The pilot and co-pilot seats were covered in sheepskin. She turned to the rear and took a step in. Six more seats in grey leather, smart carpeting in darker grey, wooden panelling in the roof. She hesitated as a huge roar announced the engine starting, and turned back. Her jaw dropped. Kamal was in the pilot's seat! The young guy was still on the tarmac, his grin even wider. He closed the door.

Kamal patted the co-pilot's seat. "Get buckled up."

She hurried to comply. "Can you actually fly this thing?"

The plane lurched forward. "Hopefully. It seems to be a Socata TBM700B."

"You devil! You never said you could fly."

"I wanted to see the surprise on your face. It was quite a picture just now!" He pointed to a mirror that reflected the plane's interior. "The property of a friend, this plane."

Kamal lined up to the runway and chatted incomprehensibly to the control tower.

"Is that why you rushed me? Did you think I wouldn't get on?"

"Something like that. In our culture, a man takes charge. I wouldn't dream of imposing that on you ordinarily..." as the engine noise suddenly increased and the plane rushed forward, "but I thought a small demonstration might be fun!" He turned and displayed a beautiful smile, which made her heart sing. Everything shook; the din beat against her ears.

"Well I'm not complaining. It's fun!"

What a way to be swept off her feet! The plane leapt into the air, rocking from side to side and leaving Abigail's stomach behind. They banked steeply as Kamal got his bearings, circling back over the runway and nearby highway. Looking out of her side window, Abigail had the unnerving impression that the window faced directly downwards. Everything on the ground was a model from a child's play-set, small and yet perfectly detailed. They were not yet high.

Then Abigail saw a lone figure dressed in black, just outside the airport's perimeter fence. He was pointing something at them. A rifle!

She screamed. "Kamal!" The ground reeled past. She spluttered, trying to say more, but her mouth wouldn't work. She felt the blood drain from her face. The angle of the sun slid around, adding to her sense of dizziness and placing Kamal's face into shadow. His eyes were full of surprise.

He reached out and shook her knee. "Abigail! I thought you were okay with flying."

"It's not... Oh..." She shook her head. "Not that!" It was a while before

175

her heart slowed and she was able to explain. By now the airport was far behind. The engine noise lessened, though Kamal was still climbing.

"If he'd wanted to shoot, he would have," stated Kamal calmly. "I'd guess he was just using the telescopic sight to get a look at us."

"But who was he? Surely the Mercedes couldn't have caught us up? And why did he have a rifle anyway?"

"It's Iran; anyone who thinks they're important has an automatic rifle, unless they have a machine gun. I have to assume he was some accomplice of the others, but I must admit I've no idea who they are. *Certainly* not government, or they'd have liaised with the airport staff to stop us. So the good news is we're unlikely to be intercepted by fighter jets."

And then she caught sight of the compass bearing and crashing upon her came the direction that Kamal was heading.

"Kamal, we can't be –! Where are we going? Stop trying to scare me more!"

"We're going into my own back yard, where you'll be perfectly safe, anywhere that *we* go. Syria, Abi, Syria, where the answer to your mystery may be –"

"*Syria!* We can't! My papa would have kittens!"

"My dear, what a picturesque phrase... Ismaili colleagues at the University of Damascus might help with your fragment, but I never make promises I cannot keep. I needed, shall we say, some pieces to be in place, as well as absolute reassurances about stability wherever we go. Besides," and he grinned, "I guessed you'd love to see a crusader castle such as Krak des Chevaliers, just for instance?"

Abigail's shock was passing. Now she felt giggly and high. Syria! Paul would give his eye-teeth as a reporter to be heading into the country! What a man Kamal was. She was in his hands, and what hands those were. Kamal stroked her thigh, with inevitable consequences.

"There there, my love."

She flushed but tried to remain serious. "You must have logged our flight path to Syria, but we never showed our passports."

"I'm known at Rasht. It makes the officialdom more... streamlined."

Kamal smiled his rakish smile and moved his hand up between her legs. Suddenly feeling wholly adventurous and deliciously naughty, Abigail didn't object.

"I detected, soon after we met, that you desired a life with more excitement."

True, very true. She'd yearned for excitement. Now here she was, headily alive and in love, with her so, *so* accomplished man thwarting pursuers and winging her over an exotic land. The Caspian shimmered, blue and turquoise like the tiles of some vast mosque conceived in the unknowable mind of Allah. To the south, a wall of mountains reached up to the altitude of the plane, gold and ochre and black in the sharp sun of late morning, seemingly above the cares of the world; like the Nizaris who'd lived there, reaching for God. Patchwork green rolled by beneath. Kamal's eyes twinkled somewhat wickedly, no doubt promising much more adventure to come.

Abigail laughed, and maybe sounded a little manic, but she didn't care. Syria! This life was rich, she had to grasp it! She relaxed her legs a little more as Kamal's gentle massage started to work its magic.

"Is this thing fitted with an auto-pilot?"

Qa'lat al-Alamut, Elburz Mountains, Persia: August 1164

Everything valuable and useful was in Alamut. Thousands of books, a tower that housed an astrolabe for measuring the positions of stars, fine carpets and wall-hangings and exquisitely patterned tiles, jewelled daggers and goblets and other rich gifts given to the Master in hope of favour, and all left out for every man to see and to touch.

Nasir watched the Fida'een being trained, those angels of destruction who would sacrifice themselves for the faith. Their training in sword craft and knife craft and acrobatics was breathtaking to see. Aiming behind the ribs, they could part a goat clean in two with a single stroke, and the best of them did this in the midst of an acrobatic leap! Tutored in languages and customs too, the Fida'een could pass unnoticed among strangers within many lands. They were human treasures, who would go to paradise, and would gladly be spent if purchasing the survival of the brotherhood.

Nasir and the other visiting leaders did not yet meet with the Master of Alamut, receiving no word of when they would. Apparently, Hasan was meditating in his well-guarded quarters. Yet on the following morning, which was the seventeenth day of Ramadan, there was sudden bustle within the great courtyard. Servants were busy setting up a pulpit; most oddly it faced south and an eighth west.

"Those in front of that pulpit," commented Umar to Nasir in slow disbelief, "will have their backs to Mecca!"

"Evidently." *Could it be, could it really be?*

Next, the servants erected huge banners at each corner of the pulpit. Red, green, yellow, and white. Tables were placed here and there, towards the edges of the courtyard.

Presently a summons to assemble was cried throughout the castle and its grounds.

As the guest leaders and their entourages arrived, the Syrians were directed to the left, visitors from other regions to the right or to the centre. Many from Alamut itself crowded around at the rear. Evidently, every detail of the forthcoming ceremony had been planned.

Excitement quickened the crowd, which waited; waited. A fleet of fluffy clouds drifted through the mountains, sailing serenely over Alamut, veiling the fierce sun which had beat upon the courtyard only minutes before.

And they waited. How could something momentous happen without there being a wait? The world had waited so many years already.

A light breeze rippled the tall banners. An eagle soared overhead.

Then at last the Master came, dressed all in pure white, a white turban upon his head, a sword in a silver scabbard at his side. He ascended the pulpit and first he greeted the crowd directly facing him, then repeated his salutations to those on the left, then to those on the right. Finally, he drew his sword and called out:

"Oh denizens of the worlds, oh *jinn* and men and angels, hear me! The Imam of our age, our holy Imam who remains aloof from vulgar sight, sends to you his blessings. He sends to you his compassion. You are his special servants. You are his children, his soldiers, his chosen ones. Accordingly, the blessed Imam frees you from all the obligations of Sacred Law. Like a broken bowl, the Shari'ah is now shattered! *The Imam brings you the Resurrection!*"

A buzz as of bees ran through the crowd.

"This very day," continued Hasan loudly, "you are all reborn, free from the burden of bygone laws. The blessed Imam has named Hasan Ali, son of Muhammad" – *himself* – "as your authority and your proof. In all matters concerning religion and concerning the world, the commands of Hasan" – *himself* – "shall be utterly obeyed. For Hasan's word is the very same as the Imam's word. Through Hasan's lips, the Imam speaks. And his very first command of *the Resurrection*, is that Ramadan ends now, this very moment!"

In the stunned silence that followed, Hasan descended from the pulpit and prostrated himself twice, praying, *away from Mecca*. After he arose the second time, he turned and cried out: "Therefore break your fast! Feast and rejoice!"

At that moment the sun blazed through dispersing clouds, upon ranks of dumbly open mouths, upon servants already hastening to the tables, bearing bread and saffron rice, spiced lamb and roasted chickens and sweetmeats made with seed and honey.

"All here are saved from death!" Hasan declared. "You now possess knowledge of the Truth. You are saved from sin, absolved of sin!"

Other servants were bringing turquoise cups, and what could only be *wine*. Wine! The first Hasan had even executed his very own son for drinking wine. Truly, the old law was utterly overturned!

"And if a man shall not eat," added Hasan, "then let stones be cast at him."

The crowd found their voice, and roared their rejoicing. "Ya Husayn!" they called out. Oh that true Imam, slaughtered at Kerbala so many centuries since. Then also they shouted, "Ya Hasan!" Nasir did so too, like a joyful prayer. "Hasan! Hasan!"

Now rich awnings and canopies were brought to shade the low tables. Nasir exulted as he and Umar seated themselves upon the dusty stone, to partake of meat and rice, *and wine, so delicious!* After enjoying a sugary and pasty sweetmeat, the world seemed aglow; the banners around the pulpit rippled luminously like a captured, writhing rainbow. Soon exultation became spiritual exaltation, a high elation, a mystical rapture.

Nasir could hear sweet music of harp and rebeck and song approaching, as if heaven had opened its gates. As indeed seemed to be so, for the players and singers were surely Houris. How else could there be so many beautiful young women, beguilingly gowned in silk? Surely they were sent from paradise by the hidden Imam. The visions of loveliness played, they sang, they danced, they enchanted, they shimmered. In part of his mind Nasir acknowledged that the women were real and that they must be servants or slaves of Hasan. Yet this knowledge did not matter in the least. In esoteric reality, paradise was in the courtyard this very day. Nasir felt that his exaltation must burst forth from him any moment, like a hawk unhooded and released, like a hunting dog unchained, like a horse given its head to run wildly.

Presently, a player set down her harp and invitingly reached out her hand to him. Her hair was silken ebony, her eyes were golden topaz, her lips were rose-petals rolled upward and downward. Nasir arose. He barely noticed that all music had hushed and that other women were offering themselves, here, there, were leading away men to one or other building around the courtyard; men who were eager yet bashful, as though their boyhood had come again, as though their sexual selfhood was reborn.

He almost seemed afloat as she led him into a small room. Sunlight blazed through a muslin-hung window and upon a bed, dappling it into a bright snakeskin.

Beside that bed, her smile showing teeth that put pearls to shame, this Houri so human divested herself slowly, entirely, while Nasir gazed. His eyes drank in the smooth blushing yoke of her shoulders, the ripe apricots of her breasts, the shallow bowl of her belly, the smooth little cave of her navel… and the shaved, cleft peach below. The hairs of modesty, or of immodesty for that matter, were all gone. He and she were beyond any veil.

Advancing, she plucked away his clothes. As his hands roved over her softness, the perfume of her hair intoxicated him so that his nostrils flared like a stallion's. She took him in hand by his stiffness, drawing him down with her upon the bed. She said nothing, yet her tongue licked the roses of her lips, so he knew that soon it would moisten him too in the place where swollen flesh raged.

After timeless touches and caresses, he lay upon her and within her, her legs wrapping him tightly, her ankles locked upon his buttocks, heels drumming like a heartbeat.

Some while after, as their breath came in great gasps like a chant, his exaltation finally erupted ecstatically into her. After this, his throbbing flesh became again like a beardless young boy's, and he found himself sliding apart from her. Beads of milk issued from her opened peach to bedew the tops of her thighs.

Ian Watson & Andy West

Damascus University, Syria: May 2008

Abigail tried to stifle a yawn. They'd been going around in verbal circles for an hour and a half, and so far the three worthy professors had offered no more than poor Walid. Damascus sun punched through slanted blinds behind Abigail's left shoulder, tattooing brilliance and shadow onto the elderly trio, making them look as if they were behind bars. Maybe they were, she thought, bars of traditional thinking.

Pedants, in other words, these profs, hardly touched by political events. Perfectly familiar to her was such an untidy, shared academic office as this, crammed with books and papers and piles of ageing data CDs. At the far end a post-grad typed slowly, his hands hovering uncertainly above the keyboard; if he was writing his thesis, it would take him a long time.

Kamal glanced her way, and she smiled back. After setting up this meeting, he'd contributed very little, doubtless hoping these professors of medieval poetry and Ismaili studies would speak their own minds spontaneously.

"It's very common," repeated Tazim in throaty cadences, "for the *Master of the Time* to be depicted as having complete judgement over us. For instance over whether we've been faithful, or whether we've *made sense of the truth*, as your fragment more or less says, even judgement over life and death itself."

"Not merely judgement, but direct power," added Hussain as he cleaned his spectacles. "Over more than just life and death too. Ra'is Hasan says of and to the Master of *his* time, something like: 'If you frown at an angel, all his works will become dust, but if you glance favourably at a devil he will transform into an angel of purity and truth.' Ra'is Hasan was a scholar for the chief da'i in Quhistan in the later years of Alamut, and almost certainly would have personally met the Master of whom he spoke."

"Was that just flattery?" asked Abigail.

Tazim shrugged. "The literature doesn't seem to have been used for flattery. More likely the loyalty and awe which such poets *genuinely felt* led to superlatives."

"The chain of command, so to speak, rises to the heavenly," added Sami. "For behind the Master is Ali, of whom Khusraw says, 'Truly no one can be saved from the fire unless he comes within Ali's protection.' And behind Ali is the Prophet himself. The poets, your poetisa included, would have been aware of this all the time."

Abigail sighed; this wasn't going anywhere.

The post-grad stole a glance at her. He'd done so quite a number of times; maybe he fancied her. Full cheeks and an innocent smile gave him a childish look, yet irises of dark-oak implied intensity.

182

"Can anyone tell me about al-Hakim?" she asked of a sudden.

"Abigail," interjected Kamal smoothly. "I already told you all about al-Hakim when we were in Cairo. You remember his mosque by the old city walls?"

"Oh, sorry, but I don't mean *him*. I meant the *other* Ismaili al-Hakim, from the twelfth century. *The sword of Allah, the shield of Allah, the possessed.*"

The room went silent. The post-grad goggled at her. Had she committed some great religious faux-pas?

"Er I... Did I say something inappropriate? I didn't..."

Tazim cleared his throat. "No no, it's just that we, that's to say I'm not sure who you're talking about."

Hussain rubbed his salt and pepper beard and gazed at his shoes. Sami scratched his neck.

"I found him in an old book, *Legends of the Elburz Mountains*," she continued hopefully. "The author is French, Professor Ruffie."

"Who?" asked Tazim and Sami in unison.

"Ah, *him*." Hussain grimaced. "He wrote a work on the Crusader castles here in Syria. Very romantic, very unprofessional. He wasn't a genuine academic."

The post-grad seemed suddenly inspired, and typed furiously.

"But he wouldn't simply *invent* al-Hakim?"

Hussain raised his eyebrows. "He may have found someone in the historical records to associate his romantic notions with. I wouldn't give much credence."

"A brilliant physician, according to Ruffie."

"Well, *Hakim* actually means *scholar* or *physician*, so that doesn't tell us more than his name already suggests." Tazim cleared his throat again, a nervous tic with him. "Is this anything to do with your poetic puzzle?"

"No... No, I'm just curious." Why did she feel that there was a connection?

Kamal lightly clapped his hands. "I think we've done enough for now." He beamed. "These gentlemen owe me a few favours, I'm sure we can rely on them to keep working on the problem?" A chorus of agreement. "Now I need to talk a while about funding, for the 'Literature of the Light' series. Tazim, can you show Abigail around for a bit?"

Tazim looked as though he didn't want to be left out of any discussions about money. "Fawzi," he called, "could you show our guest some of the manuscripts we're working on? The artefacts room might be interesting too."

The post-grad nodded and grinned nervously. "Of course, Professor."

Fawzi carefully replaced an illuminated manuscript, then his head twitched in a bird-like way as he scanned the room for something else interesting. He seemed scared to look at Abigail, yet, the couple of times he'd actually done so, his gaze pierced like a hawk's. Maybe he was uncomfortable around women, though desiring them too.

"We don't just work on poetry. This for instance," and he pointed to a stained page beneath a mounted lens, "is part of a chemistry manual. Mostly about making different kinds and colours of glass, plus glazes on pots." The page was crammed with compressed Arabic in faded ink.

He led Abigail through an airtight door to the next room, where it was cooler. On a brightly lit table lay a large dagger, in very poor condition. Next to it were dainty brushes and bottles of fluid and implements that looked like dental tools, no doubt for cleaning.

"This was unearthed inside one of the Nizari castles in the Jebel Ansariye."

"Wow. An actual Assassin's dagger!"

A fleeting smile passed over Fawzi's youthful face.

"Probably not used in earnest. See the jewels here in the hilt?" He pointed them out. "This was most likely a gift, or made for ceremonial purposes. It's good quality, or was, Damascus steel. The tools of the trade, so to speak, would be unadorned and easier to hide than this."

Romantic notions about the knife's history, already forming in Abigail's head, were swiftly quashed. Fawzi was constantly fiddling with a ring on his finger: was her womanly presence really so disturbing? Or was something else bothering him? Suddenly he snapped into action, strode to a tall tier of drawers and pulled one open.

Fawzi's hard eyes were bright as he placed a yellowy box in her hands, of a size that would hold 100 teabags. He didn't speak.

Abigail examined the object, carefully turning it around. Oddly, holes were drilled through the lid and sides, surrounded by stylised scrollwork. The material was smooth ivory, the whole box formed from separate pieces glued together. Four short lines of Arabic adorned the top, probably carved with a knife and then filled with something black. Opening the lid, she saw two curved supports, as if to hold a cylinder or small bottle.

"What is it? What does the inscription say?"

Without saying a word, Fawzi handed her a small card and looked at her eagerly. Did this box have some deep significance that he expected her to recognise? The card held some text in English, presumably a translation of the inscription. *Since he made me / the water of life / pestilence has become / quite insignificant to me.*

"This rings a bell...!"

Fawzi rewarded her with a brief grin and whispered, "The box is fourteenth century, regarded as a quaint curiosity. The inscription is either a terrible copying error, say the historians, or some artisan who didn't know the origin of the words made up his own variant for some reason. Can you guess why?"

An image of Walid's office in the Roxbury mosque sprang to Abigail's mind, then the cleric's face, his deep chocolate voice quoting... "Khusraw!" The correct words came to her. "*Since he made me / drink from the water of life / death has become / quite insignificant to me.* How odd!"

"*Very* odd. Yet too close to be a coincidence. The lines must derive from Khusraw, so this box *must* be associated with the Nizaris."

"What did it hold?"

Fawzi spoke slowly, deliberately, as if carefully choosing his words, or as if hiding something. "There are two similar examples from northern Syria made out of wood and in a very poor state. No inscription on those. There's some evidence they held bottles containing a kind of... magic potion... a supposed cure-all. Ten years ago, a visiting French medical historian proposed that this might be *Syrian Rue*."

His frown deepened, marring his youthful face. If he *did* want to hide something, why would he then show her the box at all?

"What on Earth is Syrian Rue?"

"Syrian Rue, or Assyrian Rue, is an ancient potion said to ward off or cure many diseases, made from the seeds of the Harmal flower. Some also call the flower itself Syrian Rue. Its botanical name is Peganum Harmala. The active components are still being researched, but contain complex beta-carbolides and can cause hallucinations. Apparently, the stuff does strengthen the immune system. It's also part of *the vinegar of the four thieves*, the famous magical elixir of the Alchemists."

"Goodness. Very mysterious. And you're very knowledgeable."

"Look underneath."

Abigail turned the box over and saw more Arabic script scratched into the ivory and barely visible.

"This says, *they have forty days*."

"What do you think it means?"

Fawzi ignored the question. "Some experts say that a potion kept inside this box may have been blessed by an Ismaili da'i, thus meriting the main inscription – an identity tag for a holy cure, a kind of... holy water. Others say the altered verse might convey some humour that's now lost to us, maybe something to do with a cure for sexually transmitted diseases." The postgrad stared hard at her.

Abigail was flustered. "It's all very interesting, but I don't quite see why..."

"Syrian Rue is said to cure plague," Fawzi interjected softly. "The usual word for plague is *ta'un*, but sometimes *waba* is used. *Pestilence*."

For a second or two, Abigail's blood ran cold. *Nizaris. Holy Water. Plague*. All of them connected. And the *very same* connections she herself had stumbled across by an entirely different route, via Safiyya's fragment and Sinaldin and Guy de Dieulefit. She felt she was gaping. *Get a grip, girl*; this is all just the complex tangles of history. But her obsession for the mystery of the fragment, overshadowed for a short while by passion for Kamal, was burning again.

Fawzi looked relieved. His frown had gone. He took the ivory relic back and quickly replaced it in the drawer.

"Do you know whether –?"

"No more questions, I'm afraid. Time to get back." He walked away. Abigail had little choice but to follow.

Kamal still held court with the smiling professors. She enjoyed looking at her man when he wasn't aware, appreciating his animation and natural authority. Oh yes, he was a trustee for a fund sponsoring some of the department's work; yet another notch in his first-class belt of achievements. The professors would be trying to impress him, but they certainly hadn't impressed her.

Fawzi unexpectedly and earnestly whispered, "Kushraw said: *make a sword from patience and a shield from faith*. Maybe your al-Hakim was a man of great patience and extreme faith." Then he hurried away.

She'd gained the distinct impression that he was dropping hints to her. But why be so obscure? And why was he nervous? Was there more to all this than a self-conscious young man in the presence of a more experienced woman? Had Kamal's obvious possession of her made Fawzi particularly bashful? What had Fawzi been trying to say?

Abigail pulled out her diary and scribbled his Khusraw quotation and the words on the ivory box too. As she wrote, it occurred to her that the Professors might have been holding out on her, afraid of something. She recalled the deafening silence and Fawzi's shocked look when she'd first mentioned al-Hakim. Yet Kamal would surely have spotted any evasion?

"I'm getting paranoid," she muttered. *Like ICEman Jack*

Leila's Restaurant, Damascus, Syria: May 2008

That evening Kamal took her for an Arab meal at a celebrated restaurant which no troubles could conceivably close, quoth Kamal. Leila's; in the Shi'a section of the old city of Damascus. They sat on a roof terrace, the floodlit Jesus Minaret of the Great Umayyad Mosque ascending to the starry heavens right above them like an enormous shining sword of faith.

Yet she only picked at her food, brooding about mysteries. Plague and Holy Water, or at least Syrian Rue, obscure Nizari poetry... If Ruffie was right and al-Hakim was a brilliant physician, might he have addressed himself to the curing of plague? *Everyone* seemed to be quoting Khusraw at her, yet the Persian poet died well over two centuries before Safiyya was even born... Could some of his verses have taken on a new meaning for the Nizari elite? The old reflected in the new, like Trinity Church in the Hancock Tower? And what about nowadays? Could those men trailing them in Iran have anything to do with this? Horror of horrors, might Walid's brutal death be connected too? Else, why was ICE interested? God forbid that Jack was right all along, and there *was* a modern terrorist connection!

"Doesn't Leila's food please you?" asked Kamal.

"Oh I'm sorry..." She confessed her broodings, but he was highly sceptical, and who could blame him? She'd thought Jack was raving that day the ICEman entered her office.

"Abigail, one mustn't become *superstitious* about such things! Given the medieval Nizaris' dramatic and unusual history, even the very name *The Assassins*, it's highly tempting to believe *anything* about them – even some nebulous plot that exists only in Jack Turner's mind. I really don't think the Assassins will be causing trouble eight hundred years after their demise. Academics such as us must rely upon historical facts and poetic analysis. I'm sure that given a couple of weeks our professors will come up with some perfectly viable background or precedent for your troublesome fragment."

"I'd even thought of calling Jack Turner to tell him everything I've found out, just in case..."

Kamal stopped eating and folded his hands. "Well, we could always do that later, *if* we don't crack the problem ourselves. But you said yourself he's paranoid *and* a religious nut."

"That's true. He is." She felt a little comforted.

"Have you finally told *me* everything?" Kamal raised his eyebrows in mock amusement, though beneath this mask she could tell he was serious.

"I'm sorry. Yes I think so." She blushed. "I only just came across the Ruffie book, in Qazvin." Under the table she touched wood. She hadn't told

Kamal about the ivory box and what Fawzi said. Given Kamal was a big-wig at the university, she didn't want any negative feedback going Fawzi's way.

Yet Abigail's distraction lasted throughout their lovemaking later, and her sleep was disturbed as lines of medieval poetry she frustratingly couldn't quite read flowed constantly through her dreams. A sense of great danger weighed down on her spirit, while echoes of *ring a ring o' roses* provoked her several times into panicky wakefulness.

The Omayad Hotel, Damascus, Syria: May 2008

Bright morning sun flooded past partially opened curtains to gild Abigail and Kamal's room at the Omayad hotel near the Cham Palace, a plush establishment in a quiet side-street.

Thank goodness for Wi-Fi. Abigail was still in bed, propped up on pillows and working with her laptop, searching the net. And thank goodness for room service; she refilled her cup of tea from the pot on the breakfast tray beside her. Kamal had left early on another business mission, while sleep still clutched her, so she'd only managed a muttered farewell.

It hadn't taken long to confirm Fawzi's information regarding Syrian Rue. For many centuries it was considered to confer protection against plague and other serious afflictions; in more modern times it had proved useful in treating malaria and was being analysed as a potential weapon against cancer. The seed extract had been used by various sects including the Assassins, the Sufi masters and the Templars, to enhance their inner search for secret knowledge. Abigail could find little about what these elites may have learned during their hallucinogenic trips, but there was plenty about the plant itself. The white flower had five petals arranged as a star; it seemed ancient Persians had hung dried bunches above their doors to ward off the evil eye, also burning the seeds as incense, a practice still alive in parts of the Middle East and Turkey.

Abigail crunched into another piece of toast and marmalade, and settled back on the pillows, feeling pleasantly decadent. She needed to remind herself about the ghastly tale of the Black Death, but first there were emails to send.

The first, to Paul, started with reassurances mixed with some impishness as regards her being in Syria; but House of Representatives Speaker Nancy Pelosi was here just recently to meet with President Assad, and Condi Rice was talking to the Syrian Foreign Minister, so what was to worry about in Syria? What might be going on Waters-wise took priority, plus all that had happened at the University of Damascus. After many minutes of furious typing, she wondered whether she should drastically cut it down, yet couldn't be bothered to spend time re-crafting. So she added that Kamal was sceptical, no doubt justifiably, and asked Paul what he knew about the Black Death.

Might Paul take her lengthy unburdening as romantic encouragement? She sighed, and sent the message anyway. No conversation with a man seemed ever to be free of amorous implication.

After minor updates to friends and colleagues, it was Jen's turn to hear of Abi's Syrian escapade, and receive another request for help. If anyone could track down the anonymous Ismaili poem 'The Triumph', it was Jen. Aware that her old friend ought to be rewarded for more hard work, she gave a long summary of the romantic situation with Kamal, including some pretty graphic detail. Jen was between men right now, and in that state was always voracious for news of her friends' relationships; the dirtier the descriptions, the better! Quite apart from the pleasant memories this evoked, Abigail felt for the first time in her life that she might be a bit ahead of her peers on the sexual front. As an afterthought she asked for any information on al-Hakim, the twelfth century Ismaili physician, *not* the eleventh century mad Ismaili Caliph.

Then it was on to the Black Death. Pages and pages of the familiar story slid across Abigail's screen, putting a chill down her spine despite her cosy situation in a soft bed in a warm room. The tale had always scared her. A disease so implacable, so unforgiving, killing in such a ghastly way.

People's utter helplessness scared Abigail, but also the link with rats and fleas, creatures which she'd detested from childhood. She forced herself through the details of the epidemic that entered Europe via Sicily and Provence at the end of 1347, around the date that Guy and Sinaldin would have made port in the latter region, at Marseille.

Apparently the black rat was a native of tropical India but made a home in Europe, transported on sailing ships. Hardier brown rats from Russia didn't start to displace the black variety till the early eighteenth century. Bubonic plague spread rapidly through the black rat population, and rat fleas jumped on to people after their natural hosts died, passing the curse to humans by their bites. In a small fraction of cases a pneumonic form of plague could then pass from person to person, but to keep the fire of plague fully fuelled a large reservoir of rats and their fleas was required.

Horrible fascination glued Abigail to her screen even though she was holding back an urge to pee. Finally she jumped out of bed and visited the bathroom, rushing back to ring for a hot chocolate to sustain her through medical sites.

Surprisingly, bubonic plague was still alive and prospering in the world. Yet recent outbreaks in India and Asia had claimed only 5% of the stricken populations. In the New World, the kill rate was lower still; a natural reservoir of the disease in American rodents caused occasional infections, but intervention with antibiotics usually saved people and avoided epidemics. In the end, *Yersinia pestis* was a simple bacterium. Act swiftly enough, since the time between infection and death was typically three to five days, and it seemed the monster had been tamed. Could it have become a lot less virulent? This was puzzling, though comforting.

The hot chocolate arrived, topped with cream and sprinkled chocolate. She sipped in delight as she searched for the story of plague *before* its big medieval invasion of Europe. For instance in the late twelfth century, when the mysterious al-Hakim had stayed at Alamut.

Plague had certainly launched its attacks on mankind as far back as classical times, for instance the plague that struck Athens in the hot summer of 430 BC while the crowded city was besieged by the Spartans. With no escape, mortality was extremely high. Burial rites weren't observed; bodies were simply piled in the streets and temples.

900 years later there was the Plague of Justinian, which the historian Procopius had described in dramatic detail as exploding out of the Egyptian port of Pelusium in 541 AD and devastating the empires of Byzantium and Persia. At its peak in the Byzantine capital of Constantinople a staggering 10,000 citizens were dying *every day*. Vomiting blood or violently delirious, many of the afflicted threw themselves into the sea and drowned.

This plague returned every nine to twelve years, wreaking havoc each time, until about 700 AD. And the newly risen Muslim empire recorded five great plagues up to 744 AD, one of which wiped out 25,000 of their soldiers on campaign. What's more, plague pockets persisted in Syria, so there *could* be an overlap with al-Hakim in the twelfth century if he'd ever stayed at the Nizari castles there, as well as at Alamut.

Why oh why did *all* of these epidemics, including the medieval ones, seem like hurricanes of death compared with the trivial squalls of the modern bubonic plague?

Not wanting to read any more horrors for the moment, she forced herself out of bed to take a shower. *Yet something was wrong.* Something didn't add up.

With a soft bathrobe caressing her still wet skin and a towel around her head, she returned reluctantly to the plague, this time at the desk so that her laptop's battery could recharge from the mains socket. She didn't open the curtains any further, since sunlight would make it harder to see the screen.

Reams of consistent material agreed about the terrible symptoms and huge fatalities. Plausible tales of cities losing half or three-quarters or more of their populations were common. Some cities were wiped out entirely, and often rural areas were scarcely safer.

Mass burnings and pit burials at best, priests avoiding the afflicted, mothers shunning their own daughters for fear of contact, fathers running away from their families, friendships abandoned. It must have been hell on Earth, thought Abigail...

Nordhausen, Thuringia-Meisen: May 1348

Abraham Rumbold was terrified. He'd fled from Erfurt, coins sewn into his clothes, after seeing thirty fellow Jews publicly burned on a grill. In spite of their agony, the obstinate victims sang psalms and laughed joyously. Even above the hiss of flesh and the jeers of the crowd, he'd heard them clearly, until their voices ascended to weave an inhuman web of sound, each thread a screech of silver on glass. Many others in his tight-knit community had set light to their own homes, their families, and themselves within; a terrible sacrifice to escape the rape and violence that preceded a final reckoning. Yiddish verses meant nothing to the enraged citizens, and they'd taken laughter as acknowledgement of guilt, proof of a pact with the devil on the part of the Jews to spread foul disease.

Abraham's wife and daughters were dead; brutally raped, then their throats cut.

What sort of coward am I, he sobbed to Jehovah, *to be still alive?* He asked in vain, from the filthy straw of the fetid room where he was now locked, half-naked and badly bruised, his coat and precious coin gone. Any lingering reason for living had long gone too. All he ironically retained was his reason; how much better if by now madness had thieved his mind, so he couldn't anticipate the inevitable pain to come.

In Erfurt, first had come the pestilence. He'd seen men and women, feverish and naked, running recklessly through the town before they fell. He'd seen crazed victims cast out on the streets to die, scarcely able to move and so thirsty they lapped piss from the gutters. He'd seen the fearful fragility of mankind, the bursting bags of foul blood and decaying tissue that human bodies so swiftly became. Soon after came desperate debauchery; the newly plague-marked copulating with each other in public, and healthy citizens emulating them heedlessly. In this festival of sin, the corpse-collectors violated dying women and children before looting their houses, since only the vilest of villains would accept such work, and they fully intended to profit. The world had become Gehenna, the place of torment.

"Feeling cold, are we? We'll toast your feet a bit, then yer'll tell us how you poisoned the wells. And yer'll tell us where you buried the rest of your Jew-gold. See, Landgrave Frederick ain't at all happy we ain't been doing our godly duty enough in this town."

Dressed in their dirty, blood-stained jerkins and hose, they'd brought a brazier into the room and puffed it red-hot with bellows. While Abraham trembled uncontrollably, a round-shouldered man twirled a quill and portentously read from thick parchment.

"The confessions of the Jew Abraham Rumbold, freely given before the revealed glory of the Lord. Er... Proceed."

Then an ox of a man held Abraham down, while the others...

There followed a seeming eternity of atrocious pain, and such a smell of roasting flesh that he knew he'd never walk again. He screamed nonsense: *Oh yes, I poisoned the wells, just stop and I'll tell you how. Oh yes, I buried a satchel of gold, only stop and I'll show you where.*

When he awoke from a faint, his feet, or what remained, were as charred as the coals. Fire blazed up his legs as though the stumps were still licked by its cruel tongues. Yet the room smelled so sweet, as if seraphs breathed out holy perfumes.

Somehow, incredibly, his reason *still* had not fled. From Erfurt, he well knew the cause of someone experiencing a heavenly smell. The organs inside his body were swiftly starting to rot, to liquefy. Tight red boils would soon sprout from him, like full, hot cherries. In a day or two he'd be a bag of stinking juices and bones. He'd brought the plague within him from Erfurt, was already a dead man before he'd even set out! He began to pray that his tormenters, now doomed themselves, would soon drag him out and burn him. Desperately, Abraham craved the absolution of darkness, the blessing of nothingness.

The Omayad Hotel, Damascus, Syria: May 2008

Abigail noted how local governments often tried to impose quarantine. One heroic English village, Eyam in Derbyshire, *voluntarily* sealed itself off so that plague shouldn't spread to its neighbours. She remembered the story from childhood. Whether in classical Greece or medieval Baghdad or Italian Renaissance cities, the length of quarantine seemed almost universally to be forty days, measured from the final death until the all-clear. Indeed the English word *quarantine* came via early French from the Latin for forty.

Abigail's blood suddenly ran chill, yet she didn't know why. Sun, streaming through the gap in the curtains, seemed a false friend. When she pulled the towel from her head and flung it onto the bed, motes of dust swarmed in the sunbeams. *We're all dust, swept hither and thither by the forces of history, or simply blown away.* She reread the last web-page. *Forty days!*

"Shit! Godammit!" What had the words on the bottom of Fawzi's ivory box been? *They have forty days.*

Trying to slow her racing thoughts, slowly and deliberately Abigail dried her hair then got dressed. Given that the box may have held Syrian Rue, and Fawzi's heavy hints about its purpose, need she look further for a direct connection between the Nizaris and plague?

Indeed, a *second* connection, if her guesses about Sinaldin and Guy de Dieulefit turned out to be true. But *why* had Fawzi given her this huge hint?

Never mind that for the moment! She'd read that the incubation period for bubonic plague was only a day or two, with another two or three days of suffering until the victim either died or recovered. Why on Earth was *forty days* quarantine imposed? Six days from the last death should be sufficient, seven to be on the safe side. Abigail tapped frantically into search engines to solve this little mystery, to which there surely had to be a simple answer.

But there wasn't, there just wasn't.

Gradually a terrible truth began to emerge. And once it emerged, it was so blindingly obvious that Abigail was dumbfounded not to have seen it earlier. She swore out loud and banged her fist onto the desk. *All she'd been taught at school was wrong! All the mainstream literature was wrong!*

The medieval Black Death, and similar epidemics in ancient times, *weren't* bubonic plague at all! They were something *far* more sinister and *far* more destructive, something that spread via direct human to human contact, something with a *much longer* incubation time, something for which a forty day isolation period was essential!

It was Iceland that put her on the right track. The Black Death swept across Iceland from 1402 to 1404 AD, and again from 1494 to 1495 AD, just as it repeatedly swept over other parts of Europe in that period. But at the time *there were no rats in Iceland!*

In fact, black rat experts claimed there were few such in rural Britain in the mid-fourteenth century. Black rats were *tropical*. In winter they relied for warmth on human dwellings. Their numbers needed boosting regularly by new recruits on ships sailing in from warmer climes. Yet rural Britain and its north weren't spared the scourge.

The famous story of Eyam made no sense at all if the Black Death was *bubonic* plague! Allegedly, infected fleas had been trapped in a bolt of cloth brought to Eyam. Yet everything the villagers of Eyam did presupposed that they knew the disease was *directly* very infectious, *nothing to do with rats or fleas*. And Eyam's strategy of isolation had worked, even though no one could have stopped rats from scurrying in and out of the village as they pleased! Therefore plague had arrived in Eyam within a person. Plague was spread by people, not rats.

Flabbergasted, Abigail rubbed her neck, which ached from being hunched over the screen for so long. How could so many historians and scientists believe something so wrong for such a long time?

As she pressed on, one disease seemed an overwhelmingly close fit to historical data about the Black Death: a voracious form of haemorrhagic fever. Haemorrhagic fevers typically had kill rates of thirty to eighty percent, sometimes passing ninety percent. In a population with no previous exposure, it could potentially reach a hundred percent. *This* explained the devastation in ancient cities. The Black Death must be a vicious and hitherto unidentified cousin to *Ebola*, the so-called flesh-eater, and lethal *Marburg Fever*, caused by a primitive filo-virus, worm-like and highly contagious. Ebola and Marburg themselves were rare, fortunately…

The symptoms lined up. Swellings similar to bubonic plague were often misleadingly present at the start of haemorrhagic fever, but that was *only the start*. Black pustules, blood pouring from orifices, madness, the dissolving organs ancient physicians had described: those were all completely normal for haemorrhagic fevers, if one could ever use the word *normal* for such vileness.

Then she came across an estimated incubation time for haemorrhagic fever; around thirty-two to thirty-three days. Add six days for the likely longest time between showing signs until death; giving a maximum of thirty-nine days. Another day for safety, and there you had the universal quarantine period, forty days. If somebody was infected, they'd have an absolute maximum of forty days to live. *They have forty days.*

Then Abigail discovered that a travelling tailor named George Viccars had brought those bolts of cloth to Eyam. The supposed rat fleas were *added* to the Eyam story at the end of the nineteenth century, when Yersin made his great discovery about the rat-flea-human cycle of the bacterium that caused bubonic plague, duly named after him as *Yersinia pestis*. Clearly, the tailor had arrived already infected in his *person*, not in his goods!

She did finally find a piece giving alternative explanations of the Black Death, including haemorrhagic fever as a possible candidate. So at least somebody was on the right track! Maybe the people in American military labs who were reportedly working on Ebola virus…

The laptop loudly announced 'ya got mail' in Bugs Bunny's voice, surprising her. Oh yeah, she'd recently changed the settings in an idle moment.

The mail was from Paul. She skipped through pointed comments about how romantically risky, rhymes with frisky, it must be in Syria; too much was on her mind to bother about petty jealousy, though continued help from the immature but obliging reporter could be invaluable.

…may have some good news for you soon. My buddy in France has come across something, but I need him to get off his butt and drive all the way to Montlume, Provence. Hey, do you think that Fawzi guy is for real? Do you think he was trying to help you? Or deliberately confuse you? Either way, I think something very odd is going on!

You could say that again!

I remember our conversation in the Sabra, wrote it down, remember? But I've been trying to dig up something on Guy and Sinaldin rather than concentrating on plague. So as to your question, I know zip about the Black Death, 'cept it's bubonic plague, it's nasty, it killed lots and lots of folks back when. Plague is plague isn't it?
It's raining in Boston. I'm thinking of you out in the Syrian sun. Hope you don't rue it ☺ *Paul XX.*

Paul must be up real early in Boston. She checked her watch. Just gone one in the afternoon in Syria, no wonder she was hungry again. About six in the morning for Paul! Maybe he was still at his computer. He'd sent his ID some days back, so she was able to try instant messaging. The status box claimed he was online.

Hello Paul, U there?

Yes I am, how R U Abi? How's Syrian sun?

Fine. I'm not in sun, am in hotel room. Why U up so early?

Reading up on Ismailis pre work. All for U! Kamal with U?

No he's not. Yes he's well. Yes he's wonderful. Yes we're sleeping together. Please get over it!

There was a pause.

Sorry. Is it so obvious?

Yes. Oh damn, sorry to be brutal. Just slipped off my fingers. Worried about all this Nizari and plague stuff, have very bad vibes about it. Grateful for yr support and help.

Happy to serve, sure there'll be big story in this one day. Just read that the area of Quhistan, around Alamut, definitely still Ismaili 70 years+ after Mongols took Nizari castles, because attempt was made to try convert people there to Sunnism (if that's right word). & Mamluk conquerors of Syria let Nizaris there keep some fortresses till at least mid-14th century. I'd say Nizaris survived Mongols & Mamluks also, though maybe whittled down to a desperate core.

The mid-fourteenth century, mused Abigail. When the Black Death erupted. Around the time 'The Triumph' was written. She typed:

Beginning to realise that myself. Some Ismailis also migrated to India. Listen, I don't think plague is plague. I mean, don't think Black Death is bubonic plague at all. Is something far worse, lot worse than just nasty. & is linked to ivory box by much stronger connection than speculation about Syrian Rue. I need go eat, will send email later explaining all. Want U put Ismailis aside for mo & read 'Return of the Black Death', by Scott & Duncan. Should tell you what BD really is. Can't get it out here but Brattle on West St should stock. Tell me what U think.

Sounds bit heretical Abi, but OK.

Oh, I'm very confused about Fawzi, but pretty certain not trying mislead me. Don't think F wanted the professors or anyone to find out he told me anything significant. In fact F never said anything not already public knowledge, just showed me box & hinted about stuff. All rather weird.

197

Yeah, very weird! Look, have to take shower & get off to work. Roving reporter today, outa town.

Thanks for all yr help. Really do appreciate. I'll send email soon. Abigail X.

Good to talk to you. Take care. Paul XX. Hey, this makes me sound like Pope! Paul Twentieth! You'd be Abi Tenth. Abbey, abbess, get it? One of those legendary female popes. Probably hung out in Avignon.

Aren't you overreaching a bit? Not many Pope Pauls. Abigail One.

Paul Nil. But hey, I'm ambitious. Why not Paul XXX :).

Abigail smiled. Paul was irrepressible. She was about to head out when the phone rang. It must be Kamal! She sprang back and grabbed the receiver.

"Hello."

"Hello my darling. Have you had a good morning?"

"Breakfast in bed and surfing the net. And you?"

"Alas, my meetings aren't going well. I'm in Beirut right now and I'll have to stay here late. I'll be too tired to drive back tonight, really."

"Oh, damn." Abigail struggled to hide her disappointment.

"But I have an exciting plan for tomorrow! I'll send a driver to pick you up, around midday, and we shall meet at a mystery destination."

"That sounds a bit better."

"I'm truly sorry, my love."

"Hey, it's okay. I was just looking forward to cuddling up tonight."

"I shall miss that too." Did he sound sincere? Yes, he did. "Can you bring the luggage with you? We're moving our base."

"Okay, will do. Tomorrow then. Love you."

"I love you too, Abigail. Until tomorrow…" He hung up.

Damn, thought Abigail. But her stomach overruled other thoughts. She was just reaching for the door handle, when Bugs Bunny called out again. *Double damn!* She hovered for a second, undecided, then went back to her laptop. It was Jen; the United Kingdom was only a couple of hours behind Syrian time.

Hello Abigail,

I'm in a rush right now, I'll write more later, but thanks for the lovely long update - such delicious detail! I'm jealous up to the tip of my hairs of course, or at least the tip of my tongue!

Abigail blushed. Jen could be so blatantly indelicate sometimes.

I think you're out of luck with The Triumph. I remember some distinguished Arab sponsors wanted us to ferret The T out a few years back; yours truly was put on the task. And now you're asking me to do the very same thing. Who says coincidence doesn't exist! It turns out that only known medieval copy (as you rightly say from Allah Ansari's notes) was stolen from an archive in London during the Second World War. What with everything else going on then, the theft didn't get much attention. The strange thing is, nothing else got taken. Anyhow, the poem was never published in any collected works or academic papers, so there's nowhere I could get a reproduction of the text, let alone details like ink type, script style etc. if you need those too. There may well be copies in private research notes, but there's no way to know whose, or whether they've still survived after so long. Hope you weren't depending on this. Why is this poem so important?

In haste, Jen XXX.

Abigail didn't know why it was important, *if* it was important. Yet clearly somebody had thought so about seventy years ago, risking a burglary during wartime to grab the original text, indeed perhaps the only text. It would certainly be very interesting to know what had inspired the Nizaris to such an upbeat title as 'The Triumph', while still under the heel of the Mongols!

She felt she'd learned a lot this day, yet it boiled down to only one thing of substance: the scary fact that Black Death was haemorrhagic fever, not bubonic plague. As for the bigger picture, she seemed to be chasing shadows and myths and maybe coincidence, not what a proper academic should do.

And as for tomorrow's mystery destination, time would tell. Briefly it occurred to her that she had far less notion what was going on around her in Syria in the present compared with the past, but the urgency of the past overrode all; besides which, her stomach was rumbling.

Orient Palace Hotel, Damascus, Syria: May 2008

Was it the strangely appetising smell which awoke Abdul Khaliq in his big bedroom in the Damascus Orient Palace hotel? Rather than fumbling for a lamp switch, he turned on the torch which he'd put on the bedside table and was amazed to see a little plate bearing a griddle cake.

Which was still warm to the touch!

Thoughts cascaded: long ago, he recalled, Sultan Saladin was besieging the Nizari castle of Masyaf, until one night he woke to find by his bed a plate of fresh hotcakes such as this, and a poisoned dagger too. Abdul Khaliq cursed. He should have slept safely with a member of the loyal Ismaili community! Of course he hadn't checked into the Omayad Hotel itself, which the suspect may well have chosen because he felt secure there, but even in this hotel there must be prying eyes. What a fool he'd been!

Scared by the warning from *those people*, Saladin had called off his siege. And now, centuries later, here was Abdul Khaliq's warning in the same fashion. Incredible! A fresh griddle cake, placed near his sleeping head in utmost stealth... *how long since?* A minute, or a moment? Had the click of the door closing behind a departing intruder woken him? A solitary griddle cake; though where was the warning dagger, as if out of legend?

The curtain wafted inward from the balcony. Part detached itself like a burly ghost. As Abdul Khaliq swung the torch, a long blade glinted. "No!" he cried, clutching for his mobile as though that might bring help or provide a flimsy defence.

"*False* slave of the Creator," whispered a voice. Then the whirlwind came, bringing terrible agony to Abdul Khaliq's belly.

The Omayad Hotel, Damascus, Syria: May 2008

The next morning brought more email from Paul. He'd obtained a second-hand copy of the *Return of the Black Death* book and stayed up late to read the first five chapters. Reading his mail, while yet again enjoying breakfast in bed, Abigail felt a little guilty about using so much of his time. For once there were no quips in his text.

This is turning out the scariest thing I ever read! It's horrible how BD puts its tentacles through families and friends, then rips the heart out of a town. The sheer scale of fatalities is hard to get my head around; if this monster returned in modern times, with our megacities and people jetting around the globe, the outcome would be unimaginable! I'm sensitive you know, this is going to give me nightmares!

The book hasn't got onto causes yet, but chapter 4 explains all about the 40 day quarantine, plus confirms your info about plague sweeping ratless Iceland. 70% of the population was wasted in the first plague there, numbers didn't recover for nearly 500 years!

Poor Paul, reading up on these horrors just to help her. She sent her thanks and some encouragement, for she certainly needed the help. In fact she could do with more help. The mystery of the fragment had mushroomed into other mysteries, and no doubt angry ICEman Jack would be right on her case the moment she got back to Boston.

When she got back to Boston... Would Kamal stay with her? They hadn't addressed the future, and he seemed to be an international globe-trotter. She'd abandoned stay-at-home Terry, but would she herself now receive the same treatment?

She glanced at the radio-clock. Damn! How did it get to be so late? She had to rush around and ensure everything was packed up. Easy enough for Kamal's stuff, he travelled light and was very neat. *Might that apply to her too one day?*

Qa'lat al-Alamut, Elburz Mountains, Persia: August 1164

The Summoner to Wisdom escorted Nasir and Umar and three regional leaders up a spiral stone stairway. At its base they passed a pair of impassive Nubian guards, each holding a bared scimitar across a wide and naked chest. The contrast of shining damascened steel against black skin seemed to enhance the lethal sharpness of their weapons. Up above were two more Nubians, basalt statues which by magic might suddenly move and in one motion slash the head from an intruder. Only a slow pulse in protruding veins, feeding massive muscles, revealed they were alive.

The invited yet now somewhat nervous visitors passed along a short corridor to Hasan's audience chamber, high up in his tower. Oil lamps revealed crowded gold scripts chasing across thick black cloth, which hung over every stone of the walls.

Within, gorgeous rugs strewn one above another hid the floor. Four men were already seated. Three were evidently chief da'is, or at least fully initiated superior da'is. The fourth was robed differently, and sported a trim beard. Perhaps this one was a da'i too, yet, as he stacked up some books the four must have been viewing, he had at once the quick, definite movements of a practical man, a man of action, and the frowning mien of a scholar. The Master of Alamut himself stood by a window. Bright sunlight haloed his white turban and his snow-white cloak of heavy brocade. Golden sandals adorned his surprisingly delicate feet.

The chamber contained various chests, one of which was partly held open by bejewelled silver cups, plates and other precious ornaments. Yet to Nasir's eyes the true treasure was Hasan himself, Master not only of Alamut, but of the route to paradise.

After florid courtesies were exchanged, during which the fourth man was revealed to be a notable physician, a servant brought aromatic coffee in a golden pot, then poured the warm dark fluid into exquisite glass cups.

"Coffee," said Hasan as the men sipped, "came originally from the region of Ethiopia called Kaffa." His voice was quiet, as though he merely mused reflectively to himself. "Five hundred years ago Arab traders brought its seeds and bushes from Ethiopia into Yemen, via the port of al-Mukha, sometimes called al-Mokka. Coffee flourished in Yemen, as likewise it now flourishes in Arabia too. Coffee is a precious secret of the Arabs. That same trade route brings mainly slaves these days. Not to mention ivory and such."

Why was Hasan telling them this, instead of confiding more about the revelation of the Hidden Imam? Yet Nasir and the other guests knew Hasan's reputation. He never said anything that wasn't deeply meaningful, though sometimes he spoke in riddles. They held their tongues and awaited enlightenment.

"Ethiopia," Hasan continued, "hides another secret. One which is far, far more valuable than coffee is to the Arabs. The value of coffee is in its invigoration of body and mind. The value of this other thing... is in its absolute deadliness to the body, and its power to paralyse the mind with fear. We shall capture and control this thing, as the Arabs have done with coffee."

The tone of Hasan's voice had not changed in the slightest, yet the visiting leaders felt a cold echo of fear themselves. They put down their cups. Nasir imagined a terrible beast from the jungle, or worse still an evil *jinnee*. Hasan turned from the window, casting his face into shadow while light gleamed all around him.

"What I shall tell you now, by the grace of our sacred Imam, is only for the ears of superior and chief initiates. Should you speak of this to anyone lesser, the punishment will be a very hard death. And Hell thereafter, with burnings and lashings and scalding of the flesh, a repeated crushing of the head and the stinging of scorpions, with pus as the only drink for raging thirst, *forever*. Do any of you wish to leave this chamber right now?"

Nobody moved. Nasir thought to himself that a Nubian guard might well behead anyone who departed, as soon as that person set foot upon the stairway. And that the severed man's head, perhaps still retaining awareness, would then roll step by step down to the bottom of the stairs, where another Nubian would split it in half like a melon. And this would be justice, holy justice. Nasir would cut off his own head before failing Hasan, if such a feat were possible.

After sufficient pause, Hasan nodded.

"Ethiopia harboured coffee, and the south of that same far land also harbours the source of *plague*," he announced. "The plague which reaps men like wheat, which blackens and melts the organs of the body. The plague which you, honoured physician, have informed us resides within certain animals in Ethiopia. Animals which are rarely harmed by its presence, and from which the disease can be taken rather as we take milk from a goat, though by a different means. We will indeed take the plague, and make it our weapon. Al-Hakim, kindly explain to our guests, with all *accuracy*," he instructed the savant.

Al-Hakim rose, dominating the group, apart from Hasan who remained by the window, listening attentively. Nasir struggled to hide his utter amazement. Was this thing possible? Could any hand but the divine Hand itself manipulate plague? Such a feat seemed like capturing the wind! But Hasan was *the hand of power*, his words were the Imam's words, and he said it could be done.

"Exactly as the law is overturned," and Hakim nodded to the Master of Alamut, "so, at least in the matter of plague, is medical doctrine overthrown. Most of this doctrine derives from the Greeks of old.

"What precisely is the cause of plague? We are told that it's due to foul air from swamps. Or that earthquakes cause it. Or unfortunate alignments of the stars. Yet I tell you with certainty that plague is due to *none* of these things. Furthermore, I tell you that plague can be contained, like a powerful *jinnee* in a bottle. Ay, a *frite* or a *ghoul* confined, until our Master chooses to release it to slay the enemies of our faith by the thousands, by tens of thousands!"

Al-Hakim paused for effect, but alarm galvanised Nasir's thought. Even if the wind were miraculously captured, how when released might it blow *only* in the face of their enemies? Words burst out of him. "And to slay likewise those who release this *ghoul* from the bottle?" Others in the room nodded.

The doctor took this interruption in his stride. "From the writings of Procopius about the so-called Plague of Justinian and from other observations, it is evident that a victim of plague experiences a slight fever followed shortly by black swellings in different parts of the body, which swiftly lead to an agonising death. However, physicians have opened these swellings to examine their contents, and the physicians themselves *did not* become afflicted by plague. *Therefore*, by the time a victim shows the outward signs of plague, he does not give plague to another person. *Therefore*, a person has plague within him before he shows any outward signs, otherwise it would never spread.

"How long does a man contain plague, you might ask, before he shows the signs? Plainly, the Plague of Justinian was carried on ships from Alexandria to many ports, including Justinian's own capital of Constantinople. Some of those ships needed at least two weeks to arrive at their destinations. Yet ships require strong and healthy sailors to keep sailing. *Therefore*, those sailors contained the plague in their bodies for several weeks before any signs showed."

"But how," asked Nasir respectfully, "can you remain healthy and strong if you have the plague?"

"Do you know the story of the grain of rice, my friend? Do you know the game of chess with sixty-four squares on a board, which Arab armies found in a Persian empire weakened by plague?"

"You mean the story about the wise man and the King?"

"Just so!"

"I do not know it," said one of the other da'is.

"Well now, a certain King asked a wise man what reward he would like for his good counsel. Would he like a wonderful house, or a dozen beautiful slave girls, of a sack of silver coins? No, said the wise man, a single grain of rice placed on the first square of a chess board would suffice, then two grains of rice on the second square, four on the next, and so forth. This would amply satisfy him. The King was delighted at such modesty."

Nasir grinned. "But the total number of grains of rice will exceed all the grains of sand in all the deserts of the world!"

"Exactly! By the grace of Allah, *it came to me in a dream of a chess board*, in which I played opposite Khidr himself, that maybe *thus* is the case with plague. One grain of plague on the first day, two on the second... During many days you would notice nothing significant at all, until suddenly you were overwhelmed! And during all those days of ignorance, you in turn might give spare grains of plague to whoever you met. If a man with just one grain of plague is locked alone in a dungeon and supplied with ample food and water, by the end of perhaps about thirty days, he will die from the accumulated grains of plague; and then the plague itself will die for lack of a man to feed upon. But if a man, on his fifth day of harbouring plague, unawares gives a grain to another, the plague will not die until five days beyond a month. And in the meantime..."

"Many die when plague strikes," observed the Summoner to Wisdom. "Very many, but not absolutely everyone."

"All those whom plague *can* kill, it will, thus they disappear. Those few who do not die cannot retain the plague. Thus, in time, the plague will pass away. Our magnificent castles will be our protection. Provision the castles as for a siege! It is surely men who pass the grain of plague to other men. Birds do not carry the grain in their beaks, nor do butterflies or bees. Prevent *any* man, however so healthy in appearance, from entering our citadels for six months, and we'll be completely safe."

"But what about those of our faith who till the land?" asked Umar.

"Many such seek refuge in the castles during military sieges," replied al-Hakim. "This same defence will work against plague. But instead, when the time comes, they could simply be instructed not to allow any visitors to approach. Firstly, they should warn visitors away with shouts. If these are not heeded, they must kill *anyone* who still approaches, at a distance by using arrows, even if these people are kin."

There were more questions, all of which the mysterious al-Hakim handled with ease. When presently Hasan dismissed the senior da'is, he gestured Nasir and Umar to remain...

"My excellent Syrians," he said, though mainly eyeing Umar, "in addition to receiving full news of the blessed qiyama, our protégé Sinan needs to know that I took very seriously his recommendation to me of al-Hakim, who has honed his knowledge further in our library here; and that I shall fund an expedition to Ethiopia. Al-Hakim may need to labour long in Ethiopia. This isn't an expedition that would return within one year, nor within two, nor perhaps even five. So Sinan should know that I have indeed acted, even though no further word of this matter may be heard for several years. Sinan must know this *in absolute secrecy*."

"I swear by my life," exclaimed Nasir – and Umar almost in unison.

"In your case, good Nasir," said Hasan, "that isn't necessary. I wish Umar alone to carry the news. You, I wish to accompany the expedition to Ethiopia as a sign of the entire confidence I entrust in Sinan, so that you may eventually recount everything to him as witnessed by your own eyes."

Nasir was stunned. An absence that might last *for five years*.

"But my wife..."

Hasan frowned. "I ask you which is greater, your love of your wife and the flesh, or your love of God and the true religion?"

"There can only be one answer," said Nasir. "I submit to your will."

Hasan nodded, then added in a softer, almost conciliatory tone, "I believe you enjoyed the love of the flesh to the full in acceptance of the *qiyama*. Let that suffice you. Sinan will care for your family."

The Master of Alamut had spoken, and now turned a searching gaze upon Hakim.

"I need to hear again, also for the ears of Nasir and Umar, and therefore Sinan, your explanation of how you consider the essential leaders of our faith can be *guaranteed* safety, even should the scourge enter our fortresses, which Allah forbid."

Al-Hakim seemed eager to please, as all were with Hasan, yet even so there was caution in his tone. "As I told, Master, I am sure I can place that guarantee in your hands, but not without the several years of labour you have mentioned."

Even amid his consternation, which he prayed would abate, Nasir was astounded. A *guarantee* of safety from plague, even if it raged around oneself?

"A wise answer, not the answer of a charlatan. Proceed."

Nasir listened, now enthralled, as al-Hakim began to speak about a previous sojourn in Africa, and about monkeys, and about blood...

Finally, Hasan said to Umar, "*Nothing* may be written down. So have you understood clearly? And can you rely on your memory when relating to Sinan?"

"God willing, not every exact detail, but yes. Yes, I understand."

"So," said Hasan to al-Hakim, "I guarantee *you* all the treasure needed to support your work, to fulfil the new vision which the Imam has granted me through your agency.

"Treasure with which to buy slaves, for example – slaves who will of course cost less, being nearer to their source in Africa..."

At the Hidden Imam's bidding Hasan had overthrown the law and he was still in an exalted state of mind, yet this sacred prince among men remained a master of practicalities.

A *mystery trip, Syria: May 2008*

The driver arrived promptly outside the hotel in a redoubtable-looking Toyota Land Cruiser. He clunked the rear door heavily behind Abi then threaded skilfully out of the city's clutches and headed north on the highway to Homs and Hama further onward.

After a couple of hours, Abigail was impatient to arrive somewhere, *anywhere*. Since her chauffeur seemed to speak neither English nor French, asking him anything was useless.

A flotilla of gunmetal grey clouds had begun to mar the perfect blue overhead. Tiered high like vast battleships, more gathered as the car travelled further north. Bright sun glanced off their flanks. The driver scanned the unusual sky and muttered.

Then he quit the main highway and other traffic for a side road, and soon turned off this too, bouncing along a track rather than a road. At around the point Abigail started to worry about being abducted, another highway appeared out of nowhere so the world seemed civilised and safer again. They began to climb, heading for the top of a dark line of hills.

She didn't see it until almost the moment the car stopped. She gasped. The driver hopped out and opened the door for her. She stepped into a fitful breeze.

"Qa'lat al-Husn," announced the driver. "Krak des Chevaliers."

The light was strange, touched with purple. Those fleets of hostile clouds had all but coalesced, their black reinforcements coming up from the east where Abigail could glimpse flickers of lightning. She imagined this scene as the Crusaders might see it, God's manifest vision shafting through ragged holes to illuminate patches of tawny and olive and brown on the plains below, and picking out pale walls on a high hill, the unassailable ramparts and towers of God's strength upon Earth, the fortress home of His Hospitallers.

The shaft of light passed on; the castle dimmed and blended with the natural profile of its mount.

As the driver ushered her back into the car from this viewpoint, Abigail realised that the detour on small roads must have been taken so that they could approach from the West, the only direction it seemed from which the view of the castle wasn't spoiled by nearby modern buildings.

Kamal was so thoughtful, *and there he was*, leaning against the entrance to the parking area, gazing at the sky. Abigail's heart leapt to see him. In a moment they were hugging tightly. He lifted her up and whirled her around.

Eight or nine coaches were parked, though few private cars other than

Kamal's. They'd soon paid off the driver and transferred their luggage.

After they bought their tickets inside the castle, Kamal smiled. "We won't need to wait to be guided. I know the place well." He parodied the over-emphatic voice of a tour-guide. "Occupied by the Crusading Order of the Knights of St. John, also known as the *Knights Hospitaller*, from 1144 AD until 1271 AD, *thees castle* is the most famous and strongest of all the Crusader castles. *Thees castle* was *nevvveer* taken by force, but only by *treekery*. The Mamluk Sultan Baibars laid siege to *thees castle* in 1271 AD, and that *cunning Sooltan*, he tricked those knights into surrendering. He... ow!"

Abigail had thumped him. "Okay okay, so you're clever!" She grinned and kissed him on the cheek. "But all these school children running around... They kinda spoil the atmosphere." Then she thought: how dare I, a foreign guest, presume to complain about local children enjoying themselves?

Fortunately Kamal didn't seem to take offence. "Behold, world: kids from the city of Homs are playing happily. Fear not. In about twenty minutes the coaches will magically remove all children and hopefully a lot of the adult tourists too. Till then, we can stroll around the walls."

They found their way onto the rampart walkway, admiring the architecture and gazing out over the surrounding land. Scattered huddles of buildings forming the modern village of al-Hosn surrounded the castle on three sides, as though they were edging towards their gigantic companion for protection from what had visibly afflicted them in the recent past. Accompanying the threatening weather front, a deep murmur of thunder brought to mind distant war. Abigail slipped her arm around Kamal's as they moved on.

"The Nizari qa'lat of Masyaf is only thirty kilometres due north of here," commented Kamal. "We'll go there tomorrow. Al-Kahf is about the same distance away too, but more to the west."

"It's easy to see why the Nizaris and the Hospitallers became allies. It was either that or face off with each other every week!"

Kamal frowned. "There's always been a collision of cultures and religions here in the Levant. Alliances were constantly shifting. The Nizari Brotherhood would see it as their sacred duty to survive by any means at their disposal, including temporary pacts with Christians, so that they could continue to serve Allah and later triumph in an ultimate future."

The strengthening wind had a chill edge, but still blew hither and thither as though confused. The touch of the air was electric and exciting. Abigail's skin prickled and sudden gusts pulled pleasantly at her hair.

"Maybe some alliances lasted a lot longer than originally intended. Look at Guy and Sinaldin, still chummy even after the Crusaders lost their last possessions in the Holy Land, when the Nizaris were just a shadow of their former selves."

Kamal shrugged. "Only assuming that Guy and Sinaldin represented their respective organisations and weren't just acting alone."

The restless air was pregnant with moisture. The unfulfilled storm was consuming more and more light.

"True… but look, Guy would have carried the traditions of the dispossessed Templars in his heart, as well as those of the Hospitallers who'd long since lost this castle. The Nizaris were trying to shore up their identity, clinging to the last shreds of their real power. They were all down and out together! Both Christian and Muslim were Gnostic and they'd worked together before. Mightn't they be trying to help each other out in adversity?"

Kamal laughed out loud and gave her a glance that said *silly girl.*

"You certainly have a vivid imagination!"

Abigail thumped him again.

"Listen, Abigail, the nearest Crusaders to Syria by then would be the Hospitallers on Rhodes. Their arm had grown far too weak ever to reach into the Holy Land again. No, I'm sure the Nizaris survived by their own efforts, as they had done many times before. They'd use the tactic of *taqiyyah.*"

"Tacky-what?"

"Dissimulation. Blending in. Nizaris have behaved like Twelver Shi'as or mainstream Sunnis, practising all the proper rites. Yet this behaviour was just a cloak to be discarded when the light of truth could freely shine again. The Nizaris are masters at pretending to be what they are not."

An extended flicker of lightning danced shadows briefly across Kamal's face.

An inspired thought came to Abigail.

"That's it!"

"That's what?"

"The fragment! That's why it never quite fits our theories," she shouted excitedly. "It's pretending to be what it isn't. I'll bet it isn't rooted in religion at all!" Already she was certain. And then an image forced its way into her head, Trinity church reflected in the Hancock tower. *The Khusraw-like quote on the ivory box, that's pretence too!* Or at least Khusraw's original meaning had been hijacked, the old mirrored in the new…

"Aah!" exclaimed Abigail, teetering into revelation.

A very large drop of water splattered against Kamal's forehead, startling him.

"I have it!" she yelled. "The *water of life* isn't esoteric knowledge at all, or not *just* esoteric knowledge. For the elite there's a double meaning. It's *actual fluid*, Holy Water, the stuff that Sinaldin gave to Guy!"

Kamal's mouth dropped open.

A cold hard smack of water found Abigail's skin just below her neck, then ran icily down her cleavage. Rain slanted in on the wind and splayed across the ancient flagstones.

"Abigail, we'd better find cover!"

"Which means that this is all about *plague*, or protection from plague, *not* about Ismaili beliefs! Religion is just the framework, maybe even a red herring."

A cascade of thunder assaulted their ears, as loud as if a mangonel had demolished the huge tier wall right next to them. An army of grey water advanced across the plain, the hiss and roar of its fury rolling over the castle. They ran for shelter, but didn't make it quite in time.

Just inside a stone archway, Abigail ruffled her hair, trying to shake off some water and stop the wet strands from clinging to her skin. Kamal was flustered and cursed under his breath. Maybe Syrians didn't like getting wet. Water dripped from the end of his nose. Rain sealed the entrance like a solid door and turned the floor outside to a seething pool. A stone lip blocked any flow into the tower where they'd fled. Abigail loved rain when it was dramatic and powerful like this. She laughed at Kamal for being so put out.

"It's only water!"

Kamal wasn't impressed. He glared at her, his dark brows knitted together.

"So what do you think the Holy Water could actually be?" he demanded.

"Possibly just an extract of Syrian Rue. I guess the point is that they really believed it could cure or prevent plague."

"Syrian Rue? From the flower?"

"I think it'd be an extract from the seeds, but yes."

"Why's that?"

"It's a kind of medieval cure-all. Very mysterious. Lots of odd effects, and the Gnostics have a long history of using the stuff."

"I see. We can probably find our way to the rest of the castle down this staircase. Hopefully we can get to most of it without venturing outside again."

Abigail giggled. "You won't shrivel up and die you know! Water isn't fatal."

At last Kamal smiled, although it came out more as a grimace. Abigail produced a tissue and dried his brow.

"Abigail, I'm not sure you're heading in the right direction with this little fragment puzzle. Your ideas might be considered… far-fetched."

"Oh, I know. Academics the world over will be horrified by my rash and dramatic interpretation. I'm bothered too. Nevertheless, I'm sure. I need you on my side. What do you think the Black Death is?"

Kamal shrugged. "It's a nasty plague, bubonic plague, everyone knows that."

"That's more or less what Paul said yesterday, but…"

"Paul?"

"Paul Summers, the reporter guy, the…"

"You're still communicating with him?"

Kamal's strained tone betrayed surprise and anger. Abigail sensed danger. Could her sophisticated new man be so prone to jealousy? Had she swapped one possessive boyfriend for another?

"Just a few emails," she said as casually as possible. "He's helping me out by doing a bit of research. The Black Death isn't bubonic plague," she added dramatically, "it's haemorrhagic fever. Paul's reading up some info on this for me right now."

"Abigail!" Kamal's dark eyes flashed, his voice was stern. "He's a reporter. He'll publish some bizarre version of your theories long before they're verified and without your approval. Your career could be ruined!"

Kamal turned and stalked off down the stone stairs, leaving Abigail flabbergasted. He seemed far too angry. Was he really thinking of her career? Or anticipating a stain on his own, by association? Or was it indeed simple jealousy? Paul was a much younger man, after all. *Damn!* Whatever the reason, she'd have to mollify Kamal now.

They toured the rest of the castle in a tense stand-off badly veiled by polite exchanges on history and architecture. As Kamal had predicted, the crowds had departed and what seemed only a single coach load of other tourists wandered around the vast structure, much dispersed. Lebanese? How should she know? From mundane storage systems, ovens, water channels and hidden passageways in the depths, they rose up to the King's Daughter Tower, the Command Tower, and a Romanesque chapel long ago converted to a mosque. The storm had abated somewhat, but rain still descended from a dim sky that seemed barely higher than the towers. Abigail had a feeling that the weather was re-gathering its force for another assault. Echoes of distant thunder chased around time-worn walls that once had rung to the cries of Crusaders, repulsing a siege or returning from their expeditions of conquest.

Abigail was impressed by vaulted ceilings and Gothic window seats and intricate friezes and much else, surprised by the decorative elegance in both

Arabic and Christian styles. But her favourite was the beautiful loggia fronting a colonnaded hall, to which they returned after covering all the main sights. The rain thrummed beside them, definitely picking up strength again.

"Look here," said Kamal. He led her to a window lintel on which was an inscription in Latin. "Grace, wisdom and beauty you may enjoy, but beware pride which alone can tarnish all the rest."

"Don't tell me you can read Latin too," exclaimed Abigail.

"Well, only a little. I happen to know already what it says."

He tentatively touched her arm. "Hey, I'm sorry for being so angry. That was very improper of me, and it doesn't really matter now anyway."

Abigail felt the tension snap, letting forth a flood of warm relief that seemed to map all her veins, and surprisingly was accompanied by raw passion. She grasped his midriff and pulled him closer.

"Oh, Kamal, I'm so glad you aren't still angry with me! You're right, nothing matters now but us. Do you think you were a little bit jealous?"

"Jealous? Well, maybe. You're a very beautiful woman."

They hugged tightly, and then seeing that no one was visible through the veils of rain, they kissed. Abigail felt Kamal's passion rise, and the knowledge of his state fired her own feelings still more. She clung tightly to him and nuzzled into his neck, relieved their spat was forgotten and hungry for healing contact.

Kamal responded, burying his face in her hair and deeply inhaling her scent. Then he pulled away. His eyes flashed, and for just a split second Abigail was afraid his anger was aroused once more, yet then she saw it was animal desire that consumed him. Without a word he grabbed her hand and pulled her out into the rain. They ran for a nearby doorway, then descended into the dark stone guts of the castle.

Abigail wondered where they were going, what he was doing, but, when they got to a taped-off area where renovations were in progress, realisation began to dawn. They'd passed this place earlier. Evidently, no work was going on today.

"Oh Kamal, no. Really, no!"

But he dragged her past the 'NO ENTRY' sign and under the tape, then along a short corridor and through an archway into a large cellar. It was dank. Dim light filtered in from a single slit, high above. Part of one wall was slick; rainwater must somehow be seeping through. Crowbars and pick-axes and other tools were neatly stored in a corner. A large patch of cobbles was missing from the floor; new or refurbished ones were piled nearby, ready to place. Kamal pushed her against hard stone and reached under her skirt, groping roughly between her legs. It was a little painful and she gasped, but

213

to her surprise her body responded strongly to his touch.

They kissed, Kamal thrusting his tongue into her. He seemed more than just eager. His intensity was of a different sort that she couldn't really fathom, but it seemed to harbour both sorrow and roughness, perhaps even an edge of savagery. She didn't resist, in fact she aided.

Kamal reached behind and under her buttocks and with main strength heaved her right off the ground. She took the cue and got her legs up around his waist, then yanked her knickers aside and helped him into her, before wrapping her legs tighter and linking her arms around his neck. His first proper thrust was a stab of fire, but by the fourth his member was pushing huge pulses of pleasure into her. Kamal growled and bit at her shoulder, then thrust faster and harder, becoming frenetic. He rammed against her opened flesh, grinding her spine into knobbly stone and making her yelp in distress, yet still her pleasure soared above her pain.

A massive peal of thunder up above shook the very foundations of the castle. Abigail felt nature's force in her belly even as she felt Kamal's. In this public place, it added still more to the strange sense that her legs were open to the world.

He came explosively, shuddering and crying out as though in agony. Abigail quickly forced the fingers of her right hand down between their bodies and finished herself off just a few seconds later. Ecstasy hijacked her in an extended succession of spasms. She bawled long and loud, independent of any will or control. Her contractions extracted the last of Kamal's essence and elicited a deep groan from him.

It was another two minutes before the hurt in her back resurfaced and they had to awkwardly disentangle. They smiled foolishly at each other in the thin light, finding no words to admit or describe such a total release. Kamal led her back, almost visibly returning to the sophisticated gentleman that he usually was. A swarthy elderly couple passed by as they ducked under the tape. Unknowable words in scandalised tones then drifted down the corridor from them.

"They probably heard us!" Abigail tried to sound reproving, but ended up giggling instead. They both laughed, not caring that they'd be heard yet again.

Qa'lat al-Alamut, Elburz Mountains, Persia: September 1164

Hakim was taking coffee with Hasan in his high, guarded tower. On a low table rested a rather stained book from the library, held open by a silver measuring stick laid across it. Its calligraphy was unornamented, functional. Beside the book, a map was unrolled, weighed down by two daggers.

That book was an almanac of shipping schedules, produced at the port of Siraf some years earlier. And there was Siraf on the map, half way down the Gulf of Persia. Much higher up the gulf was the port of Rishahr, which Hakim now touched with the point of a dagger.

"Many days closer to Alamut overland," observed Hasan.

"And thus avoiding the high taxes at Siraf, which may be accompanied by potential curiosity about our mission. For the same reason we should avoid putting in at the island of Qais, and make straight for Zayla on the African coast."

The Master of Alamut raised an eyebrow. "Have you tried to anticipate everything? Only God can do so."

"I don't wish to disappoint God," replied Hakim quickly, "by making an *unnecessary* mistake. When I finally start work in Africa, I know I shall make some mistakes. Those will be necessary mistakes, which cause me to learn and in the end, God willing, to succeed."

Hasan placed his hand for a few moments over Hakim's on the pommel of the dagger, an almost electrifying contact. The brief touch was akin to a blessing. "I entirely approve of your thoroughness... to which I add further insurance. You shall have the pick of the Fida'een for your earthly protection, including Rahim and Hamdullah, and Taj al-Din to lead them."

Hakim bowed his head, overcome.

"Your concept of *necessary mistakes* is a vital one, Hakim. Mistakes that assist the evolution of true wisdom. In a sense, the majority of adherents to our faith are in error, *necessarily so*. They are mistaken in their beliefs, for these are only crude approximations. Yet only thus can they advance to higher truths, just as I believe you will advance in Africa. Perhaps God permits the multitudinous mistakes of mankind, because otherwise no one might ascend to perfection."

When Hakim moved the dagger back from the map, he noticed that its point had left a tiny pit-mark. His eyes were still as keen now as during his youth, thanks be to Allah. He would need keen eyes in Africa, in search of the minuscule that could nevertheless kill multitudes.

By now Hasan was looking into an abstract distance. Which was greater: the distance to Africa and to the bottling of plague, or to the ineffable?

The Mehmet Hotel, Hama, Syria: May 2008

Abigail awoke to find an amplified call to prayer prompting continuous pain in her head. Strange. After much exposure in Cairo and Tehran, Qazvin and Rasht and Damascus, her brain normally tuned out the ritual wailing. True, their small hotel in Homs was quite close to a minaret, with its clusters of flared Tannoy speakers seemingly as much a feature of Islamic religious architecture as gargoyles on old Christian churches, but even so...

She turned her head to check the time, which immediately caused it to throb unbearably. Ah... the culprit was not so much the call to prayer then, as the sweet call of last night's wine, which had seduced her in the bar downstairs after Kamal had eagerly seduced her yet again in this very room. They'd both drunk heavily, celebrating survival after their first spat, perhaps, or maybe plunging into an orgy of avoidance in case they argued again.

It was 11.33am. She couldn't figure out why the noon call to prayer never seemed to actually be at noon. Kamal was gone, his handsome head replaced by a note on the pillow. Her befuddled brain took some time to absorb the few words. He had business matters to arrange. He'd be back to take her out before 3pm. *Love and kisses.* She clutched the note to her bosom, for once not disappointed; she'd have time to recover! What with the storm of nature and storming sex the day before, she'd likely never get to see the giant water wheels on the Orontes river, the reason for over-nighting at Hama rather than Homs.

Desperate for pills and tea and the loo, she tried to sit up, then groaned as more pain assaulted her. Not just from her head this time, but from her back too, no doubt the result of yesterday's exertions against the cellar wall at Krak. She probably had bruises right down her spine.

Later, invigorated by a shower and bolstered by medicine and fluids, Abigail searched desperately for chocolate and was rewarded with a squashed half bar in the bottom of her bag. She wolfed it down. The sugar rush seemed to restore some normality and she decided to check her email. There was no Wi-Fi in the modest hotel, but fortunately a wire snaked up through a hole in the floor. She hooked up. Among the chit-chat and spam mail, there were two from Paul. She tried to push aside feelings of guilt spawned from yesterday's argument with Kamal, and quickly scanned the first one.

Okay, I'm utterly convinced about the haemorrhagic fever theory. How could the world miss this... then there's a scary chapter on what would happen if it came back, complete collapse, corpses everywhere, you see... another chapter covers diseases as terrorist weapons, and developed diseases too… I've gained a horrible fascination for this stuff. I can't sleep anyhow, so I'm going to see what else I can find on the net…

She realised the second email had come in only recently. Paul must indeed be working on this all night! Perhaps typically for a reporter, he was searching for any betrayal or scandal or malicious intent in the story of the Black Death, especially if these may have cost many more lives.

…plenty of betrayal and abandonment, and cruelties such as many of the sick being buried alive. And apparently there were daily burnings of people in Europe, those people thought to have been spreading the disease deliberately, most often by contaminating well water. They were often Jews or other minorities, and it seems likely that enormous fear was amplifying existing jealousies or racial hate. Yet I wondered if underneath this there was any truth about deliberate intent. I came across a confession by one Abraham Rumbold from Erfurt, it's stored in a museum in Munich, but the PDF is on their documents website. It seems he was under instruction to pour the blood of an infected person into the wells at a place called Nordhausen. Pretty nasty huh?

I'll report again soon. Why aren't you up yet anyhow? Maybe you're just busy. How was Krak castle?

Pope Paul XXX

She started up instant messaging and put the kettle on for more tea. By the time she looked back at the screen, Paul had already noticed her status and started a conversation.

Hi, I thought you must have gone out for the day. How was Krak?

Just up late, hangover. Krak was great, really interesting. There was a big storm that made it more dramatic too. Kamal's doing some business for a few hours, but we're going to Masyaf this afternoon. Do you think there's really anything in that stuff about the Jews? Would putting blood in the wells actually do anything?

It might in fact. I've been digging up more info. The blood of a person infected with haemorrhagic fever is a massively toxic substance. But since I sent that email, I've read more at the museum's site too. It's highly likely that Abraham Rumbold's confession, and all others like it, were obtained under torture. The authorities needed scapegoats. But listen, Abi, I think I was only searching for this kind of thing because a weird idea was starting to form in my warped reporter's subconscious. An idea that's now crystallised. I can practically SMELL deliberate purpose. But it's not coming from the Jews, it's from the Nizaris. What if Sinaldin intentionally BROUGHT the disease to Europe??

Paul, you're completely crazy! We've no evidence for that whatsoever. I'll admit that some cloaked connection between the Nizaris and plague is emerging. But I'm still worried that we might be leaving reality behind, and now here you are making a jump into hyperspace! Kamal warned me that you might ruin my career by publicising bizarre theories. I put it down to a little jealousy, but don't let him be right!!

Abi, I'm deeply hurt and professionally offended. Well, deeply hurt anyway. And only slightly smug that he's jealous. You know I wouldn't publish anything you hadn't approved. Will you just humour me for a while and let me explain?

Abigail hissed in exasperation. The tea was forgotten. She couldn't type fast enough to express her thoughts.

Sinaldin was carrying his Holy Water, which he believed was a CURE for plague. In practice it was probably Syrian Rue and didn't work anyway. Perhaps it was blessed by an Ismaili da'i. How could he carry the disease too, unless as a victim? Yet there's no evidence he was ill in that way, only badly wounded by the Seljuk, from which he recovered. We have to stick to the evidence, or at least implied evidence, such as from the poetry. Even that is pretty tenuous!

It's the evidence that's shouting this at me! Perhaps reporters see these things in a different way. We're jaded, suspicious; lens of reality and all that.. Okay, maybe lens of lunacy, but it's served me well! I re-checked the text about Guy and Sinaldin at that French land registry weblink you sent me. Here, look: 'the Arab begged Guy to journey onward, being strangely afraid that the eastern plague would descend upon such a busy area of trade and shipping. In this his fear was soon proved true...' How soon? About the incubation time of 32 days maybe?? We have no way to know whether their ship stopped at Sicily first, but Sicily and Provence were the places where the European outbreak started. A galley from the Crimea was blamed for causing the first outbreak – notoriously so, it seems – but that boat must have been innocent. As for Sinaldin and his Holy Water, why would you constantly carry an antidote around, unless you KNEW you would need it, because you were spreading the disease too! And what about the ivory box? 'They have forty days'. WHO has forty days? The random victims of plague? Why write that on the box? You wouldn't know for sure who those victims would be. That carving implies intent, or I'm a Dutchman. Whoever wrote it, KNEW who it referred to, knew for sure who the victims would be!

Abigail's fingers hovered eagerly over the keyboard, but then withdrew. The rushing protests in her head had been derailed by Paul's persuasive speculation. She felt chilly, her stomach hollow. Probably the lingering effects of last night's alcohol. But she realised that part of her resistance to

Paul was really a fight with herself. She didn't really want to believe where all this had been leading recently. And she was caught in the middle, as Kamal clung to conventional interpretations while Paul seemed to be launching into fiction. She tried to regain some academic posture and forced herself to think logically.

Goed mijn kleine Nederlander, clever conjecture. But the antidote isn't really antidote. It's just hocus-pocus potion with a holy blessing on top. So you wouldn't mess with plague if you weren't genuinely protected, surely?

Well, you said yourself that in gratitude for his life Sinaldin would only have given a genuinely precious gift to Guy. You also said that maybe this was really about belief. Believing it worked. For someone on a mission, belief may only have to last a short while, followed by a nasty shock.

Oh Paul, really. Not terrorist missions in the fourteenth century!

Why not? The Assassins already mounted many suicide missions. But anyhow, what if Sinaldin's Holy Water wasn't Syrian Rue? That's only a theory after all.

Whatever it is, it's very unlikely to be effective against haemorrhagic fever! By all accounts, that seems like the worst disease on the planet. Oh, and I realised that the term 'water of life' was being used to refer to this stuff, to the Holy Water. It's dissimulation, a double meaning. That term in Nizari poetry usually just means 'esoteric knowledge' or 'holy knowledge'.

Very interesting. Well done! Maybe this name will reveal something more of its nature. But anyhow, I'm not done persuading you yet. I'm tenacious, like my dog. He forgets he's a Retriever sometimes. I forget I might be wrong sometimes. Woof woof! Listen to me! Apparently, parts of the Islamic world used a technique to inoculate against smallpox for centuries before Jenner's work in the West. It's not a true vaccine and more dangerous to use; basically a mild form of smallpox is induced by binding material from an infected pustule to the skin for a few days. Sounds highly horrible huh? But after the subject was ill for a little while and then recovered, he was immune. About one in 1000 times, the full-blown form would develop instead and be fatal. Not bad odds for those times. Haemorrhagic fever is viral, like smallpox. So what if your 'water of life' has some mild form of plague in it, a survivable form? The smallpox technique came from India they say, via Persia.

Via Persia where the Nizaris live, where Alamut is located, he may as well have said! Abigail struggled to touch base with facts, to resist Paul's enthusiasm for conspiracy.

Pure speculation! And without a sample of Holy Water, we'll never find out! Plus it's the case that plague was already raging in the east when Guy and Sinaldin made their landing at Marseille. ANY ship could have brought it in. From Constantinople say, or even the Crimea where that galley supposedly came from. Just 30 days or so EARLIER than the galley is all. So stop barking and fetch me a stick I can really chew on!

Well here's a stick for you. Where did the medieval plague start?

Hmmm, I can't actually remember.

Sarai, that's where. The capital of the Golden Horde Mongols. In the mid-fourteenth century, the most important Mongol city in the West. Apparently the place was devastated. For sworn enemies of the Mongols, one might regard that as quite a TRIUMPH.

The letters of the last word seemed to jump out at Abigail. He meant the poem of course. A poem about revenge. A chill ran down her spine. And then the voice of Bugs Bunny startled her. It was Jen, with an email titled: *The Triumph.*

"Oh my goodness, oh my goodness." Abigail's heart bumped. She felt reality blurring around her. Nausea nearly overwhelmed her. She managed to steady her breathing, then opened the email.

Hi Abigail,
I've been asking around, and discovered a tiny bit more. It's from just a few lines of scribble made by a don here before the war, a researcher into the continuity of Persian society under the Mongols and the Timurids. I'll send a scan, but it seems that Allah Ansari never said who wrote The Triumph, though he implied it was someone of holy rank, maybe one of the lost Imams from the Ismaili dark times during the fourteenth century. And the Don left an odd, disconnected question in the margin, which says: "could it mean 'unholy knowledge'?"
I'm going on a blind date next week, so I'll send you the full story after the event. Any more delicious news about your Kamal?
Love Jen XX.

Paul was impatient.

Hey Abigail, you still there?

Sorry, minor distraction. Look I have to go for a loo break and then get organised. I'll send again soon.

Okay. I'm going to get a bit of sleep and go in late. Take care Abi. Paul XXX.

Abigail sighed. Sometimes, she had to let her brain absorb new information in background mode. Especially obscure connections. She seemed to come to better conclusions without conscious intervention. Meanwhile, she couldn't resist a few paragraphs to Jen about a certain cellar in Krak. And since they were changing hotels, she put her camera out, ready for the ritual of the final picture; yet another cosy love-nest captured forever.

Esfahan, Persia, December 1164

Almost a month after leaving Alamut, Hakim's expedition arrived in Esfahan. The same distance awaited them before they would come to Rishahr on the coast, that great trading centre and port of seagoing dhows.

Esfahan was the capital of the harsh Saljuqs, Turkish invaders who a century before came from the east. They imposed Shari'ah law with the sword, in the past slaughtering so many pious Ismailis. Yet just seven years ago their sultan himself had no option but to crave assistance *from* Ismailis, to stand against their common enemies, the Ghuzz. The princes and warlords of the Saljuq Empire had weakened themselves by squabbling over their dynasty and territory, while the vengeful daggers of Alamut had wounded them still further, despatching high officials and commanders. So now, under Ghuzz threat, a tacit truce reigned between Ismailis and their nominal overlords south and east of the Caspian. Yet even to ease his journey, this was not a truce that Hakim intended to trust one jot. His party travelled in dissimulation, as Sunni merchants.

After a long trek through jagged sandstone mountains, they appreciated the verdant oasis of Esfahan. Even this late in the year, some roses still bloomed in its gardens. Textile workers were fixing the colours of tablecloths by washing them in the gushing turquoise river, which seemed to have burst forth from Paradise. Grey crows cawed among elegant plane trees. Within the bazaar, what treasure stores there were of enamelled and gilded glassware!

The substantial group settled for their sojourn in a welcoming caravanserai. Much-trodden carpets covered the raised brick floors of the rooms, and curtains masked off the hallway. In the courtyard where they stabled their horses and pack horses, always with a guard, a fountain pleasantly splashed. The roast camel meat and freshly baked bread were excellent.

However, the real joy for Hakim and a few others of the party was to visit others of the true faith whom they already knew were living in Esfahan. The Master of Alamut had wisely withdrawn the local headquarters of Ismaili religious activity back from Esfahan to the *eagle's nest*, but volunteers and others who couldn't easily uproot themselves had remained clandestinely in the Saljuq capital, masquerading as Sunnis or Sufis.

On the second evening of their stay, a guide from the secret community came to the caravanserai to lead Hakim to a meeting, along with Nasir and Taj al-Din, as well as Rahim and Hamdullah, who were two of Hasan's most prized Fida'een, both highly trained in killing should the need ever arise.

The guide's name was Jalal. The moon was three-quarters full, and a ghost of light sought to complete the rotundity of its shining silver plate which seemed to bear some dark figs upon it. When they came to a southern gateway, beyond which houses had sprawled, Jalal stopped and said, "We call this gate *Bab-i-batin*."

The Gate of the Hidden. Exactly! Beyond which, in a certain house, one might presume that the hidden community would meet. But that was also the name for one of the ranks of the Ismaili hierarchy. First learner, then teacher, then da'i, and then *gate of the hidden*, followed by *tongue of knowledge*, then *greatest proof*, and topmost: *hand of power*.

"And I," said Hakim to Jalal, "am the *tongue of knowledge*." For this was the rank to which Hasan, the *hand of power*, had advanced Hakim.

Immediately Jalal made an obeisance, then he gestured Hakim and his companions not through the gateway, but in a different direction down a narrow street. For this had been the final test before their guide would lead these strangers to their true destination.

Two veiled womenfolk played the harp and the lute as Hakim's group and a score of darkly bearded men enjoyed rich barley soup sprinkled with basil leaves, along with soft bread, figs, walnuts and honeyed delicacies, and they sipped sweet wine of Shiraz. Their leader, Iranshah; his deputy, Khurshah. Conversation flowed, itself like wine or honey to the soul. Between sips of wine, cool water was so much more refreshing than the salt-tainted water of Qom.

Above the lamp-lit courtyard hung constellations, mosaic fragments of God's light which also quickened the still-rising moon that caused roof-tiles to shine. At this moment the astronomers of Alamut too might be watching as-Sad al-Ahbiya, the Lucky Star of Hidden Things, twinkling in the night.

Iranshah said to Hakim, "I am also a *tongue of knowledge*. Two tongues can converse like lover and beloved, and one might steal the other's heart away."

Of course Iranshah was speaking spiritually. His curiosity as to Hakim's rapid advancement by the *hand of power* himself, as well as regarding the mission funded lavishly by the Master, was evident.

Hakim smiled and raised his cup. "I could easily become intoxicated by your tongue, as surely as by your wine. May you benefit by the fruit of the tree of life! The wine cup I hold in my hand in your home, this corner of Paradise upon Earth, is to me right now the magical goblet of Jamshid…"

"Aye, the *jam-i-jam*." Iranshah nodded.

"…wherein that king of old Persia perceived the knowledge of all things. Would you take this cup from me, Iranshah?"

The local leader gazed into Hakim's eyes almost wooingly, yet understanding all the subtleties. For if Iranshah received from Hakim knowledge of the doctor's mission, this might diminish Hakim's ability to fulfil that mission.

"Instead of that," said Iranshah, "I shall fill your cup twice over." And he clapped his for the young man who was wine-bearer. "Truly," he added, "you are the *tongue of knowledge.*"

Hakim relaxed. "If not my cup, I have at least lost my heart to you, blessed Iranshah."

At a nod from Iranshah, Khurshah began to recite rapturously, to the tune of the lute, blessings upon the names of the Imams. Others of the local community rose and whirled around and around, chanting remembrance of Allah, becoming after a while visibly intoxicated to the point of ecstasy, finally reducing *Allahu* to its last syllable, *hu*, which itself was a shorter version of *Huwa*, He, the purest form of the Divine Name.

Hu hu hu hu hu hu hu, was the chant, like the breath of life itself.

Hakim imagined the God-given puffing breath of a wind filling the sails of a dhow, propelling it towards Africa and his destiny.

Hakim and his five companions were spiritually effervescent after the evening's communion as well as heightened by the fine wine of Shiraz, as Jalal conducted them through deserted alleys in the direction of the caravanserai. The moon, now high over the city, partially illuminated their route, light and darkness stretching ahead side by side. They kept to the lane of darkness while guiding their way by the lane of light.

Of a sudden figures began emerging from a side alley, fifty paces ahead. Immediately Jalal jerked his arm to halt the party, and one of them, maybe Taj al-Din, blundered into another, maybe Nasir, and a dagger fell, pinging against a stone.

"*Who's there? Show yourselves!*" came a cry. The caller moved into the moonlight, as if this might help his sight penetrate the deep shadow. The peaked tarboosh on his head, with its upturned fur-trimmed brim and glinting triangular panel, marked him right away as a Saljuq soldier. As did the wide sash belt upon his baggy trousers, through which a scabbarded sword was tucked. There seemed to be seven or eight others with him, similarly uniformed, now releasing their swords. Or were there more?

A patrol!

"*In the Sultan's name, show yourselves!*"

The five from Alamut, and the guide Jalal, confronting maybe ten Turks.

"We can take them," whispered Hamdullah, sliding forward along the wall.

"Oh yes," agreed his fellow Fida'i, Rahim.

Apparently aware of the disparity in numbers, the patrol advanced; and so the matter was decided without any instruction from Hakim, who now must draw his sword. Moments later bright moonlit steel arced and dark blades, almost invisible, parried. Briefly, darkness and light seemed to war. Briefly, the men of Alamut were advantaged to fight from shadow, occulted, and then combat was everywhere across the alley, turbans against tarbooshes. A Saljuq lost a hand, lopped off, and only screamed after his weapon, still gripped as it seemed by loyal fingers, hit the ground. His arm flailed in vain, spurting blood. A thrust in the belly dropped him and he squirmed, groaning terribly. Steel clashed and sparked as parry followed parry.

Then from out of darkness back into the light leapt Rahim. Pirouetting with his sword, deploying incredible strength, he struck the officer of the Saljuqs in the waist; through cloth, through flesh, through bone itself, it seemed. Razor-sharp, propelled by the sheer force of Rahim's spin, the sword emerged, slowed almost to a standstill now, from the officer's other side. For several moments the officer balanced, goggle-eyed. Then his upper body toppled to the rightward, while his legs and what connected them together buckled to the leftward.

Hakim had never seen such a feat before.

Nor had the Saljuq soldiers. One of them howled, "Demon!" Another took up the cry. Disengaging, now deprived of their officer, they began to retreat and then to run.

Rahim was still holding out his sword, now in empty air, his eyes half-closed, the lids fluttering as if in a seizure or in some trance. He exhaled rhythmically, *hoo hoo hoo*.

Hamdullah saluted his fellow Fida'i, touching his fingertips in turn to his brow then his chin then his chest.

And he confided, "Our brother practised upon old goats and sheep hung from trees."

"He practised to perfection," acknowledged Hakim, before demanding, "Are any of us hurt?"

"A flesh wound," said Nasir. He was clutching his arm.

"Let me see."

Blood darkened a sliced sleeve, spreading slowly. Hakim ripped the fabric apart and contrived a tourniquet, then a wad which he bound to the wound itself.

"Now it will clot faster." He spared several intent seconds to stare at the two parts of the officer, their pools of blood converging as if to reunite, somehow, the bisected body. Then the group set off in haste for the caravanserai.

The qa'lat of Masyaf, Syria: May 2008

"Respectful locals," Kamal said, "visit this shrine before entering Masyaf castle itself."

Abigail had already observed that Kamal was a bit of a cultural snob, but then she didn't really want to be seen as just a tourist herself. She felt perspiration trickle down various parts of her and hoped it didn't look too obvious. The climb up to the summit of the ridge in blazing heat seemed to have sent her sweat glands into overdrive. The last days of May already; what would June and July be like here?

They were standing beside the modest tomb of Rashid al-Din Sinan, who from here, or sometimes from al-Kahf nearby, had ruled all the Syrian Ismailis for about thirty years in the latter half of the thirteenth century. Sinan's leadership had been inspired; he was easily the most famous of the Syrian masters. Abigail noted that the shrine was newly whitewashed and well tended.

"A great man," murmured Kamal.

Flies buzzed. Abigail's eyes smarted as sweat ran into them. She wondered if this long deceased master had ever held the *water of life* in his hands, if he'd known what it really was, if he'd met the mysterious al-Hakim. Her lack of knowledge had become so frustrating that she felt like yelling questions at the silent grave and demanding that the long-deceased master's old bones rouse up to answer her.

"I read that he was an excellent physician, good with medicines."

"Sinan was excellent at most anything he tried. A truly remarkable person. He was even said to be prescient." Kamal smiled at her, and they turned to thread their way back down the rocky ridge and over towards the pale-honey walls of the qa'lat, which rose romantically above a less romantic modern town.

Even as they approached, Kamal was enthusiastically launching into a discourse about the water catchment and storage arrangements, the piping and reservoirs and underground galleries. Abigail strongly suspected he'd once been an engineer. She nodded and smiled, but was a little melancholy inside. This would be their last castle. Soon she'd have to think about going home, and so broach Kamal about his own plans and what would happen between them. She hoped and hoped he'd stay with her.

She wanted very much to discuss Paul's latest theory too; the grotesque possibility that Sinaldin had deliberately spread plague. Yet she was afraid Kamal's scepticism and low opinion of Paul would rouse him to anger again.

They passed a simple café laid out along the rock base supporting the castle. Some tables were set in the shelter of shadowy little caves. Abigail noted it for a possible pit-stop later, pleasantly out of the fierce sun.

Even at the dark castle entrance with its worn and battered steps, Abigail could tell the masonry was mixed, probably originating from many different ages. The quality and strength of the architecture didn't look to be at all as good as at Krak des Chevaliers.

"The qa'lat has suffered greatly over the years," murmured Kamal, as though he was apologising.

Inside, when the dilapidated state became more apparent, Abigail wondered whether there'd be much to see. But in fact she enjoyed the sense of adventure and exploration as they probed dark spaces and what may once have been secret passages underground, with wind-up electric torches Kamal had brought along. The voices of some other visitors rolled eerily along unseen walls. She was briefly reminded of Terry showing her around some old vaults in Boston. How fortunate that she'd escaped his needy moods to hook up with wonderful Kamal!

In addition to having no lighting installations, there was little else to assist the curious. Scrambling over rubble and climbing very uneven stairs, which did not benefit from hand-rails even where these bordered significant drops, certainly added excitement. Kamal firmly clasped her hand most of the time, so she felt safe.

"Just think!" she exclaimed. "Maybe Guy's grandfather travelled here in his youth, to forge a pact with Sinaldin's grandfather, before the Mongols came." Abigail loved the breath of history. She reached out and touched stone that Sinaldin's grandfather might have touched.

"It's possible, the dates could stretch to it. But only if they were young at the time, and not if Sinaldin is the younger lover of Safiyya that you imagine. He'd most likely be her age at least, maybe older."

"Oh! Men always discount the exciting unlikely. But it *could* be so."

Despite the rather basic visitor experience, it was clear that the castle had been much worse until quite recently. A great deal of restoration work was going on, and a couple of the more interesting areas were already well advanced. Shovels and picks propped in a corner reminded her of the cellar at Krak, and she flushed. She asked Kamal questions to divert her mind, and her body.

"Most of the townspeople here are still Ismaili," he replied. "But alone they couldn't possibly afford to restore their castle. It's paid for by the Aga Khan's foundation."

"When you think of it," mused Abigail, "how bizarre that the ruthless Assassins of Alamut and their Syrian side-kicks should give rise to the peaceful modern Ismailis, headed by the benevolent Aga Khan! A very productive, non-political people, devoted to an Imam who does so much good in the world, yet with a descent from none other than the homicidal Hasan as-Sabah and apocalyptic Hasan the Second."

Kamal eyed her oddly.

"How much you know… *wrongly*. Much like today's Ismailis themselves, who have no idea who they are, or who they were." Strangely, softly, so that she scarcely heard, he added more. "Or who they might be."

"What do you mean, the Ismailis don't know who they are? Or who they were?"

"They're just sheep, who'd follow any shepherd obediently. They obey their Aga Khan absolutely, and absolutely believe what he says, especially in his *farmans*, which are official declarations, even if these contradict earlier *farmans*. Yet he's their God, who may change his mind as convenience serves. But it's all extremely complicated."

"Oh, I see! You mean don't bother my pretty little head? Come on, Kamal, darling, you have to tell me!"

Kamal seemed reluctant, but then shrugged, as if whatever he told her was irrelevant.

"Most of the Ismailis in India are descended from lower caste Hindus called Khojas, who centuries ago converted to Islam. Although there was some Shi'a' tradition, the great majority of these Khojas had originally and quite evidently become *Sunnis*.

"Much later, in the time of the British Empire, the original Aga Khan, literally the 'Big Chief', arrived in India from Persia with a large force of cavalry. He assisted the British Empire militarily against some Baluchi rebels, after which he manipulated the Khoja community for the best part of two decades, until in 1866 there's a court case in Bombay protesting at his interference. The British judge, who was on friendly terms with the AK…"

"You make him sound like a Kalashnikov."

"…*and* who followed the British policy of 'divide and conquer', not only banned all reporters and cleared the court when the AK testified, but ended up by declaring him the princely head of the Khoja community and sole custodian of its assets. The British didn't want to go as far as awarding the AK any actual territory, such as the Province of Sind which he wanted, but a community would serve the purpose."

"A judge can't behave like that!"

"Ha! In the days of *Pax Britannica*, he could. And, newly empowered by the British judge, this Big Chief proceeded to bully and hypnotise all the Muslim Khojas into his personal religion, a religion based loosely on

Ismailism, but really just a vehicle to enforce his own absolute power and status."

"But I've read myself," protested Abigail, "that the Nizaris founded communities where modern India and Pakistan now are, in the centuries following the Mongol invasion of their homeland in Persia. It's in that funny little book by Ruffie too."

Kamal drove his fist into his hand. He seemed quite angry. "That's all nonsense! Deliberately created myths, which even most academics haven't seen through. There are some grains of truth beneath, yes, there were probably a very few Ismailis in India before the Aga Khan came. But, for instance, the ancestors of the first Aga Khan weren't even Nizaris, they were Ithna'ashris, Twelvers, the official sect of modern Iran. Yet the AK's independent ambition was much better served by his invented brand of Ismailism, and his descendants have continued to impose this."

They sauntered out from cool shadow into a mantle of heat that Abigail felt burning her head and shoulders. She'd forgotten her sunglasses and had to squint across a dazzling courtyard of ancient sandy stone. Kamal donned his own glasses, then checked his watch. She wrapped her arm around her lover's, feeling his tension.

"Well, it's quite shocking. I don't suppose all the Aga Khan's charitable trusts know his family's dubious history, but why are you angry about it?"

Kamal shrugged. "I dislike the injustice of it all. *Real* Ismailis, like those here in Syria, have had to submit to the AK's rule. Indeed they've forgotten anything else. The Aga Khani Imams clearly *don't* descend from Alamut at all. But their genealogies have been falsified, or suppressed. Notwithstanding this, contradictions stare you in the face. 'Hidden Imams' had to be invented, scattered throughout a span of almost *three centuries*, where real historical traces are very rare or inconveniently contradict the official story.

"What's more, the Aga Khans tossed the Holy Quran overboard in favour of indoctrinatory chants called Ginans, many of dubious origin or simply concocted, setting the Aga Khans up as Allah-on-Earth, whose word is law. Why should Ismailis pay attention to an old book, when they have their own living 'Speaking Quran'? The latest Aga Khan tried to mask all this somewhat, by saying that Ismailis should now do the Hajj to Mecca, whereas before they were only required to visit *himself*, bringing tribute of course."

"Kamal, you're sounding a teeny bit biased, if I might say so."

"Oh, it's verifiable. I'm an academic at heart, like you. I've seen the research. But the ins and outs are very intricate. And Ismailis are supposed to *serve with an unsuspecting mind*, so they never notice that their supposedly eternal faith has kept changing significantly, nor that it's at variance with the

Quran, which they don't bother to read. They don't trouble their own pretty little heads."

"Most Christians don't read the whole of the Bible."

"The Aga Khans are simply impostors! Or rather, *cleverly* impostors. What you said, Abigail, about their descent being bizarre, is in fact much more bizarre than you thought. Embarrassing though it might be to claim the murderous chief of the Assassins as your conduit to holy legitimacy, the Aga Khans are in a position where they *have* to do exactly that, even though it's entirely false."

Abigail mused upon this irony as they climbed up to the topmost walls. They gazed out at the modern town over a very low parapet that made her nervous. A dull sea of heat-shimmying grey boxes washed up to dark greenery and bare rock on the hills opposite. Kamal fiddled with his mobile phone and glanced at his watch again.

Abigail shielded her eyes. "You'd think someone would expose all this. Are there any legitimate descendants of the Hasans?"

Kamal smiled evasively. "Well, if so, they haven't appeared in court in Bombay or anywhere else to claim justice." He took her hand and pulled her right up to the edge, so that they could peer over, directly downwards. Three or four other visitors in scruffy suits were hesitantly doing just the same, eight or ten metres away. Hanging back was a knot of similar tourists, including women in full concealment.

The long drop of the walls was extended by craggy foundations, the raw bones of the earth, and a steep slope beneath, altogether a cruel approach for attackers. But a strong breeze easily made the ascent, rushing upwards past Abigail and Kamal and the men in thin suits, who laughed and held their arms further out into the pleasantly cooling fountain of air.

Kamal turned and shouted something in Arabic to the knot of tourists, some of the males answering back. He let go of Abigail's hand and took a step or two away towards the venturesome suits. Surprisingly, she didn't feel afraid. The atmospheric elevator made her feel like she could step right off the edge and yet be perfectly well buoyed up.

Then she noticed a tiny figure standing on the main road near the town. A figure in black, with its arms up, surely with binoculars trained on the castle, on her. Probably just a sightseer, but suddenly she felt cooler than the breeze ought to make her.

And then her mobile rang.

It was Paul. Words spilled from him in an excited cascade that she was completely unable to decipher. She had to interject twice and slow him down. When at last she began to grasp what he was babbling about, a tingling wave of elation swept through her. At last! At last they had something solid, not just rumour and speculation and shaky theories built on fragments of poetry.

"Kamal!" Abigail shrieked. "Paul's located Guy's grave, Guy de Dieulefit." Kamal turned from his perhaps ribald conversation with the suits. "And there's Holy Water in his tomb. *Actual* Holy Water, the *water of life*, buried with him!"

Kamal's face blossomed into utter astonishment, his eyes... then her phone bleated thinly and diverted her attention. "Abi. Abigail. Listen I... maybe... Abigail!" The signal seemed to be bad, she could hardly hear Paul. She turned her back to the edge and stepped away from the low parapet, getting away from the breeze whiffling in her ears. And so she saw her killer.

Dressed from head to toe in flapping black robes, he was only a few metres away and charging straight at her. Her mind went into overdrive; it seemed she could think at light-speed, yet her body was utterly frozen with fear. The man's arms were raised; he reminded her irresistibly of a great black crow, swooping to kill her, for she had absolutely no doubt his momentum would shunt her over the edge, perhaps both of them. She physically felt the fatal drop at her back like the point of an assassin's blade, just starting to break the skin between her shoulder blades. A sickening feeling of helplessness washed through her. She saw intense determination in dark eyes, around which were wrapped wrinkles of contempt. Lips pulled back in a snarl revealed yellowy teeth. She seemed unable even to use her voice. There was something asymmetrical about his face she that couldn't quite grasp. She would go silent to her death.

Then, just before the impact, Kamal appeared from outside her field of vision and grabbed the assailant's arm. He heaved with all his might, swerving the killer off course and twisting the limb so that its owner pitched uncontrollably forward. A whirl of black swept past her like a wraith, not close enough to touch her, but close enough that she felt the wind of its passing and even caught a faint scent of sweat. A piercing shriek, suddenly curtailed, sent a massive shock into her nerves; for a split second she thought it was herself, until she remembered that her own voice was disabled. She was still alive! Fear released its grip a little, and she sank to her knees.

And then Kamal was kneeling beside her, his strong arms wrapped around her.

"It's all right my love, it's all right. You're safe now." He kissed her hair and squeezed her. People gathered around, some seemingly from nowhere, until a small crowd surrounded Abigail. They seemed shocked themselves, and babbled, offering sympathy. She saw some nervously scan the area, no

231

doubt wondering if any other madmen were loose in the castle. Her mind was foggy. Could there be more?

"I must check on the attacker," stated Kamal slowly and clearly. "I'll be back shortly." She supposed someone had to do so. There was a faint chance he could be alive. She imagined a broken black crow spread-eagled on the rocks, red gore all about it. She knew she wouldn't be able to look. In Arabic and English Kamal instructed the crowd to take care of her, and disappeared. She was suddenly aware of her mobile ringing, how long had it been doing that? Only when she tried to answer, did she realise that she was shivering uncontrollably. With difficulty, she pushed the button. Two women got her into a more comfortable position and started to rub her back and limbs. That helped. She was close to a faint. She couldn't tell what Paul was saying. Concerned smiles all around aimed encouragement at her. She concentrated on trying to speak into the device.

"SSsome…someone ttried to…to kkill me!"

"WHAT! Are you all right? WHO tried to? What happened? Who are all those people I can hear?"

Paul's questions just confused her. "Am… ssafe. Ring… later."

The mobile dropped from her hand. Her vision shrank to a curiously small circle, into which worried people peered, as though gazing through a tunnel to her soul. Yet then the tunnel lengthened, making the people recede. She felt consciousness slipping from her grasp.

Fortunately, Abigail's faint didn't last long, but when she came around some medics and a small mob of policemen were present. Kamal was by her side again too. Despite still being weak and woolly-headed, she declined an ambulance ride and a check-up at the hospital.

"It's just shock," she declared, annoyed at her own weakness. "I'm fine!" Yet she couldn't stand up without Kamal's help and leaned heavily on him for a few minutes, until her legs stopped wobbling.

"Is he dead?" she whispered into Kamal's ear.

Kamal nodded. "Very."

Esfahan, Persia, November 1164

Hakim decided the expedition would have to stay in Esfahan another day. To attempt to leave in the morning would immediately make the authorities suspect them. There would be double guards on gates, vigilance in their eyes and vengeance in their hearts. Yet he doubted they'd escape some sort of check as a formal alert spread through the city.

Indeed, towards noon, a dozen heavily armed tarbooshes entered the caravanserai and blocked the doors as Hakim hastened to present himself to their officer, a haughty sneering man, although with fat lips suggestive of depravity which he could probably not afford.

"Who are you all?" demanded the officer. "Where have you come from, and where are you going to?"

Hakim contrived to be at once unctuous and steadfast.

"Sir, I lack any notion why you should enquire, although of course that is right and proper."

"I've no need to explain myself to you! Who are you and your companions?"

Hakim explained that they were from Rayy, great and prosperous under Saljuq administration, and lied that they were heading for wondrous Shiraz, veritable rival to Baghdad. He himself was a doctor, summoned to treat a prolonged malaise of a prince's daughter, whose names he should not mention.

"Already you contradict yourself and insult my intelligence," sneered the officer. "I'm perfectly aware that Shiraz is full of subtle specialists in all the arts and sciences. Why ever summon a stranger who must travel for weeks to arrive in Shiraz?"

"Because," Hakim said in a low voice, "this is a delicate matter concerning the female anatomy. As you may know, a physician may only examine a woman, especially one of noble blood, at a prudent distance, through the intermediary of a female assistant, so that the physician's own gaze does not fall upon the intimate parts of the woman in question. I happen to possess particular expertise..."

"Do you indeed!"

"...which it appears is lacking among even the sagest medical savants of Shiraz. Do not imagine that the prince has not consulted specialists in his own city! Now, as a last recourse, being kindly advised by one of those savants of my modest accomplishments, the prince has commanded that I should make all possible haste to Shiraz, carrying medicines and equipment as delicate as a woman's tender anatomy deserves."

233

"Ha!" exclaimed the officer. "I know a thing or two about female anatomy. Maybe I should ride to Shiraz and claim your undoubtedly large fee."

Hakim rejoiced, and implored the officer to step aside with him, while calling for coffee and sweetmeats. No ransacking had taken place yet.

"As it happens, Sir, the prince has already provided travel expenses so that nothing should impede or delay us." So saying, Hakim drew out a pouch, which he emptied into his palm, displaying five golden coins from the Alamut treasury, three of them dinars, two of them the gold of Byzantium which had replaced silver dirhams as a common currency.

Hakim closed his palm into a fist. "If in your bountiful goodness you could see your way to expediting our swift departure from Esfahan, where we have no purpose beyond obtaining food and fodder."

"You want an escort to the Shiraz Gate, and passage through it?" The officer eyed Hakim. "I shall need to scatter some lesser coins among my men, and oil some other palms for a smooth departure."

"I believe, Sir," said Hakim, "I can spare a little more of the Prince's provision."

While the officer enjoyed coffee and sweetmeats with Hakim, the rest of the party must pack swiftly and prepare the horses. All in all, this venal officer's visit to the caravanserai, undoubtedly one among several such visits on his schedule for that day, seemed to have become advantageous.

South of Esfahan, Persia, November 1164

Land was becoming less green as it rose upward, four days out of Esfahan. Ahead lay the rugged ridges of the Zagros Mountains, peaks capped with snow, stretching away to the south-east for a distance as great as the width of the Caspian Sea; to be crossed by the lowest, most convenient route, although still between the grindstones of towering heights.

And now Hakim's party was being followed, at speed. Dust rose from the road behind, which could only be a sign of galloping horses; *how many?*

Constrained by the lack of speed of the pack-horses, the best policy seemed to be to wait, armed and prepared. If the oncomers were bandits, they might be deterred by the sight of calmness rather than flight.

Yet bandits, bent on robbery, seemed less likely than Saljuq cavalry.

As it proved. Presently a dozen horsemen reined in, a couple of hundred paces away, bright in embroidered brocade coats decorated in arabesque flourishes, black felt caps on their heads, double-bent bows worn aslant across their chests, arrows stuck into boots complementing quivers of many more arrows and a javelin each, little round green shields decorated with red crescents and rosettes. Their captain shielded his eyes, assessing Hakim's group.

"They can't have galloped all the way from Esfahan," observed Taj al-Din, "otherwise their horses would be dead, or in no fit state. Unless they only galloped fast at the end to impress us. To intimidate us."

Hakim tried to calculate how long ago these cavalry must have set off. Swiftly he imagined events. The greedy officer of the tarbooshes confiding to a superior his 'suspicions' the day after he was bribed? Or the day after that? Considering there was nothing to link Hakim's group to the killing by a 'demon' in that alley, it might genuinely have taken two days for his suspicions to clarify, and only after his little troop and others presumably turned up no alternate suspects. In the interim, too, the officer may already have spent more than one gold coin on becoming intimate with the anatomy of an expensive girl of pleasure. A supposition that no prince with an ailing daughter actually existed in Shiraz would likely lead to the thought that Hakim's group could be relieved of more gold. Maybe the officer's superior concurred, or was simply motivated to solve the mystery of why those men on that night of the three-quarter moon had resisted questioning so vigorously.

Satisfied with his scrutiny, the captain waved forward and the cavalry approached at a fine trot as if boastful of the stamina of their mounts. The horsemen spread out in a loose half-circle.

The swords of Hakim's party, even wielded by Fida'een, couldn't match javelins and hundreds of arrows.

"You are Hakim, who calls himself a physician from Rayy?"

Pointless to deny this. Hakim handed his sword to Rahim, his dagger too, and approached the Saljuq captain. Unlike the venal officer, the captain looked... yes, fresh, uncontaminated by vices. A pure heart.

Hakim assessed the situation. Fighting would be futile, and fatal. He sensed that bribery would no longer suffice. Either his group would be escorted back to Esfahan for interrogation, which would waste days, or else he needed to give the captain some valid information which would send him and the cavalry hot-foot back to the city. What would Hasan do in this circumstance? What would Sinan have advised?

Hakim stroked his beard.

"The only reason I can understand why you might be interested in us is a strange experience which I myself had the night before soldiers visited our caravanserai."

Protect the hidden community! No, that was not the voice of Hasan, nor of Sinan, heard magically! It was the ordinary reaction of an ordinary man.

Hakim continued, "I was returning quietly along an alley, one side in moonlight, the other in darkness when I saw an astonishing sight. Two men wearing turbans were bending over a corpse which was in two parts. The corpse seemed to be dressed similarly to the soldiers who came to the caravanserai. A dead body in itself is not uncommon in a city..."

"In Esfahan it is!"

Unless, thought Hakim, the dead bodies are those of butchered Ismailis.

Mildly he said, "I know little of Esfahan, but I have been in various cities, some less orderly. Anyway, this corpse had been divided at the waist, as if those two men had done this the better to carry away the body, even though they would soil themselves much more than if they had lifted the corpse by the ankles and wrists."

"Carry on."

Protect the community of the faith!

"I stood silent and still in the shadow, listening. The men were talking hectically about vengeance upon, pardon me, the Saljuq administration. I did not mention this to the officer in the caravanserai, firstly because he never stated the reasons for his questions, if indeed there is any connection between his visit and the sight I saw; and secondly because any supposed connection, however tenuous, between ourselves and supposed awareness of some plot against the administration could result in delay for us who are on an important medical mission." The latter, at least, was true enough;

simply, it did not involve any Prince's daughter.

Protect! Yet Hakim was faced by an *extraordinary* decision.

"One of the men called the other by name. The name was, let me see…"

Protect!

"Iranshah, yes, that was the name."

To whom Hakim had lost his heart…

And even this much information might not be quite enough. A scalpel-like clarity filled Hakim with light, with the *Nur* of God.

"For some reason, Iranshah and the other man decided against moving the body they had cut apart."

"Did you *see* them cut it apart?"

"No, but how else could that have happened?"

"Proceed."

"Those two dangerous men began to move in my direction, so that I was compelled to step quickly into another alleyway to the side, and to run along that alley almost on tiptoes to escape observation, and to conceal myself again. However, both men turned down that same alley. I seemed most unlucky in my subsequent choices of direction, although perhaps lucky for you, for finally as I was hiding myself yet again the two men entered a house."

"In which street?"

"I'm unfamiliar with Esfahan, but I did notice a knocker on the door shaped like an eagle's head."

The very door of that blessed man, to whom Hakim had surrendered his heart.

The captain called to his men, "There are assassins from Alamut in the city!" while the Fida'een in Hakim's party looked incurious, even bored. At a wave from the captain, the cavalry regrouped, wheeled, and departed.

Later, after they had camped, Hakim wept, even though when he returned triumphant to Alamut he must surely be exonerated, utterly. To bring cleansing plague to the world would protect ten thousand of the faithful for each person sacrificed in Esfahan. That is what Hasan would have decided.

Hakim's thoughts dwelled on the two veiled women who had played lute and harp, imagining them being raped repeatedly in some filthy dungeon while their imprisoned, tormented men-folk listened to their screams. The women would go immediately to Paradise, just like warriors. He imagined hot irons placed on tender parts of men and women alike, to discover the exact number of their community and the whereabouts of houses. Could one go to Paradise if insane from pain? God would restore.

Because of the truce it was not outside the bounds of possibility, God willing, that the Ismailis would be released and merely impoverished by fines and confiscations. Hakim might never even know the consequences of his betrayal, unless God willed.

After a while, Taj al-Din entered the tent, bearing a small oil lamp. He knelt by Hakim.

"Be comforted. I understand your reasons. Myself, I might not have had the courage. The courage for oneself to die is praiseworthy. The courage to cause the innocent to die for the sake of the faith is beyond the ordinary. You are the Tongue, and you spoke inspiredly, and the Saljuqs went away."

Passing through the Zagros mountains was a chilly endeavour, especially when camping overnight. The vigorous physical exercises which the Fida'een always undertook at first light and in the evenings were now something which Hakim instructed the rest of the party to imitate, although neither he nor the others could hope to match the hundred press-ups, the gymnastic leaps and crouches and spins and cartwheels. Compliant with Shari'ah law, they all now bowed in devotion a full five times a day in the direction of Mecca, Hakim the Tongue leading the prayers. The harsh austere grandeur of nature in this region seemed to complement their increased physical and spiritual exertions. Of course, comparative cold was better than the raging heat they would have encountered during summer months.

Coming towards them late one afternoon, as the hour for pitching camp approached, they met a caravan of laden mules and riders, venting a smell of Zanzibari cloves. After effusive greetings and mutual enquiries, it suited the two parties to make camp together. To proceed only a short distance further in the fast-failing light could have seemed suspect, as if one group might plan to sneak back and under cover of darkness attack and rob. Together, they could keep a better eye on one another.

Prayers were shared, the Ismailis successfully passing themselves off as Sunni.

The other party had come from Rishahr on the coast. Over food, by the flickering firelight from what scrub was available, Hakim and Taj al-Din were able to learn from the rotund merchant, who led the others, useful details of what lay ahead, especially at the port.

"Ha," said the merchant, Khalil, slapping his belly, "I must admit I feel the chill in these desolate mountains less than most people. Many of your group have no spare fat on them at all. Although a lot of muscle."

And, to reciprocate, what should Hakim or Taj al-Din *admit*?

"They like to keep fit," allowed Taj al-Din. The Fida'een had performed no exercise on that particular occasion; such an exhibition might have seemed menacing.

"Very fit," agreed Khalil. "Visibly, the best of bodyguards." How little he knew! Or did he suspect? "I'd be glad to acquire such bodyguards myself. As I already mentioned, and as your noses can probably witness, my trade is in precious spices. I wonder where I might be able to find a few more such fine fellows."

"We hired them in Rayy," said Taj al-Din.

"South from the Elburz Mountains," observed Khalil.

"They hire themselves out at Rayy," said Hakim, "because of the silk route to east and west."

"And now they are going southwards for a change."

Taj al-Din shrugged. "North, south, east, west."

"Oh, do your bodyguards go northward too?"

Northward, into the region of Alamut...

"I might need," added Khalil innocently, "to travel towards the Caspian Sea."

"The mind of man is forever inquisitive," remarked Hakim idly. "New sights to be seen."

"On the contrary, if you'll pardon me," said Khalil, "I find the bulk of mankind to be uninquisitive, more like grazing beasts. It's a pleasure to encounter intellects, which indeed I judge you both must be."

"You are *too* kind," said Hakim. Maybe the merchant was trying to assess any possible danger to his caravan. Or maybe a battle of wits amused the fat man even if this involved dicing with danger. Weeks of conveying spices must be boring; so therefore: spice up the journey a little.

Hakim diverted. "Maybe you would care for a game of chess, supposing that you have a set with you? I'm an indifferent player but I believe Taj al-Din possesses some skills."

Khalil's eyes widened with pleasure. "I would indeed."

So they went to the merchant's tent, and by lamplight the two men waged a battle that was mostly silent apart from occasional quiet compliments, while for his part Hakim recalled the seeds of plague, one on the first square, two on the second, four on the third.

The central police station, Hama, Syria: May 2008

The police closed down the castle and ferried Kamal and Abigail and all the witnesses to headquarters in Hama, where each was separately interviewed. The tourists were soon allowed to leave, but Kamal was subjected to full process; he had after all killed someone. Privately, an officer who'd obtained some hot chocolate for Abigail admitted that they were doing everything by the book because the higher-ups were hyper-sensitive about a potential effect on the tourist industry. As several witnesses had not only declared that they saw the madman charge at Abigail, but then added it was almost a miracle that Kamal had been able to save her, he was pretty certain to be freed. They'd praised Kamal's bravery too. The attacker had been brandishing a knife and was clearly berserk.

The rest of the day and most of the evening had passed before freedom was finally granted them. The police temporarily confiscated their ID documents and mobile phones. Abigail spent a lot of time in bare rooms, with little to do but think, yet her brain was too addled for thinking. It was strange how the brain worked, she mused. She didn't recall a knife at all. But she did remember the man's eyes, and she doubted very much that he'd been berserk. She didn't offer this opinion, though; any complication might delay Kamal's release, plus it was rather subjective after all. The police had obligingly transferred their Toyota Land Cruiser from the castle car park at Masyaf to the Mehmet hotel.

At times, they were allowed to sit together. They held hands, but said little. Through knowing looks and hints while travelling in the police car, they'd agreed not to mention their investigation into old poetry and Nizari culture. That would take a week to explain, Abigail told herself, and they needed to talk alone first, to figure out in their own minds whether this incident could possibly be connected. It seemed very unlikely.

"I'm so glad you're alive," said Kamal earnestly, as he kissed her on the cheek.

"I'm so glad you saved me!" She shifted closer to her saviour and took his arm.

At one point, they could hear a commotion at the station's main door.

"Reporters, demanding information and pictures," commented a grizzled plain clothes officer, who'd just entered the room to show them a photograph. His English was very good. "We're trying to keep a lid on the nature of this thing, so we'd appreciate you not saying too much about the attacker's garb."

"Yes of course, but why? I don't understand," said Abigail politely.

"Most of the people who live in the town of Masyaf are Ismaili. Maybe you've learned from the tour guides about the, errm... melodramatic nature of Ismaili history. Now this guy was dressed like some kind of medieval assassin and carrying a *genuine* medieval knife. We've had an expert verify that."

"Ah, the Assassins," supplied Kamal. "Yes, we know about them."

"Good. Well I'm not Ismaili myself, but I know that having an apparent Assassin pop up in modern times, and fall to his death from a Nizari castle, would cause a great deal of controversy indeed! Even if the man is in fact an, er... a nutcase. Apparently, the medieval guys used to specialise in jumping off castle walls, to prove their loyalty. To have this happen again, *seven hundred years later*, would be an unfortunate reminder of embarrassing history, for most Ismailis at any rate. For a very few it might be a glorious reminder, and that'd be even worse."

"Our lips are sealed," Kamal assured him.

Abigail was nearly sick when she saw the photograph. The attacker's face was damaged, but it still brought back a vivid recall. One feature she hadn't remembered, though, was a scar above the right eyebrow; it almost looked as if he had two eyebrows, one above the other. There was a haunting familiarity about the face, but then she supposed there would be; it was probably etched into her memory forever. They both declared officially that they'd never seen the man before.

Much later, the police attempted to smuggle them out of the station's back door, but a few eager reporters were lurking there too. Kamal managed to keep his head covered, but Abigail was not so quick to react as the flashlights went off. Fortunately, though, they were not followed back to the Mehmet. The grizzled officer accompanied them, handing back their personal effects.

"The main witnesses dispersed before the press smelled the story, but unscrupulous reporters will probably bribe staff at the castle," the officer commented. "We got a cover over the body as soon as possible, but someone there may have seen that damned black robe."

"Did any ticket staff recognise the photograph?" asked Abigail.

"Oddly, no. You'd think that scar would make the face very memorable. But many faces pass by them. Apart from the scar, he had nothing to identify him either. We'll trace him, eventually."

Once more, Abigail thought she'd never be able to erase the memory of that face. She shivered. They pulled up at the hotel.

"I don't expect you'll sleep well, but rest assured we'll be doing everything possible to get to the bottom of this. We Syrians are extremely professional when it comes to police work... given normal circumstances."

"Thank you, thank you for all your assistance at this most unfortunate time for us," answered Kamal. "You have indeed been absolutely professional, yet very kind too."

"Remember, you can't leave Syria for forty-eight hours, just in case. I'd prefer you remain in Hama too."

"That's no problem. Some rest and contemplation may be good for us. Really, we're both still in a state of shock."

The car drove off. At last they were alone.

Rishahr, Arabia, December 1164

At last, at long last, the salty smell of the sea at the port of Rishahr! The air was warm indeed. Oranges hung ripe on their trees. On the outskirts they promised a lad a half-dirham to guide them to the best caravanserai. As they followed winding lanes, a forest of extremely tall chimneys upon houses was an enigma until the lad explained that of course those were the wind-towers, what else, built to catch any available breeze. Another curiosity on some houses was double door-knockers shaped like hands: one larger manly hand and one delicate tapered female hand, thus to signal by different echoes the nature of a visitor.

Presently they came to a caravanserai near the southern end of the harbour. At anchor rode a number of huge dhows, while others were tied up, rocking on water that slapped their sides. Seeing the motion, it occurred to Hakim that some of his party, himself included, might suffer from seasickness. Had any of the group ever crossed a sea? Not he, for a fact. Only rivers. He hoped the vertiginous somersaults and other acrobatics performed by the Fida'een while exercising might protect them from malady. How vital that the expert killers should be able to perform their duties at all times, should the need arise.

Confronted by the open sea off shore, Hakim realised that here was an environment where he and his companions would have no control, compared with on land. Yet what control, Hakim comforted himself, did he have after plague ravished Arwe's village and he wandered through forests, delirious and lost? God had sent an angel then!

Nevertheless, it was important to be able to fully trust the captain of whichever vessel would convey them, and Hakim with Taj al-Din invested many days in locating just such a man. After initial contact, Hakim invited their new acquaintance the merchant al-Hamad and his Captain Kharki to the caravanserai for humble hospitality and more discussion.

Hakim had thought long and hard about the negotiations. He consulted Taj al-Din, then he spoke to the Fida'een.

Their guests arrived at the caravanserai escorted by two tall and muscular men armed with scimitars and daggers.

"Simply on account of..." and the merchant displayed the large ruby ring he had chosen to wear, a twin of which gem adorned his turban. "My mutes safeguard me in the streets, purely on the off-chance, as seems only sensible."

The plump-faced Al-Hamad owned an opulent mansion and at least three seagoing dhows, maybe more. Apparently the elegant wood for the mansion had been imported from Africa at a cost of 30,000 dinars, as the merchant had idly let slip. He was long established; he was substantial. As for Kharki, a puckered scar disfigured the left cheek and sunken orbit of his face, from which the eye was missing, lending him a villainous appearance that was belied by his bluff and friendly personality.

Hakim had given the proprietor of the caravanserai free rein in the matter of menu, and presently, as introductions to Hakim's companions came to a close, a feast of seafood began to arrive.

"Your proposed exploration of Africa," remarked al-Hamad, "is quite an ambitious undertaking. This may bring great profit to your patient sponsor... eventually."

"Investment," said Hakim, "doesn't always bring rapid profit. There is also the matter of knowledge. I see myself more as a man of knowledge..."

And so they talked and ate, while the Fida'een ate only sparingly. The two mutes remained standing throughout, one behind each of the two guests.

"So," said al-Hamad, "you wish to sail to a port close to the Gate of Tears?"

"Near to the Bab al-Mandab, yes. So as to travel most conveniently into south-western Abyssinia."

"We must consider *which* port carefully," urged Kharki. "Taking into account the season and regular trade cycles and current market values. For if we return fully laden with high value goods, our profits rise and your fee consequently falls. Otherwise, you'd be..."

"...subsidising our return," put in al-Hamad.

"Ah," said Hakim, "which of course..."

"Neither of us desires." Al-Hamad gave a thin smile.

Kharki expounded on the basics of trade cycles and the best possibilities. Hakim's head spun somewhat as the captain reeled off the names of ports and trade goods. Muza on the Arabian side, where much was manufactured for Africa, such as spears and small swords, axes, glassware, together with trans-shipped cotton and silk; and Okalis, further east, the narrowest crossing. On the African side, Massawa and Adulis to the north of the Gate of Tears, and, to the south, Zayla, sending spices and ivory and some myrrh, although of highest quality; and then Berbera, for ivory, rhino horn, tortoise-shell, panther skins, gemstones, camphor, bamboo, aloes, ambergris, and of course Christian Abyssinian slaves for the depot at Zabid in Yemen...

"Don't forget," added al-Hamad, "that the first great export from Abyssinia was none other than the Prophet's – blessings and peace – muezzin, Bilal."

Hakim nodded piously. In one respect, the torrent of information comforted him. The ship owner and the captain knew the whole region like the backs of their hands. In another respect, the two were weighing and calculating ports of call of best profit, and did these conform with the best port for Hakim's expedition to disembark at? However, captain Kharki then proceeded to reject Berbera on those very grounds, and plumped for Zayla as destination, short of the Gate of Tears by a good day's sailing, with 'excellent' access to the interior.

"As Allah wills," intoned Hakim with some relief.

Afterwards, with much food left uneaten, Hakim said to al-Hamad, "All I can offer by way of entertainment is some acrobatics. Several of my men are performers. Would you care to see them perform?" When al-Hamad inclined his head, Hakim clapped his hands. As the Fida'een withdrew from the table, the mutes became alert, however al-Hamad waved a calming, bejewelled hand.

And then the Fida'een performed their finest, their limbs and swords cutting arabesques through the air... for five minutes, ten. And stopped, in unison, poised on the balls of their feet.

The merchant snapped his mouth shut and slapped an appreciative hand against his thigh. A wry grin of admiration tilted the one-eyed captain's face still further.

"You aren't pirates, that's for sure, planning to capture my ship and throw the crew overboard with their throats cut, or else you wouldn't have shown off your skills! Nor," he added, "would we dream of throwing you overboard either. So don't worry. Men of honour. Long established business. We understand each other perfectly, eh?" Kharki made a comic mockery of leering. "Eye to eye, eh?"

Al-Hamad smiled radiantly. "Now, as to the cost of passage..."

The Mehmet Hotel, Hama, Syria: May 2008

The hotel managed to find some food for Kamal and Abigail, and after consuming this in their room they propped themselves up on the bed together, arm in arm and still in their clothes. Abigail had all the lights on; she didn't want to be surrounded by shadows.

"You were so heroic," whispered Abigail. "I can still hardly believe I'm alive."

"You're valuable to me. I won't let anyone hurt you."

"Do you think there's any connection? To the fragment I mean, to the old Nizaris?"

"It seems so very improbable. He probably *was* just a violent madman. But it's a very peculiar coincidence too, and not the first one, so I'm vowing to be much less sceptical about your theories from this moment on." He smiled thinly. "When someone threatens my woman, I become the man of action! So in fact I want to help you much more."

Abigail liked the sound of that, *my woman*. "Ah. Well, Paul has a new theory. I wasn't sure about telling you..."

Kamal grimaced. "Don't worry. I won't be jealous of his youth, nor angry, whatever his ideas are. We need to figure this out, before anything else strange happens. If he can help, so much the better. I won't promise to believe everything, but I will promise to leave no stone unturned!"

So, with great relief, Abigail told him of her last email exchange with Paul, and his speculation about Sinaldin deliberately bringing plague to Provence.

"An interesting and provocative theory." Kamal forcefully exhaled, as though in frustration, but then he announced decisively, "We must follow this up. We must follow everything up! We should ring Paul now and discuss it, plus get all the details of Guy de Dieulefit and his Holy Water. Let's do it right now!"

A ripple of happiness eased Abigail's unsettled mood and pushed away her weariness. Perhaps there would be peace at last between the two men in her life! It was well after midnight, so in U.S. time Paul had maybe just arrived home, or was still at work if he'd been kept late. She turned on her mobile to discover three messages from him anyway, checking on her welfare and what had happened. But she called his mobile number from the hotel landline, as this had a loudspeaker option with plenty of volume.

Paul was surprised to be talking to both of them, but desperate to know if Abigail was safe and what on Earth had been going on. Their story astounded him.

"Don't worry, Paul, I will keep her safe."

"I'm very glad you have!" Indeed Paul's voice was full of gratitude. "But hasn't it occurred to you both that this incident might not be just coincidence?"

"It has," replied Abigail, glancing over at Kamal, who confirmed with a nod. "We think it's so unlikely as to be bizarre. But neither can we rule it out."

"Do you think we should alert someone, Jack maybe? As I think I emailed you earlier, our ICEman is already all over the idea that maybe your Walid's hit-and-run wasn't a coincidence."

Kamal interjected, "I think we should try and figure this out ourselves before we invite that crazy ICEman to stomp all over medieval history; but *swiftly*. What about *your* story, what about the Holy Water? What are the details?"

"Oh, yeah. My buddy found Guy de Dieulefit's tomb in a village called Montlume, not too far from Dieulefit in fact. It's in good condition, in a sheltered chapel and surrounded by stone, so temperature-stable and protected from erosion. That means Guy's remains inside might also be in good condition, and so might something else with him, because, *get this*, I think there's Holy Water tucked up with him!"

"You think?" queried Kamal.

"I'm pretty certain. There's an inscription on the tomb. It's in Provencal, but the guide pamphlet for the village has a translation in several languages. It says: *since in me the holy water of life, plague has become quite insignificant.*"

Abigail gasped. "It's almost the same phrase as on the ivory box!"

"Ivory box?" Kamal's eyebrows rose.

"Oh, sorry. I saw it in the artefacts room at the University, while you were chatting with the professors."

"I see."

"Anyway," Paul continued impatiently, "there's a tradition in the village that some kind of Holy Water is indeed stashed in Guy's tomb, and that this cures sickness. A trickle of pilgrims used to visit, right up to the Second World War. It's all in the pamphlet. The villagers took 'in me' to mean 'inside the tomb'. More likely it's Guy speaking and means 'inside him', that's to say he drank it or whatever for his personal protection. *But that doesn't mean he took it all.* I dug further. A description of the burial survives; apparently when they sealed Guy up, he was clutching something incredibly valuable with both hands."

"Aaahh…" mused Kamal out loud. "This is good work Paul, well done!"

"It all fits!" blurted out Abigail, pleased the two men were cooperating so well. "If this stuff really does what it says on the tin…"

"Or tomb in this case…" put in Paul.

"…plus it's of genuine Holy origin as far as Sinaldin and Guy know, then it would be far and away his most valuable possession."

"Yeah, like being buried with the family jewels, only more so."

"We should meet you in Provence as soon as we can, and all of us can view this tomb," suggested Kamal.

"Yes!" urged Abigail, "what a fantastic idea!" Another travel adventure would put off the moment of going home, ensure that for a while longer at least she'd be with Kamal *every single day*, and without them having to tackle any difficult plans for the future just yet.

"Agreed. The paper owes me some time off work, but I'll have to finish my current stories. A day or two should do it."

"We're stuck here for two days anyway," put in Abigail. "Police instructions."

"And I have another idea," added Kamal. "We should retrieve this *water of life* from the tomb, *ourselves*."

Abigail gasped.

The voice from the speaker was thin and uncertain. "Er… tomb robbing is illegal, isn't it?"

"Think about it. Going through the French archaeological authorities would take months. Neither would they keep the matter a secret. If there *is* something special about the Holy Water, we need to get to it before anyone else does. If it just turns out to be Syrian Rue, why then there's little damage done. The worthies of Montlume would just put it down to vandalism and seal the tomb up again. Plus this way, we can pass the stuff over to Harvard for analysis, pre-empting the authorities from being able to veil the whole process in secrecy, or finding false justification for attacks on modern Islam in fourteenth century potions."

Abigail was speechless.

"I told you I'd become the man of action," murmured Kamal softly. "Unlikely though it seems, if there *is* a modern connection, this is the best way I can protect you."

A strange thrill of illicit excitement coursed through Abigail. "I agree," she heard herself say. Her man was a proven hero; she'd follow his lead anywhere.

"Fuck," exclaimed Paul. "I think we've all gone mad, but I'm up for it too. The two of you aren't keeping me out of this!"

A broad smile split Kamal's features. "Then it's all set! We need some sleep, Paul. Abigail's done for. We'll call you back tomorrow about detailed arrangements. You can check up on flight times in the remainder of your day."

"Okay," said Paul, like a man still recovering from a blow to the head. "Good night to you both."

"Good night Paul," effused Abigail. "Thanks so much for all your help!"

Abigail laid back against the pillow, and long-postponed weariness flooded over her. "What shall we do stuck in Hama... apart from water wheels..."

Kamal moved his hand to Abigail's lap. "I'm sure we'll think of *something.*"

But Abigail's eyelids were already drooping. Kamal pulled a blanket over them, and they slept exactly as they were, still in their clothes.

Abigail was hungry. She dragged Kamal straight into breakfast before they'd even showered and changed. They passed by the hotel lobby, where newspapers were displayed. And there was Abigail's disturbed face, lots of them in fact, a neat row all staring back at her.

"Shit!"

Kamal bought a copy, and started translating as they drank orange juice. The headline was: *Assassins Awake!* Inside was a very poor image of a figure sprawled out on rock, no doubt taken with a zoom lens from quite some distance, but certainly clear enough for the black robe to be obvious.

"That officer at the station was right. Someone at the castle sold out."

Kamal shrugged. "I doubt they ever had much chance of disguising this."

"This could go international! Right after breakfast, I'll have to ring my father. He'll be horrified I came into Syria. He'll want to – I don't know what he'll try to do."

Guests at some of the other tables were beginning to stare at Abigail.

"Tell him you'll be on a plane bound for France *before* he could do anything."

"Good idea. France is his favourite place, outside of home of course. He'll know I'm safe there."

"You're safe anywhere with me."

Abigail blushed as an odd mixture of emotions washed through her. Reminders of fear from the day before, a feeling of intense gratitude towards her powerful protector, sexual arousal.

"My hero," she jested, and fluttered her eyelids. Kamal made a mock bow. "We should check up on flights and call Paul again."

"Paul's day doesn't start for seven hours," Kamal pointed out. "And we

249

need to get clean first." He peered at her. "You look very dirty," he continued in a very matter of fact tone. "I can see that I'm going to have to scrub every little centimetre of you."

"Oh. I… Ah." Abigail blushed again.

The Persian Gulf: December 1164

An azure gulf in all directions. The world seemed perfectly simple, mused Hakim, composed only of water. There'd been no sails in sight since the other ships of the convoy put in to low-slung Qais island the day before. At this rate the dhow should arrive at Zayla on the African coast in nine days, maybe ten. And, praise God, not a one of the expedition had yet needed to vomit into the brightly decorated barrels of toilets overhanging the sides of the stern!

The boat constantly creaked and squeaked and softly thumped and quietly clattered. Coir ropes rubbed. Timbers stitched to the ribs of the vessel flexed and slid. The redoubtable rudder blade had leather hinges. Rigging blocks shifted. A moderate breeze stretched the main lateen-rigged sail, along with the aft mizzen-sail and the forward jib-sail on its long bowsprit. Water softly hissed an accompaniment. Ear cocked to the concert of his vessel, Captain Khaki was personally taking a turn at the tiller, which was the length of two men, seemingly for the sheer joy of feeling united with his boat in motion through the sea.

Hakim inhaled the faint odour of shark-oil which impregnated the timbers; shark-fat boiled with lime was the watertight caulking that also stopped the sea from rotting the wood. This seemed a good and safe ship, and the barefoot crew in their loosely flapping loincloths amenable and constantly busier than he would have expected, though certainly the rigging was complicated and the ropes heavy to handle. The Fida'een remained unobtrusively alert. Now and then Hakim caught a whiff from the stick of incense which was measuring out the three-hour watch, a careful watch due to their now travelling alone.

The captain regularly pointed his tanned and wrinkled face upwards, keeping an experienced eye on the path of the sun, also checking the compass, a magnetised hollow iron fish afloat in a bowl of water. Kharki was *mu'allim* of his vessel, Master Navigator. Not until night would he be able fully to confirm their course by using a *kamal*, a rectangle of wood attached to a knotted cord, checking the height of a certain star above the horizon. With that calibrated cord held in his teeth and the piece of wood at eye-level, its base touching the horizon, the exact knot told him their latitude. The previous evening, Hakim had marvelled at the simplicity and ingenuity of this device, and Kharki had quoted the Holy Qu'ran to him: *And He it is who appointed the stars to you, that you might guide yourselves through the darkness of land and sea.*

And Kharki had added sardonically, "I've heard that the Franks," by which he meant all Christians, "boast of a bright star guiding some camels to the birth of Isa ibn Maryam. That's about the only star those barbarians know of! They merely know the compass and dead reckoning, nothing about stellar altitudes. They'd soon be lost where we're going. What an infidel bunch of goatfucks."

Except, thought Hakim, recalling what Sinan had confided once, for a small élite who had learned to emulate the esoteric ways of the true faith...

The bows lifted and glided and dipped, lifted again from a wave and glided and dipped as Hakim gazed into the distance. The prow jutted high, unadorned unlike the barrels of glory at the stern.

Presently the captain yielded the tiller to the regular steersman, and ambled towards Hakim.

"What's more," Kharki remarked, the topic of the previous evening plainly still upon his mind, "those stupid Franks still use a long steering oar. Which, of course, can snap in a heavy sea." The captain cocked an eye at a fluffy white cloud rising up on the horizon.

"Whereas," said Hakim, "we devised the rudder."

"Oh no, we copied the hinged rudder from China. Credit where credit's due."

"Have you ever been to China?" Hakim asked idly.

Kharki shook his head. "The Chinese are a strange people, not least in their attitude to strangers. Once, they massacred all the foreign merchants. I ask you, *why do that?*"

"Maybe that's because they aren't yet united with a diversity of people in the bosom of Allah," replied Hakim piously.

The captain eyed Hakim intently. "*Is* the abode of Islam united?"

Hakim shrugged, and added by way of distraction, "We should thank al-Khidr who gave the magnetised needle to men."

"Patron of all us sailors, indeed, *as-salamu 'alaykum!*"

That was a Sufist response to the mention of al-Khidr's name, but perhaps the captain was merely invoking that mysterious, invisible presence to protect his ship, as might any sailor. Kharki seemed far from being a mystic, yet, rather as with the spice merchant they had met in the mountains, Hakim was wary of the man's intelligence. Maybe the captain spoke as he had in order to probe Hakim's beliefs. Or was he just garrulous?

Again, Kharki stared at the horizon, frowning.

In due course would come the hour for prayer, when Hakim's Nizaris would unite with the Sunni crew, pretending to believe what the crew believed, prelude to a starlit evening meal of dates and rice and eggs preserved in grease then bedded in sawdust, and water from the barrel kept on the deck for daily use. However, what came into sight before that hour were the sails of two dhows speeding towards the Omani side of the gulf.

By now that first fleecy cloud had expanded into a towering mountain range, snowy peaks darkening in silhouette against a yellowing sky. The base of the range was long and low and inky and approaching fast. Wind and sea surged, accelerating the dhow.

The other dhows were visibly changing direction to intercept Kharki's boat.

"They have to be *bedans*!" the captain cried. "Pirate ships! They must be deranged to try to take us with a storm coming out of nowhere!"

"Maybe deranged with greed," a sailor called to him.

The watch-leader called, "They think all hands will be too busy controlling our boat to defend it."

The captain agreed. "Right now we should be changing the mainsail for a smaller one! We should be fitting the heavy weather jib! *How can we?* They'd be on to us in the midst of it. Mad dogs are what they are. Thank God your *acrobats* are with us," said Kharki to Hakim; the latter had made sure early on that the entire crew saw the Fida'een practising their stunning skills. "Those dogs hope to kill us all and crew our boat, then loot it after the storm passes. Here's what we'll do. As they come close, most likely they'll shoot arrows. Half of my men must tend our boat while the other half shield them. Your men can shoot?"

"Very accurately," Hakim assured him.

"Not in these gusts, man! Not with the torrents of rain that are coming! Pirate arrows are merely to make my lads duck as the boarding begins. If your acrobats deter the archers, we have a better chance of meeting steel with steel when the pirates board. We'll be ready."

"Of course," agreed Hakim, although the tactics hadn't occurred to him. *Hasan, be with me. You would understand this in an instant.*

A flash of lightning zigzagged from the menacing mountain of fast impending dark cloud, striking the sea in the mid-distance. The further distance was now invisible, swallowed by purple storm. An icy cold presaged a tempest. Kharki shouted orders, as did Hakim to his Fida'een.

As their own dhow rose higher and dipped deeper, the other dhows diverged, one coming up near from the port side, the other in turn from starboard. Both the attacking vessels listed perilously, spray lashing their tilted sails, yet they accomplished the manoeuvre without capsizing. Baggy-trousered, bare-chested figures were visible, struggling to maintain control.

"I'll grant 'em something for seamanship," snarled Kharki.

The hostile boats were sleeker and swifter than a merchant vessel. The pirate dhow to port was drawing parallel, the starboard dhow still abaft but angling to bracket Kharki's ship. The ever rising wind hurled stinging rain. Lightning snaked from cloud to cloud, illuminating the three vessels with spasmodic brilliance in the thickening gloom. Driven raindrops were gleaming arrows, visible one moment, invisible the next. And some were real arrows now, streaking from the port side, bending in their flight across the path of the fierce wind, embedding themselves in masts, in decking, in a wooden shield held by a sailor, tangling in the straining tackle and sails. The volley faltered as the Fida'een sent their own arrows winging back, firing so quickly that there might have been twice as many defenders; yet then half of Hakim's holy warriors were forced to direct their attention to a new threat, since more arrows rained over from the dhow overhauling to starboard.

Thus far, no arrow had hit a human target, at least not on Kharki's boat. In the whip of the wet wind aiming was almost senseless. So it was foul luck when one of the sailors cried out, his hand pinned to the boom onto which the mainsail was strung. Crabbing towards him across the now slippery, pitching deck, Hakim grasped the boom, feeling such pent-up momentum in the thrumming wood as might toss him aside or even hurl him overboard if the wind veered but a fraction.

Gripping the arrow-shaft tight in his right hand, he wrenched, freeing the grimacing sailor who sank to his knees, the arrow still through his blood-soaked hand. Struggling for balance, even though down on his own knees, Hakim cut off the arrow head with his razor-sharp knife, then pulled the shaft back through the man's palm. Quickly removing his turban, he cut loose a long bandage to wrap and then tie around the injured hand. That would have to do for now.

"I'll tend to your wound later," he bellowed. "Get under cover below with the cargo!"

But the sailor gave a great gritted-toothed grin and from his belt pulled his sword, clutching the hilt in his bandaged hand.

"By Khidr, I'll give them *pain*, Great Lord." Because of the man's dialect, Hakim couldn't be sure if the 'Great Lord' was a grateful reference to himself, or to the patron of seamen.

"Khidr bless you," shouted Hakim.

At that moment a four-clawed grapnel flew over the bulwark and found a lodging. An iron chain, not a rope, stretched from the grapnel; rope could be slashed through with a sword stroke. The pirate who'd thrown the combined weight of grapnel and chain must be strong indeed. Timber creaked, audible even in the wild wind, as two plunging vessels were drawn together, lurch by lurch. A winch must have been taking up slack as the vertical motions of the two vessels permitted. Why couldn't the grapnel snap its chain or tear loose the section of gunwale it had lodged against? A second grapnel hit the deck, dragged, then lodged.

Now the bows of the joined vessels were digging deep into the sea. The scuppers went under again and again so that brine sluiced along the deck instead of draining away, sweeping some sailors from their feet as they clutched for ropes to save themselves. The rumble of the waves was thunderous.

Of a sudden, a mightier crack rent the air... as the mainsail ripped. Canvas flew away like so many banners disappearing into the darkness. A rope as thick as a man's wrist snapped. A heavy wooden block that had secured a sheet swung lethally to and fro across the deck. The jib and mizzen sails bellied out more than seemed possible; surely they too would burst.

Hakim prayed and drew his scimitar. Rain lashed at his eyes. It was impossible to take in the totality even of their own vessel in the spray and rain and lightning-riven semi-darkness. Only God is all-seeing. The world of the open sea had utterly vanished, apart from intimations of the other dhows, these acting in unison like hunting dogs manoeuvring to drag down their prey whichever way it sought to veer.

As Kharki's dhow began to dive into a trough, the dhow whose bow paced their mid-ship, still high on the crest of the wave, disgorged from its bulwark what seemed to be leaping black demons. These flew down upon their deck to the sternwards, skidding and tumbling, then righting themselves and uttering blood-curdling screams like the curses of the wind itself, swords suddenly in their hands as they leapt forward; to encounter Fida'een no less agile than themselves, and much more fanatical, utterly careless of life.

Hakim saw a demon's head fly off and bowl along the deck. The wind propelled the headless body forward as it toppled. No, those creatures were not demons sent by Iblis the Accursed Adversary to destroy the expedition! They were merely viciously avaricious men.

As Hakim strove to reach the scene of combat, the wind suddenly became a wall, just like the hand of God staying him, pushing him back however much he leaned into it, preventing him, he realised, from risking himself. Thunder crashed deafeningly. Then only a roar could be heard, rushing over their deck.

Halfway along their starboard side, the other dhow had also secured a hold, and – *flash, flash* – armed sailors were skidding and sliding to greet the arrival of more would-be boarders – *flash, flash* – who were readying themselves at the starboard dhow's bulwarks, waiting for the next crest of water to lift them high.

As the pirate dhow which had grappled them first also rose high, the fiercest jag of incandescent silver light reached instantaneously to explode its mast, shattering it, the wet sail suddenly and briefly ablaze like a steaming beacon as heavy wreckage crashed upon the dhow's deck, crippling that vessel worse than Kharki's. The disabled dhow now lagged in their reckless race through the great waves. At last its weight snapped a grapnel's chain, and only moments later the *bedan*'s other connecting chain burst. The assailant's course began to diverge.

Hakim rubbed his dazzled eyes, imprinted with the afterglow of the lightning strike. Surely the devilish pirates of the starboard dhow had not leapt, after all!

What's more, surely a chain no longer held that new grapnel taut!

Yes, the dhow to starboard was now further from Kharki's ship than it had been. The captain's vessel had been released, not boarded by yet more demon pirates. A fierce battle still continued on the deck of the merchant boat, but the sister ship had broken away, and the pirates remaining on Kharki's dhow were abandoned, to succeed or to die.

Those on the second dhow had seen the first dhow's mast destroyed by lightning, and the vessel of a sudden adrift in the convulsing sea. Maybe they were breaking off their engagement in order to give aid. Or maybe that blinding bolt had seemed a gleaming sword stroke from God, cleaving through the darkness to chastise them while His voice roared angrily. Maybe, too, they had glimpsed the supreme skill of the Fida'een. No ordinary sailors those, more like *jinn*! Inexplicable protectors of the merchant dhow.

Clinging to the sail-less mainmast, Hakim watched by glaring coruscations of lightning as a Fida'i, who was inclined into the wind in a way that would normally have made any man fall on his face, slashed at a hulking pirate whose bulk at first seemed almost immovable... until its size was bloodily reduced. Someone's severed guts slithered across the awash deck, like a live octopus trying to regain its native element. An arm rolled by, gold-ringed fingers widespread as though to catch hold of anything fixed. Peering through flying water, Hakim saw a pirate, one of whose arms had been lopped off while his other seemed crippled, squirming upon his back, his mouth wide open in a scream.

Propelled by the straining jib-sail and mizzen-sail alone, Kharki's dhow scudded under a bruised sky, where it seemed that great glowing rose-coloured angels were returning to heaven. Across the gradually calming waters, no sign remained of any other vessel.

Only one sailor had died by direct violence. One other had vanished, undoubtedly swept overboard. The sailor whose hand was injured, and a Fida'i who took a flesh wound, were the only other casualties of combat, although a sailor had broken an arm in a fall on deck and another had been badly bruised by the swinging block. In all, eleven pirate corpses lay here and there; two others had leapt into raging sea to escape from the Fida'een.

Exhaustion had followed the storm and the attack, so that sailors had simply sprawled, careless of wet and wind. Even the Fida'een had rested, but now the battered boat must be put to rights. Hakim was haunted by an anxiety that Kharki might order cargo to be jettisoned; not the additional lucrative cargo in the hold but the expedition's equipment, so that the craft might more easily limp to a port.

If Kharki gave such an order, what could Hakim and his companions do? Fight a second time, against men who had almost become comrades? Even so, the Fida'een couldn't possibly crew this vessel by themselves.

When Kharki bellowed a summons, weary sailors and Fida'een too began to gather. Hakim quickly stepped forward and presumed to address the crew.

"Al-Khidr himself sent the storm out of nowhere," he declared, "to save us from the pirates. Were it not for this miraculous storm, in calmer waters the pirates could well have succeeded. The hand of God himself, holding a radiant sword of light, reached through a dozen veils of darkness to unmast our enemy. We are safeguarded, my friends, on our journey." Indeed, in the aftermath of such deadly circumstances all must be friends and brothers, whatever the reality might be. "Let us adore Allah with our thanks."

Kharki clapped Hakim on the back. "Eloquently put! This event will be legendary. Thirteen pirates slain or drowned." His eyes gleamed. "First thing," he called out, "corpses overboard to feed the sea."

Bleakly Hakim gazed up at the sail-less mainmast.

The captain chuckled. "No, my obsessive friend, we aren't putting into port to waste time. Apart from Sohar, where we'd be safe, that's the pirate coast over there, as you may already have gathered. We keep a spare mainsail below plus spare jib, mizzen, timber, ropes, brailing lines. We never set out less than fully prepared. Nor should anyone else in their right mind, not when one deep-sea dhow in ten is regularly lost."

One in ten. The risk that sailors accepted!

A vision came to Hakim of a vast palace containing a multitude of doorways leading to a multitude of rooms which contained innumerable more choices of doorways. Hakim could only have come this far by an inner light revealing which doorway to choose next, whether in Cairo or Ethiopia, in Arwe's village or lost in the jungle, in Syria then in Persia, and the door that was his choice of Kharki for their transport; doorways not only of events but of concepts and inspirations. Several times he'd explored beyond the wrong doorway – though that was necessary at the time – always to recover the true route once more. More doorways surely awaited him in Africa, and he must never be over-confident, yet far ahead he glimpsed already the terrible glory of the Throne Room of Enlightened Power, by the agency of which nine out of ten human beings would perish.

"Of course," said Kharki to Hakim, "the risk on our return voyage is still one in ten, not two in ten; else I wouldn't be here today. And that risk is average, taking little account of the variable calibre of seamanship."

No other dire incident troubled the rest of their voyage. Angels might have been gentling the waters while wafting the dhow with their wings and sieving the sea, for hooks baited with bright feathery lures of torn cloth, cast by sailors with time to spare, brought up tuna and giant mackerel and sharks to be cooked over charcoal in the firebox on the deck.

Three weeks after setting sail from Rishahr, they made harbour at Zayla.

Provence, France: May 2008

The first thing Abigail and Kamal did after landing at Marseille Provence airport, and emerging into the Arrivals area, was to check on Paul's flight from Boston via Paris. This was due in two hours, with no signs of delay. Coincidentally, Abigail's mobile pinged. A text: BRDING @ PARIS NOW, ONTIME. CU PAUL.

The next task was to extract Euros from an ATM, then to arrange car rental, which proved to be more expensive than Abigail had expected. Kamal used a Visa card and showed an international driving licence; Abigail would be the second driver. Then Kamal indicated a branch of Cafés Debout, which proved to have a couple of tables, one free. Arrivals in an airport wasn't the best place for eateries.

A buttery croissant and hot chocolate for Abigail, a tiny espresso for Kamal; "I'm not hungry." He drank it immediately, as one should. "But," and he grinned, "I'm hungry to see the light of Provence that inspired Van Gogh, and to breathe the air. Would you excuse my impetuosity?"

So saying, he headed for the main doors.

Spotting a kiosk close by, Abigail called in her Québecois French to the woman at the food counter. "Will you watch our bags for a moment? I just want to get a newspaper." Who knows what she might find of interest in a local paper? Yet hopefully nothing about madmen on Syrian castles accompanied by her own picture! The woman merely glared, as Abigail quit the table and her coffee and croissant. Rude French people.

Twenty paces took Abigail to the kiosk and a copy of *La Provence*. Just visible from where she stood, she spotted Kamal outside, apparently exchanging a few words with a whiplash-thin dark-skinned man in jeans and a blue shirt. Hurriedly, Abigail returned to the coffee bar, in case that woman might decide to call security. Having their luggage hauled away to be destroyed would not be a good start to the mission, and she did think of this as a mission, an exciting mission.

When Kamal also returned, she beamed happily at him. "Who were you talking to outside?" she asked.

"What?" He glanced towards the exit, as though surprised. "Oh, him. A North African, I suppose. *M'sieur, aidez-moi...* He probably gets more money begging at an airport than on the streets of Marseille."

"He spoke to you in French, not Arabic?"

"An automatic chant. Ah," teasingly, "you mean, what with me looking so obviously Arab?"

Abigail flushed with embarrassment at the unintended faux pas, then reached out to clasp Kamal's hand.

She reflected that when Paul arrived, he'd encounter a very different situation from back in Boston; she and Kamal would unabashedly be sharing whatever hotel room they found in the anonymity of Montélimar, half an hour's drive from Montlume itself. They'd already decided that staying in Montlume village might draw too much attention. Would her new-found happiness bother Paul? Or had he come to terms with the situation during their email exchanges? She'd tried to be open, even blunt.

She busied herself ruffling through the pages of *La Provence* while Kamal sat contemplatively, eyelids closed as if meditating. An article claimed that the once famous nougat trade of Montélimar was recovering after many years of hard times and several factory closures.

Kamal re-opened his eyes. "It's the duty of all Muslims to be charitable," he added as though their previous conversation still continued. "So I gave the poor fellow a little money."

"I adore you," replied Abigail.

"For performing this small duty?"

"For being you, such a wonderful, clever man. And," she whispered, "*such* a clever lover too."

When Paul emerged, clad in a crumpled jacket of cream linen, a small backpack over one shoulder, he was jauntily wearing a black beret and dark sunglasses. Abigail thought he looked a little comical. Should she hug him? Would he expect that? She compromised by bowing ironically.

A handshake with Kamal, a few quick explanations – "Our hire car'll be waiting" – then they were all outside in sun-bright, sky-blue radiance. Even at an airport, the Provençal air smelled languidly sweet, with a hint of saltiness. Of the Algerian or Moroccan beggar there was no sign, so Kamal wasn't pressed to do his duty twice over.

"Wow!" exclaimed Paul. "Vive la France."

"You've been most helpful regarding the investigation," Kamal remarked to him.

"Shucks. Anything for our Abi."

Our Abi, thought Abigail. No, Kamal's Abi.

"But why," continued Kamal, "the hat?"

"Picked it up in a shop at Charles de Gaulle. To look suitably Gallic."

"Put it away, my young friend," advised Kamal. "That doesn't serve as a disguise, because you don't look French at all! The best cover is to seem like an ordinary tourist."

"So?" queried Paul. "Isn't this the very thing tourists do?"

Sun-hatted Abigail laughed. "Just *silly* tourists, Paul." She winked. "And there's our academic dignity to consider!"

"Consider me duly chastised." Hauling off the offending beret, Paul folded and crammed it in his jacket pocket. "Burglarising a tomb mightn't be so academically dignified though."

"Shhhh!"

Kamal was stern: "No more such talk until we're in the car."

Marseille Provence airport being north-west of the city, they saw nothing of France's chief seaport, but almost immediately joined the A7, which was crowded with trucks and speeding cars. As a native French speaker, although of Québecoise stripe, Kamal had asked Abigail to take the wheel of the Renault Mégane in case of any incident. He occupied the seat beside her, consigning Paul to the rear where the latter immediately began to check his messages and surf the Internet on his smartphone; how newsman! His device was the highest specification possible, he told them eagerly, with cool fourth generation features others only dreamed of. Abigail had in fact never ever dreamed of multi-touch screens or video quality roaming bandwidth or whatever else.

Abigail stole what glances she could spare from the road: at villages of shuttered houses, roofed with terracotta tiles baking in the sun and as ochre as the local soil itself; at bell towers crowned with cage-like wrought iron; at groves of gnarled olive trees.

"Ahem," said Paul eventually. "I'm still iffy about what we're planning. Tentatively planning, anyway."

"Me too," admitted Abigail.

"What is *iffy*?" queried Kamal.

"Well," continued Paul, "we know Montlume has been somewhat restored in recent years. Surely we ought to liaise with whoever's into the restoration work?"

"Quite likely," said Abigail, "there'll be an Association des Amis du Vieux Village, Friends of the Old Village, or some such organisation."

"Very likely composed of fussy pedants!" Kamal exclaimed. "People who'll need to hold five meetings before touching anything. All because of French archaeological laws. Official permits may be needed. Nothing may happen, or not soon enough." He spoke more softly, sweetly reasonable. "Don't you see that it's our duty to take the initiative? We *cannot* prove a connection with anything happening in modern times, the way ICE imagines. Yet it's possible that something *may* be happening. If what we think may be in Montlume actually *is* in Montlume, other people who are ruthless might take it first. Besides," he added debonairly, "this'll be an adventure, won't it?"

"Not quite like my adventure at Masyaf, I hope!" Despite which, a thrill coursed through Abigail. From disinterring an ancient piece of paper from a chapbook in the quiet confines of an academic library, she'd progressed to recovering solid evidence in the real world. Perhaps!

"What's more," urged Kamal persuasively, "if we do find some liquid, what a scoop for Harvard. The Medical School could analyse this substance, then hand it over to your Jack person, if need be. Even if it turns out to merely be based on Syrian Rue, that's still quite a coup for medieval historians."

"Except," mentioned Abigail, "we wouldn't be able to say where we got the stuff…"

"Frankly," said Paul from behind, "there could be nothing in Montlume. We shouldn't raise our hopes too high. I think those old-time villagers misinterpreted *since in me the holy water of life* et cetera. They thought it was a riddle, with *me* referring to the tomb rather than to Guy himself. And the description of the burial isn't accurately dateable; it *could* have been written after a rumour had already started. So it's quite possible we won't find anything."

"In that case," said Abigail, emboldened, "there's no harm in looking. Nothing ventured, nothing gained, eh?"

"That's the spirit," agreed Kamal. "The spirit of enquiry."

"I'll buy that," affirmed Paul.

"And we need to look up *Cadastres* when we get time," added Abigail.

Paul looked blank. "Sounds like a card game, or is that *Canasta?*"

Cadastres, Abigail explained, were land registry documents for tax purposes, invaluable to historians. Most related to the post-Napoleonic period, but some went right back to medieval times and many were now online. During the last two days in Syria she'd discovered some coverage for the Montlume area, but hadn't found time to take it further. Anything relating to Guy de Dieulefit could be invaluable. Paul didn't ask what she'd done with her time instead, he could guess.

As they neared Salon-de-Provence, Abigail slowed to see her first field of sunflowers, not as yet in yellow glory, only to be angrily honked as the car behind overtook impatiently.

Equipped with his smartphone and Internet maps, Paul gave an endless commentary on the route, complete with humorous mal-pronunciations of French. Abigail was content to listen and smile. Kamal frowned.

"Hey," said Paul, "about twenty miles east of here there's a place called… Ven-as-kay…"

Venasque.

"That'll be pronounced Venask. You make it sound Spanish."

"Sorry. Anyway, they built a vast wall to try keeping the plague out."

"A wall against plague?" enquired Kamal, smiling at last. "That would be something to see."

"Seems there are still some traces of it left. Apparently it's from the time of the third big plague in these parts. In the Seventeen-Twenties. There were several smaller plagues too."

"We're interested in the first one. 1348," Abigail reminded him.

"I know."

Paul's smartphone eventually proved more useful. He located a likely-looking hotel to the south of Montélimar: the Hostellerie Des Pins.

The land was ochre, aglow.

Montélimar, Provence, France: May 2008

Soon their Mégane was entering Montélimar along the Route de Marseille, amid sprawling commercial zones that not even the gorgeous sunshine could beautify. Of a sudden, Abigail signalled and turned off, coming soon into the forecourt of a large unit bearing the sign Monsieur Bricolage.

"Hardware store," she explained. "*Tools.*"

"*Good,*" enthused Kamal.

Twenty minutes later, the trunk of the Mégane was heavier by the weight of a pick, a pinch bar, a sledge hammer, a battery-powered drill, a charger for the drill, hammers and chisels, plus powerful torches and some protective gloves. Kamal had put almost 500 Euros on a credit card. Shopping had been an effervescent rush around, loading a trolley.

"What do we do with all this stuff afterwards?" asked Paul.

"Get rid of it, of course," said Kamal. "When it's of no more use."

Presently, a Pont Roosevelt took them over water, just by the confluence of two rivers that must be tributaries of the mighty Rhône. In the avenue immediately after, they passed by a confiserie advertising *Nougat de Montélimar.*

"Look, Paul, a nougat shop."

"Hey, if we pass another will you stop?"

She glanced at the car's clock. "I think we ought to get on to the hotel, then we'll have time for more research after eating…"

"Please!"

It occurred to her that Paul might be feeling a bit left out when, after all, he'd flown all the way from America to help out. Another sweetshop did appear, so she turned off.

"What are you doing?" demanded Kamal.

"This'll only take a moment."

"Will you translate for me?" asked Paul. "I want to buy you a box of nougat."

"But I don't want…"

"Pretty please?"

"Maybe some chocolate. I've run out."

"This is ridiculous. We're not here to buy candies." However, Kamal curbed himself, and stayed to guard the car with its trunkful of tools.

No sooner were they inside the little shop than Paul began to talk urgently.

"Abi, I wanted to get you on your own for a moment. Do you fully *trust* Kamal? Spending a small fortune on tools, just to throw them away! Who's bankrolling him?"

"Himself. Kamal was a very successful businessman before he became a scholar. He still maintains some business interests."

"Says who? Look, I did some checking up. His degree from that university... There's something dodgy, but I didn't have enough time."

"Oh, Paul! You're still *jealous*." Abigail apologised to the shop assistant and asked for a bar of chocolate.

"Nougat ohsi, si voos play," added Paul, pulling out his wallet and pointing at a little box adorned with roses and smiling faces under bonnets.

"Trust Kamal? I adore him."

"Okay. But that's an irrational thing, Abi. And I notice you don't say *love*."

"Paul, you and me are friends. And you've come all this way for me. I'm eternally grateful."

"But don't push it? Yeah. Got you."

Inclining herself, she kissed him on the cheek. "You're like a brother to me." No doubt the shop assistant presumed otherwise. "And if you hadn't phoned me when you did at Masyaf... maybe... maybe I wouldn't have turned around and seen... maybe we wouldn't be here at all." For a few moments Abigail felt drained and shivery, as if a hideous ghost had walked over her grave. She shook her head, to clear it. "Feed me some sweetness."

Paul ripped open his newly acquired box, tore loose some sticky white nougat, and popped the piece into Abigail's mouth.

She struggled to speak. "My teeth... getting stuck together."

Paul followed suit. "So," he mumbled, "are mine. The better... um... not to," and he chewed valiantly, "put my foot... in my mouth... again."

Giggling, the two returned to the car. Something strange had kindled, all the way from Boston. Why, Abigail wondered a few moments later, was she still holding back *any details at all* from Kamal? Such as all the stuff Fawzi had told her, and some of Jen's information too. So as to keep a card or two up her sleeve? Yet he was her wonderful and brilliant lover, the Sheikh of Araby. Had Terry been right all along, was she manipulative?

The forty or so rooms of the low-slung Hostellerie Des Pins looked out upon a pine forest. Its restaurant boasted a delectable tour of local delights, so they treated themselves, Abigail enjoying rabbit roasted with rosemary followed by crème brûlée flavoured with lavender. Paul overdosed on extra garlic, perhaps his goofy way of being Gallic, or a statement, either conscious or unconscious, that personally he wouldn't be kissing anyone that night. After eating, the trio went to Kamal and Abigail's room.

To get themselves in the medieval mood and perhaps uncover something useful for their coming thievery, they waded through the cadastre information Abigail had found online. It was hard going, the documents didn't have search tags appended and references were made to other documents clearly not yet online.

"It's a shame we can't go to the Mairie of Montlume, the town hall," complained Abigail, "or the archive office here in Montélimar."

"Out of the question," asserted Kamal. "Quite apart from the fact that they'd probably want to see our ID, if there's a big fuss afterwards they might make a connection."

"And remember our faces," added Paul.

Yet less than two hours later, they'd managed to find out that late in 1348, Guy de Dieulefit had inherited valuable land near Montlume from a half-brother, Roger, who died of plague. This seemed to be under a strict family covenant, probably made long before to stop the family's assets dispersing, though they didn't have the document itself. It also seemed that Guy survived another plague outbreak in the area, over 1361 to 1363. As did his children, who were also untouched by several more waves over the next fifty years, including one that devastated Avignon in 1382.

"A very lucky family?" questioned Abigail.

"Hey, if he gave the Holy Water to all his offspring, there won't be any juice left for us to find!" complained Paul.

"Pure speculation," answered Kamal. "There's only one way to find out, and that way we must take."

Later, warmly in bed together after urgent love-making by Kamal, Abigail was sinking softly into sleep. Yet peculiar themes in her head disturbed her. "You know that North African guy you gave money to?" she remarked sleepily. "At the airport."

"*Know* him? Of course not!"

"I mean, remember him?"

Kamal sounded strangely guarded. "Yes. What of it?"

"I just wondered... Oh, I'm half in a dream already. It was your duty to give him money. I'm curious. Suppose a man had to make," and she yawned, "had to make love as a duty... could a man do that? A lot of women must. Arranged marriage... physically less hard for women... maybe... no, maybe not..."

"What a crazy question!" Kamal arose on his elbow. "Ah, but I think I understand... Women often seek reassurance from a man who has made love to them. Abigail, you are the beautiful bright light of my later years, the sweet oil that kindles my flame to be tall."

"That's all right then," Abigail murmured, passing from half-dream towards the fullness of oblivion.

"As to your question, I'd be certain to enjoy myself," added Kamal, although most likely she no longer heard him.

Next morning, while Kamal was busy showering, Abigail took a photo of the room. Yet another cosy nest where they'd made love! True, the room was ordinary enough, and in *any* event the bed sheets would have been in disarray. Yet the light of Provence spilling through the window, and her memories of the previous night, made the ordinary luminous.

The tip of a folded white handkerchief peeped from a side pocket of Kamal's jacket… no, it was paper. Barefoot, Abigail went to inspect. She couldn't resist teasing out the paper and opening it up. Handwriting, in Arabic, laid out visibly as quatrains of verse. Could he, she wondered with a thrill, have been penning a love poem to her? Intending to read it aloud in Arabic, then render it into English. She remembered with pleasure his skilful translation of Hafiz, on the sofa at that fancy house in Qazvin, before ever they'd made love.

Maybe he wasn't satisfied with the poem as yet. Maybe he never would be, he was such a perfectionist! In which case… Quickly she laid the paper flat, took a photo of the writing, then refolded the poem and restored it exactly as before. She mustn't even hint. Put it out of her mind. Let it be a surprise.

Montlume, Provence, France: June 2008

The air was still and hazy with heat. Montlume came into sight. Its massive, almost blank-faced keep glared in the sunlight. Topped by a tall stone pigeon loft, that *donjon* dominated the white, ochre-roofed village, which descended a hillside into the green fields and meadows beyond. To the rear of the keep, the stony mountain that was its foundation rose steeply, wooded now but perhaps once kept clear, and not in the least a viable route for assaulting the Hospitaller stronghold. Montlume was one of the *villages perchés* common in Provence: perched, keeping watch. Abigail hoped that its present inhabitants weren't too vigilant. At a guesstimate of the size of Montlume, maybe a thousand souls dwelled here, give or take.

The lower village, the more modern part comparatively speaking, was negotiable by car, though most streets were narrow. A bread and cake store. A grocer's. A boutique art gallery. A china store; and another evidently specialising in faience: plumed birds and donkey musicians visible on the examples of tin-glazed earthenware in its window. Locals were about on the streets: grizzle-haired elderly women in baggy floral frocks, their faces like rutted mahogany; an old fellow with big ears in a floppy black beret, another beret on a slow oldster who might have been the first one's brother or cousin...

"Berets, berets," said Paul.

"But not on the young guys," Abigail pointed out as she nosed their car along.

An athletic-looking young man, curly jet hair shining as though oiled, sat astride a slim scrambler parked in the shade. In fact most people kept out of the sun. Such knife-sharp contrasts between deep shadows and dazzling illumination. Abigail felt a strange confusion of reality and unreality. Here she was in actual, inhabited Montlume, and yet their plans seemed to be based upon the village being uninhabited. Maybe by night it would seem so; silent and dark, with the fierce searchlight of the sun switched off.

Much narrower lanes, paved with stones, ascended crookedly towards the oldest and highest part of the village. Soon enough, Abigail was able to park in the square of the tricoleur-hung town hall, behind a modest-sized coach from Germany that was disembarking its camera-slung passengers.

"Perfect," announced Kamal. "We'll follow the tourists."

Abigail noticed some fresh-looking posters for *Festival du Rock parmi les roches* at the Théatre du plein air. A Rock festival among the rocks: the partial pun became a full pun in English. This very night would kick off the two-day event. Quickly she explained to Kamal and Paul.

"Shit," exclaimed Paul, "that'll draw in kids from all around. The village'll be swarming."

"Allah is gracious," retorted Kamal. "Rock music is usually very loud."

Soon Abigail, Paul, and Kamal were climbing up a steep dusty lane behind thirty or forty others led by a German-speaking guide. Abigail and Kamal both toted their slim cameras; Abigail also had her shoulder bag with two bottles of water inside. Reconnoitring in the heat would be thirsty work.

The ancient lanes were a labyrinth, bridged over by arched buttresses where weeds flowered. Covered passages ran aslant. Tall hollyhocks thrust from cracks by the walls, their fattest buds already burst open, mauve and pink. Stairways of stone led to even higher terraced levels. An old lady was descending painstakingly, arm in arm with an adolescent who might be her grandson and whose free hand held a basket of cherries.

Paul muttered: "Figure there's any access to the top by car? Those tools weigh..."

Kamal cut him off with a hissed "Be quiet!"

"Hey, I wasn't shouting."

"Nevertheless."

And so they came to the chapel, its bell tower doing double duty as part of the fortifications. As they gazed up at terracotta-topped limestone against lavender-blue sky, Kamal gestured higher overhead, as if in salute. An eagle was gliding in a wide, slow circle.

Most of the nave remained, and visibly an intact chancel beyond with semi-circular apse. But they were obliged to queue behind those Germans, while families and couples passed through a gateway in wrought iron railings five feet high, resembling a long rack of rusty upright spears, which stretched across the open nave from wall to wall. It looked like a 19th century addition to protect a piece of antiquity, perhaps still sacred, from vagabonds or goats.

As Kamal in turn went through the opening, his hand rested briefly on the redoubtable vintage padlock and chain which would secure the gate of spears. Probably some old man was the custodian of a bulky black key.

Towards the dim rear of the apse, on either side, were rectangular tombs, essentially tall box coffins of thick stone. In fact, two on the right side, one behind the other. It was hard not to thrust the Germans aside; they were only half-listening to their guide's comments yet resolutely occupying all the space! However, these comments weren't lengthy, and within a couple of minutes the tourists were ambling back through the gateway into the sunshine.

Paydirt. On the single tomb-slab to the left: that Provençal inscription, and some ornate medieval French, and the name of Guy de Dieulefit, worn by the centuries but still perfectly legible, just as Paul had described from the photo. Together with the raised sculpture of a double-handled sword, its hilt a fleur-de-lys pattern signifying French nobility, and a simple Hospitaller crucifix shield as coat of arms.

Abigail ran her hands across the cool slab, as if blinded by what she saw and needing to confirm by touch. Paul knelt, though not to pray. Scratched deeply on the side of the tomb were a number of initials made by vandals and even a couple of dates: *1789*, the year of the French Revolution, and *1843*. Also, a much more worn inscription in capitals: *ORA PRO NOBIS*.

"Pray for us," Abigail explained. "He'll be inside. His bones…"

The tomb-slab was a great lid secured by ancient mortar. A crack about six inches long, also mortared, shaped a little triangle at the bottom right of the slab. Kamal scraped the back of a fingernail along the line of mortar, which proved rock-hard. He took photographs, then returned to the railings and the open gate with its chain and padlock, to capture more images.

Voices nearby. Italian. Consequently the trio quit the chapel, after politely making way for its new visitors while taking the opportunity to re-hydrate themselves, Kamal and Abigail sharing the same bottle.

"Look," said Kamal. Tucked almost out of sight was a small, elderly tractor. "That got up here somehow."

They found a stony track, which they followed past ruined walls still bent upon their centuries-long tumble into oblivion. Presently, the track became grassy, hosting loud choirs of cicadas as it began to descend circuitously.

Eventually, they emerged onto the road by which they had entered Montlume. Kamal scribbled some notes in Arabic, then they walked back to their Mégane in the increasing heat, ignoring the shops, the bar, and the restaurant. It was one o'clock.

"We saw all we need," stated Kamal. "The situation looks very promising, wouldn't you say so, my fellow adventurers?" and without waiting for a reply: "Now we can drive back to Montélimar for a rest."

"Eat our sandwiches first?" asked Paul hopefully.

"Here, in full view? Abigail can stop after a few miles." Spoken in a voice of quiet authority. "Although tonight I think I should drive up the track, with your permission? I'm accustomed to primitive roads."

Montélimar, Provence, France: June 2008

Back at the Hostellerie Des Pins, Kamal set the alarm on the clock and then proceeded to fall asleep in his underwear, while Abigail was still undoing her bra, just as though he'd switched off his mind. An enviable talent, perhaps! Or was that a tad impolite, as though he couldn't even wait to admire her body? No, Kamal was right: they ought to be well rested for this evening's exertions. Abigail, however, didn't find it so easy to fall asleep and wondered for a while about Paul, in his own room. Was he also dozing, or texting? Watching TV that he couldn't understand? Ah, but there was always CNN 24 hour News, though it repeated itself so often. Maybe that's how Paul was occupying his time during the hot languor of the afternoon...

Undoubtedly Abigail did fall asleep, because she was half-aware of waking up without, however, being quite sure of this until she noticed a soft, slow throb of snoring from Kamal.. Nothing would disturb him until the alarm went off. Which would give him exactly enough time for a shower and a light dinner before setting off to commit what was certainly a crime. What composure he had!

Montlume, Provence, France: June 2008

Shortly before they arrived at Montlume for the second time, towards half-nine in the gathering dusk, a police car overtook their Mégane, followed by half a dozen dirt bikes.

"Cops!" exclaimed Abigail, at the wheel.

Kamal reassured her. "No flashing lights or siren. Doubtless they're going to monitor the concert in case of any disturbance, and the concert isn't beside our destination. Note that the bikers are following the police, not the other way round."

"Still, we could have done without police in the area."

"I believe you say: Win some, Lose some."

A couple more bikes overtook.

"Those police," said Paul, "are missing the warm-up band." Ahead, a lower area of the village was aglow with bright colour that spawned stabbing beams and the occasional flicker of strobe lights. Already, above the purr of their engine, a thumping bass was audible, pumped out in monotonous rhythm. Paul laughed. "Probably they know the warm-up band is crap."

"Any disturbances wouldn't happen until later, when young people get drunk," was Kamal's opinion. "Will you pull over, Abigail? I should take the wheel now."

She was glad to yield. Being passed by the police had made her heart thump, a bit like that bass beat up ahead.

Kamal had Paul walk ahead up the tractor route, carrying one of their torches, while the car followed slowly with lights extinguished.

On reaching the top, Kamal executed a to and fro manoeuvre, until their Mégane was semi-masked by the tractor and pointing back the way they had come, its loaded rear facing the chapel, although some forty metres away. Once outside, Kamal produced from the trunk an opaque plastic box, the size of a fat hardback book. He must have brought it all the way from Syria in his luggage, then stowed it in the car.

"What's in there?" whispered Abigail.

"Only padding at the moment. It's for whatever we might find. If anything."

"You do think ahead."

"Always. Paul, will you carry the crowbar and the sledge hammer please?"

"Crowbar? Oh, that's a pinch bar."

"Crowbar is the word I learned."

Thus Kamal apportioned tools. Rock music now reverberated from buildings and walls and even from the steep mountain slope, a heavily amplified female voice ringing out above a thundering metallic pulse. Abigail could hardly make out a word that was being sung. The situation seemed surreal. She was as jumpy as a frightened cat. By now it was ten and fully night. A half-moon had risen, enough for some weak natural light, nothing too revealing.

The chain on the gate yielded to the pinch bar, twisted clockwise by the combined force of Kamal and Paul. Then they were inside, now on the other side of the law.

They moved swiftly over to the tomb. The torchlight created looming shadows that amplified Abigail's fears, but Kamal seemed unperturbed. Protected by thick gloves, he was soon hammering a chisel against the mortar of the small crack in the tomb's slab, while Paul held a torch. To no avail. The chisel jarringly rebounded. Discarding those implements, Kamal shook his hand a few times, then rubbed both gloves together.

"If the sledge hammer fails, we'll drill, but that's a constant loud noise and we might miss any lull in the music."

Standing back, Kamal hefted the sledge hammer, raising it overhead then bringing it down with an almighty impact upon the flaw in the slab. Abigail jumped. The head of the sledge hammer sank in by an inch. It had breached the crack.

"Again."

This time Abigail saw the small triangle of slab sag inwards. Kamal was so strong, but then she already knew that from being in bed with him; those muscles on his back and shoulders! Not that he misused his strength in any scary way. And how would Paul have performed with the sledge hammer? Ironic that the older man should be wielding it, while the younger man was just a torch bearer.

Kamal inhaled and exhaled a few times, deeply, then he thrust the pinch bar into the gap and tested.

"Abigail, you should keep watch at the gate. Paul, help me."

Abigail retreated, casting glances back as, bodies pressed together, both men bore down. Her face flushed hot with guilt and nervousness at what they were doing, but with excitement too. Her breath came fast and shallow.

"We need dynamite," she heard Paul panting out. "Or plastic explosive."

"Yes we do, no matter if it's loud. But none is available in France."

"What, did you look up *dynamite* in the Yellow Pages?"

Ignoring Paul's quip, Kamal lifted the sledge hammer again, then slammed it down.

"Hey, there's another bit of crack now. Well done."

"You have a go. I shall direct the torch."

Crash. A long "Woof," from Paul, as if his breath was knocked out of him.

"You hit the edge," said Kamal accusingly. But then a moment later: "Wait, mortar has failed between the slab and the side. Hit again, the same way!"

"Okay, I'll try to make the exact same mistake."

Crash.

"Bingo. I think."

Unable to contain herself, Abigail darted back. The nearside wall of the tomb was no longer vertical. Kamal now positioned the pinch bar and forced all his weight downward on it. Hastily, she resumed her watch upon the darkness. Her heart seemed louder than the rock music as it pounded in her ears.

"It's… coming," she heard in Kamal's strained tones. The side-panel inched outward with a grating reluctance.

"And now, we must hit it hard."

Abigail had to see this. When the sledge hammer descended, very accurately considering its great weight, the metal head walloped the inside edge of the stone side-panel. A concussion seemed to split the air; Abigail and Paul jumped in shock as the panel jerked outward by six inches or more.

Kamal was unruffled, yet panting now. "Once again."

This time the side-panel opened even wider, like the swing-down writing flap of a box desk, though of hard limestone and vastly more substantial. Kamal and Paul stooped forward, bringing both torches to bear as dust eddied. Abigail crept up behind them, actually trembling with apprehension and anticipation. She leaned against Kamal's back. *At last*, her thought sang, the resolution of her medieval puzzles might begin. They all peered into an antiquity undisturbed since the fourteenth century. Powerful beams illuminated… an intact skeleton resting upon a lunar sea of dust, the desiccated debris of decomposition.

The skull had rolled to one side; empty eyes stared accusingly at them. And clutched in a cage of hand-bones upon the ribs of Guy de Dieulefit, was a dusty glass bottle.

"He has it!" rejoiced Kamal.

Abigail gasped. "It's exactly the same type of bottle as at Alamut, and in the museum!"

"Wow. Authentic then, most likely." Paul's tones were hushed, the moment had gripped them all.

"Yes, very likely, but only one bottle," answered Kamal.

"You expected two?"

Kamal didn't answer, but thrust his torch at Abigail to hold, then pulled off his workman gloves. He extracted from a pocket the surprise of surgical gloves, which he donned before resuming the thicker ones on top. Delicately, he stretched his hand into the tomb and prised metacarpal and phalange bones apart. Carefully, he withdrew the glass container, still sealed with now hardened browned wax.

"The wax remnants on the other bottles were black, I'm sure of it."

"Paul, open the plastic box."

Paul did so. Kamal reverently placed the bottle within the padding and wrapped more cushioning layers over it. Closing the lid tight, Paul withdrew from the precariously tilted side-stone.

"I guess I can take care of this for the moment."

Kamal slowly removed his double layer of gloves. Taking the torch from Abigail, he rested it on the carved top of the tomb, angling up to Paul's face.

"Better put it here on the slab for now, while we clean up." The female singer's voice attempted to soar as drums pounded and amplified guitars shrieked, and Kamal turned his head as though nevertheless he'd heard a noise from nearer by, which now caused him to move away and glance out into the night. Apparently satisfied, he turned to regard Paul, who still clutched the protective box.

"You think *you* can take care of such a treasure?"

"Oh, I think I'm competent not to drop it. A safe guy, completely reliable; not to mention an unbiased reporter. A most suitable custodian."

"Paul, don't be an asshole," hissed Abigail.

"Take care of that?" Kamal repeated loudly, coldly. "Not after I take care of *you* and," he added, "Abigail." From his jacket pocket had come a pistol, black and compact, somehow as ugly as its purpose.

"Wh-at...?" quavered Abigail.

"A treasure now restored!" Kamal clicked off the safety.

"B-but... you saved me!"

Even as Abigail spoke, the rock music suddenly ceased. All was shockingly silent after so much noise. Kamal frowned, but held the pistol steady.

"Oh... Oh God. No... No! And how did...? Oh, that Arab at the airport...!"

"Quite right. Not shocked out of all sense and control, I see. Surprising. By prior arrangement, he delivered the gun to me."

But Abigail's control was rapidly flowing out as cold realisation flooded in.

"You shit!" She screamed. "You slimy lying deceitful shit! You fucking..."

Paul was saying nothing, perhaps on the assumption that a man would more readily shoot another man, or maybe just to let Abigail fully express herself.

"...*terrorist*," was the word that ended Abigail's brief tirade, but spoken more softly as implication after terrible implication dawned. Oh God, dear Walid's death, it must've been murder! And surely the events at Masyaf weren't what they'd seemed... Her mind churned furiously...

"You arranged it!" she yelled. "You ordered me killed at Masyaf! It was *Paul* who saved me. At the last moment, he phoned to tell me about this tomb, about the *water of life*. So you killed your own fucking assassin!"

"A delay of execution." Kamal inclined his head. He was waiting for loud music to resume, to mask gunshots, otherwise police at the concert would hear those *crack crack crack* sounds and recognize what they were. "And believe me, I've enjoyed our relationship," he remarked, maybe for something to fill in the time, "including extra time."

"Are you trying to fucking infuriate me?"

Momentarily, Kamal's expression seemed regretful, though only to the extent that a *faux pas* might have caused Abigail to launch herself at him, nails to the fore, compelling him to fire the pistol before it was safe to do so.

But then Paul butted in. "What did you mean about *restoring* the thing we found?" he asked softly. "As in: to its rightful owners? That guy Sinaldin should never have given the juice to Guy, should he? I mean, to this guy here, to the dead Guy. The guy called Guy as opposed to the Sinaldin guy." He contrived to laugh. "A guy too many, I guess."

Abigail's anger was already deserting her; she just felt sick and weak at the knees. Amid the wreckage of her hopes and dreams, Paul's scatty tongue-twistedness seemed almost endearing for a moment. But then... then she wondered whether there was something beneath his joking, whether he had some kind of a plan. She'd already learned that Paul's humour masked intelligence; might it mask bravery too?

"Of course he shouldn't have given it," answered Kamal scornfully. "Sinan al-Din's compassion for the Christian was stupid."

Abigail glanced quickly away from the hypnotic muzzle of the pistol. In the direct torch beam, Paul's face was a glowing Greek icon. In the deep shadow lower down, he had the plastic box pressed against his thigh. She got the impression he was trying to manipulate it with one hand, so Kamal wouldn't see. *If he got the bottle out before the music restarted, maybe...*

"Compassion not copied by that same Christian in the matter of his half-brother," continued Paul. "I guess Guy preferred a chance to get Roger's land, over protecting his merely half kin."

"Hospitaller, have pity..." quoted Abigail, desperately trying to assist the diversion, though her thought was sinking in a chill mire of betrayal and impending oblivion. "Maybe now we know who wrote that." She tried to lock her legs straight and get more breath into her lungs. It wouldn't do to fall in a faint before the executioner, to waste her last moments of life and receive death while sprawled unconscious.

"And pity came there none!" uttered Paul dramatically. "Once the epidemic started, I bet Roger found out that Guy had some special dispensation from plague. Maybe Guy got drunk and boasted."

And still the gun pointed, while Kamal waited impatiently, unspeaking now. The silence must be an interval between sets, not just a gap between wailings by that woman.

"So," speculated Paul, "was someone on board Sinaldin's ship infected? Or... was Sinaldin carrying some *death-juice* with him, as well as the life-juice. Yeah, he was carrying the pestilence, but himself protected! A Nizari fanatic, on a mission against medieval Europe."

Kamal remained poised, staring, like an eagle. But his eyebrows briefly raised when Paul said the words Nizari fanatic. Abigail risked another glance; Paul had managed to peel back a corner of the lid and worm a finger in. *Why did Kamal wear surgical gloves?*

"Sinaldin's like you, isn't he Kamal? Aren't you on a big world-mission too? To spread something far worse than Marburg virus?"

Death-juice! Abigail wasn't religious, but she prayed it was the right stuff, or at least that the bottle's seal wasn't disturbed.

"Stop that!" yelled Kamal. The muzzle tracked to Paul's heart and Kamal's eyes narrowed with purpose.

Paul immediately swung his arm up, holding the box before his chest, perhaps just in time. He withdrew his finger and snapped the lid shut again.

"Very clever of you," he blurted out, perhaps hoping that flattery would delay the inevitable a little longer. "To get us all here together, secretly. You must've thought real fast at Masyaf. A neat removal of two loose ends, and the juice in your pocket too, despite your having to kill your own man to make it work. I guess this getting to the authorities would be a disaster for your plan, but I'd have gone straight to them if Abigail... if..."

He stuttered to a halt. Abigail had heard unmistakable desperation in his tone. But she was desperate too, worse in fact, almost uncaring.

"But if you shoot me now, you might hit the stuff," Paul continued more boldly. "And those Gendarmes will come running."

"You don't just act the fool," commented Kamal, "you *are* the fool. If the bottle is shot, its liquid dispersed on the ground with dirt and broken glass, and of course *lots* of your blood, it'll be no use to anyone, perhaps not even noticed."

Then he actually smiled, the boyish smile Abigail so adored. Something twisted horribly inside her. Her head felt strangely light, her airway painfully constricted, as though she was being strangled. She lurched, fought to stay upright.

"But this original *water of life* is indeed holy. I would like to return it…" He swung the pistol over to Abigail. "Put the box on the slab, Mr Summers, or…"

Paul didn't argue. He took a step nearer to Guy's tomb.

"Put the gun down now, or die." An American voice.

On Flight from Manchester UK to Reykjavik Iceland Onward to Halifax Nova Scotia: June 2008

How long it had been, reflected Ali. How long since he and Jafar, as he was known back then, along with Yusuf and the unfortunate Mahmoud, had located the deadly treasure in that cave up in the Elburz Mountains. Since they unearthed the miraculous medieval potions in that perilous black chest, which Jafar had so cleverly understood. *Over thirty years.* Thirty years of scientific work and careful preparation. Now at last, praise God, the plan was being fulfilled!

And *he*, Ali, none other, was chosen to be sent forth westward from Tehran, fittingly close to Alamut, as the ultimate assassin. Not just the assassin of a single leader, however important, like the Sunni Viziers or Sultans who were typical targets of old, but of millions of the faithless, *hundreds of millions, possibly billions in fact*. For this he was not furnished with the traditional poisoned dagger, but his very body was the poisonous weapon, infected with plague to form a medical time bomb. Truly, he was rewarded.

Alas that fellow discoverer Yasuf had come to such a terrible end, a great loss for the cause and for the Iranian government, otherwise there could have been perfect symmetry. The infected volunteer who'd flown eastward from Iran, Farhad, was a younger man; and indeed the task required stamina.

Ali sneezed explosively, twice, as he sat there in the wide-bodied jet. Not that he was suffering any symptoms of the genocide he carried within him; time enough yet, amply so! Not that he even had a cold. Surreptitiously, he'd taken a tiny pinch of snuff to irritate his nose. He wouldn't do so again. No need. The particles he'd already expelled would be travelling through the huge passenger space, to be caught up and recycled by the air conditioning until almost everyone should have breathed in many.

The fat woman next to him, dressed in a dowdy floral frock, darted a dirty look at Ali. He shrugged apologetically. She would die in agony the following month.

America's paranoid Homeland Security had spent a billion dollars on sensors in cities to detect the mass release of biological warfare agents, their so-called BioWatch. Ali could sneeze as he pleased right next to any of their sensors, and it wouldn't register the difference between his and a dozen other sneezes, not that the sensor would even be sensitive to an exotic filovirus spreading atmospherically as well as by contact. By the time a mass of victims was *erupting* a month after infection, it would be far too late.

Despite his criss-crossing of Europe in the closest proximity to people as possible, he had caught no cold. Maybe that was due to all the Vitamin C he was taking. More likely the hand of God protected him. And he was fit for fifty-five, although tired by the constant travelling, the need to catch most of his sleep while journeying by one means or another to establish a long trail of infection, on metros and buses, in airports and ports and shopping malls.

However, the night before this late afternoon flight he'd stayed in a hotel, Manchester's Radisson Edwardian with its Italianate frontage, apparently built on the site of some hall where an orchestra called the Hallé used to perform. So probably that name referred to the former *hall*, but Ali wasn't as polished regarding nuances of Western culture as his comrade Jafar.

And Ali had phoned out for a whore, from his large and richly decorated room, equipped with a Bang and Olufsen sound system, its mirrored slate bathroom Scandinavian-style. From an ad in the local entertainment guide he'd chosen *Intimate massage special extras slim Black Beauty*. 'High Class Escorts' mightn't be nearly as suitable. On the phone, it sounded as though the woman was chewing gum. "Radisson room 621 at 9 PM, right you are, honey."

"What is your name?"

"Sophie."

"I'll see you, Sophie."

"That's for sure."

Then Ali showered to cleanse himself, and prayed, after which he went down for dinner, something sustaining though not weighty.

He noted that in the Sienna Health Spa a beautician was wearing a mask, so he abandoned the idea of a manicure.

The restaurant's ceiling soared over him. Glossy black woodwork and velvet-red walls, goldenly adorned, exuded an atmosphere of ostentation, but he perceived the red and the black as symbolic of blood and death. The restaurant was called Opus One. This made him think of the English word *pus*. And then *pussy*. For both, how appropriate. A black maître d' seated him and brought a menu.

Nor was this the first occasion since leaving Tehran that he would fuck and slobber upon a whore as the surest way of passing on infection. An insurance policy, in case snuff and sneezing proved less effective than the minimal tests had suggested. Just a pity that the limits of a man's body at his age restricted the number of possible occasions. Of course Viagra was an option, but al-Maut ibn Hakim, the modern medical master, had forbidden the use of this chemical enhancement. None of the unfortunate test subjects had been given those blue pills while incubating plague. What unforeseen consequence, he'd demanded, might result from widening the arteries by blocking phosphodieasterase type 5, in a body under increasing covert attack?

Ali had found he could best sustain the stiffness of lust by dwelling upon the consequences for the whore a month later; at the same time embracing his own imminent death, which was the gateway to a Paradise of delights, *and* to ultimate enlightenment. Was fucking a compliant, naked female to death an anticipatory treat as well as a divine duty? Or might this besmirch his enlightened pleasures hereafter?

He ordered lobster Thermidor.

At a couple of minutes past nine, Ali opened the door to a skinny, tallish black girl of maybe nineteen. She wore a red leather coat, which slid open to reveal a cropped top and tight red leather mini-skirt. Red and black, blood and death. And pussy. Her bare navel bore a couple of cheap, goldeny rings. Her hair was short and wiry, nothing that he could clutch hold of. Once inside the room, she postured like an absurd film star or model and stuck out her palm.

"Hi. You pay in advance." And she proceeded to recite her brief menu of skills, robotically.

"Full," he specified.

"I don't do anal, and you use a condom."

"No condom. I'll pay more."

She considered, maybe assessing his likely state of health, and glanced around the luxuriously-appointed hotel room.

"No condom is fifty extra."

Money changed hands, and she stripped. Her pubes were shaved, and her breasts quite small. She looked as he imagined a completely emasculated eunuch would. Approaching Ali, she unbuttoned his shirt as he inhaled an excess of patchouli, then loosened his trousers, her hand wandering within, where his member was only partially, softly swollen. With both hands he grabbed her buttocks, pulling her against him. He wetly kissed her full lips, thrust his tongue.

She broke off. "Hey, none of that. No mouth on mouth. That's private."

As he already knew from her recital, she would suck a penis, yet he mustn't kiss her. Kisses were reserved for her boyfriend, or pimp.

"I want to kiss. I'll pay extra."

"Fifty," she said. "But right now."

So he reached into his back pocket for yet another banknote, which she quickly took bare-assed to her coat pocket while he quickly discarded trousers, shirt and briefs. He kept his socks on.

Soon she was on the bed and he was upon her, his tongue in her mouth. This assault, aided by the frottage of her hand, caused his member to stiffen sufficiently. Yet without the lubrication of a condom he could only bump, not yet enter even this whore who must be opened up several times a day, not until he slobbered upon his hand and anointed himself. Then he achieved entry, his tongue in her mouth once more, his mind upon the *water of death* that would ravage her, unravel her. Pressure built in his pump as she wrapped her legs around his rump to hasten him, panting and moaning theatrically. Yes, ravage her, and all her clients, and her clients' wives and children and their school friends, and the mothers and fathers of those friends in turn, radiating ripples from the blobs of infection tossed into a pool of unknown humanity here tonight.

After Sophie had gone away, a scant ten minutes later, he lay upon the bed in only his socks. To avoid any possible melancholy, he concentrated upon his achievements so far.

Kiev had been first, and Bucharest next, and then Budapest, the very name of that city suggesting its fate by pestilence. The crowded yellow trams of Budapest had occupied him for hours. Vienna the next day, and then Rome generously, to catch flocks of Christian tourists from all over the world, followed by a major sleep on a ferry, to Marseille as a homage, then a high-speed train onward to Paris, sneezing because of snuff.

Five whores so far, of whom black Sophie had been the latest. As well as vitamin C, Ali was eating a lot of Brazil nuts for their high content of selenium, an important component in the production of semen.

Montlume, Provence, France: June 2008

"Put the gun down now, or die." At that moment, a resounding din of music resumed. From out of the night, a gun held steadily two-handed, appeared Jack Turner in dark slacks and unzipped windcheater, moving through the gate and into the chapel. Abigail could only gape as Kamal half-turned and immediately raised both hands above his head. The sly Syrian's pistol was still in his clutch, but it no longer pointed at anybody, at the roof more like, nor was his finger on the trigger.

A moment later, very fast and unerringly, Kamal hurled his gun at the ICEman, hitting Jack full in the face. The weapon discharged and blood bloomed from Jack's nose. He staggered, one hand grasping at his damaged features, as Kamal first barrelled into Paul, elbowing him fiercely in the belly and seizing hold of the plastic box, then raced past Jack and out to be swallowed by darkness. Only seconds later: a car engine, just audible against the amplified music.

"Fuck, fuck." Jack was at the gate, wiping his eyes, gun pointed again. But he didn't fire. He dithered, maybe distracted by pain.

Abigail burst into tears. With immediate tension gone, sobs racked her. How stupid she'd been, how utterly stupid! She'd let Kamal give her orgasms that seemed now like epileptic fits, mindless frenzies, she had so surrendered herself. In the compelling ecstasy of his embrace, she'd disabled her perception, disabled her suspicion. She'd been stupefied, mesmerised, a blind fool... and a traitor too; way, way out of her depth, and so persistent in her naïvety. She hunched up. Self-revulsion shivered through her nervous system.

Still partly bent by Kamal's belly-blow, Paul nevertheless shuffled closer to Abigail. "Don't cry, Abi," he managed to utter in strained tones.

Jack lurched towards them, gun now pointing their way as if he was some black ops trooper rigidly targeted to murder. Blood stained his shirt.

"You gonna kill me?" gasped Abigail. "I can't bear thinking any more!"

"Kill you? I'd like to wallop the both of you on your sweet fucking bippies! But kill our only real specialists in what's going on? At the moment I'm just furious mad, not insane. The cunning fucker! Who shoots a man with his hands up? I mean shoots instantly! Coupla seconds, you don't know what's happening, he's surrendering, then *splat*. He could've been a pitcher for the Red Sox!"

Still snivelling and shivering, Abigail tried to straighten up.

"I... I think I owe you an apology, Mr Turner."

"Too true you do! You know how much time could've been saved if you'd only levelled with me?"

"You didn't... didn't exactly... make it easy."

"I guess not. Last days are upon us with a rush."

"Eh?" queried Paul, as Jack very gently dabbed his nose with a sleeve.

"Gotten kinda urgent lately, don't you think?" Dab, dab.

Abigail forced herself to interact. "The bullet didn't hit your nose?" she asked.

"No, my nose would've been torn off, obviously. But I'm a bit deafened. Bells ringing, or is that the music?" Jack glanced down at Kamal's gun. "Browning High Power. Fucking hard is what I'd call it."

"Is your nose broken?"

"Don't think so, though it sure hurts like hell. My rent-a-car's down below, that's why I didn't give chase, and because of you two dumbos. Where might you rush off to next?"

"So do we phone the police?" queried Paul. "Abigail speaks French."

"I *know* that Mam'zelle Smarty speaks French, but I'm not wanting to *explain* myself, ourselves, to dumb-ass police for the next six or eight hours. They could keep you criminals in custody; not at all convenient. God, I want Kamal by the balls, to squeeze."

Her lover, whose balls she had softly cupped, waggling her fingers while he fucked her, which had spurred him on so pleasurably. Or so she'd supposed. Abigail retched, but breathed hard and held down vomit.

"I'll pull out every fingernail."

Of Kamal's clever fingers, thought Abigail. He deserved that. No, he didn't. No one did. It was her own fault! She tightly clutched her stomach.

"Hang on," said Paul. "*Torture?* Haven't we learned anything yet?"

"Not nearly enough, you freaky liberal! And what would *you* do, if otherwise a few billion people were about to die, loathsomely? Weren't you just talking about him spreading *plague*, unless my hearing was already impaired?"

"Hey, who's with you, down below in your car?"

"Who's in it? Nobody."

"Do you mean you came *alone?* With no back-up?"

"Yes, you asshole."

"I'm so sorry," said Abigail to Paul. "For what I said to you. I was... deluded," she ended feebly.

"For want of a fingernail, or a few, civilization was lost. That's about it, right?"

"Fanatics can survive losing their fingernails," Paul commented.

"Yeah, well they can't claw you with them so much afterwards."

Abigail tried to shore herself up through anger. She grimaced, spreading her fingers and raking the air, enacting what she'd do to Kamal. His cheeks, but not his eyes.

"Mr Turner," she ventured, "I still think you're a bit unsuitable to be an officer of the US government."

"Oh, do call me Jack after all this time." He gazed around, at the torch burning bright on the burst tomb, at the scattered tools. "Such experiences shared, wouldn't you say?"

Abigail accepted the peace offer. "It was clever of you to find us on your own."

"Yeah, and *why* all on your ownsome?" added Paul. "And *how* did you find us?"

Jack bridled. "I'm not electronically alone. Your smartphone chirps exactly where you are all the time, so my people update me constantly."

Paul gasped "You bugged me! When you couldn't bug and follow Abi, you switched to me!"

"Got it in one. Plus another couple of tricks, which I shan't be telling an ace reporter, or it'll be all over the *Globe*." Jack turned to Abigail. "What I'm still missing is many of your e-mails, Instant Messaging or whatever, at least half the story, or maybe more. So we need to sit down together for a very long chat. This may be a chapel, but I don't notice a comfortable confessional. QED, your hotel. Besides, I need to clean up."

Jack bent and picked up the Browning High Power to pocket. "This baby makes a lot of noise. He must've got it at short notice. You two are lucky to be alive; if he'd obtained a silencer too, you wouldn't be."

Paul fought down his outrage. After all, being bugged had saved him, Abigail too. He gestured at the broken tomb. "This is gonna be in the news. Fingerprints? Take the tools with us? Oh, our car isn't here now. At least it's in Kamal's name, although Abi's listed as second driver."

"He'll abandon it as soon as possible and rent another, using a fresh card. People or cars, he'll throw away anything that's run out of use, or is useful to sacrifice. That guy is a complete professional."

These words brought more tears to Abigail's eyes; she couldn't hold them back. She felt degraded. She couldn't get a grip on her oscillating emotions.

"In fact," added Jack, "after I clean up we oughta switch your hotel, even though it's the middle of the night. I haven't got a place yet. I don't figure Kamal will come after you both again, or could get another gun so fast. But I don't care to underestimate him either, nor his colleagues as yet unknown, seeing as he had a courier waiting at the airport."

They wiped the tools.

"Right, let's go. Just keep one torch. Leave everything else."

During their steep descent to the village, the howling storm of metallic chords ceased once more. Massed clapping and cheering was just so much gentle surf by comparison. They came into the square, where a middle-aged local couple expressed shocked concern at Jack's bloodied appearance.

"Pas de problème," Abigail assured them." Il a tombé. Sur le nez."

Which must account for her red eyes and tear tracks too. Jack shrugged indifferently and headed for a parked Peugeot.

"Did you say *tomb*?" whispered Paul, aghast.

"I said he fell. *Tomber* means to fall."

"Ah."

Jack held out the car key on its rental company tab. "I got a bad headache."

Abigail accepted the key, but then a sob burst from her. She wasn't stable. Horror and disgust kept on catching up. And shame, such shame. Memories were a vivid torment. "Paul, please, will you drive?"

"Sure. Uh," he asked Jack, "am I insured for this car?"

"Just don't crash it or run red lights. Obey speed limits. Kamal probably does, no matter what hurry he's in."

Some time later, Jack cleaned up at the sink in the room that Abigail and Kamal had shared, also changing his shirt. His windcheater had fortunately escaped the worst of the blood flow, and anyhow the dried stains were hard to distinguish on its dark brown material. Then, unashamedly, Jack searched every cupboard and drawer and receptacle, yet in vain. Kamal's big travel bag was absent, so he'd dared a return visit, could conceivably be in the vicinity still.

Accordingly they transferred to the Ibis Montélimar Nord, to the north of the town on the N7 and very close to the A7 autoroute, attempting to ensure that they weren't followed along the way.

A two-storey hotel. Its windows seemed modern and robust, and Jack felt that a potential prowler would be more obvious in its few adjoining corridors than in a high-rise hotel.

Then the ICEman melted a little. Paul was dog tired, Abigail was scarcely managing to stay sane. He put off his interrogation, and let them sleep.

The Ibis Montélimar Nord Hotel, Montélimar, Provence, France: June 2008

Abigail woke to sunlight leaking through orange curtains, and a bed empty but for her. For a fleeting moment, she imagined that Kamal must have just gone in the bathroom. But memory crashed back upon her and she began to swear, "Shit shit shit shit…"

Have a shower, girl. No, soak in a bath and scrub his touch from your body. Yes, call yourself *girl*. Only a besotted teenager could have been so stupid, the sort of needy idiot who would even turn tricks for a pimp to please him. She yearned for chocolate, to banish the remembered taste of Kamal's kisses. The remaining nougat would have to do. Paul had placed the box in her room like a waiter providing complementary chocs and champagne. A dose of morphine might have been a better idea. Still, it was a kindly thought.

On impulse, she fired up her laptop before serious decontamination in the bathroom. Jack hadn't confiscated it, which she'd thought he might, or not yet anyhow. *What on Earth was she going to tell Jen?* Her need to confess was overwhelming; she must tell something, of betrayal in love at least, if not about the details of guns and deeper betrayal. An email was already waiting for her; she gasped upon reading it.

We must meet. Your life is in danger. K is not what he seems. I beg you not to tell him of this message. Are you still in Hama? Please reply. Fz.

Not what he seems… an understatement to say the least. But the warning was too late! And who was Fz? The email address was a random string of letters and numbers, but *.net.sy* ended it. Syria! It was sent from Syria. It came to her. Fz must be Fawzi; she knew no one else it could possibly be. No doubt Jack would want to dictate her reply, but she wasn't going to let him. She dabbed at the keyboard.

I'm in France, in Provence. Kamal tried to kill me, he's gone now. I can't believe I was so stupid. We found water of life, but he took it. I'm with a friend, and US aid, but what now? How can we stop him?

When Abigail emerged from the bathroom, wrapped in soft towelling, sugared up and scrubbed and glowing yet feeling only marginally better, there was already a reply.

Maybe I am talking to K. But I think not, he'd be more subtle. In any case, even your voice would not be proof of independence. But I'll trust. We will send someone, immediately, from southern Germany, arriving tomorrow. Give me an address. Though the gaze of the outside world will hurt us, the Ajaweed have agreed, it's time to expose that which has been cloaked for many centuries, but which also has riven us. Fz.

287

She immediately understood Fawzi's fear. Kamal's consummate dissimulation meant he could pretend to be just about anyone. Online, she reflected grimly, he could certainly be her. But who were the *Ajaweed*, who was *we*? She swiftly sent back.

In the artefacts room, you fiddled with the ring on the second finger of your left hand. I know this isn't proof, but it is me here. I need to consult. Stand by. Abigail.

And she sent something to Jen. Something short and simple, but also humiliating, desperate.

After another half an hour she was ready to face Jack, so she phoned his room, then Paul's. Jack's cross-examination would be embarrassing in the extreme, excruciating even, but at least she now had something to distract him with.

Whether it was Paul's idea or Jack's, coffee and a basket of *pain au chocolat* was waiting in the ICEman's room. She must stop thinking of Jack derogatively as the ICEman.

"Pain," said Paul lightly, using English pronunciation, "with chocolate. I won't ask how you feel."

"Got it in one," she told him, as he poured.

Presently, Paul was dismissed and it was Abigail's turn to pour out… explanations for Jack. He wanted their stories separately, the better to check for inconsistencies no doubt. Abigail enacted her distraction tactic and blurted out about Fawzi's email and the mysterious Ajaweed; that it was important to confirm a meeting as soon as possible. To no avail.

"Important or not, it'll have to wait. Right now I've no clue what you're babbling about! I want everything in proper order." He stared accusingly.

Abigail's heart sank. She remembered their last meeting back in Boston, how she'd wanted to tear out those hard blue eyes. But Jack was right all along, and she'd been wrong, very wrong. Fighting against bitterness and shame that bunched her jaw muscles as though to keep her words clamped inside, she started from the time she'd stayed in the department all night doing Internet research; even admitting that she'd kept some of her finds from Jack during their discussion at Totally Thai. In fact, Jack belied his ICEman label and was not as cold or probing as she'd expected; she supposed he knew much of the story already. She managed to hold back from tears until her guilty explanations were finally done, and then she did snivel as Jack's pale features twisted with scorn.

"You're an utter fool," he softly judged. "A harlot, and a traitor too."

Words that would normally have made her incandescent with rage simply made her sniffle and shiver instead. Was he being just? She was robbed of fight.

"Kamal can't have been sure how much you knew. He whisked you away to help sever your connections to authority, to me. And so he could spend time teasing out your knowledge, while he enjoyed you too of course. The panel of professors wasn't set up to help you, but to ensure they'd dragged out everything you'd discovered, to assess their potential vulnerabilities. Should it be necessary, killing you would be less risky than in America too; clearly he *did* come to the conclusion it was necessary, but Paul's phone call saved your life. Kamal couldn't let any Holy Water end up with the authorities, and also he saw a way to silence both you and Paul at the same time."

Sardonically, Jack offered her a handkerchief, but Abigail just bit on her lip. "I'm sorry, but I did find out more while I was there, in the Middle East."

"Seems likely," he continued, "that Kamal didn't know about the latest archaeological dig at Alamut. Isn't on top of everything, after all. And that Ruffie book you found was just a lucky break, *if* in fact 'The Triumph' and al-Hakim have anything at all to do with this."

"I'm sure they have! Fawzi…"

Jack laughed, a curiously high, mechanical sound, like a car trying to start when the engine wouldn't fire.

"Well well. So now *you're* trying to convince *me* that ancient history is driving modern terrorism!"

Abigail sniffed and hung her head. It was true. Kamal had wrecked her life, but her eyes were uncovered.

"God can forgive," added Jack unexpectedly, still wagging the handkerchief, "even if *I* find it hard. Just do the right thing from now on. Do as you're told."

Abigail nodded numbly.

"There's one thing I don't get. Who the hell were those guys dressed in black? They pop up as though they're on the lookout for something. Well-connected and knowledgeable. Kamal doesn't seem to have any idea, but he acts warily."

Abigail shrugged. "I've no idea either. Maybe this person coming from Germany will tell us."

"Just forget about that Fuzzy guy for the moment…"

"Fawzi."

"That's what I said. Forget about him and speculate based on what you know."

Abigail concentrated. "In Iran I thought they might be government guys, keeping an eye on foreigners. But I don't think Kamal really believed that, so in the end neither did I." She hated having to say his name. "Thinking back, I had the impression he might have made a decent guess about who they were, but he wasn't sure. He tended not to talk about things until he *was* sure about them, so I never pushed. Oh, and I think they caught up with us again at Masyaf. Just before... Well, there was a guy with binoculars."

"You didn't mention that earlier."

Abigail smiled bleakly. "I just remembered. Good interrogation technique."

"Like, pain with chocolate?" Jack's echo of Paul's little joke upset her. That'd been private, between friends! She caught herself, and breathed deeply; she *mustn't* be offended by Jack's manner. He'd saved her life, something Kamal did only for the nastiest of motives. Jack had saved Paul's life too. At least now she was making amends, siding with authority against the bad guys, against *him*, the slyest of Syrians, the slyest of men. Perhaps one day she'd get revenge; but even now, could she really hurt him?

"Well, maybe Kamal has rivals, rival terrorists that is."

"You think so?" Jack fished a photo from his pocket. "Recognize him?"

The photo wasn't good quality, a blurred image taken in some shop? But the face, the line above the eyebrow, like a double eyebrow...!

"It's the man who tried to kill me in Syria!"

"Are you sure?"

Abigail nodded vigorously. "He seemed strangely known to me, like déjà-vu, as if I'd seen him before..."

"This man murdered your cleric, Walid. The photo's cleaned up from CCTV footage taken at a car-hire counter in Boston."

Abigail's blood ran cold. Then she recalled. The CMES reception!

"I saw him. I saw him at a reception in the Center for Middle Eastern Studies, that's where!"

"He doesn't figure in the mug-shots of known terrorists at large, or he'd never have got into America, except maybe over the Mexican border. Anyhow, Kamal must have pulled him out, same time as he left himself. New mission, get in position."

"No! That shit couldn't already have...!"

"Already been planning to kill you? After he'd *squeezed* all your knowledge out of you, on honeymoon? Which yesterday were you born?"

Graven in Abigail's mind was the murderous intent on the face of her would-be assassin... Probably the very last thing dear Walid saw too... except that was at night, it was dark... and now for Walid it would *always* be dark.

Abigail pressed her nails into her palms.

"Right," said Jack. "Paul's session next. I'll phone him to come since I don't think you'll want to summon him."

Abigail fled swiftly to her room so they wouldn't pass in the corridor, in case she lost control of her tear ducts. She tried to empty her mind of everything, digging out a rarely used MP3 player from the bottom of her bag and replacing thought with ridiculously loud music, as she curled into a foetal position on the bed.

Later, Jack gathered them both together again. "And now, boys and girls," he announced, "I'm going to tell you something about the famous fragment of poetry. While Abigail was swanning around the Middle East I impounded it from the university library. "What the university couldn't pick up, well, we use better labs. Electron microscopy, for instance…"

"The university has that too," defended Paul bravely on Abigail's behalf. "I'm sure it's just a case of project priority and waiting to get some time on the machine."

"Shut up!" Jack tone was dangerously sharp. Paul visibly clamped his lips together.

"*We* gave it *top* priority. The partial words you couldn't see, Abigail, are '*water of life and more of…*' We used a prof in New York for the translation. Wouldn't have dreamed of bothering you! I've a note of the Provençal words." He produced an index card and held it out. Upon it was: *Aiga de vida e mai de mort.*

Abigail nodded, then recited slowly: "water of life and more of death, swells and overflows, while the strong eagle teacher of many lessons…, watches down from high, with the vision to judge what we make of the truth, before our term is ended…

"So, it isn't death *itself* that overflows after all! No wonder we couldn't find a religious context. It's like I said at Krak, this poem isn't primarily rooted in religion… Oh…" She realised she'd said that to Kamal, who in fact would already have known. "It's the *waters* that swell and overflow, somehow? Ah, and that means as well as *water of life*, there's *water of death*. Yes! I think that was written in 'The Triumph'," she continued excitedly, her bitterness momentarily erased by the sweet taste of academic breakthrough. "If you were an Oxford don and you absolutely knew that *water of life* meant esoteric or holy knowledge, what would you think *water of death* meant?"

"Unholy knowledge?" suggested Paul, after an awkward pause.

"Precisely! Yes! Like the *Baha'is* say. *The water of death flows from the pen of Satan.* But Jen's don was wrong, back then before the war, before 'The Triumph' was stolen. That poem references actual fluid, *not* a metaphor for knowledge. It's just the same for our fragment. Oh!" Abigail's tone collapsed to a strangled murmur. "Walid must have guessed, when he was investigating for me, that's why…"

Paul and Jack, somewhat lost, exchanged glances.

"Okay. So the *water of death* means plague, that's all I really need to know." But Jack's tone rose slightly on the last word, as though questioning.

"Without the *water of life*, plague may mean global disaster," added Paul.

"We had the *water of life* in our hands! And Kamal stole it."

"Hey," said Jack, boldly steering them away from dejection. "Now we can see about this guy that Fuzzy's sending. Paul, google for Ajaweed on that deluxe device of yours. Let's find out what we're dealing with."

"Deluxe enough to be much more useful than yours!" Paul got busy.

"We ought to get a bit further away from Montlume, somewhere with more tourists so we can mingle in."

"Avignon's not far away, to the south," Abigail put in mechanically. My translation of *de riba sort* was right after all, she thought bitterly, *overflows*. Nothing to do with the dead 'coming out from the earth' as she'd speculated with Walid. The *water of death* swells in its victims and overflows across the population. But how, in some apparently lesser way, did the *water of life* similarly spread?

"Still after your papal palace, huh?"

"It might cheer her up," Paul pointed out.

"Okay okay! Google for a hotel in Avignon as well. Book it too if you can do that online."

"Er... Are we on official expenses now?"

Jack rolled his eyes. "You ought to be in prison, not on expenses! But I guess as you've actually been co-operative *at last*...."

Paul set off a separate search window for four-star hotels. "Hey, there's all sorts on Ajaweed. It's a personal name for a start, so lots of Facebook entries and such, then stuff on Libya, various businesses, a catering service, links in Arabic script and other foreign languages, a...."

"Add Syria as a search term," cut in Jack.

"Oh, yeah... Ah... that's better. I'd say the most likely bet is the religious leaders of the Druze community. The literal meaning of their name is *the good*."

"The *what* community?" asked Jack.

"The Druze," replied Abigail wearily. "That makes a weird kind of sense. They used to be Ismailis, although that was a thousand years ago, before the two diverged. I know almost nothing about them though. They're a very tight-knit community, almost closed to the outside world."

Having found the 4-star Hotel Cloître Saint-Louis in the very heart of Avignon, Paul tried to suppress a smirk. It was both cosy and swanky together, a 17th century religious building with a modern extension by top architect Jean Nouvel. He entered details for a booking; no doubt it'd make a noticeable dint in Jack's departmental budget.

"A thousand years, huh? Well, six hundred, seven hundred, a thousand, what's the difference in this game? The ghosts of history are rising up. This Ajaweed guy better be as *good* as his name though. I'm not as gullible as Abigail, and if there's any funny business this time around, I'll be shooting first and asking questions later."

"Errm...We're all set for Avignon," Paul announced into the shocked silence. Abigail wondered whether Jack's words were just bravado, or whether he really meant them.

"Right, you both got the afternoon off. I need to think."

"Excuse me," chirped Paul, "but what about Kamal and the Holy Water? Isn't it urgent to...?"

"He'll be out of the country by now," snapped Jack, "and I already told my guys. Nothing more we can do in that department. Give the hotel address to Abi, so she can email it to Fuzzy. You," he added, fixing an imperative gaze on Abigail, "get a phone number out of them, so we can set up the time later, *and* so we at least have a lead if something goes wrong,"

Paul escorted Abigail back to her room, to the door and no further. "Hey, you *sure* you don't want to grab something to eat?" asked Paul hopefully.

"I told you, I'm not hungry. I need... to be alone."

"Did Jack ask you many questions?"

"It wasn't too awful," she lied. Well, it *could* have been worse. Not just a *harlot* and a *traitor* and *born yesterday*. Jack could have ordered her to summon Paul.

"Did he record any of it?"

Abigail looked blank. "Not that I noticed."

Paul shook his head. "Altogether, very unprofessional. And no colleague in the room either. Bad Jack. He never said why he came without back-up."

"He must have a reason."

"Yeah, but *what* reason? He clearly hasn't liaised with the French police either."

"Oh Paul, don't cast doubt on him too! I've already been down that blind alley. You were right about Kamal, so utterly right, and I was so dumb. But... please, not again." Tears started.

Paul eyed her with heartfelt concern.

"I'm sorry," he murmured, touching her arm. His goofy smile appeared. "Probably just my suspicious reporter mode kicking in. And I don't much like the guy either. He's got scary religious stuff inside; a wound-up spring of fervour, clockwork judgement."

"Paul! I don't really like him either. But we *have* to make amends."

"Okay. You're right, Abi."

Comforted, she let herself into her room.

Going on for 2pm in France, so 7am in Nebraska. Brother George was an early riser, he'd be up by now. But it was probably best to call tomorrow, after they'd visited this Aveen-yon place. The Druze big-wig might have an important angle. Besides, how to play this threat of a haemorrhagic plague pandemic? It was vaster than anything he'd suspected when he first went after Abigail. Foremost, Jack was an officer of God: In Whom We Trust. We, being the good old USA. Surely the Last Days were approaching fast, when entire countries would fold up or fall apart, preceded by the Rapture, when the godly would vanish.

What would the experience be like? A sudden, blissful surge of ecstatic communion with the highest power in the universe. To be almost instantaneously in His presence! Along with the other faithful; butt-naked, clothes left behind on Earth, yet feeling so innocent too! So many naked bodies, all repaired from the defects of ageing or illness; their angelic beauty restored, or granted anew, to men and to women alike. Able to experience pleasures, although spiritual bliss would of course far outweigh permitted enjoyments, which in any case would simultaneously be celestial communions.

Would faithful children, once raptured, *mature* as it were, to ideal adult embodiment? Would they remain forever pre-sexual, in an endless state of grace?

So much that was wondrous might soon now be discovered!

And would the faithful be able to look down upon the sordid plane of existence they'd left behind? Where the horrors and glories of the last days led inexorably towards the Battle of Armageddon; as some Antichrist arose to govern by violent dictatorship a ravaged world where relentless plagues raged, until Jesus Himself returned with his cleansing sword to put paid forever to history, and inaugurate eternity.

And, since its reason for existence had expired, would the universe cease at this point? He'd read that the structure of space-time was unstable. If it flipped to a new state, then *nothingness* could propagate outward from the redeemed Earth at the speed of light. *No*, at the speed of darkness, infinitely faster! Engulfing dark would annul the whole of creation, which had served its purpose. Stars and entire galaxies would vanish more swiftly than they could be seen to vanish; who would even be aware of this except God in His Glory?

In his bedroom in the Ibis Montélimar Nord, Jack knelt and prayed fervently.

Avignon, Provence, France: June 2008

Before breakfast that morning, and before giving Jack the phone number too, Abigail plucked up her trampled courage and called the Druze man. She'd instinctively trusted Fawzi, but remembered his hesitancy. Perhaps a messenger from Fawzi's hidden community would be hesitant too; she didn't want Jack's aggressive manner to put him off. As it turned out the guy was extremely nervous, much more so than herself, keeping his words to an absolute minimum. He would only meet in public, preferably a controlled environment with gates and security, maybe a museum.

At which point the palace of the Popes popped into Abigail's head. "Yes. Wait *beyond* the ticket barrier. Fawzi says you have a green scarf. Tie it around your wrist."

He'd hung up abruptly, leaving a cold feeling of apprehension behind. Abigail had drunk far more than her fill of cloak and dagger excitement.

Jack did the driving to Avignon while Paul used his smartphone for navigation. Rather than making straight for Rue du Portail Boquier and the Hotel Cloître Saint-Louis, Paul insisted that Jack drive most of the way around the busy periphery boulevards. As towers and toothed ramparts loomed on one side, with steeples poking up everywhere from behind this curtain of old stone, the broad river Rhône shone to the other. Abigail eagerly viewed the famous white bridge, to which clung a chapel rather like a fortification tower. She realised Paul had chosen the route just to give her this sight.

"Oh," exclaimed Paul as they passed by, "but the Pont stops in the middle of the river! What use is that? If people danced along it like the song says, they'd end up in the water."

Despite herself, Abigail laughed at his droll clownery. For the first time in quite a while. "All the rest of the bridge fell down."

"All fall down," commented Jack. "That's a different song, about plague."

"Will you shut up? We're allowed to enjoy the sights."

When they finally reached the hotel, off the tree-lined Cours Jean Jaurès, they found it enchanting. Diners were enjoying their lunch in a cloistered courtyard with a few trees, at tables with red cloths that were set along a vaulted arcade. The trio went to check in, Abigail doing the talking.

Paul eyed Jack. "It's on you, I think, being as how we're advisors to ICE."

"Wouldn't have it otherwise." Out came a credit card, doubtless government issue.

Near reception, newspapers were on sale. As they left the desk, card keys in hand, Abigail noticed a midday edition with a story: *Mystère de Vandalisme d'une Chapelle à Montlume*. The second ever coverage of her life by the popular press was even more unwelcome than the first had been. Reluctantly, she bought a copy.

As they headed to their rooms, Paul carrying her baggage, she summarised: "Police don't think the perps were vandals attracted by the rock concert, though maybe they used it as cover. That's on account of the equipment they brought. But why, the paper speculates, did they abandon all the gear? No one reports disturbing them. Did they have an accident? Local residents recount seeing a probable foreigner, white, late thirties, male, face and shirt stained with blood, accompanied by another man and by a woman who spoke French, though perhaps not the French of France. The hand bones of the skeleton in the wrecked tomb seem to have been disturbed. Maybe something was taken, like a ring? That's about it. Enquiries are ongoing."

"What did you do with your shirt?" whispered Paul, as though he feared that police were already just around the corner.

"Put it in a laundry bag from the Pines place and stuck it in here." Jack's leather travel bag. "I'll get rid of it. I need to dump my gun too before we check-in at an airport for home, Kamal's as well. I flew American, so that was fixable, but of course it's French security on the way out. Never mind about these things, my children, Uncle Jack has lots of experience. No one will notice us here, too many tourists."

Paul swiftly changed the subject. "Can we have lunch," he suggested hopefully, "in the old stone corridor here?"

"I'm not sure I'm all that hungry," replied Abigail. "It looked high-end gastronomic. Maybe drop in to somewhere while we're walking around?"

"Much better plan," agreed Jack. "A drawn-out French lunch would make us late for the meeting."

Boston, Massachusetts: June 2008

And so by the giant overnight ferry, Ali entered the most hated nation. From the port of Boston he took a cab to a Macy's department store at the very heart of the city, as a big bronze disc in the sidewalk proclaimed. Police were on horses here, cars appeared to be banned and pedestrians wandered as they pleased. At this very point, strangely, a Summer Street suddenly became a *Winter* Street. Just so, would the carefree scene of today abruptly reverse in a few weeks from now! The dying would stagger and collapse here, their bodies rotting while still alive.

Ali bought a newspaper, then sat down at a sidewalk café below the imposing façade of some department store, at the edge of which hung four bells, two by two in a niche. He imagined those bells clanging, warning of pestilence even as some people felt the first throbbing in their head, succumbing to fear as their eyes become sore. Vain peals; the time for warnings would be long past. No alarm would save them.

After the pestilence, there would be so many denuded cities around the world still full of a vast wealth of *things*, which any surviving and organised society could make use of just as it pleased, subject to the divine will. A rekindling of the triumphant early years of Islam, when invincible armies had gone forth in all directions.

What he was about to achieve would be far more potent and lethal than if he could, impractically, have smuggled in a dirty bomb to spread radioactivity around. He imagined this city almost stripped of inhabitants, *living* inhabitants at least. Thanks to the ancient skill of al-Hakim and the modern technology of al-FaQ, only privileged Ismailis and any Muslim women who'd been on the Hajj would remain untouched.

Courtesy of a pinch of snuff, he sneezed copiously, using the pages of the *Boston Globe* as a big fan to waft his nasal discharge upon its way.

After coffee and syrupy wild blueberry pancakes, Ali headed onward. Winter Street led to Park Street, the whole west side of which opened upon a huge swathe of grass and trees crisscrossed by paths, a wholly unsuitable place for spreading infection. An ornate two-tiered fountain played, as did some kids. He picked up his pace. Soon streets led uphill as the land rose, yet the architecture was too stately and distinguished for his purpose; he needed an area with a higher concentration of people.

Almost, he retraced his route, but then instead pressed on. The genteel slope pitched down again, soon becoming bohemian. The streets were busier, with cafés and grocers, pizzerias and barber shops, music issuing from the open windows of apartments. He looked along a leafy Myrtle Street where youngsters were playing stickball, then continued on for a while before deciding that hereabouts was appropriate to visit some local bar for a soft drink; and besides, he needed a pee.

The thin-faced barman was morose, maybe because Ali only ordered an apple juice, or maybe the young man was just having a bad day. Certainly no ethnic prejudice seemed to account for this sullenness. Perhaps the guy had lost a girlfriend, or he'd come down in the world recently, got himself fired from a good job so that he had to work in this dim place. Well, he might have a *much* worse day in about a month's time, unless he wore surgical gloves when it came to handling Ali's emptied glass. The man had been chewing at the skin around his fingernails. There he was, at it again, worrying at a bit of loose flesh, providing an entry point into his body.

The bar was called the Leprechaun, whatever that might be. Surely nothing to do with leprosy, a very slow disease. For some reason verdant posters advertising Ireland alternated with framed sepia photos of some city in the past. A large photo occupied prime position on the rear wall, which even Ali could recognize was President Kennedy in the company of some blonde, who might be a film star. Jaunty songs backed by raucous fiddle tones were piped through old speakers. When Ali got up to leave, he licked around the rim of his glass before considerately placing it back on the counter in front of the barman, who automatically took it with a distracted grunt.

Ali emerged from the neighbourhood into a busy, wide street with the name of Cambridge. So this must lead, sooner or later, to Cambridge where... yes, at élite Harvard University, the flower of America's brightest youth would be.

Ahead he could see a long bridge across a river, though before that a large overhead traffic sign indicated right for Massachusetts General Hospital. Why not, why not indeed? Physically vulnerable people went to hospitals; and to plant pestilence there would strike an early blow at nurses and doctors.

As he proceeded, a quartet of short towers rising from the piers of the bridge bizarrely reminded him of squat, dwarf minarets. Soon he was veering right past the Liberty Hotel, a robust, historic-looking building of granite blocks around an octagonal rotunda. A former jail, evidently, transformed luxuriously within.

The main entrance to the hospital, on a high podium, was by way of twin stairways leading up to a portico of columns. A temple to medicine! Within, many day patients, visitors, and medical staff all came and went. Information panels around the walls highlighted the first use of ether in the world, the first use of smallpox vaccine, a Nobel prize for developing the polio vaccine, the first human kidney transplant, plus the first successful replantation of a human limb, torn off some boy, and many other firsts. Plenty to read while he loitered. He saw there were public tours to the operating theatre where ether was first used.

After studying the hospital's visitor map, Ali took snuff and then roamed as much as he could. Maybe this would be the first hospital in America where the staff would succumb to plague, as if a traitor lurked within.

Then he went back towards the bridge, to the subway station nearby, so to be transported to Harvard.

True, the pestilence would strike young and old alike. Yet there'd be a poignancy to privileged young people being reaped in the earlier days, while the media might still have the capacity to transfix the populace on such a national misfortune, following soon in the wake of terrible news breaking elsewhere in the world.

The Pope's Palace, Avignon, Provence, France: June 2008

The mysterious Druze was heavily moustachioed and ruggedly handsome. Or rather, he was once ruggedly handsome, corrected Abigail. His hair was greying and his features had started to sag. He wore a dark suit.

She and Paul quickly introduced themselves, but he refused to give a name in return. Like Fawzi, his head twitched from side to side, as though he constantly expected trouble. Jack stayed silent. Rather than start straight into serious exchange, and to first get comfortable with each other, they stepped into the palace.

Inside, what a maze of marbled corridors, vaulted halls and gilded chapels, with richly appointed audience chambers for meetings with cardinals and kings! Half of the sprawling colossus was a riot of fancy ceilings and frolicsome frescos. Those popes must sure have known how to live.

Far from being more comfortable, the Druze looked overwhelmed.

"Such ostentation in the name of God!" He shook his head. "Our plain *khalwa* are all we need. Even a typical mosque is not an appropriately humble environment in which to meet God." His voice was throaty, powerful, like a wood-saw doing its work.

"You don't use mosques? Isn't your religion considered a branch of Islam?" queried Abigail, in polite tones.

"The *Tawhid*, the Unity, is what it is. But both Sunnis and Shi'a have persecuted us over the ages. The Christians too, *and* other minorities, even the Ismailis though more than a thousand years ago. Much of our path was shared with them."

"Wow," commented Paul. "Tough deal. Do you have any friends?"

The Druze grimaced. "We do what is necessary to survive."

"And just what is necessary now?" Typically, Jack's voice was sharp.

The Druze ignored him and addressed Abigail. "We acknowledge the divinity of al-Hakim, and obey his wishes as they come down to us through the ages."

"Al-Hakim the 11th century Ismaili Caliph, in Egypt?" Abigail hesitantly confirmed.

"Yes. In doing so, our shared experience with the Ismailis ceased."

"To them, he is *not* divine."

"They, ah… lack true vision."

They found some seats, in a corridor at the entrance to a vast and elegant chamber. Phalanxes of Chinese tourists marched past. Instinctively, Abigail felt she knew where the Druze was headed. "Go on," she urged.

"In the mid-twelfth century, a man who called himself al-Hakim appeared in the Syrian mountains. This was not to the liking of our ancestors, for we revered that name then just as we do now. Yet also it was of little consequence, for he was but a man, and he kept himself to the Ismaili community, separate to us, living chiefly at al-Kahf and later at Masyaf. But this man was a physician, as his name suggests…"

Abigail sucked in her breath. "A brilliant physician! *The sword of Allah, the shield of Allah, the possessed.*"

The Druze vigorously nodded his head. "Just so, just so! He had yet to earn that accolade, but his reputation grew and grew. He helped Rashid al-Din Sinan to power, he who was the most famed and able of the Syrian Ismaili leaders. Then he left, for a long time, first to Alamut, and perhaps thence to Africa. Our leaders of old were relieved, for some among the community asked why it was that God did not strike this man down for using a divine name, while others wondered at the magical nature of his cures, many of which it became clear he had lent to Sinan."

"He *was* at Alamut, though I don't know the dates." So much for Kamal's pet professors discrediting Ruffie's book.

An American tour leader stepped briskly past them, waving a small U.S. flag and calling out very loudly to the youngsters behind her: "Follow me, follow me!" Abigail checked on her companions. Jack looked bored. Paul glanced supportively back at her.

"Our real problems began when he returned, white-haired but unbent, and with the power of God in his hand!"

Suddenly, Jack was not bored but angry. "That's blasphemy! No one carries the power of the Lord!"

"Hey, chill," calmed Paul. "This was the twelfth century. Let's just hear the story."

Jack growled, but subsided.

"What power?" prompted Abigail.

"The sword of Allah, plague, which he could unsheathe at will; the shield of Allah, an ability to protect those whom he so chose. And he was possessed of a holy spirit, like a pure fire, seeing visions of things to come. He would answer to none in Syria save Sinan, because of their past relationship, and because he was still a good Ismaili."

"Er… look," said Paul. "How can you really know all this is true? I mean, after all those years."

The Druze smiled bleakly. "We have always kept a close watch on our neighbours. It is… necessary. And even among the famous dissimulators, we dissimulate. We did so then, and still we do so now. Our own people witnessed the terrible demonstrations, and recorded them. We still have the writings."

"Fawzi!" exclaimed Abigail. "He's your man dissimulating among the modern Ismailis."

"One of them, yes. He is young, but he serves us well. He also understands modern technology and the modern world. He wasn't sure who you were, but he did his best to warn, without directly giving anything away. Yet there is a greater reason than mere witness why we remember so well. It is not the part of one of the Ajaweed to instruct outsiders, yet..."

"Yet it is necessary," completed Jack.

The Druze bobbed his head. Abigail noticed that his hands were clasped tightly together. A nervous tick periodically made one of his eyes appear to wink.

"Part of our religion is a belief in reincarnation."

Jack soughed his breath and rolled his eyes, but combined glares from Abigail and Paul kept him silent.

"Some of our twelfth century community believed that no one could possess such power unless... unless they were divine. They believed this al-Hakim to be a reincarnation of He whom we worship. The heresy was never wholly stamped out. It was held at bay only by a promise to keep an open mind, and to closely monitor the impact of the *waters of life* and the *waters of death* upon the world. Over the ages, we have done just that, and although by this means the controversy was successfully sealed within the core of our leadership, a raw controversy it has remained."

Abigail was astounded. "Then you know..."

"Much," cut in the heavy saw-tone of the Druze. "But not all. In 1345 A.D. the Nizaris set plague in Sarai, the northern capital of the Mongols, at the opposite end of the Caspian to what was once their own heartlands. They targeted Europe, too; presumably they weren't sure whether a natural spread would do this job for them. But we don't know why they waited so long, almost ninety years after the fall of Alamut, until their culture in Persia was at the edge of extinction."

"A last resort?" suggested Paul.

"Perhaps. It's the most terrible and indiscriminate weapon imaginable. Whole cities were wiped out. Nations were brought to their knees, with two-thirds of their people gone. And we know the Nizaris could protect but a few of their own."

An attendant walked past them for the third time.

Abigail was both elated and scared by the sudden confirmation of so much they'd suspected over the last few weeks. A sense of unreality crept over her.

"We'd better shift," murmured Jack.

They attempted to find a quieter area, and so came across the older half of the palace, as austere as a monastery, a complete contrast.

"This house still dwarfs God's children," rasped the Druze, "which it should not. But it is nevertheless much more suitable. What caused the Popes to leave a humble path behind, and live in that garish monstrosity?"

"Power," stated Jack.

"Ah yes. That. Obscene things are often done with it. Obscene things to get it too. Our community in Europe is not large. I was one of only two European Ahl al-Tawheed, sons of Unity, who knows this story. Yet now there is just me."

"I'm sorry?" queried Abigail. "You mean…"

"Al-FaQ killed the other, a year ago. And a leader from our Syrian homeland too. They were driving through the Jebel Ansariye and were forced over the edge of a cliff."

Abigail's stomach lurched. "Oh my God!"

Jack was apparently unmoved. "Who's al-FaQ?"

The eyes of the Druze leader widened. "Do you not know the name of your enemy?" He pulled at his impressive moustache. "Al-Fida'een al-Qiyama," he whispered. "The Faithful of the Resurrection".

"The Resurrection!" breathed Abigail. "The Resurrection enacted by Hasan II in Alamut, when Shari'ah law was abandoned."

"Just so. Al-FaQ do not seriously intend to eliminate our entire leadership. It was a warning. A warning never to reveal the story I'm now telling you."

Paul whistled softly. "Then we're extremely grateful to you," he enthused.

The Druze shrugged. "More than we fear al-FaQ, we fear that this revelation, so long repressed, so explosive to us, will blow our community apart. But how will it benefit us, if the whole world is blown apart instead?"

"Can they really do that?"

The moustache was tugged again. The eye flickered. "They've already done it once, long ago."

An awkward silence was broken by Paul. "What I don't understand is how the stuff can still be active after all this time. I mean, vaccines are basically viral too, aren't they? And they have to be carried around in chilled containers, don't they?"

The Druze made a strange bobbing motion, as though praying, or asking for forgiveness. Fear stalked across his mien, as though he might bolt at any second. "*The water of death* remained active from al-Hakim's time, beyond the fall of Alamut," he whispered hoarsely, "then longer still, until it was seeded in Sarai. Over 150 years overall. In modern times, this fact has amplified our

Ian Watson & Andy West

controversy. Even some of our leaders who do *not* believe in the second Hakim's divinity, believe in the *divinity of the waters.*" He half rose, then sat back down again.

Jack gazed at him, pale faced and goggle-eyed. "Do you?"

"I must go…"

"Wait!" said Abigail. Can you tell us about Sinaldin? Sinan al-Din ibn Nasir?"

An anguished sigh, almost a groan, but then he spoke. "On the surface, it seemed that the relationship between the Ismailis in Syria and the Crusaders blew hot and cold, as you say. But underneath, channels were *always* kept open, particularly with the Hospitallers, and came to be handled very discreetly by a constant family dynasty upon each side. This was convenient for, what do you Americans say? Ah, yes, plausible deniability, at certain times.

"But these link families became powerful through their close association, and the knowledge communicated to each of what passed in the different world of the other. They formed their own alliance, a cynical alliance *within* an alliance, you might say, which eventually outlived its original purpose. This purpose survived the thirteenth century reduction in Nizari power, the Hospitallers' move to Rhodes, even the fall of the Templars. Sinan al-Din ibn Nasir was from the dynasty on the Ismaili side, of course."

"Did he carry the *water of death* into Europe?" interrupted Jack.

"We've always believed so, though we know little of his later life in the West. It was said that he led a terrorist cell in al-Andalus, co-ordinating the activities of various militant minorities. His woman there was apparently the cell's propagandist, circulating literature that contained veiled Shi'a or Ismaili messages."

"Oh!" Abigail couldn't help herself. "Oh no. Safiyya, writing terrorist propaganda!"

"I told you!" snapped Jack. "Right back at the start!"

The Druze rose, stepped away, then turned back towards them. "Secretly, our destiny has been tied to the waters for centuries, hence we have long named them *the waters of destiny.* But now the secret is out, and our destiny surely is almost upon us." He bowed his head, pulling something from around his neck, then tossed a small object into Abigail's lap.

She raised up a yellowed tooth dangling on a chain, a large molar rooted in silver, polished as though by long contact.

"On his return, the second Hakim brought a monkey with him. It's nickname was a corruption of the phrase, *the grey protector.* Make of that what you will! After it died, Hakim dissected it. Later, the remains were disposed of, but for some reason the Ismailis kept its teeth, perhaps to make into charms. Yet those lay almost forgotten in a jar for many years, until one of our people, er, liberated them. Since that time, almost eight centuries ago, the highest in our leadership has each worn a tooth, to constantly remind us of our controversy, and of our doubt.

"Now *our* problem," grated the Druze, "is *your* problem too. The world's problem!" He turned away.

"Wait!" urged Abigail once more.

"Your watchers," Jack called out tightly, "they dress in modern black gear, is that right?"

But the Druze fled, disappearing down a grey stone corridor as though pursued.

Paul displayed one of his goofy grins. "Well, that was quite an eye-opener!" The act didn't hide a tremor in his voice.

They found their way back out to sunshine, and warm reality.

After the palace, Jack let Paul and Abigail have time to themselves. They roamed cute old cobbled streets. Posters all over were advertising some festival of theatre and dance, due the next month. It looked morally suspect; that was France for you.

"Jack's being pretty lax with us now," commented Paul. "What's to stop us escaping his jurisdiction?"

"Why would we want to?" returned Abigail sharply. "We messed up. Now we've got to help him. Help him to save the world."

"Hey, maybe it's not that serious. Despite a distraught Druze, what's the real chance that these ancient potions still work?"

"Kamal thinks they do. So they must. I know him."

Paul frowned.

They stopped at a bistro to eat some lamb and eggplant, washed down with glasses of what Jack would probably call Coat of the Rhone. Then Paul bought Abigail chocs filled with oregano liqueur. People had weird tastes hereabouts, but alcohol hidden in Abigail's favourite substance was good for keeping her tipsily relaxed. Then there was more pleasant wandering, poking about in curio shops and pretending to be care-free tourists. Paul did his utmost to keep her mind away from potions and plague and Syrian lady-killers, and mostly succeeded.

Hotel Cloître Saint-Louis, Avignon, Provence, France: June 2008

Would Heaven be a strictly spiritual place? wondered Jack. Or a more fun place? Or maybe both at once, by the grace of God. Austere and luxurious together, like that palace. Time would tell. Not much time now, perhaps... He was footsore, and he needed to call Brother George. Little opportunity hitherto.

"Brother George? Yeah, Jack. I'm in France... Yes, France as in Paris and the Eiffel Tower, except I'm in the south, in the land of Van Go's dayglo sunflowers, you know? I've found out something real amazing and scary, means the last days might only be months away! My obvious duty, and as fast as possible... Well, since this is a terrorist plot that could come off worldwide, and real *big* this time... No, not rogue nuclear weapons. I'd say this is potentially a lot lot worse. Thing is, given what we know about the Temple, this might trigger the Rapture, and I heed a higher duty also. After I explain, maybe we could pray together on the phone for guidance?

"Right... Okay. Do you know anything about the Ismailis? Or the Druze? Oh...wow, that's good. Well you see, there's these waters, the *waters of destiny*, which may... Now look, I'm only relating this, they may be divinely derived... No, please, listen to the rest...listen..."

And so Jack spilled out a long tale to Brother George, whose study and knowledge of the Holy Land and neighbouring areas, Jack reckoned, were second to none.

"Yeah, that's what I said. I almost got my hands on the protection! What's *supposed* to be that anyhow, stuck away in a tomb hundreds of years old, only the Lord knows if it was still viable. Except, I was taken by surprise. Otherwise I coulda couriered a sample to you for that crackerjack lab at Faith University. Except, it was Jack who got cracked in the face... Yeah, I'm all right, thanks for your concern. Yeah, the Syrian took it. I guess the Lord can't have intended... Yeah, sure, He expects us to strive, but how... Yeah, the flock *must* be protected till the rapture happens. I get that. But I don't know where...The Lord will show me, if I believe? *But of course I believe...*

"Oh... I'm honoured, Brother George. Yeah... I'm God's agent now, not the government's. Wholly His... Holy."

They prayed, some thousands of miles apart, although that was trivial where prayer was concerned.

The next morning Jack knocked on his charges' doors, at an early if not unreasonable hour. As they headed for croissants and coffee, Paul looked at once bleary-eyed and infectiously excited, as if he had some great gift for Abigail, perhaps in the shape of an ace up his sleeve. He could barely restrain himself until they sat down.

"Abi," Paul told her, and Jack of course, "I've found Safiyya's grave!"

She could only gape, while Jack listened as if thunderstruck.

"Before I flew here, I'd been trying all sorts of web searches. My Puerto Rican pal on the *Globe*, Salvador, he was helping out with Spanish language sites. Him pitching in was a lot quicker than me working through everything using auto-translation, because Salvador could see at a glance. *Also*, he's friendly with the chef at The Jewel of Newbury. Don't know if you know the restaurant, it's Moroccan, in Newbury Street, hence the name, rather than, say, The Jewel of Tangier or Marrakesh. That was in case of us needing help with any Arabic inscriptions, although the Moors didn't exactly go in for names on graves, never mind epitaphs, as we duly found out."

The Jewel of Newbury. Did Abigail know it! Her hands gripped the edge of the table, nails indenting the cloth, before forcing herself to relax.

"Salvador writes some restaurant reviews, you see, as well as covering Latin American news, and he five-starred The Jewel of Newbury. I didn't mention any of this before in case it was a wild goose chase. But Salvador phoned me last night. He'd gone on web-searching, bless his cotton socks! Actually, he loves bright yellow ones, does Salvador. Well, we thought we'd drawn a blank. As I said, the Moors in Spain generally didn't bother putting names on stones, not unless the dead were royal or pretty important. So for instance you get some alabaster remains originating from the Alhambra palace, with prose and verse in gold letters on blue."

"But Safiyya wouldn't be anywhere like that," Abigail managed to say. "Not with her unorthodox sympathies."

"Unorthodox?" queried Jack.

"Al-Andalus in general was strongly anti-Shi'a," she explained. "Particularly anti-Ismaili, because the Ismailis were into esotericism…"

"Yeah yeah, all right, you told me about that *mystic gnostic* dualistic esoteric crap already. In your less than candid history lesson, remember? But it could as well be terrorism as esotericism; by all accounts, that's what they're really into!"

Abigail was about to launch into a devastating academic rebuttal of Jack's crude distortion, but her words died before reaching her lips. Jack had been right all along. It was she, the supposedly knowledgeable scholar, who'd been terribly wrong. She no longer felt sure of herself, no longer felt her grasp on history was firm.

At that moment a waitress arrived, so they ordered impatiently.

"Okay," resumed Paul. "Anyway, it seemed our search might be doomed, because next we found out that after the reconquest of Granada province by the Catholic monarchs, um, Ferdinand and um…"

"Isabella," supplied Abigail.

"Right. Basically, as time went by, the Christians destroyed all the Arab cemeteries. They reused the marker stones of the macabres in house walls or pigsties, whatever."

"Macabres?" queried Jack. "Like in *gruesome?*"

"It's an Arabic word for cemeteries, borrowed into Spanish. I don't know how to pronounce it. That's how we get the word macabre. And the Christians grubbed up the grounds for olive groves, or whatever they felt like growing."

"Good nutrients, I guess. Beats pushing up the daisies. Muslim corpses pushing up olives. Great recycling. So how come your Salvador found a grave when there aren't no cemeteries or headstones anymore?"

"Well, the thing is, Ferdy and Isabella rewarded their knights with big land holdings, and not all the knights were bigoted Christian fundamentalists, so to speak."

Jack darted a dark look at Paul.

"The gentling of Christian Europe!" exclaimed Abigail.

"Yeah, spot on. Whatever knight got the land where Safiyya's grave is, must've been impressed by Muslim culture, or at least respectful of it. Maybe the Alhambra amazed him, or he'd rubbed shoulders with dispossessed Moors and made a friend or two; it was a while before they got evicted from Spain. Anyhow…"

"Or maybe he had a Muslim lover. But never mind that," Jack added hastily, as if belatedly aware that he was overstepping a bound, even though Paul had offended him. Abigail kept her head high, but the invoked echo of her own Muslim lover had her blinking back tears like a silly girl. "So does he set up an ethnic reservation on his property?" continued Jack. "Like Uncle Sam for the Sioux?"

"Hardly! No, the speculation is, and this is in a Spanish newspaper piece Salvador found from six years ago, still on-line, that he incorporated a Moorish graveyard into gardens, at a walled and fortified residence he either built or adapted. Okay, now let's jump forward a whole lot of years. For most of the twentieth century, Andalucía was dirt-poor. In the *nineteenth*, goatherds and beggars were even camping out in the Alhambra. Modernity did arrive, but not for most of the countryside. Yet there were always some very rich people who owned pots of land and buildings, which could often lie quite neglected. Vast estates were handed down from generation to generation, and the dictatorship of Generalissimo Franco intensified this, until, *ka-boom*, democracy arrives. Then these huge properties get broken up at last, because they're such an obstacle to development."

"What is it with you guys?" complained Jack. "I don't need another history lesson!"

"You don't *want* it," corrected Abigail, "but you *do* need it."

Jack grunted, then looked around in annoyance for the waitress. They still had no breakfast.

Paul smirked. "Okay, a certain property, grand *casa* something-or-other, has been abandoned for fifty years. A guy buys it to restore and starts having the jungle of plants cleared. *Big swimming pool would look good over there.*" Paul got into character and pointed dramatically, mainly to annoy Jack. "Labourers hit upon this surviving Moorish cemetery. They snitch to the town hall, because they're socialists who hate the rich. Prohibitions are slapped. A newspaper in Granada gets photos. Quarrels erupt. All work ceases. The photos include inscriptions on a couple of stones, not too badly weathered; there isn't much rain there. Salvador reorients and enhances and prints. Then off he goes to the Jewel of Newbury for a chef's special translation, and bingo! Someone must have held Safiyya in high esteem to merit even her name on a stone."

"Where?" urged Jack. "*Where is it?*"

Paul couldn't resist. "The Jewel? It's on Newbury Street, like I told you." However, as Jack's pale face ominously reddened, Paul produced his smartphone and eagerly displayed a photo of a small tumbled slab, on which was a brief Arabic inscription. Across the bottom of the photo was scrawled: *Safiyya bint Yusuf al-Ballisiyya.*

"Bloody hell," breathed Abigail. "Clever Salvador. Clever *you*. My Safi, found at last! I'm proud of you."

"We aim to please." He turned unguarded puppy eyes to her; she looked down to hide a wince. "The place is called Fuente de los Árabes. That means fountain, or source, or spring, of the Arabs."

"Yes," she agreed.

He grinned. "Good thing you know Spanish! It's a pretty big village that was quite important once, about forty kilometres south of Granada. I was busy trawling the internet until the wee hours. The Archbishop of Granada had his summer palace near there. He was a son of the town, so he made it an ecclesiastic and admin centre. Earlier, the place was prominent in a rebellion of Moors living under Christian rule, after which the Moors got deported from there and finally were kicked out of Spain. So I guess the place was likewise big back in al-Andalus times. Safiyya could have been holidaying there, I dunno, or off to visit family in Málaga, or maybe more plague broke out in Granada. Anyway, she's there, what remains of her. And… whatever else too, maybe."

"Whatever else?" echoed Jack cautiously.

Paul beamed. "Like Abi said before with Guy, if any Holy Water *was* left, it'd be the most precious thing Safi owned by far; of divine origin too as far as she knew. Much more than just taking her jewels to the grave, it'd be like taking the Holy Grail or something, a key to heaven maybe. We can't be sure, but I'd say there's a high probability."

"A second chance," murmured Abigail. "*A second chance.*"

Her hand brushed against Paul's as she took the smartphone, to peer at Safiyya's little stone.

"I'm so deeply sorry," he muttered, "about the first chance."

Abigail couldn't hold back tears – of hurt and rage at Kamal's betrayal, but tears of gratitude, too. Tears might be cleansing. She tossed her head, like a Retriever after a dunking, sending salty drops flying.

"Hey," Jack exclaimed with an appearance of bonhomie, "this means *I* get a chance to rob a grave too! Hopefully with a spot of professional assistance," he added. "No amateur crap this time. Oh but shit, you said this is six years ago!"

Croissants, little pots of lavender honey, and coffee arrived. Jack got started immediately. "Didn't you say the story is *six years old*?" he repeated through a mouthful of croissant while the waitress was still in earshot. "That pool could be on top of the graves by now, or houses!"

"'Put your faith in Spanish bureaucracy,' Salvador said to me. He lived in Spain for a year. An officious town hall, local politics, regional cultural and antiquities authorities, a few lawyers, a pissed-off property investor probably with lots of other things to keep him busy in the meantime. Her stone will still be there. Have faith, Jack."

"Oh, *I do*. And the Lord helps those who help themselves. Soon as we're finished here, we're headed to Marseille, the American consulate general. Our help will come via the CIA."

Abigail, still dabbing her cheeks, looked dutifully impressed, but Paul was fiddling with his smartphone, bringing up Google Earth.

"Maybe I can find this Fuente place. Should look like a real big garden. If they couldn't build on the cemetery itself, maybe they put a pool nearby. Hmm… screen size isn't exactly…"

"Don't waste your time. In a few hours we'll have military grade satellite images. Assuming the cemetery still exists, I'll have agents meet us in Spain, with all the tools we'll need. When Jack robs a grave, it's professional!"

As crumbly flakes scattered across the tablecloth, Paul eyed the other man. "You're real eager to get to the source."

"Course I am. If your Puerto Rican can find that grave, so can Kamal."

"My god," uttered Abigail.

Paul barrelled on, "I'm almost forgetting: before Salvador phoned, I did some more digging in those cadastre files online."

"But you don't read French," protested Abigail, "let alone medieval. Is this some hidden talent?" She sagged, because her words seemed to echo similar words once spoken to that vile Syrian shit.

Paul grinned. "Auto-translator. Came out pretty odd, but mostly comprehensible. Listen, Guy inherited land from plague victims, and maybe he bought some up real cheap too, because of all the deaths… I couldn't quite tell. But he also *gave land away*, and… guess what… the people who benefited were all families of those disinherited when the Templars were forcibly disbanded!"

Abigail was back on track again. "Guy's grandfather was a Templar. So Guy must've had respect instilled in him… and maybe… quite likely… hatred for those who tortured and executed the knights of the Order?"

"No, it couldn't be…" began Paul; "So could it be…?" Abigail was saying at the very same time.

"*What?*" demanded Jack. "*What* could or couldn't be?"

Paul nodded to Abigail, and she continued. "Maybe Guy *knew* what Sinaldin was doing, still saving his life *despite* that, perhaps even *helping* to spread plague… All in revenge for the fall of the Templars… warning the survivors and descendants of the Order at the same time… so they could go to ground, ride the storm."

"Fucking traitor to the West," muttered Jack. "Maybe he could've stopped it, all those centuries ago… or at least tried. Right now *we* need to stop it! So after Marseille, we need to get to Granada neighbourhood, pronto!"

Kingdom of Granada, February 1348

"Ah, how you unman me, Safiyya! No more can I do justice to your charms!" So saying, Sinan al-Din ibn Nasir propped himself upon his elbow amid the pink silken pillows while his free fingertips slid along the fine dew of her nude perspiring flank. Her pubic hair looked dark as jet, slicked together as it was; Sinan and Safiyya had exercised lustily that morning, and the brass brazier had been putting out much heat through the vents in its lid.

He sighed. "I'm become a eunuch."

"Not exactly," replied Safiyya. "I know a *hakim* who told me how *that's* done," and she smiled at the secret they shared, of the chosen name of a certain great genius unknown to anyone outside of their faith. "It happens between six and ten years old. Either they open the boy's scrotal pouch with a red-hot scalpel to cut out the balls, or else they twist to increase the size of the testicles then they hammer the gonads to render them dead. Of course," she added, "to lessen the pain first they plunge the boy into a bath of hot water, then they squeeze his jugular veins so he passes out."

Her exotic long vowels, so typical of the city, still enchanted Sinan. "You are very... realistic, as well as a woman of the purest ideals. That's how I can totally trust you, my love. Trust you with the *waters of life* and *death*."

He reached across the bright woollen rug nearby, one of many scattered over the floor, past Safiyya's discarded sandals that were silver-embroidered with leather silk-lined, and grasped the flask of highly superior grape juice from Málaga. Then he refilled their cups that stood by the bed.

The house was no grand mansion, although it did contain a small internal courtyard with a tiny pool and pots of lilies and geraniums; as with many dwellings in Granada it was externally bare, yet a little palace within. Safiyya's uncle and aunt, who owned the place, were of the faith too, of course, and smiled upon her relationship with Sinan, even if the occasions when Sinan could possibly visit their niece were few and far between. His was an illustrious name to them; aside from matters of lineage, his name echoed that of Sinan ibn Salman ibn Muhammad, also called Rashid al-Din, who had led the Syrian Nizaris for so long and so brilliantly two centuries earlier.

Sinan noticed the eagle-talons on the bottoms of the short iron tripod supporting the charcoal-burning brazier, and was reminded of the *eagle's nest* far away in northern Persia, lost to the faith in the youth of his grandfather. After all things changed, he mused, maybe they would have the numbers and the strength to rebuild and reoccupy that hallowed site.

"You realise," said Sinan, "this may be the last time I can visit you? Soon the world will be convulsed."

"Maybe as well," Safiyya replied lightly. "I'm over forty now. I shouldn't wish you to see the effects of time and age. What is ours is now eternal."

"You're a young *lioness*, my love."

"Rather than a gazelle in the arms of a lion?"

"That must be a poetic allusion."

"My clever love, yes indeed it is. To a verse written years ago by another poetisa of this city of mine, Nazhun bint al-Qalai. I wouldn't have you be a lion, since my eyes shoot arrows at you, and I wouldn't wish you wounded."

"Your tongue can be sharp enough to others. Although not when it licks my little lance."

Safiyya laughed. "Would your little lance like to become more upstanding?"

"Impossible. For now."

"Then I shall go to the bathhouse to wash myself, and hear the gossip of women, who often know more than men about what goes on."

"Safiyya, will you go away to a safer place when the hand of the true God begins to strike?"

"Even though I cannot now succumb to plague…?"

"Here in the city there could be disorder and famine."

"We have kin in a lovely little town at the western end of the Gateway Valley, which is like a bounteous garden, on the way to the sea. I was thinking of going there anyway. Sometimes lately my heart beats strangely. I lose my breath. I feel an ache in my chest. Maybe I need the country air."

"This does not afflict you while we…?"

"No! You aren't the cause, dearest Sinan, or at least not so far. It might be poetic to sing to you how my heart beats wildly, how I fight for breath like a panicked gazelle brought down by a leopard. But no. Two months might pass, then this happens unaccountably, as God wills."

She rose naked, her buttocks a ripe cleft peach, and pulled on baggy silken trousers and blouse; paused by her desk to dip reed pen in inkwell and note something down; found a red muslin veil, then cast about for heavier woollen outdoor garments. Sinan lounged, admiring her while sipping grape juice. Within reach on the floor stood a pot of digestive marmalade, made the previous Spring by Safiyya's aunt from the bitter oranges and still delicious, remarkably, this following February. Sinan had already feasted upon Safiyya's flesh; now a dessert seemed deserved, to replenish his energies.

"This evening you lead the prayers!" Safiyya exclaimed exultantly.

Long before that, he too must go to a bathhouse to purify himself, for he had indulged in sex, long and lustily!

"Here in Granada," preached Sinan that evening, robed in green silk, "as I understand, you speak of sultans and their chief ministers dying from either the White Death or the Red Death. White, if they die in their sleep, which I understand is very rare. Red, if as usual here they are murdered, assassinated, poisoned, stabbed..." His breath, as he spoke, became faint white smoke, even though a fire of logs within a ring of bricks burned, its own smoke ascending to an opening in the thick clay covering the roof.

Including Safiyya and her uncle and aunt, a score and a half of the faithful were within the candlelit storeroom, the men separated from the women by a low wall of wheat sacks, and all wearing woollen garb against the cold. Sacks of barley, and of rye from fields at higher altitude, were piled around the walls and near the door, as if ready to barricade their meeting place or to muffle the words said within it.

"But soon a *new* death will come from God to ravage unbelievers and send them to Hell, after two or three days of terrible torments that are but a foretaste of *an-nar*, the Hell-fire whose fuel is stones and men, a fire whose burning tongues are the errors which brought their doom. May God protect us ourselves, the faithful, from this doom which is the *Black* Death. Rejoice, my loyal and true Brethren, that the scythe of God will cut down the innumerable weeds of the world and cast those into an everlasting bonfire, to purify the world for the true faith. Rejoice *silently as yet* in the deaths to come, so that others should not notice. As many deaths as there are grains in these sacks, yea multiplied by ten thousand!"

Yes, Sinan affirmed to himself. Yes.

His audience murmured in awe and appreciation.

"Soon millions of benighted Christians will die in agony, and the same fate will sweep over those who pay no reverence to Ali, peace and blessings be upon him. Yea death will ravage all the *ahl al-tadadd*, whose numbers have swollen like vermin, like lice of the Adversary, the Accursed One, till the world groans with their lies. Brethren, store food, as in this warehouse, and prepare to hide yourselves away. Shun those whose doom is coming... Keep your distance, so that their breath does not mingle with yours."

Due to some trick of light, the bright glow of certain candles illuminated Safiyya's face behind her veil. Her features were carved to absolute intensity and her eyes shone at him, the bringer and custodian of death. Sinan had seen that special intensity in her before, at her moments of orgasm.

Something else shone too, a bottle hanging from a cord around her neck, for she too was a custodian of death, and at prayer the two of them showed their power. All their *water of life* had gone, used to protect the most important among their flock, also his bosom friend Guy de Dieulefit, to whom he owed life. But should the seeded plague even now raging in Provence miraculously fail to edge around the Pyrenees, or be blocked by the precautions at ports and borders, his bold lady and he would *ensure* that the Black Death cleansed the lands of Castilla, Aragon and Portugal, and the Sunni land of Granada too!

Granada, Spain: June 2008

Abigail gazed at what might be one of the most beautiful views in any country. Rising from amid dark woods on the hill opposite, at varying elevations over hundreds of metres, honey-hued with russet hints, glowed the marvel of the Alhambra: its outer walls and linked square towers and empty windows. Beyond and away to one side, the hazy, humpbacked Sierra Nevada seemed to borrow blue from the sky. Directly below were the descending and intersecting white-walled homes of the ancient Albaicín district, their tiles like dragon scales.

"Safiyya saw this," murmured Abigail, "and now I see it."

"Pity Jack wouldn't let us take the tour," said Paul. "Two or three hours wouldn't harm the mission. But maybe *she* never got to look inside either. Don't you want to immortalise the moment?"

"I can't possibly take a photo. That would be," as a camera-toting tourist bumped against her, "banal." Abigail leaned against a wall of mortared round stones. "I'm trying to put myself into Safiyya's mind."

"Hmm, a poetical, mystical, amorous mind. Rooting for plague to teach the world a lesson. Turned on by mass-death, which her lover already set in motion. Just because she has a lovely name doesn't mean…"

"I know, I know," responded Abigail testily. "Yet it's magical here. Let's go with the magic just for a moment."

"Oh, I'm all for magic." Paul sounded plaintive. "Look, the Sultan's turret caught in a noose of light. A flask of wine and thou, dah-de-dah paradise."

"Granada had kings, but I see what you mean."

Another tourist attempted to elbow in beside Abigail. Carlos, one of their two CIA minders, fended the guy off, in the process putting his hand on Abigail's shoulder. For some reason shame and despair flooded Abigail. The feel of Kamal's skin replayed unbidden to her senses and she shivered with revulsion.

"I feel a bit light-headed," she said.

"It's the sun, Abigail," Carlos told her, "or may I call you Abi?"

"You have any chocolate in the Nissan?"

"Chocolate. Hey, you need a churrería. I know the perfect place."

"What's a choo-rare-ear?" asked Paul.

Carlos grinned. "You'll see. I'll call Jack and have him and Ryan meet us there." He offered his arm to Abigail. "Make it to the Nissan?" But she made it on her own, although swaying just slightly.

"Damn, I need to be in shape for tonight!"

"Lady, you look in very fine shape. Muy guapa."

From Paul, "What's wappa?" but Carlos seemed not to hear.

Abigail still thought of the two CIA men as minders rather than comrades in crime. Perhaps that would change. Ryan looked somewhat Hispanic and sported a thin moustache; clean-shaven Carlos had a sallower face under curly dark hair. The agents had joined them at a service station just short of Martorell, after which their black four-door Nissan Patrol had followed Jack's Peugeot hire-car for the rest of the epic drive to Granada. Jack insisted on driving; more anonymous than flying he'd said, but Abigail suspected the real reason was to hang onto his gun. After a matching epic sleep in a nameless hotel to recover from the journey, Abigail had insisted on seeing the Alhambra. Grudgingly, Jack agreed, assigning Carlos to 'look after' them.

Carlos navigated to a café near the centre of town that specialised in hot chocolate and sections of huge spiral doughnuts. At tables crowded together, local patrons of the establishment shouted at one another in Spanish as if quarrelling, though in apparent amity. What might well be flamenco music and song struggled unsuccessfully to play over the noise, yet the large TV screen suspended in one corner showed a football match.

Paul jerked his thumb at the rear wall. "That bullfight poster there. Remember Café Lorca?"

"Now we're here, where Lorca wrote."

The chocolate was so thick you could stand a spoon upright, almost. Carlos tore off a crisp greasy chunk of doughnut, dunked, and offered it to Abigail. "Like, so."

She devoured that, then tore off more and dunked her own, and devoured that too; then another.

Paul licked his fingers fastidiously, then pulled paper napkins from a small dispenser. "Cholesterol heaven, this."

"Medical emergency," protested Carlos. "Anyway, I only ordered half a wheel. They call 'em wheels. Gotta watch one's figure." He watched Abigail's.

Abigail gathered herself, now that calories had flooded her. She was done with charm, done with machismo, perhaps done with men. She inclined towards Carlos and said softly, "Don't try to romance me, macho man. Especially not in front of Paul."

Despite the din all around, Paul heard.

"No," he agreed. "I'm the official provider of nougat and things."

"Hey, this is just to stop you from fainting, being carried off back to bed."

"I'm all right now."

317

Ian Watson & Andy West

They finished their churros and chocolate, then stepped into the street. As they meandered back to the Nissan, Carlos took the opportunity for a cigarette. On the white and brown packet, *Fumar mata*, smoking kills. Could Carlos also kill? *Had* he killed?

"Are you armed?" she whispered.

By way of answer, Carlos bent and patted the calf of his baggy jeans. A leg holster, evidently. He flashed her a dazzling and somewhat suggestive smile.

Of course Jack could only have enlisted the help of the CIA by explaining the complete nature of the threat. Of course the agents on the ground would need to know that too, with full background details. But until now she simply hadn't thought that Carlos might know more than a bare outline, certainly not about her erotic dalliance with Kamal... She blushed within, feeling naked. So did Carlos think she was anyone's for the taking? Hence his coming on to her! In his view, a loose woman? For sure she was tight shut by now, and maybe she always would be.

"You okay?" asked Carlos. "Not enough sugar in the churros and chocolate?"

"Quite enough, thank you," she said. "A surfeit."

Carlos was just finishing his cigarette when Jack and Ryan pulled up in the Peugeot. Jack's voice, loud and sour, emerged the moment the doors cracked open.

"So just remember who's in charge here!"

Carlos grimaced.

"Hard to forget," murmured Paul.

They held an impromptu meeting in the Nissan, yet it seemed Jack was not done with disciplining his CIA helpers yet.

"I'm thinking you both look a tad memorable in those T-shirts."

Carlos had Bart Simpson across his chest, Ryan a white cat on black.

"Spanish love the Simpsons."

"Yeah, but Bart's a naughty boy."

"So," said Ryan, "am I, when necessary."

"Don't you have anything more neutral and forgettable? I mean, do I really need to tell you guys this?"

"Look," said Carlos, "any witnesses remember Bart and a cat, not our faces, nor you three particularly. It's distraction, Mr Turner, that's what. Right afterwards, we get rid of the T-shirts, change into ordinary dull shirts."

Was that their own idea? wondered Abigail. Or standard CIA training nowadays?

"ICE wouldn't stake out a place dressed as clowns or cowboys."

318

"We aren't doing surveillance. This is smash and grab."

Jack grunted. "What we're *grabbing* is very delicate."

"The stone pine is delicate too, but it's survived a long time," stated Ryan.

"What?" Jack's pale eyes leaked frustration.

Ryan pulled out a picture, a printout of a high resolution satellite image. "This is where we need to look." He pointed. "It's near a big pool, but that's an ancient stone reservoir. Apparently there's still some risk of the cemetery being bulldozed, the old Casa too, for new housing. Some of the locals are resisting, protecting their heritage. Especially a few Muslim locals. But there's a huge stone pine by the graves, must be very old. That species is very sensitive to frost. So whatever's buried nearby probably won't ever have been frozen. Just an observation."

"Okay okay, so you did your homework," admitted Jack grudgingly.

Carlos grinned. "And our admin, we're booked into the Miramar at Lanjarón, nearest sizeable town to Fuente."

"So we check out Fuente tonight, after everyone's gone to bed." Jack sounded eager.

"No chance they'll be in bed! Fuente's having a three-day patron saint fiesta."

"My god," said Paul. "A rock concert in Montlume, and now a fiesta. Are we blessed or cursed?"

Carlos laughed. "Blessed… though Spanish villages might put on four or five fiestas every year. Any excuse for a party! And a good excuse to be wandering around the place. Tonight, tomorrow, tomorrow night. I guess we'll identify this *casa señorial* easy enough, but the fiesta gives us leeway to study the lie of the land. Mazes of one-way alleys, that sorta thing."

Passing a sign for Fuente de los Arabes on the highway from Granada to the coast, they pushed on to Lanjarón, the Nissan Patrol leading and the Peugeot behind. The town's approaches were guarded by the ruin of a Moorish castle overlooking a plunging gorge, and too by a quartet of cannons at the municipal boundary. The main avenida, bordered by blotchy-trunked plane trees, seemed intent on evoking the spirit of some French spa town. They checked into the Miramar and rested. It was almost 8pm before they set off for Fuente itself.

Fuente de los Arabes, Granada Province, Spain: June 2008

As the five of them walked up a steep cobbled lane through the hot evening, of a sudden a thunderous explosion had Abigail clutch at Paul in shock. Jack was darting a hand inside his windcheater and Carlos was swiftly clamping that hand with a, "Just a firework!" For some seconds reverberations echoed from hilltop to hilltop. "Cool it."

Out of a side street slowly swaggered a short middle-aged fellow in white shirt and black trousers, wielding what looked like a plasterer's laying-on trowel to which were welded two little hoops. A companion who might have been the fellow's brother offered a sack. Out came another rocket, quickly slotted through those hoops. The launcher crooked his arm; a lighter flicked, and in a whoosh of orange fire and smoke the firework hurtled upward, to burst ear-splittingly. Abigail gaped at the casual nonchalance of the pyrotechnician, firing off something so dangerous, protected only by a thin metal plate.

"There'll be hundreds of rockets," Carlos advised Jack. "Day after day. Guys get competitive about who fires off most in honour of their saint."

"Aren't there ever *injuries?*" Abigail asked him.

"Sure. Hands lost, even a death now and then. That's nothing; they have a special firecracker that chases you round and blows up under you. Like a heat-seeking missile. Good thing you're in slacks. Wouldn't want a firecracker up your skirt."

Was macho-man being impertinent?

"No, I very much *wouldn't.*"

The main square was full of people at plastic tables and chairs that flooded out over the geranium-clad terrace of a café, while a rival army of seats spilled forth all around a restaurant opposite, called La Posada de Antonio. Bunting featuring the flags of many nations connected the leafy lopped branches of trees – like squids with short petrified arms – circuiting a fountain and pool, which was edged by roses and low railings.

Under awnings, Moroccan traders manned stalls selling lurid jelly sweets, watches, bangles, necklaces, toy bears that banged drums, radio-controlled racing cars. Helium balloons of cartoon characters bobbed in bunches. Bright red chorizo and blood sausages of a darker red sizzled on hot trays. A great stage backed by the precipitous wall of an ancient church sported a dozen big spotlights, tall amplifiers, microphones. Already a brass band of blue-uniformed teenagers was coming, although not to the stage, their tubas and trumpets and trombones and cymbals booming and blaring and clanging boisterously, while rockets banged overhead in competition.

The band halted outside a turreted little town hall, two flags jutting out above the doorway; one of the Junta de Andalucía and the other of Spain. Nearby stood a blue Nissan Patrol of the Guardia Civil, its pair of policeman, in their pale green shirts and dark green trousers and green caps, pistols in their leather holsters, chatting to a couple of the locals.

"Cops," muttered Jack.

"Cops got to be on duty at a fiesta," said Ryan.

Abigail stared to and fro at the sea of people, straw-hatted ruddy-faced men in checked shirts, women in gowns loaded with huge spiders' webs of lace, some others in flamenco costume, three tiers of pink from booted ankles to above the knee, rose-red camellias tucked by their ears or worn upon high buns of hair. Kids ran about clutching newly acquired toy animals or plastic guns or dolls, or handfuls of the vivid rubbery sugary confectioneries. The noise in the square was a tumult.

"Let's get a drink and a bite to eat," said Carlos.

So the two agents led the way, Jack and Paul and Abigail threading after them, until they came upon a table newly being vacated, and grabbed it. Ryan waved at one of the many part-time waiters, ordered *cañas* of Cruzcampo and a big plate of *pinchos* to share.

"On the way in, you notice the big pine tree poking up?" Carlos asked Jack, who nodded then craned.

"Can't see it from here. Got the photo?"

"Safe in Ryan's pocket." Evidently Carlos felt it unwise to pull out the satellite image amid so many possible witnesses.

"Let's go find the place now!"

"Not yet. Probably be a procession round the streets in an hour or so. We tag along." Carlos sat back, and lit a BN cigarette. "Relax. I don't notice any suspicious Arabs here so far, just a few street traders. Ryan, *benny*?" Ryan took a cigarette.

"I don't notice any Simpsons," Jack said, "except on a couple of kids."

"So?" said Ryan. "I'm just a big kid at heart."

"What does *benny* stand for?" asked Paul. "Sounds like something good that benefits you."

"*Bay-ennay. Baja Nicotina,* low nicotine."

Paul wrinkled his nose. "Those things don't smell low in *anything.* Who'd have thought it?" he added to Abigail jauntily. "Here we are at a fiesta in Spain. Doesn't seem very religious, though, does it?"

"That'll be another day," Carlos put in. "This is the warm-up."

Quite soon, pork chunks on skewers arrived with a pile of bread, and five plastic cups of beer. Jack didn't touch the food. Abigail picked at one skewer while the others ate appreciatively.

Half an hour later, a tall woman in her thirties wearing a pink flamenco dress, camellia in her hair, ascended the stage and approached the microphone, along with a man in a dark suit to introduce her.

"This'll be the *pregón*," said Carlos. "Speech in praise of the village. She's the *pregonera*."

"You guys come over almost like natives," remarked Jack.

"We're a long way from Barcelona, but we do get around. Though as regards going 'native', Mr Turner, we're patriotic Americans."

To Abigail it seemed that Carlos was developing quite a dislike for Jack, which, from Carlos's glance at her, he somehow supposed might raise him in her Canadian estimation.

Ryan nodded. "You wouldn't want ignorant agents. In your ICE outfit, say."

"Nobody's ignorant in ICE," Jack retorted, so quickly that it seemed Ryan had touched a nerve.

"Hush now." And Carlos cocked an ear.

The suited man spoke for a while, and then the woman read from pages in a high, clear voice. At the end, most in the square clapped. A mischievous smile flitted over the face of the pregonera woman. Abruptly she seemed to become even taller, and haughty. With a loud clattering of her boots, she executed intricate footwork on the planks, then threw up both arms, fingers bent back in some significant gesture. Applause erupted.

"Did you understand the speech?" Carlos asked Abigail.

"Bits," she replied. "I didn't understand *anything* the guy said."

"Yeah, he was less educated. Plus, Andalucians cut the ends off words, and they leave letters out."

Next came the coronation on stage of the Queen of the Fiesta, a plump big-bosomed teenager in a spangled yellow ball gown, and of her Dames of Honour, also dolled up to the nines, and of the suited child King and a child Queen. Strings of white light bulbs, suspended like the spokes of a huge umbrella without fabric over the fountain, glowed brightly, for the sky was by now deep purple. The band had disappeared some while since, yet now its brass jubilantly reasserted itself as the blue-clad teenagers emerged from a street behind their conductor...

"Okay," said Carlos. "Here come the *carrozas*. We can get up and follow soon."

...followed by half a dozen sumptuous, brightly-lit, flower-decked floats pulled by little tractors, the first carrying armchair-thrones for the Queen and her dames. As the royalty ascended, on the float behind them a trio of merry mermaids blew kisses while lolling with their giant sequined fish-tails on heaps of cushions, green ribbons in their hair for seaweed. The carroza behind that bore a platinum blond in a pure white gown, and seven face-painted dwarfs, no, children, wearing cardboard bowler hats and intermittently brandishing toy shovels and big hammers and axes made of inflated rubber or plastic.

"Just like a parody of us in Montlume," joked Paul. "Off to work we go, again, hey-ho…" He stopped short as he saw Abigail wince.

The brass band struck up once more and led the floats out of the square, the royalty tossing wrapped sweeties from cans to scampering children. At least a third of the seated crowd arose from the multitude of tables, to become part of the cavalcade, so Paul and Abigail, the white cat and Bart Simpson and Jack quickly joined in. Street lamps were shining by now.

A few streets later the silhouette of the pine tree came in sight, eclipsing starlight up a Calle Alberca, which wasn't the route of the procession. The five of them stopped under a lamp at the corner, looking along into semi-obscurity as people behind passed by.

"Alberca…" commented Ryan. "Means Reservoir Street. Best bet for access. Section of fence not overlooked, near as I can tell from the image and street map."

Carlos instructed Jack, "You and Abi and Paul carry on. Meet back at the square. Me and Ryan will check this out. It's what we do."

"I need to be with you two," Jack insisted.

Hurrying the opposite way through the crowd came that pregonera woman in her flamenco dress, calling out, "José Luis ¿dond'está? ¡Niño!" She stared along Calle Alberca since that was where these halted people were gazing intently, and addressed Abigail as the woman of the group."¿Ha visto a un niño llevando una camiseta de Spiderman?"

Abigail managed to process the words *seen, little boy, T-shirt, Spiderman*. The woman had pronounced the name as Speederman. But hey, Spidey did move very fast.

"No," Abigail replied, "no he visto…"

The Spanish woman smiled, and said, "Oh you are English! Sorry! I'm looking for my son. He never thinks of consequences, and all sorts of people are here. That sounds rude. I don't mean you! But other strangers. Who knows?" Such a chatterbox the pregonera seemed; no wonder the villagers chose her to give a speech.

Abigail disregarded a dark look from Carlos. "Your English is wonderful."

"Oh I teach English in the Instituto, the high school. Maybe your friends saw a little boy in a Speederman T-shirt?"

The men shook their heads and looked appropriately blank.

Jack said, "We aren't exactly together. Just following the show."

"Please do excuse me." And on she ran, searching for her son.

"Don't socialise," Ryan warned Abigail.

"I couldn't ignore her, could I?"

"I'm coming with you," repeated Jack. "*Right?*"

Carlos shrugged. "If you insist." To Abigail and Paul: "You two keep your eyes peeled. Speed up a bit, don't be last in the procession. Look like you belong. Then stay in the square."

The pregonera, whose name was María, was quick-witted, inquisitive, and loved solving the *jeroglífico* puzzle in the newspaper every school day morning in record time; although she did worry constantly about her two boys in case any harm befell them. A philology graduate of Granada University, she'd won prizes in national poetry competitions and currently was writing a series of poems called *Canciones del harén*, Songs of the Harem, fascinated as she was by that enclosed way of life, similar to a nunnery yet at the same time luxurious and sensual, if perhaps frustrating…

A neighbour, met on the way, assured María that little José Luis had gone into the house of his chum Rodrigo next to the Posada de Antonio; so María returned at a run to catch up with the cavalcade, near the head of which she ought to be, as this year's pregonera. María was forever running: to school, to the shops, to the brass band association of which she was secretary, to flamenco workshops which she taught, to the meetings with her new Arab friends Naguib and Omar – at which she usually arrived late – and of course often to locate her straying children.

But what was this? Torchlight along Calle Alberca, where of course the old mansion was, near the old Moorish reservoir. And she had faithfully promised Naguib that she'd keep a look out for any suspicious activity there; especially anyone snooping around the old cemetery. Guilty at neglecting her duty in the cavalcade, but conscious of her promise and spurred by curiosity, María sneaked quickly along the dimly-lit street to an alley from which she could peep. Activity at the stretch of chain-link fencing which blocked access to the old casa señorial. Three men, by the look of it. One of them was gesturing with a torch beam in the direction where she knew the graveyard lay, somewhat masked by vegetation. The moon wasn't due to rise for another hour or so, she thought, maybe longer.

Presently whoever it was let himself back down the fence, so the idea wasn't to climb into the property, *or not yet*, not tonight. The same three as had been loitering on the corner along with the other foreign couple? Not *necessarily*. Why should foreigners who sounded American be interested in the graveyard? Fellow Spaniards were more likely. As soon as the interlopers began to pace along the outside of the high stone wall beyond the fencing, she retreated and ran again, back urgently to catch the cavalcade of carrozas.

The Miramar Hotel, Lanjarón, Granada Province, Spain: June 2008

They slept in late at the Miramar, gathering for breakfast at eleven. Carlos led their little party out along the Avenida de Andalucía to find a café. Despite the Frenchified look of Lanjarón, on the breakfast menu in the chosen café were exclusively *tostadas*, toasted half-baguettes. With goblets of ice cubes all round, into which they poured milky coffee as fast as possible from finger-burning tumblers.

To Jack's great annoyance, Carlos insisted on reiterating most of their observations and decisions from the night before.

"…now remember, from what we saw yesterday the graves look quite close to the tree, but on the wrong side as far as we're concerned, unfortunately visible from the casa's upper windows. So torchlight has to be minimal beyond the tree. The night vision lens from the Nissan should help. The fence is climbable, but that'd be awkward if escaping in a hurry, from dogs, or worse. We'll use the bolt-cutters, slit the fence close to a pillar, hitch it closed while we're inside."

Jack hissed, or maybe he was blowing on his coffee.

Carlos continued obliviously. "We'll park the vehicles in Calle Alberca itself. There's no restrictions and there'll be plenty of other non-locals around for the festival."

"And no need," added Ryan, eying Abigail and Paul, "for you two to enter the casa grounds. We know what we're looking for. If you're on hand in the unlikely case of an, er, archaeological or identification problem, we can give you a call to come in."

"You don't have to come either, Jack," said Carlos neutrally. "Two is enough."

Jack glared momentarily. "I'll remind you that this is *my* operation."

"ICE's operation," Carlos said. "In co-operation. Then the three of us it is. Operation Hielo. Here's to it." He lifted his already clinking goblet and clinked Jack's, who looked puzzled. "*Hielo*, Spanish for ice," explained Carlos as Abigail nodded. "So I guess we stretch our legs around town, don't get too hot, late lunch, then siesta to sleep it off. We don't go into action still digesting."

Fuente de los Arabes, Granada Province, Spain: June 2008

They arrived in Fuente at 10 pm and parked the vehicles as planned.

"Okay, we'll hang out in the square for a while, until the entertainment starts," announced Carlos in a tone of command. From a leaflet which Ryan had pocketed the day before, a grand spectacle of fire and music was due in the square later, a *noche infernal* with diverse surprises. To be followed by a band playing pasadobles, sevillanas, and tangos.

"Why don't we get the job over with right away?" demanded Jack, from the off challenging Carlos and his careful planning.

"Because nothing's happening in the square yet. Anyone might come wandering by on their way there. And there'll be mass fireworks for the *noche infernal*, which will cover our noise."

"So why didn't you time it...?"

"I timed it near enough. Could have been a donkey-cart on the road."

"At night?"

"Or whatever. We need to be in position."

"Yeah, I understand *that*. I've done enough stake-outs."

"Unlike stake-outs in cities, five of us can't sit here in two vehicles for over an hour in an empty street doing nothing. We risk arousing suspicion. Also, we need to be sure what's going on. Okay, Abi, Paul, you two go by that route," jerking his thumb towards the end of the street where the pregonera had first seen them. "We'll use the other way, up and round."

As Abigail and Paul were approaching the end of Calle Alberca, under the corner street-lamp a man moved into sight, only to halt immediately. A man dressed in black trousers and a black shirt, his face swarthy and thin. Already, after a piercing long glance, he had gone.

How disconcerting, that brief scrutiny. Nerves, nerves, that was the reason, Abigail told herself. Who wouldn't be nervous in this situation? And yet... the circumstances seemed strangely familiar. Not from the previous attempt on a grave, in Montlume, no. Familiar, as in déjà-vu. Seen in a wrong place entirely.

"Paul, that man. This might seem silly, but he looked like one of those Druze watchers in Iran. The ones who were following us! Wearing black. I told you about their car."

"He'll be one of the street musicians."

"That was *last* night, Paul."

"Why not tonight as well?"

"He didn't look Spanish."

They hesitated when they reached the lamp on the corner, but the man wasn't in sight, only some women in frocks who must have come out of a house.

"He looked Middle Eastern. Out of place here."

"Unlike those Moroccans selling toys and balloons? There must be thousands of North Africans in southern Spain. Illegal workers, whatever. There is *no* way any of those whoever-they-weres in Syria can know where we are. Not unless they already know about Safi's grave. Look, Kamal didn't even know about *Montlume* beforehand."

"He didn't know *who* those other men were either. And I doubt they were Druzes."

"If somebody else knows what might be in Safi's grave, they've had six years to do what we're about to. A musician! Or a tango-freak from Argentina, who knows?"

They reached the square and found a free table squeezed up against a tree, where they might be less conspicuous. In front of the stage, which was now laden with drums, a row of tall display fireworks were mounted, separated from spectators-to-be by a token rope. The bandsmen, all smoking together in a huddle, were wearing identical lightweight blue suits. A waiter steered himself to the table.

"Uh," said Abigail, "dos cañas de Cruzcampo, por favor. I didn't know what else to order," she whispered as the waiter wheeled away.

"Beer's fine, but we'd better pay as soon as it comes. I spy the three musketeers." For Jack and Carlos and Ryan had arrived, to seat themselves ten tables away.

"You'll be pleased to know I found my son last night." It was the pregonera woman, appearing out of nowhere, wearing tight blue jeans and a red blouse bow-tied above a bare waist, a tiny mobile clipped to her belt like a side buckle. "I was so sorry to bother you on the procession. You aren't with your friends?" She glanced over to where Jack and the others were sitting.

"I'm glad all is well," Abigail struggled to put feminine sympathy into her face.

"We don't really know them, just bumped into them yesterday," said Paul almost at the same time. "Hey, that was a great procession."

Why the hell was she so observant? The waiter returned, tray overhead bearing two plastic cups, which he set down. Hastily Paul thrust some Euros at him.

Without invitation, the Pregonera sat down. "Are you on holiday?"

Damn! Not just a chatterbox, but nosy too.

"Er... yes," said Paul, who seemed to be distracted as he looked across the thronged square. Following his gaze, Abigail spied the black-clad man again, staring towards where Jack sat silently while Carlos and Ryan chattered to one another.

"I hope you've seen our beautiful Alhambra?"

"Beautiful indeed," echoed Abigail, hoping she wouldn't be asked about the inside.

"I often think," said the pregonera, "of the lives of women in the harem there in Islamic times. Some might have been poetisas, poets."

The word 'poetisa' caused Abigail to flinch. She couldn't help it. In the eyes of the pregonera, she saw her own unguarded expression had spawned surprise.

Blessedly, a young boy ducked under the rope towards the fireworks, whereupon the woman promptly leapt up, crying, "José *Luis*!" and was off like a flash to retrieve him.

"Why did she use *that word*?" hissed Abigail. "*Poetisa*."

"Abi, I have no idea! Coincidence? Or else she's telepathic?"

Abigail wrung her hands. Her confidence was still shot to pieces after Kamal. "I'm not sure I believe in coincidence. And do we warn Carlos about the guy in black?"

"Abi, Carlos and Ryan are agents. They'll know."

Two middle-aged women had engaged the pregonera in conversation, her boy duly rescued and held by her side while he fidgeted, scuffing his trainers to and fro. Distraction after distraction overtook the woman. She chatted affably with him and her, with them, with those, not even glancing back towards the table, yet Abigail felt that she and Paul remained on her radar. Maybe she could see out of the corner of her eye.

And then the drumming and cymbaling began, as a fellow wearing a fluorescent yellow jacket of the kind a road-worker might wear, a smouldering cheroot in his mouth, stood by the fireworks on their frames. Watch your boy, pregonera, when those start popping off, soon please god. *Yes*, sparkling silver was rushing up first. Then crimson and blue geysers erupted, Catherine wheels spun, golden stars rained.

Abigail barely heard her phone, cycling through its theme where she'd placed it on the table. It was Carlos.

"A man in black is watching us," she blurted out in a loud hiss, wanting to stay discreet and yet overcome the noise at the same time.

"I know. You stay here when we go. I'll phone again, when to come, then *hurry*. I got the photo of her gravestone with me. We'll be careful, and quick as we can. Now I want you to stand up and have a flaming row for the benefit of our observer. Shout, slap Paul's face. Do it now."

"Wait –" She wanted to tell him that the pregonera seemed suspicious of them, but Carlos had rung off.

"Carlos says we must stage a quarrel. *Get up*, Paul." Rising, rocking the table, spilling a beer, Abigail shouted at Paul, "Do you really think I'll stay in that fleabag hotel?"

Paul also rose and obediently bellowed, "What's with you, high and mighty?"

She slapped him on the cheek, trying to mute her blow at the last moment, though he rocked, hopefully just acting.

"You demoness!" he shouted back. Seemed he couldn't bring himself to call her a bitch or any such rude word.

Drums thundered, so their improvisations were almost drowned, though neighbouring tables were paying a lot of attention.

"Hey, sit down," Paul bellowed, "and talk this over. PLEASE!"

Abigail subsided, as did Paul, rubbing his cheek.

By now the man in black was pacing in their direction, perhaps to try and catch what they were shouting about. Carlos, Ryan, and Jack were nowhere in sight – no, she caught a glimpse of Carlos hastening away – and a Guardia Civil officer was thrusting their way. Quickly Abigail babbled, "I'm sorry, I'm sorry," and clasped Paul's hand. Since all had calmed, the Guardia Civil man paused... only for the very attentive guy in black to catch his attention instead. The Guardia man changed direction and intercepted this new target, who began fumbling in his clothes, fumbling... Finally he produced what looked like an identity card, which the Guardia man spent a while scrutinising before grinning apologetically and starting to chat at length, as if to compensate for bothering a legitimate resident of Spain.

Five more minutes passed. Ten. The pyrotechnics and accompanying percussion were dazzling and deafening. Fifteen minutes. Abigail kept her mobile in her hand so that she could feel it vibrate. A finale, practically a volcanic eruption, was followed by sudden calm, and at once came the start of the tinkling *Petrushka* theme.

"Yes?"

"Done it. Come now," Abigail heard Carlos tell her.

"Paul, let's go."

"It wasn't archaeology, but we got a little bottle." Carlos was peeling off latex gloves filthy with sandy soil. Both vehicles had been moved close to the mesh fence, part of which was folded back. The trunk of the Peugeot gaped open, empty. Jack was busy thrusting a bag – whose? – into the Nissan Patrol. "Lying next to her ribs, in a kind of string net held by a cord going around her neck, but the fibres crumbled to pieces. An *intact* bottle, sealed with something black, wax I guess, very hard. She was lying on her side, face *away* from Mecca, so confirmed as Nizari elite. Just half a meter down. Jack has the item well padded. We'll abandon the French car, cram in the Patrol. Mr Turner's decided he wants us all together."

Paul slapped the Peugeot's roof. "This is a lead to who Jack is," he pointed out. "Licence plate, rental agency. Surely we shouldn't leave it here?"

Jack had trotted up. "You think I gave my real ID?" Quickly he slammed the trunk shut and zapped the central locking.

"At least," persisted Paul, "we could lose it miles away from here."

"Already been through this," snapped Carlos. "Of course you're right, but Mr Turner insists. He doesn't want to… lose *you*."

Stood to reason, reflected Abigail, that Jack planned on riding in the Nissan now. Two CIA guards were better security for their precious find, and he'd stay glued to Safiyya's bottle. Perhaps he didn't trust her or Paul to keep up in the Peugeot, or more likely he simply didn't trust them to be on their own.

Suddenly, exactly what Carlos had said hit her. "Carlos, did you say *black* wax? *Black*? Are you sure?"

"Hurry up, get in the Nissan," urged Jack.

"Yes. We had a powerful light, and the pouch had kept the dirt off."

"What are you doing?" cried a female voice, in English.

It was the pregonera, in her jeans and knotted blouse, forty yards away, advancing quickly in shadow. Just behind her was that *watcher*.

Jack's gun was in his hand, then in both hands now outstretched. "*Stop there!*"

The pregonera hesitated… then went for… from her belt came… flipping open the mobile, she raised it to her cheek just as Jack fired.

The bullet appeared to take the pregonera in the shoulder. Without a sound she spun, colliding with the man directly behind her, collapsing sideways.

"*Gilipollas!*" Carlos bellowed, "King asshole!" He gripped Jack's wrists, thrusting the gun aside, as a result of which it discharged again, harmlessly.

The man in black was trying to drag the pregonera towards some scanty protection offered by long grass and a pile of stones while the shocked and confused woman resisted. She started screaming and desperately reached with her uninjured arm for her fallen phone.

"Get in the Nissan!"

Abigail squeezed in with Paul and Jack as Carlos started the engine. She felt the offensive hardness of the ICEman's pistol in his pocket.

"She was about to phone! I didn't intend to hit her."

"*So*, you were aiming at her *phone*, crack-shot? By that action, Mr Turner, you bought us less than a minute and turned us into armed criminals on the run."

"How far do we have to run?"

"Eighty, ninety kilometres to Málaga airport," answered Ryan as their Nissan Patrol swung sharply, scraping a corner, then raced along a narrow street, which fortunately was deserted.

"What's that in miles?"

"About fifty."

"I wasn't aiming to kill."

"That's great to know," retorted Carlos sarcastically, even though preoccupied by frantic steering. "Otherwise the Guardia would be chasing murderers. So we're *only* class two criminals, armed and dangerous, *coño*. Ryan, get talking to the office in Barça. See what ideas they might have for help with the Spanish authorities." Then he really had to concentrate as they plunged down a curving incline that was steep and rutted.

"*Black wax*," repeated Abigail. But everyone's attention was occupied as they all clung tight to the lurching Nissan.

As was very soon evident, they had no option but to return to the N323. The formidable obstacles of various Sierras between Fuente and Málaga removed any possibility of short cuts.

"You're driving insanely!" shouted Jack. "If we turn over, the goods might smash."

Ryan called back, "Don't distract the driver, por favor. Carlos has to get to the highway before Guardia from Lanjarón block off the junction. Fuente had a cuartel and..."

"What the fuck's a cuartel?"

"Small police building. Say a couple of officers on duty at the fiesta, out of a strength of four. The other pair might well live in Fuente though. Lanjarón's Guardia on duty will be haciendo la ronda, out on patrol, but on this side of Lanjarón or to the east?"

"Yeah, yeah. Why aren't our headlamps on high beam? At this speed bends rush out of nowhere!"

"You want us to shine beacons across the landscape?"

Abigail was finally able to get a word in. "*Black* wax," she shouted, "means that this isn't the protection! The wax seal on Guy's bottle in Montlume was brown; it was probably lighter-coloured in his time and then darkened with age. But it *wasn't* black. Guy was holding the *water of life*. But Safiyya was holding the *water of death*, plague itself!"

"You mean she died of plague?" demanded Ryan, who obviously hadn't understood.

"The seal wasn't broken, was it? *Carlos*, was the wax seal broken?"

"What? No, I'm sure it wasn't. Let me drive!"

"You mean," Paul's voice was loud and strained, "that rattling around with us in here is *live haemorrhagic fever?*"

The Nissan Patrol swung wildly around a bend, Carlos braking then immediately accelerating out of the curve.

"It isn't rattling," insisted Jack. "I packed it well, despite the rush."

"Fuck," said Ryan. "*¡Joder!* Carlos must still hurry."

"Okay, clever girl," snapped Jack at Abigail. "Why would the poeteaser have gotten live virus? Like, what sort of gift from a boyfriend is *that?*"

"Poetisa."

"*Terrorista*, if you're right," said Ryan. "Medieval terrorista."

"Okay. That's okay," said Jack, "That's cool. It's better to have the virus itself. The *water of life* might have turned into goo. Viruses are tough critters, aren't they? Just a few surviving, and we're there."

Abigail wished sourly that someone a whole lot better than Jack had been put forward as the official defender of society. Not only was he a bigoted nutcase, he probably had no idea what he was talking about. Her instinct was still to resist him, to tell him what a complete jerk he was. But she'd screwed up herself, screwed up *very* badly. Her only hope of rescuing some good from this was complete compliance. She held her tongue.

They were indeed *there*, having reached the N323 before any intervention. Once on the highway Carlos headed south in the Motril direction, at a much more sedate rate.

"What are you doing? Now's the time for speed! Don't be scared of the virus spilling, if it didn't already!"

"Scared?" Carlos actually slowed further. Beside Abigail, Jack smashed his fist into his other hand several times in frustration, as though his palm might be Carlos's face.

"Get ready," said Ryan, "to duck down when I say. As low as possible." And only moments later, "Now, duck! And stay put."

Abigail found herself squashed against Jack, who was ventilating heavily. Due to wearing a jacket, his sweat smelled strongly stale. Once again she felt the hard pressure of the gun in his pocket and flinched, worried in case the weapon might fire itself. As his way of fitting in low, Paul draped an arm around Abigail's back. At least he wasn't trying to hug her. Tobacco fumes drifted back.

The sound of a vehicle passed, heading north; then another, not so quickly.

"*And keep down*, keep down. Guardia Nissan passed at high speed. The second one slowed down a lot, to eyeball us. It's still lagging. Not sure if it's going to do a turn…"

Abigail caught her mind willing for invisibility, as in her childhood when she'd done something very wrong. *Grow up, Abigail,* she chided herself.

"Don't *think* so. Can't see it any more. Okay, relax."

As Abigail straightened, Ryan was scrutinising the wing mirror. Carlos nursed a mostly-consumed cigarette in his mouth.

"Do you have to smoke all the time?" came from Jack, who then thumbed his window down. Warm side-stream whistled.

"Moderate speed, driver looking casual, passenger snoozing with his mouth open," was Carlos' comment as he speeded up. "And now we should steal an anonymous car, if we can do that inconspicuously. Change of shirts for us. And Ryan will drive while I shave this moustache off."

Ryan consulted his own smartphone screen. "Vélez de Benaudalla tiene buena pinta, tio…" he suggested to Carlos.

"Speak English, will you!" the ICEman demanded.

"Village coming up soonish on the left," commented Ryan.

"Might be better to risk it all the way to Motril," suggested Carlos. "Only twenty-some kilometres further. Much bigger place, many more cars. Hey, bound to be Brits living there. Watch for a car with GB plates? Means they only arrived in the past year, won't speak Spanish, delays in explaining a car theft."

"Wrong-side drive, though."

"So it isn't what we'd reasonably switch to."

"Sí, ese es un punto interesante."

"I have a point," said Carlos. "So we look for an urbanization, rows of Lego chalets, little villas."

"Barça will call back, by the way."

"That'll take a while. Could go diplomatic, which I wouldn't appreciate. Might end up getting us expelled. Because of a hot-shot. Actually, calling Barça was a bit impulsive. In fact, Ryan, call back and stand them down for now."

"You okay?" murmured Abigail to Paul. "You're quiet. No quips for us?"

"You phoned Barcelona," emphasised Jack heavily, "because it's of world importance that we three get out *quickly.*"

"I'm fine, just quipped out I guess. Don't like people getting shot." Paul treated Abigail to his goofy smile, subdued somewhat. Oddly, this made her feel good.

"Mr Turner, I'm well aware!" retorted Carlos. "Rather than taking a compulsory trip to the nearest Juzgado de instrucción, hear your rights, involve the consulado. Talking of diplomats and Barcelona, if you hadn't screwed up by shooting, wouldn't the wisest way to sneak your item out have been in *a diplomatic pouch* from Barça?"

"We couldn't waste time driving all the way back there."

"Not half a day extra?"

"I told you, this is urgent."

"Abi," called Carlos. "Are you sure about that wax colour business?"

"It must be so," she said. "To prevent confusion between virus and protection."

"I could," growled Jack, "have appreciated this insight before tonight."

"I didn't quite realise. Now it's obvious."

"Well debriefed," Carlos commented ironically. "Well analysed. How good is your padded box for decompression in an airplane luggage hold? I hope you weren't thinking hand luggage."

"Ah," crowed Jack, "I got an airtight titanium flask with gel inside. I'll switch to that, now I know the size is right."

"Have it your way. I'm wondering, what if we *split up*? What if Ryan and I run as far as we can back Almería way? Hell, we might get further, even all the way. It was only a wounding."

"Quite so," responded Jack quickly, as if justified.

"In a GB car you'd look like a newish foreign resident delivering a couple of friends back to Málaga airport. If we steal the car after midnight, soon, nobody's likely to realise until the morning. Among your multiple plane reservations, Mr Turner, when's the earliest?"

"8.00 am, check-in 7.00 right in time for boarding. Then Madrid to the States at noon."

"Pity it isn't a lot earlier. Motril to Málaga's an hour at most. You'd best abandon the Brit car in a parking lot in town, take a taxi to the airport."

"*Which* Brit car, exactly? Aren't we getting ahead of ourselves?"

Paul had been playing with his smartphone. "Okay," he said. "English language site. Properties for sale, Southern Spain. I searched for near Motril. How about *Lobres*, just four kilometres from it?"

"Perfecto!" exclaimed Ryan. "Lobres is right beside this very road, a little further on."

"Okay. Urbanization five kilometres from the beaches. Superb sea and mountain views. Terraced villas and semi-detached. Oops, *with garages*."

"Since when does everyone put their cars in garages? Garages are for storing junk. An urbanization means a hundred, maybe hundred and fifty homes. Shouldn't be hard to spot. Let's go for it. At most we waste ten minutes."

"Good man," said Carlos. "Incidentally, Mr Turner, I'll be making a formal complaint about you discharging your weapon without adequate reason."

"I'd rather you didn't."

"Me suda la polla vino tinto, ¿quieres un vasito?" Carlos remarked offhandedly, whatever that might mean, though Ryan sniggered.

Jack declared, "For now, the fewer people who know what any of this is about, the better. Potential for panic here is enormous."

"Oh come on! You think that my superiors issue press releases? Besides, they already *do know*. How else are Ryan and I assigned to you? For the love of God, what possessed you?"

"The love of God," muttered Jack softly. "She oughtn't to have gone for her phone."

"A phone is equivalent to a gun?"

"If the call sets off a terrorist bomb. Yes. In those circumstances. And that guy in black behind her, same as those guys who were dogging Abi in Iran…"

"No, I didn't say *the same*," broke in Abigail. "I said *similar*."

"Suspiciously so, I'd say! If that Kamal guy was, *is*, the arch-terrorist, or at least *a* terrorist, what does that make guys in black who were trailing *him*? I'd say some Middle Eastern security service. Middle Eastern security services are sometimes behind terrorism themselves," Jack defended. "Sponsoring, protecting. There are factions."

"There's *behind*," pointed out Paul, "in the sense of supporting. And *behind* meaning tiptoeing after."

"Yeah, tiptoeing," said Carlos. "In order to snatch the Holy Grail of Evil from the naïve terrorist? Or from whoever gets to the Grail first? But then to *really* make use of it? You can't be suggesting that the guy behind the innocent pregonera woman was a genuine rogue-state terrorist. *He* never pulled a gun. He just tried to save her."

"No such agents," Paul speculated, "could have turned up in Fuente. How could they have possibly known?"

Jack sighed. "There's a lot of things we don't understand. Yet." He sounded back in control of himself now. Had Abigail heard him murmuring a prayer under his breath, to calm himself?

"Lobres, *coming up*," announced Ryan.

Twenty minutes later, Carlos was hauling Abigail and Paul's bags to the trunk of a white Mazda hatchback, stolen with professional ease. Its non-Spanish plate included the letters GB. Jack protectively handled his own bags, on account of Safiyya's ancient bottle.

"Bueno," Carlos told Abigail, "you'll drive. Use the coastal road rather than the motorway. Slower, and more places to duck into. After you park the car, drop the multi-key down a drain somewhere else. Special key, fancy technology; don't want it turning up. Right, Mr Turner, I won't say it has been totally a pleasure."

"I owe you guys. I'll express that through channels."

"Get driving," replied Carlos. "Me cago en tus muertos. A traditional Spanish expression of respect upon parting."

Abigail stifled a snigger. She idly wondered what Carlos would look like, very soon, without his moustache. Well, she would never know.

"Good luck," she told him. For a moment it seemed that there might be a handshake or even a hug from him; but instead there was just a long and thoughtful gaze.

"Go," he said, and turned away.

Lobres to Málaga, Spain: June 2008

Over halfway to Málaga, they pulled into a gas station with café, minimally lit since it was closed. They climbed out and stretched in the warm night air, taking care to glance around them during this innocuous action. Cicadas chirped nearby, but there was no one about. Jack opened the trunk, unzipped his bag and brought out a metal flask, then the plastic box. He donned a clean pair of latex gloves. Unscrewing the top of the flask, he set it carefully down, well lodged. Pulling the lid off the box, he folded back padding and extracted the ancient glass bottle.

"Let me see it properly," insisted Abigail. So Jack held it top and bottom, to display. Though it was hard to be certain in poor light, the seal did indeed look black, not dark brown. And Carlos *had* been certain.

This vial in its pouch had been gripped by the cold finger-bones of Safiyya for over six centuries. Before that it was in Sinaldin's care, no doubt one of two or three or more, for another just like it must have been used to devastate the population of bygone Marseille. Chill spirits clutched at Abigail's spine. Before Sinaldin's journey the potion had been in Syria, and before that most probably at Alamut; perhaps even created in that very chamber underground where the earthquake had scared her.

"It doesn't say *al-Hakim's Terrible Tincture*," remarked Paul lightly.

"Nor did the other bottle say *al-Hakim's Elixir*," answered Abigail. "What *can* he have been like?"

"Osama bin Laden with a PhD in virology," suggested Jack. "Okay, enough? Before I drop it? Hold the flask steady, Paul."

Paul knelt on the tarmac and complied. "Er, don't I get to wear gloves too?"

"You aren't handling the bottle itself."

"Just don't crack the glass then, or break the seal!"

Gently, though his hands trembled a little, Jack inserted the vial vertically into the flask, pushing slowly down as gel welled up. He pressed the tip of his forefinger upon the hardened wax, sinking it deeper into the flask, and finally scooped displaced gel back on top. After wiping his gloved fingers on a cloth, he screwed the flask up tight.

"Bit like inserting a suppository, really," commented Paul, relaxing his grip with obvious relief.

"Is that," snapped Jack, "your stupidly humorous way of alluding to Carlos calling me an asshole?"

"No, of course not. You've achieved. We've done it!"

"With the Lord's help, I've achieved. Yeah."

"Abi assisted just a bit."

"Yes," agreed Jack begrudgingly, "you too."

At that moment, they were all caught in beams from a car that turned into the gas station forecourt and coasted slowly towards them. A white car, a panel of emergency lights across its roof. Light blue chevrons ran along its side, where Abigail made out a word:

POLICIA

followed by a second word:

MUNI... MUNICIPAL.

Police! A hot bar of guilt pressed against her mind and her skin came in goose bumps. What sort of police? Was there more than one kind of police in Spain? Police, nevertheless!

"Don't speak," hissed Abigail quickly. "Just smile. Our accents are wrong for GB. I'll use my Spanish."

Two officers got out. Blue uniforms, white chequered bands on their caps. Holstered pistols at their hips.

"You have a problem?" asked one in English, quite well pronounced. He assessed Paul, now rising to his feet. He eyed the latex gloves on Jack's hands.

"No problema, gracias," said Abigail. "Necesitamos cambiar..." What was the word for driver? Oh yes, a false friend of a word. "Conductores."

Maybe she should have said *change a tyre* to explain Jack's gloves and Paul kneeling down. But then they would have needed to unload the trunk and change a perfectly good tyre while the police looked on. Why would they be burrowing in the trunk if they only needed to change drivers?

"You speak English?" asked the policeman, glancing at GB on the British licence plate.

"Oh yes, I live in England."

"But your voice is not English."

How much damned work had this policeman put in at language school? Smile, smile! Should she say she was South African, or a New Zealander? But what if they asked to see her passport? Keep smiling.

"Actually, I'm French Canadian. But I live in England at the moment."

"I see. Where in England?"

Abigail knew bits of London, as well as Oxford, Cambridge, Stratford. What if this policeman had a brother or sister who lived in England, and whom he visited? What if he regularly went to England on holiday? *He might know somewhere better than she did.* Since the other policeman was saying nothing, was it safe to assume that he didn't know as much English?

Abigail verged on panic. Seconds seemed to be sliding by. Were they really? Choose somewhere out of the way, *if only* a name would come to mind. *No*, choose somewhere big, with lots of people. No, choose... it was big enough...

"Oxford," she said, because of Jen.

The gaze of both officers drifted back to the latex gloves. An uncomfortable silence descended. God, was *that gun* weighing down Jack's pocket? Was there a bulge? *Don't look*. But Abigail looked anyway. In fact Jack had shifted, so that the suspicious side of him was facing away from the police. Had he done so soon enough? Had he moved like a gunslinger in some western, readying himself? Whatever happens, *don't* pull the gun out!

Then Jack did move, making Abigail start. But he walked calmly to the still open driver's door of the Mazda and reached in to pull the hood catch. In a couple more seconds he'd raised the hood, disappearing behind it.

"I have been to Oxford," the policeman said. "Beautiful city. I went to the pub where the Lord of the Rings drank."

He meant Tolkien, of course, not Sauron. A joke, so it seemed. Was she supposed to know the pub's name? She gave a grin that she hoped wasn't too strained.

Jack reappeared, with the dipstick in his hand.

"Do you like English beer?" she hastened to ask.

"Some is very good. And you?"

"I prefer wine. Spanish wine is wonderful."

"It's fine," called Jack, in an oddly clipped accent that he probably thought sounded like real English, instead of American.

"The oil light flickered a while back," explained Abigail rather loudly, hoping Jack could hear. "Thought we'd better check. It's probably just the light."

The policeman nodded. "I suppose you are going to Málaga airport?"

"Yes. Early flight!"

The policeman glanced at his watch.

"I'm very neurotic about getting to airports early."

"Neurotic," he repeated. "Neurótico." And he grinned. "Not erótico."

At last, she began to relax. She flashed a brief suggestive glance at the officer.

"Paul, take over at the wheel, will you?"

Paul nodded to Abigail, then reached to shut the trunk. He smiled amiably at the policemen, walked round to the driver's door. Jack closed the hood and casually stripped off his gloves.

"Many thanks for stopping!" gushed Abigail. "That was very kind of you."

"De nada," said the other policeman, who evidently understood.

"Well, let's go," Abigail said cheerfully.

When they pulled out of the forecourt, the police guys were lighting up cigarettes. Abigail had to grip the steering wheel hard to stop her hands from shaking.

Málaga, Spain: June 2008

In moonlit Málaga, they stopped for coffee and to kill time at a gas station with mini-café facilities. Finally, before even a hint of dawn was showing, a taxi deposited them at the airport. They had left the Mazda in underground parking off the Alameda Principal, hauling their bags a few blocks until they found a hotel where the man on reception had kindly phoned for a taxi. Abigail had dutifully dropped the multi-key down a grating. Then it was fruit juices and more waiting.

Finally, Jack was telling the Spanish check-in woman their reservation number; she consulted her screen. "Passengers Turner, Leclaire, Summers," she said briskly. "Madrid, Chicago, Omaha."

Jack leaned closer. "That's right."

"Did you hear *Chicago* and *Omaha*?" Paul whispered to Abigail.

"Yes. Shh."

"We packed the bags ourselves, nobody can have interfered, no one gave us anything to take."

They turned away, blessedly without bags, though in Jack's case reluctantly; his gaze followed his own bag along the conveyor belt until it disappeared through a hole in the wall.

"What's with Omaha?" hissed Paul. "I thought we were all going home to Boston!"

"There's an ace Army virus lab near Omaha, best in the country, and they're expecting our package. Plus ICE has a regional office there. It'll minimize take-offs and landings this way."

"So how many illegals does Omaha have?"

"Our Omaha facility covers the whole mid-West."

"Ice see. Hey, can we have our boarding cards? We aren't kids in your care."

"Sure."

Security presented no problems, although now and then Abigail heard Paul mutter incredulously under his breath the name of their final destination.

Zayla, East African coast: January 1165

Although on three sides sea surrounded the evidently ancient town, no saline breezes could dispel the reek of fish and of blood from camels slaughtered in its streets. Camels were also being traded, seemingly hale and hearty ones; inland lay nothing but bare desert, at least for two or three days journey. However, Zayla was the outlet for slaves from the interior, as well as for ivory and other African treasures. The slavers trail was the quickest route to Harar and onward to the south. Within a day, Hakim was negotiating with a Sheikh Abu Muhammad, a slave trader.

And so, a third of a year after they landed, they were finally where Allah willed...

Bale Region, Southern Ethiopia: May 1165

The five men rose from prayers in the cave, which seemed so like a mosque created underground especially for them by the hand of God. The river which the natives called Weyb thrummed hauntingly at the edge of their senses, rushing deeper within the seemingly endless rounded passageways and chambers of polished limestone.

Hussain, Rahim and Nasir picked up their lamps, and Taj al-Din the Persian, who had led the prayers, brought the three men and al-Hakim back through sandy intervening chambers and towards the sunlight. Next to the huge hall of the dome was a smaller space containing a natural altar, a smooth and legless limestone table that the natives used in their pagan sacrifices. Relics of their vulgar ceremonies, which appealed for health or for prosperity as regards rain or crops, were evident: dark blood-stains and scraps of hide. Then they came to the high-roofed entrance chamber, where the three men extinguished the lamps they carried, for shimmering daylight was here, dappled reflections from the river cast like spirits into the sanctity of the cave. One of several alternative passageways led to the expedition's store room.

If need be, Allah forbid, Hakim's elite company could have blocked the entrance to these caves and defended it with their swords, perhaps holding out for months. Fortunately this circumstance had showed no signs of ever happening, though the Muslims had taken care to avoid friction by ensuring they didn't obstruct the pagans' access for their rites.

And of course we shan't ever get in their way, reflected Hakim with satisfaction. He had learned useful things from the chattering and childish yet inventive pagans, almost as much as on his previous visit to the region, years earlier.

Such as the trick of catching wild monkeys to experiment upon, which, out of respect for the creatures they worshipped, Arwe and Guba had never revealed to him. Yet it was delightfully simple. Put out bowls of the local beer mixed with strong spirit, under trees where the inquisitive creatures ranged. Some monkeys would scorn the taste; others would sip and become moderately merry. But quite a number would quaff without any restraint until like Christian soldiers they sprawled senseless, and could simply be picked up and popped into bags to lug back to the village, so to the camp and waiting cages.

Daylight glared full and bright as the five men emerged from dry coolness. Under the shade of acacia trees and enclosed within a wall of thorns, were rows of stoutly-built individual wooden cages, widely spaced and each topped with an extra sun-shield of thick straw. These housed monkeys with yellowish and olive hues in their brown coats, as though moss grew in the fur. They were clearly from the same monkey tribe that Arwe's people had revered, if 'tribe' was an appropriate term for beasts, yet their white beards were a little thicker, their brow-bands fainter. Their canines were long and sharp; oh slaves who feed you, beware of those teeth!

The dozen black slaves shared adjacent tall-thatched huts of tough bamboo, harvested from higher in the hills then bound and woven with tough grasses and reeds. One hut was for men; the other that could be secured overnight, for women. During the first couple of months, slim iron shackles had linked each slave's ankles, not so as to unduly hobble and impede them, but more as a signal of their subordinate status. True, such shackles were a disincentive for any attempt to run away, but at Hakim's behest the chains were now done away with. Where would a slave run to without being tracked down? Or eaten by wild animals? Hakim didn't want his essential workers to be clumsy. Already one had been bitten by a monkey.

Hakim had bought these slaves from Sheikh Abu Muhammad, and had hired the Sheikh himself for his local expertise. He was paying for three of the Sheikh's guards besides, all with jewels from Alamut, lighter to transport and conceal than gold, although Hakim had brought gold too. The Sheikh probably couldn't be prevailed on to stay more than another couple of weeks in this area; the man was becoming restless. Yet greed if not loyalty guaranteed he'd return to them in due course.

Hamdullah and Nizam and others had accomplished their prayers out in the open, since it was unwise policy to leave monkeys and slaves unsupervised, unwise too for everyone except the Sheikh and his men to be inside the cave. Although Hakim believed that his fellow Muslim Abu Muhammad wouldn't dream of blocking the Nizaris within, while attempting to rob or blackmail them, he also believed in insurance. To that end, Rahim and Hamdullah had demonstrated certain Assassin skills and fighting techniques a few weeks earlier. The stunning display had also served to impress the natives, not that they seemed at all hostile. To cut off the head of a cow with one blow of a scimitar, while somersaulting upside-down in mid-air, made a powerful and lasting impression. Followed by a feast of cooked cow, its death munificently paid for by Hakim, everyone was *very* well aware of who should stay a friend and never become an enemy. Even so, the most valuable jewels remained on Hakim's person.

Bristle-crowned starlings, blue mousebirds, and little grey fly-catchers all congregated near the cages, from which drifted the smell of monkey-shit and food. Procuring the latter was a duty of the women slaves. The restless monkeys ate almost anything: nuts, leaves, lizards, berries, fungi, eggs, as well as any kind of leftover scraps, yet they did have a special love for fruits and flowers. Hakim required their diet to be as varied as possible, both for health reasons and also to avert madness due to the boredom of confinement, which could sometimes occur even with other confined monkeys in plain sight for token companionship. He needed healthy stock as well as stock with necessary ailments which gave rise to the seeds of plague and protection. Already they had three weeping monkeys, so experiments could start in earnest, though no young grey-hairs yet.

Hakim reflected that his own hair, which rapidly transitioned to grey six years before, was now entering its final season, turning just as swiftly to white. This was a comfort; a daily reminder that God's protection from plague ran in his own veins.

Later in the day, Hakim and three companions arduously climbed the narrow footpath to the native village, where the Sheikh preferred to pitch his tents and hobble his horses. This upper location probably allowed Abu Muhammad and his guards to more conveniently enjoy now and then the coming and going of native women, no doubt exchanging little gifts for sinful pleasures; but Hakim chose not to enquire. Sacred law may have been overthrown by the Master of Alamut, yet it was far better that the doctor's expedition functioned chastely and with absolute dedication, in which tradition the Fida'een of Alamut had indeed been previously trained, with sexual spillage severely punished. To this end Hakim had lectured his companions about certain copulatory diseases befouling the local population.

"You would not wish," he recalled telling them, "to be forever desperate to piss, yet only able to painfully discharge a few drops from your stinging prick, along with oozing yellow pus. And all due to carnal congress with a woman polluted by the putrid semen of some unclean native man!" He hadn't bothered to mention that this vile condition could be simply cured by an appropriate diet, accompanied by washing of the afflicted organ twice a day with an electuary formed from certain powders mixed with syrup and honey.

They reached the village, which was ringed by thorn-brush. Phallic wooden totems marked cardinal points of this natural fence, preventing the intrusion of local malicious spirits. The round houses were plastered with an adobe of mud and straw under steep thatch, pottery jars perched atop their centre-poles to deflect the rain.

White-robed Abu Muhammad was burly and sweaty, though perfumed. On his fingers, gold rings. Sword in an elegant scabbard of engraved brass. He spoke the native language well, and was coaching Hakim along with

Nasir and Taj al-Din and Rahim who passed on what he learned to several of the other Fida´een.

On his previous visit to this region, Hakim had relied upon an interpreter, poor Yaqob, who had died of plague. A few of the natives understood some Arabic, but Hakim and his men might be here for several years and needed direct communication, both more efficient and far safer; interpreters could develop their own agenda. So as usual each morning at this time the four men met with the Sheikh outside his tent, in the shade of an acacia. Rugs had already been laid over the sandy soil. Courtesies were exchanged. The stout Sheikh and his adult pupils seated themselves, cross-legged. One of the Sheikh's guards brought them a blackened brass pot of sweet coffee spiced with ginger.

"There will occur this afternoon a ritual important to these people," announced the Sheikh portentously, waving a stubby-fingered hand vaguely towards the village. "Their priest-witch invites you to nominate one of your group to participate. I should add that this is an honour, akin to a privileged initiation."

Immediately, Hakim recalled drinking the monkey's blood years earlier at Arwe's behest.

"If you intend to live with these people harmoniously for a prolonged period, it is wise to accept. The natives believe this ritual brings enlightenment as to the spirits that dwell in trees and streams and in certain stones, and especially in caves."

"Truly there is no enlightenment but from Allah," protested Nasir.

"True," agreed the Sheikh. "However, no worship of these pagan *jinn* takes place during this ritual, no prayers nor sacrifices, simply some temporary alteration of the mind. One of my men experienced this ritual on my behalf, just two years ago. He was unharmed."

So: a different barbaric ritual, which affected *the mind*. "Did you yourself witness the nature of this ritual?" asked Hakim.

"It employs the juice of what the natives call *the little onion*, a bulb resembling narcissus. Far in the south, said the priest-witch, men make cuts on their heads and rub the juice of the bulb into the wounds. Here, the priest-witch employs another method."

"What method?"

"That, you will discover," replied the Sheikh. "But your scalp will not need to be cut by a knife, nor any part of you."

It irritated Hakim that the Sheikh should think to play this little game, when he was being paid amply for his services. Was Abu Muhammad testing the mettle of Hakim and his men? Did he do so benevolently, so as to

347

determine whether he might safely leave them to their own devices? Or instead slyly? Was he probing at the quality of Hakim's leadership? Even probing at his religious sincerity?

Hakim thought rapidly. It would be foolish, as leader of an expedition upon which so much of enormous consequence depended, to risk his own health unnecessarily, either bodily or mentally. He had to think clearly, constantly. Immediately into his mind came what the Master of Alamut had confided about the motivating of assassins. Hakim gestured Rahim to step aside with him, then spoke in a hush.

"Rahim, in Alamut I believe that you communed with paradise after tasting a sticky brown gum; blessed by our Imam and Master," he hastened to add.

The athletic Fida'i, capable of dangerous and acrobatic feats, gazed in wide-eyed dismay at the doctor, as though this subject should not have been divulged anywhere near to a stranger. Yet absolute obedience was everything. Rahim nodded assent.

Hakim continued carefully. "You experienced an alteration of perception, revealing the hidden world beyond. I envy you and honour you. Are you prepared for an encounter which may reveal a different hidden world, one which may be…" he could not say *an illusion*, "which may be disturbing?"

Rahim replied calmly. "I am prepared to encounter the spirits of Hell in the juice of an onion, if this advances our mission." He understood.

"You are faithful beyond price."

After the two had sat once again, Hakim felt moved to add more. "Do not dwell upon Hell, in case what you dwell upon possesses your mind. Far better to contemplate Allah in the name of *an-Nur*, the Light, or *al-Basir*, the Seeing."

"Excellent advice," commented the Sheikh.

Omaha, Nebraska: June 2008

At Eppley Airport, Omaha, a black Dodge people carrier with tinted windows was waiting when they emerged from Arrivals at 7.00 pm. Dark thunder-heads towered, lightning flickering vividly. Elsewhere, the sky was a bruised dull yellow. Daylight, of sorts, still had two hours before expiry. A day already extremely long and tiring, for their noon plane from Madrid to Chicago had started its race with the sun more than twelve hours before, landing late so that they'd only just made their connection.

Abigail and Paul clutched their bags as Jack urged them into the van through its side door. Paul hesitated momentarily before climbing in, looking around as though he might prefer to call a taxi. Jack was close behind. Fat drops of rain had started to fall.

"Praise the Lord, you're lucky to land, not get diverted," announced the blond driver by way of a greeting. Something in his watery blue eyes seemed to contradict a broad smile. His attire was casual: a red and green checked shirt, jeans, and decoratively tooled cowboy boots. Beside him lounged a veritable bodybuilder, his biceps straining a white T-shirt. That fellow's lumpy bumpy shaven head might have been a joy to phrenologists. Abigail had vaguely been expecting tight-lipped agents wearing dark suits.

"Pleased to drive you, Ma'am, and Sir," the blond man added, to Abigail and Paul. A clap of thunder was followed a moment later by the loud clunk of central locking, as though thus the storm would be excluded from their vehicle.

"Take it *very* carefully, Svenson," cautioned Jack. "We're carrying something fragile."

As they pulled away from the airport rain sluiced down, blotting out urban landmarks. By the time the cloudburst dwindled twenty minutes later, the Dodge was already in open country. Huge flat fields of young corn dominated, a million cobs swelling within their hairy husks of leaf. Modest hills, more like the lumps on the muscleman's head, resisted the modern conqueror, while goldenrod in early bud infiltrated via the roadsides and burst out in occasional patches. The sky, as it cleared, seemed vast. The nameless specimen of physique passed back chilled cans of cherry Kool-Aid.

"Lots of Vit-C, caffeine free," he commented in an incongruously squeaky voice, sounding like an ad jingled by a chipmunk.

"Caffeine's what I could do with, and chocolate," replied Abigail. "Got any chocolate?"

Sorry, Ma'am."

Paul smirked and nudged Abigail. "Don't drink the Kool-Aid."

"What do you mean by that?" queried Svenson. "People hereabouts are very proud of Kool-Aid. Hastings, Nebraska, that's its birthplace. Week-long fair every summer."

"It's a common saying, didn't you know?" temporised Paul. "Meaning: whatever you're told, don't give it too much credence. Like, kooky Jim Jones giving his disciples cyanide Kool-Aid in Jamestown."

"That was *not* Kool-Aid. It was imitation stuff called Flavor Aid."

"I stand corrected. Sorry I spoke."

"No," interjected Jack, "don't be sorry about speaking. Say whatever you want, although maybe you should reserve that till we get to..." and he tailed off.

Paul couldn't help yawning convulsively, infecting Abigail likewise, although Jack seemed made of sterner stuff. After a few moments' silence, Paul piped up again. "Well, let's hope it doesn't rain, or worse, on the fair. We're in Tornado Alley here, aren't we?"

"Toto," Jack said lightly, "you sure aren't in Boston anymore."

"Yes, I've been wondering idly why Immigration Enforcement has this bureau so far from any borders or ports of entry."

"Paul," pleaded Abigail. "Hush."

"This," replied Jack, "is the electronic era, if you hadn't noticed." A tone of annoyance tightened his voice. "Everywhere is next door to everywhere else. Plus, some of ICE's work is high security stuff, so we don't nail up our colours on Main Street in Busyville. *And* there are such things as the need to sweeten a Congressman who'll vote the right way on a budgetary appropriation, provided we locate a facility in his home state. Right?"

"Right," agreed Paul. To Abigail, he said through a semi-suppressed yawn, "Kurt Cobain once dyed his hair red with Kool-Aid."

Her eyes signalled him to please shut up. What an effort. Her lids felt so heavy.

He did, though, leaning his head back against the rest, his own lids fluttering as he resisted sleep.

Presently, on a minor though monotonously straight road, they passed by a tiny community boasting COLON, SANDERS COUNTY: POPULATION 140. Ten minutes later, Svenson turned off to a broad dirt track. This passed through the thick green carpet of a cornfield before doglegging rightward through rows of pyramidal jack pines and red cedars, then switching to diagonally leftward, and finally resuming its original direction, now through masses of cottonwoods and blue spruce.

"Chicanery," murmured Paul. "Kinky."

"What you gabbing on about now?" asked Jack.

"Like chicanes on a race track. Kinks in the route, so you can't see from one end to the other."

"So you'd put a tunnel straight through the middle of a windbreak, would you, for better visibility?"

Now they could see, ahead, a steel gate topped with razor-wire barring the way; and beyond: open land, some horses grazing, sprawling ranch-style buildings, a water-tower. Svenson slowed, coming to a halt by an intercom. Overhead rose a yellow steel mast, topped by a large square-mouthed horn pointing in the direction of the buildings. A CCTV camera on the mast was angled at the gate. To right and left a high steel-mesh fence stretched away, likewise tipped with razor-wire.

Abigail struggled to stay alert. "What's that loudspeaker thing up there for?" she asked.

"Rock concerts?" suggested Paul. "Bible readings?"

"Tornado siren," said Svenson.

The great yellow horn could be a strident alarm for other eventualities, too.

"Those boxes on poles along the fence," Paul remarked. "Looks electrified."

Their driver thumbed down his window and pressed a button.

"Brothers, we're back. Consignment collected."

Smoothly, the gate swung wide.

Bale Region, Southern Ethiopia: May 1165

The sun was well on its way towards the horizon when natives came bare-chested and daubed with ochre mud, their faces painted white as though little shields masked them, except for their eyes. In their midst was the priest-witch, the *bawda* in the local tongue, his head the long-snouted and fully-maned head of a baboon. He wore beads and a skirt of grasses, a large pouch of hide at his waist. The mystic man's eyes were almost hidden by the brow-ridge of the dead animal, glinting from deep within its empty sockets. The priest-witch chanted as he drew near, while his white-masked pagan adherents ululated alarmingly.

Presently, all were sitting in a circle, including Rahim. Hakim and his armed companions and the Sheikh too stood close by the circle, watching intently.

Firstly the priest-witch produced a bowl from his pouch, then a handful of what indeed looked like small onions, and then a wooden device evidently contrived to squeeze tightly. For a moment an image came to Hakim of a man's testicle being inserted and squeezed mercilessly. One by one the baboon-man placed onions in the device and crushed their juice into the bowl.

Ah, so the juice of onions was to be drunk...

But no. The baboon-priest took one final item from his pouch, and displayed it to the now silent circle. It was part of the jaw of a viper, its curved biting teeth exposed, and, behind, the tiny bags of the poison sacs. Then the human baboon dipped the fangs into the bowl of juice and manipulated the sacs cleverly with his fingers. Hakim realised that juice was being drawn up through the hollow teeth to fill, or partly fill, the empty sacs.

The baboon-priest mimed at Rahim to bare his right arm and stretch it out. In case Rahim had not understood properly, two of the white-masked natives assisted, which Rahim allowed.

The priest chanted, then he held the fangs against Rahim's flesh, and pressed.

In that moment a blinding insight came to Hakim, almost as though it was he rather than Rahim who'd received the perception-changing juice into his blood.

This was how! How by artifice to put the seed of plague into the body of a monkey, or of a slave.

Long ago, Arwe had protected him not via *digestion* of monkey blood, but because a little of the monkey's blood had mingled with his own, due to the tooth extraction leaving an open wound in his mouth. He'd long since realised this, ever since the death of that Igwe warrior who'd nicked his lips on a befouled spear-point. Yet using a viper's sharp fangs was a cunning and efficient method of accomplishing the same effect, in fact a perfect way to insert *any* liquid into the flow of a person's blood! Then and there, Hakim termed this new technique, unknown in Muslim lands, *intravening*.

Truly, God brought him blessed revelations by way of these pagan priests. Had God permitted them to remain infidel for this very purpose? To help preserve ancient local skills until the time they were needed, until *now*.

Revelations: soon Rahim's pupils were dilated...

Hours later, Rahim related his experience to Hakim. "The world brightened and became many-fold. If I moved my head, the priest-witch was in six different places at the same time, and the natives were a multitude of jinn. A parrot that flew by was everywhere in its flight at once. The features of men and women seemed larger and cruder. Women's bodies appeared lascivious; those of men, menacing. Sometimes they were dwarfs, sometimes giants. Or else I was a giant, then a dwarf. I lost the understanding of size and of time."

"You observed very well," said Hakim, with respect, for he remembered his own delusions when Arwe had operated within his mouth. Maybe the crushed little bulbs had been part of what Arwe gave him to drink?

"I rocked between bliss and fear. The bliss was similar to what I experienced of paradise in Alamut. The fear was the possibility of being in hell. I could sway in either direction. But a Fida'i doesn't feel fear! Nor would I let myself be enchanted or seduced. I... kept my balance for what seemed an eternity, like a rock poised upon another rock while caressing winds pull at it and rainbows wrap around it. Within me I knew, with the strength of a prayer, that these sensations would finally depart."

"I salute you," said Hakim, remembering his own fevered wanderings in the jungle of brightness and dark madness. Almost, he added, as a brother. But Rahim was one of the instruments in the service of his great quest, albeit one of the finest. Rahim could never be Hakim's brother. There must always be a certain distance.

Bale Region, Southern Ethiopia: August 1165

Three months later, Hakim might well have surveyed the busy, highly organised camp with some satisfaction, had he not himself been working constantly from dawn until after dark by the light of oil lamps. Several cycles of experimentation were under way and, with the help of the Fida'een, all the camp's activities were carefully recorded. Two overseers simultaneously recorded the most crucial procedures on different manuscripts, reducing the possibility of mistakes.

Whenever Hakim inspected, it was always with vigilance, an alertness which by now he had trained fairly successfully into the increasing number of slaves. The men from Alamut were naturally alert, and knew what they must beware of. Hakim himself could work with the dangerous blood and organs of monkeys, knowing God's shield protected him, but as to the other workers... Captive monkeys were handled at all times using long sticks equipped with nooses, the workers wearing leather gloves and masks of fabric. Female slaves, who supplied the monkeys' richly varied diet, delivered their baskets likewise masked and gloved.

Although some experiments were aimed at increasing the stock of weepers, via cross-breeding of monkeys or their cross-blooding via intravention, and others were designed to improve techniques and equipment Hakim thought he'd need, there was now a most urgent requirement for human experimental subjects. The village had three abject prisoners on which to make a start, yet fulfilling his vision required a steady stream of healthy individuals to work with, prisoners of war or some other captives.

Hakim had no wish to encourage hostilities between his hosts and their immediate neighbours, since conflict might rebound, as it had done so disastrously with the Igwe during his previous expedition. Yet several large tribes a few days march away frequently engaged in disputes about territory, which often led to raids. Before Sheikh Abu Muhammad departed, and when Hakim, Rahim, Nasir and Taj al-Din had only the most basic grasp of Oromifa, Hakim accompanied by Rahim and the Sheikh had conferred with the prestigious *bawda*, whose name was Tewo, in his hut.

Unaccoutred by the baboon mask, Tewo's own nose looked squashed, evidence perhaps of some Bantu blood or of pressure in the womb, an awkward position up against a stouter sibling, or even two siblings. His dome of a forehead, under crinkly salt-and-pepper hair, seemed babyish, though around his eyes his dusky skin was meshed with wrinkles suggestive of much squinty concentration allied perhaps with a sense of inspired mischief or a certain madness. The yellowish streaking in the whites of his eyes, around shiny brown pupils, made Hakim think of polished agate.

After the usual courtesies and coffee, Hakim declared, "I need a reliable supply of unwanted people, to discover secrets about the body which I will share freely with you."

The sheikh translated. Tewo grinned.

"Tewo asks if you will cut them apart while alive."

"Never. They must be fit and healthy. Although if they die, then I will cut them open. My religion grants rights to slaves, so these people cannot be slaves. They must be prisoners. In my experience, prisoners are often tortured to death for the entertainment of their captors."

"Tewo says that such entertainment may be prolonged for weeks or even months. But if it's necessary to exchange prisoners there'll be no torture; nor if a prisoner is an important man and the enemy tribe is rich enough to buy him back."

"Ah, so a prisoner *can* be bought? That is exactly what I wish to do! I wish to buy prisoners from tribes quite far from here, paying adequately for the loss of entertainment. I'll also pay a percentage of the cost to those who expedite this. Ask Tewo if this can be arranged."

To consider the proposal, Tewo arose lithely and adopted a one-legged stance, tucking the toes of one foot behind the opposing knee so that a bony bent knee stuck out through his grass skirt. He stood stock-still, a difficult posture to maintain, in Hakim's opinion. Since the Sheikh remained cross-legged, so did Hakim.

Tewo mused a while, then grinned down at his visitors.

"He says such entertainment is often highly prized."

"I shall pay reasonable prices."

"Also, he would need to negotiate gifts for the crossing of other tribes' territory. Slave traders are usually many and well-armed, so they can risk neglecting gifts. Tewo's tribesmen couldn't neglect this aspect."

"I see."

Evidently Tewo was foreseeing quite a lot of profit. He'd also witnessed the lethal agility of Hakim's Fida'een, which excluded the possibility of robbing Hakim in any ordinary way. Perhaps his pose was a comment on this, to show that he could also be something of an acrobat, albeit a static one. Or perhaps to achieve bird-like vision, communing with the spirits of storks or flamingos.

Yet a crop of healthy subjects was desperately needed!

"Tell him I agree."

Tewo quickly dropped to all fours in front of Hakim and the Sheikh and bared his teeth, baboon-like, then he was cross-legged again. Those agate eyes gleamed.

"This," he remarked, "will result in more raids and strife than usual. But not near here. The vexatious will be distracted. We shall enjoy peace."

Was that not worth something? Rather than that Hakim should pay for it?

"And prosperity," Tewo added. "Tell me, is a *woman* prisoner of the same value to you as a man?"

"Women are not warriors, to be captured."

Tewo's reply was, "They may be more easily caught. So?"

A woman could die of plague as easily as a man. Depending on how long Hakim must remain here, women could even give birth and thus provide extra bodies free of cost.

Sanders County, Nebraska: June 2008

"Why were you needling Jack?" Abigail demanded once they were alone together in the two-bedroom chalet, where air-conditioning purred. Generous-size lounge, which they were in, kitchen with an enormous fridge-freezer, plus commodious bathroom. "He saved our lives, remember! And needling that Svenson guy too. Or was I dreaming it?"

Paul tried to open a window. "Locked," he said. "Toughened glass, no doubt in case of tornados. You notice they locked the door too? And there's no phone or computer. Given they've confiscated your laptop and mobile, my smartphone too, we're utterly incommunicado!"

"Paul, *think*… if we could phone or e-mail out, we might blab anything to anyone, word of honour or not. We could inadvertently sabotage ICE's investigation."

He raised an eyebrow. "We could've emailed from Spain. You still think this is ICE?"

"Well, there wouldn't be a sign on the gate, as Jack already pointed out. God, I have to crash out."

Paul joined Abigail by the well-stocked bookcase and peered at the shelves. "Zane Grey and lots of other Westerns. Holy Land, history of Israel, Jewish and Bible stuff. Hey, a complete set of the *Left Behind* books."

"The what?"

"What happens to our poor old planet after God raptures the righteous straight to Heaven."

"Loads of Agatha Christie too," she pointed out.

"No sex scenes, drugs, or rock 'n' roll. You know how Agatha came up with her unsolvable mysteries?"

"I've no idea."

Paul grinned. "She wrote everything except for the final chapter, and only *then* did she decide who was the most *unlikely* murderer. After which she adjusted it all accordingly."

"That's cheating!"

Paul had drifted to the lounge door. "Fooled millions of readers, she did. Jack's trying to fool us, Abi, unlikely though that seems after how he hassled you to root out the terrorists."

She shook her head. "No. I can't take this. I'm going to bed."

But inquisitive Paul had pulled back a rug in the corridor to reveal a hatch in the timber flooring. "Lookee here!"

A ring-pull raised the hinged hatch; wooden steps led down into a concrete cellar, a light switch by the topmost step. Down he went, as

357

fluorescence flickered to life, illuminating rows of shelves.

"What's down there?" she called, almost tumbling forward with tiredness.

"Canned food. Water. Radio. Bunk beds. Chemical toilet. Survivalist stuff."

Abigail forced herself to clamber half way down. "At any rate, it doesn't look much like a torture chamber. I think this has more to do with tornados."

"Uh. A storm cellar. Right."

"And on that note, for God's sake goodnight."

"Technically, it's still evening."

Early next morning, Thursday, as sunshine cheered the lounge while local TV reported on trivialities, they fixed a breakfast of cereal, toast and coffee. Presently Svenson appeared.

"Mr Turner says debriefing starts at 10.30, after some folks get here."

Paul pointed to the rug in the hall. "We noticed we have a well-equipped storm cellar underneath. Would that be good too for a nuclear war?"

Svenson shook his head. "The hatch ain't steel, and the air comes from outside."

"Aren't you missing a trick there? I mean, if the End Times are coming? Though I suppose true believers don't need protecting from whatever causes the apocalypse."

"Faith is the finest protector, Mr Summers."

"Still, a bit of technology and preparation don't go amiss."

"Trouble with some folks," observed Svenson, "is trying to be too clever. 10.30, then."

"So what was that about?" asked Abigail in exasperation after the front door had closed, locking them in again. "Are you determined to be objectionable?"

"No, just sceptical. I continue to wonder about us being debriefed so far from…"

"Civilization? Omaha's a major city, and Jack *said* about the local congressman."

"Yes, Jack's real quick-witted, for someone with a delusional belief system."

"Oh Paul! It's obvious he's very religious, but that doesn't make him disloyal. Back in Boston, he said he'd never let anything get in the way of the job. Next you'll be saying there's microphones hidden in here."

"If so, we'd need an electronic sweeper to find any. But I think not, since nothing such as us has arisen before. So I guess we can still speak freely. Abi, um," and he looked away, "have you thought through... well, how much you're prepared to tell about Kamal? I mean, how much detail? In case they want, um, everything?"

Paul was obviously uncomfortable broaching this. Somewhat impertinent too? No, he was trying to protect her, she could see that. And it hurt him to mention the *everything*. Yet he wasn't avoiding the subject... in the way she'd been pushing it aside herself... to fend off pain and humiliation. It'd been bad enough spilling generalities to Jack in Provence, awful in fact, degrading.

Was there a legitimate reason why ICE might need to know lurid detail? Would they seek insights into Kamal's personality based upon his intimate behaviour... Or did that only happen in films? Until now, she'd assumed that she and Paul would be questioned together. Yet what if questioning happened separately, one interrogator being a sympathetic woman? Debriefing: symbolically, the stripping naked of her foolish and sex-crazed self.

"I'm not," answered Abigail awkwardly, feeling herself blush, "going to make a porn confession." It was good that Paul was staring determinedly into the distance, at the horses.

As it happened, she and Paul were indeed separated for their questioning. Paul was closeted in the kitchen with a middle-aged bald man and a younger ginger-haired companion. Both had local accents; the zealous aspect of the redhead suggested a desire to evangelise on the sinful East Coast. Abigail, no doubt the star attraction, was in the lounge with Jack plus a supposed Professor of Immunology and Virology, not to mention a craggy, granitic, heavily-jowled figure whom the others seemed to hold in great respect.

That evening, left alone again after hours of interrogation, Paul and Abigail compared unwritten notes.

"They didn't," she said with obvious relief, "go into... what you were worried about. Not in any... detail. Not today, anyhow." More days of debriefing probably lay ahead.

"Um, how much actual profiling of Kamal did they go in for?"

"Much less than I feared they would." She looked away. "It was more Safiyya and Sinaldin and the Assassins and Alamut, plus whatever I knew about al-Hakim and plague plague plague. They'd been through the history of searches on my laptop."

"Oh Abi, I'm sorry to sound like another interrogator! But how much, well, physical description of Kamal did they want? Jack only saw Kamal fleetingly."

She shrugged and pursed her lips. "Not a hell of a lot."

"Me neither. Frankly, I don't think they're interested in tracking Kamal down. Or else they don't possess the capability or the contacts."

"Conspiracy theory again?" asked Abigail wearily.

"Did you query what they've done with the stuff we got from Safi's tomb?"

"I assume it's gone for analysis."

"Well, I asked. 'It's in the right hands,' was the response. So whose hands are those? While you were in Syria I was googling about haemorrhagic, Ebola or whatever. I came across the names of level-4 containment facilities, the sort of labs you need to handle hot viruses. There's *very few* of them. And our specimen is pretty much the hottest stuff there is! It should've gone straightaway to CDC in Atlanta. The Centers for Disease Control."

"Even us French Canadians know what CDC is."

"Jack mentioned an army lab near here. Maybe it's real, but that doesn't mean it's suitable. Fort Detrick is top notch, but that's Maryland, gotta be 1000 miles away, same for CDC."

"They must have access to *some* local facility, maybe a secret one?"

"Gotcha!" crowed Paul. "*They*. The nameless *they*."

"ICE," she corrected herself. "I mean ICE."

"One thing you ought to do is minimise risks en-route to any lab. You don't send one van in a rainstorm."

"When Svenson set off, it wasn't storming."

"So they don't pay any attention to weather forecasts in Tornado Alley? Plenty of time since we left Málaga for an armoured truck and a police escort."

"They didn't want attention. It never should've been on a commercial plane. You're twisting things!"

Paul whirled around, flapping his hands. "Whee, I'm a tornado."

Well into their second day of debriefing, the Professor of Immunology received a mobile phone call which he quickly went outside to continue, unheard by Abigail. Jack took the opportunity to have Svenson bring coffee and doughnuts. When the Immunologist returned a good fifteen minutes later, he carried a black leather case that he then popped open.

"Well, *Doctor* Leclaire," he said, addressing Abigail as though she were some fellow professional, or maybe he was being ironic. "I need to ask you for a blood sample, if you'd be so kind as to oblige."

"*A blood sample? Why?*" Thoughts raced through her mind. She couldn't possibly be incubating plague; Safiyya's vial had stayed sealed. If there was a risk, it'd be no different for Jack, yet the Professor wasn't requiring a sample from him! Something else then… But what? To check whether Kamal had given her a venereal disease? Oh God, that'd be a new level of treachery by the bastard. But surely Kamal wouldn't have permitted himself to pick up VD, when he needed maximum health and efficiency for his malevolent master plan? *Oh, Kamal's sheer physical efficiency… put those memories aside!* So why, why? A shiver of apprehension traced Abigail's spine. What was going on?

"I'm not at liberty to say," replied the Immunologist cum Virologist.

"Do you think I'm sick from something?"

Indeed she was sick, from the constant jogging of her memories. Sick, from the memory of sex with that man. And now she was getting frightened too.

"Would you roll up your sleeve?"

Abigail hesitated.

"Sterilised one-time needle, Dr Leclaire. I do know how to take blood."

Numbly, she complied.

No sooner did he have his sample, than the Immunologist left and didn't return. Jack continued plying Abigail with questions, some seemingly for the benefit of the craggy guy she'd christened Mount Rushmore, since Jack had been present at one or two of the events in Provence and Spain he was now quizzing her about. Occasionally Mount Rushmore inserted a few questions of his own, in a resonant voice that would carry far if he raised it. Questions especially about medieval plague.

Sunlight filled their chalet with golden optimism. Yet for Abigail, nagging worry unravelled the sun's pleasant makeover.

"Paul, did that Immunologist guy take a blood sample from you?"

"I never even saw him after he arrived this morning. He had one from you?"

"Yes, right after a long phone call. And he wouldn't say why. I suspect if I hadn't co-operated, Svenson's bodybuilder pal might have helped me sit still. Why a blood sample from *me*, but not from you?"

Paul fiddled with his curly locks while concentrating. "All I can think of is… er, how to put this? You were more, um, connected with Kamal than I was."

"*You think he might have fucked me full of plague?* That a penis can pass on plague more effectively than heavy breathing in my face? If so, I'd fucking deserve it, wouldn't I?"

Paul's face blossomed with concern. "No, no, calm down. Hey look, you don't deserve *anything* bad. And I can't imagine Kamal imperilling himself. He never seemed like a man under a death sentence, quite the opposite."

"Well what then!" yelled Abigail. "What do you mean?"

Paul's forehead creased to a deep frown as his eyes signalled distress. "I'm sorry, I'm just guessing. But maybe... maybe the Immunologist guy found some reason for thinking that Kamal could have... no not infected, but... er, immunised you, um, physically, by, well, er, sexual transmission..."

"*Fucked me immune*? I hardly think saving my life was much on Kamal's mind in Iran or Syria or France. The evidence kind of points directly the other way."

"Yeah, yeah, but what if immunity is an unintentional consequence of what happened between...? Perhaps there's something in the Safiyya vial that suggests this."

"The wax seal was black. That vial was for *infection*, not for immunity!"

"Yeah I know, but listen, this has *got* to be something connected with, pardon me... *semen*. After all, you didn't share blood. Something in the sample must have alerted them, maybe something that's common to both the *waters*, brown *and* black vials."

"That's nonsense!" protested Abigail uncertainly. "Protection granted by some kind of vaccine wouldn't be sexually transmittable, would it? Or are you suggesting that *you* can be immune too, *if* we go to bed and fuck like rabbits! Oh no, I'm forgetting," she added sarcastically, "I don't have a penis, so that mightn't work. I can't do injecting the way men do it."

Paul blushed bright red. "I wasn't thinking that at all. I wouldn't dream... It's just that..."

"Just what!" snapped Abigail rather unfairly.

"Well, injection is a big problem all on its own. But I was thinking the other day, if Guy de Dieulefit's descendants aren't just incredibly lucky, how did they get immune? There wouldn't have been enough *water of life*, especially since Guy took some to the grave. Yet if immunity can be *heritable*... and then I thought, what other characteristics might it have?"

"Oh, I see, I think. But..."

"Surely Kamal would've availed himself of protection, so... Look, I don't know the ins and outs of vaccine production. Maybe I'm adding two and two to get five. But maybe you can produce antidote from antibodies."

"Okay, I'm definitely lost now."

"I mean that you might end up being a physical resource for our... hosts, here."

"Oh, thanks for the thought!" Abigail lashed back.

Paul looked hurt.

"A resource," she repeated. Already trafficked from Spain and confined here, she now imagined herself transferred to some medical species of brothel. Her bloodstream, just goods, used repeatedly until she was exhausted and anaemic.

Then she angrily shook her head and dispelled the image. "No! We're with the authorities. They wouldn't abuse me!"

Now Paul looked crushed.

"I'm sorry," she added more gently. I appreciate your theories. But you're scaring me even more."

Paul's face immediately brightened and then moist compassion poured from his eyes. Abigail couldn't decide whether that was rather pathetic, or very beautiful.

"What did you mean when you said 'injection is a big problem'?" she asked.

Paul shrugged. "I presume you inject Holy Water, not ingest it."

"That makes sense, the word 'drink' was taken out of Khusraw's verse on the ivory box". A man became himself the *water of life*, thought Abigail, through his blood. "And oral vaccines are hard to do, aren't they?"

"Think so. But how could injections be done in medieval times? No hypodermics then, or anything else they could conceivably use instead."

On this Abigail pondered, but then a vivid image came to her, of snake-fangs jumping towards her hand in the cave under Alamut.

"Hey, let's grab a couple of beers and try to find some good news on TV. Maybe some folks won a square dance competition. Maybe someone cooked the biggest beef burger in the world! Rejoice that our fridge doesn't only stock six flavours of Kool-Aid."

On Saturday morning the debrief ceased. Jack and their other interrogators had been called away, urgently, said Svenson as he delivered fresh provisions. They left no message, nothing about what happened next.

"Relax, it's in the hands of a higher power now," called Svenson as he closed the chalet door. The bodybuilder had been lurking just outside.

"A higher power," murmured Paul. "But who?"

Abigail bit her lip, and didn't answer.

The day wore on towards evening. Abigail read Agatha. Paul read the apocalyptic popular novels of Jim Lafayette.

Bale Region, Southern Ethiopia: December 1165

And so, after several months of frustration, a supply of prisoners was finally established. The camp by the caves expanded greatly. More slaves, by now fully trained in their duties. More cages for segregated, suitable monkeys. Many new cages for segregated prisoners, both male and female. These were well cared-for and made to understand that they weren't being held for brutal torture, though on pain of death their complete co-operation was required. In truth, reflected Hakim, quite a number would suffer terrible torture as their organs dissolved and blood burst out of them; it was necessary.

Out of sight, within the caves, were special cages for prisoners who acquired plague. Further within, a subterranean river tumbled noisily over a waterfall into dark and unknown depths. Hamdullah had tossed in many white-painted sticks, each specially marked, while Rahim had promised youths and children rewards for their retrieval, inspiring a thorough search of lower watercourses far and wide. No such stick was retrieved, though a couple of imitation ones were hopefully offered up. Consequently, corpses and polluted blood could safely be disposed of in the rushing water, by torchlight as though at a barbarian funeral rite, the foul material swallowed by an insatiable black mouth. Also the expedition's glassware, so carefully transported from Alamut, could be cleansed there.

As time passed, and the camp's work rolled forth like a mighty cart pulled by the white oxen of God's vision given to Hakim and the Fida'een, triumph rode hand in hand with frustration and failure.

The elation from observing their first successful plague cases, was indescribable. *The seeds of plague deliberately transferred to men! God's sword unsheathed and ready to place in the Imam's hand!* After years of patience and effort, Hakim had at last reached the same point in his experiments that he'd achieved with the final Igwe prisoner; yet *this time* he was well equipped and prepared, *this time* plague did not escape his control and devastate the local population. After an anxious forty days to prove the truth of this, Hakim ordered a whole day of celebration.

Yet his encouraging smiles were already sabotaged from the inside. A seemingly insurmountable problem threatened his plans, haunted his thoughts; a problem he should have expected, for all material that stems from animals or plants will eventually putrefy. Indeed his blood samples putrefied very quickly, long before he could have taken them back to Alamut, let alone hold them there against a time of danger, a time to use them.

Fortunately, air deep within the caves was as cool as sherbet, a welcome contrast to the stifling heat outside. This coolness preserved samples and specimens for longer than they might otherwise have survived, yet another God-given boon of the location. Securely tethered bottles could even be suspended in the water itself, where it eddied into a tiny cove. Yet Hakim knew in his heart this was a minor reprieve, not a solution. He prayed for inspiration daily, and started a huge series of experiments to defeat putrefaction, necessarily increasing the camp's workload still further.

The capture of a young grey-hair, a prematurely aged monkey, lifted Hakim's spirits for a while. Now they could start experiments on protection in earnest; he hadn't wanted to use too much of his own blood in case he became too weak to bear the great burdens of the mission. Yet, once again, nature's resistance to being ruled spoiled the good news. Quite a number of subjects were reacting badly to their intraventions, getting infections or slipping into fevers or being wracked by strange pains. The site of a jab with the viper fangs would sometimes swell or suppurate. A couple of prisoners even died, long before plague would have taken them. While moderate illness prior to developing plague was hardly a problem, it would clearly be a barrier to granting protection, especially if accompanied by a significant risk of death!

Somewhat distraught and with his thought fully engaged on other issues, Hakim was forced to delegate work on the improvement of intraventions. He chose Hamdullah, who'd accompanied the mission not only for his supreme fighting ability, but for other invaluable skills acquired at Alamut. Then Hakim pushed the slaves hard, his Fida'een still harder and, though headaches often gripped him now and writing swam before his eyes in the lamplight, himself hardest of all.

Bale Region, Southern Ethiopia: May 1166

While Hakim was paying a visit to the village in the company of Taj al-Din, three men wearing white jellabas arrived, riding camels bearing large leather saddlebags. The camels caused a sensation among the natives. A few might have seen those snooty humped beasts before, though not many. When the villagers crowded around, two of the animals expressed their disdain and irritation by sneezing a spray of snot explosively at the natives, sending them scurrying back, wiping their faces.

Hakim immediately recognized one of the armed men, a Fida'i named Razzak. A second Fida'i was familiar, and proved to be Sadra. The third declared that he was Herith. The men looked solemn, although relieved to have arrived. Gutturally, they ordered their mounts to kneel down, slapping their necks. After dismounting, the Fida'een bowed deeply to Hakim, then without further ado, Herith presented a letter.

Hakim opened the pages and read:

I, Muhammad, son and heir of Imam Hasan, and now myself Imam and Qa'im...

What was this! Heir of Hasan! The words were like a hammer blow to Hakim's heart. The wondrous Hasan, *dead?* He could *not* be dead! God could not snatch away that king of men when sacred work in His service remained unfinished! *Whatever had become of the magnificent sponsor of their expedition?* Oblivious to the opinion of the newly arrived Fida'een, as if hamstrung, Hakim sank down dizzily upon the gritty soil.

"What is wrong?" asked Taj al-Din with great concern.

"Wait, I beg you…"

After breathing deeply for a while, Hakim forced himself to read:

...and now myself Imam and Qa'im, bringer of justice who, at the termination of this cycle of the world, completes the work of the imams preceding me, greet you, oh Tongue of Knowledge, although truly rank and degree wither away in the presence of the Imam-Qa'im, before whom all men are levelled; for even the Prophets themselves turned to the Imam-Qa'im as to their lord, aye to Khidr who drank the water of life, becoming thus the Qa'im, to be re-embodied in Imam Hasan and now in myself, Muhammad.

The difference between the terse style of Hasan and that of his son was notable… Was the flowery eloquence of Muhammad a prelude to a terrible announcement, of support withdrawn, of a recall to Alamut? Yet what news could be more terrible in itself than that of Hasan's demise! Hasan the genius, the more than a saint! Upon whom Hakim had bestowed worship, as his Imam, embodiment on Earth of the Resurrection!

Hakim struggled to concentrate. Sweat stung his eyes, or were those salty tears? The words writhed incomprehensibly, until he gathered up his sleeve to wipe his vision clear.

Let it be known that, only a year and a half after the blessed day of Qiyama resurrected the faithful, my father's brother-in-law, namely Husayn an-Namawar of the Buwayhid line of Daylaman, blasphemously knifed my father to death…

How could such a thing *happen*? Such Satan-inspired madness! Or such… treason!

…knifed my father to death, hoping thus to overthrow the miraculous revelation of the Qiyama and restore the former moribund way of Shari'ah. Verily such a man was already spiritually dead even if physically he remained, for the purpose of the world is to know and behold God, of whom I am now the Proof; so far as God may be known; for should there not be an Imam, the world would cease to exist.

Shocked, Hakim read with increasing anxiety, even while he chastised himself for allowing any personal considerations to enter his mind at such a moment. It was as if God had withdrawn His favour from the world; as if, even, part of God had died; which could not be; so therefore God had permitted this. The newly arrived Fida'een were regarding Hakim sympathetically. Taj al-Din was wringing his hands in anxious impatience.

Such a man as Husayn an-Namawar was not a man but a beast feeding only on the husks of truth, disdaining the grain; a beast fit for slaughter together with all of his family, as I decreed. For the unrepentant shall be destroyed. For the unrepentant are superfluous.

Muhammad was only nineteen, yet plainly he had laid hold on the reins of power unhesitatingly, with absolute confidence and with no qualms as to what must be done; and he wrote with the wisdom of a man older than his years. So much was clear.

For this reason I assure you that when, God willing, you return to Alamut, be it

Ian Watson & Andy West

a year from now, be it ten years from now, you will receive all that you may require. For I am Kalimah, the Word; and you have the word of the Word.

Now Hakim relaxed somewhat, even though the pain of loss remained acute.

And this is my command to you, as al-Amr, the Command of God: May you shuck off impediments to seeing the truth, and perceive the inner world within and behind the outer world!

Yes, yes, the inner world of the seeds of pestilence hidden within the body! If only there was a glass as powerful as the eye of God, by which to see this. Yet Hakim could infer such by reason, endowed in him by God.

Through me, feats impossible to ordinary mortals are made possible. Peace be upon the Chosen Prophet and his family, and God suffices us, He is an excellent guardian.

An expression of total support! And yes, of full understanding of what Hakim's mission was, without revealing such in a document which might have been intercepted. *The unrepentant shall be destroyed. The unrepentant are superfluous.*

This was a cause for joy, yet at the moment Hakim still mainly felt devastated. How *could* God have permitted Hasan to be slain? And not in battle as a martyr, which would at least have been an exalted death, but treacherously, deceitfully, at the hands of one of his own kin!

Hakim reread the epistle carefully, then he read it yet again, the words burning into his brain like the damascening upon a sword. By now Rahim and Hamdullah had arrived, hotfoot. A slave must have run down to the camp. Seeing Hakim kneeling, they hesitated to greet their brethren.

Hakim arose, dusted off his robe, and thrust the letter at Taj al-Din, for he must not let his second-in-command stand by as yet unknowing.

"Read, but I beg you, let me be with my thoughts."

Could it be that Hasan had fulfilled his purpose in life? And that God wanted Hasan back to reward him? Or that the traitor must be revealed, in order to be exterminated along with his family, lest they delay their treason until a time when their treachery might cause greater harm? That was similar to the reason why Khidr had slaughtered a seemingly innocent young boy, because Khidr could see the face of the future should that boy ever become a man.

Truly, God foresaw all! Consequently God could anticipate that Hasan's son, despite his comparative youth, would from the very outset be a powerful and devout successor to his father.

Perhaps joy *was* appropriate, after all. Right now, at this moment, though in eternity, Hasan was receiving his reward from God, *in His very presence*. Hasan's son, may he live long, had reaffirmed total support for Hakim's mission. Surely God foresaw a long reign for Imam Qa'im Muhammad. And more years of labour for Hakim himself, until he succeeded?

He heard Taj al-Din gasp. To Herith he said, "I assume you're acquainted with the contents of this? I mean, in general."

The Fida'i bowed. "Tongue of Knowledge," he declared, "I am myself, humbly and obediently, also a message and a container."

Herith switched to Persian, doubtless in case any of the natives understood Arabic. It transpired that into his garments many valuable jewels were sewn. Those saddlebags contained, among other gifts from Alamut, well-protected items of medical glassware.

"The Imam and Qa'im," said Herith awkwardly, "supposed that there may have been breakages by now."

Breakages… What were such trivia compared with the breakage in Hakim's very soul which the news had caused? Herith was, in his way, attempting to give comfort. Yet the new arrivals had already had several months to adjust to the fact of Hasan's death. Hakim himself, a scant handful of minutes. And Rahim and Hamdullah *did not yet* know! Not to mention the other companions of the camp. Taj al-Din himself looked thunderstruck.

"Few breakages," replied Hakim in Persian. Did his voice shake? "But more glass is very welcome. We have an ocean of work. And now, perhaps, three more helpers? Or must you return?"

"We are entirely at your disposal, Tongue of Knowledge."

"Good, good…" Hakim turned to his companions. His voice must not falter. Whatever he said must be correct and decisive. Later, he would cope with grief, even though God's purpose surely included within it Hasan's death. The forty days of litanies would have ended long since at Alamut. Should he decree the same length of litanies here?

"Brethren. Taj al-Din, Rahim, Hamdullah. God is great. Restrain yourselves from shock and grief while the natives witness us. Ay, the shock that I myself displayed," he added ruefully. "For God the all-wise has taken Imam Hasan to heaven."

Rahim and Abdullah, so disciplined, merely widened their eyes, merely whispered a prayer beneath their breath.

"Praise be to the Imam and Qa'im Muhammad, who sends us gifts and his absolute support. And now we should conduct his messengers to our camp, so that we may welcome them properly."

"This is not your camp?" asked Herith, gesturing around the village, where many faces peered.

"Our camp is lower down, beside caves."

"Caves... I see. As a stronghold, if need be. Our Imam and Qa'im commanded me to deliver the letter to you immediately that I found you in your camp. I shall cut off the hand that gave the letter to you here, prematurely."

"No!" burst from Hakim. "We need all possible hands."

"Then I shall hold a hot coal until it cools."

"Certainly not. You might cripple your muscles. There is no fault but mine, my weakness."

"No," intervened Taj al-Din, "not weakness at all, but the depth of your love for Imam Hasan!"

Hakim collected himself. "We shall welcome our new companions with feasting, so that the natives will know how greatly our strength has increased. Before the feast we shall each say our personal prayers. Remain here, if you would, Rahim, to arrange the killing of a cow. You may kill it yourself dramatically, to impress the villagers' minds."

"The schedule of work," murmured Taj al-Din.

"We have three more helpers," replied Hakim. "We can afford to lag slightly." Even if to him at least, he reflected, the roast meat might taste like ashes, the coffee like mud.

Sanders County, Nebraska: June 2008

Sunday morning's TV news brought a bizarre item.

"In Downtown Los Angeles at seven p.m. local time last evening, a man committed suicide with explosives which he evidently wore inside his jacket, after climbing into a fountain near the County Courthouse."

A fountain that was now switched off, no shimmering plumes rising from the big central bowl. A couple of white-suited forensics people wearing thigh-high rubber boots waded around in the much wider, ochre-kerbed basin below, scooping with what looked like square sieves. Police incident tape linked an extensive circular perimeter of barriers; officers kept an eye upon the spectators.

"According to witnesses, the man was of Middle Eastern appearance. There were no other casualties. Pizza delivery person Chuck d'Alessandro said," with a cut to another doubtless syndicated shot of a bronzed young man in spandex sitting astride a speedy-looking bicycle...

"Like the fountain gushed pink, I'm not kidding! Like with added ketchup. Gross."

Back to the blonde anchorwoman against the fountain background. "Police remain baffled as to the dead man's motive or identity, although speculation is he may have had a grievance against the County Courthouse. This is Luisa Sanchez for..."

Paul zapped off the sound. "Abi," he said hollowly, "it's started. The symbolism of it! A Middle Eastern man explodes himself and his blood in a fountain of *waters*. What else can this be? In the heart of one of America's major cities, where all the movies come from. They must have sent out *plague couriers*, Abi! Infected volunteers!"

"But... to blow themselves up without a single passer-by being hurt?"

"He'll most likely have blown himself up because he felt haemo fever breaking out in him, therefore *after weeks of spreading it*. He destroyed himself so he wouldn't end up in a hospital, or in a morgue being autopsied, which would show what he died from. He didn't want to kill people with explosives like your usual suicide bomber, he merely wanted to deny samples. And he wanted to send a signal too. Mission accomplished, over and out, Paradise here I come. Plus, of course, the sheer symbolism of the waters. Symbolic to him and his group, leastways. And to you and me."

Cold traced its way down Abigail's spine. "Oh God, Paul, I think you're right. A suicide volunteer Assassin... as fanatical as any of Hasan as-Sabah's Fida'een who jumped to their deaths so long ago. But... those forensics people we saw?"

"They were tidying up. They might test bits of flesh and the water for AIDS, hepatitis, I dunno, routinely, but never for anything so far out. And he can't be the *only* volunteer, can he? So we'll hear of others doing similar. Sent out around the same time. Ten to twelve days latency, followed by three weeks when he's highly infectious, then his own outbreak and two or three terrible days until death, unless he kills himself first..." Paul bit on his lip.

A horrible suspicion started to grow at the back of Abigail's mind. "What," she pondered, "was I doing about thirty-one days ago? I think... I think... it was about then that Kamal invited me on my travels..."

"I hoped you weren't going to think of that."

"That was just after I told him in the Sabra about ICE suspecting a plot, linked to Assassins both ancient and modern. Kamal must have phoned home *later that very evening*, ordering his plague couriers to be infected. God, he thought quickly. All because I'd told him ICE suspected... It's as if *I* pushed the button to launch plague upon the world!" Despair tightened her throat and pressed at the inside of her skull.

"No no, don't go there, Abi. Don't go back to the Sabra..." Paul halted, shocked. "Go back to the Sabra... But *we* went to that place around the same date! Abi, you dined with me at the Sabra..." he calculated, "perhaps only the evening before you ate there with Kamal."

Abigail hiccupped horribly as if trying to expel something nauseous.

"I was testing the place..." she gasped as her eyes began to water. "*Was it good enough for wonderful Kamal?*" she paraphrased bitterly. "Oh I'm sorry... I'm so sorry, Paul. What rubbish I am. And I let plague loose... at the very same time."

Paul made a move towards her, yet it was as if he met an invisible barrier. "Don't go there," he lamely repeated. "Erase the Sabra from your mind... *Just like I erase it*. Right? I'll get you some tissues."

When he returned, Abigail managed to talk in between catching her breath and holding back tears. "How did he get explosives? You can't just buy dynamite or whatever in a shop, especially if you're a stranger, a foreigner, can you? How would he do that? Maybe this is just a coincidence..."

"Maybe."

"Shit, same sort of way Kamal got a gun in Marseille." A grimace stretched her features. "It's all planned."

Svenson came later to check on them, accompanied by the bodybuilder. "Did you see the news about the man who blew himself up in Los Angeles?" Abigail immediately demanded.

"Someone mentioned something. So?"

"That Arab... he was sent out infected, to spread haemorrhagic fever! The plague signs were starting in him, so he blew himself up."

"Didn't hear he was an Arab. What's this ragic fever?"

"It's *plague*. It's the *Black Death*. I swear he was one of the terrorists Jack Turner knows all about. This means the man was *actively spreading plague* for the past three weeks. People are going to start dying soon! *Lots* of people. Then more and more!"

"Mr Turner knows all about this, it's in good hands."

"I need to be sure! Where is he today?"

"You gotta be patient."

"You don't understand," Abigail pleaded. "The whole world's at risk."

"Dunno about terrorists, but don't they usually try to blow *other* people up, like take some God-fearing Americans with them? Not just waste themselves in some fountain."

"One less Ay-rab's always good," added the body builder as though he was quoting a fundamental law. "But how do you think this guy's an Ay-rab if his body blew to pieces?"

"Because I know! Because it makes sense!"

"Don't make none to me," said Svenson flatly. "And ain't none of my business."

"I need to know that the proper authorities have been alerted!"

"Mr Turner's seeing to everything that needs seeing to. *Your* business is to keep out of the way for a while, let the *proper authorities* get their job done, without premature stories all over the media. Right?"

It was useless.

Svenson saw to some housekeeping and departed, his lumbering shadow with him. "He's just a lamebrain underling," commented Paul the moment the door closed on them. "I'm surprised you got that much response out of him."

Abigail crumpled a tissue in her fist.

"If only Jack could let us know what's going on! He must have seen the news, or been told. Hasn't he realised the significance? Do you think he mightn't?"

"Abi, do you really think Jack's doing what he's supposed to be doing?"

"I can't bear this!" And she fled to her room.

Monday came, bringing no contact from Jack, no sense from Svenson, and no further TV news about the suicide in the fountain. Maybe Californian TV was following the story, or maybe there was no story, just a one-day wonder with nothing more that could be dug up. Nor was there any report of other dramatic suicides.

"Early days yet," Paul pointed out. "There's a bit of variability in the disease's progression, isn't there? And maybe not all volunteers were infected on the same day."

"How *many* would they have sent?"

"Isn't something I'd volunteer for lightly, no matter how fanatical I was. Blowing yourself up is pretty instant, but having to experience a day or so of Black Death before you die… Well, I guess that's true total martyrdom, like putting yourself in the way of torture before the finale. I don't think I'm cut out to be a martyr." He grinned. "Mata Hari might suit me fine. Hey, just kidding. Oops, she sounds too much like hara kiri. I guess there mightn't be too many volunteers, even so. You'd have to *really* trust the martyr. And you couldn't exactly advertise. Wanted: Absolutely discreet fanatic; send CV to Box 22, Alamut."

Despite herself, Abigail had to smile… a smile that faded fast.

"If someone blew themselves up in a fountain in China…"

"China shatters. Or how about the offshore island of Porcelain?"

"…do you think we'd even hear anything about it on TV here in Omaha?"

By now they'd been enforcedly confined in the chalet for four days. Fortunately, Paul was proving a decent companion to live penned up with; his mix of provocative stimulus and wacky humour seemed, surprisingly, just right. This despite his odd conviction that Jack no longer represented authority… or maybe not so odd; she reluctantly had to admit it was looking more plausible each day. And Paul took stuff in his stride, like her awful gaff about the Sabra, which he hadn't once referred back to.

In fact, Abigail couldn't think of anyone else she'd tolerate being with in similar frustrating circumstances. Going on holiday with a person was one thing… No, don't head down that route. Terry would have driven her mad fairly soon. Paul was easy to be with, a brother she'd never had; yet having no experience of a real brother, maybe this was a spurious comparison! It occurred to her that Paul must be itching to contact the *Globe*, and his dad…

"The *Globe*? No way," he said when she enquired. "I absolutely appreciate the need to keep this under wraps. Irresponsible scoops aren't my scene. Just, I'm certain we're under the *wrong* wraps. If only someone would turn up flashing FBI or CIA credentials, just for instance."

"What if this goes on for weeks?" asked Abigail. "And us with no idea what's happening?"

"In that case, welcome to Guantanamo Bay, Nebraska. Minus hoods and handcuffs and cages. We're with End Timers, Abi, of whom Jack is one. I'm convinced of it. They're trying to work out how to protect themselves from the Assassin plague, I guess in case the Rapture doesn't happen beforehand. No doubt the rest of the faithless world can all go hang, since plague is prophesied along with a lot of other mess.

"Nutty religions perceive everything as part of their own story. *The modern Assassins will do Jehovah's righteous work, while imagining that they're doing Allah's...* I can just imagine Jack saying it."

"Impossible," defended Abigail, still unwilling to believe she'd been fooled again. "You said yourself, handling *water of death* needs a superb lab, level-4 or whatever. How could your End Timers have such a resource? And I presume a plant to make vaccines too!"

"As opposed to, say, our latter-day Assassins? Who, realistically, can only be a fanatical fringe group with modest numbers. Yet *they* seem to have such things." He paused as a wry smile crossed his face. "And America is the land of opportunity. I'd guess your Mount Rushmore guy probably has enough true believers to come up with some hurriedly upgraded university lab space, probably a pharmaceutical company into the bargain. Don't forget how much money there is in the salvation business. Hundreds of millions of dollars."

"You don't think Jack will at least have shared the *water of death* with CDC?"

"For my money he's gone back to Boston to lie and prevaricate. And Mount Rushmore looks like a guy who can take his drink, or *thinks* he can take it. But Pandora's hip flask will cause him more than a few hiccups if things go wrong!" Paul proceeded to hiccup loudly, then collapsed dramatically back onto the sofa, clutching his throat and gasping.

Abigail tried to smile at his humour, but it came out as a grimace.

Tuesday, and Abigail was desperately worried. Yet there was still nothing more on TV about dramatic suicides, so no more putting of two and two together even in the most speculative way. This didn't actually stop them speculating.

"Explosives aren't the only way to kill yourself spectacularly," hypothesised Abigail out loud. "Would we even hear if someone sick went berserk with a sword in some mega-city in India and had to be shot by the police? Just for instance."

"That would make two infected Assassins. I keep thinking, suppose on his first day of fieldwork one of them gets run over by a bus and squashed flat? Instant end of him. Don't Muslims have weird ideas about fate? If Allah wills... *success*! If Allah doesn't, nice try but no cigar. Maybe they only sent out a single Assassin. Or just two... symmetry, like esoteric-exoteric, east-west, the duality of God."

"After *years and years* of preparation?"

"If Allah wills. There's faith for you. Can't beat faith for one-off miracles. Plus, maybe a shortage of suitable candidates. Especially in a *hurry*, the date suddenly brought forward."

"What *date* will the first outbreak start?"

"Well, working back using the latency and infectious periods we got off the Internet, I'd reckoned, um, June 19th or so. Somewhere."

"That's only nine days from now."

"Okay, Abi, we have to escape from here if possible. Seize the slightest chance."

A tremor of fear passed through Abigail's gut, yet also a sense of relief and purpose strengthened her mind. Yes, the time had come to act. They had to be heard, before, like the fragment said, a drizzle of infection already blowing through the populations of the world *swelled and overflowed* into an irresistible tsunami of death.

"How?"

"For instance, Mr Universe calls in sick and Svenson delivers the groceries on his own and he falls into the storm cellar..." The unlikelihood was dawning on Paul, yet zanily he went on. "...because I removed the hatch with my screwdriver fingernails, although somehow the rug's still in place. I guess the rug would have to be glued. Do you know how to make glue?" He gestured out of the window. "I think you boil horses' hooves." He whinnied and snickered, as though the grazing horses would be lured in. But Abigail had learned to read past the humour. Escape was seriously on the agenda.

The weekend passed monotonously. Paul did press-ups, trying to reach a hundred. Despite his best efforts, and card games, Abigail was fretting ever more. She kept looking at her watch, sometimes staring at it for a minute, two minutes, five.

Wednesday went by, then Thursday. Out in the world, the implacable clock of disease was measuring an end to people's lives. Only days until the invisible wave broke all too visibly and horribly to the surface, on unfortunate victims. But alongside this, another timescale was now preoccupying Abigail.

"I'm scared," she finally confessed to Paul on Friday morning. "My period's about a week late."

"But surely you... but didn't you...?"

"Some days I forgot to take my pill. Things happened, so much happened."

"Surely you're still protected if you just miss a day. Or two."

"I don't know!" she yelled. "I'm a week late. Paul, what do I *do*?"

To imagine that a part of loathsome Kamal was attached inside her like a parasite! That it would grow inside her, leaching from her body and distorting her month by month until finally the thing burst out, with his hateful features in miniature upon it!

"Um," expressed Paul, both crestfallen and concerned. "We need a pregnancy test kit. I can ask Svenson to get one. You don't have to say a word to him."

"He'll still look at me, thinking."

"So he'd better keep his thoughts to himself! Let me ask him."

Abigail gestured uselessly. "If I test positive…"

Paul swallowed. "That… depends. Depends on you. What you want. You could pretend you'd wanted a baby and, um, that you went to a clinic for artificial… you know, from a donor, um, anonymous…"

"Paul!" Abigail practically shrieked. "I can't keep the horrible thing! How could I *pretend*… that's it's anything other than…"

He stared at her in dismay, almost panic. "Shit, okay. How could you *conceivably* pretend? Right, of course… okay." Paul rapidly went into full reverse. "Well, being entirely duped by a villainous lover… Well, I mean, it's the same as… like being raped. And so there couldn't be any stigma… I mean no one would… if you wanted it…"

"It's *me* who ought to be terminated, put down like an animal!"

"No no, don't say that. Abi, you've been through the mill, but you're coming out the other side."

Ground into flour for a burger bun, with a filling of Kamal."

"Oh *shit*. Listen, all this running around the world breaking into tombs might have thrown you off your cycle, I mean might have thrown your cycle out."

Abigail groaned. "Yes, there was I nicely balanced on my bicycle, speeding along all carefree and self-assured, till bang, I got banged and my tyres burst. I'm useless, Paul, worse than useless." A bitter memory gripped her, of confidence and elation as she ran and pranced down a sunny street in Gazorkhan.

"No, you are *not*! Never say that. Listen to me, you aren't necessarily… One week over? That's nothing. You don't know till you have a test."

Hearing a vehicle, Paul glanced, then stared. "Look, it's Svenson, on his own! There's no Mr Universe with him! What did I promise you?"

Indeed Svenson was alone at the wheel of a pick-up truck, which was now swinging round to stop by the chalet.

"Condition Red, Abi!"

"To do *what*, ask him for a pregnancy kit or trip him up?"

"Maybe both! Whatever works! Whatever throws him off balance."

The blond man with the watery blue eyes entered, key in one hand, a roll of green garbage bags in the other. "Hi, Folks," he announced. "Come to collect the laundry, put the refuse out."

Paul immediately punched Svenson hard in the stomach, caught his shirt collar as he doubled forward, tripped him and propelled him in the general direction of the rug, which due to lack of time still covered the hatch.

"Out, out!"

Paul and Abigail raced to the pick-up truck where, *yes*, Svenson had left the keys in the ignition. It was hot inside the vehicle, although the windows were open. "Fasten belts!" ordered Paul even as he revved away, bringing the pick-up around and then racing towards where they'd entered the compound over a week earlier. A few people were scattered about, working or idly strolling; at least a couple noticed them. One guy began to run towards a building, another unclipped a mobile from his belt.

"You going for the fence by the gate?"

"No, fence has elasticity. Gate itself. Accelerate, fuck you." Already they were doing 50. Then 60, bucking in their seats as the pick-up's suspension fought the uneven road. "Sit well back, for when the airbags go off."

"Won't those trap us?"

"Naw, deflate through vents in less than a second."

At the last moment Paul took his hands off the wheel. *Impact*; and the exploding bag forcefully encountered Abigail before her body was thrown more than half an inch forward. She was momentarily winded. A wave of crystals from the shattered windscreen passed over them. She felt as though her brain had carried on going, and her breasts were surely bruised. Her vision reeled for a second or two. As it steadied she was already unimpeded, except by some floppy and empty ectoplasmic ghost.

No movement nor noise; or rather, a hissing, nothing as compared with the previous roar of the engine. And maybe the impact had jerked her horrid parasite loose. The gate had burst open about a foot; the front of the pick-up was badly crumpled. Abruptly a deafening howl arose, falling and rising, falling and rising. The siren! White smoke curled inside the vehicle.

"You all right?" Paul bellowed as he thrust his ghost aside, fought his seatbelt, then rummaged on the floor among miscellanea thrown out from a shelf. The coils of smoke...

"We're on fire!"

"No, it's just talc or cornstarch, keeps the bags lubricated. No mobile here... Out! There's room to get through the gate."

They squeezed through the opening. Within moments they were running side by side along the track between cottonwoods and blue spruce. Even with blessed shade from the trees the sheer heat sapped them. Their long entrapment in air-conditioning was not good preparation.

At the dogleg, both were panting. Of a sudden the siren cut off. Distantly, bike engines were revving.

"Don't worry," gasped Paul, "can't get a bike through that gap."

Onward, sweating, through red cedars and jack pines. Don't trip, don't twist an ankle, don't get a stitch.

They paused at a huge cornfield, its ordered rows rolling away from them down a slight slope, mustering untold thousands of thriving stems not much more than a foot high. The corn was parted by the dry river of the track.

The sun beat down. Abigail and Paul began to trot, as briskly as they could by now.

"Bound to be a phone… in Colon… call 911," he managed to say.

"Population… 140," she replied with difficulty. "Might need … bang on a door."

Exactly how far away had Colon been? Five miles, ten miles, more? Can't run a half-marathon bare-headed in this heat, in fact not a chance with no water.

"Thumb a lift," panted Paul.

As if on cue, a car turned into the far end of the way through the dense ranks of corn. It shimmered in the sun and shot bright reflections towards them. Mounted across its top were roof lights, red and blue.

"Police car! Thank god."

The Ford Crown Victoria coasted towards them as they trotted faster, waving. Then it halted, fifty yards off. A peak-capped trooper climbed out, donned sun-glasses, and waited. As soon as they were close, he drew his gun.

"Police. Stop and kneel down! Put your hands on your heads!"

Of course, they complied. And what a relief it was to rest. What else would a trooper do about two strangers rushing frantically towards him, other than order them to halt?

"Thank god you're here," exclaimed Abigail raggedly.

"Heard the siren." The red badge on the trooper's jacket sported what looked like an Art Deco skyscraper surrounded by flames. "Why were you running?"

"We've been held against our will." Paul squinted to see the trooper's face. "We escaped… I'm a journalist, Paul Summers, *Boston Globe*. This is Dr Abigail Leclaire… from Harvard. We need to contact the FBI, *urgently*."

"The FBI? What about?"

"It's complicated... but vitally important. I'm still out of breath. Will you drive us away... before they come after us?"

"They?"

"The people from the compound."

Throbbing engines were loud now, must be big bikes, approaching through the woods. How had they got the machines through that narrow gap? Abigail twisted to look around. Looked like two Harleys, ridden by handsome dark-haired guys whom she'd noticed occasionally tending the horses. They were certainly brothers, possibly even twins. The bikes roared forward, raising dust as they braked to a halt right alongside the kneeling fugitives.

"Hi there, Pete," one rider called out to the trooper.

"Zeb? Or are you Norris?"

"I'm Zeb," said the one who had spoken.

"So what's going on here, boys?"

"Damn East Coast journalists is what. Made themselves out to be believers. Then Norris caught them hiding bugs."

"That's right," his brother chimed in, "'cept I only saw 'em planting *one*. For sure there'll be more."

"That's a lie," challenged Paul flatly.

Pete the trooper peered. "Didn't you just tell me you work on the *Boston Globe*? Or it's a lie there'll be more than one bug?"

"Those bugs are a complete invention." Abigail realised there was anger and panic in her own tone; she tried to stay calm.

"A fine invention indeed for snooping on innocent folks," exclaimed Zeb indignantly. "So as soon as we suss this pair, they make a run for it, guilty as hell. All we want is for them to show us where the other bugs are hid, then they're both free to *bug off*, with our blessing."

"Uh-huh," said the trooper.

"Could we please stand up?" asked Abigail. "I refuse to kneel beside these... lying kidnappers."

"You seemed happy enough kneeling beside us to praise the Lord," Norris swiftly cut back. "But I guess the Lord wasn't truly in your hearts at the time."

The trooper's brow furrowed. "Okay," he conceded. "You can both lower your hands too, now I've got backup."

Incredulity exceeded Abigail's anger. "You call *these* backup?"

"Far as I know, Zeb and Norris have always been upstanding citizens. Kidnapping, eh? You saying you were brought here 'gainst your will?"

"Being *kept* against our will, is what I meant."

"But you came here voluntarily, right? And it seems you can leave soon enough. Folks around here are patient and helpful. Perhaps you ain't being either."

"But folks around here are rather *too* hospitable," put in Paul. "Lock all the doors and then forget to give you a key."

The trooper clucked his tongue. "Reckon I'll give you both a ride back to the compound. Check on this bugging allegation."

"Pete, you might need to back your way out through the trees afterwards," warned Zeb. "These two stole an old pick-up of ours and wrecked it at the gate."

"You want to press charges about that?"

Zeb shrugged. "You'll understand we're a little pissed. But that's for Brother George to say. Pick-up might be out of the way and the gate clear soon enough."

"Officer," appealed Abigail, "please will you call the FBI? This is of national importance."

"Do you claim you were transported across a state line?" demanded the trooper. "Otherwise this is our jurisdiction. Are you saying now that they brought you here from out of state?"

"They brought us from Eppley Airport," replied Paul, "but we came…"

"Gave you a lift, do you mean?"

"We didn't realise who they were," appealed Abigail. "We thought they were Immigration and Customs Enforcement people."

The Trooper sighed. "Now why on earth should you think that? And I know Eppley is within a spit of the state line, but it was still inside Nebraska last time I paid attention. Both of you get in the back of my car."

"This is a huge mistake!" cried Abigail, gesturing as if to ward him off.

"A moment ago you *wanted* a ride. I don't wish to have to cuff you, so get in nice and peaceful."

Little alternative offered itself. Rear door locks clunked. Escorted by Harleys to front and rear, the Ford Crown Victoria proceeded through the woodland, bearing Abigail and Paul back at no great speed towards the compound.

"Listen, Officer," said Paul urgently, "this is about a terrorist plot to release a deadly plague on America."

"You calling the Christian Brothers terrorists?"

"No. *They* aren't the terrorists. But they've stolen a medical sample of the utmost importance, so as to protect themselves."

"A medical sample which you and your doctor pal here just happened to bring from Harvard all the way to Omaha?" The trooper glanced at Abigail in the rear-view mirror. What line of doctoring you in, anyway?"

"I'm, I'm… an epidemiologist. I study epidemics."

"So what's the medical word for smallpox?"

"Uh, veriola."

"Wrong, it's *vari*ola with a letter *a*. My dad's a doc, retired."

"Slip of the tongue."

"Terrorists and kidnapping…" the trooper slowly shook his head "…you two say whatever the hell comes into your heads."

"Look," persisted Abigail, "we didn't bring the medical sample from Harvard. We brought it all the way from Spain, in the custody of an officer of Immigration and Customs Enforcement…"

"Sounds like a strange custodian for a *medical* sample."

"…called Jack Turner, who fooled us into coming here, because he's in league with these people and now disloyal to Homeland Security."

"Spain, eh? Where else you been?"

"Turner and Paul and I met up in France. Before that I was in Iran and Syria with the *real* terrorist, of course I didn't know who he was then. It was only later that we discovered he's unleashing plague!"

"Consorting with terrorists, eh?"

"No! In France, the shit tried to kill us!"

"And before all this I guess you were in Timbuktu and the Mountains of the Moon. Your middle name wouldn't be Indiana?"

A heavy truck had rammed the pick-up, the gate too, shunting both right out of the way. Such was the obvious deduction from sight of the truck parked just within the compound, and the still more crumpled pick-up pushed up against a cottonwood by the side of the track. Trooper Pete idled past the gate, now wide open the wrong way, and through, picking up speed towards the spread of buildings.

A patriarchal figure of a man whom Abigail had never seen before, sporting thinning white hair and dressed in a light cream suit, was talking on a mobile by their chalet. Svenson stood by, displaying body language that Abigail assessed at somewhere between respectful and subservient. Trooper Pete parked twenty yards short of the two, then strolled over to the patriarch, who immediately ended the call and beamed at him. They talked for three or four minutes, with Svenson adding some comment.

"Doesn't look good," murmured Paul. "No doubt they all worship together, and this police guy probably thinks we're on something."

Svenson's bodybuilder shadow emerged from the chalet.

"We could do something to get arrested," suggested Abigail desperately. "Shoot someone in the foot, knife someone."

"No gun, no knife. And as for fisticuffs, Mr Universe could easily restrain us while still managing to look kind."

Then the trooper returned to the Ford, along with Svenson and the muscleman. Locks clunked open.

"Okay, I'm letting you out. Another three-four hours, I'll be out this way, make sure you're safely gone outa my county. You'll be taken back to the airport."

"Same as they came," agreed Svenson.

"But you can't release us to them!" protested Abigail.

"Yeah yeah, these terrorists. You notice I never arrested you? So I cannot be *releasing* you, Harvard Doctor lady, jus' supposing that's true either."

"Officer, you never even asked to see our ID!"

"That's something else you left behind, as well as your bugs," said Svenson promptly. "Forgot your bag, you did, the brown one. If you hadn't run off like there was ants in your pants, you mighta thought of that. What did you think we'd do, *eat* you?"

"Pat me down, officer," requested Paul earnestly. "You'll find no mobile. Does that make sense? Taken from us when we got here! Why else were we running in the sun, hot day like this, miles to go?"

Trooper Pete adjusted his shades. "Does anything you two say make sense? Your hosts are generously going to overlook the damage you did to their property." Just then, his radio came alive, calling him. "Okay, that settles it. You two get out right now." He hauled open the door on Abigail's side and vigorously assisted her out by the arm, which caused Paul to leave promptly by the other rear door.

"I'd ask you to stop for a Kool-Aid, Pete, while we're sorting things out…"

"Thanks, Sven, but busy." Trooper Pete quickly climbed in his Nebraska State Patrol car and drove off, even while replying to the call. Svenson looked at Abigail, the bodybuilder at Paul. By now the Patriarch person was heading off, using his mobile again.

"Right then," growled Svenson ominously, "back into your holiday home." And thus they were escorted to the door and inside. Abigail first, then Paul, followed by Svenson and the big fellow.

"Hey you," Svenson called out to Paul's back. And Paul turned, to meet a kick in his groin that doubled him up on the floor of the corridor, howling, clutching between his legs.

"That's for my belly," Svenson was saying, just as Abigail threw herself past Paul to tear at the blonde man's face.

"You shit!" she screamed, as Svenson tried to fend her off. But then the bodybuilder was dragging her back. Powerful arms immobilised her. Wincing, Svenson palmed blood from his cheek. "Fuck you, lady." Calmly, he twisted and kicked out sidelong at Abigail, right into *her* belly.

Through a dark wave of agony and her own gasping, she heard Paul's anguished voice from the floor. "She's pregnant," he implored, "don't!"

Bale Region, Southern Ethiopia: July 1166

Many weeks later, grief was still strong and burned like red embers in the back of Hakim's mind. But their sacred mission to capture the jinnee of plague in a bottle, and the essence of protection too, had to take precedence over all emotion, all expression of emotion.

The work of the camp made them all slaves; to crushing routines, to horrific sights, to danger, to mental strain. Hakim struggled to keep all the complex processes in his mind, keep them all rolling forward, while the constant buzz of insects seemed to tempt him with sleep and forgetfulness. He started a new intravention test of some sort twice each week, and a putrefaction trial every second day. Each was carefully planned and rigorously executed, with a wait of weeks before the results. Yet Hakim had developed a nose for putrefaction; he could be certain a sample had gone foul without any need to test its properties, which saved a great deal of time. Only long-stored samples that still seemed good needed proving with an actual intravention trial. And the blood of cows or pigs sufficed for basic putrefaction experiments, relieving the pressure for samples on their stock of monkeys and human subjects.

"That one's death was disgusting," Rahim was saying of a prisoner who had just died horribly. "To kill in battle is one thing. Even to skin alive as a punishment."

"Absolve yourself of remorse," calmed Hakim. "Purge pity, and any self-pity too, or sorrow. Now hear me: yesterday Nasir was walking beside some low chalky cliffs half an hour's walk to the west, when he suffered a gushing nose-bleed. Do you know where those cliffs are?"

"I believe so. Yes."

"Nasir says those cliffs crumble easily, and at their base lies a fine white powder that is easily blown by the wind."

Although it cost time, Hakim had recently been explaining in detail to the Fida'een everything that he was attempting, and exactly why, and his reasoning regarding successes and failures. This policy had now borne fruit with Nasir. If afflicted by a similar nose-bleed a year ago, Nasir would never have scrupulously observed what became of his blood upon the ground.

"He was stooping over to let his blood fall without staining his clothes, and he told me that the little pool of blood which he made seemed surrounded by a circle of less dark wetness. He brought a sample of the powder back with him. It's abrasive to the touch, yet very lightweight, almost as if each grain contains tiny emptinesses, little holes which the eye cannot see. I too dripped blood upon the powder, with the same result."

"Do you mean that blood is *not* one liquid?" asked Rahim in surprise. "That this powder can *divide* blood?"

Hakim himself had long been aware that blood was divisible, by the simple expedient of letting the vital fluid stand in a glass vessel. After a day or so, approximately the top quarter of the vessel contained a lighter pink liquid, above a dark red majority. He'd thought of these two parts as the *water* of blood, and the *wine* of blood.

"I'm very pleased by your question, good Rahim. Blood can indeed be divided, into two parts certainly, maybe more."

Clean water can usually be stored in a dark place almost indefinitely, Hakim had reasoned, even when exposed to air, whereas exposed wine will very soon go sour. Hence drawing off the *water of blood* might yield a long-lasting liquid which still, nevertheless, possessed the properties of blood, or at least some of those properties. Unfortunately, even the pink water spoiled eventually… Yet if there was a substance much finer than muslin, which could filter the *water of blood* until it was almost colourless, more like water indeed…

"We know that blood goes foul after a while in the heat here, even in a closed vessel. If I store blood in the caves to keep it cooler, putrefaction is merely delayed somewhat. No matter whether it's ordinary blood, or blood with the seeds of plague or protection within. I was becoming… frustrated… by how I cannot yet seem to preserve blood, and so I prayed for guidance." Hakim paused, for proper gravitas. "God gave Nasir his nose-bleed in that place to show us a sign, directing Nasir's eyes at the same time. We need a lot more of that powder which parts blood. I need to test whether a pure form of the lighter aspect of blood lasts for a longer time, and by itself can convey the essence of plague, without the red aspect."

"Nasir and I will take a couple of strong slaves with us. But the weave of sacking is too loose. Shall we use some of our silk to make bags?"

"That will be excellent."

Sanders County, Nebraska: June 2008

The bodybuilder released Abigail, who sank down groaning beside Paul.

Svenson stepped by, rubbing his boots along Abigail's body. "So that's what you get up to at nights here in your nest." He smirked at Paul, who was still clutching his genitals. "Maybe *not tonight Josephine*, like the Frenchman said." Stooping, he pulled the rug away from the hatch to the storm cellar. "And I think your whore's kinda offline anyhow," he sniped. Abigail was nursing her midriff.

Paul grimaced, but managed to hold his tongue. Abigail hung her head.

Svenson opened the hatch, then reached in to flip on the light. "Now you two get yu'selves down there, seeing as Pete says he'll come back, so you need to be gone. Hurry up now, don't waste no time. Gordo, fetch their mattresses and chuck those down." The name Gordo sounded like it should apply to some mutant Japanese monster, or a small-time pro wrestler, although maybe the bodybuilder was christened Gordon.

Awkwardly, carefully, Abigail and Paul assisted each other as they descended the stairs into the storm cellar.

"Chem latrine in the far left corner, remember," Svenson called after them. "Use the food and water down there for tonight."

Soon enough the mattresses from their beds slid down the stairs, followed by sheets and pillows and a couple of blankets. The hatch banged shut. Presently, the dragging of some big object sent vibrations through the wood. Since the only bolts were on the inside, Gordo must be positioning the heaviest piece of furniture he could find upon the hatch.

Somewhat recovered, Abigail reached out to touch Paul's arm. "Your poor... parts," she murmured.

"S'okay, I'll live. Just aching now. You?"

At that moment the light went out. It was utterly black.

"They flipped the trip off," muttered Paul. "Bound to be a torch or two down here... in case the power fails. We'll search the shelves by touch. Give us something to do. Maybe there's some residual light from an air vent, once our eyes adapt."

"Why leave us in darkness?"

"Sense of humour? Or maybe to grind us down, take away our spirit."

Abigail felt her spirit was pretty much drained already, but she didn't voice this. She tried to be positive instead. "That trooper, he's coming back. We could yell and bang on the hatch so he hears us."

"How'd we know when to bang? Down in this shit-hole we won't hear him drive up, or have any chance of catching conversation. And if we simply bang all the time, they'll just gag and bind us… Ow! Stubbed my toe."

"Oh… yeah." She didn't give up. "He'll see a sofa or something, blocking the hall."

"If he bothers to more than glance. So they'll say, 'We had to shift all the furniture about to search for more bugs. Still ain't sure we got em all.' And old buddy Pete says, 'Good luck, boys, those two were sure a freaky pair,' and off he goes."

"Fuck," announced Abigail, softly but clearly. Paul was right.

Moving very carefully in the darkness, they felt their way around their new prison. Presently welcome light beamed from a torch in Paul's hand, revealing several other torches, an electric lantern, a small battery radio and quite a cache of spare batteries.

"Bingo." Lantern on.

Next Abigail found Ibuprofen, which they both took. The day wore on, relieved somewhat by the radio. Mostly they lay on their separate mattresses, occasionally wandering around to stretch. After a few hours Paul changed the failing batteries of the lantern.

Though reception was weak underground, they still picked up quite a number of local stations when the radio was perched high on a top shelf. Fortunately, not all of these were like Station K-Love: Positive and Encouraging. There was Hip Hop, Oldies, Classic Rock, Nostalgia, Farm, Sports. They settled on switching between KKAR for news and talk, with KVNO from the University of Nebraska for classical music, and occasional bursts of Rock to invigorate. Even at full volume, there was no way trooper Pete would hear it above.

"At least they need us," remarked Abigail at one point.

"Uh," replied Paul. "Exactly *why*? Seeing as they have the *water of death* and our confessions too."

"They can't just kill us!"

"No, of course not. Shouldn't have said that, damn my tongue."

"What else *aren't* you saying?"

"Well, maybe nothing happens to us without the say-so of Mount Rushmore or Jack," offered Paul reluctantly. "I don't think Jack would… but then again, I don't think they're in charge. I dunno who is. Maybe that guy in the cream suit."

"But they're all Christians. Thou shalt not kill." Her voice softened. "Making a break for it could have worked," she added. "It almost did."

"No. My stupid idea. Now we're worse off."

"Hey, just no TV for a change."

Some Mozart interceded, courtesy of KVNO.

"There is some good news, Abi."

"Don't tell me... um... there's only one room to keep tidy."

"No. They never came back for any more of your blood. So there can't be anything in it worth having."

So, Abigail thought, she wouldn't end up being a one-woman blood-bank after all. A weight long shunted to the back of her mind, one weight among many, now lifted. "Thank you, Paul."

Dinner that evening was canned meatballs and canned spaghetti, cold.

A noise woke Paul. Lurching shadows alarmed him. It took him seconds to remember where he was. Abigail was moving around, torch in hand. Though always dark here, it had to be the middle of the night.

"What? What's up?"

"Don't look," she snapped. "I'm doing things. Private things."

"Oh, right."

"Sorry," she added. "I dropped my torch on the floor." Moments later, softly, "*Shit.*"

"What's wrong? Tell me."

"I'm bleeding. It's my period, or..."

"Or what?"

"Or that bastard's kick."

Paul reproached himself. "Or the airbag and the running. I couldn't crash the pick-up any softer. Um, I saw packs of tampons."

"I know. Already got some. A sudden sharp pain woke me, and I felt..."

"It's your overdue period, Abi."

"Yeah, probably, not an early miscarriage. Okay. Suppose it *is* a miscarriage though, which we'll never know... I guess that's my ethical dilemma out of the way. Really, I should cheer." She couldn't have sounded less like cheering. "I'm so sorry I put this on you, Paul. I shouldn't have mentioned the whole pregnancy possibility thing."

"Hey, it was preying on your mind. I didn't mind sharing. Truly."

"You're a good man. I'm rubbish."

"I told you not to say that, Abi. It hurts me."

Next morning around ten the cellar light came on, and after an audible heaving of the weight upon the hatch, Svenson looked in on them from above, Gordo looming behind.

"Okay down there? Found the pack of cards? Chem toilet should be good for a week. We'd let you out, but we can't take the risk of Pete coming back, seeing as how you involved him. I'm sure ya understand."

Both Abigail and Paul forbore to say they had serious doubts as to whether

389

Trooper Pete had ever bothered to return the day before. He wasn't likely to come back any time soon either, not after his chat with the Moses person in the cream suit. End Timers in cahoots. No doubt confinement in the cellar was as much for punishment as for concealment. But it was best not voicing anything that might provoke Svenson again, which in fact left nothing to say.

"Don't need anything? Fine. Well stocked down there." The hatch fell back into position, and was weighted down. Soon the mains light went out.

Paul turned on a torch and made ghastly faces in the upward pointing beam, then launched into a string of humorous stories. Abigail forced a smile, which for all she knew looked as awful as Paul's expressions; inside she felt used and broken and without hope. Paul meant well; he was a good companion and trying his best. But if terrible events and stifling captivity hadn't stolen her choices, she'd be as far from any man as possible. Entirely alone, in fact.

They switched to the lantern and played cards, tilting their hands toward the light to see, although they were soon bored as they'd already spent a great deal of time on the same ritual upstairs. And now too there was no outside world to glance out at between rounds. Besides, Abigail suspected Paul of inconspicuously trying to lose. The day wore on.

Days passed. A kind of torpor slipped over them; it was difficult to resist, perhaps the brain's defence against the excruciatingly slow passage of time and a lack of stimulation. Paul was heroic in attempts to brighten the darkness of their situation, but the darkness of the cellar was a constant reminder. The chemical toilet began to stink, but Svenson wouldn't empty it despite their pleas. "Naw, it's rated for a full week, three people using it. Ain't that right, Gordo?" He'd smirked, and Gordo provided his usual affirmative grunt.

As a curiosity item, the Thursday morning news on KKAR reported two small outbreaks of a mystery disease. Victims had come down with symptoms similar to Ebola fever, yet at widely separated places of which neither was in central Africa, the normal home for Ebola. The locations were Kiev in the Ukraine, and Mumbai, India. Experts were trying to establish a link, or determine whether this was complete coincidence.

"We've been stuck in this shit-hole of crazy apocalypse fools for almost a fortnight," Abigail was climbing the stairs, "when the world could've been warned!" She banged her fists on the underside of the hatch and started yelling. "Open up, open up!"

"Please stop it. You'll only bruise yourself, Abi. They aren't up there, no one can hear you."

She howled with rage and frustration, then braced her back against the hatch.

"I already tried that, Abi."

"Let's try it *together*!"

So he joined her, and, crammed together, they strained for almost a minute until the futility became all too obvious.

"Okay, okay," panted Paul, "retreat."

Abigail sank down on her mattress to recover herself, muttering, "Bloody impotence."

Momentary hurt flickered in Paul's eyes. What, speculated Abigail, was he sensitive to this time? Was he comparing with... the *potence* of Kamal? And well he might, for Kamal was busy fucking the world just as he'd fucked her! Perhaps from a male perspective, that didn't leave much for an immature guy who still lived with his dad. Paul still clung to the booby prize though... a stupid crush on a broken doll.

"You know," Paul said gently, "if we *had* shifted Mount Impossible, we'd still have been locked in a chalet inside a compound of folks who know what we tried last time."

"Yes yes, you're right. I just want to *do* something."

"You tried wonderfully. You did your very best."

"Stop patronising me!" she snapped. "If I hadn't been so fucking obstinate trying to find things out, if I hadn't been so *stupid* about Kamal, if he hadn't found out about ICE, there wouldn't be plague in Kiev and India right now. And Walid wouldn't be dead, and tens of thousands, millions more people to follow him!"

"Abi, the terror plan would've been launched anyway. Maybe next Fall, maybe next month, surely sometime soon. Kamal was going abroad on 'business' anyway, wasn't he?"

"*Was* he? Without my stupid interference?"

"ICE was already on to the *Eagle Teacher* plot, Abi. Homeland Security were."

"But without a clue where to look next."

"So then, minus you, plague would have burst upon the world without *any* prior warning whatsoever. And al-FaQ wouldn't have been forced to accelerate their plan either."

"Fuck! If only Jack wasn't so demented!"

"Irrespective of Jack's End Timer lunacy and loyalty, he might still have passed some warning on to his ICE superiors. We can't possibly know. For Chrissake, Abi, stop punishing yourself!"

Abigail pulled up her knees and hugged herself. Paul moved closer and put a tentative arm around her, but she immediately stiffened.

"You said Jack would be back in Boston, *lying and prevaricating*," she challenged ungently, as if to repel affection.

Paul withdrew his arm. "Ah… so I did."

An awkward silence prevailed.

"Oh! Kiev and Mumbai, *at the same time*," exclaimed Abigail suddenly.

"What?"

"Symmetry, like you said. Must be two carriers, or at least two. And with the most likely starting point as Tehran, Kiev is north-west, Mumbai is south-east."

"Hmm… typical Ismaili. Symmetry all right, though not like anyone else would do it. But these are small outbreaks, Abi. Maybe the virus isn't as powerful as they'd hoped."

"Oh Paul! That 'small' number of victims has already had about twenty days to spread infection around Kiev. And any people they infected have in turn had nineteen days, then eighteen, seventeen and so on. It's like that old story about the chess board and the grains of rice. The number of contacts could be in the tens of thousands."

"Okay, I admit I was trying to minimise this."

"Do you think they wouldn't have tested the *lethality* on people. Kamal's cruel enough, of course they would!"

"Well, as I understand it," Paul said levelly, "there are two aspects to a virus. There's kill-power, and then there's spreadability. A virus can only pack so many genes into a very small space, so it might need functional trade off. Less power to kill, more power to spread. Less spread, more kill. Although the Black Death did pretty damn well on both counts… I guess after however many years experimenting, they think they've got the optimum cocktail. Yet not necessarily so. They could *never* have tested spreadability on a wide scale without going public; as in starting an epidemic, which therefore everybody would've known about! So, fingers crossed."

"Sounds like whistling while Rome burns. This *is* the Black Death, original version, or perhaps even deadlier." Abigail was grim, inconsolable.

"Did you hear the news?" Abigail cried out when Svenson and Gordo visited, towards noon. "Plague has broken out in the Ukraine and India! Millions of lives are at risk, Mr Svenson. You might think you'll be safe and protected on account of the virus sample, but whoever's analysing that sample can't possibly have the resources! The plague has already begun, and this is an international emergency. *Please* let us out!"

"So the Last Days are upon us, you mean. At last. Praise the Lord."

"You won't praise the Lord when you feel the symptoms. In a month you'll be screaming with pain!"

"Pains are for disbelieving folk. Our bodies'll be raptured pure and clean by then."

"*Ruptured*, not raptured," put in Paul. "Internal organs liquefying, agonising black boils swollen to bursting point."

"You two do have a way with words. Oughta have been preachers, serving the Lord, 'stead of wasting your words on ungodly stuff. Think it's a coincidence that Darwin and the Devil both begin with a D, for Damnation? Seeing as you ain't ordering anything from room service today, we'll be off."

"The world is flat," jibed Paul.

"Now what's that s'posed to mean? Hereabouts is pretty flat, anyways." Svenson grinned. "Don't you intellect-fools go thinking I'm stupid."

After their two jailers had gone, Abigail groaned. "That's me, an intellect-fool."

"You have to admire his logic," quipped Paul. "What else does D stand for, apart from Deuteronomy? That could be our pastime today. Make up a story using all the words that start with D."

"Death," responded Abigail, flatly.

Saturday morning, on KKAR: "...medical authorities in Kiev are tentatively identifying it as an unknown strain of haemorrhagic fever. Adding to the outbreaks there and in Mumbai, India, reports of a similar disease have now come in from Bucharest, Romania, and also the Indian city of Madras. The World Health Organisation in Geneva, Switzerland, has rushed specialists..."

"At least someone's paying attention," commented Paul dully. It seemed even his hope might eventually be exhaustible, after all.

"Without the faintest idea what they're facing, or why!"

It was four in the afternoon. Their minds ached with boredom and frustration.

"When the hell's Svenson going to see to the toilet?" enquired Paul wearily. "He did say Saturday. I know it's a small matter compared with plague spreading into Europe and through India, but..."

crack-crack-crack-crack.

"That sounded like shots!" exclaimed Paul.

"Or just back-firing," cautioned Abigail.

No, I think *front*-firing! Something's happening."

"Maybe it's target-practice time. Can't be anything to do with us, Paul. Think about it... there's no way anyone can know where we are!"

"Hmm... I guess not."

Nevertheless, they strained their ears. Fifteen minutes passed by... until, incredibly, a faint voice was calling out, *"Abigail, Paul, are you here anywhere?"*

"YES, YES!" they chorused.

"We're in the storm cellar under the furniture in the hall!" bellowed Paul, as Abigail snatched up a kettle and began banging it against the wall. Whose voice *was* it? She found it familiar, yet couldn't quite place it.

"HELP, HELP!" they cried, punctuated by the percussion of the kettle, which Abigail had transferred to the underside of the hatch. "STORM CELLAR! HALL!"

A grinding and a groaning above... then the hatch opened, silhouetting... *Carlos*. CIA Carlos from Spain, wearing a blue flak-jacket and a cap bearing the letters FBI, and looking extra tough on account of a day or two of dark stubble. Behind him, another capped agent cradled a pump-action shotgun.

"Up you come." Carlos reached a hand down to Abigail but, ecstatic as she was to see that face, she didn't need a man's hand.

"*How* can you be *here*, Carlos? And FBI? I thought..."

Carlos grinned widely. "CIA doesn't do internal domestic ops. Clothing's on loan. How am I here? Several things Flash Jack said didn't make sense to me at the time, and then that supposed Middle Eastern guy blows himself up in a fountain in LA." He tapped his nose, then abruptly, and unnecessarily, reached to haul Paul up the last few steps like a cork from a bottle. Carlos wrinkled his nose at Paul – "You reeker, as the Greek guy said in his bathtub!" – before resuming, "A fountain of *waters*, uh-huh?"

Of course! Carlos *also* knew and could understand the symbolism.

"I'd put in a complaint about Jack Turner like I said I would, shooting at pregoneras for no adequate reason. Sounds almost as bad as shooting a pregnant woman, come to think of it. Strictly speaking, there wasn't any reason I oughta have heard anything yet, beyond an acknowledgement, things take time. And Turner wasn't likely to give me a chummy phone call either, Eagle and chicks landed safely, thanks. So I gave it a few days, then. But I was smelling a rat."

Paul laughed. "Probably me, even across the ocean!"

"In this case it was Jack Rat. And you two can have quick showers before we leave. Helicopter Safety Regulations."

"Helicopter?" marvelled Abigail, who seemed to have two vying jokers in her life.

"Only the best," declared Carlos, accompanied by a flourish of his hand. "Hey, you're staggering, Abi."

"Unused to so much fresh air. Tell me, tell me!"

"So I phoned to check the airline computers for the tickets Jack bought at Málaga. Destination *Omaha*. Atlanta would be the obvious recipient for a plague sample. Boston, I'd have understood. But Omaha Nebraska? Alarm bell. I phoned Boston ICE, and got what I later realised was the run-around, from a guy called Dan Siegel. Yeah yeah, no problems, but Mr Turner's very busy now. A few more days wasted. Then I put in a much fuller report to Langley… By now I'd checked up on the pregonera and guys in black, turns out they're not players. And what happens next but plague breaks out in Kiev and India? Well, I call that a definite problem. Hey, do you *know* about Kiev? Did you know about the LA business?"

"Saw that on TV," confirmed Paul. "So we tried to escape. Hence the cellar. We heard about Kiev on a radio down there."

"Okay. So I phoned FBI Omaha for any lead. And they paid attention, after a bit of explaining. And I decided to get on a plane. By the time I arrived, a few things had happened. Dan Siegel got guilty about lying to the CIA and came clean with his ICE boss. Truth was, Flash Jack had dropped out of sight."

"So he didn't go back to Boston after all…" put in Paul.

"Uh-uh. ICE got in touch with the FBI. Meanwhile, FBI Omaha reports about me to FBI HQ. Ding-dong, Feds get busy. CCTV pics of you at the airport, and who met you there, a Dodge van license plate too, traceable. So today we arrive in force."

"Hey man, top work. We're eternally grateful." Paul was earnest. "I heard shooting," he added.

"I thought I'd fire in the air a bit, maybe alert you to the cavalry arriving."

"How marvellously macho of you." Abigail almost sounded as though she meant this. Almost.

"Black looks from the Feds for shooting off, but what the hell. We didn't meet any armed resistance."

"Didn't the Spanish police try to stop you and Ryan, after we split up?"

Carlos grinned. "We lucked out. Drove all night. Ryan had some bennies with him, just in case. Okay, shower time, freshen up, before we head out?"

"Diplomatically put," said Abigail.

"You first," Paul told her.

"The perfect gentleman," remarked Carlos, with an ironic sigh.

"Yes, he *is*, actually."

"Hey," exclaimed Paul, his forehead creased by a frown, "how come you aren't wearing any protection? Biohaz suits? I mean, if plague's suspected to be here in any shape or form…"

"Tell you on the way out. We're in a hurry."

In-Air Above Nebraska: June 2008

The Gang Task Force of the FBI Field Office in Omaha came in by vehicle, but as soon as the End Timers' compound was secured, a McDonnell Douglas 530 'Little Bird' had landed. It was in this helicopter that Carlos, Paul and Abigail were now being piloted high above the course of a creek heading into the north-west of the city. Doubtless this creek fed into the wide Missouri river, a shining strip just visible beyond the sprawl of the city.

"...so the Feds already had their lady under cover on that other End Timer ranch on account of the alleged vote-rigging, and she manages to get her hands on the mobile number of one of the important dudes in Sanders County. FBI luck out overhearing a bit of talk, not enough to know where the sample went off to – guy used a code name, Patmos, which is no help – but enough to know it was treated with kid gloves and in fact shipped on without being opened. So the risk level was extremely low."

"Ah," voiced Abigail. "Patmos is the island where the author of *Revelation* hung out. You know, from the Bible."

"Full marks." Carlos' mouth betrayed a sardonic twist. "Apocalypse man, who wanted God to wipe out most of the human race as heathen sinners. Actually, Patmos is three islands linked by land bridges, and from the air it even looks like a replicating virus. So... full credit for an appropriate name. But that doesn't help us with where the End Timer's Patmos might be."

"So what was the pregonera's story? Who was her suspicious companion?" asked Paul.

"Turns out she's into ancient poetry, like you, Abigail. But she specialises in Harem stuff. Has a regular discussion group with one Naguib, who's attached to the Center for Historical Studies of Granada and its Kingdom, based in the Casa Zafir, a 14th century Arab house restored by money from..." Carlos smiled. "...*the Aga Khan*. Naguib apparently knows a *lot* about the décor and customs of harems. Third member of the group is one Omar, an Arabic friend of Naguib's and a Professor of Hydrology, so like the Ismailis into water engineering if you like, though into poetry and history too. He's researching the Moorish acequias, the irrigation channels, of the Alpujarra region. So on the surface there's Ismaili-ish links, I figured they might connect to Kamal et al. But it turns out they're innocent. All three are sworn to protect the Islamic graveyard from being bulldozed, apparently there's already been attempts to break in with digging equipment, or just to desecrate the plots. The pregonera, Maria, is their 'agent on the ground'. Must've spotted us eyeballing the place. She'd phoned Naguib. Lucky, or unlucky for us, that Omar couldn't make it to Fuente too."

"Christ. Just defending history." Abigail shuddered. "Jack shooting her seems even worse now."

"Okay guys, here we are."

And now the Little Bird was swooping over the long FBI building, two storeys of white concrete and dark windows, satellite dish and tall aerials on its rooftop, fronted by an immaculate lawn where a large piece of marble on a plinth declared the building's identity.

They landed on the lawn, to be met by heavily armed FBI agents, as though some assassination attempt might be made. Hastily, they were hustled in through the doors.

In the lobby a poster caught Abigail's attention.

Wanted by the FBI Omaha
Featured Fugitives

Underneath, a few mug-shots, annotated 'Fraud Against the Government', 'Failure to Appear (Drug Charges)'...

But next along the wall was another poster: **Most Wanted Terrorists**.

Mostly Arab names and faces, the mug-shots looking neutral or sullen, along with a more pixellated foggy one that was nevertheless very familiar...

"Kamal!"

Carlos caught Abigail's exclamation. "We can work quickly sometimes. Passport photo, scanned from the database of arrivals at Logan, Boston."

"I took much clearer photos than that... Oh!" In her camera were all the horrid embarrassing holiday snaps. Where was her camera? In her big bag, still to come from the helicopter... No, she'd delved into her bag enough times before they got locked in the cellar. Surely she'd remember *noticing* the camera, even if the contents of its memory card were anathema and she had no wish ever to see those images again.

"Carlos, Jack or someone must have taken my camera. It may still be at the ranch, or whatever you call that place. It has very clear images of Kamal." Yes, of his smiling lying face, and of beds they had shared.

"I'll phone the team. What make is your camera?"

"Cannon. I don't know which type, sorry."

Photos of beds where she'd opened her legs, delightedly.

Pull yourself together, girl! You're free. The punishment for stupidity is over. A kick in the belly, days locked in a cellar. You can spread your wings again.

Bale Region, Southern Ethiopia: November 1166

Hakim put down his quill and rubbed his temples, until dizziness passed.

The lamps flickered and the insect chorus sawed into his thought, severing any connections he might make. He'd get no more done this night, and indeed this was a good moment to stop. Although *always* some samples seemed to go wrong, no matter how much care was taken, the record showed beyond doubt that pure *water of blood* stored for much longer than undivided blood.

This pure form was straw coloured, obtained by thrice filtering through the special powder he'd named *hollow sand*, and crucially, it still passed on the seeds of plague! The power of this lighter aspect to pass on protection had still to be trialled, and yet, via the undivided blood of a grey-hair, albeit amid some unexplained deaths, three prisoners had clearly been granted invulnerability. Repeated jabs of the pestilence had no effect upon them.

To add to this tally of progress, they'd learned how to increase the stock of weeping and grey-haired monkeys, more of which had also been captured from the jungle. And the intravention of plague from man to man, not just from a monkey to a man, had been proven to work. This was not necessary to aid the spread of plague of course, for it leapt like a fire between men unless the strictest precautions were taken, but it validated Hakim's previous observations, demonstrating that, when deliberately planning to start an outbreak, the blood of a man was as good a weapon as the blood of a monkey.

Hamdullah approached, clutching a manuscript, his eyes burning. Hakim feared the Fida'i was over-worked, or had a fever.

"Good Hamdullah, it is late. You should go to bed!" he cautioned.

"Why should I sleep, when the purpose of our Imam still burns in you, and you do not cease your own labours?"

Hakim gave a tired smile. "You're a shining example to our brethren, but I need you to stay well."

Hamdullah knelt by the table and presented his manuscript. "I believe, oh Tongue of Knowledge," he declared formally, "that we have defeated the problem of bad intraventions!"

Hakim's spirit flared in sudden joy. He placed his hand on Hamdullah's head. "Oh blessed *rafiq*, if this be true, I shall see your rank raised upon our return. Your idea regarding snake venom was successful then?"

"Yes indeed. Some snakebites bleed instantly and profusely. Hence snake venom must cause this, since the worm's sharp stab inflicts only a small puncture. Mixing a little non-lethal snake venom with our samples prevents stickiness and eases the passage of fluid into the subject's veins."

Hamdullah was skilled at milking snakes of their venom, by holding the head in a precise way and pressing the fangs against a suitable receptacle. Hakim had witnessed this technique at Alamut itself, for a snake-handler from

India had been one of Hasan's guest savants, some of whom enjoyed the Lord of Alamut's hospitality rather longer than they expected or desired. Since a poisoned dagger was the preferred weapon of an Assassin, and snakes could conveniently be bought in many a bazaar, several Fida'een had learned all that the Indian guest could teach. Hamdullah had excelled in this specialist field, and also had a good working knowledge of practical medicine.

"The results exceeded my hopes," admitted Hamdullah, "and I believe the power within snake venom somehow quells any battle between a man's body and alien material. Yet still, good medicinal practice must be scrupulously conducted; as with any wound, poultices of honey and herbs must be bound over the holes that the fangs have pricked. And used fangs must be cleansed with alcohol, to remove residue and prevent clogging."

Hakim glanced over the manuscript. "This is good news indeed! In twenty-five intraventions, no deaths or serious illness, and only two prisoners with minor problems."

Hakim praised God for the gift of Hamdullah's mind. He recalled the straightforward yet brilliant technique employed by this talented Fida'i. To separate any ordinary effects of the intravention procedure, and its deep puncture wound, from the possibly stronger effects caused by introducing foreign blood, he'd started by intravening blood taken earlier *from the same subject*, via a small cut. This approach had also proved helpful in the putrefaction trials.

The manuscript told that the amount of venom required was tiny, and of itself caused no illness, only some sweating in the subject for a few hours.

Hakim bent and kissed Hamdullah's forehead. "Sleep now, good Hamdullah."

Minutes later, Hakim retired exhausted to his fern-stuffed mattress within the entrance to the caves. Yet, despite all the recent good news, still the putrefaction problem haunted him. He needed samples that would last at least a year, even in transit, not just a few months while benefiting from the cool air or water further inside. He feared that God's challenge surpassed his mortal skill, he feared failure. He prayed, even as sleep took him...

The next morning, Hakim awoke with a fresh idea. Perhaps he could take the coolness of the caves back to Alamut with him! Straight away, he sought out Rahim.

"Rahim, when we succeed and leave here, since indeed we shan't leave until we *do* succeed, we'll need a way of carrying our samples in such a way that they may be kept cool. I'm thinking of wooden boxes with holes in their lids. Within each, cloth wrapping a bottle, to protect it from shocks; so also

399

that dampness may constantly surround the vessel, by at times dribbling liquid through the holes. Would you make such a box yourself, so that we may appraise its suitability?"

"Also," offered Rahim, "those holes will let hot air escape, for I've noticed that hot air rises above a fire. Although that must mean that hot air is less heavy than cooler air... Hmm, maybe the hot air within a box will be less in amount, and thus convey less heat to the bottle, than the warm air from outside that will enter the box..."

Hakim frowned, but then said, "We shall see. Good Rahim, you're developing the mind of a natural philosopher."

Rahim duly made a box from local hardwood and carved holes in the lid and sides, adding two crescents within as a stand, to keep firm a glass vessel wrapped in its cloth. They experimented by soaking the cloth around a bottle of *water of blood*; a slave keeping it damp for several weeks until the *water of blood* finally putrefied, long after a similar sample which was *not* soaked had done so. Next, alcohol was used instead of water as the dampening agent, and a second slave watched the first slave to ensure that he poured none of the alcohol into himself. It was just as well that this second slave was present, otherwise Hakim mightn't have believed how quickly alcohol disappeared from the cloth. This time, the *water of blood* lasted even longer; yet the amount of alcohol required! Finally, Hakim settled upon a mixture of alcohol and water.

Tehran, Iran: May 2008

A new age approaches, to be ushered in by a time of momentous upheaval. Yet blessed or not, no man can know what will happen to him as dangers peak. So now it is time to break Jafar's prohibition, and set down what has for so long been locked inside my mind, lest our brethren lose the knowledge. I have made the password to this document, *Hujjah*, signifying the act of witness of Hasan, on whose memory be peace; for this is my witness.

– Al-Maut ibn Hakim.

1.0 Overview

Allahu Akbar. So the great work is almost all done! It is over two decades now since Jafar, known otherwise these days, recovered the *waters of life*, and of *death*, from that perilous chest buried in a cave in the Elburz Mountains. And with each passing year I have become more humbled by how the ancient al-Hakim accomplished his goal within a comparable period, or even less. Him, lacking our modern laboratories and technology! Him, without our biochemical and virological knowledge! More than ever, it cannot now be doubted that the hand of Allah assisted him; consequently our completion of al-Hakim's work is most blessed. Yet too Hakim was assuredly a genius upon whose shoulder I merely perch, as a dwarf upon the shoulder of a giant. If only, *if only*, a record of his methods had survived, beyond the legend, beyond the sheer physical proof of the plague fluid itself, and too the wondrous fluid that provides protection.

Why did he blend blood products and seminal fluid? What means did he use for his filtrations? How did he intuit that complex cationic lipids will preserve viruses? Or indeed grasp that they also enable non-viral vector vaccines! Did he derive his basic lipids, mainly phosphatidylcholine alias lecithin, from *milk*? Chemical traces strongly support this supposition.

Bound by the conceptual framework and primitive technology of his epoch, it is absolutely *inconceivable* that he could deliberately aim for cationic mediums similar to the modern choices, say for instance (and praise be for macro keys!): *2, 3-dioleyloxy-N-[2 (sperminecarboxamido) ethyl]-N, N-dimethyl-1-propanaminium trifluoroacetate*, or perhaps: *dipalmitoyl phosphatidylethanolamyl spermine (DPPES)*, or: *1, 3-dioleoyoxy-2-(6-carboxy-spermyl)-propylamide (DOSPER)*, or even the rather easier: *dioctadecylaminoglycyl spermine (DOGS)*, by extracting spermine from seminal fluid (hard enough without a lab!) and then taking all the other necessary steps to attach this amine to long chains, so arriving at such highly complex lipids! Hakim did not have a flask with a magical jinn inside it, to simply shake.

Yet suppose indeed he started with seminal fluid *already doped with virus*, and of course containing spermine and spermidine? Even so, the process to release natural lipids from the cells in this seminal fluid would then destroy the virus, likewise as regards the protection. But what if, instead, Hakim added in the lipids extracted from milk...? Or rather, added such lipids that were *pre-processed* in a way which allowed progression to the more complex components observed...? Plus he would have needed to add the cationic detergent, as well as much else...

Bale Region, Southern Ethiopia: February 1167

In Hakim's dream, strong young men bore old Arwe on his carved throne of black wood to the great bamboo cage of the sacred monkeys. Oh the outcry of the monkeys, followed by their strange silence! Oh the vivid blue scrotal sacs and red penises of the males. In the dream, Arwe addressed the silent monkeys incomprehensibly, then he went into a trance, eyelids fluttering. Monkeys rushed to the bamboo bars, baring their teeth and crying out.

And one of the male monkeys masturbated, jerking semen from itself towards Arwe and Hakim. And this signified that the Gods smiled upon Hakim; that he could stay and work...

Hakim awoke, the masturbating monkey and spurt of pale semen vivid in his mind.

Semen: that sticky white juice which produced new life, in conjunction with the semen of the woman hidden within her; together creating a baby with skin so fresh, usually with perfect limbs and organs, even if the father's skin was flabby or wrinkled, even if the mother was far beyond her youthful beauty, her complexion corrupted, her body worn. From old flesh: fresh new flesh! Surely, something in semen acted like an elixir.

Even the purest *water of blood*, thrice filtered through *hollow sand*, would eventually still go foul. Yet had not the Greek Hippocrates written that sperm, a foam like the froth of the sea, was refined from blood? Might this essential white fluid, which turned back the years as regards the condition of flesh, accordingly help to further refine the *water of blood*? And perhaps prevent it from putrefying? This might be analogous to the double distillations of the alchemists who sought a liquid conferring eternal youth, without, however, any boiling that would extinguish all living essence.

Hakim recollected cautioning the Fida'een against the possible copulatory diseases of native women, "polluted," as he'd put it, "by the putrid semen of some unclean native men." Prior to the proclamation of the qiyama by the blessed Hasan, any sexual spilling on the part of Fida'een was severely punished, and absolute righteous chastity was a rule of the current expedition. Absolutely, he couldn't ask or require the Fida'een, or himself, to spill their seed into a beaker for experimentation. So, must he pay *the natives* to donate their semen? Their possibly *putrid, unclean* semen? Surely this was an inconsistency!

Perhaps the semen of native boys, who were still virgin... The semen of youths was more voluminous than in adulthood...

Hakim and Taj al-Din sat before Tewo, who regarded them with those beady yellow-webbed agate eyes while Hakim did his best to confide a few secrets of the body.

"I have need," continued Hakim in Oromifa. "Need white liquid of penis, from youths not been with woman." Did his words convey his meaning properly?

Tewo chuckled. "In the past an Arab man with Sheikh Abu Muhammad had such a need. He paid well to satisfy his need with a boy. I observe none of you has ever tried to bed our daughters."

Hakim flushed. Memories of the brothel in Cairo returned to him.

"Not need boy for sex. *We* not need. All vowed be without sex. Need white liquid from youth into glass vessel."

"How will a glass vessel excite a youth to gush?" queried Tewo. He gazed at them, curious as to what the answer might be. When neither Hakim nor Taj al-Din replied soon, the priest-witch stroked his dome of a forehead as if cogitating deeply, then announced: "I see a way. A beautiful naked women must excite the youths by hand. Such as my youngest wife who uses the *gifti bandu* on her skin."

Taj al-Din translated the Oromifa words. "Lady... beautiful?"

"What is *Lady Beautiful*?" Hakim demanded.

"That is a cream made of many items, some very rare. Such as the venom of bees, and a special honey. Therefore, it is very costly to buy from traders. All my wives demand it for their faces."

Hakim growled in Persian, "This old fox intends to sell us good semen expensively!"

"If we don't pay his price," suggested Taj al-Din, "he'll have some pagan reason why milking youths is taboo."

"No doubt. Of course there's always the more copious semen of our horses, although that might perhaps be alien to human *water of blood*."

"What about our prisoners?"

"Whose semen may be tainted by rampant copulation with every woman and beast imaginable!"

Taj al-Din grimaced. "These natives do not know God, so they do not know restraint."

FBI Field Office Omaha, Nebraska: June 2008

The head of the FBI Field Office Omaha was a tall, ample black woman named Orchid Jones. She wore a purple pinstripe trouser suit and ruffly pink blouse; her accent was robustly southern.

"Welcome, welcome." Without the slightest hesitation she embraced Abigail comfortingly, then shook hands with Paul. It wasn't the reception Abigail expected from an FBI boss. Enveloped in a cloud of Orchid's perfume, she felt immediately at ease.

"No resistance, Ma'am," Carlos reported. "Your task force are processing for kidnapping charges, depending on the evidence."

"What we need to do now," declared Orchid Jones, immediately in control, "is start hearing your story right away, Abigail, assuming you're up to talking, over, I think, some coffee and sandwiches?"

"And chocolate for the lady," added Paul helpfully.

"And your story to supplement where necessary."

"It's so urgent," broke in Abigail.

"Honey, I realise. CIA Langley are fully aware, and ICE and CDC, and Washington. Mr Gutierrez," nodding at Carlos: *so that was his other name*, "already did a report on how much he knows. Now we need the full picture, so we can circulate a lucid synopsis. An APB is out on Mr Turner. Questioning at the End Timer compound is urgently aimed at resolving where the plague sample is."

"How soon do you think you'll know that?" asked Paul.

"Synchronous with our swoop on the compound, agents went in to the three most likely labs, one academic, two commercial, but no news yet. It's best if you don't ask us unknowns, and that we ask you about your own knowns, okay?"

"Makes sense," Paul said.

Orchid Jones cocked her head. "Just you dampen those reporter instincts for the time being. Regarding which, you'll understand we do need to control your communications for a while."

Paul grinned. "I'm not even going to ask about being first to file a Pulitzer story. This is too major."

"By the way, I don't want to stick you in a hotel after your unfortunate experience of Nebraskan hospitality. So I'm inviting you both to stay at my home, seeing as my two kids are away visiting their dad." Orchid Jones beamed. "You're welcome too, Mr Gutierrez."

Was this, reflected Abigail, to be a friendlier form of modified captivity? Of course the FBI couldn't let them have the run of a hotel with unmonitored phones in every room. What better way to keep an eye on them than in the Field Office head's own house? Yet already, she instinctively trusted Orchid.

"Thank you, Ma'am," answered Carlos for them all.

"Just so you don't get stir-crazy," added Orchid Jones, "I've booked a good restaurant for this evening, once," and she beamed again, "you've sung for your supper. So: something to look forward to. I reckoned as how Ahmad's Persian Cuisine mightn't have much appeal in the circumstances, so we'll go to my favourite Italian place, Lo Sole Mio. So… let's get on with it."

So this, so the other: everything was planned out in Orchid Jones' mind.

The debriefing took place in a room with dark louvres closed, evidently set up for video-conferencing, though no such seemed intended as yet. A bald tubby senior agent, Phil Bergman, was in charge of videoing the proceedings. A lean swarthy CIA man called Charlie Abu-deeb, Lebanese-American, a Middle Eastern analyst, had flown in from Chicago earlier that afternoon. "My parents thought of Americanising our name," he joked when introduced, "but the closest they could come up with was Scooby Doo, so we stuck with the old name."

Then any joking ceased as Abigail related all that had happened, guided by interventions from Charlie Abu-deeb and occasionally by Orchid Jones, who had a razor of a mind although she used it gently, as for instance, "We don't need to know intimate details, Abi, but assuming Kamal might disguise himself, does he have any concealed identifying features, such as scars or birthmarks or abnormalities…?"

Then it was Paul's turn to be vectored in, in tandem with Abigail, and presently Carlos was exchanging glances with Abu-deeb regarding the black-clad pursuers in Iran.

"Black T-shirts and jeans. Silver Mercedes. In Gazorkhan. I took a quick photo of them." Yes, and in the background would be the hotel-house with one room where she and Kamal had stayed and first made love, as she had deludedly thought of it.

"All the more reason to find your camera," emphasised Carlos. "That picture could turn out to be crucial."

"I imagine," said Orchid Jones, "the, um, woman in Fuente you thought was consorting with one of those wild cards was righteously livid. So –"

Carlos cut in, though respectfully. "The US consul we got to go from Fuengirola, by Málaga, to mediate told her this was in connection with possible international terrorists, so she wouldn't freak and phone the police again on the spot. She co-operated but she high-mindedly refused compensation and actually said of her own accord she had no intention of contacting the media. We decided to trust this, the alternative being to eat humble pie with the Spanish government, which wouldn't go down well with the State Department. So far so good."

A tentative knock at the door. In came a tanned young woman bearing a loaded tray that rattled, which she deposited near Orchid Jones and hastily began unloading. A couple of doughnuts slipped from a laden plate. Coffee slurped out of the top of the pot.

"What's with you, Amy?" hissed Orchid Jones.

The young woman looked panic-stricken. "Ma'am," she began, then whispered something to her boss.

"Come with me," said Orchid Jones, promptly rising and taking Amy by the arm to propel her towards the door. "Would you'all serve yourselves?" she called back as she left.

"Can you get regular TV on that video-conference screen?" Carlos asked Bergman.

Bergman could. Satellite news. CNN.

"...reports of a hundred and fifty cases of the so-called 'haemorrhagic fever' in the Indian city of Mumbai, formerly Bombay, rising steeply from twenty yesterday, in addition to the outbreak in Madras." The footage showed a bustling Indian city, choked with pedestrians and pedal rickshaws and laden three-wheelers, then an over-packed train leaving a station, passengers perched on the roofs and clinging to the sides of carriages.

"Irresponsible journalism," commented Abu-deeb. "Makes that seem like a panic flight from the city, but Indian commuter trains often look just so."

"Top of the news again are newly reported cases of a similar serious illness in Hungary's capital, Budapest, following the outbreak in Romania's capital Bucharest..."

"He must've moved real quick," observed Paul.

The anchor woman was now on split-screen, questioning a spokeswoman for CDC Atlanta. "So how serious is this 'haemorrhagic fever', and what are the first signs?"

"We don't know the criticality of the strain yet. And we don't know the incubation period either." Doubtless the spokeswoman added this, gambling on attention span, to avoid going into lurid depth about the Black Death, or naming it thus.

"So far, there are outbreaks in the Ukraine, Romania, and Hungary. And in India too. Might this suggest a *deliberate* spreading of the disease?"

The Spokeswoman shook her head. "Much more likely it's due to the sheer volume of international air traffic. A victim in the terminal stages of a

407

haemorrhagic fever is scarcely capable of rational planning."

"That's an evasion," commented Paul.

"Do you think international air travel should be temporarily suspended, at least by the US government?"

"That certainly isn't the recommendation of CDC at this stage."

"One expert says that this disease may be the Black Death, which decimated Europe in the Middle Ages."

"Strictly speaking, 'decimated' means one in ten deaths, whereas…"

"Ha!" cried Paul. "She shouldn't have said that." However, the spokeswoman recovered, barely avoiding the PR disaster that was the logical end of her sentence.

"…whereas the medieval 'plague' was spread by rat fleas. Our own experts are busy analysing samples flown to Atlanta from the Ukraine. The Ukrainians reacted very promptly, realising there was a serious situation and prioritising this. I guess, in the long aftermath of Chernobyl, they're sensitive to medical abnormalities."

"But this could be *plague*, then, though of a different sort?"

Just then Orchid Jones returned, so Bergman cut the sound on the news though he left the visuals running. "My apologies! Particularly to you, Abigail. Seems there's been some scuttlebutt, which I've had to, hmm… control. Before we sent our task force in, I reckoned I had to brief them fully about the nature of the sample Turner stole, *in confidence* of course, the better to retrieve it from wherever."

Carlos was nodding assent, for of course he'd been at that briefing.

"Also," continued Orchid Jones, "one agent whom I respect raised the point that we didn't want another Waco siege, especially with apparently upstanding and righteous, well-heeled citizens taking the place of those Koresh nutters. Well, after my briefing the team fully understood this wasn't merely a question of kidnapping. And of course as you're seeing right now, plague, quote unquote, is top of the hour.

"In light of all that, Amy just confessed to me that her devoted boyfriend was on the team. He told her an hour ago, by mobile, that they'd freed and sent right here a woman who'd been in contact with the disease, and so to take care." Bitterness crept into her voice. "That's what Amy *understood* he'd said, anyhow! But fear and misunderstanding can spread like wildfire in a situation like this, even in our own ranks, and I guess you just saw," she gestured towards the screen, "what the TV channels are making of this already."

"Hey," complained Paul, "don't I get a look in as the *guy* closest to plague?"

"If there'd been any perceived risk, we'd have sent agents in full biohazard-suits," Orchid continued, "and I'd hardly be inviting the two of you home, now would I?" Silence reigned for a few seconds; Paul failed to provide a quip. "*Home* is where I've sent Amy, after a very severe warning. She swears she didn't tell anyone else. But the Black Death is *such* a spectre in our culture, many will share her anxieties."

"I think," said Abigail, "anxiety is just the start."

"I'd advise anyone prone to nightmares, *not* to read the literature," added Paul.

Lo Sole Mio Restaurant, Omaha, Nebraska: June 2008

The meal didn't go well. Abigail wasn't hungry. Paul ate minimally too, perhaps out of solidarity? Orchid's phone constantly interrupted and she had to leave the table several times. She only drank soda, but Carlos and Paul and Abigail emptied a bottle of Primitivo del Salento. Only Carlos did justice to the excellent food, ploughing through fried breaded beef-stuffed ravioli, followed by salsiccia and pepperoni with angel hair pasta tossed in olive oil and garlic. Abigail couldn't shake from her head an image of a chain of explosions, like volcanic eruptions marching across the map of the world. Two chains at least. Biological blasts worse than bombs, for these al-FaQ explosions were self-sustaining, devouring ever more human food.

Just as coffee was served, a phone call sent Carlos hurrying to the door, where undoubtedly he would avail himself of a BN. When he returned, he was beaming.

"Ryan has found your camera, Abi! It was lodged in a corner of the Nissan. Must have slid out in the rush in Fuente, or when you switched to the Brit car. Jack Turner doesn't have it at all!"

"How soon can it get here?" demanded Abi, whereupon Carlos and Paul uttered an almost simultaneous groan.

"Abi," said Carlos, amused, "all your images are being emailed to CIA Langley, FBI Washington, FBI Omaha."

"That means…"

"That means, honey," interjected Orchid, picking up her own phone, "we'll be able to view your holiday pics this very evening in the comfort of my home. Unless of course you're exhausted."

Paul was eyeing Abigail uncertainly.

Intimacies… the holiday pics of a deluded dumb doll. Yet that shot of the mystery guys in Gazorkhan could be important; the recent images of Kamal would be useful too. How could she make any excuses not to view them? Of course she couldn't. Accordingly, Abigail squared her shoulders and nodded.

Orchid Jones' House, Omaha, Nebraska: June 2008

Orchid Jones had provided more excellent coffee for wakefulness. On the plasma screen in her exuberant lounge of brocaded scarlet and purple sofas littered with gold and silver cushions, huge images of Abigail's time in Iran succeeded one another quite rapidly. Abigail felt as though she was drowning and her life was flashing by before her eyes... then she was staring at the photo of the silver Mercedes in that street in Gazorkhan, almost life size. 'Very good girl,' she heard again in her head.

Don't remember Kamal, remember anything else!

Play the *Jungle Book* game: how many items can you remember that were on the tray; that were *in the car* for example...? Binoculars, yes of course. Cans of soft drinks...

"I've just remembered something else," she exclaimed. "Inside the Merc I spotted a pamphlet in English headed, let's see, yes, it was '...ional Water Projects.' But I was much more focused on the binoculars they'd been using to spy on us."

Paul winked at Abigail. "Binoculars and focus do go together."

Meaning he wasn't upset at beholding the very place where Kamal had first ravished a very willing Abi? Ravished: No! Don't think of that, don't sink beneath a sea of guilt and memories.

"Ional water projects," mused Orchid Jones aloud, "would either be for water softening or for various industrial uses. Calcium ions are replaced by sodium using an ion exchange resin. I majored in chemistry."

"No no," protested Abigail, "'...ional' looked like the end of a word which was folded over. I thought the word could have been 'national' or 'international'."

"Aha. Well, there wouldn't be any pamphlet about your *waters of life* or *death* lying around in a car! But I do wonder what you saw."

"It's," said Abigail. "It's... Kamal was very keen on explaining the water system at Alamut. No, that isn't it, quite..." She paused while facts linked up. "Got it!"

I'm not drowning, I'm swimming...

"We passed a water project sponsored by the Aga Khan Foundation, according to a sign. Aga Khan means *Ismaili* sponsorship. After all those centuries they still do water engineering! The Aga Khans head the modern Ismailis and claim direct descent from the rulers of Alamut, and way back earlier to the time of the Prophet, although Kamal was pretty disparaging about *that* claim. He would be, wouldn't he, if the only true believers he heeds are latter-day assassin fanatics! I recall Kamal once – *was* it him? –

411

saying that the Aga Khan Ismailis broke with the old Nizari traditions, they even ditched the Quran itself in favour of concocted Ginans, poems. Yet some of them, especially in Syria, certainly have a real Nizari heritage. The Aga Khan Ismailis are like, like the good side of the coin, of which Kamal's lot are the mad, evil side."

"We'll check the plate," said Carlos, "if it's not false, maybe it'll turn up an Ismaili connection. But why…?"

"Perhaps the Aga Khan's organisation, well, some of its leaders anyway, got wind of what al-FaQ might be up to? Perhaps they're doing their own investigating? Maybe the good Ismailis are attempting to police the bad ones!"

"Abigail," declared Orchid Jones, making a note on a pad, "that's a bright intuition. But if you knew that a gang of terrorists were planning to release plague upon the world, wouldn't you warn the security services *somewhere*?"

Carlos backtracked to the previous photo. They all stared at two unremarkable men of middle-eastern appearance. Out of context, Abigail thought they looked much less suspicious than she remembered.

"The Aga Khan's people may not have known how advanced the plans were," she replied to Orchid. "Maybe they were hoping to nip this in the bud themselves. But in the meantime, can you see how downright *embarrassing* this would be to them? The Ismailis are famously progressive. Educational and social and architectural projects all over the world. Yet coming from the very same heritage are these mass-murdering mad fanatics. What a stain on the flag of progress and sanity!"

Her own personal flag was distinctly stained, come to think of it.

"Wash the dirty laundry out of sight," murmured Carlos, as if intuiting her thought; or maybe that was plain on Abigail's face. "Excuse me, I'm going to phone Charlie Abu-deeb. I think he should put out powerful feelers regarding the Aga Khan connection, on the assumption that Abi's right."

Carlos was back from the hallway five minutes later, a hallway which from the outside had looked like a small chapel: tall pillared porch and trios of slim stained-glass-effect windows to either side. By now they were clicking through photos taken in Syria.

As yawns were beginning to engulf Paul and Abigail, despite the caffeine, she found herself staring glazedly at a hotel bedroom in Provence, *oh god no*, then at a sheet of paper, groups of four lines inked upon it in Arabic handwriting.

"Oh my god, that's what Kamal had in his pocket. I took a picture. He never showed the paper to me."

"Looks like a poem," offered Carlos. "Some golden oldy, like your Safi poem? No, surely that would be photocopied. If he scribbled it out of a book it sure looks neat, more like it's all his own work. I guess we'll know tomorrow. Langley'll be having it translated."

Shit! Any second now someone would ask why she was snooping on her lover. 'Was it her habit to do this kind of thing?'

"Oh," continued Carlos, "I'm wondering if they copied all the photos to Charlie Abu-deeb's laptop as well. His Arabic oughta be good enough, depending when his parents immigrated over here. Of course Langley'll be getting an expert translation."

Paul stared studiously at the floor, Orchid at the elegant words she couldn't possibly understand.

The poem in *his* pocket.

It could be *ever so* intimate.

Even if the bastard had ordered her killed in Syria. Even if he would have shot her personally in Montlume.

The room seemed to shrink around Abigail, trapping her. She felt hot and realised she was blushing. She wanted to escape, to somewhere safe, familiar. "Orchid, I know it's late, but do you think I could possibly phone my dad in Montreal, just briefly to let him know I'm in the land of the living? He must be pretty worried by now, all the time it's been. I promise I won't say anything about what's going on. I'd so like to hear his voice, let him hear mine."

Orchid considered.

"If I was your dad, I'd be bombarding you with questions. And not answering his questions might make him *more* anxious."

"I can handle it."

Orchid mused.

"Late night calls can be worrisome too."

"Papa stays up late. I won't use any French. You can even hold the phone."

"Phone in my study, I can put it on speaker."

"Oh thank you!"

"I'll need to cut the call if I don't like something, you understand?"

Orchid Jones' smallish study was illuminated by soft lamps and lined with books. History, biography, civil rights, some older volumes on chemistry tucked into a corner, a surprising amount about drama including Shakespeare. Orchid shut the door to muffle any background noises as Abigail seated herself in a black leather swivel chair at a crowded desk. Abigail tapped the number which was etched in her memory; it hadn't changed in over thirty years, from before phones themselves had memories.

Orchid hovered, with a ready finger held lightly over the cut-off button.

"Hello Papa."

"Ma mignonne!"

"Papa, will you speak English? I can't talk for long. I just want you to know I'm fine and I love you. Are you all right, Papa?"

"All right? It's been weeks! Where are you? Why didn't you answer my latest messages?"

"I'm in America, don't worry. I lost my phone." More or less true.

"Abigail, that's like saying you're in Asia or in Europe. Do you mean Boston? You promised you'd come home after your jaunt with the Sheikh of Araby."

"I can't just yet, I'm sorry, Papa. The trip became complicated."

"Are you in trouble?"

"No no, in fact I've just had a lovely Italian meal."

"With the Sheikh?"

"No, I won't see him again."

"Did he take advantage of you, ma Mignonne?"

"Don't use any French. There are simply too many things to tell you to even *start*, and it's late and I need some sleep. I just wanted to say all's well, and hear your voice, and I love you, Papa, and you mustn't worry if I'm out of touch a bit longer."

"Where in America is French forbidden? By whom? As to 'all's well', have you heard that there's some deadly disease rampant in the world? I didn't know whether you were still in Iran of all the crazy places, uncomfortably close to India, there was even a report about some cases closer still, in Pakistan."

Thank mercy, Papa hadn't learned what happened to her in Syria! The story could only have made local Arabic papers, and maybe spreading it further had been discouraged.

"Yes, I've heard. Look, I do really have to go now. It's been wonderful to hear your voice."

"Are you in some hospital?"

"I'm at a friend's house. Honestly. But I've had a long day. And I have to go. Bye-bye, Papa, bye-bye, love you."

"But…"

Orchid cut the call. "Hmm, thanks for the friend bit."

"You are, you are."

"Within limitations, honey."

Orchid Jones' House, Omaha, Nebraska: June 2008

The morning's news on CNN reported numerous more cases of

haemorrhagic plague; the word *plague* was now being used openly. India and Pakistan had outbreaks, as did the cities of Kiev, Bucharest, Budapest and now Vienna, in addition to what might or might not be an outbreak in Bangkok. Cases had also spread to the Hungarian and Romanian countryside, since whatever the currently unknown infectious period might actually be, some percentage of the infected had obviously been travelling around their home countries as normal, infecting others in turn before showing signs themselves and soon succumbing. Anomalous single cases were even reported from places as far apart as Iceland and Australia, no doubt due to collateral infection while in an airport or on a flight.

"Where do you think is next after Vienna for the main push?" asked Paul as they addressed flapjacks and waffles with butter and maple syrup. "Where's next after Bangkok?" Except for Orchid, they were all half-hearted about breakfast.

"There must be at least two of the bastards," remarked Carlos. "Or maybe three, perhaps even four…"

"I figured just two. Gnostic duality, religious symmetry."

"Well, Allah sure seems to be smiling on their project so far."

"Only the Allah of the lunatics," replied Abigail firmly.

"Yeah, right," agreed Carlos.

Worst hit so far in the West, Ukraine had mobilised its masked and gloved army, also imposing a total internal and external travel ban. Several phone-videos from the stricken country were of course circulating the web already, showing horribly disfigured corpses and victims dying in agony. TV stations, probably under government influence, were being more selective, mainly using emotive stills taken from these videos and other sources, prefaced by warnings to viewers.

"Blessedly," concluded the anchorwoman, "there's been no cases in America or Canada so far, although this might only be a matter of time."

"Except that we know otherwise!" exclaimed Paul. "LA, the pink fountain."

"It's nine-twenty now," said Orchid Jones. "Per my phone call, agents should be visiting the LA Coroner Office in about forty minutes. Pacific Time there, but we're getting them out of bed to open an hour early."

"Coroner Office?" queried Paul. "Don't you mean Medical Examiner's Office?"

"Same thing in LA County, apparently. Director's the Chief Medical Examiner Coroner. Maybe nothing much was left from the explosion to examine. But," and Orchid Jones grinned, "you never know. Okay, troops, since you aren't in much of an eating mood, let's get you on the job."

In the conference room, Abigail, Paul and Carlos, with Orchid Jones, Charlie Abu-deeb and Phil Bergman, all gazed at the CIA translation of Kamal's poem on-screen. Abigail was hugely relieved. Thank god the poem didn't consist of amatory, erotic lies penned to reinforce her naïve bamboozlement! In fact it was something else entirely…

> *Holy poet, you wrote in your Triumph:*
> *Waters of Death welled up from hiding*
> *With poison to smite the great horde*
> *Who savaged our faith abiding.*
>
> *Again Eagle Teacher calls forth*
> *Deadly Waters to purge this Earth*
> *For the faithful, with godly brides*
> *Who tasted the Waters of Life.*
>
> *The boils are black roses budding*
> *Dark blood pouring out in libation*
> *Ruby eyes gape from alabaster faces*
> *Behold beauty in God's retribution.*
>
> *Hearts, lungs, livers, weeping gore*
> *So feast, ye innocent crows; celebrate*
> *ahl al-tadadd in their billions reaped*
> *As God wills their faithless fate.*

"It's quite hypnotic in Arabic," Abu-deeb said. "Like an incantation. Poetry's central to Arab culture, so a terrorist writing poems isn't too weird. The Qu'ran being eloquent *proves* it's divine, unquote. I did a more pedestrian version," and he shuffled paper, "but our man at Langley kept a poetic feel to it; as best he could."

"It's pretty powerful even in English," pointed out Carlos.

"The *ahl al-tadadd* is literally *the people of opposition*, meaning those beyond the pale, kind of like infidels, although most Muslims would be included, certainly Sunnis. It's a complex concept to pin down in an English word."

"So," exclaimed Paul, "that's what was going through his head all along; ring-a-ring-a-roses, crows feasting on our corpses! If that *taqiyyah* stuff is a Nizari speciality, Kamal is the grand master."

"Taqiyyah?" queried Carlos. "I think I missed out."

"Pretending to be something you ain't, for the good of the cause. That's how the Nizaris survived for so long."

"So who's the 'Holy poet' meant to be?" Abu-deeb asked Abigail.

"Someone who wrote 'The Triumph' in the fourteenth century; that poem I mentioned in the debrief," she answered, relieved to give a technical response. "Maybe an Imam, hence 'Holy', one of the lost ones from the Nizari dark times, after Alamut and the other fortresses were smashed in the Mongol invasion. Professor Ruffie, whose book I came across in Iran, he assumed 'The Triumph' implied a *spiritual* victory, perhaps an Ismaili religious resurgence, um... maybe associated with the Mongols converting to Islam. Yet Ka... *this* poem confirms there was an *actual* vengeance attack upon the Mongols, using plague, though we'd already deduced that 'The Triumph' must have referred to the *water of death*."

"Or rather, *Abigail* deduced," corrected Paul. "And Mongols weren't the only target, the Nizaris took a swipe at infidel Europeans for good measure."

"A very lethal swipe," added Abigail. "And now it's coming again. Like the fragment said, swelling and overflowing. This time, world-wide. And the perpetrators and all their kin are protected."

"Original vintage Black Death, killer of nations. Maybe even enhanced a bit on the lethal original. I wonder how many fortunate 'faithful' there are. A thousand, five thousand? I guess they've had years to inoculate under the pretence of some health programme; would be bad security to explain themselves."

"The poem says that the faithful *tasted* the *waters of life*," pointed out Abigail. "Not *got inoculated*."

"It's a poem," said Abu-deeb. "Poems use metaphors."

Abigail studied the words once more.

> *Again Eagle Teacher calls forth*
> *Deadly Waters to purge this Earth*
> *For the faithful, with godly brides*
> *Who tasted the Waters of Life*

"The faithful *tasted* the *waters of life*," she repeated. "Oral, they drank the stuff." She frowned. "That's different to before. The word 'drink' was deleted from Khusraw's words on the ivory box."

Charlie Abu-deeb raised his eyebrows. "Some vaccines are oral," he suggested. "Polio, typhoid, cholera."

"And the Aga Khan's people are involved in water projects..." continued Abigail. "Could there be some literal connection?"

"*That*," said Abu-deeb, "we hope to learn soon. I acted on your call right away last night, Carlos."

Carlos scratched his head. "This is probably a dumb question, but if the Assassins were already geared up to spread Black Death, why didn't they hit the Mongols earlier? Why wait until *after* the Mongols had zapped them? I understand resistance terrorism following an invasion... just remember Iraq... but this seems a very excessive wait. When exactly was Alamut destroyed?"

"1256." Abigail calculated dates. "Almost 90 years before the outbreak of plague. I can't explain such a long delay until their revenge, until 'The Triumph' was written to record it. Remember, Paul, that Druze guy with the weird voice couldn't either."

"We're trying to get in touch with him," put in Charlie Abu-deeb. "No luck so far."

"No chance," remarked Paul. "Gone back to his hibernation. But I reckoned the long delay was simply fear; the Nizaris must have lost thousands of their own. And it wasn't total victory; use of the term 'poison' in 'The Triumph' must mean they still couldn't afford to be too open about what they'd done..."

"We don't know the original context," cautioned Abigail, "though this author," she waved vaguely at the screen, "seems to be echoing the original poem." She cringed. What a prissy academic way to phrase it: 'this author'. Yet she couldn't bring herself to say Kamal's name. "But it was probably written such that, like Ruffie, you'd think of poisonous words or culture, or perhaps if you *did* make the leap to something physical, the poisoned daggers of the Assassins. The original poet must have been security-conscious, even while rejoicing."

Orchid's mobile rang. She listened to her caller for a while.

"A foot, why that's..."

"What?"

"Say that again..."

She fell silent again, until finally:

"Uh-huh... uh-huh. You'll send a report through to Washington? Right. Okay. Thank you. The good news," she relayed, pocketing her phone," is that an intact right foot was recovered, protected by a shoe. As well as some scraps of flesh and bone, though those got incinerated because they already had the foot. The bad news is that a senior official of Immigration and Customs Enforcement, with all the right ID, paid a visit a couple of days after the fountain incident. You can guess his name. He was very plausible, according to whoever he saw at the Coroner's Office. *Boston ICE had been keeping an eye on a dodgy Middle Eastern guy,* he said, *who they thought flew to LA.*

So the ingenious Mr Turner borrowed the foot, allegedly to run DNA tests for identification of a known terror suspect, unquote. Signed for it, took it away in a freezer box."

"The bare-faced cheek!" cried Abigail.

"DNA tests, eh?" said Carlos. "So there's a database of terrorists' DNA? Obtained *how*, unless they've been captured? ¡No me cortes el pelo!"

"Excuse me?" said Orchid.

"Don't pull my leg. Hair, in Spanish."

"Maybe," suggested Paul drolly, "undercover agents pose as waiters and sneak off with used coffee cups to screen the saliva? Alternatively, you just bribe the waiters."

"Hmm," voiced Carlos. "You think Jack Turner actually uttered any such bullshit?"

"Since you can't take fingerprints from a foot, you wouldn't believe a database of toe prints. But at least we now know where Jack was roughly twelve days ago."

Orchid's phone rang again.

"Oh *yes*," she uttered after just a few seconds. She glanced around those in the room, as though wondering whether to take this call privately; decided there was no need.

A full two minutes passed before Orchid spoke again. "Very well done. I want you to summon all resident agents from across Iowa to hurry to Waterloo. Meanwhile use the local police to isolate the place, but nobody get too near, just observe! Check our manual on best procedure. I'll fly down to take charge, be with you in couple, three hours... No. We can't spare many agents from Omaha, bearing in mind we're still processing the many kidnappers of Dr Leclaire and Mr Summers, but I'll request some back-up assistance from Illinois and Wisconsin. Okay, Simons, you're in charge till I get there... Yes. Good."

"Well," said Orchid, beaming, "we might know where Jack Turner is *today*. That was our resident Omaha Field Office agent in Waterloo, Iowa. Looks like he's located 'Patmos'. The Reverend Abraham Collins is hanging out at an agricultural biochemistry facility there with an unspecified number of his End Timers, apparently armed, also a man fitting Turner's description. The place is called AgroPharm. Phil, set up a conference link to FBI Washington, then will you implement what I just said? Assistance from Illinois and Wisconsin. And charter a chopper too."

The conference call that followed speedily enough brought the Deputy Director FBI himself onto the screen, spruce and silver-haired, steely-blue-suited, and from the glimpses they could get, in a palatial office.

"Congratulations," he said after hearing Orchid out, "on lassoing the broken-off bit of the *ice*berg." His stress was surely a barbed one. "What sort of place is Waterloo? Apart from being voted fourth best place in the nation to play golf, so I heard, though I never got around to playing there yet. Why *there*, Jones?"

"Nice enough place to be, sir, so long as you aren't black and you don't live where the flood defences might fail. Importantly from Reverend Collins and Turner's point of view, it's a thriving center of biotech business and research due to the number of agro-industrial companies based there, ConAgra Grocery Products, Tyson Foods and so on. Iowa Biotech. And it ain't the sort of campus or medical school place we'd go hunting for a lab first off."

"But they can't have very high bio-security there. Tailoring tomatoes isn't like playing with plague. Sounds like a recipe for disaster."

"Quite likely, sir. They couldn't have known that Mr Gutierrez here would tip us off, so perhaps they chose Waterloo and AgroPharm because of stronger End Timer connections. Maybe they've drafted in some sympathetic specialists from higher calibre labs, where they mightn't have felt so safe from scrutiny. My resident agent said the place where they're at is into genetic engineering to modify plants, but they're also tweaking bacteria to convert tough woody non-food plants into bio-ethanol. Modified bacteria implies some level of security."

"Who knows," whispered Paul to Abigail, "maybe they have a secret sideline persuading cows to produce coloured milk to entice kiddies."

"And who else am I seeing here?" asked the Deputy Director.

"Dr Abigail Leclaire and Mr Paul Summers, and our guests from the CIA, Charlie Abu-deeb and Mr Gutierrez." Orchid pointed to each in turn. Out of shot, Phil Bergman fiddled with the remote, panning back the lens to fit them all in more comfortably.

"Ah. Indeed. Dr Leclaire, Mr Summers, my commiserations to you both regarding your incarceration. And our thanks for your full disclosure of this matter. Very cogent report you sent, Jones.

"It's essential of course that we expose civilians and indeed precious informants to no danger." The Deputy Director gazed at Abigail, then Paul. "Yet you do have an insight into Jack Turner's mind and behaviour, assuming that he's there in Waterloo."

"*I'll* go," Paul broke in promptly. "I want to see that crazy bastard nailed. I want to see Safiyya's bottle of evil recovered. *Yes*, thank you."

"Me too," added Abigail. "Definitely."

"Of course I'm aware from the report that you're a journalist, Mr

Summers. You'll appreciate the need for certain restrictions."

"Orchid Jones already mentioned as much. She's been *very* genuinely hospitable, by the way, er, sir."

"I'm delighted to hear that."

Carlos chipped in. "Sir, I take it this invitation includes me."

"You're also acquainted with this renegade ICEman. And I value inter-agency co-operation. So, Jones, my prayers for a peaceful and productive outcome."

The Deputy Director was replaced by an FBI logo and a 'site offline' message.

"That was a stiff shirt," Paul murmured to Carlos. "I guess life gets political up at those heights."

"Looked expensively comfortable to me, that shirt," replied Carlos.

"Gentlemen," rebuked Orchid mildly, "I'd say the Deputy Director was being, well, gentlemanly." Then her good cheer returned, as it well might in view of the Deputy Director's approval, and she winked. "Why, of course you can come along to Waterloo, Abi and Paul. We could hardly keep an eye on you in Omaha while our attention's diverted urgently elsewhere, could we now? As for you, Carlos, sometimes I indulge naughty boys who get things done. But an agricultural science lab – cows and corn – can't handle plague safely in a place like that! So I'll want you three to keep well back anyhow, aside from the obvious risk of gunfire." She picked up her phone. "I need the executive Sikorksy. Yes... the 3-76, that's the one honey."

Tehran, Iran: May 2008

3.2.2 The cationic polypeptide component

Allahu Akbar. Even after the realisation of a non-viral vector vaccine dawned, long before such a concept appeared in research papers, I wondered for years how the incomparable al-Hakim had arrived at the use of cationic polypeptides. Along with the small cations provided by free spermine and spermidine, their detergent-like properties assist transfection, the non-viral vaccine action via which the *water of life* protects. Even modern researchers haven't tried this, although synthetic detergents such as trimethylammonium bromide are used.

When Hakim realised the need for such a substance, though I'm tempted these days to question *whether he even did*, he would surely have turned to the detergent traditionally used in Ethiopia. This is the 'soap-berry plant', *Phytolacca* (or *Sarcoca*) *dodecandra*. Its dried and ground berries produce a foaming detergent when added to water. However, the active component of these soap berries is *anionic*, not cationic. What's more the saponins in them, those glycosides with their foaming action (which incidentally stun fish and kill the snails that vector schistosomiasis; so aside from use for general hygiene the natives were probably very familiar with this plant), those very glycosides haemolyse red blood cells. They break open and release haemoglobin into the surrounding plasma fluid. True, al-Hakim's filtration technique appeared to be excellent; no red blood cells remained. Yet even so, this didn't alter the anionic nature of his most obvious plant source regarding detergents.

So where indeed had Hakim found his cationic polypeptides? No synthetics for him, his sources must be natural. Though I cannot be sure, my theory is that he may have resorted to the cationic polypeptides in bee venom, though this was surely very labour intensive to obtain, and thus expensive. Yet whatever can have guided him towards *bees*? Truly, I would say, the hand of Allah. As well as incredibly thorough methodology and a soaring intellect, once bees had captured his attention. Truly, in Sura 16 of the *Holy Quran*, "The Bee" (and the male honey-bee has *sixteen* chromosomes, which cannot be a coincidence!) it is written: 'And your Lord inspired the bee.' Whatever inspired al-Hakim? Did a swarm appear as a sign?

Bale Region, Southern Ethiopia: February 1167

Shimbi, Tewo's lovely youngest wife, concentrated as she applied her face cream from a small ceramic pot. Hakim looked on, nursing a glass beaker with a ground-glass stopper. An hour earlier, that beaker had been in boiling water…

A week before, alert slave workers had noticed Prisoner 21 showing early signs of plague. However, Prisoner 21 had not been intravened with plague, but with the *protection!* Hakim had been distraught. Were his scrupulous records *wrong?*

Along with Taj al-Din, Rahim and Nasir, Hakim had checked and rechecked. The heat had been intense that day, humidity high.

"Prisoner 21 is scheduled to be intravened with plague ten weeks from now," Hakim had summed up. "Agreed?"

"Definitely," stated Rahim.

"And thirty-two days ago he received *protection*. Agreed?"

"This is certain," said Nasir emphatically. "I countersigned the record myself as witness, see here. And protection bottles are clearly numbered in blue ink, as against red."

Hakim wiped sweat from his eyes to better see the manuscript. "So *how* can plague have become confused with protection?"

"Maybe a jinnee sneaked into the cleansed bottle while you were filling it, carrying with it some seeds of plague?"

Exotic birds in a nearby tree squawked with a kind of devilish laughter that seemed to deride the concept.

The cleansed bottle…

"Was the bottle *properly* cleansed?"

Rahim consulted the record, and stabbed a finger. "Yes. Look."

So it had been washed for re-use in the river within the cave, using a lather of soap-berry, which of course also removed the ink…

And prior to that…?

"I believe," stated Hakim, "that the bottle was previously used for plague fluid. If this is so… a brush and soap-berry lather and rushing water *cannot* be enough to cleanse. A few seeds of plague might still cling within, perhaps only in a droplet of water lodged in some roughness in the glass, which our eyes cannot see. The great Ibn Sina himself said that such foreign bodies can live in water. And a few can become many, invisibly."

"Shall we clean away what is invisible by putting poison in the washed bottles and shaking?" asked Taj al-Din. "Surely not, for then poison might linger too. Maybe we should rinse with diluted honey?"

Hakim thought about employing the cleansing properties of alcohol, but then a better idea struck him, a less expensive one!

"What will kill any ant or spider or beetle? Or *any* creature? If a creature is dropped into boiling water, it will surely die. We must imagine the seeds of plague as being like some mite so small that we cannot see it. We must boil all our glassware."

"But the glass may shatter!"

"Not if we begin with merely warm water, over the flame. We shall contrive tongs of bamboo for the slaves to extract hot vessels and stopper them without much delay..."

So the beaker which Hakim now held couldn't possibly pollute the chosen youth's semen. Shimbi completed her facial massage, rubbing any remaining trace of that costly cream between her fingers, and grinned, showing perfectly white teeth set in a deep crescent of gums the colour of lamb liver. She wore belts of bright beads and a blue-striped robe and a turban of a headscarf. She was slim and dusky. Of course she needn't have rubbed the cream onto her face at this particular juncture. Doubtless it amused Tewo to demonstrate the use of Hakim's money, and the need for it. Yet Hakim noted that the skin of the woman's face was indeed flawless; perhaps he should show more interest in this display of feminine vanity.

"Venom of bees truly preserve skin of face?" he asked in Oromifa. "Miracle does not sting you! Who could think such ingredient?"

And then he realised what he'd said: *an ingredient that preserves skin*. He must think about this later. He held out the beaker. "Now, with regard to handling..."

Shimbi giggled, and Tewo guffawed.

The chosen youth was already waiting in an adjacent hut. Only a few minutes later, Tewo's wife returned with a little pool of semen in the bottom of the stoppered beaker.

Tehran, Iran: May 2008

4.3 The Modern Delivery Mechanism for Protection

Allahu Akbar. It was clear right from the start that we'd need a subtle mass-delivery system, to spread the benefit of the *water of life* to the true adherents of our faith. Injecting millions of people could hardly be kept secret, and attempting to disguise this within a mass vaccination program for flu, or some other ailment, was really a non-starter. Quite apart from the funding, all sorts of permissions would be required, all sorts of questions would be asked, and sooner or later someone would analyse our medicine.

So instead, what better way than to use the medium of water? A transparent medium, ingested by everyone, unquestioned. And ever since supplying the lofty qa'lats of old, we've been water engineers at heart, still involved in many projects around the world.

The problem thus became one of leaping from the stomach to the bloodstream, before indeed *digestion* destroys our delicate protection. Yet Allah provides a tool for every purpose, the best one in this case being the cholera virus. Back then, splicing vaccine material to neutered cholera was an entirely theoretical procedure, but, after many attempts, we made it work. The cholera outbreaks in east Africa were unfortunate; we might have been discovered. Yet Allah protected us, and the victims were not of our faith. We underestimated the disease's ability to mutate backwards into its native form, but since then we have put in more barriers to prevent this possibility. The formulas and flow-charts in Appendix B summarise our final solution.

For years delivery was our focus; we had no need to know how protection worked, as long as our procedures didn't destroy the active structures, as long as our test subjects still showed *water of life* in their veins. Neither could we guess how the *waters* had survived their long journey through time. Deeper knowledge only came later.

Access to the water supplies of the faithful Ismaili communities was straightforward. I hardly need to say that inadvertently protecting the false Khan and his hierarchy was easily avoided. Much of the time, he hides in the West. No doubt, too, he prefers their wine to water.

Later, after we discovered sexual targeting and our plans evolved accordingly, it proved much harder to dose the water of the Zamzam well in Mecca. Our most persuasive means had to be employed to gain agents in the production plant and inspection teams.

AgroPharm Building, Waterloo, Iowa: June 2008

The AgroPharm building was a long fortress of almost featureless grey brick walls, set in its own verdant mini-park. Some guns poked out of high windows, covering the approaches. Their Sikorsky descended beyond a masking row of trees towards a nearby couple of acres of tarmac marked out with car-bays, which was now occupied by police cars, large camper vans, and other vehicles.

Abigail, Paul, Carlos, and Charlie Abu-deeb were ushered to one of several palatial campers, room after room inside, blessedly air-conditioned.

"Your quarters," said Orchid. "Now don't you two go wandering off, just because I have to." Her eyes flicked between Abigail and Paul. "Relax. Chill out. Sorry there'll only be soft drinks in the fridge."

In the meantime a local police car had drifted over, to park by the camper, two sun-glassed officers inside, presumably to ensure Orchid's wishes.

Carlos switched on a plasma screen, flipping through channels to CNN. On a main street in Kiev, banks seemed to alternate with casinos, as if from one you naturally went to the next, or vice versa if lucky. That street was deserted except for an armed patrol dressed in white biohazard suits with breathing gear; the film shot from the height of an upper window. An ambulance raced by...

In Bucharest, from a type of clunky jeep, masked soldiers opened fire on a gang of mongrels feeding on a human corpse...

Somewhere in India, as rain fell lightly, a bulldozer was pushing disfigured half-naked bodies mixed with wreckage from shanties towards a large open muddy grave, its driver protected by a handkerchief tied over mouth and nose. Elsewhere in that country, bright flames and sooty smoke rose from what looked like a barbecue of human beings...

In the Danube passing under Budapest's Chain Bridge, a corpse floated downstream, followed by another as though the pair might have jumped in together. Deliberate suicides, or the burning delirium of plague? A police launch approached, circled, then went away... Maybe the police were merely confirming the signs of plague just in case a murderer might have taken advantage of the situation. Maybe all the available morgues were filling up fast. The two bodies drifted onward.

"In breaking news, isolated instances of suspected haemo-fever are reported from Kenya's capital Nairobi, also in St Petersburg, Lisbon, and in several other cities worldwide..."

Said Carlos, "So haemo-fever's what CNN have settled on as a friendlier name than Black Death, because you usually get over fevers, despite the evidence on film."

"CNN, or the US government," said Paul. "Minimize panic while the footprints head towards us. Vienna today, and where tomorrow?"

"He sure must have racked up frequent flyer points, whoever he was, *coño*, and his pal or pals."

"But they'd have needed to use all sorts of passports and credit cards," began Abigail.

"I *realise* that," Carlos said gently, and headed for a large fridge, pulled the door open. "Steaks!" he declared. "Wonder if the police'll let us barbecue outside later on."

Abigail, Paul, and Carlos whiled the time away with games of cards, a third player lessening the monotony of the previous confinement.

"Getting back," said Paul, "to the Pregonera's Moslem friends. History center in Granada supported by Ismaili money, one of the guys there specialising in *water* studies…"

Charlie Abu-deeb tapped two fingers on the table of the camper like some judge calling for order. "That's suggestive, though they couldn't have known what was in that grave. We'll hear from the Aga Khan organisation pretty soon. They know it's urgent, and why."

"Of course they couldn't have known," said Abigail. "How could they?"

"Only you guys did. That's what I call good research." He inclined his head in acknowledgement to Abigail. "When this is all over: instant professorship, consultancies. Whatever."

"Assuming," said Paul, "there are any universities left with staff or students. The plague's begun, and it's going global. We're a few months late."

"At least we're putting the pieces together."

"Die well informed, eh?"

"We still need to verify the Safiyya sample to know this all knits together. Also, see if there's any difference between the virus in its original state, supposing any survives, and any tweaks the New Assassins might have added. My god, to think that some Arab scientist achieved this 800 years ago! Almost makes me extra proud of my heritage, in a manner of speaking. My folks are Maronite Christian, incidentally. Still seems unbelievable unless the sample matches what CDC now has…"

"Are some people *doubting* this?" asked Paul.

Abu-deeb shrugged, then he jerked his thumb in the direction of the siege.

"The answer's inside there. Probably. Let's hope it doesn't get destroyed in some Waco-style inferno."

"I'm going to phone Ryan," said Carlos, rising.

"Why?" challenged Abu-Deeb.

"He's my buddy."

"*No*," said Abu-Deeb. "No need to know."

"How useful to have a phone," observed Paul.

"You know I can't lend you mine."

"I wonder if the missing foot's over there too?" said Paul.

"Well, it can't run away on its own," said Carlos.

Orchid had been elsewhere for several hours by now. Doubtless she had a lot of organising to do. Abu-deeb had gone away. By 5pm Carlos decided he was hungry, so he carried a fold-up barbecue out of the camper, followed by Paul and Abigail bearing aluminium chairs and a collapsible table. Good to stretch one's legs. The two local officers quickly emerged from their patrol car forbiddingly.

"I can't barbecue inside," said Carlos.

"Well okay, set it up *behind* the camper." Away from the trees and the biotech building barely visible some way beyond.

"Some End Timer could have thermal sights, I suppose," agreed Carlos affably, "however blind in other regards."

"Anything wrong with believing in the Bible?" asked the cop.

"*Me suda la polla*," Carlos replied in a tone of devout apology, crossing himself as if his words were a prayer.

Paul went to fetch the steaks, and salad, and cutlery. The same officer loitered watchfully while his partner returned to the car.

"You guys want some food?"

"Not while on duty, no thank you."

"I'll throw an extra steak on the grill, case you change your mind."

Presently, Paul had seen to the salad, and food was served, just as Orchid herself arrived fortuitously.

"Looks good," she said. She herself appeared hot and tired, and was wearing a protective vest.

"I'm telepathic," said Carlos, uncollapsing a spare seat for her, then pronging the extra steak on to a plate. "Secret CIA implant, although I oughtn't to be telling you."

"Maybe you can use it to read the minds of those inside the building. Our negotiator has phoned them in vain on all lines we got numbers for. Don't want to use a bull-horn in the open; press could hear that from half a mile. We're bringing in an armoured half-track to get closer safely. ETA, an hour from now. By the way, that was useful input from your colleague in Spain."

Orchid sat and forked up salad, then cut a chunk of steak, knifed cucumber and tomato relish on to it.

"Land a team on the roof?" asked Carlos.

She waved her loaded fork, ate before answering.

"They have a couple of guys up there with assault rifles. An airborne marksman could try to pick them off, but we oughta aim to establish some dialogue first. Not everyone in that building can be a hundred per cent, I hope. Exit to the roof might be booby-trapped, too. I'm kinda haunted by the image of flames rising up from Koresh's compound in Waco." And Orchid paid attention to her steak and salad. Before long she thought to unzip the vest and hang it on the seat back.

"Should have taken this off already." Yes, she was tired.

"Is that one of the spider-silk high performance polymer things?" Carlos asked her.

She nodded. "More comfortable than Kevlar, but it still heats up." A glance at the sky, where in the distance an anvil of cloud was rising into view.

Paul slapped his brow. "Do you have Abi's mobile here? I'm almost sure Jack phoned her in Provence or Spain some time. About meeting up or whatnot. Her phone'll have the number."

"Nice one, press corps," she said; at which Paul looked hurt. "I did bring your bits and pieces, but ICE already gave us Turner's numbers and his mobile's been switched off for days."

"Wait a minute," said Abigail, "If Jack had the idea of defecting in the back of his mind all along, he might have had a *second* phone that ICE knows nothing about... Maybe kept for contact with his End Timer nutters, and in haste or whatever he used the second phone to call me, or he was already planning on putting Paul and me on ice in Nebraska if necessary, so it wouldn't matter anyway which phone he used to call me!"

"Which means," Paul joined in, "Jack *may* have a phone over there that we can call."

Orchid nodded slowly, then stabbed her steak and sawed. "Which *I* can call. Which you can call. Or which Abi can call, in the hope. Heads or tails, which is better?"

"You need a three-sided coin to decide that," said Paul.

Twenty minutes later, as they sat at the table, accompanied now by an FBI negotiator, Phil Kowalski, Abigail made the call on her restored mobile, to which was attached a speaker so that they all could hear. And the number was ringing and not failing. Facing her on the table was a screen to display in large capitals any silent comments Kowalski typed; he'd briefly demonstrated how fast he was.

"Why you calling me?" she heard Jack's voice say; of course he had caller display. "Where you calling from?"

Kowalski's fingers flickered.

NEAR BLDNG YR IN.

"I'm quite near the building you're in."

"Which building would that be, then?"

WTRLOO. WITH FBI. RAP WITH HIM.

"In Waterloo, the AgroPharm building the FBI are surrounding. Jack, would you say a prayer with me for all the people dying in Europe and India because of Kamal's terrorists?"

Kowalski made a thumbs-up.

"You aren't a believer, Abigail." NAME, GOOD. "You can't be saved."

"I'm afraid, Jack, when I hear the word *saved* I think of millions of innocent fellow Americans dying very horribly and agonisingly, just because they haven't chanced to have the opportunity you had."

"They coulda paid attention to their Bibles. And you're Canadian, so what's with 'fellow' Americans?"

Abigail swallowed. "We share America, the continent. Just as you and I shared a great adventure, Jack, and you saved my life. Jack, imagine me screaming with boils and black blood. Is that what you want?" KEEP IT UP. "Is that what you want for babies too young to be saved yet? For little children who haven't yet had the chance? Is that what God would want you to choose?"

"Hell, *we* didn't make this plague! We didn't release it!"

SATN'S DSCPLES DID.

"Satan's disciples did that. *Satan's*. Why should Satan rejoice when all the FBI want is to get that sample safely to a real hazard-containment laboratory to try to fight Satan effectively and give the children a chance to be saved?" NICE DBLE MEANING. U CANT HANDLE PLAGUE. "Jack, what you have can't be handled with the sort of facilities you have here."

"Got X-ray vision, now, have you?"

"I can guess well enough. Jack, your brethren are actually… hampering themselves. Contrary to their own devout interests."

"You whore of Babylon," he said softly. "Spreading yourself for the Babylonian."

Earlier, Abigail might have flushed. Now she bit at her lip to stifle fury. Anyway, the shit was Syrian, if ethnicity mattered. Gently: "I repented of that, believe me, Jack."

"In the arms of a wise-guy reporter?"

HUMILITY.

"No, he's been down on his knees, as I have." Scarcely had she spoken, and saw the expressions fleet across Paul's face, of stifled hilarity followed by horror, than she realised how this might be misinterpreted. "Do you want to ask him?" she said hastily. "He's grateful to you for his life too."

"I reckon," said Jack, "what we need in here is an actual hostage to keep the Feds from any foolish actions, and *you* are too serpent-tongued. You'd distract us."

"I'll go," called out Paul immediately, rising. Though Kowalski waved him back and though Abigail shook her head fiercely, Paul snatched the phone from her. "Paul Summers here, Jack. I'll be your hostage."

"Be here within six minutes," Jack's voice said promptly. "You don't come wired, you don't swallow anything electronic, you just don't have time to. That's five minutes fifty seconds now. You better run, boy. Get here late, we shoot you." And the phone cut off.

"Oh Paul, what have you done?" cried Abigail, expressing the visible, unvoiced feelings of Orchid, Carlos, Kowalski.

"Someone has to get deep inside," said Paul.

Orchid took an instant decision. "Right. Run to the right side of the trees there, over a little road you'll see the main gate. Go!"

And Paul set off forthwith at speed, Abigail hurling herself after him, shouting "Come back!" and her arms reaching out, until Carlos overtook Abigail, caught her, held her struggling, way out beyond the camper. Paul didn't look back as he diminished, legs pumping.

Carlos led a shuddering Abigail back, frustration and grief in her eyes. Orchid was finishing phoning orders to let Paul pass.

"That," Kowalski said to her, "may have been an unfortunate judgement call. He isn't trained. You're exhausted."

Orchid shrugged. "Well, it was my call. And, Mr Kowalski, I can do my duty in my sleep. Mr Summers has proved himself resourceful, as well as brave. He knows exactly what the sample looks like. He knows the background to all this. He knows Turner. Also, there's gonna be a storm." She eyed the approaching, upheaving anvil, cumulonimbus rising behind it, a long line of darkness beneath. It looked as though a mountain had been dropped into a sea, sending enormous slow billows of tidal wave towards Waterloo. The sun, now sunk behind, made a serrated buckled framework of gold and red and dirty yellow.

"Storm's a good cover for putting our armour and guys in that lobby."

"Glad you don't suggest seizing the roof at the same time. Choppers don't much like lightning and hail. Our armour isn't here yet."

"Why didn't you give Paul your special vest?" demanded Abigail.

"Don't worry, he'll be there well within the six minutes. I guess they can make out our vehicles through the trees. Honey, I had to act decisively on the spur of the moment when Turner gave us that chance to infiltrate someone."

"But... Paul! Didn't your boss tell you to keep us *out* of danger?"

"Yeah, there's that," allowed Orchid, "but like I say. Guess I'll be carpeted whatever the outcome. However, we're in a bio-war situation."

"Is Paul more expendable than me?"

"Nobody is expendable, dear."

"I'd have gone," said Carlos, sitting Abigail down with gentle emphasis. Cloud towered now.

Kowalski was far from satisfied. "Usually hostages get *taken* rather than sprinting opportunistically for the chance to be the *only* one. Newsman, remember? Inside story?"

Carlos turned and, in derisive and elegant parody, softly slapped Kowalski on the cheek.

"What the heck do you...?"

"Just saving Abi from needing to stand up to do that. Paul's standing in for millions of people, like Orchid said, all hostages to those fools. He's their voice."

"But," said Kowalski, "surely..."

Preliminary raindrops spattered the table, hissed on the barbecue. Almost immediately white bullets of hail rattled down, bouncing, dancing, drumming at the camper.

"Inside, everyone!" ordered Orchid, gathering up Abigail's phone and the flat screen and speaker and keyboard in a precarious enfolding. "Somebody bring my vest!"

Heart pounding, breath ragged, Paul was racing towards the great glass porch just as the skies exploded, and for a moment he thought he'd been shot again and again and again, a veritable fusillade ricocheting around him, from machine guns, yes, cannoning off his head, impacting his shirt and trousers stingingly, so why wasn't he thrown around like a bloody rag doll? But he *was* being tossed, skidding crazily on slippery balls, tumbling chaotically, crashing to the dancing ground, and then *realizing*, although the fall winded and hurt him, that some of the bombarding ice was the size of blanched cherries, and even bigger, and he might indeed die from another crack on the head like the last one, as he clawed to his knees, to his feet, to stumble onward, slithering, arms waving, legs trying to do the splits, pirouetting, aiming for what now offered sanctuary rather than captivity, unless that great porch itself burst into glass daggers, must be of strong glass, maybe armoured, and a door was open, and he was through it, blessedly sheltered all of a sudden; and a bearded man with a powerful hunting rifle consulting his wristwatch was actually laughing as Paul skidded one final time and bent over, hands on knees, gasping.

"Crikey Moses, what a *clown*. Five minutes fifty-five."

"Would you... really... have shot?" Paul panted.

"Maybe around your feet to liven the show up even more. Couldn't have spoiled that performance. Priceless." The bearded man, who wore what looked like a flak jacket in jungle camo colours, poked the rifle at Paul. "Talk about dancing bears. You do encores?"

At least Paul's clothes weren't soaking, since most of the incoming had bounced. "Take me," he hammed, still panting as he straightened up, a trouser knee torn, palms grazed, "to your leader."

"Don't watch those kind of films nowadays," the hunter said, clamming up somewhat. "All the Sci-Fi we need is in God's book, and without the Fi bit."

Another flak-protected man, shaven and skinny, closed the door. At the left of the lobby was a receptionist's desk, to which he returned, and knelt down on a cushion, laying his rifle with sights across the top. He steepled his hands, resting his brow against the pitch of his thumbs and forefingers, and muttered. Behind the desk hung a hugely magnified photo of some plant's first twin baby leaves on an upwardly questing stem, the first embryonic sprouting of growth from a seed. A companion artwork had been photo-shopped so that the twin leaves continued upwards in a green DNA spiral, implying that here the genetic code could visibly be manifested, developed. Cool science.

Beard gestured Paul towards an open elevator at the rear, under a CCTV camera.

"Stairs?" suggested Paul. "They might cut power to the building."

"Well, aren't you Mr Helpful." Beard veered Paul away towards other doors.

The FBI almost certainly wouldn't cut power in view of temperature control of bio-samples, negative pressure pumps, visibility, and all else; but controlling his own situation in any minor way was good for morale, although the march up false marble stairs was no pleasure so soon after his run.

At the top, steel cabinets almost blocked the way, another cabinet waiting ready to be toppled into place. Paul slipped through a gap which Beard the hunter needed to squeeze through behind him. Turning back on themselves, these stairs would run up to the roof.

"Push the door on your left quite hard."

The door resisted briefly, like a freezer door if you try to re-open it immediately, then unsuctioned open, though it wasn't part of an airlock, just a firm fit. Paul stared into a large open laboratory area of microscopes, computers, manipulators, autoclaves, shelves of chemicals, devices unknown to him, racks of young plants in numbered cloches with their own special lighting. No windows, not on this level of the building. Strip lights, mumble of a TV, smell of disinfectant, hum of a couple of big column-mounted fans angling to and fro to provide some breeze; otherwise, the air was quite hot and stifling. Why wasn't the air-con working?

Part way along, heavy plastic sheeting hung across the whole width, duck-taped to walls and ceiling and floor, plastic behind plastic by the look of it, an impromptu airlock being part of the assembly, near which hung an array of what must be some firemen's protective clothing and breathing equipment, a couple of rubber Scuba-diving suits, a crop-sprayer's outfit most like, and a hooded suit marked SEWAGE DEPT. Like the wardrobe for a bizarre fancy dress party of extreme allergy-sufferers who wouldn't be able to drink anything. Someone must have used his ingenuity. Fortunately for prospective wearers that ingenuity was unnecessary, since alongside hung several of those neck-to-ankle white polyester bunny suits from the microchip manufacturing industry, used in clean-rooms 10,000 times more filtered, Paul recalled, than a hospital operating theatre. Year ago, the *Globe* ran a feature on the Intel Museum at Santa Clara.

So that's what their devout tame bio-scientists were using to protect themselves. Soft helmets, with long hoses attached low down to their rears, and gloves and booties rested on a shelf above, along with a large heap of disposable face-plates in sealed plastic bags. Now what had those face-plates been called? Ah, scope shields... Also, a number of filter units and battery packs, plus a pile of spare filters in individual bags, and rolls of tape.

Might work as well as any biohaz suit. In fact those *were* biohaz suits, except that in their case the hazard was to vulnerable microchips from skin flakes, hairs, detritus and exhalations of a human body. With suitable HEPA filters installed, for high efficiency particle management, and maybe something extra slipped in, they could probably guard the body from inhalations of virus, although had the kit yet faced such a challenge?

Was work of whatever sort still going on beyond the wall of plastic sheeting, or had the arrival of the FBI put a halt to that?

Two figures, clad in bunny suits, though minus helmets or gloves or any gear clipped to their waists at the moment, rose in unison from behind a partition. Mount Rushmore, him being the Reverend Collins; and Jack Turner.

"Why did you bring him in *here*?" Mount Rushmore demanded.

Take me to your leader, thought Paul. Hey, neurolinguistic programming works.

Beard the hunter said, "I assumed Mr Turner wanted to see him."

"Hullo-o," Paul said to Mount Rushmore. "Nice to see you again. I like your costume, but aren't you supposed to have an independent air supply rather than just a battery-operated filter?" Yes, that was *it* about bunny suits, normally worn when the external environment wasn't in the least hostile to the wearer, quite the contrary, being the cleanest on the planet. Probably the microbiology guys would have improvised *suit*ably, they'd be dumbos otherwise. But there was no harm in sowing doubts.

"Don't mock the Lord's work."

"No, I mean seriously. And this room's like a hothouse, which is bug heaven… Sorry, Reverend. That's what I meant," turning to Jack, "about exposing yourself to terrible hazard because this isn't a biohaz lab."

"Since when are you any sort of expert?" said Jack. "This floor's air-con's off so as not to churn lab air around the rest of the building."

"And where *is* everyone?" Paul pursued. "Oh right," and he upped his finger, "manning the sniper windows."

To the hunter Jack said, "Take him up the next level and shut him in the mandatory mother-and-baby-and-breastfeeding toilet. Diaper-changing shelf oughta bear your weight as a bunk," he told Paul, "if you curl up. All home comforts, food in the morning."

"Mr Summers educated himself quite a lot," interrupted Mount Rushmore, "judging by what I heard concerning his debriefing. Are you suggesting," he asked Paul, "that the air filter units in the helmets…"

"…which you aren't even wearing right now…"

"…are the wrong way round or the wrong kind or something?"

"Well," Paul improvised, "air's coming *in* through them, the opposite of real biohaz. But I wouldn't worry too much. Maybe they're okay if you couldn't afford genuine biohaz gear."

"You make do with what God gives you, boy."

"Yeah, ingenious, and better than a fireman's or a sewer worker's suit for delicate manipulations. In fact, can I have one, since I'm your guest? No, I'm remembering… Ah, that's why you haven't taken them off! It takes about twenty minutes to put them on correctly, unless you're an ace fabricator…"

"What do you mean by *that*? *Making something up*?"

"No, making a microchip, fabricating. What does really worry me is the millions of innocent children in the world, who haven't had any chance yet to be saved, and who haven't *any* protection, and meanwhile you're sitting on one route to that protection, *blocking it*, like, pardon me, the canine in the manger, when CDC in Atlanta or Fort Detrick can only be sure what they're up against if they get what we took from that grave in Spain. I'm begging you, Reverend Collins, don't murder the children like Herod did. Suffer little children to come unto me, okay, but not suffering agonies. Surely *suffer* means let, allow, permit, release. You can release the sample and you'll still have me as a safeguard while you negotiate an exit. The authorities are going to be very preoccupied by other things, if only you let them be."

"That's total bullshit," said Jack. "Haven't you caught any news? CDC Atlanta already got the virus in analysis from Kiev. Fresh virus, at that! All our sample can serve CDC for is verification that it's the same strain as the new outbreaks."

"No, listen: verification means that the *water of life*, the protection, is authentic too, and already *available*."

"Yeah, from the Kamal Kemistry Korporation?" The sarcastic emphatic Ks were very audible.

"I mean, the protection *exists*. Weeks and months could be saved."

"Seems to me that CDC and the CIA should take your story on trust *anyway* and go hunting for the other water soonest, *just in case*, without waiting for *verification*. Like, if someone phones that there's a nuclear weapon ticking in Manhattan and you can switch the bomb off, you don't sit around checking you all know how to spell nuclear. You go swarming right away. Seems to me that you've obsessed and intoxicated yourself and you're really here to vindicate your girlfriend's quest!"

A biblical thunderbolt could have struck Paul, worse than any of the balls of hail. To a great extent Jack was *right*. The Safi sample probably couldn't lead to faster countermeasures. The FBI were here in force not to verify the Safi sample but because religious loonies had stolen plague virus and were holing up with it in this fine town in the American heartland. Sure, recovering the Spanish sample would assist in confirming Abigail's and his own story of a medieval source rediscovered and amplified by Kamal's terrorist cronies. Sure, that should validate the existence of the *water of life*. But it certainly wouldn't produce the *water of life* like a rabbit from a top hat. Amid the helter-skelter of the past couple of days Paul had indeed obsessed himself. As Jack said: he was here to authenticate Abigail's quest, to authenticate *her*.

Paul had propelled himself here on pumping legs and slithering shoes to be a hostage, based on a false assumption born of, yes, *obsession*. He and Abi had been so frustratedly focused upon the value of the vial from Safiyya's grave because of how much they'd both put in to the quest. How much *he'd* put in, because of how much he cared for her! No, not cared. *Loved.*

Was her final shout of 'Come back!' because Abi had simply been improvising on the phone about those millions of children dying – because millions very likely *would* anyway – and suddenly she understood that he seemed to be taking this literally in the tension of the moment? And Abi's would-be knight in shining armour had promptly galloped off.

Okay, Don Quixote tilted at windmills because they looked like giants to him; but that was still a brave and chivalric thing to do! Admittedly, Don Quixote wasn't a seasoned investigative journalist...

Abi's quest had obsessed him because it was *hers*. Validating what she'd discovered was worth risking his life for, especially when she'd almost lost her own precious life.

"Cat got your tongue, boy?" asked Mount Rushmore.

"The sample you have *proves* who's responsible for the new plague! It's the smoking gun, to nail them. And what's in it'll give clues to how it was made, eight centuries ago, and maybe clues to potential protection as well! Every bit of evidence is vital, and what you have here is the *only* historical evidence."

"*Historical* evidence?" jeered Jack. "You mean, as in an appendix to Mam'zelle Gabby's next history opus, *The Black Death: A Solution*?"

That was too close to the bone.

"*History*," said Mount Rushmore, "is over. Verily the Last Days are upon us."

"And you want that you and your congregations *survive* those days? Or just the big boys who have ranches?"

"We must be enabled to preach the Lord's message, so that souls are saved. For He cometh, wielding a bright sword."

"You're much more likely to release plague right here, never mind your bunny suits and Scooby-Doo rubber outfits. Do you realise how long it takes, and how complicated, to derive a protection from a live sample?"

"If a heathen Ayrab could accomplish this, in the Queen of Sheba's land, with resources a hundred times less than we have in this building here today, with God's mandate we shall surpass that heathen, Mister Summers."

"A heathen who had God on his side too, no doubt. Funny guy, God."

Mount Rushmore darkened. "Blasphemy betrays your deceitful tongue."

"Do you have the foot you stole here too?" Paul jibed at Jack, utterly furious perhaps because Jack had caught Paul out, wrong-footing him. "That could look good as a coat of arms. The frozen foot of Sir Jackoff the traitor."

"Take Paul Summers to the toilet," Jack told Beard the hunter, who momentarily looked non-plussed.

Hesitantly, "What do I work him over *for*?"

At that moment Jack's phone burbled.

"Yes?" he asked angrily. "Of course he's here. Who are you? Oh, a hot-shot hostage negotiator, are you? Well, thank you for the hostage. We are remaining in here for forty days and forty nights."

"Not long enough," chipped in Paul. "That's only the quarantine period…"

"Shut up, you. If you try to assault the building, Mr Kowal-whatever, then Mr Summers suffers. Yes, I *was* addressing him then. No, there's no need for you to talk to him. Obviously he's capable of stupid wisecracks, so he must be in good condition. And we don't require phone calls every hour regarding his welfare… What do I mean by *suffer*?"

"You used the word," suggested Paul, "because I used it."

"Jerk! If we want anything, I'll call you."

The toilet. The breast-feeding diaper-changing toilet. Something bulky up against the door which would open outwards in case the breast-feeding diaper-changing mother was also in a power wheelchair, say, or at least needed to push out her buggy or baby-carriage. Something like the furniture over the hatch to the storm cellar. Paul rebelled.

Taking a deep breath, for all *that* was worth, he ran headlong at the improvised airlock in the multiple veils of plastic sheeting.

Bale Region, Southern Ethiopia: August 1167

The camp continued its experimentation like a huge, slow mill, with regular rotations tied to the 32-day period of ripening for plague. Its raw grist was the flesh and blood of monkeys and men, processed and winnowed to extract the foreign bodies that no one but God could see.

Rumour of strange magics and grisly deaths leaked out to the nearby village. Tewo was not the only one to observe that space within the cages was never exceeded, despite a constant supply of prisoners. Yet no villager was harmed, and Hakim's men were a source of great profit. Nor could the fearsome Fida'een conceivably be ejected or overcome.

Hakim was gratified to discover that the *water of blood* did indeed pass on protection, yet, just as with undivided blood, this was far from guaranteed. Protection didn't always seem to take; an uncomfortably high proportion of treated subjects could still develop plague. And other problems beset Hakim.

It had proved very difficult to blend sticky semen with *water of blood*. And, as regards quantities for experimentation, even those lusty village youths produced comparatively small amounts; they didn't gush like excited stallions. Furthermore, Shimbi could hardly be asked, and paid, interminably; she had other interests than milking boys, such as gossip and applying Lady Beautiful to herself, and more gossip, and titivation.

Consequently, Hakim wondered whether the seminal fluid could somehow be diluted, both to make it go further and to make it more miscible. But diluted with what? Pure distilled water? Trials were unsatisfactory. However, recalling that blood tastes salty, he reasoned that a mild salt solution of about the same taste might assist a mingling with blood. So Hakim added just such a solution to semen, squeezed the mixture through a cloth, then filtered the product and added this to pure *water of blood*.

As he waited weeks for the results, further justifications heightened his expectations of success. He remembered that a salt solution was good for cleansing wounds... Its slight sting, compared with distilled water, signalled some combative activity taking place. If the seeds of plague were far too small to see, there might also exist invisible seeds of many other misfortunes such as fevers and... festering. Salt must fight these invisible seeds that had fallen upon the torn flesh of a man, an unseen battle experienced as a pricking by minuscule daggers. A crystal of salt was sharp. Dissolved, salt must still retain its quality of sharpness. Surely all this must assist in defeating the problem of putrefaction!

Yet the outcome was perplexing. Most samples lasted no longer than before, yet just two out of the seven survived a *lot* longer before becoming foul. Although Hakim was disappointed, he was simultaneously encouraged. He prayed for guidance, then played with dilution ratios and salt strength. Milder seemed better. And he mercilessly wrung his mind for fresh ideas as he tossed about on his mattress in the sultry nights.

Might alcohol serve the purpose instead? An organ cut out of the body, and submerged in strong alcohol, never rotted. Alcohol might bulk out the seminal fluid and strengthen its preservation characteristics too. Yet alas, this was not so! Some samples of a final mix failed hopelessly. Although others did indeed putrefy less quickly, none passed on protection. Even the ability to pass on plague was severely diminished.

In despair he returned to basics and dissected the body of a plague victim, deliberately awaiting the death of a pregnant female they'd infected. God *must* have provided a substance to help him, if only Hakim could find it. To his great surprise, many liquids from the ruined cadaver turned out to carry the seeds of plague, including unlikely candidates such as bile and also aqueous humour, the fluid behind the lens of the eye. Yet after many weeks of frustrating trials, it transpired that *none* provided a weapon against putrefaction. He'd exhausted all possibilities, including urine, the fluid around the lungs, the fluid around an unborn child in the womb, and even the fluids of the foetus itself.

Hakim's main medium remained the water of blood. And his only faint hope of fighting putrefaction was from those two long-lived samples, each fortified by the semen of virgin youths in a very mild salt solution, which he'd named seminal solution. Bereft of inspiration and with the pressure for success almost bursting his temples, he took some juice of the poppy, brought from Alamut. Then he awaited visions from God.

Tehran, Iran: May 2008

5.4 Complex Cationic Lipids as Viral Storage Mediums

Allahu Akbar. As I write, I see that the West has achieved viral storage up to 5 years at 12 Celsius, up to 2 years at room temperature. We must assume they could do better; the timescales were only the length of these particular trials. Yet how pitifully far behind the incomparable Hakim they are! 800 years behind!

What works for preserving viruses, works still more for preserving the protein chains that provide protection; these cannot be considered alive in the same way that viruses usually are. Yet we must note that Hakim has different ratios of active components in the *water of life* and the *water of death*; we will return to this later.

Patents on viral preservation now proliferate, but modern efforts on this subject date back to the late 1980s, soon after Jafar and Ali and the others returned triumphant from the cave near Alamut...

Bale Region, Southern Ethiopia: November 1167

Hakim awoke drenched in sweat. Vivid and disorientating dreams remained with him. His soul was bound to a wooden post planted immovably in sweltering Ethiopia. The cruel putrefaction problem, a festering presence with Guba's bulging eyes, drew out all his ideas and ambitions and burned them in an agony of doubt, even as years ago the Igwe's innards were burned while the victim yet lived. But then Shimbi appeared, fresh and naked. Running to Hakim's aid, she rubbed Lady Beautiful onto his tormentor's stinking skin. The putrefying Guba disappeared, and the fires of doubt went out.

And so, part out of curiosity, in part perhaps clutching at straws, Hakim's thought turned to *gifti bandu*, the famed preserver of complexions. By now he'd observed its effect on Tewo's older wives, whose skins were almost as flawless as Shimbi's, even though his chief wife was surely quite advanced in years, having sired several children. To freshen the skin of the young was one thing, to make smooth the skin of the old was quite another.

What was the formula of this impressive cream? What else was within, apart from bee venom and a special honey? Of course some ingredients, maybe used minutely, might make no sense except just to raise the price, which he'd now discovered and which indeed seemed exorbitant. He had to know more; here was a potential source of profit for Alamut, and perhaps something that might indeed emerge to assist his great work.

"Rahim, tell all the others, the slaves too; when a trader comes to visit Tewo, they must tell me immediately."

Such a visit occurred only three weeks later. In view of Tewo's increasing prosperity, and its source, his older wives may have clamoured for additional pots of Lady Beautiful, causing a message to be sent. Powerful women, those.

Nasir, alerted by a slave, took it upon himself to intercept the trader on his way to Tewo's hut, before he dashed over to report to Hakim down in the caves.

"...so I asked if he carried the *gifti bandu* with him, and at first the man was suspicious and his two bodyguards put their hands on their swords."

"Only two bodyguards, for a trader carrying such a precious commodity?"

"The man probably has a regular route. If he's robbed by any of his customers, they'll be the losers as time passes. If he's killed, other angry customers might exact vengeance upon whoever deprived them. I persuaded the man to reserve two pots of the *gifti bandu* for yourself, at a slightly higher price than usual, for which I beg your pardon. He'll come down here after trading with Tewo. Now I should return to the village, to ensure he complies."

"Excellently done, good Nasir."

An hour later the trader presented himself, led by Nasir and escorted by two warriors with rich nut-brown skin. On their heads were skull-caps of white cloth. At their loin-clothed waists hung scabbarded swords and a dagger apiece. Their scanty clothing not only revealed a redoubtable musculature, but also a tally of scars from superficial wounds, none apparently recent. Heavy leather bags hung from their shoulders. The trader himself was darker skinned and hook-nosed, yet blue-eyed. Might his mother have been some exotic Ferengi slave?

Hakim clapped his hands so that a waiting slave would provide necessary hospitality, but the trader shook his head.

"If you forgive me," he said in adequate Arabic, "some cool water suffices. My name is Othman." He provided no lineage. "How may I serve your Excellency?"

Hakim and Othman sat down on mats facing one another, as if about to play a game, which indeed was the case. The trader looked around the cave at all the laboratory equipment.

"I'm curious as to why your Excellency desires two pots of *gifti bandu*. Presumably not for your own complexion, nor the complexions of your associates! Seeing all that I see here, I also reject the notion of a precious gift for a lady, or ladies, in your homeland far away."

"Persia," said Hakim. "Far away indeed. So you needn't fear that I could in any way undermine your trade here in this part of Africa. But yes, I'd like to introduce the remarkable cream into my homeland. I'm speaking as one man of commerce to another. I believe the ingredients are no great secret. The venom of bees, a certain honey, various other items."

Othman raised an eyebrow. "Your excellence, a man of commerce?"

"Strictly speaking my sponsor is the man of commerce, whereas I have an enquiring mind."

"Enquiring into blood and semen and how plague kills a person?" Evidently Tewo had been talking.

Hakim spread his hands to show that he would conceal nothing.

"In that respect I'm seeking an elixir of protection against plague, analogous to the protection which the *gifti bandu* provides against ageing of the skin."

"Analogous," repeated Othman in a neutral tone. "This would be analogous in the sense that a minnow is analogous to a whale? So that if one swallows a minnow alive, a whale will not swallow you in the sea?"

The implication might be that there were limits to what Othman himself would swallow.

"Perhaps my example is ill-chosen. To be frank, my master, who sponsors me, seeks immortality."

Of course the Imam-Qa'im was already spiritually immortal, even though a mortal man. It pained Hakim to misdescribe Muhammad in such a way, and by implication the blessed Hasan, yet the trader might well believe such a quest. Never should Hakim even hint that he was seeking to capture pestilence as a weapon.

"Immortality," repeated Hakim, "by protecting himself against all the major threats which imperil life." Hakim warmed somewhat to his theme. "Others such as myself," he added, "study how to prepare elixirs against the bites of serpents."

Othman shrugged. "And after your master is fully protected, no doubt he'll cut his finger on some broken glass and bleed to death. I don't say this as a curse or prophecy, you understand! Merely as an analogy. I believe the main difference between an elixir that defeats pestilence and the *gifti bandu*, is that the *gifti bandu* performs what it promises. So you'd be well advised to present some to your master, to indicate at least a degree of success in your travels."

What a cynical realist this blue-eyed Othman was; and his mind was as sharp as broken glass.

"Once your master finds how effective the cream is," added the trader, "he'll require constant supplies, which you must accordingly provide."

Hakim compelled himself to smile. "You have too bright a mind for me. You perceive immediately. But of course a cream for skin is trivial compared with an elixir of life." *Do not overvalue the cream!*

"But it would," persevered Othman, "be something actual. So you presume that I know the exact ingredients and proportions, rather than simply being a trader who buys then sells? Why, I might even invent the answer!"

The image came to Hakim's mind of Othman being tortured until he shrieked out the correct information. An unrealistic, entirely impractical image. He should determine whether Othman was a Moslem, since God might assist.

"Will you join us in our prayers?" invited Hakim. "It seems that time of day."

Othman sipped water. "Please feel free to pray," he then responded. "I prefer to obscure my own perspective when travelling among my clients in these parts."

Dissimulation! Taqiyyah! No, the man couldn't possibly be a fellow believer. He'd made no reference to faith. Perspective, indeed! Even pagans *believed*, albeit falsely, for instance that spirits inhabited stones and trees; therefore one day pagans might progress to believe the truth revealed by the Prophet, peace be upon him.

"I witness many things," said Othman. "I accept what I witness. You might say I became a trader from curiosity about the various ways of mankind."

This was certainly not the kind of trader Hakim had expected to meet. An honest rogue like the slaver Sheikh Abu Muhammad was one matter; honest in the sense that he earned his pay. But this Othman, seeking to fill an emptiness inside himself with the knowledge of strange customs... Yes, that was it: the man was quick-witted, but empty.

Since Hakim was committed to prayer, he now knelt upon the mat, as did Nasir upon bare stone, and both commenced the witnessing affirmation of the *Shahadah* just as any Sunni Moslem would...

After they had prayed, Othman said, "I'll instruct you, accurately, so that you don't entirely disappoint your master and perhaps lose your head. So much effort merits some small success. Though first you must vow in the name of your God not to export the cream outside of Persia, by saying 'As Allah is my witness.' And secondly, the price of the two pots will reflect the cost of instruction, as a man of commerce would expect."

Hakim imagined the blue-eyed trader dying of plague.

AgroPharm Building, Waterloo, Iowa: June 2008

What they heard on the speaker in the camper was: "Shoot him!" "No, don't shoot a hole in the plastic! Tackle him, bring him down!" "I'm not going in there! You guys got the suits on!" Then the phone cut off.

Already Orchid was on her own phone, staring out of a window at gloom, melting hail and resumed rain, albeit not torrential and with no cracking booms of thunder yet.

"Armour's here? Great. Paul Summers has caused a distraction incident. Team One, go in *now*. Two, take out the windows with high velocity, follow with gas grenades. Mortar the roof with nausea too, I *know* it's raining. Do it! Try to get a chopper on the roof, pilot's discretion, doesn't need to take off again. I'm on my way. Out." She closed her phone, grabbed and donned her protective vest, gestured at the combo of screen, speaker, keyboard, and Abigail's phone. "Kowalski, *bring*. Carlos, umbrella and open the police car for him. Abi, 'fraid you'll have to come along. Turner might phone, wanting you."

Carlos tore open a wardrobe of the camper, found an anorak, tossed it to Abigail, *"Put that on."* But he tore off his own shirt exposing tanned musculature, and next he had a red and yellow golfing umbrella.

"What's with the *Rambo?*" Orchid demanded.

"Bodies are waterproof, sodden shirts give you cold, Ma'am."

Oh it's his macho thing, thought Abigail as she struggled into and zipped the anorak; for an identical anorak hung in the wardrobe, but Carlos wasn't about to put that on himself, while donating it to Kowalski might seem patronising.

To Orchid, "A vest for Abi, soon as can be, seeing as you're leading the troops into the valley of death, *coño.*"

"I'm well aware, Mr Gutierrez."

"Okay, and I agree. Gotta adapt, and fast." Already Carlos, bare to the waist, was out of the camper, thrusting the golfing umbrella open, awaiting Kowalski.

"Can I help?" asked Abigail.

"No, stuff's all linked. Got 'em!"

At the car, as Carlos held the umbrella over the rear door he'd torn open, Orchid shouted, "Sorry officers, outa your vehicle please, use the camper, coffee break. Into the back, Abi, duck down, bad hair day for you and me, I'm afraid." At that moment thunder cracked and cracked again and again. No, that must be those high velocity rounds aimed at the sniper windows to make access easy for the nausea grenades. Then Orchid was behind the wheel as the two officers made for the camper and she had switched on engine and main beams while Abigail followed Kowalski and his equipment into the rear, and Carlos with collapsed umbrella, jutting like a lance wrapped in gaudy pennants, joined Orchid in the front as she immediately started the police car rolling, rain lancing through its bright beams. Clinging to the back of Carlos's seat, Abigail craned defiantly to see flashes beyond the trees.

The airlock relied on the weight of dangling, overlapping plastic rather than on seals and air pumps. The next stage inwards featured a couple of upright sun-beds bearing the logo HI-UV. Oh, that was the *bright* idea: stand between those in your Bunny suit and zap any viruses with powerful ultraviolet. Definitely less messy than showers, though industrial cartons of EnvironChem and sponges also stood nearby.

Paul fought through into a work-space of large clear perspex sheets, ceiling-mounted from hooks, and duck-taped together to form conical containment tents, which were taped to sections of lab bench, and within which a medley of apparatus and dishes and jars and test tubes stood. A throbbing portable air-con unit was rigged so as to vent to the outside through a well-taped hole high in the wall. To spread any escaping virus into the air over Waterloo? Naw, the output looked heavily filtered... Aha, that must be to create some negative pressure in the work area.

Access to the interior of the cones was by way of long elastic sleeves bonded to gloves. Perched on stools, arms plunged within, a couple of figures in bunny suits, tape doubly sealing the scope shields to their helmets, were manipulating flasks. Another sat at a bench adjusting a large microscope linked to a screen on which lurid pond life seemed to writhe and wiggle. The presumed microbiologist raised his helmeted head at Paul's intrusion, revealing a deeply tanned face.

Voice only slightly muffled, "Hey, what you doing here without a suit? *Who are you?*"

No sign of the severed foot, nor of any sliced-off defrosted toes. But inside an unattended containment cone, among much else, Paul spotted Safiyya's vial in a rack of its own, a red plastic stopper in place of the wax that had been; the bright red catching his eye. Just along, a bookbinder-style guillotine was clamped to the bench amid off-cuts of perspex, oh yes for the construction of the cones. He spied duck tape in dispensers.

As the microbiologist rose, Paul thrust one arm deep into an access sleeve of the cone, wriggled his fingers into its glove, reached out and took Safiyya's vial. Reversing his action, he pulled the vial with him, bringing his gloved hand along with vial out of the cone, followed in turn by the sleeve.

The elastic sleeve stretched considerably as he yanked his way to the guillotine. *My god, I'm Elastic Man.* Positioning himself, he slammed the blade down. The vast majority of sleeve jumped back to the cone, to dangle. Some severed sleeve flopped back around his protruding fist, the red stopper poking out like a panic button.

The microbiologist halted, horrified. Paul stared at what he held. He shook his hand but couldn't tell if the vial still contained any *water of death.* So he moved his free hand towards that panic button.

"You madman, *stand still,* don't move!" At which, the man's two colleagues broke from their intense concentration, turned their helmeted heads, then put down beakers carefully before withdrawing...

Judging by the panic reaction, probably the vial did still hold some *water of death*, though in any case the inside must be contaminated.

"Give it to me slowly," appealed the microbiologist.

"Won't," said Paul. "If you come any closer, I'll crush it." Driving infected splinters through his glove into his skin? That would be clever. From behind, Jack's blurred boomy voice: "Hold it right there."

Jack had come through the stiff triple veils, a pistol in his now-gloved hand, helmet on head, its skirt tucked into the neck of the Bunny suit, booties in place over his shoes, filter unit and battery pack up and running. He'd completed his protection in double quick time before venturing after Paul. Must have practised, although he'd neglected to tape his scope shield in place; maybe that needed help and he was in too much of a hurry.

Paul brandished the vial. "You look dressed to kill, but I wouldn't advise it. One crunch and the genie's out of the bottle."

"Guys, restrain him."

"*You* wouldn't dare shoot, or even come closer."

"Guys, I forgot to put in a new fucking filter! There's no filter. You grab him."

A glance showed the three microbiologists staying where they were for the moment.

"Aside from getting infected," Paul added, guessing, "you can't afford to lose a drop of the sample. And a drop in the wrong place is all it takes to infect someone."

Perhaps. He was making the *water of death* sound like VX nerve gas, but the effect of his words was what mattered, not absolute accuracy.

"The moment you pull that trigger, Jack, I'll crush the bottle. I'm watching your fingers. If you miss, who knows what you'll hit, or who? Listen to me, the FBI are outside in force. Checkmate next move." Paul waggled the vial. "It's time to resign."

"You mean stalemate," said Jack. "You look half asleep on your feet. Why don't you sit down?"

Crack crack crack. Muted by being heard in the windowless middle of the building, surely that was gunfire. Jack glanced back at where the sound seemed to have come from, through the sheets of plastic.

"Fuck," he said, and turned to push his way back.

"Remember to get a tan!"

No vertical sun-beds for Jack, apparently. Paul followed him, clutching the red-topped vial, shouldering through the obstacles. Unsuited, was he infected by air that had spilled from the ruptured perspex cone? Mount Rushmore had also attired himself. Beard the hunter was pointing his rifle towards the exit door. At that moment came a crash as of a violent vehicle collision with much glass. A few moments later a stocky man dressed in camo tumbled through the door and sank to his knees to vomit, blocking the door from shutting, a faint sweet sickly odour accompanying him. Try to haul him aside one-handed? Unlikely to succeed! Grab a helmet and try to put it on likewise one-handed? Without an accompanying suit, though, that would merely imprison Paul's head along with whatever was coming. Mount Rushmore swung round, to stare at Paul and at what he held, his face thunderous behind its clear shield. He stepped back, so that the mesh-shield of a swinging fan pushed into the air hose at his waist.

"God hath numbered thy kingdom, and finished it," declared the Reverend Collins. "Cometh the wrath of God upon the children of disobedience."

"Cometh the FBI," retorted Paul.

"We have a building of God eternal in the heavens," Mount Rushmore stated.

"But not *this* building here," said Paul.

"In my flesh I shall see God." Mount Rushmore paused, as if he expected to be raptured away any moment, his Bunny suit falling empty to the floor. Yes, he *was* awaiting that, exerting will power that it should be so, praying inwardly with utmost force, his face reddening with effort. What did fall loose was the air hose.

Through the door, stepping past the vomiting man, pistol in butyl-gloved hand, elastic-wristed, goggle-eyed, came a figure in a white nylon chemical suit and hood, from which jutted a snouty hard black plastic mask linked by a hose coiled over his shoulder to large filter ports belted to his back. The suit man seemed to drag greeny yellow vapour in with him, as if it clung.

"Weapons down!" he shouted, and fired immediately twice at Beard the hunter. Chest shots. The hunting rifle dropped, as did Beard, to his knees;

then the hunter toppled sideways. Already the agent was covering Jack, whose pistol now only dangled from one finger. Jack let the gun clatter to the floor. "Hands on head!" Jack complied.

A second agent followed the first, swinging his handgun left, right, before bringing it to bear on Paul. "Don't make a move, mister."

More of the vapour was entering, perhaps pulled by the negative pressure in the work area. Paul felt intimations of tightness in his chest, and the buzz of a headache, mild as yet.

"He's gotta be the Summers guy," said the other agent. "*That right?*"

"Yes, I'm Paul Summers." He shivered. "This I'm holding is the plague sample they stole."

"How the hell did you…?"

"It needs secure containment. Got to be an airtight box somewhere here or in the lab behind me. Three science guys in there, but I don't think they're armed."

The agent spoke into a radio clipped to his shoulder, relaying this. The other agent hesitated, then he said, "Fuck, *fuck*," and advanced on Paul, pulling off his own gasmask. "Don't move your head." To which he fitted that gasmask, to be followed around Paul's waist by the big powered-air system, then the goggles over Paul's eyes. "Gonna hold my breath and try to run to the roof." So saying, he was gone.

Jack was shivering now. Hands still on head, he pulled off the helmet, and abruptly he buckled, coughing, helmet discarded. On his knees he retched, then of a sudden he seized his fallen pistol and stuck the barrel into his mouth pointing upward. The pistol banged; blood, bone and brain tissue burst from the top of his head. And he fell forward like a dropped sack. Not an agent of actions any longer, never ever again.

Looking away from the thing that had been Jack Turner, Paul spied on a shelf a sandwich box, clamps on the four sides of the lid to clip down airtight, left loose fortunately. Whatever it had been used for, when he knocked the lid aside within he discovered some bubble-wrap. Depositing Safiyya's vial, he wrapped it over, replaced and clamped the lid.

Mount Rushmore was stooping over, gloved hands groping at his bowed helmet as he vomited. He might have remembered to install a fresh filter, but his hose was loose. Whereas the powered air-purifying respirator Paul wore was clearing his head and his lungs.

"Get that helmet off of him!" the FBI man ordered. "Else he'll choke on his vomit and never get to court." Only the one FBI person present; he needed to keep hold of his pistol.

As Paul moved to assist the rocking Mount Rushmore, abruptly the suited reverend clutched at his chest and then toppled backwards as if he'd been invisibly kicked. Paul tugged the Bunny suit helmet free, vomit dribbling out of it, turned the reverend's head, then felt for a pulse.

"I can't find a pulse." Paul thrust a hand upon Collins's chest; felt no movement there.

"You know CPR?"

At least the kiss of life on a stenchful vomit-stained mouth was, in the circumstances, ruled out.

"Never did till now." Reviving someone to be able to breathe more vomit gas seemed like waterboarding, the simulated repeated drowning done to terrorist suspects.

"Both hands. Arms straight, not bent. Abdomen below the ribs, not the chest. Hundred per minute. *Defibrillator to the middle lab!*" This last, radioed to colleagues.

As Paul laboured, pushing pushing pushing, the FBI man stepped closer.

"Yeah good, keep it up. Keep with the force. Pushes the blood from the abdomen to the heart. Lot of blood in the abdomen. And you don't crack ribs this way."

"How *thrust* come *thrust* you *thrust* have a *thrust* defib *thrust* rillator?"

"Sicky gas ain't standard civilian law enforcement practice. Risk of heart attack."

"There *thrust* but for *thrust* the grace of *thrust* go I."

"Johnny's the name of the guy gave you his mask. Hope he made it to the roof okay."

"This *thrust* guy *thrust* here *thrust* was all *thrust* heart." After the crazy sprint to the biotech building, now Paul was doing a version of vigorous press-ups. Would exercise never cease?

Just then, a Bunny-suited figure half-emerged from the plastic veils to gape at the sight of two dead bodies and another being pumped; it was one of the three microbiologists.

"Get back where you were!" ordered the FBI agent, gesturing with his gun, which ensured compliance. Moments later, two more suited and snouted FBI men came through the door, one lugging the yellow plastic suitcase of a portable defibrillator, his armed companion serving as escort. The suitcase came open, grey egg-box foam filling its lid. Out came the machine itself: neat control panel and ECG screen, two big black shock-giving paddles with insulated rubber hoses, powerful batteries within the casing for sure. As Paul moved aside, his initial liberator headed for the plastic sheets curtaining off the improvised containment lab.

Trying to ignore what had become of Jack Turner's head, Paul knelt and unclipped the agent's mobile from the corpse's belt, distanced himself, then fumbled with gloved hand through the menu, pressed to call.

"Abi, thank God! Yeah, I'm fine." Apart from maybe having caught plague. "My voice? Oh, I'm wearing a gas mask so I don't start vomiting. Listen, Jack has shot himself dead. I got Safi's sample safe. The reverend's had a heart attack."

"But this is wonderful…" he heard her blessed tones say. "I don't mean the deaths! *You being safe*. I was worried frantic. And the sample, *how* could you possibly get the sample?"

"I stuck in my thumb and pulled out a plum. So to speak. Right place, right time."

"It seems almost no time at all, yet it also seemed hours to me! Are you *sure* you're okay?"

"Right as rain. Or as hail. Hale and hearty. I guess I should have a check-up, though."

"*Why why why* a check-up?"

"To be on the safe side; I mean, their lab being so slapped-together. In fact, uh, maybe we'd better not touch or anything when we meet up, in case you, um, feel so inclined."

"Paul, you went in somewhere special without protection, didn't you?"

"That sounds like an accusation of unprotected sex."

"Somewhere dangerous. To get the sample."

Kowalski's voice intruded. "Sorry to butt in, Mr Summers. The lady has the good news now." Clearly he'd taken the phone away from Abigail. "Look, I need to speak to any FBI agent near you."

Paul's liberator was returning from the isolated lab. "They have oxygen cylinders releasing slowly, to freshen the air in there."

"I never noticed," said Paul. He'd had no time, spying the treasure and going for it. He held out the phone. "Agent Kowalski wants to speak to you."

"Who?"

"From Omaha. What I mean is, he's outside somewhere."

The FBI man took the phone, listened, acknowledged, switched off, and slid the mobile into an external suit pocket which he sealed.

"Hey," protested Paul.

"I'm to retain Turner's phone. Address book, call log, texts, you know. It's evidence."

So indeed, no doubt, it was. But to be cut off at this moment! Did Kowalski imagine that Paul might phone the *Globe* next, given half a chance? Ah well, this way there was no need to reply to Abi's question with an answer which might scare her… He'd see her soon enough.

"*Stand away!*" he heard for what must have been the fifth time.

But nothing, it seemed, would restore the heartbeat to Mount Rushmore.

The storm had passed over, stars had come out, and Carlos was driving the police car back towards the camper, Abigail still hyped-up in the passenger seat. By now it was ten at night. Paul, whom at least she'd been able to wave to, was being flown in a 'containment suit' to Omaha's Alegent Health Lakeside Hospital, the most technologically sophisticated for hundreds of miles around.

"Looked quite the astronaut, didn't he?" said Carlos. "About to blast off for the Moon. Moon could be the safest place for the next few months."

"How long do you think they'll keep him shut up? The full quarantine period? Forty days? At least he'll be safe!"

Carlos considered. "I doubt it'll be that long, assuming his blood tests are clean. Oughta be able to tell if any virus is multiplying in him, even if he's still latent. I'd guess so, at any rate! Now that the sample's in safe hands for analysis. 'Course if the sample's dead, no worries."

"The End Timers wouldn't have been working with a dead sample."

"They also had the foot, remember. Hospital won't quarantine full-term without very good reason. All biohaz facilities in the nation are going to be in *great* demand pretty soon."

"As in: overwhelmed?"

Another occupied police car was parked in almost the same place from which they had departed in such haste hours earlier. When they stopped and climbed out, Abigail gazed back through the trees towards the glow of lights.

"My hero," she murmured.

Carlos chuckled. "Find me a burning house and I'll run into it? Ah, maybe that isn't quite in the same league."

FBI Field Office Omaha, Nebraska: June 2008

It was going on for noon, and the conference room in the FBI building in Omaha was about to be used to the full. Paul was already on the huge main screen from his isolation room at Lakeside, where IT systems were state of the art. Bergman had explained that once the screen went multi, each sub-display would be labelled with user identity, at least in most cases. In front of Orchid, Abu-deeb, Carlos, and Abigail, were input-display tablets with optical character-recognition.

"Well," Paul was telling Abigail, "at least I oughtn't to go stir-crazy here. I can access thousands of movies, download any book. But it's *very* strange to be tended by staff in biohaz suits, as though I'm radioactive or straight out of a flying saucer. You heard about Rome? I guess he couldn't miss out on the centre of the Holy Catholic Church."

"And Hong Kong too..."

"Yeah. I don't think that other courier would've risked entering mainland China, but there's so much travel to and fro there in any case. I've been looking at the map of Europe. Vienna, Rome, where next? Catholic Spain?"

"Please don't say Barcelona," chipped in Carlos. "That's the closest part of Spain to Rome, much nearer than Madrid."

"Do you think he might conceivably have followed in the footsteps of Sinaldin," suggested Abigail, "as a kind of commemoration...?"

"So hit Marseille, you mean?" said Carlos. "Then maybe ignore Spain..."

"You hope," the room speakers voiced loudly on Paul's behalf.

"That's a definite idea!" Carlos turned to Orchid. "Listen, lots of people are gonna be trying to second-guess his route, but they mightn't appreciate the Sinaldin connection."

"Sinaldin is in the report for sure," said Orchid.

"Yeah, but symbolically this guy chooses a fountain of *waters* to blow himself up in. So he might also have chosen Marseille as a plague entry point because Sinaldin did likewise. Abi can see that, but will other people?"

"So what do you want me to do?"

"The health authorities in Marseille should be put on alert, thus giving them twenty-four hours to anticipate an outbreak. Not a collateral one but a targeted one, which could be bigger. I mean, it ain't much help compared with nailing the now dead bastard in real time a month ago, but it could be better than nothing."

Orchid mused, glanced at her watch. Eight minutes until conference time. "Right, as the host I'll state this, straight after the preliminaries."

"And he only had so much time in Europe before heading out to

454

America, which no doubt deserved his prolonged special treatment. So after Marseille, where next but London for a real big target favoured by terrorists? Probably via Paris, to infect another major population en-route; and the train from Marseille is quick plus great for anonymity." Carlos smacked his fist into his palm. "Yes, yes! And then which US gateway airport would *I* fly to myself? Certainly not New York or Washington, because that's too predictable…"

Once again Abigail ran her gaze down the list of participants prepared by Bergman.

State Department representative; top presidential advisor at the White House; Deputy Director FBI, him again; Deputy Director CIA; Deputy Secretary of Homeland Security; Under-Secretary of State for Political Affairs of the State Department; the deputy head of the National Disaster Management System; the Director of ICE in person; clusters of medical specialists coordinated by the Surgeon General's office; the Centers for Disease Control and Prevention's Viral Special Pathogens Branch; the US Army Medical Research and Materiel Command at Fort Detrick Maryland; the plague lab at Fort Collins Colorado; the National Institute of Allergy and Infectious Diseases in Bethesda; plus a foreign cluster: ECDC, the European Centre for Disease Control in Stockholm, the Pasteur Institute in Paris, the World Health Organisation in Geneva which liaised with high security labs all over the world, the London Institute of Hygiene and Tropical Medicine, and the UK Health Detection Agency which shared its site with the British military's Porton Down bio-warfare lab.

"That's a lot of voices to be heard."

"Don't I know it, honey. I can pass host status around the list, and we can do sideline chat comments with text during the talking. That's what the tablets are for, front of you. Key in the number that applies to the name on-screen."

"Did you get into trouble yet about Paul?"

Orchid grinned. "My DD said something like, 'All the better to focus on your teleconference. That's one reporter who won't go running around for a while.' I think the DD was irked but he didn't want to throw me off my stride. As host I'm kinda representing him, even if he's part of the teleconference too."

Orchid checked her watch again. "Now I think we oughta have a few moments of meditation. I don't mean praying for guidance, although that might help and can't do any harm, but just some quiet clarity and silence, a couple of minutes to compose ourselves."

"Can I pop out for a cigarette?" asked Carlos.

"*Run.* On second thoughts just use the corridor outside."

At thirty seconds to noon red lights lit on the squat black cams before Orchid and Charlie Abu-Deeb and Carlos and Abigail, showing they were active. Phil had gone wild with the technology and wasn't just squeezing the whole Omaha contingent onto a single cam. Paul diminished to bottom left as the great screen became multi-facetted, showing many persons. As the first main speaker, Orchid's image was centred and larger.

Considering the high status of a number of the participants, and accordingly the respect due, Orchid handled the introductions briskly yet very well; otherwise those might have been interminable. Assorted buzzes and clicks were only a mild nuisance, occasional feedback echoes rather more so; it was hard to frame words when you could hear your own voice a split-second delayed. Paradoxically, all of the overseas contributors came in at full strength, whereas the Deputy Director of Homeland Security was faint, a problem unresolved for half an hour, and the General heading the US Army Medical Research and Materiel Command would remain faint throughout, although since the General was to concede that the army wasn't best organised for civilian emergencies he soon became marginalised. At least half of the participants lacked the large screen capacity of FBI Omaha, thus in a sense missing the big picture, relying on thumbnails on laptops, and in one case resorting to a smart-phone at an airport, flight calls clearly audible until Orchid reminded that man to mute his phone...

"If you'll all pardon me," Orchid announced, "before all else we have a fairly solid inference that the next target after Rome is Marseille, France. Mr Gutierrez, please."

Carlos quickly explained, ending, "and after Paris it must be London."

"This is sheer guesswork," objected the State Department representative, a burly hairy Hispanic-looking man with his purple tie loosened. "If our government advises foreign governments incorrectly, causing them to concentrate resources in the wrong places..."

"Excuse me," cut in the Deputy Director CIA, a priestly-seeming figure on account of his black attire and a white bow-tie lending his shirt an almost clerical appearance. "This inference seems reasonable to me. Time is of the essence. I'll take the responsibility if our agency is wrong regarding Marseille."

Our agency. A feather in his cap if Carlos was correct? And, if wrong, surely not a resigning matter amid such an emergency...

"This, based upon as yet unverified medieval history in the exotic Leclaire-Summers debriefing?" said State.

Exotic, indeed.

"There's *also* Agent Gutierrez's report."

"Which merely endorses the former."

"If I may," said the President's advisor, a redoubtable-looking black woman with a Deep South accent, "I advise the CIA to contact their French counterparts immediately, so that we can pass onward." Might she be on Orchid's side, because of affinity? *Why should there be sides at all?*

"But that's the job of State."

"Immediately, I'd say. One city or another is a minor detail."

Moments later, the DD-CIA was talking softly into a phone.

At one point during the ensuing hour and a half, Abigail found herself insisting, "The *waters* swelling and overflowing refers, in the case of the infectious agent, to plague swelling in its victims and then overflowing across populations. Likewise in the case of protection from plague, this must somehow spread too, in a lesser manner, both back in Hakim's time and nowadays in Kamal's time. I don't mean via a production line, even if that has to be the starting point, but via some *natural* way. We believe the protection is heritable, so it would multiply or 'swell' within a chosen protected subject, then spread to his or her descendants."

"And this craz... guesswork," the red-headed freckled woman responding was from CDC Special Pathogens, "is all based on a scrap of *medieval poem*, plus a modern terrorist's take on a different, and in fact *lost* medieval poem?"

"Plus all I've learned since, in Iran and Syria, from the Druze and in French historic records," defended Abigail.

"All you've learned as a *doctor*, however, *of medieval history*. Social, not scientific. And mainly French, I gather, not Middle Eastern. True, with some *privileged* insight into a modern Middle Eastern terrorist; who, according to your own deposition, completely pulled the wool over your eyes."

"But now you have the Safiyya sample! Don't you...?"

"Arrived three hours ago. We're hoping to start preliminary analysis tomorrow. The samples of *demonstrable* plague virus from Ukraine as well as, now, India and Hungary have to take priority."

"If that sample had come to us," said the uniformed and startlingly blue-eyed officer from Fort Detrick, "we'd have been sequencing already."

"Without," the redhead cut back, "Kiev and Indian samples as control."

"So squirt us the sequences. Fly the sample to us. We can have that in three hours, maybe four. Or divide it and share. A 'natural' baseline is critical, because by comparison we'll be able to identify if the modern terrorists made any genetic modifications, and if so start analysing what these might do."

"Not a good idea to shuttle something so old and fragile around. Nor to divide it, in case any remaining active virus is only very minimally present."

Exasperated, Abigail spoke up. "If I were you, with Iran's permission, since this is a *world-wide* emergency involving all of humanity, I'd grab all the bottles and jars and monkey bones and snake fangs you can find at the Alamut dig and analyse the hell out of them. *That* was a medieval lab. The DNA of the monkeys might show if the species is still around. If so, you could start to capture and experiment on the original source of the material. And there may be some residue left in the snake teeth, which have only *one possible purpose* that I can see. Also I'd strongly suggest exhuming and analysing Guy de Dieulefit, even if there are only bones and some hair left, because he *did* take the *water of life,* and Safiyya's remains likewise for exactly the same reason. Here's a start," she added sharply, taking off the charm the Druze gave her and which she'd worn around her neck ever since, then slapping it upon the table. "One authentic monkey tooth from Alamut!"

"It's *impossible,*" protested the white-haired man at the Pasteur Institute, "that an Arab doctor in the 12th century could have isolated and preserved haemorrhagic plague, *or* created a valid protection. The idea is simply absurd."

"Yet this is what happened," insisted Abigail. "There's no other explanation of the link between the Assassins of Alamut and the modern al-FaQ, and for instance their intense interest in such things as the Holy Water within Guy de Dieulefit's tomb."

"Perhaps," commented Freckles, "they found King Arthur's round table and used it for a séance." A few participants laughed, although others looked grim.

Orchid pursed her lips at Abigail. "I'm yielding host status to the DD-FBI regarding the role of ICE and Jack Turner."

Well of course, the Director of ICE himself could hardly host this aspect. But soon, for the benefit of the FBI, CIA, and Homeland Security, the Director of ICE, a man of owlish countenance, was exonerating his organisation regarding the unforeseeable behaviour of their maverick renegade, now deceased and accordingly unquestionable. He rather implied that Jack Turner's suicide reflected adversely upon the FBI for not preventing it.

"I note," the head of ICE added, "that we have in this conference the journalist who already published harmful material about Immigration and Customs Enforcement. I regard that as highly inappropriate." Another slap at the FBI, in the person of Orchid. "Indeed this constrains me from venturing upon certain urgent security considerations."

"I'd say," intervened the presidential advisor, "that this situation transcends inter-departmental concerns, *if* it's of the potential gravity that we're being led to believe. At this stage I must emphasize *if.* Analysis of bones and bottles from the distant past suggests an archaeological timescale rather than an imminent crisis requiring massive mobilisation of resources." So she, who had authorised the urgent warning to Marseille, now seemed less supportive.

"With respect," said Blue Eyes from Fort Detrick, employing a phrase which usually means its opposite, "that's a blatant misinterpretation of a well-meant suggestion which could be very helpful in the medium term. And it doesn't diminish the fact that we and the other nations of the world are clearly facing *right now* a major crisis precipitated by indiscriminate biological warfare."

A text appeared on the tablet in front of Abigail. From Paul.

You're off hook coz military labs want big injection money.

Shameful, she stylused back. *Vested interests scoring points. Why can't set up united task force immediately?*

Isn't what government task force usually does. Task force takes months, even years, then produces report.

Oh.

The CDC redhead was consulting a laptop.

"However," she said, "we can now confirm active virus in the foot of the suicider stolen by the other suicider." Was she being ironic? "The strain is identical with the Ukraine and Indian samples which, I should perhaps have added, though this seemed unnecessary, isn't in our own genetic database or in GenBank at Los Alamos or GenInfo at the National Library of Medicine nor Harvard Medical School."

"It wouldn't be in those," pointed out Blues Eye, "if it's the medieval plague. Fort Detrick also has a data base."

"Thus," continued the redhead, unperturbed, "the Los Angeles suicider would seem to be an intentional virus vector. The foot's DNA has Arab markers, specifically Syrian."

"And the medieval Assassins were Iranian and Syrian, as I understand."

The redhead changed tack. "Whatever the provenance, effective serum production on a large scale will still take several months even if the government waives corporate liability as per the Swine Flu immunization program in the 1970s, to place legal culpability on the shoulders of taxpayers rather than upon the pharma companies; which I'd remind you *isn't* in hindsight regarded as a good precedent, although personally I'd defend our preventive vaccination program back then strenuously."

"Can Homeland give us an overview of realistic national emergency measures," interjected the DD-FBI, "for if the worst should come to the worst?"

But the question was never answered, as the Director of ICE intervened. "For reasons already stated, a separate conference is in order for even touching on hypothetical emergency measures. A conference most appropriately under the aegis of Homeland, *not* the FBI merely because its agents successfully liberated Dr Leclaire, which is a main reason for our impromptu format today." Noticeably he didn't mention Paul; those stories in the *Boston Globe* must have really galled.

"Were it not for the testimony of Dr Leclaire and Mr Summers," the bow-tied DD-CIA pointed out, "and for the initiative of our own Mr Gutierrez, I'm sorry to admit we'd have very little notion of the nature of the threat facing us."

"Which ICE *was* investigating," the Director of ICE responded acidly, "even if our Mr Turner unfortunately turned out to be pursuing a different agenda."

"A turncoat agenda. Keeping vital information of national importance to himself. And for his religious apocalypse colleagues. A vote of thanks to Dr Leclaire and Mr Summers seems appropriate."

Such jockeying for position, appeared on Abigail's tablet.

In his section of the screen the DD-CIA said, "Excuse me," and picked up a phone, listened, spoke too softly to hear, listened again, spoke, then put down the phone. For once, the conference had fallen silent, since a phone call interrupting the proceedings could only be directly relevant. Charlie Abu-deeb in particular was looking anticipative.

"I'm delighted to announce," the Deputy Director resumed, "that we will be joined very shortly by a senior representative of the Shi'a Imami Ismaili Council."

The spokesperson for the Aga Khan, on screen from New York, was named Hussain Kassam. Even sitting, dark-suited, wearing a chartreuse-green tie, he was obviously a large man, both in height and girth. His short-cut curly dark hair was oiled.

"His Highness," he said in British-sounding English, "is deeply disturbed by the revelations in the confidential report kindly, and wisely, made available to us. At the moment His Highness is in East Africa. I'm authorised to say that for some years now we have indeed been discreetly watching the activities of a radical group which came to our attention in various Middle Eastern countries. When I say 'radical group', this is our *interpretation* rather than a demonstrable fact, since in most cases we lack the authority to pursue investigations rigorously; nor would we wish to ally ourselves with the methods which a security service, for instance, might employ. Nevertheless, we have compiled a dossier, which we will immediately make available. In brief, the group in question, which skilfully does its best to hide its existence..."

"*Taqiyyah*," exclaimed Abigail, a little too loudly, for Hussain Kassam heard.

"Yes indeed, dissimulation. However, we have detected at least part of a network of connections. The presumed group goes by the name al-Fida'een al-Qiyama, which means 'The Faithful of the Resurrection.' This actual term isn't in your report, though I suspect that your Dr Leclaire is aware of its source." An eyebrow rose invitingly.

"Indeed," responded Abigail, "Hasan the Second's overturning of Shari'ah law in 1164 at Alamut."

The redhead from CDC looked momentarily peeved.

"Correct. Recently we've become fairly certain that members of The Faithful of the Resurrection have been tampering in some manner with the water supplies of Ismaili communities. I should note that there's been no further sighting for almost a month of those individuals whom we suspect are responsible, a fact which may be significant. Tampering in *what* manner? This puzzled us, since there have been no unusual outbreaks of cholera, for instance, nor typhoid. *Now* we have a valuable clue, thanks to the persistence of Dr Leclaire."

The Deputy Directors of the FBI and the CIA smiled.

Hussain Kassam spread his hands wide, invitingly once again. A flood of questions followed.

"Congratulations," Abigail said to Orchid when the screen was once again displaying only Paul, still minimised. "You handled that very well."

Carlos proceeded to clap, as did Paul and Charlie Abu-deeb and Phil Bergman.

"Once upon a time I did some amateur theatre," Orchid confided. "That helped. At times I thought we were in for a roasting. But the Aga Khan's man turned that around. You're a star, honey."

"The rivalries!" exclaimed Abigail.

"Question is, what happens next, apart from Marseille having a day or two of warning?"

Tehran, Iran: May 2008

5.6 Lipid Production

Allahu Akbar. Working backwards to Hakim's formulas has been so hard, so tremendously hard. Night after night, for year upon year. I thought this task would break me, especially as I could risk only minute fractions of the precious fluids to test. Still all is not clear, but I was able to discover just enough. I couldn't have done it alone; Allah guided me, even as he once guided Hakim.

Phosphatidylcholine and sphingomyelin, and other basic lipids, may easily be obtained from starting materials such as soy or dairy cream. A rough and ready method is to mix the material with a strong alcoholic solvent and then boil down to a residue, which in turn is slowly dissolved in water. For alcohol, we might now use isopropanol, or 3 parts ethanol with 1 part methanol, or even a methanol and chloroform mix. If boiling is terminated early and the water content increased as the temperature falls, filtering off the resulting precipitate can result in the capture of more complex lipids, which total evaporation might destroy. An initial process of this sort seems almost certain, though Hakim's later steps elude me.

Oh the resourcefulness, the skill, the surprises. Still they dazzle me! The profile of fatty traces not only suggest a starting base of milk, but possibly human milk! Mothers as well as men gave their essence to the *waters of life* and *death*. And for strong alcohol? The genius Hakim returns to bees!

Today, the Ethiopians make a drink called *tej* from honey, reported to be powerfully alcoholic; a similar drink almost certainly existed centuries ago. One wonders whether pious Hakim might have tasted this *tej* himself, experimentally of course. Not for nothing does the word alcohol come from *al-gawl*, 'the demon'.

Only a century and a half after the emigration of the Prophet, peace be upon him, from Mecca to Medina, Jabir ibn Hayyan, the father of chemistry, observed that the flammable vapour of wine was "of little use, though of great importance to science." And how that science shone! Al-Kindi, ar-Razi, al-Zahrawi, so many more great names over the passing centuries.

Jabir's very own teacher, Ja'far as-Sadiq, declared that the universe was born from a tiny particle which gave rise to an atom, from which all matter diversified. The infidels think themselves so clever to have arrived at the same explanation, twelve hundred years later! Why, Ja'far understood the sheer multitude of elements when the benighted ancestors of those infidels imagined that only fire, water, earth, and air existed indivisibly. And what of

Nasir al-Din al-Tusi, with his law of conservation of mass, eight centuries before the Jew Einstein!

Soon the infidels will learn their lesson, learn the potency of a very special product of Islamic science from centuries ago, blessedly passed down to our time by the ingenuity and perseverance of Hakim. And not just the infidels, but *all* the betrayers of the Prophet too, all *the people of opposition!*

But the times overwhelm me. I digress. So stills and distillation had been known for centuries by Hakim's time. And no doubt he'd seen natives made silly by drinking honey-alcohol. Yet then he increased its strength, perhaps threefold or fourfold. This would more than suffice. And honey has many complex properties, even after fermentation and boiling.

Alas, then he loses me, I do not possess his vision. There is juice from an exotic fruit, most likely, also a number of more complex plant extracts, and who could ever know what further processes?

Bale Region, Southern Ethiopia: December 1167

"Yes, the stronger the better," emphasised Othman.

Hakim took a sip of the *tej*. It had a sweet taste and a healthy bite, but he knew how to make it stronger still, much stronger, so that it would burn far too fiercely to drink.

The trader's eyes gleamed purple as he leaned over the fire and peered into the steaming pot. Protecting his hand with a thick cloth, he grasped the handle.

"This part is critical. We must add water, but *slowly* as the mix cools, then ready the muslin over a second pot."

"So... the more complex process produces a more potent product."

"Yes, that is so, to be sold at a higher price! Yet for the very finest grade of *gifti bandu*, one must start with the milk from women, not cow's milk as I have used here."

Hakim raised his eyebrows. Was this another trick to drive up the price, or did it genuinely matter?

After half an hour, Othman warmed the second pot somewhat, then added the oils of certain herbs and various other liquids, in strict order, explaining as he went along.

"This last is to take out all colour, so that customers will perceive the product as pure."

Minutes later, Hakim rubbed a slippery fluid between his fingers. Immediately they felt soft and smooth, like the fingers of a rich woman that had never seen work. He was truly impressed. It was almost magical.

Wonder must have shown on his face, for the trader grinned. "The liquid is too rich and powerful to use alone. Its effect goes a long way, and must be used sparingly in each pot. Otherwise the great expense of production is wasted. Bee venom is especially hard to get in quantity, so especially expensive! The rest of the cream is made up of honey and powders and perfumes, with a little high-quality fat."

But Hakim knew he wouldn't need the other ingredients. Othman had earned his pay, and already Hakim was imagining sample mixes with *water of blood* and *seminal solution*. But what proportions to try?

His mind raced onward, attempting to assess the role of bee venom. The breathing of a man stung many times often becomes paralysed. Paralysis was the stopping of activity. In the case of a man, if his bellows stop moving, he quickly dies. Perhaps bee venom in the slippery fluid paralysed some imperceptible constant activity of the skin, which led eventually to visible wrinkles. He named Othman's essential ingredient *arresting fluid*.

Obsessed by putrefaction and decay, Hakim dared to hope for more. Bread becomes foul when mould grows on it. *Grows*. Only living things grow. So mould must be alive, he reasoned. Perhaps *living* things enable the process of putrefaction! Yet if the mould could be paralysed, arrested, its activity stopped...

Also, he now recalled, a certain wasp stung caterpillars, paralysing and preserving them as food for its offspring. In some instances, perhaps to arrest was to preserve!

Then he frowned. Othman was right, bee venom was not easy to get!

Orchid Jones' House, Omaha, Nebraska: June 2008

It was four days since the teleconference and Abigail was feeling disconnected and helpless in Orchid's home, despite major forces were now engaged against catastrophe. Carlos was staying on at Orchid's basically to keep Abigail company, and chaperone her as regards phones and general security. To her relief, he hadn't – or hadn't yet – indulged in any hint of a play for her; presumably he realised the utter implausibility of any such prospect. Or maybe she was flattering herself even to imagine with disdain any such possibility… and certainly Carlos didn't deserve any disdain after rescuing her! That had taken brains and boldness and persistence. But he wasn't Paul, who had really proved himself heroically as well as in so very many smaller ways.

My God, girl, are you weighing up men when we might all be horribly dead soon? What's with you? Some primitive urge to mate and perpetuate the species when threatened by catastrophe?

Marseille had broken out the day before with haemo fever, just as predicted, along with Osaka; and today had come the turn of Paris, likewise as predicted, along with Tokyo.

"It seems so self-centred," Abigail said to Carlos over coffee and choc-chip cookies in Orchid's kitchen, "really self-centred when so many people are actually dying, but I can't help thinking that Paul and I were in Marseille a week after the assassin started infecting people."

"You know that's before the latency period ends, Abi. The people he infected wouldn't themselves be infectious. Even if you'd overlapped for longer and were statistically unlucky enough to meet the few doomed at that date, how would this somehow be fairer?"

"I read in Orchid's *Omaha World-Herald* this morning that most people don't understand statistics. Say you design a building to withstand everything except a once-in-a-hundred-year super-tornado, and the building only needs to last 60 years, that sounds very safe, but actually the building can be destroyed by just such a tornado in the very first year, even during the very first week it's in use. And even if another such tornado happens only a couple of years earlier! So long as such tornados average out over 500 years, say."

Carlos shrugged. "That's plain bad luck. But it isn't self-centred to escape a tornado or a very ugly death. It's just good luck. This is your guilt speaking."

Abigail glanced at the Art Deco-style clock on the kitchen wall, its yellow face surrounded by Capiz shell petals hand-painted in pastel orange and red. Still a while to go before her hook-up with isolated Paul via Orchid's computer.

"It's not just guilt. I'm sure I'm missing something… but I don't know what it is. I keep going through all the events and timings to try figure out what's nagging me."

"Hey, should I cook us a proper Spanish paella for tonight? Orchid ordered in pizza last night. Let's surprise her."

"Can you?"

"So long as we drive out after lunch and buy the ingredients. Gambas, chicken, saffron, suitable rice, chorizo if possible."

"But we don't know when she might get back."

"A paella will simply carry on simmering." Dismounting from his padded high-back stool, Carlos began searching cupboards. "Looking for a big enough frying pan. Aha!"

"Oughtn't I to be the one proposing cooking?"

Proposing: she shouldn't have used that word. Paul's gastronomic skill in opening cans during captivity gleamed in her mind once more, endearingly.

"Well, you didn't," said Carlos, "and it'll be fun. Take our minds off other things."

However, during the subsequent cooking late that afternoon, Abigail's subconscious mind at least must have been fretting away, like a tongue at a chipped tooth…

"Why, this is *extraordinary!*" exclaimed Orchid, surveying the steaming expanse of succulent yellow rice, giant prawns in their pink shells, squid, chopped sausage and chicken, pimento, peas, and red juices, as Carlos poured glasses of a Gran Reserva Rioja he'd opened in good time in case it needed to breathe.

They ate. They talked. Orchid updated Abigail and Carlos on such developments that she *could*, for she herself was now somewhat on the fringe, regardless of the proceedings against the End Timers.

"Do you think," asked Abigail, "the Aga Khan's people have found out any more yet?"

"I just don't know, honey. No idea."

Something, something…

And of a sudden it was clear.

"Al-FaQ tampering with the Ismaili waters supplies! You'd automatically think that must mean *mischief*. That's what Hussain Kassam thought. But what if it's *something else?* What if they've been doping the water with *protection* against plague?"

"Why would they want to protect their rivals?" said Orchid. "As I understand it, didn't the Aga Khans hijack Ismailism or whatever the word is? Nizari-ism? Then do a sort of brain-washing?"

"Yes but," persisted Abigail, "if you're wanting to take over the world, you need a population base! One that hasn't been plunged into chaos. A grateful one, a fairly educated one. You just need to get rid of the existing leadership, which plague might do anyhow given the close connections the Aga Khan and his élite have with Europe, as I understand it. You revert the sect to its origins. To do that, you need to protect the Ismaili population against the plague! The Aga Khan's people should be analysing water they suspect has been tampered with for traces of *water of life*, assuming it can be identified. More… more, they shouldn't be looking at their medical records for gross things such as cholera or typhoid, but for much more subtle signs…"

"Like what?" asked Carlos, eyebrows raised.

"Like… like… I don't know, exactly." Abigail banged her fist on the table in frustration. "Like …well many strong vaccines or medicines have some strange side effects. Maybe this one especially as it can't have been tested too much. These might be subtle or merely seem like *statistical* anomalies, something a bit out of the ordinary but not so as you'd pay a lot of attention or red-flag them. A few people might even be allergic and so get quite ill. That's what the Aga Khan's people should be sifting for: medical anomalies in Ismaili populations reported to clinics in different countries, but which never got cross-correlated."

"I'm going to phone Charlie," said Carlos.

"Charlie Abu-deeb?" asked Orchid.

"The very man. He can talk to the DD. We should have a lot of credit after getting Marseille and Paris spot on. Excuse me for a few minutes… Oh," he added to Abigail, "and credit where it's due, to you too."

When Carlos came back, he said, "Right, that's under way. Charlie absolutely agrees." He sat back down at the dinner table, lifted his glass, stared at it.

"Revert the sect to its origin, right… To Hasan and Sinan. To Alamut. *Mierda*, that sounds like some victory toast. Doubtless drunk with coffee in their benighted case."

Orchid grinned. "In that case we ought to drink an anti-toast to Abi's inspiration, whatever an anti-toast might be."

"Paul might have a notion," replied Abigail. "You drop toast into an anti-toaster and up pops soft white bread, unblemished. If only the world could be likewise, though it's a bit late."

Orchid Jones' House, Omaha, Nebraska: June 2008

By now London was infected and horrors were escalating in the places first affected. Rumours that *plague* had been spread deliberately were flooding the web. But spread by whom? Islamic fundamentalists, other sorts of fundamentalists, Russia or China to control their own populations? America itself to wrest control of the world once again, the international Jewish conspiracy? Speculation was rife, yet mostly bizarre.

Orchid went off early to her headquarters. Though Jack Turner was found and the Waterloo siege ended, this had caused a Niagara of paperwork to add to that springing from the raid on the End Timer compound. What's more, tele-evangelists had been sermonising, calling for a rally against FBI assaults upon righteous Christians, to be held this same day in Omaha's Civic Auditorium Arena. There might well be trouble.

At noon the President addressed the nation, urging calm and also co-operation with whatever emergency measures might have to be introduced at short notice, such as quarantines or restrictions on travel or anti-hoarding legislation. But he denied any need as yet for a state of emergency or ban on flights, except on a temporary, precautionary basis so far, to India and Ukraine and Romania. Even though there were serious problems in several other countries, US health authorities were coping perfectly well with all stray cases of the infectious fever brought in by international passengers, he soberly assured the nation. Let us pray, my fellow Americans, while offering as much assistance as we can.

At two, Abigail and Carlos tuned in to the rally at that venue on Capitol Avenue, which according to the announcer was more accustomed to indoor pro-football games of the Omaha Beef team as well as women's basketball and volleyball from nearby Jesuit Catholic Creighton University, along with dog-shows and concerts. Today the arena was configured concert-style, with extra seating filling the space where games were played. However, huge swathes of the available seats were empty as an evangelist began orating from *The Revelation of St. John the Divine*.

"Ha," exclaimed Carlos, "they goofed! Must be room for eight thousand or more there. What they got? A thousand? Folks mustn't be wanting to rub shoulders in crowded places, even devout believers in doomsday. Like us, just watch it remotely. Or try to forget doomsday altogether, watch the National Geographic channel instead, cute animals in exotic places."

That evening after Orchid had returned to microwaved paella leftovers, minus any seafood and chicken on safety grounds but with added fried bacon, Carlos received a phone call which he took in the hall.

"Okay," he announced on his return, "that was Charlie. The worldwide Aga Khan organisation is *very* organised. Preliminary report already. We should look at your computer, Orchid, for what downloads."

"It's being sent here?" said Abigail.

Carlos sketched a bow. "Actually, because *you're* here. What you'd suggested led to some curious data emerging. Significance as yet unknown. So you need to be in the loop, in case the significance occurs to you; just as so many other things have occurred to you, quoth Charlie."

"I'd rather some of those things never occurred at all."

"The world might think otherwise, honey," replied Orchid. "If it ever gets a chance to know."

Soon they were gathered around the computer screen as Orchid scrolled through a summary.

An Aga Khan Foundation clinic in India had been treating unusual skin and liver complaints over the last dozen years, including occasional liver failure. The hair of some sufferers had whitened prematurely. An urgent survey had revealed clusters of similar problems reported throughout the Indian subcontinent, the Middle East, and North Africa too. Some facilities claimed a preponderance of their patients were women. While most of the doctors had assumed they were dealing with a local phenomenon, according to one hepatologist already realising otherwise, the highest incidence was in Mecca, of all places. Overriding patient confidentiality, forceful requests for all the medical records had been made, as had some further blood tests. The initial returned data was appended.

"I can't read a blood test," said Abigail, bewildered.

"*You* don't have to, honey. Just, all the data's coming here for you anyhow, as well as to CDC and the rest of the bunch."

"Oh, I see. Hmm..." A sudden recall shivered through Abigail. "That Druze guy said Hakim returned from Africa *'white-haired yet unbent*, and with the power of God in his hand'. So... premature white hair, skin and liver problems. I'm betting on side-effects caused by the *water of life* in water supplies..."

"Yes! Though I'd think twice about drinking it," said Carlos.

"Better than plague. And these are just a small percentage of people who are sensitive. Never enough for the problems to have seemed major, especially as no one was looking."

Orchid mused aloud. "Creighton University right here in Omaha has a first class medical school. I know the faculty dean there. Maybe I'll copy this over to him, see what they make of it."

"The Jesuit place?"

"How do you know that?" Orchid asked; so Carlos explained about the screening on TV of the ill-attended rally.

"Creighton's Jesuit Catholic, yes, but it takes students of any religion, or no religion I guess, from the whole of the States and a lot of other countries besides. Oh darn, I'd need to do altogether too much explaining about how I'm involved with medical reports from the Aga Khan! Even then secrecy would be compromised. There's me trying to join in like you, honey, have some effect."

How Abigail yearned to see Paul in the flesh, and in private! Not just on Orchid's computer screen. There could be nothing intimate about the link to Lakeside. Someone would surely be monitoring their conversations, if only to check whether she or Paul recalled some useful detail, the significance of which might even pass themselves by. Some clue, say, to the current whereabouts of Kamal and his group, who must surely have laid plans for seizing power somehow somewhere during the chaotic aftermath of plague rampaging through the world; whatever might be left of civilization. Unless al-FaQ was simply leaving that in the hands of God.

Naturally she'd told Paul as soon as she could, on their regular call, about the medical input from the Ismailis. "These days," he'd remarked, "the news is enough to turn anyone's hair white... Keep digging, Abi."

Scenes from Osaka and Tokyo on the morning news had concentrated on commuter crowds of Japanese, still behaving in an orderly manner but all of them masked. No faces, only a multitude of wary eyes above blunt white snouts. In London, despite being summer, the majority of people wore scarves hitched up above their noses, a host of wools and silks and sometimes what even appeared to be torn-up pillow cases, like innumerable bank robbers in some movie which at first glance seemed comic, then a moment later deeply sinister. Other individuals were wearing industrial respirators, modified biker helmets, even diving masks in some cases. Police looked as though they were involved in a poison gas incident.

Apparently the British government, although still reluctant to extend access to its face-mask stock beyond medical and security workers just yet, was considering temporarily closing their subway system, the Tube. Yet this would virtually paralyse the British capital, even more so than Paris; the French had closed the Paris Metro several hours earlier.

And of course if one wanted to watch horrors, especially from India, many videos were on the web...

More Ismaili medical data and analyses were coming to Orchid's computer, as they would be to all organisations and agencies involved, yet could one see the wood for the trees? Maybe a super-computer might...

Abigail turned over in her mind yet again swinish Kamal's poem, imprinted there in the way that Safiyya's fragment was.

> *Again Eagle Teacher calls forth*
> *Deadly Waters to purge this Earth*
> *For the faithful, with godly brides*
> *Who tasted the Waters of Life…*

"Godly brides who tasted the *waters of life*. What does it mean, Carlos? Why *godly brides?* Godly brides tasting *the waters…*"

"Traditional Arab society's quite male chauvinist. Maybe this is just a way of saying 'men and women both'. Or maybe it's like the cliché Islamic heaven for martyrs, except here on Earth instead, for the faithful. If the majority of the world population dies, you need extra brides to breed more good future Nizaris from. Hey, do you want a coffee?"

"No, it has to be something special about *women*, compared with the faithful protected men, some difference…"

"Coffee stimulates the brain."

"You just want to pop out for a cigarette while the percolator's on."

"Oh, two cigarettes. Nicotine stimulates *my* brain. Ever read Sherlock Holmes? 'This is a three pipe problem, Doctor Leclaire.' Maybe this is a three cigarette problem."

"Godly brides," she repeated.

"Suppose," said Carlos, "the Ismaili community in general has been protected… *Suppose?* No, I'd say you proved that because of those side effects turning up. But as regards numerical superiority afterwards… well, aren't Ismailis only a tiny proportion of Muslims, to the extent that they're true Muslims at all? So for accelerated population growth afterwards, you'd need to get nubile young females or widows from somewhere; like I said before, new brides. And maybe from the wider Muslim community, the hated majority Sunnis, eh? But any families that survived plague won't take kindly to fanatics waltzing up and demanding their daughters to breed from. So, some other way… *Maybe many more of the men will die?*' He shrugged. "But that doesn't make sense. Men and women in Romania or wherever are dying at the same horrible rate. And why are the brides Godly? I'm going nowhere."

"Have those cigarettes… but maybe you are making sense! About some protection for women, and Ismailis being only a part of the Muslim community… That report last night… Oh, my brain's like mush, I could almost use a cigarette myself."

"I think your brain is rather fine. And feel free, even if they're only Marlboro."

"I'd just be sick or light-headed. But a proportion of the clinics reported many more women patients, so in some way protection *is* biased towards women."

"But that makes even less sense," protested Carlos. "This is data from the Aga Khani network, for which read Ismailis. Surely they'd want to preserve women *and* men? The future faithful."

"No, listen," urged Abigail. "Is it *purely* data on Ismailis? Most likely not! That first clinic in India was owned by the Aga Khan Foundation, so it services *only* the local Ismailis. But many other facilities are probably shared, taking patients from across the Muslim community, of which only *some* are Ismailis. But they've returned *all* of their data, so it's mixed data! *For non-Ismailis*, I'll bet you any money that *only* the women are protected."

Carlos gave a lop-sided grin. "I've learned enough about your intuition not to bet against it. So as well as Ismailis, some non-Ismaili Muslim *women* get to survive, as long as they don't get liver failure that is."

"Maybe lots of women. Those reports are probably the tip of a clinical iceberg. "

"Yet how could al-FaQ have achieved that exactly...?"

"Maybe link some sex specificity to the protection? But how could they possibly get controlled delivery on a large scale? It's all very well tampering with Ismaili water supplies, they're small, tight communities... but Sunnis outnumber all Shi'as by ten to one, and outnumber Ismailis by far, far more. And why are the brides especially *godly*...? Oh my God, the clue for that's in the report too! That guy who mentioned *Mecca* as having the highest incidence of skin and liver problems in women."

"The herpetologist."

"Hepatologist. A herpetologist is a specialist on reptiles."

"You know, Abi, it's a real education being with you."

"What does every good Muslim do once in a lifetime, if possible? The Hajj to Mecca, the pilgrimage! *Where they drink special water!* More than two million Muslims a year. Fifty million after twenty years. Say 40% women... *twenty friggin million* protected females! And *that's* why the women are godly," she exclaimed, eyes shining. "They've done the Hajj! We need the Internet... and to tell Paul."

"Paul," Abigail told him urgently, "there's a well in Mecca called the Zamzam. It's very close to the Ka'aba in the Grand Mosque, and it's a ritual requirement to drink its waters after you've run to and fro seven times between a couple of hills. Or walked, in the case of women who mustn't jog or run."

"That'll work up a thirst in the Saudi heat."

"There's enough water naturally for thousands of thirsty people every day, but in any case during the off-peak seasons the Saudis pump the Zamzam water into big storage tanks to make sure there's enough to go around."

"Er… how do you mean, off-peak?"

"I mean when it isn't the Hajj itself, although actually you can perform a quickie one-day pilgrimage called the Umrah at any time of year. Five million people do the Umrah thing during the course of the year, and it includes drinking Zamzam water. So about seven and a half million pilgrims in total take the waters yearly, about 150 million over 20 years, maybe *60 million women…*"

"Ah… why… oh, sex specificity, you said. Still getting my head around that."

"Anyway, the water's pumped to a number of fountains, and there are special taps for filling up a flask to take home with you as a present, although exporting it is otherwise forbidden. In fact scams even operate in lots of countries, in which bogus 'genuine' Zamzam water is sold to the naive."

"Tut tut. Where's the water source, again? What sort of supervision is there?"

According to what she'd learned from the Internet, all noted down by Carlos, the angel Jibril, alias Gabriel, had allegedly generated the source when Abraham's wife Hajar was desperately searching to and fro for water for her thirsty infant son Ishmael. The angel obligingly stamped his foot for Hajar, and lo, water poured forth. And maybe Hajar cried out, "Zamë Zamë," meaning 'Stop flowing', as she heaped up stones in her anxiety that the miraculous water might all run away. But she needn't have worried.

Apparently several springs fed the well, relying on the local aquifer system recharged from rainfall absorbed in the Valley of Abraham and through rock fractures in the mountains around Mecca. In the old days, the product of the well was available to pilgrims only sixty feet from the Ka'aba itself; but, what with cheap air travel and the huge increase in pilgrims performing the obligatory circumambulation of the Ka'aba, now the historic well itself was in a basement room of the Grand Mosque, behind glass panels, entry to visitors forbidden.

The water had no colour nor smell nor distinct taste, and would remain crystal clear for a very long time.

"Quite like the *waters of life* and *death*," Paul had commented.

This being the modern age, digital analysis, available on-line, tracked the water level, its electrical conductivity, its pH, Eh, and temperature. The water contained some calcium, magnesium, chloride, and sulphur, as well as traces of iron, manganese and copper.

"But listen, Paul, these days the water's treated with UV, ultraviolet, to control bacteria. Would that knock out the plague protection?"

"I've no idea. Maybe the al-FaQ guys do the doping *after* that Zamzam water's been zapped. Al-FaQ could have infiltrated whatever the water treatment set-up is ages ago, by dissimulating, by *taqiyyah*, you know? Before UV was even dreamed of. Hey, the Ismailis said *their* suspect guys disappeared weeks ago. So Ismaili water isn't being tampered with any longer. So analysing it *now* might show nothing unusual. But would our infiltrators have bugged off from Mecca *too*? That might seem strange if they were a long-term part of the Zamzam monitoring system. Hey, Hussein and Abdullah haven't turned up for work today. Ring-ring. Wow, they've abandoned their apartments! Ring-ring. That's weird, they both flew to Iran. Just when we have a Hajj coming up, and need all hands to the taps."

"Never mind about when this year's Hajj is or was. A lot of pilgrims must still have bottles of the water they took home with them from previous years before your Hussein and Abdullah guys buzzed off and stopped tampering with the Zamzam water."

Abigail became aware that Carlos was in the room; he'd come in softly. Minimising Paul, her fingers danced upon the keyboard, and she declared: "Ah, they're little fat round terracotta-look jars with a couple of rounded handles up top at the sides, and a big seal imprinted on the front, Arabic words above and lines of water spraying out of a fountain basin below. I wonder if they're plastic nowadays?"

"Can you run this past me?" said Carlos. "I didn't catch everything, not being an intrusive chaperone."

Abigail explained in a great rush, ending, "Someone can easily get samples of water doped with protection!"

"Wouldn't those storage tanks still have doped water in them?"

"Not necessarily. And this way's a lot easier than asking permission in Mecca."

"Assuming that Mecca *has* been doped, based on the side-effects cluster there. I'm wondering about that. Locals don't usually go tour the big sight in their own home town, unless they have guests to show round. Would the regular inhabitants of Mecca all be going to this Grand Mosque to drink Zamzam water?"

"Oh, come on Carlos. It's a religious obligation of Islam. Statistically not everyone in Cairo or Damascus might have drunk Zamzam water, but surely everyone in Mecca must have done so, as soon as possible in their lives! Listen to this: 'If children perform Hajj, it will be obligatory for them to perform Hajj again when they attain puberty. Likewise, if a slave performs Hajj and then gains his freedom, he will have to perform Hajj again if he is able to finance the journey.'"

"*Slaves?* I guess slavery still exists nowadays in some parts…"

"That's a reported saying of the Prophet. Surely the children of Mecca must drink Zamzam water early. Maybe there are school trips! That gives them a head start as regards side effects."

"Okay," said Carlos, "I'll pass this up the line *muy pronto*. Bottles of Zamzam water acquired at Mecca more than, say, three months ago, huh? I guess the CIA can manage that."

"It's possible that no one has made the Zamzam connection yet."

"You can probably bet, in the words of Orchid, your sweet bippy."

"And are they looking at heritability yet?" challenged Abigail.

"Erm… I'm thinking they might still believe you're crazy on that one. Are you figuring that the *water of life* works through the milk from godly brides?"

"She's thinking of Guy de Dieulefit's lucky little knights," put in Paul's small face from a corner of the screen.

Guy's offspring, yes, she *was* thinking of them. But there was no evidence that Guy's lady was ever protected. Abigail wasn't a scientist, but she was thinking something genetic maybe, something to do with sperm maybe. Could Kamal really have fucked her immune?

Orchid Jones' House, Omaha, Nebraska: July 2008

Every day brought inevitable terrors on the news. Today's extended noontime coverage was of multiple plague cases in England's Manchester, to which, by the evening, was added their city of Birmingham as regards a few cases, although maybe those were only collaterals.

"He's sure giving England the treatment," said Carlos.

"*Was*," Orchid corrected him. "Don't forget he already blew himself up in LA. Oh my dear God… and what day is it the day after tomorrow, please? July 4th. Independence Day. What's the betting he timed his arrival on our shores so we'll have a little gift on July 4th."

Carlos was calculating, "I think he'd have time to do it. Flying the Atlantic doesn't add much."

Also infected was Mexico City.

"Third courier?" said Abigail. "Or the same one as hit Tokyo? He's had time to cross the Pacific. There's been nowhere major in the east hit dramatically since Tokyo."

"How about," said Orchid, "Manchester England to Mexico City, to enter the States by what he thinks is a softer underbelly route?"

"I don't think so," said Carlos. "The first courier goes out of his way to hit the heart of the Catholic Church. I bet this other one aims to infect Catholic South America, starting from up above in Mexico. Only, he ends up getting trashed in some slum in Rio, just for instance, instead of blowing up Christ the Redeemer on Sugarloaf Mountain, as well as himself, for a finale, say. So that's why we never heard what became of him. Just one more slum death."

"It sure is a theory," said Orchid. "And now, family, we must eat, whatever the state of the world."

Since Orchid's own two children remained absent, this might have seemed ironic if it weren't definitely heartfelt and touching. Helped by Abigail, Orchid produced a spaghetti carbonara.

Tehran, Iran: May 2008

Jafar takes risks! He brought *her* here to the Islamic Republic! And who are those men? The Supreme Leader's intelligence is getting far too close to us, though these do not look like his merciless fixers. Spies of the Revolutionary Guards perhaps? Or could the false and deluded Aga Khan finally be alert?

I must quell my anger. Jafar has given more to the cause than anyone, except perhaps for Yasuf, who died so horribly of the disease he developed for government masters. His control of the laboratory was critical during the nineties. Now only Jafar and Ali remain from those who visited the cave.

In any case, we evacuate this building tomorrow. I must hurry to finish my records, for soon the world will turn upside down, and once more for a while I may need to pursue the path of Allah with a gun, not with a keyboard and a pipette.

6.1 Epigenetic Switches

Allahu Akbar. The Greek prefix 'epi' means 'on' or 'over'. Epigenetic information modulates gene expression without modifying the actual DNA sequence, essentially via a control system of 'switches' that turn genes on or off. As the various epigenetic mechanisms are ultimately environmental, experiences such as stress and disease, or even diet, can cause heritable effects, in humans just as in other creatures. Thus epigenetics adds a whole new layer to inherited characteristics, beyond that from DNA alone.

The letters and traditions of the old elite, certain poems too, mysteriously eluded to protection from the *water of life* passing down the generations. From the precious letter of Muhammad II of Alamut, to Sinan in Syria, how the following line had taunted me!

And likewise [do protect] *their families, yet not those born subsequently, for God is all-powerful and His cup brims over in its bounty, as your acquaintance of old shall explain.*

Note: the full letter is in Appendix D.

Blinded by the science of the West, by strict Darwinism, ashamedly weak in my faith, I was tempted to dismiss this as a fanciful legend. Yet truly, Allah's mechanisms are far more complex and wider in scope than anyone imagined, as belatedly the West began to realise. In 1992, a paper opened my eyes. I have prayed for forgiveness every day since.

Toward the end of World War II, a food embargo imposed by the Germans in western Holland, coupled with already scarce supplies and the onset of an unusually harsh winter, led to around 30,000 people dying of starvation. Birth records from this time provided scientists with rich data for

478

analyzing the long-term health effects of prenatal exposure to famine. But the data held a great surprise. Not only could researchers link such exposure to disorders in offspring such as low birth-weight, diabetes, coronary heart disease, obesity, and certain cancers, but they also stumbled across an association between exposure and the birth of smaller-than-normal *grandchildren*. This remarkable finding suggested that a pregnant mother's diet affected her health in a way such that not only her children, but also her grandchildren, and possibly great-grandchildren, etc. had inherited health problems too.

It was later proved that birth weight is inversely associated with a cluster of metabolic disorders such as obesity, hypertension, hyperlipidemia, and type 2 diabetes. Moreover, these maladies *are* transmitted transgenerationally. Epigenetic mechanisms such as DNA methylation and chromatin remodelling, RNA transcribing and Prion catalysation were slowly uncovered. Yet with knowledge from the *water of life*, finance from Jafar, and access to the biological warfare labs of Iran, we have kept ahead of the West. Soon, we will know what we might switch on *and off* at will, and how. Meanwhile, the inheritance mechanism of the *water of life* is finally laid bare, lasting an estimated twelve generations. A coincidence? Or matching the twelve divinely inspired guides from long ago? Those twelve great Imams after the Prophet Muhammad, peace be upon him, who were descended in a line of his blood. Regarding this aspect of his potion, truly Hakim must have had divine assistance.

Via tests on the children of early volunteers we have our own direct proof, for one generation at least; the *water of life* runs in them! The protection possessed by the elite of old would have faded from their descendants after about 300 years, by which time knowledge of the hidden *waters* had also faded, so replenishment was not possible.

Orchid Jones' House, Omaha, Nebraska: July 2008

And so, inevitably, to Independence Day. In Omaha today there'd be an 'optimist fun run', or for less speedy citizens a fun walk of a mile, a picnic in a park, a pie-baking contest with live music, a quilt show, a children's parade, a grand parade, fire department water fights, a modern Christian music concert, a square dance, a family street dance, and a public chicken dinner, topped off by a fireworks spectacular. The city was on holiday, apart from hospitals and police and FBI and airports and such. Thus it was across the nation.

"Plenty to do today," said Carlos after Orchid had departed in her car, somewhat later than usual.

However, she hadn't been gone more than an hour before she returned and bustled into her home, beaming.

"Great news, Abi! Lakeside is sure that Paul's blood's clean. They could discharge him at noon."

"Oh!"

"Hallelujah," said Carlos, "*but?*"

"No buts. You can both return to Boston, right away. We've kept you away from home long enough, and the word is that flights may be terminated soon... Well, sure, I know strictly speaking home in your case is Canada. The DD still wants you on tap to consult..."

"Is there anything yet about the Zamzam water?"

"I don't know. But I've been told CDC's own work towards protection is going slowly, so your clue might prove invaluable. Especially as the plague's marching so fast! Even in Hungary, with fine hospitals, they say fatality is over seventy per cent; nearer ninety in India."

"*¡Joder!*" swore Carlos.

"Of those who catch it," she added bleakly, then paused and seemed to gather herself. "There's been a policy decision by the new Emergency Co-ordinating Committee that Paul is free to publish your experiences in the *Boston Globe* as soon as possible, to what extent he chooses, subject to not mentioning anything about Zamzam water or such while that's speculative."

To what extent he *chooses*...

Oh, yes, copulation with Kamal...

"So that'll need to be vetted, but that'd be done quickly. It's a story of... Did I forget, CDC are affirming that the Safiyya sample is virtually the same as the present virus? Yours is a story of North American initiative and can-do and intelligence, I mean in the personal sense, solving an awesome world-threatening puzzle, like before anyone else *even knew*."

"Canada-do, perhaps?" suggested Carlos wryly.

"*North* American. North America is the name of our continent. And all starting in Harvard University, Mass. It'll give the country a sense of hope and heroism. That's what the ECC feels, the Emergency Co-ordinating Committee. Fair enough, Abi? They say this could be like a special edition of the *New Yorker* seventy years ago that was all devoted to John Hersey's *Hiroshima*. Except quite different, and a *Boston Globe* special, which of course promptly goes worldwide in every medium. Or maybe serialised over two or three days, given that Paul has to write it all first, and speedy publication seems desirable."

"Be careful of this, Abi," advised Carlos. "Soon as any such thing's published, you'll be besieged."

"As soon as it's about to be published, FBI Boston can easily find you a safe house in the city or nearby."

"I can already think of a safe house," said Abi, though she had never been to it yet. What was the name of Paul's dog? Heavens, he'd never told her... A Golden Retriever, yes, but why never mention it by name? Was the name something she might think silly, like Pluto?

And Paul would have his chance at a Pulitzer, after all.

Assuming such things survived.

Lakeside Hospital, Omaha, Nebraska: July 2008

They pulled in to the manicured frontage of Lakeside hospital. On the way, Carlos had drawn Abigail's attention to some military trucks on the move, but, if a precautionary deployment was going on, it was low key.

In the glass flying-saucer that was the hospital's foyer, the Salute to the Union was booming out on a TV, guns fired in turn at some military installation for each of the fifty states. Paul emerged, clutching his bag, to hasten towards Abigail. She ran into his arms as he dropped the bag. She hugged him, kissed him, mussed his hair, while Paul enthusiastically hugged her back and returned her kisses. Orchid looked on approvingly, custodian for the moment of Abigail's bag, which now included laptop and mobile phone restored. Carlos took out a pack of Marlboro and inserted a cigarette behind his ear, as if ready for a speedy smoke between the doors and Orchid's car waiting outside.

"*Hombre*," Carlos said as Abigail and Paul disentangled, then he too embraced Paul, clapping him on the back. "I missed you, and I'll miss you."

"Surely that's my line," said Abigail, wreathed in smiles.

"Minus the second part, I hope," said Paul, with a wink.

"Definitely minus the second, my hero. By the way, you never told me the name of your Golden Retriever."

Paul looked sheepish. "He's... Rudolph."

Abigail giggled. "Reindeer? Or Valentino?"

"It sounded like a *reliable* sort of name, at the time."

"Rudolph the reliable Retriever. I look forward to meeting him."

"I'm going to Washington, for Langley," mentioned Carlos. "Later flight, though."

"Promotion?" asked Abigail.

Carlos shrugged. "Personally I'd rather be back in Barcelona. *Aunque me lleve a la muerte*," he added softly.

Although it leads me to death, thought Abigail. But he hadn't actually said he was going back there.

Orchid advanced. "Paul, here's your smartphone back."

"Ah, I can phone my dad at last. Not to mention the *Globe*, see if I still have a job."

"You certainly have a job," she assured him, "quite a big one."

As the last gun sounded, the TV switched to a concert hall where a buxom middle-aged blonde wearing a star-spangled gown proceeded to give voice with heaving bosom:

> *"O! Say can you see by the dawn's early light*
> *"What so proudly we hailed at the twilight's last gleaming…"*

Inevitably Orchid and Carlos and Paul, and therefore Abigail as well, felt obliged to stand still and silent, until:

> *"…banner yet wave*
> *"O'er the land of the free and the home of the brave!"*

"We'd better head for the airport," urged Carlos. However, at that moment a bubbly brunette anchorwoman appeared, doing her best to look and sound calm.

"We interrupt this transmission to bring you a newsflash. Within the past fifteen minutes al-Jazeera, the independent Arab television station based in Qatar, has transmitted a video received by them from an organisation calling itself The Faithful of the Resurrection, which claims responsibility for the worldwide seeding of haemorrhagic fever. This is that video, which is in English."

On the TV screen, a banner with black Arabic words as background, dressed in a white robe, appeared…

"Kamal!"

He looked supremely composed, assured, sophisticated, even if his words were madness.

"Unfaithful of the world, God has declared your time to be at an end in accordance with His will. With His blessing and assistance, we, the Faithful of the Resurrection, al-Fida'een al-Qiyama, have resurrected a plague from ancient days preserved by the genius of Nizari medical science and by the hand of God, that very same plague which reaped Europe during the Middle Ages, namely the true Black Death, slayer of nations. America especially be humbled, for the sword of God is upon you within hours. The victorious sword of God's truth, which will purge the world of false beliefs. The *waters of death* have welled up from hiding. Faithful of the world: behold the beauty of God's retribution. This could not have been accomplished by God's servants without His hand, therefore this is destiny."

The video ended, and for a short while the anchorwoman said nothing. In the stunned silence, Paul was first to speak.

"He does rather try to spoil everything, doesn't he? Well, he damn well won't ruin fireworks over the Charles River Esplanade, with the Boston Pops playing in the background."

"That," said the anchorwoman, "was the communication broadcast by al-Jazeera…"

"Not as yet, anyway," said Paul. "Let's go."

Although this sounded like a forlorn hope, they went.

Bale Region, Southern Ethiopia: May 1168

To Hakim's surprise and enormous relief, it seemed that *arresting fluid* was clearly the right weapon to slay the putrefaction problem. Yet there were still erratic results and optimum formulas to work out. And, though improving techniques had removed many of their early problems, still Hakim did not always trust the camp's work. To check for consistency, he repeated every experiment. He also found that splitting every procedure down to its most basic actions, along with more documentation upon each of these, led to less capricious results.

He became obsessive about records, poring over sheaves of manuscripts during the day as his eyes often refused this task by lamplight, trying to recognise any patterns beneath the thousands of close and spidery lines. For longevity and potency, some proportion of all his three main ingredients seemed to be required, namely *water of blood, arresting fluid* and *seminal solution*. Protection especially had a much poorer record of establishing itself within subjects when mixed without *seminal solution*.

Supplies of fresh semen were adequate now that virgin boys were travelling, escorted, from other villages to be milked by giggling girls, an amusement which Tewo was fostering for some priest-witch motive of his own, although Hakim still paid a fee for each sticky white dollop. Maybe Tewo planned to foster marriage alliances, and these encounters were tests of the virility of future husbands, introductions to future brides.

Yet a discovery prompted by Hakim's earlier work, which showed that practically every fluid in the body carried the seeds of plague, lessened his cost-burden in respect of Tewo's supplies. It seemed that the unclean semen from prisoners passed on plague, when intravened as *seminal solution*. He called this *unclean seminal solution*, and used it within plague fluid, cutting down his dependency on Tewo, and finding too that he could cut down the proportion of *water of blood*, which in turn seemed to increase longevity. Yet *unclean seminal fluid* did not pass on protection, nor would he ever have considered using it in a fluid that would be intravened into the veins of the faithful! *Water of blood* remained the main medium in this case, which the other ingredients seemed to preserve and greatly enhance.

The addition of *arresting fluid* also made the final mixes clear like water, removing the predominant straw colour of the *water of blood*, also the tint from juice of the jungle fruit called *kamba*. Hakim gazed proudly at the powerful water of his own making, sealed with wax in a bottle marked with blue ink, sparkling like a jewel as he held it up to the sun.

Hakim trembled, in awe. Khidr himself stood by the fountain of the *water of life*, that blessed source of ultimate knowledge and religious experience. He beckoned. The waters glistened with the light of God, and burbled in several languages at once of things far beyond Hakim's ken. Nervously he approached and bowed. Khidr smiled, but did not speak; his face was radiant. He picked up a small bottle at his feet, then filled it at the fountain, afterward holding it aloft. Hakim gasped, for it sparkled with power and he knew the fluid was his own formula for protection. God's formula, he humbly corrected in his mind, for nothing so potent could have been achieved without God's assistance at every step. Then al-Khidr picked up another bottle and walked away a few paces, signalling Hakim to follow. They came to a different fountain, this one as black as ink and chattering evil. Hakim shuddered but, undaunted, Khidr filled the second bottle from the unholy source. This bottle he held aloft too, and lo, inside the water was no longer black, but clear! Yet the vessel did not shine, for indeed sunlight seemed to shun it. Khidr smiled again, and held both bottles out towards Hakim.

Hakim jerked awake, breathless and inspired. It was late, sunlight streamed through the entrance to the cave. He swiftly levered himself to a sitting position, Khidr's smile still blessing his thoughts.

Taj al-Din knelt by the bottom of his mattress, worry creasing his forehead.

"You do not look well," he said, respectfully but firmly. "I thought more sleep might grant you some ease."

"I am grateful for your concern, and indeed glad you did not wake me, for al-Khidr visited me within a dream."

Taj al-Din's eyes widened. "Did he speak?"

Hakim smiled. "He demonstrated. From now on, our plague mixture shall be known as the *water of death*, our protection mixture the *water of life*. It is Khidr's will. In addition to markings in ink, we will seal bottles containing *water of death* only with black wax, while the honey colour of natural wax will indicate the *water of life*."

"It shall be so, oh Tongue of Knowledge."

Omaha to Boston, USA: July 2008

The FBI had booked them into first class. Paul worked on the story, frantically typing into Abigail's laptop, frequently consulting her and also referring to tattered pages of notes dug from various pockets. Abigail resisted a strong urge to simply cling to him throughout the whole flight. She'd so nearly lost her brave and foolhardy companion; more than companion, more than friend, for he truly believed in her, even after all her terrible mistakes, even after her oh so willing and so total surrender to Kamal. Shamefully, it was only when Paul was confined to Lakeside that she'd realised the depth of her reliance on him, how emotionally wrapped up with him she was.

In the cab from Logan airport she gave up her resistance, placing her head on his shoulder and a hand over his heart. He hadn't really known what to do, of course, but that was a part of why he was so endearing. He'd put an arm awkwardly around her and joked his way through it. His touch and the familiar smell of his cologne, his innocence too, all washed through her like a revitalising tonic. Yes, despite being a reporter, despite all they'd been through, despite being much more aware of certain dangers than herself, Paul was somehow still an innocent. She felt a peculiar desire to teach him… something. Perhaps it didn't matter what, perhaps just more about herself.

She was very glad of Paul's company for other reasons too. The streets of Boston were quiet, especially so considering this day of all days. Yet suspicion stalked those streets and an impending sense of doom threatened the city like a gathering winter storm, denying July warmth and still evening airs and the lavish gilding from a gloriously sinking sun. Many shops were closed. The few pedestrians, all gloved and wearing facemasks, or improvised substitutes, cast worried glances around and carefully distanced themselves from others. Patrol cars were much in evidence, constantly cruising in order to prevent any outbreaks of looting. Despite legislation, hoarding had already created some shortages.

Paul's earlier optimism proved unfounded. In muffled tones through his own mask, the cab driver told them that most of the normal celebrations were cancelled, including the Boston Pops. Even for national pride, no one wanted to court death by congregating in large crowds. The fireworks were going ahead, when it was darker.

"The people aren't stupid," muttered Paul. "They know what's coming."

"It seemed more normal, back in Omaha."

"In the face of the unthinkable, no one knows what to think. Some believe the state will save them, some'll clean their guns and try to survive at any cost, others prefer buckets of sand, for wearing on heads. The nation's got multi-personality disorder. I'll bet some city folks are already driving out to the hills."

Abigail found Paul's hand, and clutched it tight.

"Orchid said work on protection was slow. Surely it'd normally take a couple of years to get a vaccine for a deadly new virus into production? But we need something inside weeks, days, now! Kamal's going to win, isn't he."

This last was not really a question.

"Listen, Abi, Kamal's not infallible!" Paul spoke in hushed tones so that the cabby wouldn't hear. "He didn't know about that new dig at Alamut, or about the *water of life* in Guy's tomb. He can't predict wild cards, like Jack. Some potential solution *will* have escaped him, just like *we* escaped him. He didn't manage to kill us!"

"That error is very likely to be rectified soon," pointed out Abigail calmly.

Paul had no answer to this.

Of course Paul *could* go back home to Rudolph and his dad, but by unspoken consent, he wouldn't. So soon they were unceremoniously dumping their bags and coats on the floor of Abigail's little apartment in the Cronkite Graduate Center.

Cronkite Graduate Center, Cambridge, Massachusetts, July 2008

Abigail touched some familiar objects. "It's weird to be back." Her whole world had been transformed since leaving this room, more than once. Heck, the whole real world had been transformed! Returning here felt like stepping back in time.

"Very cosy," mumbled Paul. They were both exhausted.

They snacked on packet soup and biscuits, deliberately leaving the TV and radio off. After so long steeped in the crisis, they wanted to pretend it didn't exist, just for a while. Abigail topped off with chocolate from her reserve stash, which was still intact only because she hadn't been in the apartment. Paul accepted a couple of squares; he was struggling to keep his eyes open.

"Showers and sleep, you'll get no more writing done tonight."

"I should ring my dad again. These last weeks, even when I *have* managed to contact him, I had to conceal so much."

"Me too. But that's also for clear minds and the morning." Abigail paused, barely able to stop a knowing smile from creasing her features, waiting for the inevitable. There was very obviously no couch in the apartment and only one bed; neither did she have a sleeping bag or an airbed.

Long moments later, it happened; embarrassment washed over Paul's features.

"Hey, er where..."

"With me. In the bed. I'm keeping a T-shirt and my knickers firmly on. So are you. Nothing's going to happen except sleeping." Did she really mean that? Yes. She desperately needed to sleep. So did Paul. Nor did she yet feel worthy of him, she still felt used and dirty. But it'd be nice to fall asleep next to him, protected. She softened her tone. "A little cosiness maybe."

Paul recovered his drooping jaw. "Holding hands? Good-night stories?"

She smiled. "Perhaps. The stories could be risky though."

Honesty and desire struggled for control of Paul's features. She liked that he was so transparent; it made her feel safe. No hidden agenda like... She put that thought aside.

"But what if..."

"It's all right, I trust you," she said sweetly. "We've already spent weeks locked in a cellar together!"

And after turns in the tiny bathroom, so it was. They cuddled up tightly together, in the spoons position. Within two minutes, sleep had swept them away.

Abigail woke. She felt safe and pleasantly dreamy. The edge was gone from her exhaustion. She glanced at the clock; just two hours gone. Paul still slept, his breathing deep and even, his hand around her midriff. And then she smiled; almost laughed. Neither of them had moved at all, they were still tightly coupled, so she had a shrewd idea just what he was dreaming about. Even through material, she felt a firm warmth pressing insistently at her behind.

She wondered if it was *her* in the dream; she'd like that very much, very much indeed. Then it occurred to her that maybe she could slip right into his dream! Gently, slowly, she pulled up her T-shirt and moved his hand onto her breast. Even his sleeping touch felt so wonderful, sent such a thrill through her! Whether she was worthy or not, she decided then and there that he would get what he wanted. They might both be dead in days; she could not risk endangering their consummation.

After a while Paul's breathing pattern changed. He became more animated, squeezing her breast, brushing his lips against her neck, though she still wasn't sure he was quite awake. The darkness lent a different geography to their bodies. She felt wrapped by him. Darkness also provided a magic veil that hid away protocol and embarrassment and sexual mechanics. Natural instinct held sway. Abigail was wet and ready. Perhaps Paul's innocence would cleanse her.

She reached down and, with some difficulty, got her knickers past her knees, finally sloughing them off with her feet. Then she wriggled her bottom as firmly as she could into Paul's lap.

He was definitely awake now; he moaned softly and nibbled at her neck. His hand grasped her breast urgently, ungently, but she didn't mind, she revelled in the feeling. Neither of them spoke. Silence and the dark were their allies.

His hand was withdrawn, to reappear only a moment later. Now she could feel the hard velvet of his hot member against her buttock, pressing, inexpertly probing. Her muscles ached to contract around something. She had to have him inside her! She lifted one leg to part herself, then reached under to guide him in. There were a few moments of fumbling, of hot, slippy skin and urgency and frustration. Then it all worked, naturally, beautifully, a perfect fit. At last she was filled. At last he could thrust. They both sighed in relief and ecstasy.

His pumping was soon fast and hard; he gripped her pelvis for a better purchase, pushing her breath out of her in short gasps. It was so liberating, so sweetly urgent that at first she let him. Yet after a minute or so she reached around, resisted with her palm, signalling him to slow down. He groaned, trying to find some control. Then she took his hand from her pelvis and placed it firmly between her legs.

His fingers fumbled and pulled, lost in moist folds of skin, lacking good geography and experience. His thrusts became erratic.

Abigail smiled. Well there certainly seemed to be some things she could teach him. She took hold of his forefinger and used it as a tool against herself, picking up lubrication from further down and then sliding it over her place of pleasure. Paul let the muscles of that hand relax, wholly compliant to her usage. She found a rhythm, and Paul followed it with his member; they slowly speeded up together.

She felt Paul's throbbing inside her and his warm gush, even as his low guttural moan resonated within her lungs. She frantically rubbed his finger harder and faster against herself, accelerating her body to climax almost by sheer force, unwilling to lose the moment. She made it only seconds late, squealing involuntarily, her muscles gripping Paul's still firm shaft in paroxysms of pleasure. Release was blissful.

Paul's hand moved back to cup her breast, his soft kisses moved to her back. Neither of them attempted to find words, or change their position. They settled back down, Paul's softening member still gripped firmly inside Abigail. Warmth and security bathed them like amniotic fluid. Soon, they slept.

When Abigail woke again, her small bedroom was flooded with sunlight. It was too bright to make out the LCD digits on the clock. The smell of toast was luring her invitingly away from sleep, but the warm duvet still pulled in the other direction.

"It's late," said Paul. His familiar face appeared right before her, complete with goofy grin.

"I love you." The words escaped Abigail before she was conscious enough to keep them in. Or conscious enough to disbelieve them.

"I've always loved you," he replied, bending forward and kissing her. "Have some toast." He placed a small tray on the bedside cabinet. Steam above the hot coffee revealed lancing rays within the general wash of light.

"Thanks, that's sweet of you."

"I've been up for two hours already. Got to write furiously today. The paper wants their first instalment by 7pm. They're keeping editorial staff on into the early hours, so they can hit the streets tomorrow. And we've yet to get FBI clearance too."

"I'll help, soon." Disaster threatened the world, but inside her bubble it was warm and beautiful. She didn't want to break the spell just yet.

It was after ten when Abigail made it to the small kitchen table where Paul was working; easier for constant supplies of coffee. He'd already divined her favourite chair; the Shaker was left free. Every surface seemed to be covered with scrappy papers. Exercise books littered the floor; she remembered these from their time inside the cellar in Omaha.

"Good afternoon," Paul quipped. "I probably haven't described all the discoveries from your perspective right, and certainly not fully enough. You've got just hours to correct your part and beef it up. We'll need another computer."

"My old desk-top is on a trolley, I can wheel it in here."

In the following hours, Abigail worked more intensely than she'd ever done in her life. Paul in his professional mode was transformed to an inspired and stunningly efficient writing machine, driving her hard to keep up.

At 2pm they used the encryption program provided by Amy, Orchid's assistant, and emailed a draft to the FBI, pleading for a two hour turnaround.

Paul grasped Abigail's hand. "We've got to carry straight on, I'm afraid, and hope they don't change too much, so we can merge the different versions back together."

Abigail sighed. "I know, it's important. And I wouldn't want to get in the way of your Pulitzer."

Paul grimaced. "If there's anyone left to hand it over."

In fact they paused for emergency calories, in the form of Pizza and coke. The delivery guy was masked, but at least such services were still working, unlike the airports. They briefly watched a local TV channel. All commercial passenger flights had now been cancelled until further notice; all large gatherings were banned. This included football and baseball matches, which would still be played, but only to television audiences. Most of the bulletin was taken up by details of the wrangling over TV rights, now that these had leapt up in price.

"Typical!" harrumphed Paul. Then it was back to work. And neither had made the slightest mention of their lovemaking. In one sense, it was as though it never happened; a beautiful dream. In another, it was as though this would always happen now, forever. Abigail liked that feeling, very much. It helped to lighten the growing weight of despair at the back of her mind, a weight that surely the whole world was now feeling.

The FBI didn't reply in two hours, but they did after about three. Although Paul had already disguised the names and characteristics of all official persons, it was clear, even within this first instalment, that Jack's connection to the End Timers and his turncoat action, were to be suppressed.

"I expected this," sighed Paul. "With the country on the edge of chaos, they don't want an official of the state picking up any blame."

"Well," commented Abigail grimly, "it's not as though he needs exposure and punishment. He already applied the maximum sentence to himself."

"You must imply," Paul read from the FBI instructions, "that information leaks, not necessarily from official bodies, and minor failures in procedure, are the only mechanisms by which the End Timers became involved."

Abigail groaned. "Just think of how much text we need to change!"

"IT IS ABSOLUTELY IMPERATIVE," continued Paul, "that you maintain the mystical nature of the *waters* throughout; some specifics are labelled in your text."

"What's that all about?"

Paul grinned. "They've got something up their sleeve. Or at least an idea about something. A hopeful idea. My reporter's instinct is never wrong! Anyhow, it won't be hard to comply with that particular instruction; I've no clue about the science or how al-Hakim performed his miracles, all those centuries ago."

"I heard some experts talking to Orchid while you were in Lakeside. About complex cat something lip something. A technique for preserving viruses, only researched in the last decade or so."

"Cats and lips. May as well be slugs and snails and puppy-dog tails! He was still 800 years ahead of his time. *Why not* the hand of God? Or more likely the Devil's! Well, if that's the kind of thing they want, we won't contradict them. It'll make for more dramatic reading anyhow."

Paul scanned rapidly through the text, noting red markers and struck-through lines.

"Not too bad at all, I thought there'd be much more censorship."

Abigail coloured. She'd taken the opportunity to do a little censorship herself. Paul had already written sympathetically regarding her part, but her father would read this, and eventually all the world. She didn't want anyone to guess how fully Kamal had possessed her, how willingly she'd complied. Paul had accepted the changes without comment.

"One hour and fifty-six minutes to deadline," announced Paul cheerfully. "We've got our own miracle to perform!"

They almost made it. Paul pushed the send button at 7.28pm.

"It's up to the *Globe* now. Very special edition. They'll be all over it."

Abigail opened one of the two bottles of wine in the apartment. Pino Grigio rosé. Then it was long phone calls to fathers, more packet soup and chocolate, finishing off the wine.

"We've got to do it all again tomorrow," grumbled Paul.

"You love it really, you'll be a star."

"A shooting star, most likely. The *Globe's* circulation might soon collapse, along with that of every other newspaper."

They avoided the TV and retired early. Paul was shy and tentative, then eager once Abigail had gently aroused him. She slowed him down, encouraged him to explore, yet still they finished with a sense of urgency. How many times might they have left?

The following day was a repeat of the day before, except that Abigail was up earlier. She liked the work, which kept her mind away from the unthinkable. This time they used Chinese food for brain-fuel, yet it took them four attempts. Two places didn't answer the phone. A third did, but couldn't do delivery anymore. "My drivers deserted me, went back to their families," complained the guy at the other end.

Finally, while they ate, they couldn't resist the TV. The world news was grim, the local news ominous. There were confirmed cases in Canada, though possibly from independent travellers, and a small but unspecified number of cases of individuals in Boston itself, with worrying symptoms though not yet confirmed.

"This could be the start," suggested Paul quietly. "Thirty-two days back... um... we were driving towards Barcelona." He shook his head. "We could never have stopped this. They were so far ahead of us!"

Since al-FaQ's transmission, newsreaders had been using *the Black Death* as their preferred term for the global epidemic. And now channel after channel featured historians and professors of medicine arguing heatedly about mortality rates and bubonic symptoms and rat populations, while jabbing fingers at giant medieval maps of Europe. Abigail and Paul were losing interest in this red herring, which they'd long since discounted themselves, when their own faces appeared on the screen.

Despite the gravity of the situation, Paul smiled. Abigail was shocked.

The prime channels had picked up the *Boston Globe's* story. A *sensational* story. Paul's smile broadened. "It'll be nationwide by the end of today, worldwide by tomorrow when the second part comes out too."

Abigail turned the TV off. "We've got to get that instalment sent off!" There was a note of panic in her voice.

Paul grinned. "I'll make a reporter out of you yet. Deadlines are good for the soul!" Then his tone became more serious.

"Hey, we'll have to get out of here tomorrow. Too many people at the University know this place, and your phone number. We could get mobbed by the well-meaning, but there'll be nutters too, there always are."

"Does this mean I'll get to meet Rudolph?"

Paul made a mock grimace. "I'm predicting I'll have a rival for your love again."

Abigail winced, but Paul's eyes shone knowingly at her. She recovered; she even laughed. He was right; part of getting over something bad was being able to laugh about it.

Paul's point about fleeing was proved just seconds later, when the phone rang.

"University admin, asking if they can give out my contact details. I said no, of course."

"That won't last long," replied Paul. "Let the answering machine pick up any more calls. We'll leave in the morning, finish the last part of the story at my dad's. *The Globe* protects the whereabouts of their journalists extremely well, we'll be safe."

Abigail frowned. "No one is safe."

They made the deadline for the instalment, by which time there'd been a dozen more calls; people Abigail had never heard of who urgently needed to speak to Dr. Leclaire. She disconnected the phone.

"I think, Paul," Abigail ventured as she poured from the last bottle of wine, "you made us too heroic."

"Yes." The reply was bold. "Newspaper stories aren't like historical research. They aren't just cold facts. The facts they contain need to be accurate, but the story elements will capture people's minds, will develop and amplify and diverge within society, becoming part of society in themselves, essentially memetic."

"Hmmm I never thought of them like that…"

"Most people don't." Paul frowned. "The power they have can be abused, can create despair or fear, which in fact often sells more copies. But now we need hope, mountains of hope! I aim to put some truths in part three about all that departmental infighting but, even if the FBI don't censor most of it, I'll keep it light so people aren't too dismayed. This story has to help us fight back! Despite your brilliant theories, we don't know whether all the stuff about water doping has led anywhere, nor are we allowed to mention it. So I'm trying to figure out how to end on a note of optimism, with authorities world-wide apparently making progress, or at least *working* on a brilliant theory." He aped steepled hands.

Abigail tried to digest this. The more she learned about Paul, the deeper he went.

"I'm sure you'll think of something." She topped up his glass. "You're very professional."

They were too tired to make love that night. They compensated for this in the morning sunlight, when Abigail's cosy bedroom was all warm gold and sharp shadow, and reality seemed suspended for this most optimistic of acts.

They lingered longer than they should. Paul was dumbly fascinated by the sight of Abigail's nakedness which, despite their love-play so far, he had never experienced. Abigail luxuriated and let his eyes drink their fill.

They were interrupted by banging on the door of the apartment, interspersed with muffled shouts. Some instinct alerted Abigail to familiarity, yet not quite identifiable. She leapt out of bed and grabbed her robe.

"No!" yelled Paul. "It could be anyone out there, a religious maniac!" He managed to grab her arm. The banging stopped, to be replaced by a quiet scraping sound.

Abigail freed her hand.

"I think it's…" *What? Who?*

Then a shout from *inside* the apartment.

Abigail darted out of the bedroom to face this challenge to her territory. Paul swore and glanced around for something to cover his body.

Standing at the end of her tiny hall was Terry.

Abigail vividly remembered the last time she'd seen him, tears streaming over his pasty cheeks. Yet now his face was alabaster and his tears ran ruddily. Flaming pustules were bursting up from his skin; his glazed eyes were terribly bloodshot.

"Bee, help me," he mumbled. He raised his right hand, in which there was a ragged copy of the *Boston Globe* from the day before. Abigail was frozen in terror; words failed her. She felt rather than saw Paul come up behind her; she couldn't avert her eyes from the shocking apparition that her ex-lover had become.

"Felt… sick, just yest'day… Bee… help!"

Terry sank to his knees, gazing up in bloody supplication.

Abigail couldn't make her throat work. "I…"

Terry issued a gurgling cough, then dark fluid gushed from his mouth, almost black rather than red. He dropped the paper. "Bee!" a wet whisper. Then he fell forward. His head hit the hardwood floor with an almighty thump, spattering blood.

A few drops landed on Abigail's green silk robe, one on the cuff. She stared at it in horror, recalling her ride of the subway while fighting guilt, with a drop of Terry's blood on the sleeve of her blouse. Now his death-blood was on her; she had killed him, along with millions of others, perhaps hundreds of millions!

Her thought was overwhelmed. She screamed and screamed, tearing off the soiled robe and flinging it away from herself. Paul grabbed her, wrapping the sheet he'd held over his midriff around them both, quietening her. He pressed Abigail's face against his chest, stroking her hair and making soothing noises.

Paul had divined this must be Terry. He'd seen a picture, though apart from the narrow features there wasn't much resemblance right now. He gazed over Abigail's shoulder at the bloody intrusion of reality, the sharp end of their plague story, the leaking corpse, for surely Terry was dead. Dark stains were in the seat of the tatty jeans; a foul smell in the air. Disgusting fluid, the ancient venom of the Nizaris, crept ever so slowly towards their bare feet. Paul discreetly shuffled them away a couple of steps.

"I killed him."

"No! Kamal killed him, and all the others too. Terry must have crashed out within just twenty-four hours. We know that can happen sometimes."

"Must've kept his key," sniffed Abigail. "He'd never been to a doctor or a hospital in his life, he's afraid of them. *Was* afraid of them."

Paul shrugged. "It wouldn't have helped him."

"The Assassin came *here* first, not Washington or New York, for *us*."

"*Not for us*. My guess is, he played it safe. Less chance of coming to ICE attention in Canada, then slip into New England by train or ferry. Short stop in Boston on the way to New York. But he missed the Fourth for a major US outbreak."

"Not much before Terry felt ill. Are we..." Abigail couldn't bring herself to use the word *infected*.

"Look, we should be safe, everything we read said it wasn't infectious at the very end; and no blood touched our skin, though we should shower straight away, just in case." He hoped all this was true.

"I can't stay here Paul, I can't!"

Paul seized the chance; action would keep her from thinking.

"Pack everything you need, right after a shower, as fast as possible! We're leaving for my dad's in half an hour."

"But... Can we just..."

"When we're safely away, I'll call that local FBI number Orchid gave us. They can smooth things over regarding police and university admin and notification of death and... moving him. We don't want to get tangled up in all that officialdom, we've got a story to finish!"

Abigail slipped off towards the bathroom, her eyes shunning what was once Terry.

"Did you notice," Paul called after her, "that you screamed pretty loud but nobody came to see what's wrong? That's weird. Sooner we leave here, the better."

"So shall I skip the shower?"

"No no, go ahead."

As soon as Abi was out of sight, Paul addressed the problem of the corpse messily blocking their exit.

First: get some clothes and shoes on himself. Next... Terry had fallen forward. One of his trainers looked clean. It'd take a hop, skip, and jump to get past. But doable.

Moments later, Paul was hurtling towards the open door. Absurd acrobatics again, just as at the AgroPharm place! He stabilised, swung round, inspected that trainer, then grasp Terry's ankle and hauled.

Revere Beach, Boston, Massachusetts: July 2008

Paul's dad Philip was lanky, at once weather-beaten and tanned from many long walks on Revere Beach with Rudolph the Retriever. Frequent use of electric clippers kept Philip's receding hair at a mere tenth of an inch, matching the stubble on his cheeks and chin. Quite a tough beachcomber look, his, even if he didn't actually bring back driftwood or stinky seaweed these days, although he might drag wood and weed for a while to keep Rudolph interested. Apparently Philip cultivated the look because parts of the neighbourhood were tough. How different from Abigail's own patrician papa, and how utterly welcoming.

The two-storey wooden house, facing across Revere Beach Boulevard to the great sweep of sands, those rather more creamy-grey than yellow, and the curving blue bay, was likewise weather-beaten, yet at least it had successfully resisted the pounding of winter storms which had put paid to other similar beachfront properties, yielding their plots of land to the occasional smart new condo. Some of the newer condos along the shoreline were deluxe indeed, although high prices didn't protect against youths with blaring radios shrieking with laughter outside late at night and revving bikes. Then, just a street or three inland, you'd find ramshackle taverns that were sheer dives full of crazies and freaks, or noisy Spanish discos, and one place even controlled by Russian mafia, and what looked like hillbillies supping their suds on front porches. Some of Revere Beach had up-marketed; much had resisted being gentrified. Was that why the State Police barracks were nearby?

"The thing is," Philip had explained to Abigail, "when I was a kid this was the Coney Island of New England, giant funfair rides and all. Then the place really degenerated, though it's been revitalising for the best part of a decade. Juice bars and swank things. That's decade as in ten years, not decayed. I never saw reason to move. Look at the sea view I have here."

A Honda Civic roared along the lazily steaming asphalt, equipped with huge mufflers and spoilers out of all proportion. Italianate local men ambled, wearing lurid tank-tops, sweatpants and boots. Numbers of oldsters were soaking up sun in deckchairs on the wide sidewalk opposite, prettified with planters and flower boxes, and a fair number of guys stripped to the waist were strolling with girls in bikinis, while more ample citizens with variously ample and skinny kids were availing themselves of the beach, but really there ought to have been tens of thousands of people and more milling about, using the ice cream and pizza stands, drawn to Revere Beach this week in particular by the New England Sand Sculpting Festival only half a mile to the north. The extraordinary castles and fairyland palaces and larger-than-life fantasy figures and Minutemen and Pharaohs and Pirates and Indian chiefs in full headdresses, all sculpted from sand, should attract three hundred thousand spectators during the course of the week; but this week people weren't coming, though the sand sculptures had already been made.

Philip Summers, now past sixty, had raised Paul since his mother was hit fatally by a car when the boy was five, and the house was a double bachelor delight of unwieldy crowded bookcases, old toys and games and train sets, dusty green fish-floats hung up with stubs of candles inside, old appliances, things kept because they'd come in useful, a nautical telescope upstairs at one window. Philip had been a history teacher until he retired. Out front was a small untidy garden fenced with paling in need of a lick of paint; Philip had proudly pointed out a visiting Manx Shearwater, longest-living bird species in the world, he'd said; a Shearwater had been retrieved 55 years after being ringed.

As for Rudolph, Abigail's advent delighted the dog. She was a new companion and a novelty. Soon her clothes seemed to bear as many shed hairs upon them as the carpets and upholstery, even though Philip and Paul did vacuum frequently.

"Not *in* the bedding too, Paul, please," she'd soon had to beg, so that eager Rudolph, to his chagrin, was exiled from Paul's room, although Rudolph didn't seem to blame Abigail in the least for this. Rudolph was determined to be her tail-thumping friend.

Meals were a shared occasion, since the best diet for Rudolph dictated the human diet: chicken, turkey, beef, brown rice and oatmeal, lots of veg and fruit, eggs, cottage cheese, yoghurt. No kibble was ever bought.

"Dad," said Paul, two days since he and Abigail had arrived from the horror of Terry's demise, the *Globe* story now all done, "I think we ought to change our house policy."

"You mean insurance? In case of civil disturbances caused by plague? You wouldn't get any company to underwrite that."

"No, I mean canned food, including canned dog food."

"But canned dog food is especially bad for Retrievers. It's all meat and grain that can't be sold for human use, plus chemical additives."

"Okay, canned *human* beef and chicken and turkey. And vegetables and fruit. Lots of it, in case distribution breaks down. And we ought to store water."

Abigail said affectionately, "There was me thinking you were an ace at opening cans."

"Where available, Abi. Dad, we need availability. And we can't necessarily rely on power for the freezer or the fridge."

"You really think things might get that bad? Even unto cannibalism?"

"What do you mean, *cannibalism?*"

"You just said cans of *human beef.*"

"Obviously I mean beef for human consumption, Dad."

"I just thought of a new definition of *can*nibalism: eating food out of *cans*. Highly undesirable!"

You're both as bad as each other, thought Abigail, amused; and she needed some light touch after the hideous Terry experience. She'd slept with Terry, she'd been fond of him, before she became fed up. Those were bygone bonds, yet such an appalling outcome still jerked them painfully.

Terry's fate still came back repeatedly to haunt her, besides which there was the ongoing news of the growing number of plague patients in hospitals, and of fatalities, many of those in Boston by now, about fifty in New York, and this was only just the beginning. Look to India and Europe for the continuation. That morning the Massachusetts National Guard Reserve, both Army and Air Guard, had been called up, as well as the Coast Guard reservists.

"Okay," conceded Philip, "we'll drive over to Shaw's on the Parkway."

"When?"

"Right away, of course."

Just as well that they did so, wearing dust masks which Philip had bought a year or four ago when thinking about borrowing a sander to rejuvenate the peeling picket fence.

Two masked policemen were controlling the entry of a twenty-yard queue, variously kitted out in dust masks and scarves, to Shaw's Supermarket, and there was a maximum spend of eighty dollars.

Likewise at Tedeschi, and at the Stop & Shop on Squire Road, where they also stocked up to the permitted maximum after queuing, not always of cans they would necessarily have bought even reluctantly, but shelves were becoming bare; resupply was promised overnight. Philip didn't wish to call in at all at Foodmaster. "I hate that shop," he said. And by then Philip's ten-year-old green Chrysler Cruiser was fairly well laden for a compact car with three people in it, since Paul had felt obliged to help his dad, and Abigail hadn't much wished to stay behind on her own, away from Paul.

That afternoon Abigail's mobile played *Petrushka*, jaunty and urgent. Her papa, yet again. He'd heard from her twice already since Omaha, and by now seemed almost to have committed the *Boston Globe* story to memory.

"Come home, *mignonne*," he urged, "while there's time. You can drive from Boston. We can go to the cottage. We'll have all the supplies we could need. Remember the generator. You can bring your Paul, if you like."

"But Papa," she improvised, "I need to stay in America to be available to the authorities, if they need me."

Although was that such a bad idea of her papa's? Paul and Philip and Rudolph and herself and Papa, safe in true seclusion among forests and fresh streams.

"Are you not available to anyone anywhere in the world on this phone?"

"It's four hundred miles from Boston, and the border might close to stop an exodus of Americans who might be infected."

"Yet surely not of Canadians returning home. Even so, I'm certain I could have a word and prevail."

"Paul is American and so is his dad. And his dog."

The conversation went nowhere. When *Petrushka* tootled again a few minutes later, Abigail was sure that it was her papa returning to the fray, having talked to someone in government circles in the meantime.

But it was Carlos.

Bale Region, Southern Ethiopia: June 1168

Prisoners continued to die of plague, their oozing corpses fed to the black mouth in the cave, while others, intravened beforehand with the *water of life*, survived. A few of the latter showed no signs of plague at all, while others exhibited various degrees of illness which nevertheless they overcame, proving that they too were adequately protected. Some variance was expected, for it was well known that seven people in every ten often perished during an outbreak of the pestilence. Of the three who survived maybe one was blessed by God, another might merely be lucky enough to recover, and perhaps, speculated Hakim, perhaps something akin to the *water of life* was already in the blood of the third one naturally, and so saved him.

Identical putrefaction trials, on the *water of death* and the *water of life*, revealed a tendency for the latter to maintain its properties longer, even when neither had obviously gone foul. Hence Hakim transferred his main efforts to the former fluid. Yet, for both, the timescales he had to wait for proof were now long indeed, a measure of success yet a great inconvenience to further progress.

And then came another astonishing gift from God. Hakim ordered women prisoners protected by the *water of life* to be forcefully impregnated by male slaves, so that experiments could be performed on their offspring. Four months after birth, the babies were intravened with the *water of death*, yet lo, they survived. Protection had passed from mother to child! Below the age of four months, though, babies tended to react adversely and died, not being robust enough. This was a great sorrow for the mothers, who found consolation in a healthy infant. Yet soon they'd be made pregnant again, and their next baby *would* survive. Slaves milked the mothers for as long as possible, yielding input for the production of *arresting fluid*. Only one mother went mad and hanged herself from her loincloth.

At last, after many years of contemplation, Hakim believed he had a grand theory that explained the workings of plague and protection. God's weapon required a means to engulf men like a forest fire. Hakim believed the seeds of plague leaked out in all men's fluids, and must somehow, perhaps via the thin membranes of the nose, find their way into the veins of new victims. Yet a similar model for protection would be nonsensical, largely neutralising the plague while each competed in swiftness to capture men's bodies. So God required protection to be deliberately passed among the faithful, yet thereafter allowed its blessing to follow their bloodlines indefinitely. Or probably indefinitely, mused Hakim. He couldn't afford the years for tests on grandchildren!

Tehran, Iran: June 2008

Allahu Akbar. True knowledge of the *waters* and their origin faded surprisingly quickly after al-Hakim's death. Or perhaps unsurprisingly, without the hand and mind of the great genius to guide and explain.

Fragmentary documentation possessed by the elite suggests that the laboratories at Alamut were sealed up at the end of the long reign of Mohammed II, around 605 (1210AD). From then monkeys were no longer bred, though as late as 617 (1222AD) a diplomatic visitor from Baghdad (exploring an alliance against the first Mongol incursions) noted the presence of pet monkeys.

In Syria, after the death of Rashid al-Din Sinan around 585 (1190), true knowledge faded still more swiftly. Yet the Nizari elite did not forget *the power* of the *waters*, only their formulas and in some sense that they were made by the hand of a man, rather than gifted directly by Allah, or at least by Khidr. In fact this is only a mild inaccuracy, for it was Allah, and Allah only, that granted Hakim his vision and his success.

Caution and extreme secrecy assisted this forgetfulness; while encoded into religious verse for those who could read it correctly, the real *waters* were revealed only to a very small circle, and the last actual demonstration of their power occurred during the time of Hasan III. Yet this secrecy, coupled with a canker of fear and unfaith that blighted the Nizari leadership, effectively robbed our ancient brethren of their castles.

If only Ala al-Din had been able to set aside his nomination of Rukn al-Din as his heir, while the latter was yet a young boy! *If only* the faithful had not in their innocence refused this, believing that only the first nomination could be valid unless God willed the death of the nominated heir. *If only* Rukn al-Din had not feared for his very life and therefore fostered rebellion, claiming that his own sire's misconduct was inviting attack by the Mongol horde!

If only, if only...!

The stream of history is turbulent, hard to read.

Who was it who murdered Ala al-Din in his bed while the heavy sleep of excess wine rendered the Nizari master defenceless? Rukn al-Din likewise lay abed, yet incapacitated and so exonerated of the deed by his illness. Was the murderer actually Ala al-Din's trusted favourite and confidant? Whose wife happened to be the Imam's mistress! Can a favourite bear that situation indefinitely, paying for his high position by the unvirtue of his wife opening her legs? Certainly the blame was assigned to that same Hasan, who was quickly executed along with his children and all their bodies burned, perhaps indeed to utterly destroy any evidence. Yet with the hindsight of history, Rukn al-Din was very much the most likely instigator of murder.

But I digress. This time is still painful to us, shameful to us, and the lesson is learned. We will never again tolerate the flawed, even at our heart. And though enjoying the fruits of this earth, we will always stay focussed and vigilant.

In summary, Ala al-Din, the *hand of power*, mistrusted his son, as did many others of the elite. While still a boy Rukn al-Din was deemed weak and unworthy, hence he was not initiated into many of the leadership rites, including those associated with the *waters*. Just one year before, locust-like, the Mongol hordes swept in from the east; Ala al-Din was preparing to strike them. He would have sent ambassadors, hostages and unarmed Fida'een among the Mongols, all poisoned with plague! This while their armies were concentrated, poised outside Nizari lands yet awaiting the fighting season, thereby inflicting the maximum damage. He would have played the card that wins all tricks!

Yet, alas, it was not to be, for Ala al-Din was slaughtered. His son and inheritor did not possess the key of the Imams, nor the locations of those cold caves high in the Elburz where the *waters* were hidden. Furthermore, Rukn al-Din thought the magical *waters* just a legend or an esoteric symbol, not a real weapon. Those few chief da'is with true knowledge likewise had no key and indeed no permission, also each kept just a portion of the map of the location of the caves. And Rukn al-Din did not allow them to gather together, for he feared rebellion. Time passed all too swiftly, as swift as ponies' hoofs thundering across the steppes; the next year brought the Great Horde.

Ala al-Din's sin was not to be under the sway of alcohol; much may be discovered in the realms to which wine and other substances may grant access. His sin, for which many of his people paid the same price as he, was not to lay traps against the machinations of his son, or not to strike first.

That traitorous worm Rukn al-Din behaved far worse than those past European politicians who appeased Adolf Hitler, although in my view Adolf Hitler... but I shall not set this thought down. Rukn al-Din *revelled* in appeasement; wooed by a hundred female Bactrian camels, becoming besotted with a Mongol girl for whom he said he would give up his kingdom, even accompanying the Mongol Khan Hülegü on expeditions to arrange the surrender of scores of Nizari castles. Of those fortresses that refused the orders to surrender, only two held out for any length of time; Lamasar heroically for a year, Girdkūh amazingly for *fourteen* years.

So Alamut was burned and wrecked, levelled to its foundations. And of course by his appeasement Rukn al-Din merely earned the reward of being kicked to a pulp as of no further use. An appropriate end to a life worse than worthless. Perhaps at the last he even tried to appease his own guilt; certainly he sought an audience with the Mongol overlord Möngke, yet to no avail.

For over eighty years, access to the Elburz caves was well nigh impossible, and to make matters worse contact with the Syrian Nizaris was broken. Only when the Mongol watch on the mountains finally lapsed, and messengers from the pressured yet still intact Nizari communities in the west slipped into Persia, was full knowledge deployed and the hidden card played at last. Sarai, capital of the Golden Horde Mongols, was chosen to be the first victim. It was felled by the sword of Allah in late 740 (1345), after which the flesh of much of the civilised world was reaped. The massive body-blow to Mongols, Sunnis and Christians alike, allowed our ancient brethren some breathing space, allowed their communities to hang on, even to grow again while the ignorant populations that had tried to expunge them pitched into a terror that was followed by a century and more of convalescence. The heavy grip of the Mongols loosened considerably, some parts of Persia even regained autonomy, at least until the coming of Timur. Nizari continuity was no longer in jeopardy; and revenge, while secret, was sweet. The ignorant world thinks that rats and fleas were responsible for all the carnage; so much the better, for their surprise will be absolute.

Blessedly preserved, the ultimate Nizari card is to be played again, thanks to Allah. And this time to much greater effect. Khidr would have known that all those 'if onlys' were the wrong alternatives, for centuries later, even as I type, the true destiny comes to pass.

Allahu Akbar. An amazing thing has happened, even as I work at this keyboard. Of a sudden, just after I typed 'comes to pass', the whole of my screen flooded with green light, the very colour of Khidr himself. The green light remained for a minute before disappearing, and then returned brightly… as though I might have failed to notice the transformation!

Because I am a scientist, I tried to think about this supernatural light in a natural way. Is my monitor screen perhaps failing? This may well be so, in a merely mundane way. Yet that the green of Khidr should illuminate my screen immediately after I invoked his name, seems to me, esoterically, to be remarkable.

7.4 Verification of Black Death Equivalence

Although the observed latency and infectious periods and symptoms in our test subjects matched the historical records well, no explicit work was at first undertaken to prove that the disease contained in the water of death was in fact the Black Death. Our faith and our ancestral poetry told us this; it would be sacrilege to doubt. Yet doubt some eventually did, especially those brethren far from the work, who contributed not of themselves but only with funding. Despite the devastating nature of the disease, confidence in our plans became tied with authenticity as to its nature. Perhaps this is forgivable, considering the intervening mist of centuries and the tenuous path the true faith has had to follow. God sends us tests.

Indeed this was exactly a test. A brother managed to obtain a research position in London, whereby he could gain access to the 490 skeletons excavated in the 1980s from a Black Death cemetery in east Smithfield, these having been stored for the benefit of future projects. Given that the bones and teeth had already been tampered with by other researchers, our own tiny samples, taken over a two year period at the end of the nineties, were not missed. Inside just two bones, RNA fragments matching the filovirus in the *water of death* were identified. All doubt disappeared, and funds shamefully held back once more started to flow. The test results are listed in Appendix F.

About ten years later, the same skeletons were used by an American team who vainly tried to show that the extraordinarily high death-rate, not at all typical of bubonic plague, occurred because the Smithfield population were malnourished and subject to other illnesses. Their theory was that the Black Death just delivered a final knock-out blow. How stupid! Do they really think that the entire population of Europe, North Africa, the Near East and Asia, rich and poor and any in-between, were all just clinging to life before the plague struck?

Yet the blindness of western science has aided us, and will continue to do so even as God's marks appear on the scientists themselves. Concurrent with our own efforts above, a team in Marseille found *Yersinia pestis DNA* in human teeth from 1348, 1522 and 1722. As well they might, because unlike London, Mediterranean Marseille is within the *bubonic* disease's normal range, and thus its unfortunate citizens were subject to the lesser plague as well as the greater. But those researchers never undertook to look for anything else!

Bale Region, Southern Ethiopia: November 1168

Hakim himself witnessed the horror of Nasir's death in the forest.

Scattered around the outskirts of the village were a score of bee hives. Yet these could not be raided to gather stings, no matter what inducements Hakim offered. The natives were too fond of their honey, and of the merry-making drink they fermented by adding water and hops from the gesho shrub.

However, one of the bee-keepers had been willing enough to guide Nasir and a slave to show where wild bees made their nests. After marking several locations, the pair presented themselves to Hakim late one afternoon, gloved and wearing the local version of a hood as woven by women, a voluminous veil of yellow and darker fibres. Nasir's uncle in Syria had been a bee-keeper, so from boyhood Nasir was familiar with the wearing of a hood for protection. The slave carried a net on a pole and a small, tightly woven sack.

"We're ready to collect some bees," Nasir told Hakim, "if this is a suitable occasion to dissect their stings."

Hakim was working at a table in the open, concentrating hard. He *knew* his fluid components largely worked. But the problem of subtle differences between the *water of life* and the *water of death*, the precise balances within each of *seminal solution* and *arresting fluid* and *water of blood*, was occupying vast tracts of time, and test subjects too. He foresaw another year, at least. He sighed and scrutinised the height of the sun.

"By the time we reach the place," Nasir explained, "the bees will all be back in their nest."

"Bees come and go constantly during daylight," Hakim pointed out.

"This is the time of day the native keeper assures me is best to raid *these* bees. They can be fierce, yet they'll be tired by the time we arrive."

Hakim knew that gathering bee venom was important for the mission. He must support Nasir.

"Very well. Rahim and I shall accompany you. And an additional slave, to carry spare torches if darkness falls. I need to see all stages of any process. Are those veils *adequate*?"

"They're less rigid than those in Persia, but the idea is less of a cage around the head than a net, in which bees that attack tangle themselves and can be plucked off."

For the time being, Nasir and the slave divested themselves.

Half an hour later, in the forest, a veiled Nasir was pointing towards a nest on a low bough of a tamarind tree. Around, were acacias and woody euphorbia, as well as a solitary fig tree. Already, several bushbucks and golden antelopes had scurried away through the undergrowth of globe thistles and shrubs.

The nest was a large muddy egg, lying on its side where the branch met the trunk.

A few bees still circled lazily in the growing dusk, like aerial guards.

"See," said Nasir, "just like the village hives it's horizontal, not upright as the nests I knew. That's because bees in cooler regions waft heat upwards in their homes, but here they need to keep temperature down."

Since neither Hakim nor Rahim nor the second slave were wearing veils, they stayed well back, peering as Nasir approached the nest, the slave behind him, both stooping to lessen their profile so that the veils hung shaggily down their chests.

The lion erupted from a ragged thicket, its muscular body tawny, its mane half black. Launching itself snarling at Nasir, the beast twisted in mid-air and caught his head in its open mouth. Poor Nasir shrieked briefly as he was bowled over, the lion's claws raking his sides. For a moment, Hakim saw what the lion must have seen: an interloper, *two* interlopers into its territory, with manes just like its own and therefore *also* lions, intruding where it had been stalking those bushbucks or gazelles. The veiled and unarmed slave was in fast retreat as Hakim clumsily tried to draw his blade. Rahim thrust past, sword already in hand, picking up speed and issuing a blood-curdling cry, preparing to strike.

"Rahim, stop!" bellowed Hakim. "Nasir's neck is broken! He's already dead! Stop where you are!"

Obediently Rahim halted his charge, as the lion tossed Nasir's head sideways almost casually, and scrambled around to face… a man. Rahim didn't turn tail; that might have provoked the lion to pursue him. Instead he swung his sword around and around in front of him in a swift circle of steel, shouting at the beast as slowly he stepped backward. A stone hit the side of the lion. The slave with the torches had dropped those, to throw missiles. Another stone hit its target. Abruptly the lion flinched away, to vanish among bushes. Whereupon the slave took the leaf-wrapped smoulder of charcoal from the little metal box on his belt, snatched up an oil-soaked torch and lit it, then threw this to his fellow slave, who had torn off his veil by now. He lit another and brandished it as his only weapon, although a good one, for the flame flared fiercely.

Presently, Hakim and the two slaves joined Rahim and advanced towards where Nasir lay, below the tamarind tree with its huge muddy egg containing poison and sweetness. His white robe was ripped and bloodied, his face and neck were punctured, still oozing vital red onto the clinging veil. His head was at an impossible angle to the body.

"*It is not given to any soul to die,*" recited Hakim, "*save by the leave of God, at an appointed time.* Nasir shall remain unwashed before burial, since his wounds are as those of a martyr. Come, Rahim, let us carry our brave brother between us." Although anguish clawed at Hakim's soul, just as the lion had clawed at its victim's flanks, he instructed the slave who'd been spared: "Gather up the net and bag and veil you threw off. Next time, before anything else, you'll beat all the area near to a bees' nest."

Revere Beach, Boston, Massachusetts: July 2008

"¡Hola, chica!" It was Carlos on the phone.

"Hi kid, to you."

"Good write-up in the *Globe*. Much admired in Langley. You two all right? FBI told us about the Terry incident. Traumatic! But they're non-infectious by the time they're doing ring-of-roses, remember."

"I know."

"You still in Boston?"

"North Boston by the beach, at Paul's dad's."

"A tip: I'd get away from populated areas. We're gonna ride this. Worst case scenario is that largish sections of infrastructure might fail, like the lights going out, but authority structures will mainly stay in place. Infrastructure failures could cause temporary loss of control. To be less officialese about it, like as in killing for food."

"Good thing we just shopped."

"Food includes what's in people's own homes. *However*, to cheer you up, and I'm going out on a limb here, but what the hell you deserve it, Abi, your info about the double-zee liquid is bearing a lot of fruit. Directly and laterally."

The Zamzam water, she thought. A little bit of coded talk.

"Yes?"

"We can't replicate protection or ramp up its production anywhere near soon enough. Way too complex. And Ismaili help on its own won't be enough. So we'll need a miracle. But we're gonna get one of those, although miracles take a while to arrange. So keep on watching the news for a week."

"As if I'd stop, unless the news itself stops."

"And we're not talking jet injector here, like for flu. Has to be volume injection, so hypodermics. In the whole world there aren't enough needles, so that means reusing them over and over. Risk of AIDS, yet that's long term…"

"Carlos, what are you talking about?"

"Abi, I'd love to send you some *blooms* right now, red roses, say. And just you keep reading your Bible, say Exodus seven, verses seventeen and nineteen. I'll let your nimble mind work that one out. We're into damage limitation now. Damage'll be awful, but we *will* limit it. And now I gotta go. This call never happened, as they say. Hasta la vista."

Why had Carlos used the word 'blooms' for flowers? What was in Exodus 7, 17 and 19?

As soon as Abigail told Paul what Carlos had said, he was dashing upstairs to find a Bible, and back down again.

"Here we are. Exodus seven... uh huh... behold I will smite thee with the rod that is in mine hand, sounds like a real rant, upon the waters which are in the river... and they shall be turned to blood."

"Waters and blood."

"And verse nineteen is longer: And the LORD spake unto Moses, Say unto Aaron, Take thy rod, and stretch out thine hand upon the waters of Egypt, upon their streams, upon their rivers, and upon their ponds, and upon all their pools of water, pretty comprehensive zapping, that they may become blood; and that there may be blood throughout all the land of Egypt... both in vessels of wood, and in vessels of stone. I guess they didn't have any Tupperware." Finger on the page, Paul showed her.

"Water and blood again," mused Abigail. "This is the first of the plagues of Egypt, the plague of blood; water into blood."

"I prefer water into wine myself. Better taste, unless you're a vampire. What's Carlos getting at? There's a way to turn water into blood... using a rod... or a magical wand. And this has something to do with the Zamzam water?"

"And right before that he said he'd like to send 'blooms' to me."

"Red roses, cheeky of him."

"Red *blooms*."

Philip, who'd been listening interestedly, said, "Sounds toxic to me. My pal Bill Emsley, lives in Swampscott and goes sea-fishing..."

"Just up the coast, six miles or so," Paul explained.

"Yes, Bill who taught geography. He was mentioning about red tides sometimes in Massachusetts Bay, caused by dino-somethings."

"Dinosaurs?" Paul suggested mischievously.

"I'm thinking about whipping."

"What, me?"

"Son, I never whipped you once, not even when you... Never mind about that right now. Whatever will Abi think? Of course there's a first time for everything.... Aha, dino-flagellation, that's it. Tiny critters called something *like* dino-flagellations. I guess they have tiny tails like whips. You can get fatal poisoning if clams accumulate them. Paralytic Shellfish Poisoning, that's what it's called. Is somebody planning on *poisoning* water?"

Paul consulted the Bible again.

"...and all the waters that were in the river were turned to blood. And the fish that was in the river died; and the river stank, yuck, and the Egyptians could not drink of the water of the river, da-di-da, all the Egyptians digged around the river for water to drink; for they could not drink of the water of the river. And seven days were fulfilled after that the LORD had smitten the river."

"Seven days is a week," said Abigail.

"Well counted, my Professor of Provencal Poetry!" agreed Paul solemnly.

"No, I mean Carlos mentioned a week. As a time-scale. Surely they can't be planning to *poison* the Zamzam water with toxins, killing off Muslims! That wouldn't accomplish a miracle! Read that last bit again."

Paul obliged.

"Okay," said Abigail, "all the fish died. So the river stank. But it doesn't say that people died too."

"The fish would die," suggested Philip, "because I guess dinos going into population overdrive, so that they colour all the water, would use up all the oxygen in the river."

"Right," said Paul, "but, if people ate the fish, they'd die of your paralytic poisoning."

"Hmm, I don't think fish accumulate stuff as much as clams that are sifting the water all the time. Should I phone Bill and ask him about this? I think he'd know. Of course I won't mention why I'm asking. It's a reasonable query, out of curiosity."

"Phone Bill," said Paul, "but don't pay it."

Philip chuckled, and went to the house phone to pick up the handset.

"Hi Bill, it's Phil – we rhyme… How's my boy? He's here… Ah, you read it… He's with… Yes, Abigail, that's right… Heroes? Well, to me he's still the same old Paul… Hell's bells seem more likely than wedding bells given the situation… Yeah, terrible… Fact is, I phoned to ask about something you mentioned a few months ago." Philip duly explained, then listened, chatted a bit more, finally cradled the handset.

"Aha. There's a difference between red *tides*, which are usually toxic, and red *blooms* which needn't cause any harm except for exhausting the oxygen. Blooms can happen in salt or fresh water if algal species, um, phytoplankton, suddenly get a lot of nutrient, such as phosphorus or iron. Bill said a few years ago there was a red bloom off North Carolina thirty miles long by half a mile across. Looked just like currents of bright red blood in the sea. Apparently the red pigment in the tiny algae, which you'd never normally notice, protects them from the sun's ultraviolet light. When there are billions of them, that looks just like fresh blood."

"Protects them from UV!" exclaimed Abigail. "Paul, remember they use UV on the Zamzam water."

"To kill bacteria, right. And I bet it's a quick dose, given the volume of water that gets used."

"And Carlos hinted about something lateral... as in lateral thinking I guess. Are they planning, are we, is *someone* planning... to cause a red bloom in the Zamzam water, so that it looks like blood? The Holy Water itself running as blood? A miracle to inspire Muslims? How could you go about that? Introduce algae and phosphorus and iron into the system? Dope the water table itself, the, um, aquifer?"

"Wouldn't that need hundreds of thousands of gallons, pumped in, or whatever?"

"And with Saudi consent?"

"Or," hazarded Paul, "as a sort of black op, in this case red op? I'm trying to imagine this. Maybe the area around Mecca is fairly deserted. Being desert, natch. But still... And all this to cause a miracle in the eyes of the credulous, I mean the faithful...?"

"Of course! To back up an appeal for blood with protection in it!"

"Could work, I guess. Surely it's easier to dump blooming algae in water much nearer the site... I guess in the present circumstances though, whatever offers any real possibility of manoeuvring religious minds might be tried to the utmost, with no expenses spared."

"A manufactured miracle..."

"I think, Abi, a lot of miracles have been manufactured ones."

A couple of hours later, someone rang the bell, banged on the door as Abigail was passing by.

"Who is it?" she called.

"Army Signals Corps, Ma'am," she heard. "Package for a Dr Abigail Leclaire."

Opening the door, she found a soldier in combat helmet and goggles, a grey patch with the black letters MP on the left arm of his grey, green and tan motley uniform; saw an open-top military Jeep parked on the road, a second soldier in the vehicle cradling a carbine.

The MP saluted swiftly. "Dr Leclaire? Do you have ID?"

"Yes, wait." She hastened to find her passport, and returned. The MP verified.

"I have equipment to bring in, Ma'am."

"Equipment?"

"Thales JTRS Radio, vehicle adaptor, power-boosting base station, SINCGARS interface tray, Ma'am."

"But I've no idea..."

"No problem. I'll stay to give you half an hour's basic training, and key codes."

"Paul!" she called out.

Forty minutes later, Paul was kneeling among equipment in the lounge, repeating to himself, "So the carrier wave's generated by software on fast processors, *not* frequency oscillators. So it moves constantly between frequencies during a transmission... and the key codes enable both ends of a conversation to continuously hop to the right places..."

"And you need the base station thingy to boost power," added Abigail.

"Yeah, and the radio can be put on standby to wait for incoming, when it will alert you. On standby it scans any desired bands and only wakes up when there's specifically a message for this radio and this radio alone."

"Which is what the corporal set up just now, as well as..."

"...as well as the default place to transmit, supposing we want to *initiate* conversation, as he put it..."

"...and when that starts, the frequency jumps every few milliseconds..."

"What a piece of kit," marvelled Philip. "So are you going to try it?"

"No no," said Paul. "That won't be the idea. Only if Abi has a new and startling insight. It's for us to receive a message, if the need arises. Or, like I say, if we suddenly realise something crucial."

Almost certainly the military radio was here on account of Carlos, who could have phoned if he wasn't undoubtedly deeply busy. Landlines and mobiles still worked. The radio was a way of saying: you aren't forgotten, you're still in the loop. Although it also implied that phones might possibly fail in future.

Four days had gone by, and latterly TV reports had changed in tone and content. No longer was there nearly so much news from overseas. What there was generally sounded positive: masked uniforms of the Chinese People's Armed Police calmly patrolling largely deserted streets in Hong Kong, or escorting food trucks; masked British Army soldiers driving in the early morning through Trafalgar Square where a normality of pigeons flocked. A fair number of cars on the Champs Elysées in Paris. *Heroic efforts are being made worldwide to contain the epidemics...* Likewise in those parts of the United States so far affected; which weren't named, nor were the numbers of fatalities. Government announcements advised such and such. The Pope appeared on his balcony to pray in several languages before a somewhat sparse masked throng in St Peter's Square. In Russia, bearded priests swung incense as though to purify the air. The hunt for the al-FaQ perpetrators was nearing its goal, supposedly.

Amid which was the consoling joy of nights with Paul.

Abigail stood naked behind net curtaining at the window of their bedroom, outlined by the morning sun, as the portable TV showed Pope then Patriarch. On Revere Beach a solitary sailboarder was speeding along the firm sands of low tide, pulled by what looked like an orange parachute. Paul lay in bed, revelling in the sight of her. Then she turned to her laptop and connected to the internet.

"Paul, Google's down… Suspended, it says. For advice, go to… it's the government website."

She tried other search engines.

All suspended.

"Now people can't find out what's really going on," she said.

"We still need to walk Rudolph, or he'll beat up on the house to use his energy. I'd better get dressed and take him on the beach while it's still early. Coming?"

"Every night and every morning," she assured him, not that he needed confirmation.

"Oh yes! Oh Indeed! I love you so much, Abi."

A siren wailed as a Boston EMS Advanced Life Support ambulance, white with orange stripe, passed by, escorted by a motorbike cop. The TV picture zigzagged, blanked, then came back to life spluttery with static.

When they returned with waggy panting Rudolph, Philip was on the phone.

"…magnificent of you, Bill. I utterly appreciate it. They're back now, so I'll tell them and phone you in ten minutes, okay?"

Just then the lounge lighting flickered a couple of times.

"That was Bill. He wondered whether the US Government has taken you two off somewhere safe yet. No, I said, no such offers. 'Bright shining heroes!' he said, and he offered us all a place on his boat, because he's going to put to sea to ride this out. Some guys with boats, they've already loaded and gone. Not to go anywhere else special, just to sea to stay isolated for a few weeks or more. Bill's kids and grandkids are in Kentucky and New Mexico, he doesn't have any woman, so two berths are free for bright shining heroes, one for an old pal too. How about it?"

Philip's eyes gleamed as if tears were in them, tears of gratitude no doubt.

"Where *is* the boat?" asked Abigail.

"Swampscott, just six miles up the coast. That's where Bill lives. His boat's moored off Fisherman's Beach."

Abigail tested the name. "Swamps-cott."

"Mightn't sound pretty, say it that way, but it is. Attracted hordes of holiday-makers in the past. Big hotels there; all gone, now. These days mostly it's a pretty white-collar commuter town. Stroll along Fisherman's Beach at sunset and so on. Listen, the *lobster pot* got invented in Swampscott! The place boomed, and Mary Baker Eddy lived there for a while. You know, founder of Christian Science."

"So Swampscott should still be, um, orderly?"

"Enough to board a boat. I get what you're thinking. Bill says we ought to make our minds up right now, and *go*. He's a Vietnam vet," Philip added, as if that was an endorsement of his advice and his offer. "Drafted in '69. Two tours. So: how about it?"

"Hang on a moment," said Abigail. "Paul, it's highly unlikely that Terry infected us, right?"

"Absolutely. When you start dying, you aren't spreading infection any more. You've served the virus's purpose."

"But if there's the slightest possibility… I'm thinking about this generous guy Bill."

"And how about *me?*" enquired Philip, mock-dolefully. "There's nothing like keeping it in the family, say I."

"There's no way Terry can have infected us," said Paul firmly. "I really don't think this is an ethical dilemma, so we shouldn't even mention the matter."

"I agree," said Philip. "All honour to Abi, but a surfeit of scrupulosity can be fatal. Okay, get packing your personal stuff while I ask Bill about food and water."

Revere Beach to Swampscott, Massachusetts: July 2008

Half an hour later they were finishing loading the Chrysler Cruiser while Rudolph gallumphed enthusiastically to and fro.

"Laptop, check," said Paul. "Batteries, military radio… Dad, what about the kibble we got from Stop & Shop?"

"Forget it. Bill has lots of cans of meat to put on board. C'mon, Rudolph, *up, in*."

Into the back with Abigail and a mass of things.

"Goodbye house, for a while," said Paul.

"It'll be okay," said Philip. "I'm leaving the door unlocked. If people come hunting for food, then they won't need to break in. I doubt they'll want anything but food."

"Maybe you should have a sign inside: Looters, enjoy, but please shut the door."

And so they set off along the coastal road, passing the unvisited sand sculptures which the next heavy rain would slump, leaving Revere presently to cross the out-flowing confluence of rivers at Point of Pines, open sea to their right under a cloudy unmenacing sky. Traffic was light, some vehicles speeding urgently and overtaking, others dawdling along as if to conserve gas or because their goal was uncertain. After the bridge, the town of Lynn started. Philip cut down to Lynn Harbour, just beyond which a peninsula jutted southward several miles into Massachusetts Bay like an island linked by a long slim neck to the shore, a natural wall protecting Lynn Harbour. But Nahant Road, leading out along that neck, signposted to Nahant Lifeboat Station and Nahant Dory Club, was barricaded by cars linked by coils of wire. Men in lumber-jackets and baseball caps stood guard with rifles. Far beyond: a glimpse of camper vans, mobile homes, a long refrigerated truck, the rest of what might be out there lost to view.

"Makes sense," said Philip. "It's like a big island you can drive out on to."

"And then you block the drawbridge," said Paul, "so to speak."

"They might be lucky, if they acted early enough."

Immediately afterwards came Nahant Bay, and then they were in Swampscott, heading along a Humphrey Street by the sea. Dull green rocks, seaweed-crowned and tasselled. Gentle bend of bay, and then a sharper swerve of shore to a headland bearing some smart homes, in between which nestled Fisherman's Beach. Such a seemingly idyllic setting for an evacuation.

Numerous yachts and various cruisers were moored to some of the many

517

white buoys in the harbour. A simple pier ran out a hundred yards into the water, wood-planked and blue-railed, seemingly only for strollers, unless a ferry called at the end of it. In the shallows just offshore people were loading dinghies, their little motors tipped up temporarily. One laden plastic dinghy was heading out, a rubber one had arrived inbound, empty. All was bustle upon the sandy shore and in the shallows.

Cars and 4x4s and pick-up trucks were parked about, attached to low trailers which must have carried those dinghies from wherever was home; maybe it took too long to inflate and deflate dinghies, even using power? Ah, one departing cruiser far out had its dinghy lashed across the stern. Standing in the back of one pick-up truck was a tall man in camo and shades, eyeing the pleasant nearby streets, cradling an assault rifle which he brought to bear upon the Chrysler Cruiser as they approached.

"Is that Bill?" asked Abigail.

"No, Bill's a tad older. Same as me."

Some shouted words caused the sentry to wave them closer urgently. He wasn't wearing a mask. Hardly anyone was. A matter of recognition? And self-diagnosis as untainted? So they didn't don theirs. They parked, got out; Rudolph bounded around, sniffing.

"You here to join Bill Clements?"

"That's right," said Philip.

"So you're Paul, and you're Abigail. I salute you, I truly do." And a few men and women nearby even applauded, causing Abigail to flush. How could people think this way? It was downright unjustified! She hadn't stopped al-FaQ's murderous scheme. She hadn't prevented that *shit* from stealing the Safi sample, the only known clue to a cure, known in the sense that Paul hadn't been allowed to include anything about the Zamzam water in his story for the *Globe*, and besides, despite Carlos's hints about red blooms, she no longer had any idea what was going on. Fundamentally she'd *failed*.

"No no," she protested. "I don't deserve that. I only did what I could, and it hasn't been nearly enough."

"Lady," the man on guard called down to her, "without you we'd have had no warning at all, no knowledge of this thing, no chance. Because you persevered, at least the authorities got some warning and some knowledge, so we all got some hope!" Glancing out from his vantage point, "Bill's coming ashore right now. We've heard that some others might be on the way here, whom we don't want to see. Faster you unload, the better." And he resumed vigilance.

Bill Clements was well-built, bespectacled, with a big ruddy nose. Sandily barefoot, his jeans were soaked to the knees. He slapped Philip on the back, pumped Paul's hand, raised Abigail's hand and kissed her knuckles with brief formality as if he was a queen. Then he eyed Rudolph, who'd just come dashing around the Chrysler.

"Ahm," he said. "Ahm."

"Don't worry," said Philip. "I got to look after him, so I shan't be coming along."

"Dad!" exclaimed Paul.

"Even I know a four-berth boat's no place for an exercise-mad Retriever. Chihuahua maybe. Rudi would get on with other dogs fine, but I'm not releasing him to join a starving feral pack, which is how it would be."

"That's why you said bring no kibble... I'm not leaving you alone, Dad."

"Oh, you are, now you have a lady to take care of. I'll be fine."

"You tried to trick us!" cried Abigail.

"I succeeded. You're here with no arguing to hold us up. What would you *want* to happen to Rudi, son?"

"Why are you calling him Rudi all of a sudden? ...Oh."

Bill said, "Phil's trying to be diplomatic."

Of course. Bill's nose. Rudolph the...

"Always did wonder why you called him that."

"It was *me* who named him," declared Paul. "And it had nothing to do with, um, anything. He was a Christmas puppy."

Bill guffawed. Then, "Better hurry up."

"I'll be *all right*, son! Let's get moving." Philip quickly loaded himself with luggage and strode towards the beach, leaving Abigail and Paul little choice but to follow suit with as much as they could carry, assisted by Bill who must have finished packing his own gear by now. Maybe his boat had already been provisioned the day before, in view of the guard.

From behind, Bill said, "My boat's the... well, it's like Henry Ford said about cars: you can have any boat so long as it's white. Mine's that Shannon Brendan out there, 30-footer, 12-foot beam, twin Cummins 210 hp turbo diesels."

"Sounds good," said Paul vaguely. "Um, a whole lot of yachts are still here."

"Too little space in those. You'd need to be really desperate."

Naturally, Rudolph was keeping pace, sending sand flying.

"Got bags with you?" asked Bill as they neared the waterline. Since Abigail's and Paul's bags were plain to see, the question seemed odd. "Plastic bags for your shoes and socks," he clarified.

"Hell, I forgot about that," said Philip.

"Just throw them in, though dinghies tend to get wet."

"No don't," said Paul to Abi, as she put her burdens down. Depositing his own, he pulled off his shoes, quickly inserted his socks, waded out, returned, then gathered himself.

"Going to carry you aboard, shoes and all."

"I don't think that's a... What if you drop me? Let me take off..."

But Paul was already seizing her manfully.

"Hail to the bride!" sang out Philip.

A horrid momentary image came to Abigail of that vile shit hoisting her inside Krak des Chevalier to fuck her. Begone, demon-ghost! No choice but to co-operate and clutch Paul tightly around the neck as he heaved up her, by her knees and under the small of her back, into his arms, then half-slid and half-staggered into the rising lick of the sea, not exactly vertical.

The guy on guard must have let off shots at that moment, and gulls took wing screaming. Paul pitched Abigail unceremoniously into the dinghy, like a big sack of potatoes delivered, so that she banged against a long canvas bag, something hard inside it, while the dinghy rocked.

"Stay down!" – and Paul himself was ducking low – as she raised her head...

...to see half a dozen armed men in black gear come racing to the far side of the pier, taking cover behind the slim props supporting the pier, and taking aim, and firing just over the heads of those on the beach, and two of them at the guard in the pick-up, rifles on full automatic, a terrifying percussion. Everyone on the beach, apart from Bill, threw themselves down, some women shrieking although not with the sounds of pain, just pure panic. Crouching, Bill raced into the water, stopping by Paul, both kneeling waist-deep.

"They won't hole a dinghy." Bill's hand groped into the dinghy, gripped Abigail's ankle, rejected it, found the canvas bag, pulled it on to the side, tore Velcro open, and slid out... That must be an M-16, thought Abigail, maybe not a Vietnam souvenir, although the know-how would be a souvenir from South-East Asia. The gun had sights. Now Bill was leaning across the side of the dinghy, butt tucked into his shoulder, one hand outstretched to the grip at the front. "Keep as still as you can and *low*."

A voice shouted from under the pier, "Stay down, all people! If any move, shoot you!" *What was that accent?* "Only want boats! You up in the truck, shoot once, we kill people fast!"

Tehran, Iran: June 2008

8.0 Allah's Dynamic Balance

Allahu Akbar. The filoviruses can be highly selective, as two lucky workers at a monkey quarantine unit discovered. In 1989, dozens of monkeys in the unit, at Reston near the U.S. capitol Washington, crashed out with Ebola. The poor animals degenerated rapidly to bags of skin holding bone and mush. There was blood and vomit everywhere around their cages, which was probably how the two workers caught the virus, yet it caused them no detectable problem whatsoever. The particular strain was later named Ebola Reston. Other strains, though, can equally devastate an infected population of monkeys or gorillas or men. Such differences in viral expression are not yet understood, but the expression of the filovirus in the *water of death* is different again.

Scientists have proposed that Ebola cannot be naturally hosted by monkeys, because it does them far too much damage. Hence, they argue, the natural host must be some other species, for which the disease is benign. The most popular candidates, completely without proof so far, are bats, but insects have also been suggested. For Ebola perhaps this is true, but at least one filovirus *is* hosted in monkeys, and causes the Black Death in men, the Black Death which has *nothing* to do with any fleas from rats.

The intricate mechanisms of its life-cycle are wondrous to behold, a dynamic balance only Allah could conceive, and one with signs that Allah opened Hakim's mortal eyes to see.

In a monkey population not exposed to the virus for many generations, an outbreak will be swift and brutal, much like the Black Death among men. But this attack causes (via a populational trigger as yet unknown), some individuals to manufacture protective protein chains. In turn, these cause protection to pass down the generations via epigenetic switches. So the disease slowly loses its hold, hanging on within weakly protected individuals and causing them flu-like symptoms, with permanently weeping eyes and noses. But eventually finding no further victims, it dies out in a particular population (having probably leapt to an adjacent one by now). After twelve generations the epigenetic switches fall away, and protection is withdrawn. This is important, because the monkeys are disadvantaged by the protective proteins. Our tests on men and monkeys reveal liver and skin problems, probably significantly shortened life-spans. Protection has a cost, which is not paid unless it is needed.

In a few individuals, perhaps linked to the trigger mechanisms, the protection also leads to early greying or whitening of the hair. These individuals are in fact the most potently protected, and their blood may be used to manufacture non-viral vaccine. Perhaps now we know why Hakim returned from Africa white-haired, and certainly why his pet monkey was named *the grey protector.*

The balance mechanisms probably don't translate to mankind. But via our shared ancestry with apes, the same filovirus certainly reaps men like wheat, and the same protein chains, albeit artificially introduced, protect them. Truly, Allah presented Hakim with an ancient and devastating weapon.

Bale Region, Southern Ethiopia: March 1170

By the records, it was a year since Hakim had sealed up the sample bottle of the *water of death*, numbered 1927. It had been stored in the cave, but not in the coolest part nor tethered in the water, for Hakim desired a harsher test. Already a sample had lasted for nine months, and who knew how much longer it might have endured, had it not been opened and used?

"If this Water remains good," asked Taj al-Din, "have we succeeded? Can we contemplate returning to Alamut?"

Contemplate, yes… Taj al-Din wouldn't have presumed to say: *Can we go home?*

The years in this fecund yet festering land, swarming with insects and a haven for strange maladies, had not been kind. His strength had been sapped by overwork and a serious fever a year earlier, while Razzak had contracted plague due to a failure of procedure, though he'd survived, impaired. After that incident Hakim intravened protection into the Fida'een, one by one over many months, so that any mistakes or bad reactions could only debilitate a single helper.

After carefully cutting off the seal with his knife, Hakim raised the bottle in gloved hands, and sniffed. By now he could tell so much from an odour. This one contained the faint but unmistakable traces of the more aromatic components, the plant extracts, but no hint of putrefaction.

"The sample seems untainted. If it induces plague in the test subject, I think yes, we can prepare for the return journey. Good Rahim, see to the intravention, will you?"

Rahim hesitated. "Am I worthy, at such a climactic moment?"

"You are absolutely worthy! You've proved yourself a hundred times. Why should I myself claim distinction at this moment, when all of us have co-operated under the guidance of God? Use the oldest of the males from the pen of healthy stock. Taj al-Din can assist you."

Yet even as Rahim took the bottle, Hakim realised the likely truth. After so many crushing disappointments, he was afraid to proudly assume *anything* until it was utterly proven. That thought led once more to his plans for insurance. In case the *waters* didn't survive the journey, he'd determined to take the whole production paraphernalia back with him. The ability to make more, especially *water of life*, would in any case be highly advantageous. And at the high altitudes of the Nizari qa'lats, keeping bottles very cool all year round was easy.

So the return to Alamut was a massive challenge. They would need many of Rahim's special boxes, supplies of alcohol to make them work, sacks of

---

hollow sand, sacks of dried plant extracts and seeds, including *kamba* seeds, plus various living plants too that they might introduce into Persia for a more convenient supply, their roots bound into leather bags. Then quite a number of bulky cages for monkeys, with attendant food supplies and slaves… *So many items*, borne in a huge train on horses and camels. If they got home inside a year with most of their goods still intact, they'd be very fortunate. Oh Khidr, may the seas be calm!

Yet for the first time in years, Hakim allowed himself to relax a little.

Tehran, Iran: July 2008

I will scan the most precious of our documents into my statement for posterity, for some have been preserved only in their original form on manuscript, and, Allah forbid, might be lost. Encrypted copies on media can easily be hidden in places that only the faithful, only the *akhass-i khass*, will know of.

Sadly, the death of the incomparable Hasan II brought some division between the Nizaris of Persia and Syria, as is clear from the text below. Division has dogged us ever since, yet soon now we will triumph, and once more be united in single purpose.

Appendix D - The letter from Muhammad II of Alamut to the Syrian Master Rashid al-Din Sinan, sent in the year 572 (1177AD)

Allahu Akbar.

I, Muhammad, being Imam and Qa'im before whom all should be levelled, yet being aware with deep regret of your own disinclination to comply, nevertheless greet you, oh Sinan ibn Salman ibn Muhammad, whom the world also knows as Rashid al-Din Sinan, just as the world knows full well of your famous courtesy, for which reason I commend to you an acquaintance long gone from your presence, whom I know has been close to your heart.

I beseech you to hear all that is recounted by this acquaintance of yourself and of my father, peace be upon him, whom you indeed honoured as Imam and Qa'im, and to care for your acquaintance of old in his elder years, and to provide all that he may require, so that he may live at peace in his homeland, and work as he may care to.

For he has accomplished a great work of many years, receiving from the hand of God a terrible power which God Himself obliges me in turn to confide to you as a leader of our true faith, all be it in the present years sadly not compliant with your Imam and Qa'im. Not to share this fearful power with you, oh Sinan, would be to disobey God himself!

Nor is it a power which may be used except if the existence of our very faith itself is threatened, since this power is voracious and would kill multitudes of people, including many of our own. It is a weapon of ultimate resort, far more potent than the poisons on any daggers of Assassins. I present this to you to safeguard in the name of God, in the trust that it should be withheld from use except in the most exceptional circumstance.

I also present you, accompanying your acquaintance and this letter, with a protection of which I urge you, without any dissembling in my mind, to avail yourself and your most trusted circle, keeping supreme secrecy in this matter. And likewise their families, yet not those born subsequently, for God is all-powerful and His cup brims over in its bounty, as your acquaintance of old shall explain. Also I urge you, oh Sinan, for the common good of our brethren, to look now to your Imam and Qa'im, for through none other could such potency be delivered to your hand.

Peace be upon the Chosen Prophet and his family, and God suffices us, for He is an excellent guardian and has presented to us of the faith both an invincible sword and a stout shield.

Swampscott, Massachusetts: July 2008

A long cartridge case ejected upward from the barrel of Bill's rifle almost simultaneously with a bloody burst from the speaker's chest. Another case, another, another, another, as Bill shifted the gun marginally, hitting one man's shoulder, pitching him aside, another in the thigh, and likewise tumbling, whatever was most visible behind those slender uprights, and in every case part of a body was visible. Some cries rang out in a language... it sounded like Russian. Russian Mafiosi from Revere. But there was simply no time to carry out any threat. A final body lurched sideways, rifle still clutched, Bill's next shot taking the man full in the face. All happened within seconds. Then silence, except for gulls.

"Accurized M16A4," said Bill chattily, "with ACOG, that's Advanced Combat Optical Gun-sight, fibre-optic by day, tritium-illuminated reticle for night-time so it needs no batteries. I was trained as a marksman."

"So I see," said Paul, soaking.

"Damn fools thought those pier supports were enough cover." Bill rose, and called out, "Okay, folks! All over! For now."

People began picking themselves up. Then cheering started. Applause richly deserved in this case, thought Abigail, even if it was for killing... well, armed attackers. Blood stained the sand under the pier.

How much more blood before this is over? Blood in an LA fountain, blood on the shore. A whole sea of the stuff, like the End Timers' vision of Armageddon, the red grapes of wrath crushed underfoot to make delirious wine.

Yet of course, too, the possibility of redemptive water resembling blood...

If only.

Now that the fire-fight was over, Rudolph, who had also crouched, alert but confused, with his ears back, untucked his tail and ran to investigate, stopping a few yards short of a corpse, to bark at it. He went closer, shied to one side, barked at another body. What thoughts might be in the Retriever's head? Surely the incident couldn't be comprehensible. The smell of blood no doubt was. But the cause?

Up on the road, the sentry man stood up again in the pick-up truck, turned his back on the beach, scanned to north and west and south. Bill returned his marksman's rifle to the canvas bag and resealed it.

The rubber dinghy was loaded now, Abigail and Bill waiting within as Paul plodged back to his father to give him a farewell hug. With Paul on board too, it was going to be a tight squeeze, though not for long.

Imitating a curlew's cry, Philip called for Rudolph, a fluting burbly melancholy sound, *mine-notmine*, *mine-notmine*, and the Retriever bounded back, to raise its paws to the two men, one dry, one soaking, balancing against them. Paul ruffled Rudolph's russet head.

"Look after him," Paul said, voice unsteady.

"That's the general idea," agreed Philip.

"I was talking to the dog, Dad."

"Okay, get going."

At Sea Off Massachusetts: July 2008

"Where are we heading for?" Abigail asked Bill at the helm as they steered north.

"Ipswich Bay. That's up around Cape Ann, though we don't need to go round the Cape. The Annisquam, I guess you could call it a sort of sea-river, divides the Cape from the mainland, so we take a short cut through there. Ipswich Bay's usually a good sheltered anchorage at this time of year. It's a shallow, semi-enclosed embayment sheltered from the east and south by the Cape. Wind's mainly from the south-west. You *can* get stormy nor'easters any time of year, and, if that happens, they blow directly into the bay, which isn't good at all. But nor'easters mainly come in the winter and spring."

"You've really thought this out," said Paul.

"Well, one of our guys was for heading down to Provincetown harbour at the tip of Cape Cod. That's probably the best anchorage in all these parts, since it lies inside of a large recurved spit, but it's at least eighty nautical miles, and the harbour could be crowded with others of like mind. Another guy, Jim Turnbull, he was adamant for Cape Cod Bay. The Bay's big, it's shallow, within the arm of Cape Cod, generally sandy bottom. You can anchor anywhere in there and be several miles from shore. Lots of sandy beaches, if you need to land. If storms come, there's always shelter nearby depending on wind direction. Move closer to Plymouth on the west side of the bay if a strong south-westerly or north-westerly blows. Move to the east side near Provincetown in the case of a nor'easterly. *However*, every damn boat from Boston southwards will be heading there, assuming that others decide it's a lot safer being at sea. Could be thousands of boats in Cape Cod Bay. So, as the weeks pass by, if food or water run short, I was thinking there could be intimidation or violence."

"I'd think *you* could cope with any," said Abigail.

Bill nodded. "But I wouldn't want to. If shooting starts, things can go chaotic. And it's a longish way to Cape Cod Bay. So the majority of us prefer taking our chances around Ipswich Bay. Those are *good* chances."

Off-Shore in Ipswich Bay, Massachusetts: July 2008

Three days later, and the sea was calming after a squall. Dirty clouds had chased each other away, and Paul was replacing a fishing rod in one of the built-in receptors on the deck of the *Salem Swan* after casting the herring-baited line seawards into the cool south-flowing Labrador Current. There was still rich fishing in these parts, despite depletion. Cod, pollock, haddock, wolffish, enough herring left for lobster-bait and other bait, though hardly any whiting these days, and dogfish were protected. Those aboard certainly wouldn't starve, and Bill had at least two months' worth of water on board, though would that be nearly enough?

They were anchored by Ipswich Bay, with the many moored yachts of its Yacht Club; granite cliffs of Cape Ann to the east, the southerly stretch of long Plum Island to the north-west. According to Bill the north of Plum Island, especially the backside opposite Newbury and Newburyport, birthplace of the US Coast Guard, had a handful of businesses and a fair number of residences and inns and cafés and rental cottages. Access was by a causeway with an actual drawbridge; for sure that would be raised! Geographically speaking, Plum Island was a barrier island, a long strip of offshore dunes raised by the sea. Doubly a barrier now, no doubt.

Numerous other vessels had also gathered in this area, though all kept their mutual distance: cruisers such as their own, somewhat larger fishing safari boats, and mid-water trawlers, seiners, harpoon boats. Less a flotilla, perhaps, than a very spacious trailer park, going nowhere so as to conserve fuel, all fishing with rods from their decks. The day before, they'd caught a pollock, thinly white-striped along its side, that Bill said was less than a third its potential size. Even so, it must have weighed ten pounds. Three years back, Bill had won a trophy in the pollock category of the Saltwater Fishing Derby with a whopping 35-pounder, not to mention his trophy for a 42-pound striped bass. Just as well their yesterday catch wasn't any bigger; a shame to have to throw surplus fish-flesh overboard to be on the safe side. Bill had cooked most of the pollock to a treat in the LPG oven of the roomy portside galley; cold pollock scattered with dried fruit for breakfast.

Bill had offered Abigail and Paul a choice of the V-berth in the master cabin up in the bows, or the guest sleeping quarters in the starboard dinette, where the table-top dropped to become the base for green suede upholstery slid together. They'd opted for the dinette since it was more obvious at first glance how they'd lie cupped together… after making love, gently rocking to the motion of the boat. Fans above the bedding remained switched off, to conserve the *Salem Swan's* batteries, and therefore diesel.

Some radio stations played endless repeats of music; others had gone off the air. The radio news that there was had been bleak and formal, like a commentary on an ongoing funeral, and obviously wasn't relating the whole of the unfolding disaster. The government continued to counsel calm and patience and caring for one's neighbours and community. We shall see this through and emerge stronger from the present ordeal; we trust in God. Tune to your local station for local advice on emergency regulations, emergency services, sanitation, food distribution, interruptions to power supplies.

"Paul, Paul!" shrilled Abi, below deck. "Come here!"

He rushed.

"Listen, it's started!"

"…and this astonishing event is already being described by religious leaders in the Muslim world as a miracle of God. Every day in the Grand Mosque of Mecca thousands of gallons of waters flow from that sacred well. The Zamzam well has been in use for centuries. Millions of pilgrims drink from many fountains nearby. Yet now those abundant waters are as red as fresh blood. Never before has any such phenomenon been witnessed. In the holy city of Mecca there is sensational excitement. Saudi Arabia Radio reports…"

"Ya-*hoo!*" whooped Paul.

"Excuse me?" said Bill. "But you two seem to have been expecting whatever this is! And whatever the hell is it, anyway? And is there any connection with you bringing a military radio on board?"

"Ah," said Abigail slowly. "I think we may owe you a bit of an explanation…"

"There's something," chipped in Paul, "that wasn't in my story in the *Globe*. It wasn't there on account of national security. It's related to something Abi discovered, something very important."

"What… you mean *yet another thing?* As important as all the others?"

"Part of it's very secret," said Abigail softly, "and I don't know the precise details that led to what's on the radio. So I guess I'd be speaking out of turn… I got a bit overwhelmed at what I heard just now."

And indeed was still half-hearing.

"…miracle…"

"Meaning," said Bill, "that *I* oughtn't to be told… Look, I can live with that. I wouldn't *want* to know whatever that secret is. People who know things that they shouldn't, well… sometimes their lives get shortened, even under democratic governments… and even without the state of emergency we have nowadays."

"Bill, I can tell you what that well in Mecca signifies. Though something *else* needs to happen now too…"

"No no, don't tell me anything. Please! It would be wrong, and unfair to the both of you to want to know. Let the radio tell me what it wants to, when it wants to." Bill let out a long slow whistle, of what seemed like sincere appreciation. "The two of you… I never dreamed. There was me thinking the story in the *Globe* was *it*. And that was mighty enough. Enough it'll be, for me! Until maybe you rewrite history one day, if you're allowed, and if sufficient people are around to read it."

"It's something, this," said Abigail, "that never can be written. Must never be. Oh don't look so robbed, Paul! You know why."

"I guess," Paul admitted, "I do."

Half-way through the next morning, the military radio came alive.

"*Hombre* calling historian," came a familiar voice. "*Hombre* calling historian…"

"Historian here," replied Abigail only moments later.

Bill said hastily, "I'll skedaddle. Check the fishing rod." And off he went.

"I'm alone now, with Paul," Abigail said. "We're alone, I mean… Two people can't be alone, not us two." She darted a gaze of such intensity at Paul. "Carlos! Thanks so much for this radio. Without it we'd have felt… disconnected."

"That's why I had it sent. The whole country feels disconnected, without Google and gang. And it's better that way, believe me. What you don't know can't scare the *mierda* out of you."

"Carlos, the Zamzam water running red! You did it!"

"Not personally. But it got done. Where are you both, by the way?"

"At sea off Massachusetts, in a cruiser belonging to a pal of Paul's dad."

"Best place to be. Plenty of water on board?"

"Water. Food. We fish. *How* did you do it? The Zamzam miracle?" Tears of joy were welling in Abigail's eyes, like some miniature of the miracle, minus the colour red.

"I hope you won't feel, um, disconnected, if I don't explain the ins and outs. Bright Abi, you'd have realised, soon as you heard the news, that this isn't the usual sort of miracle, even if I hadn't dropped that hint earlier to cheer you up. But the less that's *ever known* about exactly what we did, and how, and with whose secret consent, and who co-operated, the better."

"We understand. This has to stay secret forever. At least I can say: thanks so much for the bloom!"

"Now for our next trick, tomorrow – well no, this isn't a trick at all – there'll be a joint announcement, an appeal, by key religious leaders of both Sunni and Shi'a communities around the world, and the Aga Khan too for the Ismailis. It's utterly unheard of, but after the Zamzam event they were only too keen to associate themselves with the miraculous… I mean… heed the Word of God. They're already on board. *Islamic scientists working super-overtime have found that the faithful who drank Zamzam water over the last twenty years, mainly the women, have protection against plague in their blood, which they can pass on.* Not the Zamzam water that's spilling out red right now, of course. I guess God can't provide protection and a bloody sign at the same time; so to speak." She heard the irony in his voice. "*The water looking like blood is a divine sign, to pay attention to all the water bestowed in the past, and to tell us that all those who are protected should step up and protect others by donating their own blood.* Somewhere down in the details it'll only be women who are asked to step up and do their religious duty, Godly Brides giving of life, unless in the Ismaili community, where on the quiet blood will be taken from the men too."

"It's wonderful," said Abigail, her voice trembling. "Like a nightmare becoming an angelic dream."

"All thanks to you, really. Even if we *aren't* exactly out of the woods yet."

Clasping Abigail's hand, Paul interrupted:

"Will it work?"

"It *has to*." Carlos sounded inspired now, all irony banished from his voice. "And, you know, this may mean a coming together of Islam as never before. United Islam to the rescue! The world saved by the good kind of Islam, not Kamal's twisted mass-murderous version. This could heal the world in more than one sense. In a hundred years from now this might seem like an epochal moment. Or so we're hoping."

Abigail hesitated. "Is there any… trace… of him?"

Was the trace within herself *indelible*? No. Paul's love was erasing that day by day.

"He could be hiding out in any hole that his people prepared in any hills… You do realise, Abi, when I said that we aren't out of the woods… even with the wonderful water *you* revealed, even if tens of millions of Muslim women co-operate by blood donations which *you* gave the key to, even if there are ten thousand donation points worldwide and ten thousand inoculation centres, this is going to take *months and months*. But it'll fill in until they can replicate the protection properly, from scratch, especially the water-borne protection. Looks like it's spliced with a virus, probably cholera. But that'll be close to two years. Meanwhile, with many millions of donors you don't have to understand how it works, you can ramp up production real fast by just isolation and some amplification, so the CDC guys say."

"How bad will it be," asked Paul, "before it gets better?"

"Frankly, we're guesstimating the probable death toll, even with protection rolling out, at ten per cent of the human race. That's as many or more as were killed in all the wars and genocides and famines of the Twentieth Century combined."

"That's…" Abigail tried to calculate in her head.

"It's *seven hundred million* people. Give or take a few million. But if it wasn't for you, Abi, it would've taken far too long to get protection properly tested and manufactured. Instead we can start rolling it out in days. Given how virulent this virus is – which I guess is the ambition of viruses! – we guesstimate you've saved *three billion lives*. That's three billion people owing their lives to you, Abi! Three billion human beings. That's at least three Nobel prizes you won't ever get. For Peace, and Medicine, and of course History."

"There isn't a Nobel for History," Paul pointed out.

"Well, there ought to be. I know who I'd vote for, if I was the King of Sweden or whoever."

"Me too," agreed Paul wholeheartedly.

Strange sensations turned in Abigail's gut. "What about heritability?" she demanded, to bridge the moment.

"Ah. At last there's official admission that you're not crazy. May take a couple of years to unravel and prove, though. Something called epigenetics. It'll mean there's less chance of plague reoccurring as the years pass, the next generation are already protected."

"Good!" She'd figure the details later. There was too much to take onboard right now. "Oh, I should have asked. How's Ryan? Do you know?"

"Alive and well, last I heard. Assigned to Granada and Fuente. Your Safi's grave is being sifted grain by grain, just in case. Her bones are being examined very thoroughly in Granada. Again, just in case. Look, I gotta go. My blessings, since the world at large won't get the opportunity to bless you."

The next day dawned sunny. At ten in the morning, radio stations still on the air were all carrying the same news, with recorded highlights, of an astonishing message to the world from the *united* Islamic religious leaders of all branches of the faith, calling upon their flocks to help, and revealing great hope. As the sun was setting, the President addressed the nation. He could relay already that the first responses from secular leaders, lesser religious figures, and most importantly the women of Islam, in droves, were all affirmative.

Scarcely had the President finished speaking than music followed, neither national nor religious, but the climax of Beethoven's *Ode to Joy*. Presently those aboard the *Salem Swan* heard the foghorns of the larger anchored fishing boats sounding off, one after another, like the deepest notes of tubas. Up on deck in the fading light, as Paul clasped her hand, Abigail's tears for the 700 million she'd failed flowed over her smile for the thousands of millions saved.

The Jebel Bahra, Syria: May 1180 AD

Al-Hakim padded along the dusty path, his heart light, as it always was these days. He was held in high honour here, his homeland, and revelled in his close companionship with Rashid al-Din Sinan. He felt like a child again, free of his great burden, for his dreams were achieved and the *hand of power* in Alamut now held a truly devastating *worldly* power, in addition to spiritual supremacy.

Amid purple mountain spinach, the older leaves fading to green, white flowers like stars caught his eye. He stopped to collect the seeds of Assyrian Rue and then dig up some nearby roots, executing these tasks without thought, for gathering medicines from the wild had been his lifelong habit. He wrapped the specimens carefully and placed them in his empty food satchel, then resumed his way back to Masyaf, Sinan's headquarters for the last three months. The Master forever moved from stronghold to stronghold, though favouring al-Kahf and Masyaf. The sun was still high in the cloudless azure sky; there was plenty of time.

These last three years back in Syria had perhaps been the happiest of his life. The six years prior to that at Alamut had been rewarding, but still hard work and, with Hasan's light extinguished upon Earth, Hakim no longer felt wholly comfortable at the highest shrine of the Nizaris. Yet the monkeys and exotic plants were now installed there, many more Fida'een were trained in procedures, and utterly convincing demonstrations had been given several times to the elite and their guests. Also, stock of the *waters* had been accumulated and hidden in the chilly heights.

Along with one monkey who'd become almost a pet, some of that stock was transferred to the Jebel Bahra, where Hakim verified its undiminished potency. After the bloody decline and terrible deaths of unfortunate Druze and Sunni prisoners, Sinan had ordered protection for the Syrian elite. Hakim himself intravened his Master and friend.

All now waited on the word of Muhammad at Alamut, to be given when the time was ripe, when any great power or alliance of powers threatened Nizari survival. God's chosen could now shake the world, and Hakim had long known that one day they would have to. Come that day, the *ahl al-tadadd* would be reaped in uncountable numbers, the heaps of their bodies rising everywhere in a new landscape of death throughout Christian and Sunni and barbarian empires alike.

Hakim froze. So did the viper, a blunt-nosed creature the length of his hand and wrist, grey with alternating brown spots.

A few paces would put him far from any danger, yet it came into Hakim's mind to capture the snake, just as he had done often in his youth; its venom would be useful.

Slowly he circled, picking up a stick as he moved. The serpent tracked him warily, slim tongue flickering. Hakim moved closer. Holding the stick at the full stretch of his left arm, he used the thin wood to distract the creature. As the snake was gathering itself to bite at the taunting lure, Hakim lunged with his right hand and grabbed just below the broad triangular head. Swiftly discarding the stick, he seized the writhing body with his left hand. A small enough creature, as snakes went, though deadly.

He smiled, pleased to know that he still had the knack. Yet just as he was about to begin the tricky operation of transferring the viper to his satchel, he heard the unmistakable snort of horses and the clink of tack.

Still clutching the snake, he headed for the only sparse cover he could find, a modest cane-break. He kept absolutely still as two knights on horseback came into view, their black linen surcoats with white crosses identifying them as Hospitallers, the leather bags for their chainmail slung alongside. Their coursers were restless, fighting the reins. A dozen dirty men at arms followed on foot, visibly sweating beneath their padded jackets and half-armour, their mail helmets covered by kerchiefs. They clearly intended to move quietly, yet were making a poor job of it. Perhaps the viper sensed heightened danger; it too stayed still.

On a crossbowman's neck were scrofula sores; may his thumbs be sliced by whoever captured him! Hakim's nose wrinkled; he could easily smell these disgusting Christians, God curse them. He hoped their scent wouldn't alarm the snake. A muscular, barrel-chested sergeant brought up the rear. Quiet and keen-eyed, he could be a veteran of many campaigns. Even so, the soldier didn't perceive Hakim.

A solitary raven cawed, high above. The sergeant turned to look, eyes aloft. Yet when his gaze lowered again, it swept the ground behind, probably from long habit, and so discovered Hakim only four paces away.

Hakim rose, proudly, unafraid.

Yelling, the sergeant raised a spear, but he waited for an order from his masters as the other men crowded back down the path, yanking out their swords, spreading out to encircle this Arab who could be a look-out.

Hakim understood no Frankish. Yet when one of the knights uttered a couple of words, in the peremptory tone and within the sergeant's pale eyes, he divined the meaning.

If God the Exalted so willed, then let this be His servant's last day! Glory to Him Who determines the length of our days! The last day, likewise, God willing, for the slayer of His servant!

Hakim flung the viper as the sergeant advanced. Constrained for many minutes and now maltreated, the angry viper hit the sergeant on the neck and bit, hanging like a twitching tassel even as the sergeant followed through, driving his spear deep into Hakim's belly.

Hakim buckled to the ground, dragging the spear down with him, his hands involuntarily clutching the haft, only half-held now by the sergeant as he tore the viper loose with his freed hand, hurling the snake aside, swearing foully.

Strangely, Hakim felt little pain as he stared up. Against the blue sky and in place of the uncouth Frankish Christian, he saw Hasan, light streaming from white raiment and golden slippers. The Holy one beckoned to Hakim.

Confident of his rightful place in heaven, Hakim tarried a while, delivering a dreadful curse to the Franks, now clustering closer. Even if they couldn't understand his words, his terrible tone was clear to all. The bitten sergeant who stood above him, one fist still gripping the spear, began to tremble.

"For the *waters of death* will overflow and devour all Christendom," proclaimed Hakim, "until mountains of putrid flesh and rivers of dark blood submerge your cities, until the few who are left cast away their swords and civilisation and run into the wild like beasts, yet begging for God's mercy, *which will be withheld!*"

Behind loomed one of the mounted knights. From that one's countenance, he was learned and understood the curse of the white-haired magician, which might haunt him for the rest of his life.

Hasan beckoned again, and reached out. Hakim raised his hand.

As if this signalled the curse starting to act, the sergeant panted in panic, tottering and clutching at his barrel chest. The side of his neck was luridly swollen, the venom's action upon him swift and powerful. From the reek of it, the Frank beshat himself. His bulk toppled forward, driving the spear, spilling agony into Hakim's gut as though from red hot coals.

With his last thought upon the Earth, forever a doctor, Hakim wondered which of his own organs had been ruptured.

Postscript by the Humanity Futures Institute

Extract from the December 2016 interview with Samih Fadul, a Damascus Druze

"I don't remember how he first came to us. We're a close community here in Jaramana... for our safety you understand... But about the war, he thought very much like us."

"Is this him?" [I showed an image on my phone.]

"Yes. Yes, I'd say so. But he's younger there... It's odd to see Jafar young, and smiling."

"So he didn't smile much. What sort of man was Jafar?"

[Samih drew down the corners of his mouth and shrugged.]

"He was many men, you know. A complex man... deep. Underneath, obsessed."

"Obsessed? About what?"

[Samih displayed a wry smile.]

"A man can behave obsessively without revealing the cause. But sometimes he ranted, mostly when flushed with spirits. It was jumbled, occasionally utter nonsense. Yet very... charged. Very repetitive. His eyes blazed at such times."

"Can you remember roughly what he would say?"

"Some of it was poetic... old words, traditional rhymes, wine and water and light and death. It all meant something to him. Or years ago it did."

"Did he ever talk about his past?"

"The cleverer you are, the less you speak. I think Jafar was a very clever man, except late at night after imbibing."

"But surely he let something slip, some hint?"

[Samih waved himself out, as the dealer of his card circle set up a new game.]

"Men wear their past like clothes."

"And what sort were Jafar's clothes?"

"Well... how shall I say? He reminded me of an old lion. One now rejected by his pride, yet once powerful. He had... poise. When occasion demanded, and he wasn't drunk, he took charge with ease. Although he was older and grizzled and damaged by alcohol, women's eyes strayed often to him."

[Samih laughed lightly.]

"More often than they stray to me!"

"Anything else?"

"He wore expensive rings. And once when we were discussing what's left of our economy, he mentioned that the war had ruined his businesses. Maybe this helped to make him bitter. Yet underneath, I'm guessing there was something much darker. He seemed very deeply disillusioned."

"Lost love? A woman?"

"No, no..."

[A waiter arrived with boiling water. The dealer refilled and stirred the maté, added sugar, and then passed it to Samih who sucked the drink through a silver straw, clearly relishing it.]

"Women wanted him, or at least wondered what he would be like. But women held no mystery for him. His heart, I believe, was hopelessly tangled with something far more serious, for better or worse. Something that maybe failed or rejected him, but he couldn't let go. What could it be but spiritual?"

"I think that's a good guess. What were his views about the war?"

"As I said, he thought like us."

[Samih paused to suck more maté, and looked uncomfortable.]

"Yes, but can you explain more? I'm not familiar with the position of the Druze here in Damascus."

"That's not part of our agreement. I'm just telling you about Jafar. I guessed he was once a big man, a player in some big game. Maybe behind the scenes. I expected someone to come asking, eventually."

"Really?"

"Yes. Like I can feel bad weather coming in my bones. And I don't mind telling. In fact it feels like a loose end that I wanted to tie off. It was nagging. But the war is something else... Talk is dangerous."

"Samih, I assure you I'm not at all interested in this war. Only in a much older one. I just wanted to get the best possible picture of Jafar as you knew him. His views on the conflict, just generally, might be helpful."

[Samih sucked at the bottom of the maté, causing burbling noises. Then he looked me in the eye for half a minute, assessing.]

"None of us like any of the foreign fighters, Sunni or Shi'a, Turkic or Kurdish or Iraqi. None of them care about the Druze. Where we sit is less than four kilometres from the old city, but the district of Jaramana is like a town in its own right. We keep ourselves to ourselves here. Although Christians share our streets, we've lived together for centuries. There's no trouble. The Iraqis coming in since 2003 are a different story. There's far too many of them. Jafar was not Druze, but he thought just the same. He didn't belong to any of those incoming faiths or sides."

"What about Assad? What did Jafar think of *him*?"

[Samih's brown forehead creased in a frown.]

"Not contempt, yet at best only grudging acceptance. Jafar was passionate about Syria as a united country, one of the few topics he was open about. And Assad still represents the legitimate government of all of this country. As such he's aligned with Jafar's hope of a return to a single Syria. But Jafar also believed that Assad had caused a huge amount of damage."

[Samih's tone suggested that his own views were similar. He thoughtfully rubbed his moustache and then added more.]

"Nor did Jafar seem to hold *any* political leaders in esteem. Though who or what he did believe in, I never discovered. A unified Syria was only a minor hope, that's why he was able to talk about it."

[I thought it best to shift from the politics of the war. And I offered something in return for Samih's candour.]

"Jafar was an Ismaili."

"Ah... that explains much. I presume then, not the Aga Khan brand."

"Correct."

"So... dissimulation."

"Exactly."

"And he wouldn't think the likes of Assad had ultimate legitimacy to rule."

"Did you have any inkling? Did you trust him?"

"There was a big car bomb here back in 2012, two cars in fact. Just a few streets from here, in a small alley near a petrol station. Terrible, terrible. An orange ball of fire came out the alley, walls collapsed. Terrible. Everyone was running away. There were body parts and blood blown out over the street. Can you believe it?

"Jafar wasn't afraid. He strode straight into the alley, and he came back with a girl in his arms. Pulled her out of a burning car. I'd wanted to run too, everyone thought there'd be follow-up explosions. But seeing Jafar stayed me. I couldn't follow him, my knees were like jelly, my ears were ringing. But he gave me the girl and he went back in. He helped many people then, and organised those who eventually overcame their fear, like me, and came back to do what they could before the ambulances and the army arrived in force.

"After that I did... Yes, I did trust him. But with Jafar, there was always something hidden, you know. Something powerful underneath. I somehow knew that anything on the wrong side of that power would see no mercy. And I wondered how he knew so much about us.

"Now I know. The Ismailis stem ultimately from the same root as ourselves. And we have many centuries of shared experience as persecuted minority sects in Syria."

"A terrible incident, as you say. Appalling. And yet it brought out the *man of action* in Jafar."

"Very much. His whole mood changed. He was confident. He gave orders. He was not at all affected by fear, nor by the awful carnage around him."

[The dealer took the maté cup from Samih, repeating the ritual of refreshing it and then handing the cup to another of the card players. I asked about the drink and the formal way it seems to be consumed, one at a time in a circle. Samih filled me in with some history].

"So how did things go after the car bomb? With you and Jafar, I mean. Did you become close?"

[Samih paused for a couple of seconds, having a far-away look in his eyes.]

"No one got close to Jafar. But yes, we shared some friendship. Jafar seemed to enjoy telling me about all the foreign places he'd visited. Perhaps he was a little boastful. For my part, I relished listening. When I was young I wanted to travel, but..." [and Samih shrugged his shoulders] "I ended up travelling only once, to Greece. Nowhere else. My roots slowly became fixed here in Damascus. Even the war does not make me want to leave."

[Samih shook his head slightly, as if even he found this truth hard to believe.]

"Yet you still enjoyed the stories."

"Yes, very much. What might have been, maybe.' [Samih smiled.]

"Where had he been? What were your favourite places?"

"Where hadn't he been! All over the Arab lands just to start with. I enjoyed tales of all the grand Mosques and other sites, I appreciate such things separately from their brands of faith. And it was good to know about Iraq and Iran. Things you don't get from the papers. You know, to fill in some context behind the fighters who come here and the political forces behind them. Yet I liked his tales of the cold places too, which I can scarcely imagine though they are often on TV. He'd seen the glorious Northern Lights, and tramped through streets in Canada and the US where they thought nothing of two meters of snow.

"He often had errands near the old city, though he never said what they were for. I go there about once a month for my own business, and to pick up gifts. So we met regularly in Bab Touma at a favourite restaurant of his. That was what killed him."

"You mentioned before that you were there?"

"It was last July. I was late, which would always make Jafar frown. So I was practically running towards the restaurant, when its windows blew out.

I found out later that a mortar shell had landed right inside. You know his name disappeared from the official list of casualties in the paper?"

"No. But then I didn't know until today that's where he died."

"He was recorded at first, on the provisional police list. Then not. I knew then he'd been someone important, perhaps in hiding. Just in case he had different names, I checked all the photos. Not there either."

"Long ago, associated with a major project in Tehran, for a few years he took the alias *Kamal.* But all the high hopes for that project came to nothing. Samih, can you tell me carefully what happened at the very end?"

"I remembered Jafar's courage and though I was cold inside with fear, I went in. There was dust and smoke. My eyes hurt. I could barely see the chequered pattern on the floor. I tripped over debris, and people. Dead or alive, I don't know. Jafar always booked the same table, so I knew where he'd be. His table was still upright, and he was sitting there as though ready to eat. But something had pierced him and his shirt was drenched with blood. I guessed there was little time, but he was still alive. He even spoke."

"What did he say?"

[Samih didn't appear to hear me, no doubt lost in vivid memories of the event.]

"His eyes were shining, as though in victory not in death or defeat. And he was clutching tight at the talisman he always wore around his neck, as though, as though..."

"A talisman? You never mentioned that! What talisman?"

"Syria is a spiritual place, many people have talismans. Jafar wore a very small phial on a gold chain. It looked like crystal glass, probably with liquid inside. But it could only have been a tiny amount. His hand reached to this phial often, especially when he was... distant. He spoke of it once as 'life', although he was rambling that night."

"Thank you Samih, this is very important. I don't suppose you know what happened to Jafar's body?"

"No. There was no funeral at which to let out my grief. It was as though he'd never been."

"I'm sorry I interrupted. What did Jafar say?"

"He seemed to draw strength from the talisman, as though it was a passport to... well, where he was going. And from his face he seemed to recognize me straight away. But when he spoke I realised that in his shock he'd mistaken me for someone else, an old friend maybe. His words are etched in my mind, I'm never free of them. *Mahmoud*, he said, *you did not die in vain. At last I've seen what you must long have known. Separated by only a thin veil, there is a world where by our hand the waters flowed. Where death swells and overflows, while the faithful are protected. Where the teacher of many lessons, judges from on high. I... I come to join you."*

[I was overwhelmed and had to control myself.]

"Samih, your faithful recall is critical. I can't thank you enough. These words are hugely important to our understanding."

[Samih looked very relieved.]

"For months they've weighed upon my mind. I knew someone high up should be told, but I had no idea who to approach. Despite all that I know about Jafar, his last words seared into me like... like a white hot truth. It was the strangest experience. I'm more than glad to be free of the burden, which I could not put from me no matter how I tried."

"Don't worry any more, Samih. You were absolutely right. But I'll handle it from here. Have no fear, people will come to know of Jafar's works and Jafar's words."

[Extract Ends.]

Acknowledgements

We gratefully acknowledge assistance from Pascal J. Thomas with the Occitan language, Walter Barnhardt of Woods Hole Oceanographic Institution regarding sailing in the Boston area, Dr Stephen Longworth and Dr Peter Winstanley as regards medical matters, snakes and virology, Faisal Qureshi regarding Syrian Arabic, Nigel Furlong regarding emergency planning, David Shaw regarding Boston and biology, Gene Parker and Luisa María García Velasco and Kris Black as readers, Ana Díaz Eiriz for artwork on the original eBook release, Tim Taylor for previous technical advice, and Cristina Macía for a brilliant idea.

About the Authors

Ian Watson splashed out in 1973 with his debut novel of psycholinguistics, *The Embedding*, which won amongst other awards the Prix Apollo in France and the John W. Campbell Memorial Award. After a first degree and a research degree in English Literature mixed with French from Balliol College, Oxford, he lectured at universities in Dar es Salaam, then in Tokyo, then in the History of Art school in Birmingham, UK, before becoming a full-time writer in 1976. Numerous novels of science fiction, fantasy, and horror and a dozen story collections followed, all of them now available as eBooks through Gollancz´s www.sfgateway.com – apart from Ian´s four delirious gothic space operas set in Games Workshop´s Warhammer 40K universe, but including the first full-length genre fiction book by two transgressive European authors with different mother tongues, *The Beloved of My Beloved*, co-authored with Italian Roberto Quaglia, one story from which won the British SF Association Award for Best Short Fiction of 2009. Nine months spent eyeball to eyeball with Stanley Kubrick resulted in screen credit for the Screen Story of *A.I. Artificial Intelligence* made by Steven Spielberg after Kubrick´s death. These days Ian lives in Asturias in Spain, where goblins swig cider while playing bagpipes in the green rainy hills. With his wife, ace translator Cristina Macía, he co-authored a historic cookery book and is busy on a Young Adult SFF novel. Both co-organised the first ever European SF convention in Barcelona in 2016 because... Why not?

Ian Watson's website with lots of photos is www.ianwatson.info

Andy West has a degree in Physics and 35 years experience working in the embedded computer industry, specialising in computers to be used in extreme conditions of temperatures and pressures high and low, such as in outer space. His debut novel, *The Outcast and the Little One*, was published by NewCon Press, UK, in 2012. Set on a largely tamed Venus, it tells of the struggle by an impoverished society of intelligent robots against their cruel suppressers, an exotic race of post-humans. Into the midst of the robots comes a post-human child, who grows by physical and mental augmentations to become their kinsperson, with dramatic consequences for both races. Andy's SF stories (several shorts also published by NewCon and a collection by Greyhart Press) deploy to the full his fascination with the dynamics of evolution, cultural development, and historical patterns. A keen folk music devotee, he plays Irish whistles. He lives in England in North Bucks.
https://www.amazon.co.uk/Andy-West/e/B004TSI73G/
https://www.amazon.com/Andy-West/e/B004TSI73G/

Also from NewCon Press

The 1000 Year Reich – Ian Watson

with introduction by Justina Robson
Ian Watson, author of the very first novels in the Warhammer 40K universe, makes a long-anticipated return to military SF with "In Golden Armour", one of three original stories in this fabulous new collection from the man who wrote the screen story to *AI: Artificial Intelligence* for Stanley Kubrick (later filmed by Steven Spielberg). 18 stories of brilliance and wonder.

Saving for a Sunny Day – Ian Watson, *with introduction by Adam Roberts*

Ian Watson is widely recognised as one of Britain's most influential genre writers. *Saving for a Sunny Day* showcases Ian at his best: fifteen previously uncollected stories selected by the author, each with comments regarding their inspiration. In his detailed introduction, Adam Roberts, takes the opportunity to assess Ian's entire oeuvre. A must for anyone who enjoys high quality, thought-provoking fiction.

The Outcast and the Little One – Andy West

In a distant future, humanity has diversified into several races, two of which struggle for supremac on a largely-tamed Venusy. The robotic, pacifist Aumons find themselves ever more suppressed by the exuberant, vital and exotic Clonir. Arkhend, a new arrival at the Aumon's Southern Arc, has first-hand experience of their enemy and is determined that the Brotherhood should not sink quietly into extinction but rather rouse themselves in defiance of the Clonir before it's too late…

www.newconpress.com

New from NewCon Press

Andrew Wallace – Celebrity Werewolf

Suave, sophisticated, erudite and charming, Gig Danvers seems too good to be true. He appears from nowhere to champion humanitarian causes and revolutionise science, including the design and development of Product 5: the first organic computer to exceed silicon capacity; but are his critics right to be cautious? Is there a darker side to this enigmatic benefactor, one that is more in keeping with his status as the Cleberity Werewolf?

David Gullen – Shopocalypse

A Bonnie and Clyde for the Trump era, Josie and Novik embark on the ultimate roadtrip. In a near-future re-sculpted politically and geographically by climate change, they blaze a trail across the shopping malls of America in a printed intelligent car (stolen by accident), with a hundred and ninety million LSD-contaminated dollars in the trunk, buying shoes and cameras to change the world.

Rachel Armstrong – Invisible Ecologies

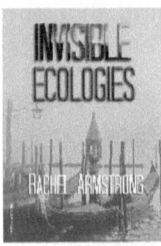

The story of Po, an ambiguously gendered boy who shares an intimate connection with a nascent sentience emerging within the Po delta: the bioregion upon which the city of Venice is founded. Carried by the world's oceans, the pair embark on a series of extraordinary adventures and, as Po starts school, stumble upon the Mayor's drastic plans to modernise the city and reshape the future of the lagoon and its people.

Ian Creasey – The Shape of Strangers

British SF's best kept secret, Ian Creasey is one of our most prolific and successful short fiction writers, with 18 stories published in *Asimov's*, a half dozen or more in *Analog*, and appearances in a host of the major SF fiction venues. *The Shape of Strangers* showcases Ian's perceptive and inventive style of science fiction, gathering together fourteen of his finest tales, including stories that have been selected for *Year's Best* anthologies.

IMMANION PRESS

Purveyors of Speculative Fiction

Venus Burning: Realms by Tanith Lee

Tanith Lee wrote 15 stories for the acclaimed *Realms of Fantasy* magazine. This book collects all the stories in one volume for the first time, some of which only ever appeared in the magazine so will be new to some of Tanith's fans. These tales are among her best work, in which she takes myth and fairy tale tropes and turns them on their heads. Lush and lyrical, deep and literary, Tanith Lee created fresh poignant tales from familiar archetypes.
ISBN 978-1-907737-88-6, £11.99, $17.50 pbk

A Raven Bound with Lilies by Storm Constantine

The Wraeththu have captivated readers for three decades. This anthology of 15 tales collects all the published Wraeththu short stories into one volume, and also includes extra material, including the author's first explorations of the androgynous race. The tales range from the 'creation story' *Paragenesis*, through the bloody, brutal rise of the earliest tribes, and on into a future, where strange mutations are starting to emerge from hidden corners of the earth.
ISBN: 978-1-907737-80-0 £11.99, $15.50 pbk

The Lightbearer by Alan Richardson

Michael Horsett parachutes into Occupied France before the D-Day Invasion. Dropped in the wrong place, badly injured, he falls prey to two Thelemist women who have awaited the Hawk God's coming, attracts a group of First World War veterans who rally to what they imagine is his cause, is hunted by a troop of German Field Police, and has a climactic encounter with a mutilated priest who believes that Lucifer Incarnate has arrived...*The Lightbearer* is a unique gnostic thriller, dealing with the themes of Light and Darkness, Good and Evil, Matter and Spirit. ISBN 9781907737763 £11.99 $18.99

http://www.immanion-press.com
info@immanion-press.com

www.ingramcontent.com/pod-product-compliance
Lightning Source LLC
Chambersburg PA
CBHW031022030726
47497CB00004B/963

9 781912 950102